ELEPHANT SONG

Wilbur Smith was born in Central Africa in 1933. He was educated at Michaelhouse and Rhodes University. He became a full-time writer in 1964 after the successful publication of *When the Lion Feeds*, and has written over thirty novels, all meticulously researched on his numerous expeditions worldwide. His books are now translated into twenty-six languages.

Find out more about Wilbur Smith by looking at his own author website, www.wilbursmithbooks.com

The novels of Wilbur Smith

THE COURTNEYS
When the Lion Feeds
The Sound of Thunder
A Sparrow Falls
Birds of Prey
Monsoon
Blue Horizon
The Triumph of the Sun
Assegai

THE COURTNEYS OF AFRICA
The Burning Shore
Power of the Sword
Rage
A Time to Die
Golden Fox

THE BALLANTYNE NOVELS
A Falcon Flies
Men of Men
The Angels Weep
The Leopard Hunts in Darkness

THE EGYPTIAN NOVELS
River God
The Seventh Scroll
Warlock
The Quest

also
The Dark of the Sun
Shout at the Devil
Gold Mine
The Diamond Hunters
The Sunbird
Eagle in the Sky
The Eye of the Tiger
Cry Wolf
Hungry as the Sea
Wild Justice
Elephant Song

WILBUR SMITH

ELEPHANT
SONG

PAN BOOKS

The author wishes to make grateful acknowledgement to Colin
Turnbull's *The Forest People*, published by Jonathan Cape, which
he found invaluable in his research for his novel.

First published 1991 by Macmillan

This edition published 1992 by Pan Books
an imprint of Pan Macmillan, a division of Macmillan Publishers Limited
Pan Macmillan, 20 New Wharf Road, London N1 9RR
Basingstoke and Oxford
Associated companies throughout the world
www.panmacmillan.com

ISBN 978-0-330-51934-2

1 3 5 7 9 8 6 4 2

A CIP catalogue record for this book is available from
the British Library.

Photoset by Datix International Limited
Printed and bound in Great Britain by
CPI Mackays, Chatham ME5 8TD

Visit **www.panmacmillan.com** to read more about all our books and to buy
them. You will also find features, author interviews and news of any author
events, and you can sign up for e-newsletters so that you're always first to hear
about our new releases.

This book is for my wife and the jewel of my life, Mokhiniso, with all my love and gratitude for the enchanted years that I have been married to her

IT WAS A windowless thatched building of dressed sandstone blocks, that Daniel Armstrong had built with his own hands almost ten years ago. At the time he had been a junior game ranger in the National Parks' administration. Since then the building had been converted into a veritable treasure house.

Johnny Nzou slipped his key into the heavy padlock, and swung open the double doors of hewn native teak. Johnny was chief warden of Chiwewe National Park. Back in the old days, he had been Daniel's tracker and gunbearer, a bright young Matabele whom Daniel had taught to read, write and speak fluent English by the light of a thousand campfires.

Daniel had lent Johnny the money to pay for his first correspondence course from the University of South Africa which had led much later to his degree of Bachelor of Science. The two youngsters, one black and one white, had patrolled the vast reaches of the National Park together, often on foot or bicycle. In the wilderness they had forged a friendship which the subsequent years of separation had left undimmed.

Now Daniel peered into the gloomy interior of the godown, and whistled softly.

'Hell, Johnny boy, you have been busy since I've been away.'

The treasure was stacked to the roof beams, hundreds of thousands of dollars' worth of it.

Johnny Nzou glanced at Daniel's face, his eyes narrowed as he looked for criticism in his friend's expression. The reaction was reflex, for he knew Daniel was an ally who understood the problem even better than he did. Nevertheless, the subject was so emotionally charged that it had become second nature to expect revulsion and antagonism.

However, Daniel had turned back to his cameraman. 'Can we get a light in here? I want some good shots of the interior.'

The cameraman trudged forward, weighed down by the

1

heavy battery packs slung around his waist, and switched on the hand-held arc lamp. The high stacks of treasure were lit with a fierce blue-white light.

'Jock, I want you to follow me and the warden down the length of the warehouse,' Daniel instructed, and the cameraman nodded and moved in closer, the sleek Sony video recorder balanced on his shoulder. Jock was in his middle thirties. He wore only a pair of short khaki pants, and open sandals. In the Zambezi valley heat his tanned bare chest was shiny with sweat and his long hair was tied with a leather thong at the nape of his neck. He looked like a pop star, but was an artist with the big Sony camera.

'Got you, guv,' he agreed, and panned the camera over the untidy stacks of elephant tusks, ending on Daniel's hand as it stroked one elegant curve of glowing ivory. Then he pulled back into a full shot of Daniel.

It was not merely Daniel's doctorate in biology, nor his books and lectures, that had made him an international authority and spokesman on African ecology. He had the healthy outdoors looks and charismatic manner that came over so well on the television screen, and his voice was deep and compelling. His accent had sufficient Sandhurst undertones remaining to soften the flat unmelodious vowel sounds of colonial speech. His father had been a staff officer in a Guards regiment during World War II and had served in North Africa under Wavell and Montgomery. After the war he came out to Rhodesia to grow tobacco. Daniel had been born in Africa but had been sent home to finish his education at Sandhurst, before coming back to Rhodesia to join the National Parks Service.

'Ivory,' he said now, as he looked into the camera. 'Since the time of the pharaohs, one of the most beautiful and treasured natural substances. The glory of the African elephant – and its terrible cross.'

Daniel began to move down between the tiers of stacked tusks, and Johnny Nzou fell in beside him. 'For two thousand years man has hunted the elephant to obtain this living white gold, and yet only a decade ago there still remained over two million elephant on the African continent. The elephant population seemed to be a renewable resource, an asset that was

2

protected and harvested and controlled – and then something went terribly, tragically wrong. In these last ten years, almost a million elephant have been slaughtered. It is barely conceivable that this could have been allowed to happen. We are here to find out what went wrong, and how the perilous existence of the African elephant can be retrieved from the brink of extinction.'

He looked at Johnny. 'With me today is Mr John Nzou, chief warden of Chiwewe National Park, one of the new breed of African conservationists. By coincidence, the name Nzou in the Shona language means elephant. John Nzou is Mr Elephant in more than name alone. As warden of Chiwewe, he is responsible for one of the largest and healthiest elephant herds that still flourish in the African wilderness. Tell us, Warden, how many tusks do you have in this store room here at Chiwewe National Park?'

'There are almost five hundred tusks in store at present – four hundred and eighty-six to be exact – with an average weight of seven kilos.'

'On the international market ivory is worth three hundred dollars a kilo,' Daniel cut in, 'so that is well over a million dollars. Where does it all come from?'

'Well, some of the tusks are pick-ups – ivory from elephant found dead in the Park, and some is illegal ivory that my rangers have confiscated from poachers. But the great majority of tusks are from the culling operations that my department is forced to undertake.'

The two of them paused at the far end of the godown and turned back to face the camera. 'We will discuss the culling programme later, Warden. But first can you tell us a little more about poaching activity in Chiwewe. How bad is it?'

'It is getting worse every day.' Johnny shook his head sadly. 'As the elephant in Kenya and Tanzania and Zambia are wiped out, so the professionals are turning their attention to our healthy elephant herds further south. Zambia is just across the Zambezi river, and the poachers that come across this side are organised and better armed than we are. They shoot to kill – men as well as elephant and rhino. We have been forced to do the same. If we run into a band of poachers, we shoot first.'

'All for these . . .' Daniel laid his hand on the nearest pile of

3

tusks. No two of the ivory shafts were the same; each curve was unique. Some were almost straight, long and thin as knitting-needles; others were bent like a drawn longbow. Some were sharp-tipped as javelins; others were squat and blunt. There were pearly shafts, and others were of buttery alabaster tone; still others were stained dark with vegetable juices, and scarred and worn with age.

Most of the ivory was female or immature; a few tusks were no longer than a man's forearm, taken from small calves. A very few were great curved imperial shafts, the heavy mature ivory of old bulls.

Daniel stroked one of these, and his expression was not simply for the camera. Once again, he felt the full weight of the melancholy that had first caused him to write about the passing and destruction of the old Africa and its enchanted animal kingdom.

'A sage and magnificent beast has been reduced to this,' his voice sank to a whisper. 'Even if it is unavoidable, we cannot escape the inherently tragic nature of the changes that are sweeping through this continent. Is the African elephant symbolic of the land? The elephant is dying. Is Africa dying?'

His sincerity was absolute. The camera recorded it faithfully. It was the most compelling reason for the enormous appeal of his television programmes around the world.

Now Daniel roused himself with an obvious effort, and turned back to Johnny Nzou. 'Tell us, Warden, is the elephant doomed? How many of these marvellous animals do you have in Zimbabwe and how many of those are in Chiwewe National Park?'

'There are an estimated fifty-two thousand elephant in Zimbabwe, and our figures for Chiwewe are even more accurate. Only three months ago, we were able to conduct an aerial survey of the Park sponsored by the International Union for the Conservation of Nature. The entire area of the Park was photographed, and the animals counted from the high-resolution prints.'

'How many?' Daniel asked.

'In Chiwewe alone, eighteen thousand elephant.'

'That's a huge population, something approaching a third of all the remaining animals in the country – all in this area.' Daniel raised an eyebrow. 'In the climate of gloom and pessimism that prevails, this must give you a great deal of encouragement?'

4

Johnny Nzou frowned. 'On the contrary, Doctor Armstrong, we are extremely concerned by these numbers.'

'Can you explain that please, Warden?'

'It's simple, Doctor. We cannot support that many elephant. We estimate that thirty thousand elephant would be an ideal population for Zimbabwe. A single beast requires up to a ton of vegetable matter each day, and he will push over trees that have taken many hundreds of years to grow, even trees with trunks four feet in diameter, to obtain that food.'

'What will happen if you allow that huge herd to flourish and to breed?'

'Quite simply, in a very short period they will reduce this park to a dust bowl, and when that happens the elephant population will collapse. We will be left with nothing – no trees, no park, no elephant.'

Daniel nodded encouragement. When the film was edited he would cut in at this point a series of shots he had taken some years previously in Kenya's Amboseli Park. These were haunting vistas of devastation, of bare red earth and dead black trees stripped of bark and leaves holding up their naked branches in agonised supplication to a hard blue African sky, while the desiccated carcasses of the great animals lay like discarded leather bags where famine and poachers had destroyed them.

'Do you have a solution, Warden?' Daniel asked softly.

'A drastic one, I'm afraid.'

'Will you show us what it is?'

Johnny Nzou shrugged. 'It is not very pretty to watch, but, yes, you may witness what has to be done.'

Daniel woke twenty minutes before sunrise. Even the intervening years spent in cities out of Africa, and the passage of so many other dawns in northern climes, or in the fluid time zones of jet aircraft travel, had not dulled the habit that he had first acquired in this valley. Of course, the habit had been reinforced during the years of that terrible

5

Rhodesian bush war, when he had been called up to serve in the security forces.

For Daniel the dawn was the most magical time of each day, and especially so in this valley. He rolled out of his sleeping-bag and reached for his boots. He and his men had slept fully clothed on the sun-baked earth, with the embers of the campfire in the centre of the huddle of their prostrate forms. They had not built a *boma* of thorn branches to protect themselves, although at intervals during the night lions had grunted and roared along the escarpment.

Daniel laced up his boots and slipped quietly out of the circle of sleeping men. The dew that hung like seed pearls upon the grass stems soaked his trouser legs to the knees as he moved out to the promontory of rock at the head of the cliff. He found a seat on the rough grey granite knoll and huddled into his anorak.

The dawn came on with stealthy and deceptive speed and painted the clouds above the great river in subtle talcum shades of pink and grey. Over the Zambezi's dark green waters the river mist undulated and pulsed like ghostly ectoplasm and the dawn flights of duck were very dark and crisp against the pale background, their formations precise and their wing-beats flickering quick as knife-blades in the uncertain light.

A lion roared, near at hand, abrupt gales of sound that died away in a descending series of moaning grunts. Daniel shivered with the thrill of that sound. Though he had heard it countless times, it always had the same effect upon him. There was no other like it in all the world. For him it was the veritable voice of Africa.

Then he picked out the great cat shape below him at the edge of the swamp. Full-bellied, dark-maned, it carried its massive head low and swung it from side to side to the rhythm of its stately arrogant walk. Its mouth was half open and its fangs glinted behind thin black lips. He watched it vanish into the dense riverine bush and sighed with the pleasure it had given him.

There was a small sound close behind him. As he started up, Johnny Nzou touched his shoulder to restrain him and settled down on the granite slab beside him.

Johnny lit a cigarette. Daniel had never been able to talk him out of the habit. They sat in companionable silence as they had so often before and watched the dawn come on more swiftly now, until that religious moment when the sun thrust its burning rim above the dark mass of the forest. The light changed and all their world was bright and glazed as a precious ceramic creation fresh from the firing oven.

'The trackers came into camp ten minutes ago. They have found a herd,' Johnny broke the silence, and the mood.

Daniel stirred and glanced at him. 'How many?' he asked.

'About fifty.' That was a good number. They would not be able to process more, for flesh and hide putrefy swiftly in the heat of the valley, and a lower number would not justify all this use of men and expensive equipment.

'Are you sure you want to film this?' Johnny asked.

Daniel nodded. 'I have considered it carefully. To attempt to conceal it would be dishonest.'

'People eat meat and wear leather, but they don't want to see inside the abattoir,' Johnny pointed out.

'This is a complex and emotional subject we are examining. People have a right to know.'

'In anyone else I would suspect journalistic sensationalism,' Johnny murmured, and Daniel frowned.

'You are probably the only person I would allow to say that – because you know better.'

'Yes, Danny, I know better,' Johnny agreed. 'You hate this as much as I do, and yet you first taught me the necessity of it.'

'Let's go to work,' Daniel suggested gruffly, and they stood up and walked back in silence to where the trucks were parked. The camp was astir, and coffee was brewing on the open fire. The rangers were rolling their blankets and sleeping-bags and checking their rifles.

There were four of them, two black lads and two white, all of them in their twenties. They wore the plain khaki uniform of the Parks Department with green shoulder flashes, and though they handled their weapons with the casual competence of veterans they kept up a cheerful high-spirited banter. Black and white treated each other as comrades, although they were just old enough to have fought in the bush war and had probably been on opposing sides. It always amazed Daniel that so little bitterness remained.

7

Jock, the cameraman, was already filming. It often seemed to Daniel that the Sony camera was a natural excrescence of his body, like a hunchback.

'I'm going to ask you some dumb questions for the camera, and I might needle you a little,' Daniel warned Johnny. 'We both know the answers to the questions, but we have to fake it, okay?'

'Go ahead.'

Johnny looked good on film. Daniel had studied the rushes the previous night. One of the joys of working with modern video equipment was the instant replay of footage. Johnny resembled the younger Cassius Clay before he became Mohammed Ali. However, he was leaner in the face and his bone structure finer and more photogenic. His expression was mobile and expressive and the tones of his skin were not so dark as to make too severe a contrast and render photography difficult.

They huddled over the smoky campfire and Jock brought the camera in close to them.

'We are camped here on the banks of the Zambezi River with the sun just rising, and not far out there in the bush your trackers have come across a herd of fifty elephant, Warden,' Daniel told Johnny, and he nodded. 'You have explained to me that the Chiwewe Park cannot support such numbers of these huge animals, and that this year alone at least a thousand of them must be removed from the Park, not only for the good of the ecology, but for the very survival of the remaining elephant herds. How do you intend removing them?'

'We will have to cull them,' Johnny said curtly.

'Cull them?' Daniel asked. 'That means kill, doesn't it?'

'Yes. My rangers and I will shoot them.'

'All of them, Warden? You are going to kill fifty elephant today?'

'We will cull the entire herd.'

'What about the young calves and the pregnant cows? Won't you spare a single animal?'

'They all have to go,' Johnny insisted.

'But why, Warden? Couldn't you catch them, dart and drug them, and send them elsewhere?'

'The costs of transporting an animal the size of an elephant

8

are staggering. A big bull weighs six tons, an average cow around four. Look at this terrain down here in the valley.' Johnny gestured towards the mountainous heights of the escarpment and the broken rocky kopjes and wild forest. 'We would require special trucks and we would have to build roads to get them in and out. Even if that were possible, where would we take them? I have told you that we have a surplus of almost twenty thousand elephant in Zimbabwe. Where would we take these elephant? There simply isn't space for them.'

'So, Warden, unlike the other countries to the north such as Kenya and Zambia who have allowed their elephant herds to be almost wiped out by poaching and unwise conservation policy, you are in a Catch 22 situation. Your management of your herds of elephant has been too good. Now you have to destroy and waste these marvellous animals.'

'No, Doctor Armstrong, we won't waste them. We will recover a great deal of value from their carcasses, ivory and hides and meat which will be sold. The proceeds will be ploughed back into conservation, to prevent poaching and to protect our National Parks. The death of these animals will not be a complete abomination.'

'But why do you have to kill the mothers and the babies?' Daniel insisted.

'You are cheating, Doctor,' Johnny warned him. 'You are using the emotive, slanted language of the animal rights groups, "mothers and babies". Let's rather call them cows and calves, and admit that a cow eats as much and takes up as much space as a bull, and that calves grow very swiftly into adults.'

'So you feel—' Daniel started, but despite his earlier warning, Johnny was becoming angry.

'Hold on,' he snapped. 'There's more to it than that. We have to take out the entire herd. It is absolutely essential that we leave no survivors. The elephant herd is a complex family group. Nearly all its members are blood relatives, and there is a highly developed social structure within the herd. The elephant is an intelligent animal, probably the most intelligent after the primates, certainly more intelligent than a cat or dog, or even a dolphin. They know – I mean, they really understand . . .' he broke off, and cleared his throat. His feelings had overcome

9

him, and Daniel had never liked nor admired him more than he did at that moment.

'The terrible truth is', Johnny's voice was husky as he went on, 'that if we allowed any of them to escape the cull, they would communicate their terror and panic to the other herds in the Park. There would be a swift breakdown in the elephants' social behaviour.'

'Isn't that a little far-fetched, Warden?' Daniel asked softly.

'No. It has happened before. After the war there were ten thousand surplus elephant in the Wankie National Park. At that time, we knew very little about the techniques or effects of massive culling operations. We soon learned. Those first clumsy efforts of ours almost destroyed the entire social structure of the herds. By shooting the older animals, we wiped out their reservoir of experience and transferable wisdom. We disrupted their migratory patterns, the hierarchy and discipline within the herds, even their breeding habits. Almost as though they understood that the holocaust was upon them, the bulls began to cover the barely mature young cows before they were ready. Like the human female, the elephant cow is ripe for breeding at fifteen or sixteen years of age at the very earliest. Under the terrible stress of the culling the bulls in Wankie went to the cows when they were only ten or eleven years of age, still in puberty, and the calves born of these unions were stunted little runts.' Johnny shook his head. 'No, we have to take out the whole herd at one stroke.'

Almost with relief, he looked up at the sky. They both picked up the distant insect drone of an aircraft engine beyond the towering cumulus clouds.

'Here comes the spotter plane,' he said quietly, and reached for the microphone of the radio.

'Good morning, Sierra Mike. We have you visual due south of our position approximately four miles. I will give you yellow smoke.'

Johnny nodded at one of his rangers, who pulled the tab on a smoke marker. Sulphur-yellow smoke drifted in a heavy cloud across the treetops.

'Roger, Parks. I have your smoke. Give me an indication on the target, please.'

Johnny frowned at the word 'target' and laid emphasis on the alternative word as he replied. 'At sunset yesterday evening the *herd* was moving north towards the river five miles south-east of this position. There are fifty-plus animals.'

'Thank you, Parks. I will call again when we locate them.'

They watched the aircraft bank away eastwards. It was an ancient single-engined Cessna that had probably served on fire-force duties as a K-Car, or killer car, during the bush war.

Fifteen minutes later the radio crackled to life again.

'Hello, Parks. I have your herd. Fifty-plus and eight miles from your present position.'

 The herd was spread out down both banks of a dry river-course that was gouged through a low line of flinty hills. The forest was greener and more luxuriant here in the drainage where the deep roots had found subterranean water. The acacia trees were in heavy pod. The pods looked like long brown biscuits, clustered at the tips of the branches sixty feet above ground level.

Two cows moved in on one of the heavily laden trees. They were the herd matriarchs, both of them over seventy years of age, gaunt old dowagers with tattered ears and rheumy eyes. The bond between them was over half a century strong. They were half-sisters, successive calves of the same mother. The elder had been weaned at the birth of her sibling and had helped to nursemaid her as tenderly as would a human elder sister. They had shared a long life, and had drawn from it a wealth of experience and wisdom to add to the deep ancestral instinct with which they had both been endowed at birth.

They had seen each other through drought and famine and sickness. They had shared the joy of good rains and abundant food. They knew all the secret hideaways in the mountains and the water-holes in the desert places. They knew where the hunters lurked, and the boundaries of the sanctuaries within which they and the herd were secure. They had played midwife to each other, leaving the herd together when the time was

11

come upon one of them, and by their presence had fortified each other in the tearing agony of birth. They had stripped the foetal sac from each other's newborn calves, and helped discipline them, instruct them and rear them to maturity.

Their own breeding days were long past, but the herd and its safety were still their duty and their main concern. Their pleasure and their responsibility were the younger cows and the new calves that carried their own blood-lines.

Perhaps it was fanciful to endow brute animals with such human emotions as love and respect, or to believe that they understand blood relationships or the continuity of their line, but no one who had seen the old cows quieten the boisterous youngsters with raised ears and a sharp angry squeal, or watched the herd follow their lead with unquestioning obedience, could doubt their authority. No one who had seen them caress the younger calves with a gentle trunk or lift them over the steep and difficult places on the elephant roads could question their concern. When danger threatened they would push the young ones behind them and rush forward to the defence with ears spread wide and trunks rolled ready to fling out and strike down an enemy.

The great bulls with towering frames and massive girth might overshadow them in size, but not in cunning and ferocity. The bulls' tusks were longer and thicker, sometimes weighing well over one hundred pounds. The two old cows had spindly misshapen ivory, worn and cracked and discoloured with age, and the bones showed through the scarred grey skin, but they were constant in their duty to the herd.

The bulls kept only a loose association with the breeding herd. As they grew older they often preferred to break away and form smaller bachelor groups of two or three males, visiting the cows only when the heady scent of oestrus drew them in. However, the old cows stayed with the herd. They formed the solid foundation on which the social structure of the herd was based. The tight-knit community of breeding cows and their calves relied heavily upon their wisdom and experience for its everyday needs and survival.

Now the two sisters moved in perfect accord to the giant acacia laden with seed pods, and each took up her position on either side of the trunk. They laid their foreheads against the rough bark. The trunk was over four feet in diameter, unyielding as a column of marble. A hundred feet above the ground the high branches formed an intricate tracery and the pods and green leaves a cathedral dome against the sky.

The two old cows began to rock back and forth in unison with the tree-trunk between their foreheads. At first the acacia was rigid, resisting even their great strength. The cows worked on doggedly, pushing and heaving, first one then the other throwing her weight in opposite directions, and a tiny shudder ran up the tree and, high above them, the top branches trembled as though a breeze had passed.

Still they worked rhythmically and the trunk began to move. A single ripe pod came loose from its twig and fell a hundred feet to crack against the skull of one of the cows. She closed her watery old eyes tightly but never broke the rhythm of her heaves. Between them the tree-trunk swayed and shuddered, ponderously at first and then more briskly. Another pod and then another plopped down as heavily as the first drops of a thunderstorm.

The younger animals of the herd realised what they were up to, flapped their ears with excitement and hurried forward. The acacia pods, rich in protein, were a favourite delicacy. They crowded gleefully around the two cows, snatching up the scattering of pods as they fell and stuffing them far down their throats with their trunks. By now the great tree was whipping back and forth, its branches waving wildly and its foliage thrashing. The pods and loose twigs showered down thick as hail, rattling and bouncing from the backs of the elephants crowded beneath.

The two cows, still braced like a pair of book ends, kept doggedly at it until the shower of falling pods began to dry up. Only when the last one was shaken from the branches did they step back from the tree-trunk. Their backs were sprinkled with dead leaves and twigs, bits of dry bark and velvety pods, and they stood ankle-deep in the fallen débris. They reached down and delicately picked out the golden pods with the dextrous fleshy tips of their trunks and curled them up into their gaping mouths, their triangular bottom lips drooping open. The ooze from their facial glands wetting their cheeks like tears of pleasure, they began to feed.

The herd was pressed closely around them at the feast that they had laid. As their long serpentine trunks swung and curled, and the pods were shovelled into their throats, there was a soft sound that seemed to reverberate through each of their great grey frames. It was a gentle rumbling in many different keys, and the sound was interspersed with tiny creaking gurgling squeaks barely audible to the human ear. It was a strangely contented chorus, in which even the youngest beasts joined. It was a sound that seemed to express joy of life and to confirm the deep bond that linked all the members of the herd.

It was the song of the elephant.

One of the old cows was the first to detect a threat to the herd. She transmitted her concern to them with a sound high above the register of the human ear and the entire herd froze into utter stillness. Even the very young calves responded instantly. The silence after the happy uproar of the feast was eerie, and the buzz of the distant spotter plane was loud in contrast.

The old cows recognised the sound of the Cessna engine. They had heard it many times over the last few years and had come to associate it with the periods of increased human activity, of tension and of unexplained terror that they felt transmitted telepathically through the wilderness from the other groups of elephant in the Park.

They knew that the sound in the air was the prelude to a popping chorus of distant gunfire and to the stench of elephant blood on the currents of heated air along the rim of the escarpment. Often after the sounds of aircraft and gunfire had faded, they had come across wide areas of the forest floor caked with dried blood, and they had smelt the odour of fear and pain and death exuded by members of their own race which still mingled with the reek of blood and of rotting entrails.

One of the old cows backed away and shook her head angrily at the sound in the sky. Her tattered ears flapped loudly against her shoulders, a sound like the mainsail of a tall ship filling with wind. Then she wheeled and led the herd away at a run.

There were two mature bulls with the herd, but at the first threat they peeled away and disappeared into the forest. Instinctively recognising that the herd was vulnerable, they sought safety in solitary flight. The younger cows and the calves bunched up behind the matriarchs and fled, the little ones racing to keep up with the longer stride of their dams; in different circumstances their haste might have been comical.

'Hello, Parks. The herd is breaking southwards towards the Imbelezi pass.'

'Roger, Sierra Mike. Please head them towards the Mana Pools turn-off.'

The old cow was leading the herd towards the hills. She wanted to get off the valley bottom into the bad ground where pursuit would be impeded by the rock and severe gradients, but the sound of the aircraft hummed across her front, cutting her off from the mouth of the pass.

She pulled up uncertainly and lifted her head to the sky, where tall silvery mountains of cumulus cloud were piled up as high as the heavens. She spread wide her ears, riven and weathered by time and thorn, and turned her ancient head to follow that dreadful sound.

Then she saw the aircraft. The early sunlight flashed from its windshield as it banked steeply across her front, and it dived back towards her, low over the tops of the forest trees, the sound of its engine rising to a roar.

The two old cows spun together and started back towards the river. Behind them the herd wheeled like an untidy mass of cavalry, and as they ran the dust rose in a fine pale cloud even higher than the treetops.

'Parks, the herd is heading your way now. Five miles from the turn-off.'

'Thank you, Sierra Mike; keep them coming nice and easy. Don't push them too hard.'

'Wilco, Parks.'

'All K-Units.' Johnny Nzou changed his call-sign. 'All K-Units, converge on the Mana Pools turn-off.'

The K-Units, or kill teams, were the four Landrovers that were deployed along the main track that ran down from Chiwewe headquarters on the escarpment to the river. Johnny had put them in as a stop line, to head off the herd if it broke awkwardly. It did not look as though that would be necessary now. The spotter plane was working the herd into position with professional expertise.

'Looks as though we'll make it on the first try,' Johnny muttered as he reversed the Landrover and swung it in a full 180-degree turn, then sent it flying down the track. A ridge of grass grew between the sandy wheel-tracks, and the Landrover rocked and rattled over the bumps. The wind whipped around their heads and Daniel pulled his hat from his head and stuffed it into his pocket.

Jock was filming over his shoulder as a herd of buffalo, disturbed by the sound of the Landrover, came pouring out of the forest and crossed the track just ahead of them.

'Damn it!' Johnny hit the brakes and glanced at his wristwatch. 'Stupid *nyati* are going to screw us up.'

Hundreds of the dark bovine shapes came in a solid phalanx, galloping heavily, raising white dust, grunting and lowing and splattering liquid green dung on the grass as they flattened it.

Within minutes they had passed and Johnny accelerated into the standing dust-cloud and rattled over the loose earth that the herd had ploughed up with their great cloven hoofs. Around a bend in the track they saw the other vehicles parked at the crossroads. The four rangers were standing in a group beside them, rifles in their hands and faces turned back expectantly.

Johnny skidded the Landrover to a halt and snatched up the microphone of his radio. 'Sierra Mike, give me a position report, please.'

'Parks, the herd is two miles from you, just approaching Long Vlei.'

A vlei is a depression of open grassland, and Long Vlei ran for miles parallel to the river. In the rainy season it was a marsh, but now it made an ideal killing ground. They had used it before.

Johnny jumped down from the driver's seat and lifted his rifle from the rack. He and all his rangers were armed with cheap mass-produced .375 magnums loaded with solid ammunition for maximum penetration of bone and tissue. His men were chosen for this work on account of their superior marks-

16

manship. The kill must be as swift and humane as possible. They would shoot for the brain and not take the easier but lingering body shot.

'Let's go!' Johnny snapped. There was no need to give instructions. These were tough young professionals, yet even though they had done this work many times before their expressions were sombre. There was no excitement, no anticipation in their eyes. This was not sport. They clearly did not enjoy the prospect of the bloody work ahead.

They were stripped down to shorts and velskoen without socks, light running gear. The only heavy items they carried were their cheap weapons and the bandoliers of ammunition strapped around their waists. All of them were lean and muscled, and Johnny Nzou was as hard as any of them. They ran to meet the herd.

Daniel fell into position behind Johnny Nzou. He believed that he had kept himself fit with regular running and training, but he had forgotten what it was like to be hunting and fighting fit as were Johnny and his rangers.

They ran like hounds, streaming through the forest effortlessly, their feet seeming to find their own way between scrub and rock and fallen branches and antbear holes. They barely touched the earth in passing. Daniel had run like that once, but now his boots were slamming down heavily and he stumbled once or twice in the rough footing. He and the camera man began to fall behind.

Johnny Nzou gave a hand signal and his rangers fanned out into a long skirmish line, fifty yards separating each of them. Ahead, the forest gave way abruptly to the open glade of Long Vlei. It was three hundred yards wide; the dry beige-coloured grass was waist-high.

The line of killers stopped at the edge of the forest and looked to Johnny at the centre, but his head was thrown back, watching the spotter plane out there above the forest. It was banking steeply, standing vertically on one wing.

Daniel caught up with him, and found that both he and Jock were panting heavily although they had run less than a mile. He envied Johnny.

'There they are,' Johnny called softly. 'You can see the dust.'

17

It lay in a haze on the treetops between them and the circling aircraft. 'Coming on fast.'

Johnny windmilled his right arm and obediently his skirmish line extended and shifted into a concave shape like the horns of a bull buffalo with Johnny at the centre. At the next signal they trotted forward into the glade.

The light breeze was in their faces; the herd would not scent them. Although originally the herd had instinctively fled into the wind so as not to run into danger, the aircraft had turned them back downwind.

The elephant's eyesight is not sharp; they would make nothing of the line of human figures until it was too late. The trap was set and the elephants were coming straight into it, chivvied and sheep-dogged by the low-flying Cessna.

The two old cows burst out of the tree-line at full run, their bony legs flying, ears cocked back, loose grey folds of skin shuddering and wobbling with each jarring footfall. The rest of the herd were strung out behind them. The youngest calves were tiring, and their mothers pushed them along with their trunks.

The line of executioners froze, standing in a half circle like the mouth of a gill net extended to take in a shoal of fish. The elephants would pick up movement more readily than they would recognise the blurred man-shapes that their weak, panic-stricken eyes disclosed to them.

'Get the two old grannies first,' Johnny called softly. He had recognised the matriarchs and he knew that with them gone the herd would be disorganised and indecisive. His order was passed down the line.

The leading cows pounded down directly towards where Johnny stood. He let them come on. He held the rifle at high port across his chest. At a hundred yards' distance the two dowager elephants started to turn away from him, angling off to the left, and Johnny moved for the first time.

He lifted his rifle and waved it over his head and shouted in Sindebele, '*Nanzi Inkosikaze* – here I am, respected old lady.'

For the first time the two elephants recognised that he was not a tree-stump but a deadly enemy. Instantly they swung back towards him, and focusing all their ancestral hatred and

18

terror and concern for the herd upon him, they burst together into full charge.

They squealed their fury at him, extending their stride so that the dust spurted from under their colossal footpads. Their ears were rolled back along the top edge, sure sign of their anger. They towered over the group of tiny human figures. Daniel wished vehemently that he had taken the precaution of arming himself. He had forgotten how terrifying this moment was, with the nearest cow only fifty yards away and coming straight in at forty miles an hour.

Jock was still filming, although the angry shrieks of the two cows had been taken up by the entire herd. They came down upon them like an avalanche of grey granite, as though a cliff had been brought rumbling down with high explosive.

At thirty yards Johnny Nzou mounted the rifle to his shoulder and leaned forward to absorb the recoil. There was no telescopic sight mounted above the blue steel barrel. For close work like this he was using open express sights.

Since its introduction in 1912, thousands of sports and professional hunters had proved the .375 Holland & Holland to be the most versatile and effective rifle ever to have been brought to Africa. It had all the virtues of inherent accuracy and moderate recoil, while the 300-grain solid bullet was a ballistic marvel, with flat trajectory and extraordinary penetration.

Johnny aimed at the head of the leading cow, at the crease of the trunk between her myopic old eyes. The report was sharp as the lash of a bull-whip, and an ostrich feather of dust flew from the surface of her weathered grey skin at the precise point upon her skull at which he had aimed.

The bullet sliced through her head as easily as a steel nail driven through a ripe apple. It obliterated the top of her brain, and the cow's front legs folded under her, and Daniel felt the earth jump under his feet as she crashed down in a cloud of dust.

Johnny swung his aim on to the second cow, just as she came level with the carcass of her sister. He reloaded without taking the butt of the rifle from his shoulder, merely flicking the bolt back and forward. The spent brass case was flung high in a glinting parabola and he fired again. The sound of the two rifle shots blended into each other; they were fired so swiftly as to cheat the ear into hearing a single prolonged detonation.

Once again the bullet struck exactly where it had been aimed and the cow died as the other had done, instantaneously. Her legs collapsed and she dropped and lay on her belly with her shoulder touching that of her sister. In the centre of each of their foreheads a misty pink plume of blood erupted from the tiny bullet-holes.

Behind them the herd was thrown into confusion. The bewildered beasts milled and circled, treading the grass flat and raising a curtain of dust that swirled about them, blanketing the scene so their forms looked ethereal and indistinct in the dust-cloud. The calves huddled for shelter beneath their mothers' bellies, their ears flattened against their skulls with terror, and they were battered and kicked and thrown about by the frantic movements of their dams.

The rangers closed in, firing steadily. The sound of gunfire was a long continuous rattle, like hail on a tin roof. They were shooting for the brain. At each shot one of the animals flinched or flung up its head, as the solid bullets cracked on the bone of the skull with the sound of a well-struck golf ball. At each shot one of the animals went down dead or stunned. Those killed cleanly, and they were the majority, collapsed at the back legs first and dropped with the dead weight of a maize sack. When the bullet missed the brain but passed close to it, the elephant reeled and staggered and went down kicking to roll on its side with a terrible despairing moan and grope helplessly at the sky with lifted trunk.

One of the young calves was trapped and pinned beneath its mother's collapsing carcass, and lay broken-backed and squealing in a mixture of pain and panic. Some of the elephant found themselves hemmed in by a palisade of fallen animals and they reared up and tried to scramble over them. The marksmen shot them down so that they fell upon the bodies of those already dead, while others tried to climb over these and were in their turn shot down.

It was swift. Within minutes all the adult animals were down, lying close together or piled upon each other in bleeding mounds and hillocks. Only the calves were still racing in bewildered circles, stumbling over the bodies of the dead and dying, squealing and tugging at the carcasses of their mothers.

The riflemen walked forward slowly, a tightening ring of gunmetal around the decimated herd. They fired and reloaded and fired again as they closed in. They picked off the calves, and when there remained not a single standing animal, they moved quickly into the herd, scrambling over the gigantic sprawling bodies, pausing only to fire a finishing bullet into each huge bleeding head. Most often there was no response to the second bullet in the brain, but occasionally an elephant not yet dead shuddered and straightened its limbs and blinked its eyes at the shot, then slumped lifelessly.

Within six minutes of Johnny's first shot, a silence fell over the killing ground on Long Vlei. Only their ears still sang to the brutal memory of gunfire. There was no movement; the elephant lay in windrows like wheat behind the blades of the mower, and the dry earth soaked up the blood. The rangers were still standing apart from each other, subdued and awed by the havoc they had wrought, staring with remorse at the mountain of the dead. Fifty elephant, two hundred tons of carnage.

Johnny Nzou broke the tragic spell that held them. He walked slowly to where the two old cows lay at the head of the herd. They lay side by side, shoulders touching, with their legs folded neatly under them, kneeling as though still alive with only the pulsing fountain of life-blood from their foreheads to spoil the illusion.

Johnny set the butt of his rifle on the ground and leaned upon it, studying the two old matriarchs for a long regretful moment. He was unaware that Jock was filming him. His actions and his words were completely unstudied and unrehearsed.

'Hamba gahle, Amakhulu,' he whispered. 'Go in peace, old grandmothers. You are together in death as you were in life. Go in peace, and forgive us for what we have done to your tribe.'

He walked away to the edge of the tree-line. Daniel did not follow him. He understood that Johnny wanted to be alone for a while now. The other rangers also avoided each other. There was no banter, nor self-congratulation; two of them wandered amongst the mountainous dead with a strangely disconsolate air; a third squatted where he had fired his last shot, smoking a cigarette and studying the dusty ground between his feet, while the last one had laid aside his rifle and, with hands thrust in his pockets and shoulders hunched, stared at the sky and watched the vultures gather.

At first the carrion birds were tiny specks against the glaring alps of cumulus cloud, like grains of pepper sprinkled on a tablecloth. Then they soared closer overhead, forming circling squadrons, turning on their wide wings in orderly formations, a dark wheel of death high above the killing-ground, and their shadows flitted over the piled carcasses in the centre of Long Vlei.

Forty minutes later Daniel heard the rumble of the approaching trucks, and saw them coming slowly through the forest. A squad of half-naked axemen ran ahead of the convoy, cutting out the brush and making a rough track for them to follow. Johnny stood up with obvious relief from where he had been sitting alone at the edge of the trees, and came to take charge of the butchering.

The piles of dead elephant were pulled apart with winches and chains. Then the wrinkled grey skin was sliced through down the length of the belly and the spine. Again the electric winches were brought into play and the skin was flensed off the carcass with a crackling sound as the subcutaneous tissue released its grip. It came off in long slabs, grey and corrugated on the outside, gleaming white on the inside. The men laid each strip on the dusty earth and heaped coarse salt upon it.

The naked carcasses looked strangely obscene in the bright sunlight, wet and marbled with white fat and exposed scarlet muscle, the swollen bellies bulging as though to invite the stroke of the flensing knives.

A skinner slipped the curved point of the knife into the belly of one of the old cows at the point where it met the sternum. Carefully controlling the depth of the cut so as not to puncture the entrails, he walked the length of the body drawing the blade like a zipper down the belly pouch so that it gaped open and the stomach sac bulged out, glistening like the silk of a para-

22

chute. Then the colossal coils of the intestines slithered after it. These seemed to have a separate life. Like the body of an awakening python, they twisted and unfolded under the impetus of their own slippery weight.

The chainsaw men set to work. The intrusive clatter of the two-stroke engines seemed almost sacrilegious in this place of death, and the exhausts blew snorting blue smoke into the bright air. They lopped the limbs off each carcass, and a fine mush of flesh and bone chips flew in a spray from the teeth of the spinning steel chains. Then they buzzed through the spine and ribs, and the carcasses fell into separate parts that were winched into the waiting refrigerator trucks.

A special gang went from carcass to carcass with long boat-hooks, poking in the soft wet mounds of spilled entrails to drag out the wombs of the females. Daniel watched as they split open one of the engorged wombs, dark purple with its covering of enlarged blood vessels. From the foetal sac, in a flood of amniotic fluid the foetus, the size of a large dog, slid out and lay in the trampled grass.

It was only a few weeks from term, a perfect little elephant covered with a coat of reddish hair that it would have lost soon after birth. It was still alive, moving its trunk feebly.

'Kill it,' Daniel ordered harshly in Sindebele. It was improbable that it could feel pain, but he turned away in relief as one of the men struck off the tiny head with a single blow of his panga. Daniel felt nauseated, but he knew that nothing from the cull should be wasted. The skin of the unborn elephant would be fine-grained and valuable, worth a few hundred dollars for a handbag or a briefcase.

To distract himself he walked away across the killing-ground. All that remained now were the heads of the great animals and the glistening piles of their entrails. From the guts nothing of value could be salvaged and they would be left for the vultures and hyena and jackal.

The ivory tusks, still embedded in their castles of bone, were the most precious part of the cull. The poachers and the ivory-hunters of old would not risk damaging them with a careless axe-stroke, and customarily would leave the ivory in the skull until the cartilaginous sheath that held it secure rotted and softened and released its grip. Within four or five days the tusks could usually be drawn by hand, perfect and unmarked. However, there was no time to waste on this procedure. The tusks must be cut out by hand.

The skinners who did this were the most experienced men, usually older, with grey woolly heads and blood-stained loincloths. They squatted beside the heads and tapped patiently with their native axes.

While they were engaged in this painstaking work Daniel stood with Johnny Nzou. Jock held the Sony VTR on them as Daniel commented, 'Gory work.'

'But necessary,' Johnny agreed shortly. 'On an average each adult elephant will yield about three thousand dollars in ivory, skin and meat.'

'To many people that will sound pretty commercial, especially as they have just witnessed the hard reality of the cull.' Daniel shook his head. 'You must know that there is a very strong campaign, led by the animal rights groups, to have the elephant placed on Appendix One of CITES, that is the Convention on International Trade in Endangered Species.'

'Yes, I know.'

'If that happens it would prohibit the trade in any elephant products, skin, ivory or meat. What do you think of that, Warden?'

'It makes me very angry.' Johnny dropped his cigarette and ground it under his heel. His expression was savage.

'It would prevent any further culling operations, wouldn't it?' Daniel persisted.

'Not at all,' Johnny contradicted him. 'We would still be forced to control the size of the herds. We would still be forced to cull. The only difference would be that we could not sell the elephant products. They would be wasted, a tragic criminal waste. We would lose millions of dollars of revenue which at present is being used to protect and enlarge and service the wildlife sanctuaries ...' Johnny broke off and watched as a tusk was lifted out of the channel in the spongy bone of the skull by two of the skinners and laid carefully on the dry brown grass. Skilfully one of them drew the nerve, a soft grey gelatinous core, from the hollow end of the tusk. Then Johnny went on, 'That tusk makes it easier for us to justify the continued existence of the Parks and the animals they contain to the local tribespeople living in close contact with wild animals on and near the boundaries of the national wilderness areas.'

'I don't understand,' Daniel encouraged him. 'Do you mean the local tribes resent the Parks and the animal population?'

'Not if they can derive some personal benefit from them. If we can prove to them that a cow elephant is worth three thousand dollars and that a foreign safari hunter will spend fifty or even a hundred thousand dollars to hunt a trophy bull, if we can show them that a single elephant is worth a hundred, even a thousand of their goats or scrawny cattle and that they will see some of that money coming to them and their tribe, then they will see the point of conserving the herds.'

'You mean the local peasants do not place a value on wildlife simply for its own sake.'

Johnny laughed bitterly. 'That's a First World luxury and affectation. The tribes here live very close to subsistence level. We are talking about an average family income of a hundred and twenty dollars a year, ten dollars a month. They cannot afford to set aside land and grazing for a beautiful but useless animal to live on. If the wild game is to survive in Africa it has to pay for its supper. There are no free rides in this harsh land.'

'One would think that living so close to nature they would have an instinctive feeling for it,' Daniel persisted.

'Yes, of course, but it is totally pragmatic. For millennia primitive man, living with nature, has treated it as a renewable resource. As the Eskimo lived on the caribou and seal and whale, or the American Indian on buffalo herds, they understood instinctively the type of management that we have never achieved. They were in balance with nature, until the white man came with explosive harpoon and Sharpe's rifle, or, here in Africa, came with his elite game department and game laws that made it a crime for the black tribesman to hunt on his own land, that reserved the wildlife of Africa for a select few to stare at and exclaim over.'

'You are being a racist,' Daniel chided him gently. 'The old colonial system preserved the wild game.'

'So how did it survive for a million years before the white

man arrived in Africa? No, the colonial system of game management was protectionist, not conservationist.'

'Aren't they the same thing, protection and conservation?'

'They are diametrically opposed. The protectionist denies man's right to exploit and harvest nature's bounty. He would deny that man has a right to kill a living animal, even if that threatens the survival of the species as a whole. If he were here today, the protectionist would prohibit us from this cull, and he would not want to look to the final consequence of that prohibition which, as we have seen, would be the eventual extinction of the entire elephant population and the destruction of this forest.

'However, the most damaging mistake that the old colonial protectionists made was to alienate the black tribesman from the benefits of controlled conservation. They denied him his share of the spoils, and built up in him a resentment towards the wild game. They broke down his natural instinct for management of his resources. They took away his control of nature and placed him in competition with the animals. The end result is that the average black peasant is hostile towards the game. The elephants raid his gardens and destroy the trees he uses for firewood. The buffalo and antelope eat the grass on which he feeds his cattle. The crocodile ate his grandmother, and the lion killed his father . . . Of course, he has come to resent the game herds.'

'The solution, Warden? Is there one?'

'Since independence from the colonial system we have been trying to change the attitude of our people,' Johnny told him. 'At first they demanded that they be allowed to enter the National Parks that the white man had proclaimed. They wanted to be allowed to go in and cut the trees and feed their cattle and build their villages. However, we have had a great deal of success in educating them to the value of tourism and safari-hunting and controlled culling. For the first time they are being allowed to participate in the profits, and there is a new understanding of conservation and sensible exploitation, especially amongst the younger generation. However, if the protectionist do-gooders of Europe and America were to force a ban on safari-hunting or the sale of ivory, it would set back all our efforts. It would probably be the death knell of the African elephant and eventually the end of all the game.'

'So in the end it is all a matter of economics?' Daniel asked.

'Like everything else in this world, it is a matter of money,' Johnny agreed. 'If you give us enough money we will stop the poachers. If you make it worth their while, we will keep the peasants and their goats out of the Parks. However, the money must come from somewhere. The newly independent states of Africa with their exploding human populations cannot afford the First World luxury of locking away their natural assets. They must exploit them and conserve them. If you prevent us doing that, then you will be guilty of contributing to the extinction of African wildlife.' Johnny nodded grimly. 'Yes, it's a matter of economics. If the game can pay, then the game can stay.'

It was perfect, Daniel signalled Jock to stop filming and clasped Johnny's shoulder.

'I could make a star out of you. You're a natural.' He was only half joking. 'How about it, Johnny? You could do a hell of a lot more for Africa on the screen than you can here.'

'You want me to live in hotels and jet aircraft instead of sleeping under the stars?' Johnny feigned indignation. 'You want me to build up a nice little roll around my belly.' He prodded Daniel's midriff. 'And puff and pant when I run a hundred yards? No thank you, Danny. I'll stay here where I can drink Zambezi water, not Coca-Cola, and eat buffalo steaks, not Big Macs.'

They loaded the last rolls of salted elephant-hide and immature calf tusks by the glare of truck headlights, and climbed back up the rough winding road to the rim of the escarpment and the headquarters of the Park at Chiwewe in the dark.

Johnny drove the green Landrover at the head of the slow convoy of refrigerator trucks and Daniel sat beside him on the front seat. They talked in the soft desultory manner of old friends in perfect accord.

'Suicide weather,' Daniel wiped his forehead on the sleeve of his bush shirt. Even though it was almost midnight, the heat and the humidity were enervating. 'Rains will break soon.'

'Good thing you're getting out of the valley,' Johnny grunted.

27

'That road turns into a swamp in the rain and most of the rivers are impassable.'

The tourist camp at Chiwewe had been closed a week previously in anticipation of the onslaught of the rainy season.

'I don't look forward to leaving,' Daniel admitted. 'It's been like old times again.'

'Old times,' Johnny nodded. 'We had some fun. When are you coming back to Chiwewe?'

'I don't know, Johnny, but my offer is genuine. Come with me. We made a good team once; we would be good again. I know it.'

'Thanks, Danny.' Johnny shook his head. 'But I've got work to do here.'

'I won't give up,' Daniel warned him, and Johnny grinned.

'I know. You never do.'

In the morning, when Daniel climbed the small kopje behind the headquarters camp to watch the sunrise, the sky was filled with dark and mountainous cloud and the heat was still oppressive.

Daniel's mood matched that sombre dawn, for although he had captured some wonderful material during his stay, he had also rediscovered his friendship and affection for Johnny Nzou. The knowledge that it might be many years before they met again saddened him.

Johnny had invited him to breakfast on this, his last day. He was waiting for Daniel on the wide mosquito-screened verandah of the thatched bungalow that had once been Daniel's own home.

Daniel paused below the verandah and glanced around the garden. It was still the way that Vicky had planned it and originally laid it out. Vicky had been the twenty-year-old bride that Daniel had brought to Chiwewe all those years ago, a slim cheerful lass with long blonde hair and smiling green eyes, only a few years younger than Daniel at the time.

She had died in the front bedroom overlooking the garden

that she had cherished. An ordinary bout of malaria had turned without warning to the pernicious cerebral strain. It had been all over very swiftly, even before the flying doctor could reach the Park.

The eerie sequel to her death was that the elephants, who had never entered the fenced garden before, despite its laden citrus trees and rich vegetable plot, came that very night. They came at the exact hour of Vicky's death and completely laid waste the garden. They even ripped out the ornamental shrubs and rose bushes. Elephant seem to have a psychic sensitivity to death. It was almost as if they had sensed her passing, and Daniel's grief.

Daniel had never married again and had left Chiwewe not long after. The memories of Vicky were too painful to allow him to remain. Now Johnny Nzou lived in the bungalow and his pretty Matabele wife Mavis tended Vicky's garden. If Daniel had been able to choose, he would have had it no other way.

This morning Mavis had prepared a traditional Matabele breakfast of maize porridge and sour milk, thickened in a calabash gourd, the beloved *amasi* of the Nguni pastoral tribes. Afterwards, Johnny and Daniel walked down towards the ivory godown together. Halfway down the hill Daniel checked and shaded his eyes as he stared towards the visitors' camp. This was the game-fenced area on the river bank where the thatched cottages with circular walls stood under the wild fig trees. These structures, peculiar to southern Africa, were known as rondavels.

'I thought you told me that the Park was closed to visitors,' Daniel said. 'One of the rondavels is still occupied, and there's a car parked outside it.'

'That's a special guest, a diplomat, the Ambassador of the Taiwanese Republic of China to Harare,' Johnny explained. 'He is extremely interested in wildlife, particularly elephants, and has contributed a great deal to conservation in this country. We allow him special privileges. He wanted to be here without other tourists, so I kept the camp open for him—' Johnny broke off, then exclaimed, 'There he is now!'

Three men stood in a group at the foot of the hill. It was still too far to make out their features. As they started towards them, Daniel asked, 'What happened to the two white rangers who helped with the cull yesterday?'

'They were on loan from Wankie National Park. They left to go home early this morning.'

Closer to the group of three men Daniel made out the Taiwanese ambassador.

He was younger than he would have expected a man of such rank to be. Although it was often difficult for a Westerner to judge the age of an oriental, Daniel put him at a little over forty. He was tall and lean with straight black hair that was oiled and combed back from a high intelligent forehead. He was good-looking with a clear, almost waxen, complexion. There was something about his features that suggested that his ancestry was not pure Chinese, but mixed with European blood. Though his eyes were liquid jet-black in colour, their shape was rounded and his upper eyelids lacked the character-istic fold of skin at the inner corner.

'Good morning, Your Excellency,' Johnny greeted him with obvious respect. 'Warm enough for you?'

'Good morning, Warden.' The ambassador left the two black rangers and came to meet them. 'I prefer it to the cold.' He was wearing an open-necked short-sleeved blue shirt and slacks, and indeed looked cool and elegant.

'May I present Doctor Daniel Armstrong?' Johnny asked. 'Daniel, His Excellency the Ambassador of Taiwan, Ning Cheng Gong.'

'No introduction is necessary, Doctor Armstrong is a famous man.' Cheng smiled charmingly as he took Daniel's hand. 'I have read your books and watched your television programmes with the greatest of interest and pleasure.' His English was excellent, as though he were born to the language, and Daniel warmed to him.

'Johnny tells me that you are very concerned about the African ecology, and that you have made a great contribution to conservation in this country.'

Cheng made a deprecatory gesture. 'I only wish I could do more.' But he was staring at Daniel thoughtfully. 'Forgive me, Doctor Armstrong, but I did not expect to find other visitors at Chiwewe at this time of year. I was assured that the Park was closed.'

Although his tone was friendly, Daniel sensed that the question was not an idle one.

'Don't worry, Your Excellency. My camera man and I are leaving this afternoon. You will soon have the whole of Chiwewe to yourself,' Daniel assured him.

'Oh, please don't misunderstand me. I am not so selfish as to wish you gone. In fact, I am sorry to hear you are leaving so soon. I am sure we would have had a great deal to discuss.' Despite the denial, Daniel sensed that Cheng was relieved that he was leaving. His expression was still warm and his manner friendly, but Daniel was becoming aware of depths and layers below the urbane exterior.

The ambassador fell in between them, as they walked down to the ivory warehouse, and chatted in a relaxed manner, and then stood aside to watch as the rangers and a team of porters began to unload the newly culled ivory from the truck parked at the door to the warehouse. By this time Jock was there with his Sony camera filming the work from every angle.

As each tusk was brought out, still crusted with freshly congealed blood, it was weighed on the old-fashioned platform scale that stood at the entrance to the warehouse. Johnny Nzou sat at a rickety deal table and recorded the weight of each tusk in a thick leather-bound ledger. He then allocated a registration number to it and one of his rangers stamped that number into the ivory with a set of steel dies. Registered and stamped, the tusk was now legal ivory and could be auctioned and exported from the country.

Cheng watched the procedure with a lively interest. One pair of tusks, although not heavy or massive, was of particular beauty. They were delicately proportioned shafts with fine grain and elegant curves, an identical and perfectly matched pair.

Cheng stepped forward and squatted beside them as they lay on the scale. He stroked them with a lover's sensual touch. 'Perfect,' he purred. 'A natural work of art.' He broke off as he noticed Daniel watching him.

Daniel had been vaguely repelled by this display of cupidity, and it showed on his face.

Cheng stood up and explained smoothly. 'I have always been

fascinated by ivory. As you probably know, we Chinese consider it to be a highly propitious substance. Few Chinese households are without any ivory carving; it brings good luck to its owner. However, my family interest goes even deeper than common superstition. My father began his working life as an ivory-carver, and so great was his skill that by the time I was born he owned shops in Taipei and Bangkok, Tokyo and Hong Kong, all of them specialising in ivory artefacts. Some of my earliest memories are of the look and feel of ivory. As a boy, I worked as an apprentice ivory-carver in the store in Taipei, and I came to love and understand ivory as my father does. He has one of the most extensive and valuable collections ...' he stopped himself. 'Forgive me, please. I sometimes get carried away by my passion, but that is a particularly beautiful set of tusks. It is very rare to find a pair so perfectly matched. My father would be ecstatic over them.'

He watched longingly as the tusks were carried away and packed with the hundreds of others in the warehouse.

'Interesting character,' Daniel remarked, after the last tusk had been registered and locked away, and he and Johnny were making their way up the hill to the bungalow for lunch. 'But how does the son of an ivory-carver get to be an ambassador?'

Johnny chuckled. 'Ning Cheng Gong's father may have come from a humble background, but he didn't remain there. I understand he still has his ivory shops and his collection, but those are merely his hobbies now. He is reputed to be one of the richest men, if not *the* richest man, in Taiwan – and that, as you can imagine, is very rich indeed. From what I hear he has his fingers in all the juiciest pies around the Pacific rim as well as some in Africa. He has a large family of sons and Cheng is the youngest and, they say, the brightest. I like him, don't you?'

'Yes, he seems pleasant enough, but there is just something a little odd. Did you notice his face as he fondled that tusk? It was,' Daniel searched for the word, 'unnatural?'

'You writers!' Johnny shook his head ruefully. 'If you can't find something sensational, you make it up.' And they both laughed.

Ning Cheng Gong stood with one of the black rangers at the foot of the hill and watched Daniel and Johnny disappear amongst the msasa trees.

'I do not like the white man being here,' said Gomo. Under Johnny Nzou, he was Chiwewe's senior ranger. 'Perhaps we should wait until another time.'

'The white man leaves this afternoon,' Cheng told him coldly. 'Besides which you have been well paid. Plans have been made that cannot be altered now. The others are already on their way and cannot be sent back.'

'You have only paid us half of what we agreed,' Gomo protested.

'The other half when your work is done, not before,' Cheng said softly, and Gomo's eyes were like the eyes of a snake. 'You know what you have to do,' Cheng went on.

Gomo was silent for a moment. The foreigner had indeed paid him a thousand US dollars, the equivalent of six months' salary, with the promise of another year's salary to follow after the job was done.

'You will do it?' Cheng insisted.

'Yes,' Gomo agreed. 'I will do it.'

Cheng nodded. 'It will be tonight or tomorrow night, not later. Be ready, both of you.'

'We will be ready,' Gomo promised, and climbed into his Landrover, where the second black ranger waited, and they drove away.

Cheng walked back to his rondavel in the deserted visitors' camp. The cottage was identical to the other thirty which during the dry cool season usually housed a full complement of tourists. He fetched a cool drink from the refrigerator and sat on the screen porch to wait out the hottest hours of the noonday.

He felt nervous and restless. Deep down he shared Gomo's misgivings about the project. Although they had considered every possible eventuality and planned for each of them, there was always the unforeseeable, the unpredictable, such as the presence of Armstrong.

It was the first time he had attempted a *coup* of this magnitude. It was his own initiative. Of course, his father knew about and thoroughly approved of the other lesser shipments, but the risk was far greater this time, in proportion to the rewards. If he succeeded he would earn his father's respect, and that was more important to him even than the material profits. He was the youngest son, and he had to strive that much harder to win his place in his father's affections. For that reason alone he must not fail.

In the years that he had been at the embassy in Harare, he had consolidated his place in the illicit ivory and rhino-horn trade. It had begun with a deceptively casual remark at a dinner-party by a middle-ranking government official about the convenience of diplomatic privilege and access to the diplomatic courier service. With the business training that his father had given him, Cheng recognised the approach immediately for what it was, and made a non-committal but encouraging response.

A week of delicate negotiations followed and then Cheng was invited to play golf with another higher official. His driver parked the ambassadorial Mercedes in the car park at the rear of the Harare golf club and as instructed left it unattended while Cheng was out on the course. Cheng was officially a ten-handicap golfer but could play well below that when he chose. On this occasion he allowed his opponent to win three thousand US dollars and paid him in cash in front of witnesses in the club house. When he returned to his official residence he ordered the driver to park the Mercedes in the garage and then dismissed him. In the boot he found six large rhino horns packed in layers of hessian cloth.

He sent these out in the next diplomatic pouch to Taipei and they were sold through his father's shop in Hong Kong for sixty thousand US dollars. His father was delighted with the transaction and wrote Cheng a long letter of approbation and reminded his son of his deep interest in, and love of, ivory.

Cheng let it be known discreetly that he was a connoisseur of ivory as well as of rhino horn, and he was offered at bargain prices various pieces of unregistered and unstamped ivory. It did not take long for the word to spread in the small closed world of the poachers that there was a new buyer in the field.

Within months he was approached by a Sikh businessman from Malawi who was ostensibly looking for Taiwanese investment in a fishing venture that he was promoting on Lake Malawi. Their first meeting went very well. Cheng found that

Chetti Singh's figures added up attractively, and passed them on to his father in Taipei. His father approved the estimates and agreed a joint venture with Chetti Singh. When the documents were signed at the embassy, Cheng invited him to dinner, and during the meal Chetti Singh remarked, 'I understand that your illustrious father is loving very much the beautiful ivory. As a token of my utmost esteem I could be arranging for a regular supply. I am sure that you would be forwarding the goods to your father without too much scarlet tape. Most miserably the ivory will be unstamped, never mind.'

'I have a deep distaste for red tape,' Cheng assured him.

Within a short time it became obvious to Cheng that Chetti Singh was head of a network that operated in all those African countries that still had healthy populations of elephant and rhino. From Botswana and Angola, Zambia, Tanzania and Mozambique, he gathered in the white gold and the horn. He controlled all aspects of his organisation down to the actual composition of the armed gangs who raided regularly into the National Parks in those countries.

At first Cheng was merely another customer of his, but once the fishing partnership on Lake Malawi began to flourish and they were netting hundreds of tons of tiny kapenta fish each week, drying them and exporting them to the east, their relationship began to change. It became more cordial and trusting. Finally Chetti Singh offered Cheng and his father a proprietary stake in the ivory trade. Naturally he asked for a substantial investment to allow him to expand the scope and range of the partnership's operations, and another larger payment for his share of goodwill in the enterprise. In all, it amounted to almost a million dollars. Cheng, on his father's behalf, was able by astute bargaining to reduce this initial fee by fifty per cent.

Only once he was a full partner could Cheng appreciate the extent and range of the operation. In each of the countries which still harboured elephant herds, Chetti Singh had been able to put in place clandestine circles of accomplices in government. Many of his contacts went as high as ministerial level. Within most of the major National Parks he had informers and officials on his payroll. Some were merely game scouts or rangers, but others were the actual chief wardens in charge of the Parks, those appointed as guardians and protectors of the herds.

The partnership was so lucrative that when Cheng's original term of appointment as ambassador expired, his father arranged through friends high in the Taiwanese government for it to be extended for a further three-year term.

By this time Cheng's father and brothers had become fully aware of the investment opportunities that Africa offered. Beginning with the small but profitable fishing venture and then the ivory partnership, the family had been attracted more and more to the dark continent. Neither Cheng nor his father had any scruples about apartheid and began investing heavily in South Africa. They were well aware that world condemnation and the policy of economic sanctions had depressed the prices of land and other valuable assets in that country to a point where no sensible businessman could resist them.

'Honoured parent,' Cheng had told his father on one of his frequent returns to Taipei, 'within ten years apartheid and white minority rule will have passed from the face of the land. Once that happens, prices in South Africa will rise to find their true levels.'

They purchased great ranches of tens of thousands of acres for the same price as a three-room flat in Taipei. They purchased factories and office blocks and shopping centres from American companies forced by their government to disinvest from South Africa. They paid five and ten cents for a dollar's worth of value.

However, Cheng's father, who had been among other things a steward of the Hong Kong race club, was too astute a gambler to place all his bets on a single horse. They invested in other African countries. An agreement had just been negotiated between South Africa and Cuba and Angola and America for the independence of Namibia. The family invested in property in Windhoek and fishing licences and mineral rights in that country. Through Chetti Singh, Cheng was introduced to ministers of government in Zambia and Zaïre and Kenya and Tanzania who for financial considerations were inclined to look favourably on Taiwanese investment in their countries, at prices which Cheng's father found acceptable.

Nevertheless, despite all these other major investments, Cheng's father, for sentimental reasons, was still drawn to the original ivory venture which had first provoked his interest in the dark continent. At their last meeting he had remarked to Cheng, as his son knelt in front of him to ask his blessing, 'My son, it would please me greatly if, once you return to Africa, you were able to find a large quantity of registered and stamped ivory.'

'Illustrious father, the only sources of legal ivory are the government auctions—' Cheng broke off as he saw his father's expression of scorn.

'Ivory purchased at government auctions leaves very little margin of profit,' the old man hissed. 'I had expected you to show better sense than that, my son.' His father's censure rankled deeply, and Cheng spoke to Chetti Singh at the very next opportunity.

Chetti Singh stroked his rolled beard thoughtfully. He was a handsome man and the immaculate white turban added to his stature. 'I am now thinking of but one single solitary source of registered ivory,' he said. 'And that is being the government warehouse.'

'You are suggesting that the ivory might be taken from the warehouse before the auction?'

'Perhaps . . .' Chetti Singh shrugged, 'but it would be calling for great and meticulous laying of plans. Let me run my mind over and around this vexing problem.'

Three weeks later they met again at Chetti Singh's office in Lilongwe.

'I have occupied my mind greatly, and a solution has occurred to me,' the Sikh told him.

'How much will it cost?' Cheng's first question was instinctive.

'Kilo for kilo, no more than the acquisition of unregistered ivory, but as there will be only opportunity to procure a single and solitary shipment we will be wise to be making it as large as possible. The contents of an entire warehouse, never mind! How would your father be struck by that?'

Cheng knew his father would be delighted. Registered ivory had three or four times the value of illicit ivory in the international market-place.

'Let us consider which country will provide us with this merchandise,' Chetti Singh suggested, but it was obvious that he had already decided. 'Not Zaïre or South Africa. Those are two countries where I do not have an effective organisation. Zambia and Tanzania and Kenya have very little ivory remaining. We are left with Botswana, where there is no large-scale culling, or finally Zimbabwe.'

'Good,' Cheng nodded with satisfaction.

'The ivory is accumulated in the game department warehouses at Wankie and Harare and Chiwewe until is being undertaken the bi-annual auction. We would acquire the merchandise from one of those centres.'

'Which one?'

'The warehouse in Harare is too well guarded.' Chetti Singh held up three fingers of his one hand and, having discarded Harare, he folded one down, leaving two fingers raised. 'Wankie is the largest National Park. However, it is far from the Zambian border.' He folded down another finger. 'Which leaves Chiwewe. I have trustworthy agents on the Park's staff there. They tell me that the warehouse is almost full of registered ivory at the present time, and the Park headquarters are less than thirty miles from the Zambezi River and the Zambian border. One of my teams could cross the river and be there in a day's march, never mind!'

'You intend to rob the warehouse?' Cheng leaned forward over his desk.

'Without the shade or fraction of a doubt.' Chetti Singh lowered his raised finger and looked surprised. 'Was that not also your intention all along?'

'Perhaps,' Cheng replied carefully. 'But is it feasible?'

'Chiwewe is in a remote and isolated area of the country but it lies on the river, which is an international boundary. I would send in a raiding party of twenty men armed absolutely with automatic weapons and led by one of my best and most reliable hunters. In darkness they cross the river from Zambia in canoes and in a day's hard marching they reach the Park's headquarters and fall upon it. They dispose of all witnesses . . .'

Cheng coughed nervously and Chetti Singh paused and looked at him questioningly. 'These would not amount to more than four or five persons. The permanent rangers are in my pay. The visitors' camp will be closed against the rainy season and the bulk of the staff will have returned to their villages on leave. The only remaining personnel will be the Park warden and two or three other skeleton staff.'

'Still, is there no way that we can avoid disposing of them?' It was not a matter of scruples that made Cheng hesitate. It was prudent not to take unnecessary risks, if they could be avoided.

'If you can be suggesting alternatives, I would be pleased to cast my mind over them,' Chetti Singh told him, and after a moment's thought Cheng shook his head.

'No, not at the moment, but please go on. Let me hear the rest of your plan.'

'Very well. My men dispose of all witnesses and burn down the ivory warehouse and then immediately retreat across the river.' The Sikh stopped speaking, but he watched Cheng's face with ill-concealed glee, anticipating his next question. It annoyed Cheng that he must ask it, for it sounded naïve even to his own ears.

'But what about the ivory?'

Chetti Singh smirked mysteriously, forcing him to ask again.

'Will your poachers take the ivory? You say they will be a small party. Surely they will not be able to carry that much, will they?'

'That is the absolute beauty of my plan. The raid is a dead herring for the Zimbabwe police.' And this time Cheng smiled at the solecism. 'We want them to believe that the poachers have taken the ivory. Then they will not think to look for it inside their own country, will they?'

Now, as he sat on his verandah in the midday heat, Cheng nodded grudgingly. Chetti Singh's plan was ingenious, except, of course, that it did not take into account the presence of Armstrong and his television crew. In fairness, however, none of them could have foreseen that.

Once again he considered delaying or cancelling the operation entirely, but almost immediately rejected the idea. By this time, Chetti Singh's men would be across the river and marching on the camp. There was no way he could reach them, and warn them to turn back. They were far past the point of no return. If

Armstrong and his camera man were still here when Chetti Singh's men arrived, then they would have to be disposed of along with the warden and his family and staff.

Cheng's train of thought was interrupted by the ringing of the telephone at the far end of the verandah. The VIP cottage was the only one in the visitors' camp equipped with a telephone. He jumped up and went to it quickly. He had been expecting the call. It had been prearranged and was part of Chetti Singh's plan.

'Ambassador Ning,' he said, and Johnny Nzou answered.

'Sorry to trouble you, Your Excellency, but there is a call from your embassy in Harare. A gentleman calling himself Mr Huang. He says he is your *chargé*. Will you take the call?'

'Thank you, Warden. I will speak to Mr Huang.' He knew that it was a party line that crossed a hundred and fifty miles of wild bush from the district telephone exchange at the little village of Karoi, and the voice of his *chargé* relayed from Harare was a whisper that seemed to come from some far corner of the galaxy. The message was the one he had expected, and afterwards Cheng cranked the handle of the antiquated telephone and Johnny Nzou came on the line again.

'Warden, my presence is required in Harare urgently. It is most unfortunate; I was looking forward to a few more days of relaxation.'

'I also regret that you are forced to leave. My wife and I would have liked you to have dinner with us.'

'Perhaps some other time.'

'The refrigerator trucks are taking the elephant meat up to Karoi this evening. It might be best if you travelled in convoy with them. Your Mercedes does not have four-wheel drive, and it looks as though it might rain at any time.'

That also was part of Chetti Singh's plan. The raid had been timed to coincide with the elephant cull and the departure of the refrigerator trucks. However, Cheng hesitated deliberately before he asked, 'When are the trucks leaving?'

'One of them has engine trouble.' Gomo the ranger had sabotaged the alternator. The object was to delay the departure of the convoy until the arrival of the raiding party. 'However, the driver tells me that they should be ready to leave around six o'clock this evening.' Johnny Nzou's voice changed as a thought struck him. 'Of course, Doctor Armstrong is leaving almost immediately, you could drive in convoy with him.'

'No. No!' Cheng cut in quickly. 'I cannot leave that soon. I will wait for the trucks.'

'As you wish.' Johnny sounded puzzled. 'However, I cannot guarantee when the convoy will be ready to leave and I am sure Doctor Armstrong would agree to delay an hour or so.'

'No,' Cheng told him firmly. 'I will not inconvenience or delay Doctor Armstrong. I will travel with your convoy. Thank you, Warden.'

To end the conversation and forestall any further discussion, he hung up the receiver. He frowned. Armstrong's presence was becoming increasingly troublesome. The sooner he disappeared the happier Cheng would be.

However, it was another twenty minutes before he heard the sound of a diesel engine coming from the direction of the warden's bungalow. He stood up and went to the screen door of the verandah and watched the Toyota Landcruiser coming down the hill. On the door of the truck was painted the logo of Armstrong Productions, a disembodied arm with the wrist encircled by a spiked bracelet, and the elbow bent and tensed in a body-builder's stylised pose to raise a heroic bulge of biceps. Doctor Armstrong was at the driver's wheel and his camera man was in the front seat beside him.

They were leaving at last. Cheng nodded with satisfaction and glanced at his wristwatch. It was a few minutes after one o'clock. They would have at least four hours to get well clear before the attack on the headquarters was launched.

Daniel Armstrong saw him and braked the truck. He rolled down the side window and smiled across at Cheng.

'Johnny tells me you are also leaving today, Your Excellency,' he called. 'Are you sure that we can't be of assistance?'

'Not at all, Doctor.' Cheng smiled politely. 'It is all arranged. Please do not worry about me.'

Armstrong made him feel uneasy. He was a big man with thick curly hair that gave him a tousled outdoors appearance. His gaze was direct and his smile was lazy. Cheng thought that to the eyes of a Westerner he might appear extremely attractive,

41

especially if the Westerner were female, but to Cheng's Chinese eye, his nose was grotesquely large and his wide mouth had a mobile childlike expression. He might have dismissed him as offering no serious threat, except for the eyes. Those eyes made Cheng uneasy. They were alert and penetrating.

Armstrong stared at him for a full five seconds before he smiled again and thrust his hand out of the Toyota's rolled-down window.

'Well then, I'll say cheerio, Your Excellency. Let's hope we get an opportunity for that chat one day soon.' He engaged the gear-shift, raised his right hand in salutation and drove down towards the main gates of the camp.

Cheng watched the truck out of sight and then turned and stared down along the crests of the hills. They were jagged and uneven as a crocodile's teeth.

Twenty miles or so to the west, one of the dark cumulus thunder-heads was abruptly shot through by vivid lightning. Even as he watched, rain began to fall from the drooping belly of the cloud mass, first in pale blue streamers and then in a sullen deluge, as impenetrable as a sheet of lead, that obscured the far hills.

Chetti Singh could not have timed it better. Soon the valley and its escarpment would be a morass. A police team sent to investigate any suspicious occurrence at Chiwewe would not only find the road impassable, but if they did succeed in reaching the Park headquarters, the torrential rain would have scoured the hills and washed away all clues and signs of the raiding party's progress.

'Just let them arrive soon,' he hoped fervently. 'Make it today and not tomorrow.' He checked his wristwatch. It was not quite two o'clock. Sunset at seven-thirty, although with the dense cloud cover it would probably be dark before that. 'Let it be today,' he reiterated.

He fetched his binoculars and his battered copy of Roberts' *Birds of South Africa* from the table on the verandah of the cottage. He was at pains to demonstrate to the warden that he was an ardent naturalist. That was his excuse for being here.

He climbed into his Mercedes and drove down to the warden's office behind the ivory godown. Johnny Nzou was at his desk. Like any other civil service employee, half the warden's work was made up of filling in forms and requisitions and registers and reports. Johnny looked up from his piles of paper as Cheng stood in the doorway.

'I thought that while I was waiting for the refrigerator truck to be repaired, I might as well go down to the water-hole at Fig Tree Pan,' he explained, and Johnny smiled sympathetically as he noticed the binoculars and field guide. Both were the paraphernalia of the typical bird-watcher, and he always felt well-disposed towards anybody who shared his love of nature.

'I'll send one of my rangers to call you when the convoy is ready to leave, but I can't promise it will be this evening,' Johnny told him. 'They tell me that the alternator on one truck is burned out. Spare parts are a terrible problem in this country; there just isn't sufficient foreign exchange to pay for everything we need.'

Cheng drove down to the man-made water-hole. Less than a mile from Chiwewe headquarters a borehole had been sunk at the head of a small vlei. From it a windmill pumped a trickle of water into a muddy pond to attract birds and animals to the proximity of the camp.

As Cheng parked the Mercedes in the observation area overlooking the pool, a small herd of kudu that had been drinking from it took fright and scattered into the surrounding bush. They were large beige-coloured antelope, striped with pale chalk lines across their backs, with long legs and necks, and huge trumpet-shaped ears. Only the males carried wide corkscrewed horns.

Cheng was too agitated to use his binoculars, although clouds of birds descended to drink at the water-hole. The fire finches burned like tiny scarlet flames, and the starlings were a shining iridescent green that reflected the sunlight. Cheng was a talented artist not only with ivory carver's knives but also with water colours. One of his favourite subjects had always been wild birds which he depicted in traditional romantic Chinese style.

Today he could not concentrate on them as they settled at the water. Instead he fitted a cigarette into his ivory holder and puffed at it restlessly. This was the spot he had chosen as the

43

rendezvous with the leader of the poachers, and Cheng scanned the encroaching bush anxiously as he fidgeted and smoked.

Still, the first indication he had that someone was there was the sound of a voice through the open window of the Mercedes beside him. Cheng started uncontrollably and turned quickly to the man who stood beside the motor car.

He had a scar that ran down from the corner of his left eye into the line of his top lip. The lip was puckered upwards on that side giving him an uneven sardonic smile. Chetti Singh had warned Cheng about the scar. It was an infallible point of recognition.

'Sali?' Cheng's voice was breathless. The poacher had startled him. 'You are Sali?'

'Yes,' the man agreed, smiling with only half his twisted mouth. 'I am Sali.'

His skin was almost purple black, the scar a livid pink upon it. He was short in stature but with broad shoulders and muscular limbs. He wore a tattered shirt and shorts of faded khaki drill that were crusted and stained with sweat and filth. He had obviously travelled hard, for his bare legs were floured with dust to the knee. In the heat he stank of stale sweat, a goaty and rancid odour that made Cheng draw away fastidiously. The gesture was not wasted on the poacher and his smile broadened into a genuine grin.

'Where are your men?' Cheng demanded, and Sali prodded his thumb towards the dense encircling bush.

'You are armed?' he insisted, and Sali's grin became insolent. He did not deign to reply to such a fatuous question. Cheng realised that relief and nervousness had made him garrulous. He determined to contain himself, but the next question slipped out before he could prevent it.

'You know what has to be done?'

With a fingertip Sali rubbed the glossy streak of scar tissue down his cheek and nodded.

'You are to leave no witnesses.' Cheng saw from his eyes that the poacher had not understood, so he repeated, 'You must kill them all. When the police come there must be no one for them to talk to.'

Sali inclined his head in agreement. Chetti Singh had explained to him in detail. The orders had been agreeable. Sali had a bitter feud against the Zimbabwe Parks Department. Only a year previously Sali's two younger brothers had crossed the Zambezi with a small group of men to hunt rhinoceros. They had run into one of the Parks anti-poaching units who were all ex-guerrilla fighters and armed, like them, with AK 47 assault rifles. In the fierce fire-fight that ensued, one of his brothers had been killed and the other shot through the spine and crippled for life. Despite his wound they had brought him to trial in Harare and he had been sentenced to seven years' imprisonment.

Thus Sali the poacher felt no great affection for the Parks rangers and it showed in his expression as he agreed. 'We will leave nobody.'

'Except the two rangers,' Cheng qualified the threat. 'Gomo and David. You know them.'

'I know them.' Sali had worked with them before.

'They will be at the workshops with the two big trucks. Make sure all your men understand that they are not to touch them or damage the trucks in any way.'

'I will tell them.'

'The warden will be in his office. His wife and their three children are at the bungalow on the hill. There are four camp servants and their families in the domestic compound. Make sure it is surrounded before you open fire. Nobody must get away.'

'You chatter like a monkey in a wild plum tree,' Sali told him scornfully. 'I know all these things. Chetti Singh has told me.'

'Then go and do as you have been told,' Cheng ordered sharply, and Sali leaned in through the Mercedes' window forcing the Chinaman to hold his breath and draw away from him.

Sali rubbed his thumb and forefinger together in the universal sign for money. Cheng reached across and opened the cubbyhole in the Mercedes' dashboard. The ten-dollar bills were in bundles of a hundred, each secured by a rubber band. He counted them into Sali's open hand, three bundles of a thousand dollars each. It would work out to approximately five dollars a kilo for the vast store of ivory in the camp warehouse, ivory that would be worth a thousand dollars a kilo in Taipei.

On the other hand, to Sali the sheaves of green bills represented an enormous fortune. He had never in his entire life held that amount of money in his hand at one time.

His usual reward for poaching a good elephant, for risking his life against the anti-poaching teams by penetrating deep into forbidden territory, for risking his life again by firing at the great beasts with the light bullets of the AK 47, for cutting out the tusks and carrying their galling weight back over heavy broken ground – his usual reward for all that risk and labour amounted to around thirty dollars an elephant killed – say, a dollar a kilo.

The treasury bills that Cheng placed in his hands represented the reward he could expect from five years of hard and dangerous labour. So, compared to that, what was the killing of a few Parks officials and their families? It entailed very little additional effort and minimal risk. For three thousand dollars, it would be a pleasure indeed.

Both men were mightily pleased with their bargain.

'I will wait here until I hear the guns,' Cheng told him delicately, and Sali smiled so broadly that he showed all his large brilliant white teeth right to the wisdoms in the back of his jaw.

'You will not have to wait long,' he promised, and then as silently as he had appeared, he vanished back into the bush.

Daniel Armstrong drove at a sedate pace. The road was fairly good by central African standards; it was graded regularly, for few of the visitors to the park drove four-wheel-drive vehicles. Nevertheless, Daniel was in no hurry and did not push it. His Toyota was equipped with a full range of camping equipment. He never stayed at motels or other formal lodgings if he could avoid them. Not only were they few and far between in this country, but in most cases the food and comforts they offered were much below the standard that Daniel could provide in his own temporary camps.

This evening he would keep going until a little before sunset and then find some inviting stand of forest or pleasant stream at which to pull well off the road and break out the tucker box and Chivas bottle. He doubted that they would get as far as Mana Pools, and certainly they would not reach the main metalled highway that ran from the Chirundu bridge on the Zambezi, south to Karoi and Harare.

Jock was pleasant company. It was one of the reasons that Daniel had hired him. They had worked together on and off over the past five years. Jock was a freelance cameraman and Daniel called him up on contract whenever he had a new project signed up and financed. They had covered huge tracts of Africa together, from the forbidding beaches of the Skeleton Coast in Namibia to the drought and famine-ravaged mountains and ambas of Ethiopia and the depths of the Sahara. Although they had not succeeded in forging a deep or committed friendship, they had spent weeks together in the remote wilderness and there had seldom been any friction between them.

They chatted amicably as Daniel took the heavily laden truck down the twisting escarpment road. Whenever a bird or animal or unusual tree caught their attention Daniel parked the truck and made notes and observations while Jock filmed.

Before they had covered twenty miles they came to a section of the road over which a large herd of elephant had fed during the previous night. They had pulled down branches and pushed over many of the large mopane trees. Some of these had fallen across the roadway, blocking it entirely. From those trees still standing they had stripped the bark, leaving the trunks naked white and weeping with sap.

'Naughty beggars,' Daniel grinned as he contemplated the destruction. 'They seem to delight in blocking the roads.' Yet it was clear demonstration, if any were needed, that regular culling of the herds was absolutely necessary. The mopane forest could survive only a limited amount of this destructive feeding.

They were able to pull off the road and detour around many of the fallen trees, although once or twice they were forced to hitch up a tree-trunk to the Toyota's tow chain and bodily haul it aside before they could pass. Thus it was after four o'clock before they reached the valley bottom and turned eastwards through the mopane forest towards the Mana Pools turn-off, near which they had filmed the elephant cull.

At this stage both of them were engrossed in a discussion of how best Daniel could edit the huge volume of film that they now had on tape. Daniel was experiencing the heightened anticipation he always felt at this stage of a production. It was all in the can. Now he could return to London where, in a hired editing room at Castle Film Studios, he would spend long weeks and months sequestered in a dark room absorbed in the exacting but infinitely rewarding labour of cutting each scene into the next and composing the commentary to support it.

Even though the forefront of his mind was focused on what Jock was saying, he was fully aware of his surroundings. Nevertheless he almost missed it. He drove over it and went on for almost two hundred yards before it fully registered that he had passed something unusual. Perhaps it was a relic of his experiences during the bush war when any extraneous mark on the roadway could give warning of a land mine and violent death buried in the tracks. In those days he would have been much quicker to register and react, but the intervening years had blunted his reflexes.

He braked the truck and Jock broke off what he was saying and glanced at him quizzically.

'What is it?'

'Don't know.' Daniel swivelled in the seat as he reversed the Landcruiser back down the track. 'Probably nothing,' he murmured, but there was a tiny niggling doubt in the back of his mind.

He stopped and pulled on the handbrake and climbed down out of the cab.

'I can't see anything.' Jock hung out of the window on the far side.

'That's just it,' Daniel agreed. 'There is a blank spot here.' He pointed down the dusty roadway whose surface was dimpled and pocked by the marvellous graffiti of the bush. The tiny v-shaped spurs of francolin and other birds, the serpentine tracks of insects and lizards, the larger hoof-prints of various species of antelope and hare, mongoose and jackal were woven into an intricate tapestry of sign except at one point in the roadway where the soft surface was smooth and unblemished. Daniel squatted beside it and studied it for a moment. 'Somebody has swept sign,' he said.

'So what's so bloody extraordinary about that?' Jock climbed down out of the truck and came to join him.

'Nothing, perhaps.' He stood up. 'Or everything. Depends on how you look at it.'

'Shoot?' Jock invited him.

'Only human beings cover their tracks, and only when they're up to no good. Besides that, there aren't supposed to be people wandering around on foot in the middle of a National Park.'

Daniel skirted the area of soft earth that had been carefully swept with a leafy branch and stepped off the track into the stand of tussocked grass on the verge. Immediately he saw other signs of anti-tracking. The grass clumps had been crushed and flattened as a party of men on foot had used them as stepping stones. It seemed to be a large party and Daniel felt the hair on his forearms and at the back of his neck prickle and lift.

Contact! he thought. It was like the old days with the Scouts when they first picked up the sign of a group of guerrilla terrorists. He experienced that same breathless feeling of excitement and the same stone of fear heavy in his bowels.

It took an effort to thrust those feelings aside. Those dangerous days were long past. Still he followed the sign. Although the chase had taken some elementary precautions, they were perfunctory. A cadre of ZANU in the war days would have been more professional. Within fifty yards of the road Daniel found the first clear print of a shod human foot, and a few yards further on the band had joined a narrow game track and formed up in Indian file, abandoning all further attempts at anti-tracking. They had struck out in the direction of the escarpment and Chiwewe base camp with determined stride. Daniel was amazed to find how large the band was. He counted the tracks of between sixteen and twenty individuals in the group.

After following them another two or three hundred yards Daniel stopped and thought about it carefully. Considering the size of the group and the direction from which they had come, the most obvious assumption was that they were a band of Zambian poachers who had crossed the Zambezi River on a raid for ivory and rhino horn. That would also explain the precautions they had taken to cover their tracks.

What he should do now was to warn Johnny Nzou so that he could get an anti-poaching unit in as fast as possible for a follow-up action. Daniel pondered the best way to do this. There was a telephone in the ranger's office at Mana Pools only an hour's drive ahead, or Daniel could turn back to Chiwewe headquarters and take the warning in person.

The decision was made for him as he made out the line of telephone poles in the forest not far ahead. These were cut from native timber and steeped in black creosote to discourage the attack of termites. Between the poles the draped copper telephone wires gleamed in the late sunlight, except between two of the poles directly ahead.

Daniel hurried forward and then stopped abruptly.

The telephone wires had been cut and dangled from the white ceramic insulators at the top of the nearest pole. Daniel reached out for the end of one wire, and peered at it. There was no question about it. It had been deliberately cut. The shear marks made by the cutting edge of a pair of pliers were evident in the malleable red metal of the cable. There were the milling tracks of many men at the base of the pole.

'Why the hell would a poacher want to cut the telephone lines?' Daniel wondered aloud, and his sense of unease turned to alarm. 'This begins to look really ugly. I have to warn Johnny. He has to get on to these gentlemen damned quickly. Only one way to warn him now.'

At a run he started back to where he had left the Landcruiser.

'What the hell is going on?' Jock wanted to know as he jumped up into the cab and started the motor.

'I don't know, but I don't like it, whatever it is,' Daniel told him as he reversed off the road and then swung back on to it, headed in the opposite direction.

Daniel drove fast now, ripping up a long bank of dust behind the Landcruiser, slowing only for the fords through the steep dry water-courses and then accelerating away again. As he drove, it occurred to him that the gang could reach the head-quarters camp by cutting across the loop that the road made down the pass of the escarpment. It would be a steep climb up on to the plateau, but on foot they could cut almost thirty miles off the longer route that Daniel was forced to follow. He estimated that the telephone lines had been cut about five or six hours earlier. He arrived at that estimate by a process of fieldcraft deduction which included a study of the erosion of the spoor and the recovery time of trodden-down grass and vegetation.

He could not think of any reason why a gang of poachers should want to visit Chiwewe headquarters. On the contrary, he would expect them to give it the widest possible berth. However, their tracks were headed resolutely in that direction, and they had cut the telephone wires. Their conduct was brazen and aggressive. If Chiwewe was indeed their destination then they could be there already. He glanced at his wristwatch. Yes, they could have climbed the escarpment and, by hard marching, have reached the headquarters camp an hour or so ago.

But why? There were no tourists. In Kenya and other countries further north the poachers, having depleted the elephant herds, had taken to attacking and robbing foreign tourists. Perhaps this gang had taken a tip from their northern counterparts. 'But there are no tourists at Chiwewe. There's nothing of value—' he broke off as the fallacy of that assumption occurred to him. 'Shit!' he whispered. 'The ivory.' Suddenly dread chilled the sweat on his cheeks. 'Johnny,' he whispered. 'And Mavis and the kids.'

The Landcruiser was flying down the track now and he slid her into the first hairpin bend that led on to the slope of the escarpment.

As he came through the corner at speed a huge white vehicle filled the road directly ahead of him. Even as Daniel hit the brakes and swung the Toyota hard over he realised that it was one of the refrigerator trucks. He missed its front wing by a foot as he went up on to the verge and tore into a patch of scrub. He came to rest with the nose of the Toyota almost touching the trunk of a big mopane. Jock was thrown up against the dashboard by the deceleration.

51

Daniel jumped out of the Toyota and ran back to where the refrigerator truck had managed to pull up, blocking his tailgate. He recognised Gomo, the senior ranger, at the wheel and called to him.

'Sorry! My fault. Are you okay?'

Gomo looked shaken by the near collision but he nodded. 'I'm okay, Doctor.'

'When did you leave Chiwewe?' Daniel demanded, and Gomo hesitated. For some reason the question seemed to disconcert him. 'How long ago?' Daniel insisted.

'I don't know for sure . . .' At that moment there was the sound of other vehicles approaching down the escarpment road and Daniel glanced around to see the second truck come grinding through the next bend.

It was running in low gear to combat the gravity of the steep gradient. Fifty yards behind the truck followed Ambassador Ning Cheng Gong's blue Mercedes. The two vehicles slowed and then pulled up behind Gomo's truck and Daniel strode towards the Mercedes.

As he approached, Ambassador Ning opened his door and stepped out into the dusty track.

'Doctor Armstrong, what are you doing here?' He seemed agitated but his voice was soft, barely audible.

'When did you leave Chiwewe?' Daniel ignored the question. He was desperate to know that Johnny and Mavis were safe and the Ambassador's reaction puzzled him.

Cheng's agitation increased. 'Why do you ask that?' he whispered. 'Why are you returning? You were supposed to be on your way to Harare.'

'Look here, Your Excellency. All I want to know is that there has been no trouble at Chiwewe.'

'Trouble? What trouble? Why should there be trouble?' The ambassador reached into his pocket and brought out a hand-kerchief. 'What are you suggesting, Doctor?'

'I'm not suggesting anything.' Daniel found it hard to conceal his exasperation. 'I picked up the tracks of a large party of men crossing the road and heading in the direction of Chiwewe. I am worried that they may be a gang of armed poachers and I am on my way back to warn the warden.'

'There is no trouble,' Cheng assured him. Daniel noticed that a faint sheen of perspiration bloomed on his forehead. 'Everything is well. I left there an hour ago. Warden Nzou is just fine. I spoke to him when we left and there was no sign of any trouble.' He wiped his face with the handkerchief.

'An hour ago?' Daniel asked, and checked his stainless steel Rolex. He felt a vast sense of relief at Ambassador Ning's reassurance. 'So you left there at about five-thirty?'

'Yes, yes.' Cheng's tone sharpened with affront. 'Are you questioning my word? Do you doubt what I am telling you?'

Daniel was surprised by his tone and the strength of his denials.

'You misunderstand me, Your Excellency. Of course I don't doubt what you say.'

Cheng's prestige as an ambassador was the main reason that Chetti Singh had insisted that he be present at Chiwewe. Cheng's natural inclination had been assiduously to avoid the scene of the raid, and even to fly to Taipei while it was in progress to give himself an infallible alibi. However, Chetti Singh had threatened to call off the operation unless Cheng was present to vouch for the fact that the raid had taken place after the convoy of trucks had left Chiwewe. That was the whole crux of the operation. As an accredited ambassador, Cheng's word would carry enormous weight in the subsequent police investigation. The testimony of the two black rangers alone might not have been accepted implicitly. The police might even have decided to give them a little earnest questioning in a back cell at Chikurubi prison and Chetti Singh was not confident that they would have withstood that treatment.

No, the police must be made to believe that when Cheng had left Chiwewe with the convoy all had been well. That way they must assume that the raiders had carried the ivory away with them or that it had been destroyed in the fire that consumed the godown.

'I'm sorry if I gave you the impression that I was doubting your word, Your Excellency,' Daniel placated him. 'It was just that I am worried about Johnny, about the warden.'

'Well, I assure you that you have no reason to worry.' Cheng stuffed the handkerchief in his hip pocket and reached for the packet of cigarettes in the top pocket of his open-neck shirt. He tapped one out of the pack but his fingers were slightly unsteady and he let the cigarette drop into the dust between his feet.

Daniel's eyes were instinctively drawn down as Cheng stooped quickly to retrieve the fallen cigarette. He wore white canvas training shoes and Daniel noticed that the side of one shoe and the cuff of his blue cotton slacks were smeared with a stain that looked at first glance like dried blood.

This puzzled Daniel for a moment, until he remembered that Cheng had been present that morning when the fresh tusks had been unloaded from the truck and stored in the godown. The explanation for the stains on his clothing was obvious; he must have picked them up from a puddle of congealed elephant blood in which the tusks had lain.

Cheng noticed the direction of his gaze and stepped back quickly, almost guiltily, into the driver's seat of the Mercedes and slammed the door. Unthinkingly Daniel noticed the unusual fish-scale pattern that the soles of his training shoes left in the fine dust of the roadway.

'Well, I am happy to have been able to set your fears at rest, Doctor.' Cheng smiled at him through the window of the Mercedes. He had regained his composure and his smile was once again suave and charming. 'I'm glad to have saved you an unnecessary journey all the way back to Chiwewe. I am sure you will want to join the convoy and get out of the Park before the rains break.' He started the Mercedes. 'Why don't you take the lead position ahead of the trucks?'

'Thank you, Your Excellency.' Daniel shook his head and stepped back. 'You go on with the trucks. I won't be joining you. I want to go back anyway. Somebody has to warn Johnny Nzou.'

Cheng's smile evaporated. 'You are giving yourself a great deal of unnecessary trouble, I assure you. I suggest you telephone him from Mana Pools or Karoi.'

'Didn't I tell you? They cut the telephone wires.'

'Doctor Armstrong, that is preposterous. I am sure you are mistaken. I think you are exaggerating the seriousness of this—'

'You think what you like,' said Daniel with finality. 'I'm

'going back to Chiwewe.' He stepped back from the window of the Mercedes.

'Doctor Armstrong,' Cheng called after him, 'look at those rain clouds. You could be trapped here for weeks.'

'I'll take the chance,' Daniel told him blithely, but to himself he thought, Just why is he being so insistent? Something is starting to smell distinctly rotten here.

He walked quickly back towards the Landcruiser. As he passed the trucks he noticed that neither of the rangers had dismounted from the driver's cabs. They were both looking sullen and neither of them said anything as he passed close beside them.

'All right, Gomo,' he called, 'pull your truck forward so I can get past you.'

Without a word the ranger obeyed. Then the second truck rumbled past and finally the Ambassador's Mercedes came level. Daniel lifted a hand in farewell. Cheng barely glanced in his direction but gave him a perfunctory salute before following the trucks around the bend and heading on down towards the Mana Pools turn-off.

'What did the Chink have to say?' Jock asked as Daniel reversed back into the roadway and put the Toyota to the steep gradient.

'He says it was all quiet at Chiwewe when he left there an hour ago,' Daniel replied.

'That's a fair do.' Jock reached into the cold box and fished out a can of beer. He offered it to Daniel who shook his head and concentrated on the road ahead. Jock opened the can for himself, took a long slug, and belched happily.

The light began to fade and a few heavy drops of rain splattered against the windscreen but Daniel did not slacken speed. It was completely dark before they reached the crest of the escarpment. The lightning blazed through the darkness, illuminating the forest with a crackling blue radiance and thunder rolled across the sky and cannonaded the ridges of granite which rose on each side of the road.

The rain began to fall like silver arrows in the headlights, each drop exploding in a white blur against the glass then streaming down it so copiously that the wipers could not clear the windshield fast enough. Soon it was oppressively humid in the closed cab and the windscreen began to mist over. Daniel leaned forward to wipe it clear with his hand but when it smeared he gave up the effort and opened his side window a few inches to let in the fresh night air. Almost immediately he wrinkled his nose and sniffed.

Jock smelt it at almost the same moment. 'Smoke,' he exclaimed. 'How far are we from the camp?'

'Almost there,' Daniel replied. 'Just over the next ridge.'

The odour of smoke thinned out. Daniel thought that it might have come from the cooking-fires in the servants' compound.

Ahead of them in the path of the headlights the gates of the main camp sprang out of the darkness. Each whitewashed column was crowned by the bleached skull of an elephant. The sign read:

WELCOME TO CHIWEWE CAMP
THE HOME OF THE ELEPHANTS

and then in smaller letters,

All arriving visitors must report immediately
to the Warden's Office.

The long driveway, lined on each side with dark casia trees, was running ankle deep with storm water and the Toyota's tyres threw up a dense fog of spray as Daniel headed for the main block of buildings. Suddenly the reek of smoke was thick and rank in their nostrils. It was the smell of burning thatch and wood with a foul underlay of something else, flesh or bone or ivory, perhaps, although Daniel had never smelt ivory burning.

'No lights,' Daniel grunted as he saw the loom of dark buildings in the rain ahead. The camp generator was not running; the entire camp was in darkness. Then he became aware of a diffused ruby light that shimmered over the wet casia trees and played gently on the walls of the buildings.

'One of the buildings is on fire.'

Jock sat forward in his seat. 'That's where the smoke is coming from.'

The Toyota's headlights cut a broad swathe through the gloom and then focused on a huge amorphous dark pile ahead of them. The misted windscreen obscured his vision and for some moments Daniel could not decide what it was. The strange glow seemed to emanate from it. Only as they drove closer and the lights lit it more clearly could he recognise it as the blackened, smouldering ruins of the ivory godown. Horrified by what he saw, Daniel let the Toyota roll to a halt and he stepped down into the mud and stared at the ruin.

The heat of the flames had cracked the walls and most of them had collapsed. The fire must have been an inferno to have produced such heat. It still burned and smouldered despite the cascading rain. Oily streamers of smoke drifted across the headlights of the truck and occasionally the flames flared up fiercely until the heavy raindrops beat them down again.

Daniel's sodden shirt clung to his body and the rain soaked his hair, smearing his thick curls over his forehead and into his eyes. He pushed them back and scrambled up on to the tumbled masonry of the wall. The collapsed roof was a thick mattress of black ash and charred beams that clogged the interior of the devastated godown. Despite the rain the smoke was still too dense and the heat too fierce to allow him to approach any closer and discover how much of the ivory still lay under that blackened pile.

Daniel backed away and ran to the truck. He climbed into the cab and wiped the rain out of his eyes with the palm of his hand.

'You were spot-on,' Jock said. 'It looks as if the bastards have hit the camp.'

Daniel did not answer. He started the engine and gunned the Toyota up the hill to the warden's cottage.

'Get the flashlight out of the locker,' he snapped. Obediently Jock knelt on the seat and groped in the heavy tool-locker that was bolted to the truck bed, and came out with the big Maglite.

Like the rest of the camp the warden's cottage was in darkness. The rain streamed down from the eaves in a silver torrent so that the headlights could not illuminate the screened verandah beyond. Daniel snatched the torch from Jock's hand and jumped out into the rain.

'Johnny!' he yelled. 'Mavis!' He ran to the front door of the cottage. The door had been smashed half off its hinges and hung open. He ran through on to the verandah.

The furniture was shattered and thrown about in confusion. He played the torch-beam over the chaos. Johnny's cherished collection of books had been tumbled from their cases along the wall and lay in heaps with their pages fanned and their spines broken.

'Johnny!' Daniel shouted. 'Where are you?'

He ran through the open double doors into the sitting-room. Here the destruction was shocking. They had hurled all Mavis's ornaments and vases at the stone fireplace and the broken shards glittered in the torch beam. They had ripped the stuffing out of the sofa and easy chairs. The room stank like an animal cage and he saw that they had defecated on the carpets and urinated down the walls.

Daniel stepped over the reeking piles of faeces and ran through into the passageway that led to the bedrooms.

'Johnny!' he shouted in anger and despair, as he played the torch-beam down the length of the passage.

On the end wall was a decoration that had not been there before. It was a dark star-shaped splash of paint that covered most of the white-painted surface. For a moment Daniel stared at it uncomprehendingly and then he dropped the beam to the small huddled shape that lay at the foot of the wall.

Johnny and Mavis had named their only son after him, Daniel Robert Nzou. After two daughters, Mavis had finally given birth to a son and both parents had been overjoyed. Daniel Nzou had been four years old. He lay on his back. His eyes were open but sightlessly staring into the beam of the torch.

They had killed him in the old barbaric African way, in the same way that Chaka's and Mzilikazi's impis had dealt with the male children of a vanquished tribe. They had seized little Daniel by the ankles and swung him head-first against the wall, crushing his skull and beating his brains out against the brick-work. His splattering blood had daubed that crude mural on the white surface.

Daniel stooped over the little boy. Despite the deformation

of the crushed skull his resemblance to his father was still marked. Tears prickled the rims of Daniel's eyelids and he stood up slowly and turned to the bedroom door.

It stood half open but Daniel dreaded pushing it all the way. He had to force himself to do it. The hinges of the door whined softly as it swung open.

For a moment Daniel stared down the beam of the Maglite as he let it play around the bedroom and then he reeled back into the passageway and leaned against the wall, gagging and gasping for breath.

He had witnessed scenes such as these during the days of the bush war, but the years had eroded his conditioning and softened the shell that he had built up to protect himself. He was no longer able to look dispassionately on the atrocity that man is able to perpetrate on his fellows.

Johnny's daughters were older than their brother. Miriam was ten and Suzie almost eight. They lay naked and spread-eagled on the floor at the foot of the bed. They had both been raped repeatedly. Their immature genitalia were a torn and bloody mush.

Mavis was on the bed. They had not bothered to strip her entirely, but had merely pushed her skirts up around her waist. Her arms were pulled up above her head and tied by the wrists to the wooden headboard. The two little girls must have died of shock and loss of blood during the prolonged assault upon them. Mavis had probably survived until they were finished with her, then they had put a bullet through her head.

Daniel forced himself to enter the room. He found where Mavis kept her extra bed-linen in one of the built-in cupboards and covered each of the corpses with a sheet. He could not bring himself to touch any of the girls, not even to close their wide staring eyes in which the horror and the terror was still deeply imprinted.

'Sweet Mother of God,' Jock whispered from the doorway. 'Whoever did this isn't human. They must be ravaging bloody beasts.'

Daniel backed out of the bedroom and closed the door. He covered Daniel Nzou's tiny body.

'Have you found Johnny?' he asked Jock. His voice was

hoarse and his throat felt rough and abraded with horror and grief.

'No.' Jock shook his head, then turned and fled down the passage. He blundered out across the verandah and into the rain.

Daniel heard him retching and vomiting in the flowerbed below the stoep. The sound of the other man's distress served to steady Daniel. He fought back his own repugnance and anger and sorrow and brought his emotions back under control.

'Johnny,' he told himself. 'Got to find Johnny.'

He went swiftly through the other two bedrooms and the rest of the house. There was no sign of his friend, and he allowed himself the first faint hope.

'He might have got away,' he told himself. 'He might have made it into the bush.'

It was a relief to get out of that charnel house. Daniel stood in the darkness and lifted his face to the rain. He opened his mouth and let it wash the bitter bile taste from his tongue and the back of his throat. Then he turned the torch-beam on to his feet and saw the clotted blood dissolve from his shoes in a pink stain. He scrubbed the soles in the gravel of the driveway to clean them and then shouted to Jock.

'Come on, we have to find Johnny.'

In the Toyota he drove down the back of the hill to the domestic compound that housed the camp servants. The compound was still enclosed with an earthen embankment and barbed-wire fence from the war days. However the fence was in a ruinous state and the gate was missing. They drove through the gateway and the smell of smoke was strong. As the headlights caught them Daniel saw that the row of servants' cottages was burnt out. The roofs had collapsed and the windows were empty. The rain had quenched the flames, although a few tendrils of smoke still drifted like pale wraiths in the lights.

The ground around the huts was sown with dozens of tiny objects which caught the headlights and sparkled like diamond chips. Daniel knew what they were, but he stepped down from the truck and picked one of them out of the mud. It was a shiny brass cartridge case. He held it to the light and inspected the familiar Cyrillic head stamp in the brass. 7.62 mm, of East European manufacture, it was the calibre of the ubiquitous AK 47 assault rifle, staple of violence and revolution throughout Africa and the entire world.

The gang had shot up the compound, but had left no corpses. Daniel guessed that they had thrown the dead into the cottages before torching them. The breeze shifted towards him so that he caught the full stench of the burned huts and had his suspicions confirmed. Underlying the smell of smoke was the odour of scorched flesh and hair and bone.

He spat out the taste of it and walked down between the huts. 'Johnny!' he shouted into the night. 'Johnny, are you there?' But the only sound was the creak and pop of the doused flames and the sough of the breeze in the mango trees that brought the raindrops pattering down from the branches.

He flicked the torch left and right as he passed between the huts, until he saw the body of a man lying in the open.

'Johnny!' he shouted, and ran to him and fell on his knees beside him.

The body was horribly burned, the khaki Parks uniform burned half away, and the skin and flesh sloughing off the exposed torso and the side of the face. The man had obviously dragged himself out of the burning hut into which they had thrown him, but he was not Johnny Nzou. He was one of the junior rangers.

Daniel jumped up and hurried back to the track.

'Did you find him?' Jock asked, and Daniel shook his head.

'Christ, they've murdered everybody in the camp. Why would they do that?'

'Witnesses!' Daniel started the truck. 'They wiped out all the witnesses.'

'Why? What do they want? It doesn't make sense.'

'The ivory. That's what they were after.'

'But they burned down the warehouse!'

'After they cleaned it out.'

He swung the Toyota back on to the track and raced up the hill.

'Who were they, Danny? Who did this?'

'How the hell do I know? Shifta? Bandits? Poachers? Don't ask stupid questions.'

Daniel's anger was only just beginning. Up until now he had been numbed by the shock and the horror. He drove back past the dark bungalow on the hill and then down again to the main camp.

The warden's office was still standing intact; although when Daniel played the beam of the torch over the thatched roof he saw the blackened area on which someone had thrown a burning torch. Well-laid thatch does not burn readily, however, and the flames had not caught fairly or perhaps had been extinguished by the rain before they could take hold.

The rain stopped with the suddenness which is characteristic of the African elements. One minute it was falling in a furious cascade that limited the range of the headlights to fifty yards, and the next it was over. Only the trees still dripped, but overhead the first stars pricked through the dispersing thunder clouds that were being carried away on the rising breeze. Daniel barely noticed the change. He left the truck and ran up on to the wide verandah.

The exterior wall was decorated with the skulls of the animals of the Park. Their empty eye-sockets and twisted horns in the torch-beam gave a macabre touch to the scene and heightened Daniel's sense of doom as he strode down the long covered verandah. He now realised that he should have searched here first, instead of rushing up to the bungalow.

The door of Johnny's office stood open and Daniel paused on the threshold and steeled himself before he stepped through.

A snowstorm of papers covered the floor and desk. They had ransacked the room, sweeping the stacks of forms off the cupboard shelves and hauling the drawers out of Johnny's desk, then spilling out the contents. They had found Johnny's keys and opened the old green-painted door to the Milner safe that was built into the wall. The keys were still in the lock but the safe was empty.

Daniel's torch-beam darted about the room and then settled on the crumpled form that lay in front of the desk.

'Johnny,' he whispered. 'Oh, Christ, no!'

'I thought that while I was waiting for the refrigerator truck to be repaired, I might as well go down to the water-hole at Fig Tree Pan.' Ambassador Ning's voice interrupted Johnny Nzou's concentration, but he felt no resentment as he looked up from his desk. In Johnny's view one of his major duties was to make the wilderness accessible to anybody who had an interest in nature. Ning Cheng Gong was certainly one of those. Johnny smiled at his accoutrements, the field guide and the binoculars.

He rose from his desk, glad of the excuse to escape from the drudgery of paperwork and went with the Ambassador out on to the verandah and down to his parked Mercedes, where he stood and chatted to him for a few minutes, making suggestions as to where he might get a glimpse of the elusive and aptly named gorgeous bush shrike that Cheng wanted to observe.

When Cheng drove away, Johnny walked down to the vehicle workshops where ranger Gomo was stripping and reassembling the alternator of the unserviceable truck. He was dubious about Gomo's ability to effect the repair. In the morning he would probably have to ring the warden at Mana Pools and ask him to send a mechanic to do the job.

One consolation was that the elephant meat would keep indefinitely in the cold storage of the hull. The truck's refrigerating equipment was plugged in now to the camp generator and the thermometer registered twenty degrees below freezing when Johnny checked it. The meat would be processed and turned into animal feed by a private contractor in Harare.

Johnny left ranger Gomo to his labour over the dismembered alternator and went back to his own office under the casia trees. No sooner had he left the workshop than Gomo looked up and exchanged a significant glance with David, the other black ranger. The alternator he was tinkering with was a worn-out piece of equipment that he had retrieved from the scrap heap in Harare for just this purpose. The truck's original alternator, in perfect working order, was hidden under the driver's seat in the cab. It would take less than ten minutes to bolt it back in place and reconnect the wiring.

Back in his office Johnny settled to the monotony of his

forms and ledgers. Once he glanced at his wristwatch and found that it was a few minutes before one o'clock, but he wanted to finish the week's reports before knocking off for lunch. Of course, it was a temptation to go up to the house early. He liked to be with the children for a while before lunch, especially with his son, but he resisted the impulse and worked on conscientiously. Anyway he knew that Mavis would probably send the children down to fetch him soon. She liked to serve his lunch promptly. He smiled in anticipation of their arrival as he heard a sound at the door and looked up.

The smile faded. A stranger stood in the doorway, a stocky man with bow legs, dressed in filthy rags. Both his hands were behind his back as though he was concealing something.

'Yes?' Johnny asked shortly. 'Who are you? What do you want?'

The man smiled. His skin was very dark with purple black highlights. When he smiled the scar that ran down one cheek pulled his mouth out of shape and the smile was malicious and humourless.

Johnny stood up from the desk and went towards him.

'What do you want?' he repeated, and the man in the doorway said, 'You!' From behind his back he brought out an AK 47 rifle and lifted the barrel towards Johnny's belly.

Johnny was caught totally off guard in the centre of the room. However, his recovery was almost instantaneous. His reflexes were those of a hunter and a soldier. The armoury door was ten paces to his left and he went for it.

The Parks weapons were kept in there. Through the door he could see the rack of firearms on the far wall. With despair turning his legs as heavy as concrete, Johnny realised that none of the weapons in the rack was loaded. That was his own strict safety rule. The ammunition was kept in the locked steel cupboard under the gun-rack.

All this passed through his mind as he leaped for the door. From the corner of his eye he saw the scar-faced brigand swing the AK 47 on to him and halfway across the room Johnny tumbled forward like an acrobat, ducking under the blast of automatic fire that swept across the room.

As he rolled smoothly to his feet he heard the man curse and

Johnny dived forward once more for the doorway. He realised that his assailant was good. He had seen that he was a killer in the practised way he handled the rifle. It was a miracle that he had been able to evade that first close-range volley.

The air was filled with a haze of plaster dust that the bullets had battered from the wall and Johnny dived through it, but he knew he was not going to make it. The man with the AK 47 was too good. He could not be fooled again. The shelter of the doorway was too far for Johnny to reach before the next burst came.

The clock in Johnny's head was running; he anticipated how long it would take for the man to recover his balance. The muzzle of the AK 47 always rode up uncontrollably in automatic fire; it would take him the major part of a second to bring it down, and line up for the second burst. Johnny judged it finely and twisted his body violently aside, but he was a fraction late.

The gunman aimed low to compensate for the rise of the AK. One bullet sliced through the flesh of Johnny's thigh, missing the bone, but the second cut through the lower curve of his buttock and smashed into the joint at the femur, shattering the head and the cup of bone of the pelvis.

The other three bullets of the burst flew wide as Johnny threw himself to one side. However, his left leg was gone and he fell against the door jamb and tried to hold himself from falling. His impetus sent him sliding sideways along the wall, and his fingernails screeched as they gouged the plaster. He ended up facing back into the room standing on one leg. His left leg hung from the shattered joint, and his arms were flung open like a crucifix as he tried to hold his balance.

Still smiling, the gunman clicked the rate-of-fire selector on to single-shot. He wanted to conserve ammunition. A single round cost him ten Zambian kwacha, and had to be carried hundreds of miles in his pack. Each cartridge was precious, and the warden was maimed and completely at his mercy. One more bullet would be enough.

'Now,' he said softly. 'Now you die.' And he shot Johnny Nzou in the stomach.

The bullet drove the breath from Johnny's lungs with an explosive exhalation. He was slammed hard against the wall and doubled over by the brutal force of the impact and then he toppled forward. Johnny had been hit before, during the war, but he had never received a full body strike and the shock of it was beyond his worst expectations. He was numbed from the waist down but his brain stayed clear, crystalline, as though the rush of adrenalin into his bloodstream had sharpened his perception to its limits.

Play dead! he thought, even as he was going down. His lower body was paralysed, but he forced his torso to relax. He hit the floor with the loose unresisting weight of a flour sack and did not move again.

His head was twisted to one side, his cheek pressed to the cold cement floor. He lay still. He heard the gunman cross the floor, the rubber soles of the combat boots squeaking softly. Then his boots entered Johnny's field of vision. They were dusty and worn almost through the uppers. He wore no socks and the stink of his feet was rancid and sour as he stood within inches of Johnny's face.

Johnny heard the metallic snick of the mechanism as the Zambian moved the rate-of-fire selector again, and then felt the cold hard touch of the muzzle against his temple as the man lined up for the *coup de grâce*.

'Don't move,' Johnny steeled himself. It was his last despairing hope. He knew that the slightest movement must trigger the shot. He had to convince the gunman he was dead.

At that moment there was a burst of shouting from outside the room, and then a volley of automatic fire, followed by more shouting. The pressure of the rifle muzzle was lifted from Johnny's temple. The stinking boots turned away and retreated across the floor towards the doorway.

'Come on! Don't waste time!' the scar-faced gunman yelled through the open door. Johnny knew enough of the northern Chinianja dialect to understand. 'Where are the trucks? We must get the ivory loaded!'

The Zambian ran out of the office leaving Johnny lying alone on the cement floor.

Johnny knew that he was mortally hit. He could feel the arterial blood squirting out of the wound in his groin and he rolled on his side and swiftly loosened the top of his trousers.

Immediately he smelled his own faeces and knew that the second bullet had ripped open his intestines. He reached down into his crotch and pressed his fingers into the wound in his groin. Blood spurted hotly over his hand.

He found the open artery and pinched off the end of the severed femoral.

Mavis, and the babies! That was his next thought. What could he do for them? At that moment he heard more firing from up the hill, in the direction of the domestic compound and his own cottage.

It's a gang of them, he realised with despair. They are all over the camp. They are attacking the compound. And then, My babies. Oh, God! My babies!

He thought about the weapons in the room next door, but he knew he could not get that far. Even if he did, how could he handle a rifle with half his guts shot away and his life-blood spreading in a pool under him?

He heard the trucks. He recognised the beat of the big diesels and knew that they were the refrigerator trucks. He felt a surge of hope.

Gomo, he thought. David . . . But it was short-lived. Lying on his side, clinging to his severed artery, he looked across the room and realised that he could see through the open door.

One of the white refrigerator trucks pulled into his view. It reversed up against the door of the ivory godown. As soon as it parked, Gomo jumped out of the cab and began a heated, gesticulating discussion with the scar-faced leader of the gang. In his confused and swiftly weakening condition, it took Johnny several seconds to work it out.

Gomo, he thought. Gomo is one of them. He set it up.

It should not have come as such a shock. Johnny knew how pervasive was the corruption in the government, in all departments, not only the Parks Administration. He had given evidence before the official commission of enquiry that was investigating the corruption, and had pledged to help stamp it out. He knew Gomo well. He was arrogant and self-seeking. He was just the type, but Johnny had never expected treachery on this scale.

Suddenly the area around the godown that Johnny could see

was teeming with the other members of the gang. Swiftly Scar-face organised them into a work-party. One of them shot the lock off the door of the warehouse and the bandits laid aside their weapons and swarmed into the building. There were shouts of greedy joy as they saw the piles of ivory and then they formed a human chain and began passing out the tusks, and loading them into the truck.

Johnny's vision began to fade. Clouds of darkness passed across his eyes and there was a soft singing in his ears.

I'm dying, he thought without emotion. He could feel the numbness spreading from his paralysed legs up through his chest.

He forced the darkness back from his eyes and thought that he must be fantasising, for now Ambassador Ning stood in the late sunlight below the verandah. He still had the binoculars slung over his shoulder and his manner was impossibly cool and urbane. Johnny tried to shout a warning to him, but it came out of his throat in a soft croak that did not carry beyond the room in which he lay.

Then to his astonishment he saw the scar-faced leader of the gang come to where the ambassador stood and salute him, if not respectfully, at least with recognition of his authority.

Ning. Johnny forced himself to believe it. It really is Ning. I'm not dreaming it.

Then the voices of the two men carried to where he lay. They were speaking in English.

'You must hurry your men,' Ning Cheng Gong said. 'They must get the ivory loaded – I want to leave here immediately.'

'Money,' answered Sali. 'One thousand dollars . . .' His English was atrocious.

'You have been paid.' Cheng was indignant. 'I have paid you your money.'

'More money. More one thousand dollars.' Sali grinned at him. 'More money or I stop. We go, leave you, leave ivory.'

'You are a scoundrel,' Cheng snarled.

'Not understand "scoundrel", but think you also "scoun-drel", maybe.' Sali's grin widened. 'Give money now.'

'I haven't any more money with me,' Cheng told him flatly.

'Then we go! Now! You load ivory yourself.'

'Wait.' Cheng was obviously thinking quickly. 'I haven't got money. You take the ivory, as much as you want. Take everything you can carry.' Cheng had realised that the poachers would be able to take only a negligible number of tusks from the hoard. They could not possibly manage more than a single tusk each. Twenty men, twenty tusks – it was a small price.

Sali stared at him while he considered the offer. Clearly he had milked every possible advantage from the situation, so at last he nodded.

'Good! We take ivory.' He began to turn away.

Ambassador Ning called after him. 'Wait, Sali! What about the others? Did you take care of them?'

'They all dead.'

'The warden and his woman and children? Them too?'

'All dead,' Sali repeated. 'Woman is dead, and her piccanins. My men make jig-jig with all three women first. Very funny, very nice jig-jig. Then kill.'

'The warden? Where is he?'

Sali the poacher jerked his head towards the door of Johnny's office. 'I shoot him boom, boom. He dead like a *n'gulubi*, dead like a pig.' He laughed. 'Very good job, hey?'

He walked away with the rifle over his shoulder, still chuckling, and Cheng followed him out of Johnny's field of vision. Anger came to arm Johnny and give him just a little more strength. The poacher's words conjured up a dreadful vision of the fate that had overtaken Mavis and the children. He could see it as clearly as if he had been there; he knew about rape and pillage. He had lived through the bush war.

He used the strength of his anger to begin to wriggle across the floor towards his desk. He knew he could not use a weapon. All he could hope for now in the few minutes of life that remained to him was to leave some sort of message. Papers had spilled off his desk and littered the floor. If he could just get to a single sheet, and write on it and hide it, the police would find it later.

He moved like a maimed caterpillar, lying on his back, still clutching the severed artery. He drew up his good knee, dug in his heel and pushed himself painfully across the floor, sliding on his back a few inches at a time, his own blood lubricating his passage. He moved six feet towards the desk and reached out for one of the sheets of paper. He saw then that it was a sheet from the wages register.

He had not touched it when the intensity of the light in the room altered. Somebody was standing in the doorway. He turned his head and Ambassador Ning was staring at him. He had come up on to the verandah. His rubber-soled training shoes made no sound at all. Now he stood petrified with shock in the doorway, and for a moment longer he stared at Johnny. Then he yelled shrilly, 'He is still alive. Sali, come quickly, he is still alive.'

Cheng disappeared from the doorway and ran down the verandah still shouting for the poacher. 'Sali, come quickly.'

It was all over, and Johnny knew it. Only seconds remaining to him. He rolled on his side reached out and snatched up the register sheet. He pressed the sheet flat on the floor with one hand, and then released the severed artery and drew his blood-drenched hand out of the front of his trousers. Immediately he felt the artery begin to pulse and fresh blood jetted from the wound.

With his forefinger he scrawled on the blank sheet of paper, writing in his own blood. He formed the letter N in a large lopsided character, and dizziness made his senses swirl. NI. It was more difficult to concentrate. The down stroke of the I was elongated and curved, too much like a J. Painfully he dotted the letter to make its meaning clearer. For a moment his finger was glued lightly to the paper with his sticky blood. He pulled it free.

He started on the second N. It was crude and childlike. His finger would not follow the dictates of his mind. He heard the ambassador still calling for Sali, and the poacher's answering shout filled with alarm and consternation. NIN — Johnny began the G but his finger wandered off at an angle and the wet red letters wiggled and swam before his eyes like tadpoles.

He heard running feet come pounding down the verandah and Sali's voice. 'I thought he was dead. I finish him good now!' Johnny crumpled the sheet of paper in his left hand, the hand that was clean of blood, and he thrust his closed fist into the front of his tunic and rolled over onto his belly with his arm trapped under him, concealing the balled note.

He did not see Sali come in at the door. His face was pressed to the concrete floor. He heard the poacher's boots squeak and slip on the blood, and then the click of the safety-catch on the rifle as he stood over Johnny's prostrate form.

Johnny felt no fear, only a vast sense of sorrow and resignation. He thought about Mavis and the children as he felt the muzzle of the rifle touch the back of his head. He was relieved that he would not be left alone after they were gone. He was glad that he would never see what had happened to them, would never be forced to witness the signs of their agony and degradation.

He was already dying before the bullet from the AK 47 tore through his skull and buried itself in the concrete under his face.

'Shit,' said Sali. He stepped back and shouldered the rifle, a faint feather of gunsmoke still drifting from the muzzle. 'A hard man to kill. He made me waste *miningi* bullets, each one ten kwacha. Too much!'

Ning Cheng Gong advanced into the room. 'Are you sure that you've finished the job – at last?' he asked.

'His head gone,' Sali grunted as he picked up Johnny's keys from the desk and went to ransack the Milner safe. '*Kufa!* He dead, for sure.'

Cheng moved closer to the corpse, and stared at it with fascination. The killing had excited him. He was sexually aroused, not as much as if it had been a young girl who had died, but aroused, nevertheless. The smell of blood filled the room. He loved that smell.

He was so absorbed that he did not notice that he was standing in a puddle of blood until Gomo called him from below the verandah.

'All the ivory is loaded. We are ready to go.'

Cheng stepped back and exclaimed with disgust as he saw the stain on the cuff of his crisply ironed blue cotton slacks.

'I'm going now,' he told Sali. 'Burn the ivory godown before you leave.'

In the safe Sali had found the canvas bank bag that contained the month's wages for the camp staff, and he grunted without looking up from the contents.

71

'I burn everything for sure.'

Cheng ran down the verandah steps and climbed into the Mercedes. He signalled to Gomo and the two refrigerator trucks pulled away. The ivory was packed into the holds and then covered with the dismembered carcasses of the culled beasts. A casual inspection would not reveal the hoard, but there was nobody to stop the convoy. They were protected by the badges of the National Parks Board painted on the trucks, and by the khaki uniforms and shoulder flashes of Gomo and David, the two rangers. Not even one of the frequent road-blocks was likely to delay them. The security forces were intent on catching political dissidents, not ivory-runners.

It had all gone as Chetti Singh had planned it. Cheng glanced at the rear-view mirror of the Mercedes. The ivory godown was already ablaze. The poachers were forming up into a column for the return march. Each of them carried a large tusk from the hoard.

Cheng smiled to himself. Perhaps Sali's greed would work to his advantage. If the police ever caught up with the gang, the disappearance of the ivory would be neatly explained by both the fire and the loads the poachers were carrying.

At Cheng's insistence they had left forty tusks in the burning godown, to provide traces of charred ivory for the police forensic laboratory. As Chetti Singh might have said, 'Another dead herring . . .'

This time Cheng laughed aloud. He was elated. The success of the raid and the thrill of violence and death and blood warmed his belly and filled him with a sense of power. He felt masterful and sexually charged, and suddenly he was aware that he had a hard throbbing erection.

He determined that next time he would do the killing himself. It was quite natural to believe that there would be a next time, and many more times after that. Death had made Cheng feel immortal.

'Johnny. Oh, God. Johnny.' Daniel squatted beside him and reached out to touch the side of his throat just below the ear feeling for the pulse of the carotid. It was an instinctive gesture, for the bullet entry wound in the back of Johnny's skull was conclusive.

Johnny's skin was cool and Daniel could not yet bring himself to turn him over and look at the exit wound. He let him lie a little longer and rocked back on his heels, letting his anger flourish to replace the enervating chill of grief. He cherished his rage, as though it were a candle flame on a dark night. It warmed the cold empty place in his soul that Johnny had left.

Daniel stood up at last. He played the torch-beam on the floor ahead of him, and stepped over the pools and smears of Johnny's blood as he went to the armoury.

The remote control for the generator was on the mains panel beside the door. Daniel threw the switch and heard the distant clatter of the diesel engine in the power house down near the main gates to the camp. The diesel engine ran up to speed and settled at a steady beat, then the generator kicked in and the lights flickered and bloomed. Through the window he saw the street lamps lining the driveway light up and in their glow the casia trees were vivid green and shiny with raindrops.

Daniel fetched the bunch of keys that still hung in the lock of the Milner safe and strode through into the armoury. Along with the .375 culling rifles, there were five AK 47 assault rifles on the rack. These were used on anti-poaching patrols when the rangers needed equivalent fire-power to take on the gangs of poachers. Ammunition was stored in the cupboard below the gunrack. He unlocked the steel door. There were four magazines of AK ammunition in each pouched webbing belt hanging on the hooks.

He slung one of these over his shoulder, then lifted an automatic rifle down from the rack and loaded it with deft movements; the old warlike arts once learned were never forgotten. Armed and angry, he ran down the verandah steps.

'Start with the ivory godown,' he decided. 'They'll have been there for sure.'

He circled the burned-out building, searching for sign by the light of the street lamps, flashing his torch at anything that caught his attention. If he had allowed himself to think about it, he would have realised he was wasting his time. The only prints that had withstood the erosion of the rain were those protected by the overhanging verandah roof, a set of heavy tyre tracks in the mud at the front entrance to the ivory godown. Even these were almost erased and only just recognisable.

Daniel ignored them; he was after the gang and they would not be using vehicles. Quickly he widened the circles of his search, trying to pick up an outgoing set of tracks, concentrating on the northern side of the camp's perimeter, for the gang would almost certainly head back to the Zambezi River.

It was useless, as he had known deep down that it would be. After twenty minutes he gave it up. There were no tracks to follow. He stood under the dark trees and raged with frustration and sorrow.

'If only I could get a shot at the bastards,' he lamented. It meant little to him in his present mood that he was one man against twenty or more professional killers. Jock was a camera-man, not a soldier. He would be of no help in a fight. The memory of those mutilated bodies in the bedroom of the bungalow and of Johnny's shattered head overpowered all rational thought. Daniel found that he was physically shaking with the strength of his anger, and that put him on the road to recovering his scattered wits.

'While I'm wasting time here, they're getting clean away,' he told himself. 'The only way is to cut them off on the river. I need help.'

He thought of the Parks camp at Mana Pools. The warden there was a good man. Daniel knew him well from the old days. He had an anti-poaching team and a fast boat. They could get downstream and patrol the river crossing to catch the gang as it attempted to get back on to the Zambian side. Daniel was already starting to think logically as he started back towards the warden's office. From Mana Pools they could ring Harare and get the police to send in a spotter plane.

He knew that speed was vital now. Within the next ten hours the gang would be back across the river. However, he could not leave Johnny like that, lying in his own blood. It meant wasting a few more minutes, but he had to show him some last respect and at the very least cover him decently.

Daniel paused in the doorway to Johnny's office. The overhead lights were brutally explicit; they left nothing of the horror concealed. He set aside the AK 47 and looked around for a covering for his friend's corpse. The curtains over the front windows were green government issue, faded by sunlight, but they would do as a makeshift shroud. He took one of them down, and went with it to where Johnny lay.

Johnny's attitude was tortured. One arm was twisted up under his chest and his face lay in a pool of thick congealing blood. Gently Daniel rolled him over. The body had not yet stiffened in rigor mortis. He winced as he looked at Johnny's face, for the bullet had come out through his right eyebrow. He used a corner of the curtain to wipe his face clean, then arranged him in a comfortable attitude on his back.

Johnny's left hand was thrust into the front of his tunic and his fist was tightly clenched. Daniel's interest quickened as he saw the balled up sheet of paper in his hand. He prised Johnny's fingers open and freed the wad.

He stood up, crossed to the desk and spread the paper on it. He saw at once that Johnny had scrawled on it, using his own blood, and Daniel shivered at the macabre characters.

NJNC. The letters were childlike and crude, smeared and barely legible. They made no sense, although perhaps the J was an I. Daniel studied it. NINC. Still there was nothing obvious in the message. Either it was gibberish or had some obscure meaning that only made sense to a dying man.

Suddenly Daniel felt a stirring in his subconscious, something was trying to surface. He closed his eyes for a minute to give it a chance. Often it helped to let his mind go blank when searching for an elusive idea or memory, rather than to harry the point and drive it further under. It was there, very close now, a shadow just below his conscious mind like the shape of a man-eating shark under the surface of a turgid sea.

NINC.

He opened his eyes again and found himself looking at the floor. There were bloody footprints left by his own boot soles and by those of the killer. He was not thinking about them; he was still grappling with that single cryptic word that Johnny had left for him.

Then he found his eyes had focused on one of the footprints, and his nerves jumped tight and shrieked like the strings of a violin slashed with the bow. The footprint was chequered with a fish-scale pattern.

NINC. It resounded through his mind and then that distinctive footprint turned the sense of it and the echo came back, altered and compelling. NING. Johnny had tried to write NING! Daniel found that he was cold and trembling with the shock of the discovery.

'Ambassador Ning – Ning Cheng Gong.' How was it possible? And yet there were the bloody footprints to confirm the impossible. Ning had been here *after* Johnny was shot. Ning had been lying when he said that he had left ... Daniel broke that train of thought as another memory struck him like a bolt from a cross-bow.

The blood on the cuff of the blue cotton slacks, the tracks of Ning's training shoes and the blood – Johnny's blood. At last his rage had a target on which to focus, but now it was a cold constructive rage. He pressed the bloody note back into Johnny's hand and folded his fingers around it for the police to find. Then he spread the green curtain over Johnny's body, covering the shattered head. He stood over him for a few seconds.

'I'll get the bastard for you, old friend. For you and Mavis and the babies. I promise you, Johnny, on the memory of our friendship. I swear it.' Then he snatched up the rifle and ran from the office, down the steps to where Jock waited beside the parked Landcruiser.

In the few seconds that it took him to reach the truck, the last details fell into place in his mind. He remembered Cheng's perturbation when he thought Daniel might be staying longer at Chiwewe, and his obvious relief when he learned that Daniel was leaving.

He glanced back towards the ruins of the ivory godown and the tyre treads were still just visible in the mud. It was simple and ingenious. Let the gang of poachers draw the pursuit, while they ferried the ivory out in the Parks Board's own trucks. Daniel remembered the surly unnatural behaviour of Gomo and the other driver when he had met them on the road. Now it made good sense. They had been sitting on a load of stolen ivory. No wonder they were acting strangely.

As he slipped behind the wheel of the Landcruiser and ordered Jock to climb aboard, he glanced at his wristwatch. It was almost ten o'clock, nearly four hours since he had passed Cheng and the trucks on the escarpment road. Could he catch them before they reached the main highway and disappeared? He realised that it had been so carefully planned that they must have worked out an escape route and some means of disposing of the ivory. He started the Landcruiser and hit the gear-lever. 'You aren't going to get away with it, you dirty bastard!'

In many places the recent storm waters had scoured the escarpment road, gouging knee-deep gulleys across the tracks and exposing boulders the size of cannonballs. Daniel pushed the Landcruiser over them so violently that Jock seized the grab handle on the dashboard for support.

'Slow down, Danny, damn it. You'll kill us both. Where the hell are we going? What's the rush?'

In as few words as possible Daniel told him the bare outlines.

'You can't touch an ambassador,' Jock grunted as the bouncing truck slammed the words out of him. 'If you're wrong, they'll crucify you, man.'

'I'm not wrong,' Daniel assured him. 'On top of Johnny's note, I feel it in my guts.'

The rain waters had rushed down the slope of the escarpment, but when they reached the floor of the valley they slowed and piled up upon themselves. Only hours before, Daniel had crossed and re-crossed a dry river-bed at the foot of the escarpment. Now he pulled up on the approach to the ford and stared down the beam of the headlights.

'You'll never get through there,' Jock muttered with alarm.

Daniel left the motor running and jumped down into ankle-deep mud. He ran to the edge of the crazy water. It was the colour of creamed coffee, racing past in a muddy blur, carrying small tree-trunks and up-rooted bushes with it. It was almost fifty yards across.

One of the trees growing beside the ford draped its branches out over the torrent, in places just touching the swirling waters with its lowest twigs. Daniel grabbed the main branch for support and let himself down into the river. He edged out across the flood and it took all the strength of his arms to prevent himself from being swept away. The drag of the water was overpowering and his feet were continually lifted clear of the bottom. However, he worked himself out to the deepest section of the river.

It was as deep as his lowest rib. The branch to which he was clinging was creaking and bowing like a fishing-rod to the strain as he began to work his way back to the bank. He emerged from the torrent with water streaming down his lower body, his sodden clothing clinging to his legs and his boots squelching.

'It'll go,' he told Jock, as he clambered back into the cab.

'You're crazy mad,' Jock exploded. 'I'm not going in there.'

'Okay! Fine! You've got just two seconds to get out,' Daniel told him grimly, and changed the gearing of the Toyota into four-wheel drive and low ratio.

'You can't leave me here,' Jock howled. 'The place is lousy with lions. What happens to me?'

'That's your problem, mate. Are you coming or going?'

'Okay, go ahead! Drown us!' Jock capitulated and grabbed the sides of his seat.

Daniel rolled the Landcruiser down the steep approach to the ford, and into the brown waters. He kept her rolling at an even pace and within a few yards the water was above the level of the wheels, but still the nose of the truck was tilted steeply downwards as the bottom fell away.

There was a whoosh of steam as water rushed through the engine compartment and swamped the hot metal of the block. The headlights were obscured as they sank below the surface, becoming two luminous glows in the turgid water. A bow wave rose ahead of the bonnet, as the water came up to the level of the windshield. A petrol engine would have swamped and stalled, but the big diesel pushed them stolidly forward into the flood. Water was pouring in around the door posts. They were calf-deep where they sat.

'You really are crazy,' Jock yelled, and put his feet up on the dashboard. 'I want to go home to mother!'

Now even the Landcruiser was faltering as the air trapped in the body floated her high and her spinning tyres lost traction on the rock-strewn bottom.

'Oh, my God!' Jock cried, as a huge up-rooted tree came hurtling down upon them out of the darkness.

It crashed into the side of the truck, hitting one of the windows, and slewing the whole chassis around. They were hurled downstream, spinning slowly under the weight of the floating tree. As they made one full revolution the mortal embrace of the tree mass was broken.

Released from its grip, they floated free, but they were sinking fast as the trapped air was expelled from the Landcruiser's body. Water began to seep in, and soon they were sitting waist-deep.

'I'm getting out,' Jock yelled, and threw his weight against the door. 'It won't budge.' He was panicking, as the pressure of water held the door tightly closed.

Then suddenly Daniel felt the wheels touch bottom again. The flood had swept them into a bend of the river and pushed them in against the far bank. The engine was still running. The modified air-intake pipe and filter reached up as high as the cab roof. Daniel had installed it for just such an emergency. In the shallows, the wheels caught at the jagged rock bottom and heaved the Landcruiser's bulk forward.

'Come on, darling,' Daniel pleaded. 'Get us out of here.' And the sturdy truck responded. She shuddered and bounced and tried to drag herself from the waters. The headlights pushed through the surface and blazed out suddenly, lighting the far bank. The flood had cast them up on the shelving mudbank and the truck canted steeply nose-up as her spinning front wheels clawed up the slope.

Ahead of them was a low spot in the riverbank. The Landcruiser slipped and slewed and crabbed up it, the engine roaring, ferociously tearing out small bushes that had survived the flood and ploughing deep ruts in the soft earth, until suddenly her lugged tyres gained full purchase and hurled her forward up out of the flood. Sheets of water streamed from her bodywork like a surfacing submarine and the big diesel engine bellowed triumphantly as they roared into the mopane forest.

'I'm alive,' Jock whispered. 'Hallelujah!'

Daniel turned parallel with the riverbank, weaving the Landcruiser back and forth between the tree-trunks of the standing mopane until they bumped over the verge on to the roadway. He kicked her out of low ratio and gunned the motor. They sped away towards the Mana Pools turn-off.

'How many more like that?' Jock asked with trepidation. For the first time since Johnny's death Daniel smiled, but it was a grim little smile.

'Only four or five,' he answered. 'A Sunday afternoon stroll. Nothing to it.'

He glanced at his watch. Cheng and the refrigerator trucks had almost four hours' start on them. They must have got through the fords before the drainage of storm waters off the slope of the escarpment had flooded them. The earth beneath the mopane trees was melted like warm chocolate by the rain. This black cotton soil was notorious for bogging down vehicles when it was wet. The Landcruiser slithered and laboured and left deep glutinous ruts behind the churning wheels.

'Here's the next river.' Daniel warned, as the road gradient altered and thick dark riverine bush pressed in close on each side of the narrow track. 'Get your life-jacket on.'

'I can't stand another one like the last.' Jock turned to him, pale-faced in the glow of the instrument panel. 'I promise ten "Hail Mary's" and fifty "Our Father's" . . .'

'The price is right – it'll be a breeze,' Daniel assured him as the headlights lit the ford.

In Africa a flash flood drops almost as abruptly as it rises. The rain had stopped almost two hours earlier, and the slope of the valley was by now almost drained. There was a high-water mark on the far bank of the river almost six feet above the present surface of the shrunken waters, to show how swiftly they had subsided. This time the Landcruiser made light of the crossing. The waters did not even cover the headlights before she triumphantly climbed the far bank.

'The power of prayer,' Daniel grunted. 'Keep it up, Jock. We'll make a believer of you yet.'

The next river had fallen even lower, to the level of the tops of the wheels, and Daniel did not bother to change gear ratios as they splashed through. Forty minutes later, Daniel parked the truck at the front door of the warden's bungalow at Mana Pools Camp. While Jock leaned on the horn button and sounded a long urgent peal, Daniel pounded with both fists on the warden's door.

The warden came stumbling out onto the screened verandah, dressed only in a pair of underpants. 'Who is it?' he called in Shona. 'What the hell is going on?' He was a lean, muscled forty-year-old named Isaac Mtwetwe.

'Isaac? It's me,' Daniel called. 'There's big trouble, man. Get your arse into gear. You've got work to do.'

'Danny?' Isaac shaded his eyes against the glare of the Landcruiser's headlights. 'Is that you, Danny?'

He flashed his torch into Daniel's face. 'What is it? What has happened?'

Daniel answered him in fluent Shona. 'A big gang of armed poachers has hit Chiwewe camp. They wiped out Johnny Nzou and his family, and the entire camp staff.'

'Good God!' Isaac came fully awake.

'My guess is that they're from the Zambian side,' Daniel went on. 'I reckon they're heading back to cross the Zambezi about twenty miles downstream from here. You've got to get your anti-poaching team there to head them off.'

Swiftly Daniel gave him all the other information he had gleaned, the estimated size of the gang, their weapons, the time that they had left Chiwewe and their probable line and speed of march. Then he asked, 'Did the refrigerator trucks come through here from Chiwewe on their return to Harare?'

'At about eight o'clock,' Isaac confirmed. 'They just got through before the rivers flooded. There was a civilian with them, a Chinese in a blue Mercedes. One of the trucks was towing him. The Mercedes was no good in the mud.' Isaac was dressing as he spoke. 'What are you going to do, Danny? I know Johnny Nzou was your friend. If you come with us you might get a shot at these swine.' Although they had fought on opposite sides during the bush war, he knew Daniel's reputation.

81

However, Daniel shook his head.

'I am going on after the trucks, and that Mercedes.'

'I don't understand.' Isaac looked up from lacing his boots and his tone was puzzled.

'I can't explain now, but it's all part of Johnny's murder. Trust me.' Daniel couldn't tell Isaac about the ivory and Ambassador Ning, not until he had proof. 'Trust me,' he repeated, and Isaac nodded.

'Okay, Danny, I'll get those murdering swine for you before they get away across the river,' he promised. 'You go ahead. Do what you have to do.'

Daniel left Isaac on the Zambezi bank, assembling his strike force of anti-poacher rangers and embarking them into the twenty-foot fast assault craft. There was a big ninety horsepower Yamaha outboard on the stern. Like the rest of them, the boat was a veteran of the bush war.

Daniel drove on westwards into the night, following the track that ran parallel to the Zambezi. Now the tyre tracks of the convoy were even more deeply ploughed into the muddy earth. In the headlights they looked as fresh as if they had been laid only minutes before. Certainly they had been made since the last downpour of rain. The pattern of the treads was clearly moulded in black cotton clay of the roadway.

Obviously one of the trucks was still towing the Mercedes. Daniel could pick out the scuff-marks where the tow rope had touched the earth at intervals. The tow would slow them down considerably, Daniel thought with satisfaction. He must be gaining on them rapidly now. He peered ahead eagerly, half expecting to see the red glow of the Mercedes's tail-lights appear out of the darkness, and he reached out to touch the AK 47 rifle propped between the seats.

Jock noticed the gesture and warned him softly, 'Don't do anything stupid, Danny. You don't have any proof, man. You can't just go blowing the ambassador's head off on suspicion. Cool it, man.'

It seemed that they were further behind the convoy than Daniel had hoped. It was after midnight when they intersected the Great North Road, the metalled highway that crossed the Chirundu bridge over the Zambezi to the north, and to the south climbed the escarpment of the valley on its serpentine route to Harare, the capital of Zimbabwe.

Daniel pulled the Landcruiser into the verge at the road junction. He jumped out with the Maglite in his hand.

In all probability the convoy would have turned south towards Harare. They couldn't have hoped to get two huge government trucks loaded with fresh game meat and ivory through both the Zimbabwean and Zambian customs posts, not even with the dispensation of the most princely bribes.

Daniel found confirmation of his deduction almost immediately. The tyres of the trucks and the Mercedes had been caked with clinging black clay. They left clear tracks on the tarmac of the highway. The tracks gradually faded out as the last vestiges of clay were spun off the tyres, but for almost a mile further the moulded bars of mud from between the treads of the tyres littered the tarmac like squares of chocolate.

'South,' said Daniel, as he climbed back behind the driving-wheel. 'They're heading south, and we're catching up with them every minute.'

He pushed the Landcruiser hard and kicked in the Fairey overdrive. The speedometer needle touched 90 miles per hour and the heavy tyres whined shrilly on the black tarmac surface of the highway.

'They can't be much further ahead,' Daniel muttered. As he said it he saw the glow of headlights in front of them.

He touched the stock of the AK rifle again, and Jock glanced at him nervously.

'For Chrissake, Danny. I don't want to be an accessory to bloody murder. They say Chikurubi prison isn't exactly five-star accommodation.'

The lights were closer now and Daniel switched on the Landcruiser's powerful spotlights, then exclaimed with disappointment. He had expected to see the distinctive hull of the refrigerator truck standing up tall and polar white in the beam of the spotlight. Instead he found a vehicle that he had never seen before. It was a gigantic MAC truck, a twenty-tonner, towing an equally large eight-wheel trailer. Both the hull of the truck and the body of the trailer were covered by heavy-duty green nylon tarpaulin and roped down with a hook-and-eye arrangement that securely protected the cargo. This massive road-rig was pulled off the highway and parked in a lay-by at the roadside facing back northwards towards Chirundu Bridge.

Three men were working around the trailer, adjusting the ropes that held the tarpaulin in place. The beam of the spotlight froze them, and they stared back at the approaching Land-cruiser.

Two of the men were black Africans dressed in faded overalls. The third was a dignified figure in a khaki safari suit. He was also dark-complexioned but bearded and wearing some sort of white headgear. It was only when Daniel got closer that he realised that it was a neatly bound white turban and that the man was a Sikh. His beard was carefully curled and rolled up into the folds of the turban.

As Daniel slowed the Landcruiser and pulled in in front of the parked truck, the Sikh spoke sharply to the two Africans. All three of them turned and hurried back to the front of the truck and climbed aboard.

'Hold it a second!' Daniel shouted, and jumped out of the Landcruiser. 'I want to talk to you.' The Sikh was already seated behind the wheel.

'Hold on!' Daniel called urgently, and came level with the cab.

The Sikh was five feet above the level of his head and he leaned out of the window and peered down at Daniel.

'Yes, what is it?'

'Sorry to trouble you,' Daniel told him. 'Have you passed two large white trucks on the road?'

The Sikh stared down at him without answering and Daniel added, 'Very big trucks – you couldn't miss them. Travelling together in convoy. There might have been a blue Mercedes saloon with them.'

The Sikh pulled his head in and spoke to the two Africans in a dialect that Daniel could not understand. While he waited impatiently for a reply, Daniel noticed a company logo painted on the front door-panel of the truck.

CHETTI SINGH LIMITED
IMPORT AND EXPORT

Malawi was the small sovereign state that nestled between the three much larger territories of Zambia, Tanzania and Mozambique. It was a country of mountains and rivers and lakes, whose population was as prosperous and happy under its octogenarian dictator Hastings Banda as any state on the poverty- and tyranny-ridden continent of Africa.

'Mr Singh, I'm in a desperate hurry,' Daniel called. 'Please tell me if you've seen those trucks.'

The Sikh popped his head back out the window in alarm. 'How do you know my name?' he demanded, and Daniel pointed at the logo on the door.

'Ha! You are one very observant and erudite fellow, never mind.' The Sikh looked relieved. 'Yes, my men reminded me that two trucks passed us one hour ago. They were heading south. We did not see a Mercedes with them. I am totally certain of that salient fact. No Mercedes. Absolutely.'

He started the engine of the MAC truck. 'I am happy to have served you. I am also in desperate haste. I must return home to Lilongwe. Farewell, my friend, safe journey and happy landings.' He waved cheerily and let the huge truck roll forward.

Something about his airy manner struck a false note in Daniel's mind. As the heavily loaded trailer rumbled past him, Daniel caught hold of one of the steel slats and swung himself up on to the footplate below the trailer's tailgate. The headlights of the parked Landcruiser gave him enough light to peer between the steel slats of the bodywork and the edge of the tarpaulin cover.

The trailer seemed to be packed with a full load of gunny sacks. Stencilled on one of the sacks that he could see was the legend 'Dried Fish, Product of . . .' The country of origin was obscured. Daniel's nose confirmed the contents of the sacks. The smell of half-rotten fish was powerful and unmistakable.

The truck was gathering speed swiftly and Daniel dropped off and let his own momentum carry him forward as he hit the ground. He ran with it for a dozen paces and then pulled up and stared after the dwindling tail-lights.

His instinct warned him that something was as fishy as the stink from under the tarpaulin of the departing trailer, but what could he do about it? He tried to think. His main concerns were still the convoy of refrigerator trucks and Ning in his Mercedes which were heading southwards, while the Sikh in his MAC truck was rumbling away in the opposite direction. He couldn't follow both of them even if he could prove a connection between them, which he could not.

'Chetti Singh,' he repeated the name and the box number to fix it firmly in his mind. Then ran back to where Jock waited in the Landcruiser.

'Who was that? What did he say?' Jock wanted to know.

'He saw the refrigerator trucks heading south about an hour ago. We're going after them.' He pulled out of the lay-by and they raced on southwards at their top speed.

The road began to climb the hills that led up on to the high central plateau, and the Landcruiser's speed bled off slowly, but still they were doing around 70 miles an hour. Jock had not spoken again since they had met Chetti Singh, but his features were drawn and nervous in the light reflected from the instrument panel. He kept glancing sideways at Daniel as if he were about to protest, but then thought better of it.

The road went into a series of gentle curves as it followed the gradient of the hills. They came through the next curve and without warning one of the white refrigerator trucks blocked the road ahead of them. It was travelling at half the speed of the Landcruiser and diesel smoke belched out of its exhausts as it laboured upwards in low gear. The driver was holding the middle line of the highway, not leaving sufficient space for Daniel to pass him.

Daniel sounded his horn and flicked his spotlights on and off to induce the truck to move over, but it never wavered.

'Move over, you murdering bastard,' Daniel snarled, and hit the horn button with another prolonged blast.

'Take it easy, Daniel,' Jock pleaded. 'You're going over the top. Cool it, man.'

Daniel swung the Landcruiser out on to the far verge of the road, into an overtaking position, and he sounded the horn again. Now he could see the wing mirror on the cab of the truck, and reflected in it the face of the driver.

The driver was Gomo. He was watching Daniel in the mirror but making no effort to give way and let him pass. His expression was a mixture of fear and ferocity, of guilt and bitter resentment. He was deliberately blocking the road, swinging wide on the corners and weaving the truck back and across when Daniel tried to pass him on the wrong side.

'He knows it's us,' Daniel told Jock angrily. 'He knows we've been back to Chiwewe and seen the bloody business there. He knows we suspect him, and he's trying to hold us off.'

'Come on, Danny. That's all in your head, man. There could be a dozen explanations for why he's behaving like this. I don't want any part of this crazy business.'

'Too late, my friend,' Daniel told him. 'Like it or not, you're part of it now.'

Daniel pulled the Landcruiser sharply back in the opposite direction. For once Gomo was slow to react and get across the road to block him. Daniel dropped a gear and thrust the accelerator flat. The Landcruiser jumped forward and got round the truck's tall tail-end. Still holding the accelerator flat to the floorboards, Daniel drew level with the cab, squeezing through the gap between the steel side of the hull and the edge of the road.

Only the nearside wheels of the Landcruiser had purchase on the tarmac surface, the off-side wheels were on the verge of the highway, throwing up a spray of loose gravel, dangerously close to the edge that fell away steeply into the Zambezi valley below them.

'Danny, you mad bastard,' Jock yelled angrily. 'You'll get us both killed. I've had enough of this bullshit, man.'

The Landcruiser hit one of the concrete road-markers with its reflective cat's-eye that warned of the dangerous drop. With a crash they snapped off the road sign, and swayed dangerously, but Daniel held grimly to the outside berth and inched up alongside the cab of the lumbering truck.

Gomo stared down at the Landcruiser from the vantage point of the high cab. Daniel leant forward to see him, lifted one hand from the wheel and made a peremptory hand signal for him to pull over and stop. Gomo nodded and obeyed, swinging the truck back to the left, giving way to the Landcruiser.

'That's more like it,' Daniel grated, and edged back into the space alongside the truck that Gomo had opened for him. He had fallen into the trap and let down his guard. The two vehicles were still grinding along side by side, and Gomo suddenly spun the driving-wheel hard back in the opposite direction. Before Daniel could react, the truck crashed into the side of the Landcruiser and a shower of sparks blazed from the violent contact of steel against steel. The weight and momentum of the huge truck flung the smaller vehicle back over the verge.

Daniel fought the wheel to try and resist the thrust but the struts flew through his fingers and he thought for a moment that his left thumb was dislocated. The pain numbed him to the elbow. He hit the brakes hard and the Landcruiser slowed and allowed the truck to pull ahead, with a shriek of metal between the two vehicles as they disengaged. The Landcruiser came to rest, half over the embankment with one front wheel hanging over the cliff face.

Daniel wrung his injured hand, tears of agony welling into his eyes. Gradually he felt strength return, and with it his anger. By now the truck was five hundred yards ahead and pulling away rapidly.

With the Landcruiser in four-wheel drive, Daniel flung her into reverse. Only three of her wheels had purchase, but she heaved herself gamely back from the drop. Her near side was scraped down to bare gleaming metal where the truck had struck her.

'Okay,' Daniel snarled at Jock. 'Do you want any more proof? That was a deliberate attempt to write us off. That bastard Gomo is guilty as hell.'

The truck had disappeared from view around the next curve of the highway, and Daniel hurled the Landcruiser in pursuit.

'Gomo isn't going to let us get ahead of him,' Daniel told Jock. 'I'm going to get on to that truck and take him out of it.'

'I want no more part of this business,' Jock muttered. 'Leave it to the police now, damn it.'

Daniel ignored his protest and pushed the Landcruiser to its top speed. As they came through the bend the refrigerator truck was only a few hundred yards ahead. The gap between them closed swiftly.

Daniel studied the other vehicle. The scrape marks down its side were not as extensive as the damage to the Landcruiser and Gomo was making better speed now as the slope of the hill eased away towards the crest of the escarpment. The double rear doors into the cargo hold were locked with a heavy vertical bar. The airtight seals were black rubber around the edge of the doors. On the nearside of the hull a steel ladder gave access to the flat roof where the cooling fans of the refrigeration equipment were housed in fibreglass pods.

'I'm going to get on that ladder,' Daniel told Jock. 'As soon as I'm gone, you slide over and grab the wheel.'

'Not me, man. I told you, I've had a gutful. Count me out.'

'Fine.' Daniel did not even glance at him. 'Don't steer! Let her crash and you with her. What's one stupid prick less in this naughty world?'

Daniel was judging the speed and distance between the two converging vehicles. He opened his side door. The retaining catch on the door had been removed to allow unimpeded photography through the opening so the door hinged fully open, to lie flat against the side of the bonnet.

Steering with one hand, Daniel leaned out of the open door. 'Take her, she's yours,' he shouted at Jock. Daniel hauled himself up on to the roof, the pain in his thumb forgotten. At that moment Gomo once again swung across to block the Landcruiser.

As the two vehicles came together Daniel leaped across the narrow gap. He caught the rung of the side ladder and hauled his lower body out from between the steel sides of the vehicles as they clashed together again.

He had a glimpse of Jock at the driver's wheel, pale-faced and sweating in the reflected headlights. Then the Landcruiser swerved away and fell behind the white truck, Jock steering it erratically, letting the slope slow it, finally bringing it to a halt on the side of the road.

Daniel clambered upwards, hand over hand, agile as an ape

on the narrow steel rungs, and reached the flat roof of the truck. The fan housing was in the centre of the roof and a low grab-rail ran the length of the hull, fore and aft. On hands and knees Daniel worked his way forward, falling flat on his belly and clinging grimly to the rail when the centrifugal force of the truck through the bends threatened to throw him from the roof.

It took him fully five minutes to get forward above the articulated driver's cab. He was pretty certain that Gomo had not seen him come aboard. The bulk of the cargo hold would have blocked his rear view. By now he must be fairly confident that he had discouraged the driver of the Landcruiser, for its headlights were no longer visible on the empty road behind the truck.

Daniel worked his way gingerly across to the passenger side of the cab and peered over. There was a running-board below the passenger door, and the sturdy wing mirror standing out from the side of the cab would give him a secure handhold. It only remained to find out if Gomo had taken the precaution of locking the passenger door. There was no reason why he should, Daniel comforted himself, as he looked ahead down the beams of the truck's powerful headlights.

He waited until the road turned left. The pull would hold him against the side of the cab, rather than throwing him clear. He slid over the side and clutched at the wing mirror. For a moment his feet were kicking in air, then they hit the wide steel running-board and found a hold. He was facing inwards, hanging on to the mirror and peering in through the side window of the cab.

Gomo turned a startled face towards him and shouted something. He tried to reach across to the locking handle of the door, but the full width of the passenger seat separated him from it and the truck slewed wildly and nearly left the road, forcing Gomo to grab the wheel again.

Daniel jerked open the side door and threw himself into the cab, sprawling half across the seat. Gomo punched at his face. The fist caught Daniel under the left eye and stunned him for only a moment, then Daniel seized the handle of the vacuum brake control and heaved it full on.

All the gigantic wheels of the truck locked simultaneously and, in a shrieking billow of blue smoke and scorching rubber, the truck skidded and swayed down the highway. Gomo was hurled forward out of his seat. The steering-wheel caught him in the chest and his forehead cracked against the windshield with enough force to star the glass.

Then the next wild swing of the vehicle flung him back, only semi-conscious, into his seat. Daniel reached across him and seized the steering-wheel. He held the truck straight until it came to a halt, half off the highway, with its offside wheels in the drainage ditch.

Daniel switched off the ignition and reached across Gomo to open the driver's door. He grabbed Gomo's shoulder and shoved him roughly out of the cab. Gomo fell the six feet to the ground and ended up on his knees. There was a lump the size and colour of a ripe fig in the centre of his forehead where he had hit the windscreen.

Daniel jumped down and stooped to catch hold of the collar of his uniform tunic.

'All right.' He twisted the collar like a garotte. 'You killed Johnny Nzou and his family.'

Gomo's face was swelling and turning purple black in the vague light reflected from the truck's headlamps.

'Please, Doctor, I don't understand. Why are you doing this?' His voice was a breathless whine as Daniel choked him.

'You lying bastard, you are as guilty—'

Gomo reached under the hem of his tunic. He wore a skinning knife in a leather sheath on his belt. Daniel heard the snap of the buckle as he released the retaining strap and caught the glint of the blade as it came free of the sheath.

Daniel released his collar and jumped back as Gomo slashed upwards. He was only just quick enough, for the blade caught in a loose fold of his shirt and sliced it like a razor. He felt the sting of it as it nicked his skin and left a shallow graze up across his lower ribs.

Gomo came to his feet, holding the knife in a low underhand grip.

'I kill you,' he warned, shaking his head to clear it, weaving the glittering blade in the typical knife-fighter's on-guard stance, aiming the point at Daniel's belly.

'I kill you, you white shit-eater.' He feinted and cut in a side-arm slash and Daniel jumped back as the blade hissed an inch from his stomach.

'Yah!' Gomo chuckled thickly. 'Jump, you white baboon. Run, you little white monkey.' He cut again, forcing Daniel to give ground, and then rushed at him in a furious prolonged attack that forced Daniel to scramble and dance to keep clear of the darting blade.

Gomo changed the angle of his thrusts, going lower, trying to cut Daniel's thighs and cripple him, but always keeping the knife well covered so that Daniel could not grab at his wrist. Moving backwards, Daniel pretended to stumble on the rough footing. He dropped on one knee and put his left hand to the ground to regain his balance.

'Yah!' Gomo thought he saw his opportunity and came in to finish it, but Daniel had snatched up a handful of gravel and now he pushed off and used his momentum to hurl the handful into Gomo's face. It was an old knife-fighter's trick, but Gomo fell for it. The gravel slashed his eyes, and deflected his thrust. Instinctively he threw up his hands to cover his face, and Daniel seized his knife-hand and wrenched it over.

They were chest to chest now, the knife held above their heads at the full stretch of their arms. Daniel snapped his head forward, butting for Gomo's face, and caught him with the top of his forehead across the bridge of his nose. Gomo gasped and reeled backwards, and Daniel brought up his right knee into Gomo's crotch, catching him squarely, crushing his genitals. This time Gomo screamed and his right arm lost its force.

Daniel swung it down and slammed the knuckles of the clenched knife-hand against the steel side of the truck. The knife spun from Gomo's nerveless fingers, and Daniel hooked him behind the heels with one foot, and heaved him backwards so that he tripped and went sprawling into the drainage ditch beside the highway.

Before Gomo could recover his balance and rise, Daniel had snatched up the knife and was standing over him. He placed the point of the blade under Gomo's chin and pricked the soft skin of his throat so that a single droplet of blood welled out on to the silver steel like a bright cabochon ruby.

'Keep still,' he grated, 'or I'll cut your gizzard out, you murdering bastard.' It took a few seconds for him to recover his breath. 'All right. Now get up, slowly.'

Gomo came to his feet, clutching his injured genitals. Daniel forced him back against the side of the truck, the knife still pressed to his throat.

'You've got the ivory in the truck,' he accused. 'Let's have a look at it, my friend.'

'No,' Gomo whispered. 'No ivory. I don't know what you want. You are mad, man.'

'Where are the keys to the hold?' Daniel demanded, and Gomo swivelled his eyes without moving his head.

'In my pocket.'

'Turn around, slowly,' Daniel ordered. 'Face the side of the truck.'

As Gomo obeyed Daniel whipped his arm around his throat in a stranglehold from behind and shoved him forward so that his lumped forehead cracked against the steel hull. Gomo cried out with the pain.

'Give me an excuse to do that again,' Daniel whispered in his ear. 'The sound of your pig squeals is sweet music.'

He pressed the knife into Gomo's back at the level of his kidneys, just hard enough to let him feel the point of it through the cloth of his tunic.

'Get the keys.' He pricked him a little harder and Gomo reached into his pocket. The keys tinkled as he brought them out.

Still holding him in a strangler's grip, Daniel frog-marched him to the rear of the truck.

'Open the lock,' he snapped. Gomo fitted the key and the mechanism turned easily.

'Okay, now get the handcuffs off your belt,' he ordered. The steel manacles were regulation issue for all rangers on anti-poaching duty.

'Snap one link over your right wrist,' Daniel told him. 'And give me the key.'

The cuffs dangling from his wrist, Gomo passed the key over his shoulder. Daniel slipped it into his pocket, then snapped the second link of the handcuffs over the steel bracing of the hull.

Now Gomo was securely chained to the bodywork of the truck and Daniel released his grip on him and turned the locking handle of the rear double doors.

He swung them open. A gust of icy air flowed out of the refrigerated interior and the smell of elephant meat was gamey and rank. The inside of the hold was in darkness, but Daniel jumped up on to the tailgate and groped for the light switch. The striplight on the roof flickered and then lit up the refrigerated compartment with a cold blue glow. Hunks of butchered carcass streaked and marbled with white fat hung from the rows of meat-hooks along the roof rails. There were tons of flesh, packed in so closely that Daniel could see only the first rank of carcasses. He dropped on his knees and peered into the narrow space below them. The steel floor was puddled with dripping blood, but that was all.

Daniel felt a sudden swoop of dismay in his guts. He had expected to see piles of tusks packed beneath the hanging carcasses. He scrambled to his feet and pushed his way into the compartment. The cold took his breath away, and the touch of the raw frozen flesh as he brushed against it was loathsome and disgusting, but he wriggled his way deeper into the hold, determined to find where they had concealed the ivory.

He gave up after ten minutes. There was no place where they could have hidden such a bulky cargo. He jumped down to ground level. His clothing was stained from contact with the raw meat. On hands and knees he crawled under the chassis of the truck, searching for a secret compartment.

When he crawled out again, Gomo crowed at him gleefully, 'No ivory, I tell you, no ivory. You break government truck. You beat me. Plenty trouble for you now, white boy.'

'We haven't finished yet,' Daniel promised him. 'We haven't finished until you sing me a little song, the song about what you and the Chinaman did with the ivory.'

'No ivory,' Gomo repeated, but Daniel grabbed his shoulder and swung him around to face the side of the truck.

With one deft movement he unlocked the link of the cuffs from the bodywork, twisted both Gomo's wrists up behind his back and locked them there.

'Okay, brother,' he muttered grimly. 'Let's go where we have a little light to work in.'

He lifted Gomo's manacled hands up between his shoulder-blades and marched him to the front of the truck. He hand-cuffed him to the front fender between the headlights. Both Gomo's hands were pinned behind his back. He was helpless.

'Johnny Nzou was my friend,' he told Gomo softly. 'You raped his wife and his little daughters. You beat his son's brains out all over the wall. You shot Johnny—'

'No, not me. I know nothing,' Gomo screamed. 'I kill nobody. No ivory, no kill . . .'

Daniel went on quietly, as though Gomo had not interjected.

'You must believe me when I tell you that I'm going to enjoy doing this. Every time you squeal, I will think of Johnny Nzou, and I'll be glad.'

'I know nothing. You mad.'

Daniel slipped the knife-blade under Gomo's belt and sliced through the leather. His khaki uniform trousers sagged down around his hips. Daniel pulled the waistband open and thrust the blade into his trouser top.

'How many wives have you got, Gomo?' he asked. 'Four? Five? How many?' He slit through the waistband and Gomo's trousers slid down around his ankles. 'I think your wives want you to tell me about the ivory, Gomo. They want you to tell me about Johnny Nzou and how he died.'

Daniel pulled the elasticised top of Gomo's underpants down around his knees.

'Let's have a look at what you've got.' He smiled coldly. 'I think your wives are going to be very unhappy, Gomo.'

Daniel took the front tails of Gomo's tunic and ripped them apart so violently that the buttons popped off and flew away into the darkness beyond the headlights. He pulled the separate flaps of the tunic back over Gomo's shoulders, so that he was naked from the throat to the knees. Gomo's body hair covered his chest and paunch with tight black balls of wool. His genitals were massively bunched at the base of his belly, nestled in their own flocculent pelt.

'Sing me a little song about the ivory and Mr Ning,' Daniel invited, and used the flat of the blade to separate Gomo's dangling penis from the bunch.

Gomo gasped and tried to shrink away from the cold metallic

touch, but the radiator grille pressed against his back and he could not move.

'Talk, Gomo, even if it is only to say goodbye to your own *matondo*.'

'You are mad,' Gomo gasped. 'I don't know what you want.'

'What I want,' said Daniel, 'is to cut this off at the root.'

The thick tube of flesh was draped over the flat of the blade. It looked like the trunk of a new-born elephant, long and dark, knotted with veins and with a wrinkled and hooded tip.

'I want to cut this off and force you to kiss it goodbye, Gomo.'

'I didn't kill Johnny Nzou.' Gomo's voice broke. 'It wasn't me.'

'What about his wife and daughters, Gomo? Did you use this big ugly rod of yours on them?'

'No, no! You are mad. I didn't . . .'

'Come on, Gomo. All I have to do is turn the knife a little, like this.' Daniel rolled his wrist slowly, bringing the razor edge uppermost. Gomo's organ was dangling over it, and then the thin skin split. It was just a scratch, but Gomo screamed.

'Stop!' he bleated. 'I will tell you. Yes, all right, I will tell you everything I know. Stop, please stop!'

'That's good.' Daniel encouraged him. 'Tell me about Chetti Singh . . .' He introduced the name with assurance. It was a flier, but Gomo accepted.

'Yes, I tell you about him, if you don't cut me. Please don't cut me.'

'Armstrong.' Another voice startled Daniel. He had not heard the Landcruiser come up. It must have arrived while he was searching the cold compartment of the truck, but now Jock stood in the peripheral shadows of the headlights.

'Leave him, Armstrong.' Jock's voice was rough with determination. 'Get away from that man,' he ordered.

'You keep out of this,' Daniel snapped at him, but Jock stepped closer and with a start Daniel saw that he carried the AK rifle. He handled it with surprising competence and authority.

'Leave him alone,' Jock ordered. 'You've gone too far – much too far.'

'The man is a murderer and a criminal,' Daniel protested, but he was forced to step back before the menace of the AK 47. Jock was pointing it at his belly.

'You haven't any proof. There is no ivory,' Jock told him. 'You don't have anything.'

'He was confessing,' Daniel told him angrily. 'If you just keep out of it—'

'You were torturing him,' Jock answered as angrily. 'You had a knife to his balls. Of course, he was confessing. He has rights; you can't abuse those rights. Unchain him now; let him go!'

'You are a bleeding heart,' Daniel fumed. 'This is an animal—'

'He is a human being,' Jock contradicted. 'And I have to stop you abusing him, or else I'm as guilty as you are. I don't want to spend the next ten years in prison. Turn him loose.'

'He will confess first, or I'll cut his balls out.' Daniel seized a handful of Gomo's genitals and pulled. The loose skin and flesh stretched like shiny black rubber and Daniel held the knife-blade threateningly over it.

Gomo screamed, and Jock lifted the AK 47 and fired. He aimed a foot over Daniel's head. The muzzle blast whipped through Daniel's thick sweat-soaked curls and sent him reeling backwards clutching his ears.

'I warned you, Daniel.' Jock's expression was grim. 'Give me the keys of the handcuffs.'

Daniel was dazed by the blast, and Jock fired again. The bullet ploughed into the gravel between Daniel's boots.

'I mean it, Danny. I swear it. I'll kill you before I let you suck me any further into this business.'

'You saw Johnny . . .' Daniel shook his head and held his ears, but the muzzle blast had temporarily stunned him.

'I also saw you threaten to emasculate this man. That's enough. Give me the keys or the next shot is through one of your knee-caps.' Daniel saw that he meant it and reluctantly tossed him the keys.

'All right, now stand well back,' Jock ordered. He kept the rifle pointed at Daniel's belly as he unlocked one of the cuffs from Gomo's wrist, and handed him the key.

'You bloody idiot,' Daniel swore with frustration. 'Another minute, and I would have had him. I would have found out who killed Johnny and what happened to the ivory.'

Gomo unlocked his other wrist and swiftly pulled up his trousers and closed his tunic. Now that he was unchained and dressed, Gomo recovered his bravado. 'He is talking shit!' His voice was loud and defiant. 'I didn't say nothing. I don't know about Nzou. He was alive when we left Chiwewe—'

'All right. You can tell all that to the police,' Jock stopped Gomo. 'I'm taking you to Harare in the truck. Fetch my camera and bag from the Landcruiser. They are on the front seat.'

Gomo hurried back to where the Landcruiser was parked.

'Listen, Jock. Just give me another five minutes,' Daniel pleaded, but Jock waved the rifle at him.

'You and I are finished, Danny. First thing I'm going to do when I reach Harare is make a full report to the police. I'm going to give them chapter and verse.'

Gomo came back, lugging the Sony video recorder and Jock's canvas duffel bag. 'Yes, you tell the police you saw this mad white shit-eater cut my cock,' Gomo shouted. 'You tell them no ivory . . .'

'Get in the truck,' Jock ordered him. 'And start up.' When Gomo obeyed he turned back to Daniel. 'I'm sorry, Danny. You're on your own. You get no more help from me. I'll give evidence against you if they ask me to. I've got to cover my own arse, man.'

'You can't help being a yellow belly,' Daniel nodded. 'But weren't you the one always sounding off about justice – what about Johnny and Mavis?'

'What you were doing didn't have anything to do with justice,' Jock raised his voice above the rumble of the truck's diesel engine. 'You were playing the sheriff and the posse and the hangman, Danny. That wasn't justice; it was vengeance. I want no part of it. You know my address. You can send the money you owe me there. So long, Danny. Sorry it had to end this way.'

He climbed up to the passenger side of the cab. 'Don't try to stop us again.' He brandished the AK 47. 'I know how to use this.'

Jock slammed the door and Gomo swung the truck back on to the highway.

Daniel was left standing in the darkness, staring after the bright red gemstones of the tail-lights until a bend in the road hid them. His ears were still singing from the concussion of the rifle blast. He felt dizzy and nauseous. He staggered slightly as he walked back to where Jock had left the Landcruiser parked, and slumped into the driver's seat.

For a little longer his anger sustained him, anger at Cheng and his accomplices, at Gomo, and most of all at Jock and his interference. Then slowly his anger evaporated and the seriousness of his own predicament began to sink in. He had acted wildly and dangerously. He had made accusations which he could not support; he had damaged property, and he had endangered life and committed aggravated assault on a government official, if not grievous bodily harm. They could get him on half a dozen charges.

Then once again he thought of Johnny and his family, and his personal peril was of no significance.

I was so close to breaking the whole scheme, he thought bitterly. Another few minutes with Gomo and I would have had them. I almost had them for you, Johnny.

He had to decide on his next actions, but his head was aching, and it was hard to think logically. There was no point in chasing after Gomo. He was alerted, and he had somehow managed to get rid of the ivory.

What other courses of action were open to him? Ning Cheng Gong, of course. He was the key to the entire plot. However, the only connection to him, now that the ivory had disappeared, was Johnny's cryptic note and the footprint he had left at the murder scene.

Then there was Chetti Singh. Gomo had tacitly admitted that he knew the Sikh. What had he said when Daniel had tried him with the name? 'Yes, I tell you about him, if you don't cut me . . .'

There was also the band of poachers. He wondered if Isaac Mtwetwe had been able to intercept the gang on the Zambezi crossing, and take prisoners. Isaac would not have the same scruples as Jock. Johnny had also been Isaac's friend. He would know how to get information out of a captured poacher.

'I'll ring Mana Pools from the police post at Chirundu,' he decided, and started the Landcruiser. He U-turned and headed back down the escarpment. The Chirundu bridge police station was closer than Karoi. He had to make a statement to the police and make sure that a police investigation was under way as soon as possible. The police must be warned about Johnny's note and the bloody footprints.

Daniel's head still ached. He stopped the Landcruiser for a few minutes while he found a bottle of Panadol tablets in the first-aid kit and washed down a couple of them with a mug of coffee from the vacuum flask. While he drove on the pain abated and he started to put his thoughts into order.

It was almost four o'clock in the morning when he reached Chirundu bridge. There was a solitary corporal in the police charge office. His arms were folded on the desk in front of him, cradling his head. He was so soundly asleep that Daniel had to shake him vigorously, and his eyes were swollen and bloodshot when at last he raised his head, and blinked uncomprehendingly at Daniel.

'I want to report a murder, a multiple murder.' Daniel began the long laborious process of getting the official machinery in motion.

When the corporal seemed unable to decide upon the correct procedure, Daniel sent him to call the member-in-charge from his rondavel at the back of the station house. When the sergeant came into the charge office at last, he was dressed in full uniform, including Sam Browne belt and cap, but he was still half asleep.

'Ring CID in Harare,' Daniel urged him. 'They must send a unit to Chiwewe.'

'First you must make a statement,' the sergeant insisted.

There was no typewriter in the charge office; this was a remote rural station. The sergeant took down Daniel's statement in halting childlike longhand. His lips moved as he spelled out each separate letter silently. Daniel wanted to take the ballpoint away from him and get it down himself.

'Damn it, sergeant. Those dead people are lying out there. The killers are getting away while we sit here.'

The sergeant went on placidly with his composition, and Daniel corrected his spelling and fumed with exasperation.

However, the pace of the dictation allowed him to phrase his statement carefully. He set down the timetable of the previous day's events: the time that he had left Chiwewe and said goodbye to Johnny Nzou; the time he had found the signs of the raiding party and decided to return to the headquarters camp with a warning; and the time that he had met the refrigerator trucks on the road in company with the ambassador's Mercedes.

He described his conversation with Ambassador Ning and hesitated, wondering whether to mention the bloodstain that he had noticed on his blue slacks. It would sound like an accusation.

'The hell with protocol,' he decided, and described in detail the blue slacks and the training shoes with fish-scale patterned soles. 'They'll have to investigate Ning now.'

He felt a grim satisfaction, as he went on to describe his return to Chiwewe and the carnage he had found there. He made sure to mention the note in Johnny's hand and the fish-scale pattern of the bloody footprint on the office floor without specifically relating either to the Taiwanese ambassador. Let them make their own inferences.

He had a great deal of difficulty when it came to describing his pursuit of the Mercedes and the refrigerator trucks. He had to give his motives without incriminating himself, or pointing too definitely at the suspicions he entertained towards Ning Cheng Gong.

'I followed the convoy to ask them if they had any knowledge of the missing ivory,' he dictated. 'Although I was unable to catch up with Ambassador Ning and the leading truck, I did speak to Ranger Gomo whom I met on the Karoi road and who was driving the second refrigerator truck. He denied any knowledge of these events and allowed me to inspect the contents of the truck. I found no ivory.' It galled him to have to admit this, but he had to cover himself against any charges that Gomo might bring against him later. 'I then determined that my duty was to contact the nearest police station and report the deaths of the Chiwewe warden, his family and staff, and the burning and destruction of buildings and other property.'

It was well after daybreak when Daniel could at last sign the handwritten statement, and only then would the police sergeant respond to his urging to telephone CID headquarters in Harare. This led to a protracted telephone discussion between the sergeant and a series of increasingly senior detectives in Harare as one passed him on to the other. This was the pace of Africa and Daniel gritted his teeth. 'AWA,' he told himself. 'Africa Wins Again.'

At last it was ordered that the sergeant should drive out to Chiwewe camp in the station Landrover while a team of detectives flew down from Harare to land at the Park's airstrip.

'Do you want me to come out with you to Chiwewe?' Daniel asked, when the sergeant finally relinquished the telephone and began preparations for his expedition to the camp.

The sergeant looked nonplussed by the question. He had received no instructions from CID as to what to do with the witness. 'You leave an address and telephone number where we can contact you if we need you,' he decided, after a great deal of frowning thought.

Daniel was relieved to be turned loose. Since arriving at the Chirundu police station, he had had many hours in which to consider the situation, and make his plans to cover every contingency.

If Isaac Mtwetwe had been able to capture any of the poachers, that would still be the swiftest path to Ning Cheng Gong, but he had to talk to Isaac before he handed over his prisoners to the police.

'I want to use your telephone,' he told the police corporal as soon as the station commander and his unit of armed constables had driven away in the green Landrover, heading for Chiwewe.

'Police telephone.' The corporal shook his head. 'Not public telephone.'

Daniel produced a blue ten Zim dollar note and laid it on the desk in front of him. 'It is only a local call,' he explained, and the banknote vanished miraculously. The corporal smiled and waved him towards the telephone. Daniel had made a friend.

Isaac Mtwetwe answered the call almost immediately the Karoi telephone exchange made the connection to Mana Pools.

'Isaac,' Daniel blurted with relief. 'When did you get back?'

'I have just walked into my office this minute,' Isaac told

him. 'We got back ten minutes ago. I have one man wounded. I must get him to hospital'

'You made contact, then?'

'Yes, we made contact. Like you said, Danny, a big gang, bad guys.'

'Did you get any prisoners, Isaac?' Daniel demanded eagerly. 'If you managed to grab a couple of them, we're home and dry.'

Isaac Mtwetwe stood at the wheel of the twenty-foot assault craft and ran downriver in the night.

His rangers squatted on the deck below the gunwale and huddled into their greatcoats, for it was cold out on the water with the wind of their passage accentuating the chill of the river mist.

The outboard motor was running rough and cutting out intermittently. Twice Isaac had to let the boat drift while he went back to work on it. It badly needed a full overhaul, but there was never enough foreign exchange available for spares to be imported. He got her running again and pointed the bows downstream.

A thick slice of moon spiked up above the dark trees that lined the bank of the Zambezi. It gave Isaac just enough light to push the boat up to top speed. Although he knew each curve and stretch of the river intimately for the next fifty miles, right down to Tete and the Mozambique border, the shallows and rocky outcrops were too complex even for him to run in complete darkness.

The glow of moonlight turned the patches of river mist to iridescent pearl dust and gave to the open water a lustre like polished black obsidian. The subdued hum of the motor and the speed of their progress gave no advance warning. They drew level with the hippopotamuses feeding in the reedbanks before the monstrous amphibians were aware of their arrival. In panic they tobogganed down the steep and slippery paths into the river, and went through the surface in a welter of spray. The flocks of wild duck roosting in the lagoons and quiet backwaters were more alert. The assault boat's approach sent them aloft on whistling wings, silhouetted against the rising moon.

Isaac knew exactly where he was heading. He had been a freedom fighter during the bush war and he had crossed this same river to raid the white farms and harass the security forces of Ian Smith's illegal regime. He knew all the techniques and tricks that the poachers employed. Some of them had been his comrades-in-arms in the struggle, but they were the new enemy now. He hated them as much as he had ever hated the Selous Scouts or the Rhodesian Light Infantry.

The Zambezi was almost half a mile wide along this stretch below Chirundu and Mana Pools. The raiders would need craft to cross its mighty green flood. They would get them the same way the guerrillas once had, from the local fisherfolk.

The Zambezi supports an itinerant population of fishermen who build their villages upon her banks. The villages are impermanent, for the tenor of their lives is dictated by the Zambezi's moods. When the river floods her banks and inundates the flood plains, the people must move to higher ground. They must follow the migrations of the shoals of tilapia and tiger fish and barbeled catfish on which they live, so every few months the clusters of rude thatched huts with their fish-smoking racks and smouldering fires are abandoned and allowed to fall into decay as the tribe moves on.

It was part of Isaac's duty to monitor the movements of the fisherfolk, for their exploitation of the river had a profound effect on the river ecology. Now he smelled the smoke and the odour of drying fish on the night air, and throttled back the motor. Softly he crept in towards the northern bank. If the poachers had come from Zambia, that was where they would return.

The odour of fish was stronger and tendrils of smoke drifted out low across the water to mingle with the mist. There were four huts with shaggy thatched roofs in an angle of the bank, and four long dugout canoes drawn up on the narrow beach below them.

Isaac nosed the assault craft on to the beach and jumped

ashore, leaving one of his rangers to hold the bows. An old woman crawled out of the low door of one of the huts. She wore only a skirt of lechwe antelope skins around her waist and her breasts were empty and pendulous.

'I see you, old mother,' Isaac greeted her respectfully. He always took pains to maintain good relations with the river-folk.

'I see you, my son,' the old woman giggled, and Isaac smelled the rank odour of cannabis on her. The Batonka people pound the weed into a paste, then mould it with fresh cow-dung into balls which they dry in the sun and smoke in clay pipes with reed mouthpieces.

The Government had granted them special dispensation to continue the tradition. It was particularly prevalent amongst the old women of the tribe.

'Are all your men in their huts?' Isaac asked quietly. 'Are all the canoes on the beach?'

The old woman blew her nose before she replied. She blocked one nostril with her thumb and from the other shot a shaft of silver mucus into the fire. She wiped the residue from her upper lip with the palm of her hand.

'All my sons and their wives are asleep in the huts, and their children with them,' she cackled.

'You saw no strange men with guns who wished you to ferry them across the river?' Isaac insisted, and the old woman shook her head and scratched herself.

'We saw no strangers.'

'I honour you, old mother,' Isaac told her formally, and pressed a small paper packet of sugar into her withered paw. 'Stay in peace.'

He ran back to the assault craft. The ranger cast off and jumped aboard as soon as Isaac started the motor.

The next village was three miles further downstream. Once again Isaac went ashore. He knew the headman of this village and found him sitting alone in the smoke from the fish-drying fires to keep off the singing clouds of malarial mosquitoes. Twenty years before, the headman had lost one of his feet to a crocodile, but he was still one of the most intrepid boatmen on the river.

Isaac greeted him and gave him a packet of cigarettes and squatted beside him in the smoke.

'You sit alone, Baba. Why can't you sleep? Are there things that trouble you?'

'An old man has many memories to trouble him.' The headman was evasive.

'Like strangers with guns who demand passage in your canoes?' Isaac asked. 'Did you give them what they wanted, Baba?'

The headman shook his head. 'One of the children saw them crossing the flood plains and ran to warn the village. We had time to hide the canoes in the reedbeds and run away into the bush.'

'How many men?' Isaac encouraged him.

The old man showed the fingers of both hands twice. 'They were hard men with guns, and faces like lions,' he whispered. 'We were afraid.'

'When was this, Baba?'

'The night before last,' the headman replied. 'When they found no people in the village and no canoes, they were angry. They shouted at each other and waved their guns, but in the end they went away.' He pointed with his chin, eastwards down the river. 'But now I am afraid they will return. That is why I sit awake while the village sleeps.'

'Are the people of Mbepura still camped at the place of the Red Birds?' Isaac asked, and the headman nodded.

'I think that after these hard men left here, they went down to Mbepura's village.'

'Thank you, old father.'

The place of the Red Birds was named for the flocks of carmine-breasted bee-eaters which burrow their nests into the steep cut-away bank of the river at that point. Mbepura's village was on the north bank, across the river from the clay cliff of the breeding colony. Isaac approached it with the engine idling softly, allowing the flow of the Zambezi to drift him down. All his rangers were alert. They had discarded their greatcoats and now crouched down below the gunwale with their weapons ready.

With a soft burst of the engine, Isaac pushed in closer to the bank. Mbepura's village was another tiny group of shaggy huts near the water's edge. They seemed deserted and the drying fires below the fish-racks had been allowed to burn out. However, he saw in the gleam of the moon that the mooring poles for the canoes were still standing in the shallow muddy landing, but the canoes were missing. The fisherfolk lived by their canoes, their most precious possession.

Isaac let the assault craft drift on downstream well below the village before he gunned the motor and cut back across the flow of the Zambezi, crossing half a mile of open water to the south bank. If the gang had crossed here, then they would be coming back the same way.

Isaac checked the time, turning the luminous dial of his wristwatch to catch the moonlight. He calculated the distance from Chiwewe headquarters and divided it by the probable rate of march of the poachers, and made allowance for the fact that they were probably carrying heavy loads of plundered ivory. He looked up at the moon. Already it was paling at the approach of dawn. He could expect the returning raiders to get back to the Zambezi bank any time within the next two or three hours.

'If I can find where they have cached the canoes,' he muttered. His guess was that they had commandeered Mbepura's entire flotilla of canoes. He recalled that on his last visit to the village there had been seven or eight of these frail craft, each of them hollowed out from a massive log of the kigelia tree. Each of them could accommodate six or seven passengers for the journey across the great river.

The gang would probably have dragooned the men from the village to act as boatmen. The handling of the canoes required skill and experience, for the canoes were cranky and unstable, especially under a heavy load. He guessed that they would probably have left the boatmen under guard on the south bank while they marched on to Chiwewe.

'If I can find the canoes, I've got them cold,' Isaac decided.

He turned the assault boat in towards the south bank a little downstream from where he judged that the canoes would have crossed. When he found the entrance to a lagoon he pressed the sharp bows into the dense stand of papyrus reeds that blocked the mouth. He cut the engine and his rangers used handfuls of the tough papyrus stems to pull themselves deeper into the reedbed while Isaac stood in the bows and sounded for bottom with a paddle.

As soon as it was shallow enough, Isaac and one of his senior rangers waded ashore, leaving the rest of the party to guard the boat. On dry land Isaac gave his ranger whispered orders, sending him down-river to search for the canoes and check the bank for signs of the passage of a large party of marauders. When he had gone, Isaac set off in the opposite direction, upstream. He went alone, swiftly and silently, moving like a wraith in the river mist.

He had judged it accurately. He had not gone more than half a mile upstream when he smelt smoke. It was too strong and fresh to originate from the village on the far side of the broad river, and Isaac knew that there were no habitations on this bank. This was part of the National Park.

He moved in quietly towards the source of the smoke. At this point the bank was a sheer red clay cliff into which the bee-eaters burrowed their subterranean nests. However, there was a break in the cliff directly below where he crouched. It was a narrow gulley, choked with riverine bush that formed a natural landing-place from the river.

The faint glimmer of coming dawn gave Isaac just sufficient light to make out the encampment in the gulley below him. The canoes were drawn up well out of the water so that they would be concealed from anyone searching from a boat. There were seven canoes, the entire flotilla from Mbepura's village across the river.

Nearby, the boatmen were lying around two small smoky fires. They were wrapped in karosses of animal skin and, as protection from mosquitoes, each of them had drawn the covering completely over his head, so they looked like corpses laid out in a morgue. An armed poacher sat at each fire with his AK 47 rifle across his lap, guarding the sleeping boatmen and making certain that none of them sneaked away to the beached canoes nearby.

'Danny figured it exactly right,' Isaac told himself. 'They are waiting for the return of the raiding party.'

He drew back from the cliff edge and silently circled inland. Within two hundred yards he intersected a well-trodden game trail that left the river and headed directly southward in the approximate direction of Chiwewe headquarters camp.

Isaac followed it for a short distance until the game trail dipped through a shallow dry water-course. The bed of the water-course was of sugary white sand and the prints that it held were plain to decipher even in the uncertain pre-dawn light. A large party of men in Indian file had trodden the sand deeply, but their tracks were eroded and overlaid by the tracks of both large and small game.

'Twenty-four hours old,' Isaac estimated. This was the route the raiding party had taken on their outward march. Almost certainly they would use the same trail on their return march to rejoin the waiting canoes.

Isaac found a vantage point from which he was able to overlook a long stretch of the trail while remaining well concealed in a patch of dense Jesse bush. At his back there was a secure escape route for him down a shallow donga, the banks of which were screened with a heavy growth of rank elephant grass. He settled in to wait. The light strengthened swiftly and within minutes he could make out the full length of the game trail winding away into the mopane forest.

The sunrise chorus of birds began with the noisy duet of a pair of Heughlin robins in the donga behind him, and then the first flight of wild duck sped overhead. Their arrowhead formation was crisp and black against the tangerine and heron blue of the dawn sky.

Isaac crouched in his ambush position. There was no way that he could be certain how long the poachers might take on the return march from Chiwewe. Danny had reckoned on ten hours or so. If he were correct they would be arriving any minute now. Isaac checked his wristwatch again. However, Danny's estimate might be wildly inaccurate. Isaac prepared himself for a long wait.

During the war, they had at times lain in ambush position for days on end, once for five days when they had slept and eaten and defecated without rising from where they lay. Patience was the hunter's and the soldier's single most important virtue.

In the distance he heard a baboon bark, that booming alarm call with which the wily ape greets the appearance of a predator. The cry was taken up by other members of the troop, and then gradually silence returned as the danger receded or the baboons retreated deeper into the forest. Now Isaac's nerves were strung out with tension. He knew that the apes might have barked at a leopard, but they would have reacted the same way to the passing of a file of human beings.

Fifteen minutes later and much closer he heard a grey lourie cry 'Go away! Go away!' in a harsh screech. Another one of the sentinels of the bush was reacting to the presence of danger. Isaac never stirred, but he blinked his eyes rapidly to clear his vision.

Minutes later, he picked out another less obtrusive sound from the subtle orchestra of the wilderness. It was the whirring chatter of a honey guide. The sound told him where to look and he spotted the small nondescript brown bird in the top branches of a mopane far ahead.

It flitted above the game trail, flicking its wings, darting from tree to tree and uttering seductive entreaties. If they were prepared to follow the bird, it would lead the honey badger or man to a hive of wild bees. While they robbed the hive the honey guide would hover in close attendance, waiting for its share of the comb and the grubs that it contained. The bird's specially adapted digestive system was capable of breaking down the beeswax and deriving nourishment where no other creature could. Legend maintained that if you failed to leave the bird his portion of the spoils, then the next time he would lead you to a deadly mamba or a man-eating lion.

The honey guide drew closer to where Isaac waited, and suddenly he discerned obscure movement in the forest below the fluttering bird. Swiftly the shadowy shapes resolved into a column of men moving down the game trail. The head of the column drew level with the head of the donga where Isaac lay.

Although they were dressed in tattered and filthy clothing with an eclectic selection of headwear that ranged from baseball caps to faded military floppies, each of them carried an AK 47 rifle and an elephant tusk.

Some of them carried the tusk balanced upon their heads, the natural curve of the ivory drooping down fore and aft. Others carried it over the shoulder, using one hand to balance the burden while the other hand held the assault rifle. Most of them had woven a pad of bark string and soft grass to cushion the galling weight of the ivory on their scalps or collar-bones. The agony that their loads were causing after all these hours and miles of trek was evident on their contorted faces. Yet to each of the raiders the tusk they carried represented an enormous fortune, and they would suffer permanent physical damage rather than abandon it.

The man leading the column was short and squat, with thick bow-legs and a bull neck. The mellow early light caught the glossy scar down the side of his face.

'Sali,' Isaac hissed as he recognised him. He was the most notorious of all the Zambian poachers. Twice before their paths had crossed, and each time it had cost the lives of good men.

He passed close to where Isaac lay at a swinging jog-trot, carrying the thick honey-coloured tusk balanced on his head. He alone of all his men showed no signs of distress from the long march.

Isaac counted the poachers as they passed his position. The slower and weaker ones had fallen far behind the killing pace that Sali set, so the column was strung out. It took almost seven minutes by Isaac's wristwatch for all of them to go by. 'Nineteen.' Isaac counted the last pair as they limped past. Greedily they had selected tusks too heavy for their own strength and they were paying the price now.

Isaac let them go, but the moment they disappeared in the direction of the river, he rose from his ambush position and slipped away into the donga. He moved with extreme caution for he could not be certain that there were not still other members of the gang on the trail behind him.

The assault boat was where he had left it, moored in the reeds at the entrance to the lagoon. Isaac waded out alongside the boat and swung himself in over the gunwale. He noticed that the man he had sent down river had returned.

Quietly he told his men what he had found, and he watched their expressions. They were good men, all three of them, but the odds were formidable even for them, and the enemy were 'hard men with faces like lions', as the headman had described them.

'We will take them on the water,' Isaac told them. 'And we will not wait for them to fire the first shot. They are armed, and they are carrying ivory in the Park. That is enough. We will take them by surprise when they expect us least.'

Robert Mugabe, the president of Zimbabwe, had issued a directive that was unequivocal. They had the right to shoot on sight. Too many Parks men had been killed in these clashes to justify the usual niceties of a formal challenge.

The expressions of the listening rangers hardened and they hefted their weapons with renewed confidence. Isaac ordered them to work the boat out of the reeds and as soon as they reached open water he cranked the starter motor. The engine baulked and fired roughly and cut out. He cranked it again and again until the battery became sluggish. They were drifting away swiftly downstream.

Muttering angrily, Isaac hurried back and pulled the cover off the motor. While he worked on it he was vividly aware that upstream the gang would be loading the plundered ivory into the canoes and preparing to cross back into their own territory and safety.

He left the motor uncovered and ran forward to the controls. This time the motor fired and ran, surged and then faded. He pumped the throttle and she surged again and then settled to a steady beat. The engine whined shrilly as he turned across the current and ran back upstream.

The sound of the unmuted motor carried far ahead, and it must have alerted the gang. As Isaac drove the assault boat around the next bend, all the canoes were strung out across the river racing for the north shore.

The rising sun was behind Isaac's back and the broad stretch of water was lit like a theatre stage. The Zambezi was bright emerald green, the papyrus beds were crowned with gold where the sun's rays struck them. The canoes were starkly lit. Each of the frail craft carried a boatman and three passengers, together with a full load of ivory. Their free-board was only the width of a man's hand, and they lay so low in the water that the men seemed to be crouched on the very surface.

The boatmen were paddling frantically. Their long spear-shaped paddles flashed in the sunlight as they drove for the far bank. The leading canoe was already within a hundred yards of the Zambian papyrus beds.

The propeller of the Yamaha carved a lacy wake from the glossy green surface as Isaac swung the boat in a long curving trajectory to head off the leading canoe from the sanctuary of the reeds.

As the two vessels closed, Isaac made out the scarred visage of Sali. He squatted in the warped bows, turning his head awkwardly to glare back at them, unable to move without upsetting the delicate trim of the canoe.

'This time we've got you,' Isaac whispered, as he pushed the throttle forward to the stop, and the Yamaha shrieked.

Suddenly Sali rose to his feet and the canoe rocked wildly under him. Water slopped in over the wooden sides and the canoe began to flood and settle. Sali shouted a threat at Isaac; his face was contorted into a mask of fury and he lifted the AK and fired a long continuous burst at the boat racing down on him.

Bullets slammed into the fibreglass hull and one of the instrument gauges on the control console in front of Isaac exploded. He ducked, but held her on course to ram the canoe.

Sali flicked the empty magazine out of the rifle, and loaded another from his bandolier. He fired again. The bright brass cases sparkled in the sunlight as they were spewed from the breech. One of the rangers in the front of the assault boat cried out and clutched at his stomach as he tumbled to the deck, and at that moment the bows of the assault boat crashed into the side of the canoe at thirty knots. The brittle kigelia wood shattered, and the men in her were hurled into the river.

At the last moment before the collision, Sali threw the AK 47 aside and dived overboard. He tried to force his body deep beneath the water to escape the speeding hull. He thought he could cover the last few yards to the edge of the reedbed without surfacing and showing himself again. However, his lungs were full of air and the buoyancy prevented him diving deeply enough. Although his head and body were angled downwards, his feet were only a few inches below the surface.

113

The propeller of the Yamaha was spinning at peak revolutions as it passed over his left leg. It took his foot off cleanly at the ankle and went over his calf muscles like the blade of a bread-slicing machine, shredding the meat down to the bone.

Then the assault boat was past, turning back steeply with Isaac spinning the wheel. She leaned out into the turn as he lined up the bows for the next canoe in the straggling line. He hit it without a check, steering into the fragile hull and spilling its crew into the river, driving it under and running on, swinging into the next turn like a slalom racer weaving through the poles.

The men in the third canoe saw them coming and threw themselves over the side an instant before the bows struck and then they were splashing and screaming as the swift green current carried them away.

Isaac spun the wheel back the other way, and the next canoe was dead ahead. The crew were shouting and pleading and firing wildly. The volleys of bullets kicked up fountains of spray all around the approaching assault craft in the moments before it struck and trod the shattered canoe under.

The remaining canoes had turned back and were paddling desperately for the south bank. Isaac overtook them effortlessly and smashed in the stern of the nearest vessel. He felt the engine check and shudder as the spinning propeller bit into living human flesh and then it surged forward again.

The last canoes reached the south bank and the poachers spilled out of them and tried to clamber up the sheer cliff. The red clay crumbled under their clawing fingers.

Isaac throttled back and turned the bows upstream holding the assault boat against the current.

'I am a Parks warden,' Isaac yelled across at them. 'You are under arrest. Stand where you are. Do not try to escape or I will fire upon you.'

One of the poachers still clutched his rifle in his hand. He almost reached the top of the bank before the clay broke away under his feet and he slid down to the water's edge. Sitting in the red mud, he threw up the rifle and aimed at the men in the assault boat.

The two unwounded rangers were kneeling at the rail, their rifles cocked and levelled.

114

'*Bulala!* Kill!' Isaac snapped, and they opened up together, a massed volley of fire that swept the riverbank. They were hand-picked members of the anti-poaching unit, both good marksmen, and they hated the gangs that plundered the elephant herds, savaged their comrades and threatened their own lives.

They laughed as they shot the panic-stricken gang members off the bank. They made a game of allowing them almost to reach the top of the red clay wall before bringing them flopping and kicking back into the river with a short crisp burst of fire.

Isaac made no effort to restrain them. He had a long-outstanding score to settle with these men, and a few years' imprisonment was not enough punishment for their crimes. As the last of them rolled down the bank and sank slowly into the clear green water, he spun the boat and raced back across the river.

Scar-faced Sali was the leader. These others were mere brainless thugs and cannon-fodder. Sali could recruit a new regiment of them for a few dollars a head. Sali was the brains and the guts of the trade, and without him this day's work would count for little. Unless Isaac stopped him now, Sali would be back again next week or next month with another gang of ruffians. He had to crush the head of the mamba or it would strike again.

He raced in close to the edge of the reeds on the north bank, to the spot at which he had rammed the first canoe. Then Isaac turned into the current and throttled back the Yamaha and allowed the current to drift them downstream, using bursts of engine to keep within a few yards of the edge of the reeds.

The two rangers stood at the port rail, and eagerly scrutinised the reedbed as they drifted by.

There was no telling how far the Zambezi current had carried the poacher before he had been able to reach the cover of the papyrus. Isaac would make only one sweep from the boat for a mile downstream. Then he would go ashore with his men and beat back along the north bank on foot to pick up any sign that Sali might have left as he dragged himself from the reeds on to dry land and tried to escape. Then they would follow him, for as far and as long as it took.

Strict interpretation of the law gave Isaac no powers of arrest on the Zambian side of the river, but this was a hot pursuit of a murderer and a notorious bandit. Isaac was prepared to fight if challenged, and put a bullet through his prisoner's head if the Zambian police tried to intervene and take Salí away from him.

At that moment something caught his eye in the reedbed directly opposite the drifting assault boat. Isaac touched the throttle and held the boat stationary against the current.

A small area of reeds had been disturbed, as if something had been dragged through them, a crocodile possibly, or a large leguan lizard, except that clumps of reeds had been twisted and broken as though used as handholds.

'Crocodiles don't have hands,' Isaac grunted, and man-oeuvred the boat in closer. The disturbance must have taken place only minutes before, for under his eyes the flattened reeds were still straightening and rising into their original upright position. Then Isaac smiled thinly.

He reached over the side and snapped one of the reeds and held it to the sunlight. The smear of colour along its fibrous stem came away wet and red on Isaac's fingers and he showed it to the ranger who stood at his shoulder.

'Blood,' the ranger nodded. 'He is hurt. The prop—' before he could finish the sentence somebody screamed in the reeds ahead of them. It was a high ringing cry of utter terror that froze them all for an instant.

Isaac recovered first and nudged the throttle, forcing the bows into the dense stand of reeds. Somewhere ahead of them the human voice screamed and screamed again.

Deep in the river Sali felt the boat run over him. His head was filled with the deafening shriek of the spinning propeller blades. The sound had no direction but assaulted his senses from every angle.

Then something struck his left leg a blow that seemed to dislocate his hip and the force of it spun him end over end in the water and disoriented him. He tried to lunge for the surface but his left leg would not respond. There was no pain, just a great heavy numbness as though the limb was encased in a block of concrete that was drawing him down into the green Zambezi depths.

He kicked out wildly with his good leg and suddenly his head broke the surface. Through streaming eyes he saw the assault boat weaving and zigzagging across the river, smashing up the flotilla of canoes and throwing their crews, splashing and screaming, into the river.

Sali welcomed the respite that this attack on the other canoes had afforded him. He knew that he had a few minutes before the boat came roaring back to find him. He turned his head. The edge of the reedbed was close. With the strength of his fighting anger and outrage still strong upon him, he struck out for it. His leg was a dead weight, a heavy drogue anchor that hampered and slowed him, but he swam with great sweeping overhead strokes of his powerful arms and seconds later grabbed the first handful of papyrus stems. Desperately he dragged himself into the cover of the reeds, sliding his body over the springing mattress of papyrus, the maimed leg slithering after him.

Deep in the reeds, he paused at last and rolled on to his back to look back the way that he had come. His breathing whistled in his throat as he saw the trail of blood that he had laid through the water. He grabbed his own knee, lifted the wounded leg above the surface and stared at it in disbelief.

His foot was gone and white bone protruded from the mangled flesh. His blood spurted and dribbled from the severed vessels so that he floated in a red-brown cloud. Tiny silver fish, excited by the smell of it, darted through the stained water, gobbling the strings and morsels of tattered meat.

Quickly Sali lowered his good leg and tried to touch bottom. The water closed over his head, but his right foot groped unavailingly for the Zambezi's mud bed. He came to the surface again coughing and choking. He was well out of his depth, with only the thick reeds to support him.

Far away across the river he heard the sound of gunfire, and then the high-pitched whine of the returning assault craft. It drew closer and closer, until abruptly it sank to a faint burbling sound and he heard voices. He realised that they were searching the edge of the reedbeds for him, and he shrank down lower in the water.

A cold lethargy was stealing over him as his life-blood leaked away into the river, but he forced himself to rally and began to edge away, deeper into the reeds, towards the Zambian bank of the river. He pushed gently into an opening in the reeds. It was the size of a tennis court enclosed by a palisade of tall swaying papyrus. The surface was paved with the flat circular green leaves of the water-lilies and their blooms raised lovely cerulean heads to the early sunlight. Their perfume was sweet and delicate on the still air.

Suddenly Sali froze with only his head above the surface. Something moved beneath the water-lilies. The water pushed and bulged while the blossoms nodded their heads to the weighty and stealthy movement passing beneath them.

Sali knew what it was. His thick liver-coloured lips split open and he drooled with terror. His blood drifted away on the lily-strewn waters and the thing beneath moved with greater authority and determination, homing in on the tantalising taste of blood.

Sali was a brave man. Very few things in this world could frighten him. However, this was a creature from another world, the secret cold world beneath the waters. His bowels evacuated uncontrollably as terror released his sphincter muscle, and this fresh odour in the water brought the creature to the surface.

A head like a log, black and gnarled and shiny with wetness, pushed through the lilies. Its beady saurian eyes were set on protruding bark-like knobs and it grinned at Sali, with ragged fangs protruding over uneven lips. The wreath of lily blossoms draped across its hideous brow gave the creature a sardonic menace.

Suddenly the great tail broke the surface, double-ridged and crested as it threshed the surface to foam, driving the long scaly body forward with astonishing speed.

Sali screamed.

Isaac stood at the control console and drove the long hull deeper into the papyrus. The tough fibrous stems wrapped around the propeller shaft and slowed the boat, bringing it to a gradual standstill.

They ran to the bows and, grabbing handfuls of papyrus, dragged themselves forward until abruptly they burst into a small patch of open water. Directly in front of the bows there was an enormous disturbance in the water. Sheets of spray were thrown into the sunlight, and splattered over their heads.

In the foam an enormous scaly body rolled and roiled, flashing its butter yellow belly, the long tail cockscombed with sharp scales thrashing the water white.

For an instant a human arm was flung upwards. It was a gesture of entreaty, of terrified supplication. Isaac leaned over the side and seized the wrist. The skin was wet and slippery but Isaac reinforced his grip with both hands and leaned back with all his weight. He could not hold Sali and the weight of the reptile together. The wrist began to slip through his grip until one of the rangers leapt to his side and grabbed Sali's arm at the elbow.

Together, inch by inch, they dragged the man's body from the water. Sali was a man on the torture rack. He was stretched out between the men at one end and the dreadful reptile below the surface.

The other ranger leaned out over the gunwale and fired a burst of automatic fire into the water. The high-velocity bullets exploded on the surface as though they had hit a steel plate and had no effect except to send needles of spray into the eyes of Isaac and the ranger at the rail.

'Stop it!' Isaac panted at him. 'You'll hit one of us!'

The ranger dropped the rifle and seized Sali's free arm.

Now there were three men taking sides in the gruesome tug-of-war. Slowly they dragged Sali's body from the water, until the reptile's huge scaly head was exposed.

Its fangs were buried in the front of Sali's belly. The crocodile's teeth lack shearing edges. It dismembers its prey by locking on and then rolling its entire body in the water to twist off a limb or a hunk of flesh. As they held Sali stretched over the gunwale, the creature flicked its tail and rolled. Sali's belly was ripped open. The crocodile heaved backwards with its fangs still locked in his flesh and stripped Sali's entrails out of him.

With the release of the strain at one end, the three men were able to heave Sali's body on board. However, the crocodile still held its grip. Although his writhing form lay on the deck, Sali's entrails were stretched over the side, a glistening fleshy tangle of tubes and ribbons like some grotesque umbilical cord that linked him to his fate.

The crocodile jerked again with the full weight and strength of the long tail. The ribbon of guts snapped and Sali screamed for the last time and died on the bloody deck.

For a while there was silence in the boat broken only by the hoarse panting of the three men who had tried to rescue him. They stared in horrified fascination at Sali's mutilated corpse until Isaac Mtwetwe whispered softly, 'I could not have chosen a more fitting death for you.' He spoke in formal ceremonial Shona. 'Go not peacefully, O Sali, evil one, and may all your foul deeds accompany you on your journey.'

 'There were no prisoners,' Isaac told Daniel Armstrong.

'Did you say none?' Daniel shouted. The telephone connection was scratchy and faint, with heavy atmospheric interference from the thunderstorm raging further down the valley.

'None, Danny,' Isaac raised his voice. 'Eight dead ones, but the rest of the gang were either eaten by crocs or escaped back into Zambia.'

'What about ivory, Isaac? Did they have tusks with them?'

'Yes, they were all carrying ivory, but it was lost in the river when the canoes went down.'

'Damn it to hell,' Daniel muttered. It would be much more difficult now to convince the authorities that the bulk of the ivory was taken out from Chiwewe in the refrigerator trucks.

The trail to Ning Cheng Gong was growing colder with every hour that passed.

'There is a police unit on its way from here to the head-quarters camp at Chiwewe,' he told Isaac.

'Yes, Danny. They are here at the moment. I'm going to join them as soon as I have made arrangements to fly my wounded ranger out to Harare. I want to see what these bastards did to Johnny Nzou.'

'Listen, Isaac, I'm going to follow up the only lead I've got on who was responsible for this business.'

'Be careful, Danny. These people don't mess about. You could get badly hurt. Where are you headed?'

'I'll see you around, Isaac.' Daniel avoided the question. He dropped the telephone back on its cradle and went out to the Landcruiser.

He sat behind the wheel and thought about it. He realised that this was merely a respite. Pretty soon now the Zimbabwean police were going to want to talk to him again, a little more seriously than before. There was only one place to be, and that was outside the country. In any event that was where the trail was leading him.

He drove down to the customs and immigration post and parked in the lot before the barrier. Naturally, he had his passport with him and the papers for the Landcruiser were all in order. The departure formalities took less than half an hour, which by African standards was almost record time.

Daniel drove out across the steel-girdered bridge that spanned the Zambezi and he was aware that he was not entering para-dise.

Zambia was, after Uganda and Ethiopia, one of the poorest and sorriest countries on the African continent. Daniel grim-aced. A cynic might put that down to the fact that it had been independent from British colonial rule longer than most others. There had been more time for the policies of structured chaos and ruination to take full effect.

Under private ownership the great mines of the Copperbelt had once been amongst the most profitable on the continent, rivalling even the fabulous gold mines further south. After independence, President Kenneth Kaunda had nationalised them

121

and instituted his Africanisation policy. This amounted to firing those skilled and experienced engineers and managers who did not have black faces, a kind of affirmative action. Within a few short years he had miraculously transformed an annual profit of many hundreds of millions into a loss of the same magnitude.

Daniel steeled himself for his encounter with Zambian official-dom.

'Can you tell me if a friend of mine passed through here last night on his way to Malawi,' he asked the uniformed officer who sauntered out of the customs building to search his Land-cruiser for contraband.

The man opened his mouth to protest his outrage at being asked to divulge official information but Daniel forestalled him by producing a five-dollar bill. The Zambian currency, the kwacha, named for 'the dawn of freedom from colonial oppression' had once held value equivalent to the US dollar. Numerous subsequent devaluations had readjusted the official exchange rate to 30:1. The black-market rate was closer to 300:1. The customs officer's scruples evaporated. He was looking at a month's salary.

'What is your friend's name?' he asked eagerly.

'Mr Chetti Singh. He was driving a large truck with a cargo of dried fish.'

'Wait.' The officer disappeared into the station and was back within minutes.

'Yes . . .' he nodded. 'Your friend passed through after mid-night.' He showed no further interest in searching the Land-cruiser and stamped Daniel's passport. His step was jaunty as he returned to his post.

Daniel felt a little chill of unease as he left the border post and headed northwards towards Lusaka, the territory's capital. In Zambia, the rule of law ended at the edge of the built-up areas. In the bush the police manned their road-blocks, but were never so foolhardy as to respond to appeals for assistance from travellers on the lonely rutted roads.

During twenty-five years of independence, the roads had fallen into an interesting state of disrepair. In some places the potholes through the eroded tarmac were almost knee deep.

Daniel kept the speed down to twenty-five miles an hour and weaved his way around the worst patches as though he were negotiating a minefield.

The countryside was lovely. He drove through magnificent open forests and glades of golden grass known as 'damboes'. The hills and kopjes seemed to have been built in antiquity by a giant's hand. The walls and turrets of stone were tumbled and eroded into spectacular chaos. The numerous rivers were deep and clear.

Daniel came to the first of the road-blocks.

A hundred yards from the barrier Daniel slowed down to a crawl and kept both hands on the wheel. The police were jumpy and trigger-happy. As he stopped, a uniformed constable wearing mirrored sunglasses thrust the barrel of a sub-machine-gun through the window and greeted him arrogantly.

'Hello, my friend.' His finger was on the trigger and the muzzle was pointed at Daniel's belly. 'Get out!'

'Do you smoke?' Daniel asked. As he stepped down into the road he produced a packet of Chesterfield cigarettes and thrust it into the constable's hand.

The constable withdrew the barrel of the machine pistol while he checked that the packet was unopened. Then he grinned and Daniel relaxed slightly.

At that moment another vehicle drew up behind Daniel's Landcruiser. It was a truck owned by one of the hunting safari companies. The back was piled with camp stores and equipment, and the gunbearers and trackers sat on top of the load.

At the driving-wheel was the professional hunter, bearded, tanned and weatherbeaten. Beside him his client seemed urbane and effete despite his new safari jacket and the zebra skin hatband around his stetson.

'Daniel!' The hunter leaned out of the side window. 'Daniel Armstrong,' he shouted happily.

Then Daniel remembered him. They had met briefly three years previously while Daniel was filming the documentary on hunting safaris in Africa, 'Man is the Hunter'. For a moment he couldn't remember the fellow's name, but they had shared a bottle of Haig at a campfire in the Luangwa valley. Daniel remembered him as a blow-hard, with a reputation more as a hard drinker than a hard hunter. He had consumed more than his fair share of the Haig, Daniel recalled.

'Stoffel.' The name came back to him with relief. He needed an ally and a protector now. The hunters of the safari companies were a class of minor aristocracy in the deep bush. 'Stoffel van der Merwe,' he cried.

Stoffel climbed down from the truck, big and beefy and grinning. Like most professional hunters in Zambia, he was an Afrikaner from South Africa.

'Hell, man, it's good to see you again.' He covered Daniel's hand with a hairy paw. 'They giving you any uphill here?'

'Well . . .' Daniel let it hang there, and Stoffel rounded on the police constable. 'Hey, Juno, this man is my friend. You treat him good, you hear me?'

The constable laughed agreement. It always amazed Daniel to watch how well Afrikaners and blacks got along on a personal level once politics were left out of it; perhaps it was because they were all of them Africans and understood each other. They had been living together for almost three hundred years, Daniel smiled to himself; by this time they damned well should.

'You want your meat, don't you?' Stoffel went on to tease the constable. 'You give Doctor Armstrong here a hard time and no meat for you.'

The hunters had their regular routes to and from the hunting concessions in the remote bush, and they knew the guards manning the road-blocks by name. Between them they had set up a regular tariff of *bonsela*.

'Hey!' Stoffel turned to shout at his trackers on top of the truck. 'Give Juno here a leg of fat buffalo. Look how skinny he's getting. We have to feed him up a bit.'

From under the tarpaulin cover they dragged out a haunch of buffalo, still in its thick black skin, dusty and buzzing with bluebottle flies. The hunters had access to unlimited supplies of game meat, legally hunted and shot by their clients.

'These poor bastards are starved for protein,' Stoffel explained to his client as the American sportsman came to join them. 'For a leg of buffalo he would sell you his wife; for two he would sell you his soul; for three he would probably sell you the whole bloody country. And any one of those would be a bad bargain!' He roared with laughter and introduced his client to Daniel. 'This is Steve Conrack from California.'

'I know you, of course,' the American interjected. 'Great honour to meet you, Doctor Armstrong. I always watch your stuff on TV. Just by chance I've got a copy of your book with me. I'd love an autograph for my kids back home. They're great fans of yours.'

Inwardly Daniel winced at the price of fame but when the client returned from the truck with a copy of one of his earlier books, he signed the flyleaf.

'Where are you headed?' Stoffel asked. 'Lusaka? Let me go ahead and run interference for you, otherwise anything could happen. It could take you a week or all eternity to get there.'

The police guard, still grinning, lifted the barrier and saluted them as they drove through. From there onwards their progress was a royal procession, with lumps of raw meat appearing regularly from under the tarpaulin.

'Roses, roses all the way – and buffalo steaks strewn in our path like mad.' Daniel grinned to himself and put his foot down to keep up with the safari truck.

They were driving through the fertile plains that were irrigated from the Kafue River. This was an area of sugar and maize and tobacco production and the farms were owned almost entirely by white Zambians. Prior to independence, the farmers had vied with each other to beautify their properties. From the main road the white-painted homesteads had glistened, set like pearls in the green and lovingly tended home paddocks. The fences had been meticulously maintained and sleek cattle had grazed within view of the road.

These days the dilapidated appearance of the properties was a deliberate attempt by the owners to divert envious and acquisitive eyes.

'If you look too good,' one of them had explained to Daniel, 'they're going to take it away from you.' He didn't have to explain who 'they' were. 'The golden rule in this country is: if you've got it, for God's sake don't flaunt it.'

The white farmers lived as a tiny separate tribe in their own little enclave. Rather like their pioneering ancestors, they made their own soap and other commodities which were simply unobtainable from the bare shelves of the local trading stores. They lived mostly on the products of their own lands, yet they enjoyed a reasonably good life with their golf clubs and polo clubs and theatrical societies.

They sent their children to school and university in South Africa with the small amounts of fiercely rationed foreign exchange they were granted; they kept their heads down below the parapet and took care not to draw attention to themselves. Even the powers that presided in the government halls in Lusaka realised that without them the precarious economy would collapse completely. The maize and sugar they produced kept the rest of the population from true starvation and their tobacco crops eked out the tiny dribble of foreign exchange brought in by the ruined copper mines.

'Where could we go?' Daniel's informant put the rhetorical question. 'If we leave here, we go in our underclothes. They won't let us take a penny or a stick with us. We've just got to make the best of it.'

As the two-vehicle convoy approached the capital town of Lusaka, Daniel was given a demonstration of one of the many distressing phenomena of the new Africa – the mass movement of rural populations to the urban centres.

Daniel smelt the slum odour as they passed the outskirts of the town. It was a miasma of smoke from the cooking-fires, the stench of pit latrines and festering garbage heaps, of sour illicit beer brewing in open drums, and human bodies without running water or rivers in which to bathe. It was the smell of disease and starvation and poverty and ignorance, the ripe new smell of Africa.

Daniel stood Stoffel and his client a drink in the bar of the Ridgeway Hotel, then excused himself and went to the reception desk to check in.

He was given a room overlooking the swimming-pool, and went to shower away the grime and exhaustion of the past twenty-four hours. Then he reached for the telephone, and called the British High Commission. He caught the telephonist there before the close of the day's business.

'May I speak to Mr Michael Hargreave, please?' He held his

breath. Mike Hargreave had still been in Lusaka two years previously, but he could have been transferred anywhere in the world by now.

'I'm putting you through to Mr Hargreave,' the girl replied after a few moments, and Daniel let his breath out.

'Michael Hargreave speaking.'

'Mike, it's Danny Armstrong.'

'Good Lord, Danny, where are you?'

'Here in Lusaka.'

'Welcome back to fairyland. How are you?'

'Mike, can I see you? I need another favour.'

'Why don't you come to dinner tonight? Wendy will be charmed.'

Michael had one of the diplomatic residences on Nobs Hill, within walking distance of Government House. As with every other house in the street it was fortified like the Maze Prison. The ten-foot perimeter walls were topped with rolled barbed wire and two *malondo*, night watchmen, guarded the gate.

Michael Hargreave quieted his pair of Rottweiler guard dogs, and greeted Daniel enthusiastically.

'You aren't taking chances, Mike.' Daniel gestured towards the security precautions and Michael grimaced.

'On this street alone we average one break-in a night, despite the wire and dogs.'

He led Daniel into the house and Wendy came to kiss him. Wendy was a rosebud, with soft blonde hair and one of those incredible English complexions.

'I had forgotten that you are even more handsome in the flesh than on television.' She smiled at him.

Michael Hargreave resembled an Oxford don more than a spook, but he was indeed an MI6 man. He and Daniel had first met in Rhodesia towards the end of the war. At the time Daniel had been sick and dispirited with what he had come to realise was not only a lost cause, but an unjust one. The breaking point had come when Daniel led a column of the Selous Scouts into the neighbouring state of Mozambique. The target was a guerrilla camp. Rhodesian intelligence had told them it was a training camp for ZANLA recruits, but when they hit the cluster of huts they found mostly old men and women and children. There had been almost five hundred of these unfortunate people. They had left none of them alive.

On the return march Daniel had found himself weeping uncontrollably as he staggered along in the darkness. Years of ever-present danger and endless call-up for active service had worn his nerves thin and brittle. Only much later Daniel realised that he had suffered a breakdown, but at that critical moment he was approached by the clandestine Alpha Group.

The war had dragged on for so many years that a small group of police and army officers had come to realise the futility of it all. Even more they had realised that they were on the side, not of the angels, but of the devil himself.

They decided that they must strive for an end to the bitter civil war, that they must force the white supremacist Smith government to accept a truce negotiated by Great Britain, and thereafter agree to a democratic and free election and the process of national reconciliation between the races. All the members of the Alpha Group were men whom Daniel admired; many were senior officers and most of them had been decorated for their courage and leadership. Daniel was drawn irresistibly to them.

Michael Hargreave had been the head of station for British intelligence in Rhodesia. They had first met once Daniel had committed himself to the Alpha Group. They had worked together closely and Daniel had played a minor role in the process that finally led to the end of those dreadful sufferings and excesses, and that culminated in the Lancaster House Agreement.

Daniel had not been in Zimbabwe when Ian Smith's white regime finally capitulated. His disloyalty had been discovered by Rhodesian intelligence. Warned of his impending arrest by other members of his group, Daniel had fled the country. Had he been captured he would certainly have faced a firing squad. He had only dared return once the country had changed its name to Zimbabwe and the new order, led by Robert Mugabe, had come to power.

When first he had met him, Daniel's relationship with Michael had been detached and professional, but mutual respect and trust had finally transformed it into genuine friendship, which had survived the years.

Michael poured him a whisky and they chatted and reminisced until Wendy called them to the dinner-table. Home cooking was a treat for Daniel, and Wendy glowed with gratification at his performance with knife and fork.

With the brandy Michael asked, 'So what about this favour?'

'Two favours, actually.'

'Runaway inflation — speak up, my lad.'

'Could you possibly arrange to have my film tapes sent back to London in the diplomatic bag? They are more valuable than life itself. I wouldn't trust them to the Zambian post office.'

'That's an easy one,' Michael nodded. 'I'll get them away in tomorrow's bag. What about the other favour?'

'I need some information on a gentleman named Ning Cheng Gong.'

'Are we likely to know him?' Michael asked.

'You should. He's Taiwan's ambassador to Harare.'

'In that case, we will certainly have a file on him. Is he friend or foe, Danny?'

'I'm not sure — not at this stage, anyway.'

'Don't tell me, then.' Michael sighed and pushed the brandy decanter across to Daniel. 'I should have a computer print-out for you before noon tomorrow. Shall I send it around to the Ridgeway?'

'Bless you, old son. I owe you another one.'

'And don't you forget it, Danny boy.'

It was an enormous relief to get rid of the tapes that Jock had shot. They represented a gruelling year's labour and almost Daniel's entire worldly wealth. He believed so strongly in this new project that he had decided that, contrary to his usual practice, he would not seek outside financing. He had put everything he owned at risk, almost half a million dollars that he had painfully accumulated over the last ten years since he had become a full-time author and television producer.

So Daniel's tapes went out the following morning with the diplomatic courier on the British Airways flight and would be in London within twelve hours. Daniel had consigned them to Castle Studios where they would be in safe keeping until he could begin the editorial work to transform it into another one of his productions. He had almost settled on a title for the series, 'Is Africa Dying?'

Rather than entrust it to a messenger, Michael Hargreave personally delivered the computer print-out on Ning Cheng Gong to Daniel at the hotel.

'Nice lad you've picked on,' he commented. 'I haven't read it all, just enough to find out that the Ning family is not one to trifle with. Take it easy, Danny; these are big boys.'

He handed over the sealed envelope. 'Just one condition. As soon as you have read it, I want you to burn it. Do I have your word on that?'

Daniel nodded in agreement and Michael went on, 'I've brought along an askari from the High Commission to guard your Landcruiser for you. You daren't leave a vehicle untended on the street, not in Lusaka.'

Daniel took the envelope up to his hotel room and ordered a pot of tea. When it arrived he locked the door, stripped to his underpants and lay on the bed.

The print-out ran to eleven pages, all of them fascinating. Johnny Nzou had given him only an inkling of the wealth and importance of the Ning family.

Ning Heng H'Sui was the patriarch. His holdings were so diversified and cross-pollinated with international companies and offshore holdings in Luxembourg, Geneva and Jersey that the author of the report admitted laconically at the end of this section, 'List of holdings probably incomplete.'

Going over the data more attentively, Daniel thought he perceived a subtle shift in investment emphasis dating from about the time of Ning Cheng Gong's appointment to his ambassadorial post in Africa. Although the Ning family holdings were still centred on the Pacific rim, the investments in Africa and in Africa-based companies had risen to a significant percentage of the entire portfolio.

Turning the page, he discovered that the computer had analysed this and determined that within six years the African section had increased from zero to just under twelve per cent of the total. There were large holdings in South African mining conglomerates, and in African land and food production companies, and even larger holdings in forestry estates, paper pulp mills and cattle and sheep ranches, all in Africa, south of the Sahara. It didn't take any clairvoyant gift to surmise that Ning Cheng Gong had pointed the family in this direction.

On page four of the computer print-out, Daniel read that Ning Cheng Gong was married to a Chinese girl from another rich Taiwanese family. The marriage had been arranged by the respective families. The couple had two children: a son born in 1982 and a daughter in 1983.

Cheng's interests were listed as oriental music and theatre and collecting oriental art, especially jade and ivory artefacts. He was an acknowledged expert on ivory netsuke. He played golf and tennis and sailed. He was also an expert in the martial arts, having reached the Fourth Dan. He smoked moderately and drank alcohol socially. He did not use any type of narcotic and the only weakness which the report suggested might be used as leverage or influence was that Ning Cheng Gong regularly patronised the high-class brothels of Taipei. His special sexual tastes seemed to lean towards acting out elaborate fantasies of an overtly sadistic nature. In 1987 one of the brothel girls had died during one of these performances. The family had obviously been able to quell any scandal, for no charges were ever brought against Cheng.

'Mike was right,' Daniel conceded as he laid aside the print out. 'He is a big boy and well protected. Best take it one careful step at a time. Chetti Singh first. If I can establish a connection, that might be the key.'

As he dressed for dinner he kept turning the pages of the report on the dressing-table to make certain he had not over-looked any connection with Malawi or with Chetti Singh.

There was none and he went down to dinner feeling depressed and discouraged. The role he had chosen for himself as Johnny Nzou's avenger was daunting.

There were both smoked Scotch salmon and roast sirloin of milk-fed Charollais beef on the five-page menu. However, when he ordered these the waiter shook his head regretfully.

'Sorry, no got.'

It swiftly developed into a guessing game. 'Sorry, no got.'

The waiter looked genuinely distressed as Daniel worked his way unsuccessfully through the menu until Daniel noticed that everyone else in the dining-room was eating stringy roast chicken and rice.

'Yes, got chicken and rice.' The waiter beamed approval. 'What you want for dessert?'

By now Daniel had learned the trick. He checked the other tables. 'How about banana custard?'

The waiter shook his head. 'No got.' But Daniel could tell by his expression that he was getting warm.

Daniel stood up and crossed to a Nigerian businessman at the next table.

'Excuse me, sir, what is that you are eating?'

He returned to his own table. 'I'll have Banana Delight,' he said, and the waiter nodded happily.

'Yes, tonight got Banana Delight.'

This little comedy restored Daniel's good humour and sense of the ridiculous.

'AWA,' Daniel reassured him. 'Africa Wins Again.' And the waiter looked delighted at such obvious praise and encouragement.

 The next morning Daniel headed eastwards towards Chipata and the Malawi border. There was not much point in expecting a sustaining breakfast from the hotel and anyway he was away long before the kitchens opened. He had covered almost a hundred miles before the sun rose, and he kept going most of the day, stopping only to eat beside the road.

He reached the border the following morning and crossed into Malawi with a lightening of his spirits. Not only was this tiny country even more spectacularly beautiful than the one he was leaving, but in comparison the mood of its people was contented and carefree.

Malawi was known as the Switzerland of Africa for its grand mountains and highland plateaux and its lakes and lovely rivers. Its people were famous throughout the southern continent for their intelligence and adaptability. They were sought after at every level of employment from domestic servants to miners and industrial workers. Lacking viable mineral deposits, Malawi's most valuable asset and export were her people.

Under the benevolent despotism of their octogenarian president-for-life, the special talents and strengths of the Malawian people were encouraged and fostered. The rural areas were not neglected and the urban migration was checked. Each family was ordered by the leader to build its own home and make itself self-sufficient in food. As cash crops they grew cotton and ground-nuts. On the large mountainside estates they raised a superior leaf of tea.

As Daniel drove towards the capital, Lilongwe, the contrast with the country he had just left was striking. The villages he passed were clean and orderly and prosperous. The people on the roadside were sleek, well dressed and smiling. Most of the handsome women favoured a full-length skirt printed with the national colours and a portrait of 'Kamuzu' Hastings Banda, the president. Short skirts were forbidden in Malawi by presidential decree, as was long hair on men.

Along the roadside, food and carved wooden curios were offered for sale. It was strange to see a surplus of food in any African country. Daniel stopped to buy eggs and oranges, mandarins, luscious red tomatoes and roasted ground-nuts, and also to exchange cheerful banter with the vendors.

After the misery and deprivation he had witnessed in the country he had so recently left, his mood was uplifted by these delightful people. Given the circumstances to make a good life, there are few peoples on earth so friendly and charming as those of Africa. Daniel found his regard for them strengthened and renewed.

'If you don't like black people, then you shouldn't be living in Africa,' Daniel's father had once said to him. It was a remark that had remained in his memory all these years, the validity of it growing ever more evident.

As he approached Lilongwe Daniel was struck even more forcefully by the contrast with other capitals of the continent. It was a recent capital, planned and built with architectural advice and financial help from South Africa. There was no slum stench here. Instead it was a pretty town, modern and functional.

Daniel found it good to be back again.

The Capital Hotel was surrounded by parks and lawns but conveniently situated close to the centre of the town. As soon as he was alone in his room, Daniel checked the local telephone directory which he found in the bedside drawer.

Chetti Singh was a big man in town and obviously enjoyed the sound of his own name. There was a string of numbers listed. He seemed to have his fingers in every honey pot: Chetti Singh Fisheries, Chetti Singh Supermarkets, Chetti Singh Tannery, Chetti Singh Sawmills and Lumber, Chetti Singh Garages and Toyota Agency. The list took up half the page.

Not a difficult bird to point, Daniel admitted to himself. Now let's see if we can get him to flush for a good sporting shot.

While he shaved and showered an attentive room servant carted his travel-stained clothing off to the laundry and ironed a clean but crumpled bush jacket to starchy perfection.

'Good excuse. I need to restock the tucker box,' Daniel told himself as he went downstairs and asked the receptionist directions to Chetti Singh's supermarket.

'Across the park.' The man pointed.

With assumed nonchalance Daniel sauntered across the park. It occurred to him that he was hardly the most inconspicuous visitor in town, with his London tailored bush jacket, silk scarf, and the spectacularly travel-dusted and battered Landcruiser with his strong-arm motif emblazoned all over it.

'Let's pray that Chetti Singh never got a good look at me or the truck that night.'

Chetti Singh's supermarket was on Main Street in a new four-storey building of modern layout, with clean tiled floors and walls. The shelves were piled with abundant wares, all reasonably priced, and the premises were thronged with customers. In Africa this was unusual.

While Daniel joined the relays of housewives wheeling their shopping trolleys down the aisles between the shelves, he was studying the building and its staff.

Four young Asian girls sat at the cash registers guarding the exit. They were quick and efficient. Under their graceful brown fingers the registers tinkled to the sweet music of Mammon.

'Chetti Singh's daughters,' Daniel guessed as he noted the family resemblance. They were pretty as sunbirds in their brightly coloured saris.

In the centre of the floor a middle-aged Asian lady sat at a tall dais from which she could keep a beady eye on every corner of the shop. She wore her hair in an iron-grey plait and though her sari was more subdued in colour, it was edged with gold thread and the diamonds on her fingers ranged from the size of peas to sparrows' eggs.

'Mama Singh,' Daniel decided. When it came to handling the cash, Asian businessmen liked to keep it close to home, which was probably one of the reasons for their universal success. He took his time selecting groceries, hoping for a glimpse of his quarry, but there was no sign of the turbaned Sikh.

At last Mama Singh left her seat on the dais and made an elephantine but dignified progress down the length of the store, until, with her long silken sari sweeping the treads, she mounted a flight of stairs set so discreetly in a corner of the food hall that Daniel had not noticed them before.

She entered a door at a higher level and now Daniel noticed a mirrored window in the wall beside the elevated door. It was obviously a one-way glass. An observer in the room beyond the door would have a clear view over the supermarket floor and Daniel had no doubt that it was Chetti Singh's office.

He turned away from that inscrutable square of glass, aware that he might have been under observation for the past half hour, and that the precaution was probably too late. He made his way to one of the girls at the cash registers and while she totted up his purchases he kept his face averted from the window in the rear wall.

Chetti Singh stood at the observation window as his wife came into the office. She saw instantly that he was disturbed. He was plucking thoughtfully at his beard and his eyes were slitted.

'That white man.' He nodded towards the store floor below the window. 'Did you notice him?'

'Yes.' She came to his side. 'I noticed him as he came in. I thought he might be a soldier or a policeman.'

'What made you think that?' Chetti Singh demanded.

She made an eloquent gesture with those lovely hands that were so incongruous on a female of her bulk. They were the hands of the young girl he had married almost thirty years ago, and the pale palms were dyed with henna.

'He stands tall, and walks with pride,' she explained. 'Like a soldier.'

'I think I know him,' Chetti Singh said. 'I saw him very recently, but it was at night and I cannot be absolutely certain.' He picked up the telephone from his desk and dialled two digits.

Standing at the window, he watched his second daughter pick up the telephone from beside her cash register.

'Treasure,' he spoke in Hindi. 'The man at your till. Is he paying with a credit card?'

'Yes, father.' She was the brightest of all his children, as much value to him as a second son, almost.

'Get his name and ask him where he is staying in town.'

Chetti Singh hung up and watched the white man pay for his purchases and leave the store heavily laden. As soon as he had gone, Chetti Singh dialled again.

'His name is Armstrong,' his daughter told him. 'D. A. Armstrong. He says that he is staying at the Capital Hotel.'

'Good. Let me speak to Chawe quickly.'

Below him his daughter swivelled her seat and called one of the uniformed security guards from the main doors. She held out the telephone receiver to him and as he placed it to his ear Chetti Singh asked, 'Chawe, did you recognise the *malungu* who has just left? The tall one with thick curly hair.' Chetti had switched to Angoni.

136

'I saw him,' the guard replied in the same language. 'But I did not recognise him.'

'Four nights ago,' Chetti Singh prompted him. 'On the road near Chirundu just after we had loaded the truck. The one who stopped and spoke to us.'

There was silence as Chawe considered the question. Chetti Singh saw him begin to pick at a nostril with his forefinger, a sign of uncertainty and embarrassment.

'Perhaps,' Chawe said at last. 'I am not sure.' He removed the thick forefinger from his nose and inspected it minutely. He was a man of the Angoni, a distant relative of the royal line of Zulu. His tribe had migrated this far north two hundred years ago at the time of King Chaka. He was a warrior, not a man given to deep thought.

'Follow him,' Chetti Singh ordered. 'Do not let him see you. Do you understand?'

'I understand, *Nkosi*.' Chawe looked relieved to be ordered into action and he left through the main doors with a spring in his step.

He returned half an hour later, hangdog and crestfallen. As soon as he came in through the main doors Chetti Singh telephoned his daughter again.

'Send Chawe up to my office right away!'

Chawe stood in the doorway at the head of the stairs, as big as a gorilla, and Chetti Singh demanded, 'Well, did you follow him as I ordered?'

'*Nkosi*, it is the same man.' Chawe shuffled his feet. Despite his size and strength, he was terrified of Chetti Singh. He had seen what happened to those who displeased the master. In fact, it was Chawe himself who was usually responsible for enforcing his master's discipline. He did not look directly into his eyes as he went on. 'It is the man who spoke to us on the night,' he said, and Chetti Singh frowned quickly.

'Why are you sure now, when you were uncertain before?' Chetti Singh demanded.

'The truck,' Chawe explained. 'He went to his truck and put the goods he had bought from us into it. It is the same truck, with a man's arm painted on the side, *Mambo*.'

'Good.' Chetti Singh nodded approval. 'You did well. Where is the man now?'

'He drove away in the truck.' Chawe looked apologetic. 'I could not follow him. I am sorry, *Nkosi Kakulu*.'

'Never mind. You did well,' Chetti Singh repeated. 'Who is on duty at the warehouse tonight?'

'I am, *Mambo* . . .' Chawe grinned suddenly, his teeth were large and even and very white, 'and, of course, Nandi.'

'Yes, of course.' Chetti Singh stood up. 'I will come down to the warehouse this evening after business is closed. I want to make sure that Nandi is ready to do her job. I think we may have trouble tonight. I want everything prepared. Have Nandi in the small cage. I don't want any mistakes. Do you understand, Chawe?'

'I understand, *Mambo*.'

'At six o'clock, at the warehouse.' Sometimes it was as well to repeat instructions to Chawe.

'*Nkosi*.' Chawe sidled from the room, still not looking directly at his master.

After he had gone, Chetti Singh sat staring at the closed door for many minutes before he picked up the telephone again.

Direct-dialling to an international exchange was always a lottery in Africa. Zimbabwe was almost a neighbouring state; only the narrow Tete corridor of Mozambique separated them. Nevertheless, it took him a dozen attempts and twenty frustrating minutes before he heard a ringing tone at the other end of the line and was through to the number in Harare.

'Good afternoon. This is the embassy of the Republic of Taiwan. May I help you?'

'I wish speech with the ambassador.'

'I'm sorry. His Excellency is not available at present. May I take a message or put you through to another member of the staff?'

'I am Chetti Singh. We are abundantly acquainted.'

'Please hold on, sir.'

A minute later Cheng came on the line. 'You are not to telephone me at this number. We agreed.'

Chetti Singh told him firmly, 'This is urgent, absolutely.'

'I cannot speak on this line. I will call you back within the hour. Give me your number there and wait for me.'

The private unlisted telephone on Chetti Singh's desk rang forty minutes later.

'This line is secure,' Cheng told him as he picked it up. 'But be discreet.'

'Do you know a white chap named Armstrong?'

'Doctor Armstrong? Yes. I know him.'

'This is the one you met at Chiwewe, and who accosted you on the road regarding certain stains on your clothing, is it not?'

'Yes.' Cheng's tone was non-committal. 'It's all right, don't worry. He knows nothing.'

'Then why has he pitched up in Lilongwe?' Chetti Singh demanded. 'You still want me not to worry?'

There was a silence. 'Lilongwe?' Cheng said at last. 'Did he also see you that night on the Chirundu road?'

'Yes.' Chetti Singh tugged at his beard. 'He stopped and spoke to me. He asked if I had seen the Parks trucks.'

'When was that? After we had transferred the ivory to you—?'

'Careful!' Chetti Singh snapped. 'But yes, it was after we had parted our separate ways, never mind. My men and I were tying down the tarpaulins when this white chap in a truck pulled up—'

Cheng cut in, 'How long did you speak to him?'

'A minute, no more than that. Then he went south towards Harare. I think he was following you, without a morsel of doubt.'

'He caught up with Gomo and forced him off the road.' Cheng's voice was sharp and agitated. 'He searched the Parks truck. Of course, he didn't find anything.'

'He is suspicious, indubitably.'

'Indubitably,' Cheng agreed sarcastically. 'But if he spoke to you for only a minute, he cannot connect you. He doesn't even know who you are.'

'My name and address are boldly imprinted upon my truck,' Chetti Singh said.

Cheng was silent again for a slow count of five. 'I did not notice. That was imprudent, my friend. You should have covered it.'

'It is no good closing the stable door after the bird has flown,' Chetti Singh pointed out.

'Where is the—' Cheng broke off. 'Where are the goods? Have you shipped them?'

'Not yet. They will go out tomorrow.'

'Can't you get rid of them sooner?'

'That is beyond the bounds of possibility.'

'You will have to deal with Armstrong then, if he becomes too curious.'

'Yes,' said Chetti Singh. 'I will deal with him most firmly and resolutely. Your side? Is everything taken care of? Your Mercedes?'

'Yes.'

'The two drivers?'

'Yes.'

'Have the authorities visited you?'

'Yes, but it was routine,' Cheng assured him. 'There were no surprises. They have not mentioned your name to me. But you must not telephone me at the embassy again. Use this number only. My security people have cleared this line.' He gave Chetti Singh the number and he wrote it down carefully.

'I will let you know about this chap. He is an absolute nuisance,' Chetti Singh went on.

'I hope not for too much longer.' Cheng cradled the receiver and instinctively reached for one of the assembly of ivory netsuke that were arranged on his desk top.

It was an exquisite miniature carving of a young girl and an old man. The beautiful child sat on the old man's lap staring with a daughter's adoration into his noble, lined and bearded face. Each tiny detail had been executed three hundred years ago by one of the great artists of the Tokugawa dynasty. The ivory had been polished by the touch of human fingers until it glowed like amber. Only when the group was inverted was it disclosed that beneath their flowing robes the couple were naked and that the old man's member was buried almost to the hilt between the girl's thighs.

The humour of it appealed to Cheng. It was one of his favourite pieces from all his vast collection, and he caressed it now between thumb and forefinger like a worry bead. As always, the silken feel of the ivory soothed him and encouraged him to think more clearly.

He had been expecting to hear more of Daniel Armstrong, but this had not lessened the shock of Chetti Singh's message.

The Sikh's questions aroused old doubts and for the thousandth time he went over all the precautions that he had taken.

After leaving the headquarters camp at Chiwewe he had not noticed the blood on his shoes and clothing until Daniel Armstrong had drawn his attention to it. This evidence of his guilt had preyed on his mind for the rest of that arduous journey out of the Zambezi valley. When at last they reached the main highway and found Chetti Singh waiting at the rendezvous, he had confided his worries to the Sikh and showed him the stains on his clothing.

'You were not supposed to go near the scene of the killing. That was foolish, never mind.'

'I had to make sure the job was done, and it was just as well I did. The warden was still alive.'

'You will have to burn that clothing.'

It was unlikely that there would be other traffic this late at night but they took no chances. They reversed the trucks well off the highway and transferred the ivory from the Parks trucks to Chetti Singh's pantechnicon behind a screen of trees. Even with Chetti Singh's gang of men to assist the two drivers, the removal took almost two hours. It was a huge quantity of ivory to move.

In the meantime Chetti Singh watched Cheng build a small fire. When it was burning hotly the ambassador stripped to his underwear. As he dressed again in fresh clothing from his luggage, Chetti Singh squatted beside the fire and burned all the soiled items. The rubber soles of the training shoes flared up fiercely when they caught. He used a stick to poke the charred scraps into the centre of the flames and make certain that they were reduced to fine ash.

'There will still be abundant traces of blood in the Mercedes,' Chetti pointed out as he stood up from the fire. 'On the floor, on the accelerator and brake pedals.' He removed the floor mat and the rubber covers from the control pedals and burned these as well. The stink of the black smoke made his eyes run, but still he was not satisfied.

'We will have to get rid of that car.' He told Cheng what to do. 'I will arrange the rest of it.'

Cheng was the first to leave the rendezvous. Even before the transfer of the ivory to the Sikh's truck was complete, he was on his way back to Harare.

He drove fast, as though trying to escape from his involvement with the raid. The reaction was setting in now. It was the same after one of his sexual pantomimes in the Myrtle Blossom Lady's house in Taipei. Afterwards he felt shaky and nauseated. He always promised himself it would never happen again.

The ambassador's residence was one of many large sprawling colonial buildings in the avenues near the golf club. He reached it well after midnight. He went directly to his own bedroom suite. He had arranged for his wife and the children to fly back to Taiwan the previous week to stay with her family. He was alone in the residence.

He stripped once again and, even though he had not worn it at the scene, placed all his clothing in a plastic bag. He was concerned that the faintest trace of blood might linger upon it. Then he showered. He stood under the steaming spray for almost half an hour, shampooing his hair twice and scrubbing his hands and fingernails with a stiff brush.

When he felt that he had washed away every last trace of blood or gunpowder, he dressed in fresh clothing from his dressing-room and carried the plastic bag containing his clothing back to the Mercedes parked in the residence garage. He placed the plastic bag in the boot beside his canvas grip. He was anxious to get rid of every single item that he had taken to Chiwewe, even his binoculars and his bird-book.

He reversed the Mercedes out of the garage and parked it in the front driveway of the residence. The gates were open and he left the key in the ignition.

Although it was by now after two in the morning and it had been a day and night filled with activity and intense nervous strain Cheng could not sleep. In a brocaded silk robe he paced his bedroom restlessly, until he heard the starter of the Mercedes whirl. He switched off the bedside lamp and darted to the window overlooking the front driveway. He was just in time to see his car, with darkened headlights, pull out of the driveway and turn into the deserted street. He sighed with relief and at last went to bed.

As he composed himself to sleep he thought how swiftly Chetti Singh had arranged it. Chetti Singh's son managed the

Harare branch of the family interests. He was almost as astute and reliable as his father.

In the morning, after breakfast, Cheng telephoned the police and reported the theft of the Mercedes. They found it twenty-four hours later, out near Hatfield on the way to the airport. It had been stripped of tyres and engine and set on fire. The fuel tank had exploded and nothing was left of the vehicle but the soot-blackened carapace. He knew that the insurance company would pay out in full, without too much delay or protest.

The following morning an anonymous caller on Cheng's unlisted line spoke without introduction or explanation.

'Look at page five of today's *Herald*,' he said, then broke the connection, but the accent had been Asian, very similar to Chetti Singh's manner of speech.

Cheng found the article at the foot of the page. It was six lines under an insignificant heading, 'Stabbed in Drunken Brawl'. Gomo Chisonda, a ranger employed by the National Parks Service, had been stabbed to death by an unknown assailant during an argument in a township beerhall.

The next day the same anonymous caller told Cheng, 'Page seven.' This time Cheng was certain that he recognised the voice of Chetti Singh's son.

The heading of the newspaper article was 'Railway Accident', and the squib read, 'The body of David Shiri, an off-duty ranger in the National Parks Service, was found on the railway line near Hartley. The dead man had a high blood alcohol level. A spokesman for Zimbabwe Railways warned the public of the danger of using unguarded crossings. This is the fourth accident of the same kind on the Hartley line since the beginning of the year.' As Chetti Singh had promised, there were no longer any surviving witnesses or accomplices.

Three days later, Cheng received a telephone call from the commissioner of police in person.

'I am very sorry indeed to disturb you, Your Excellency. I presume you have read about the murderous attack on Chiwewe Camp. I believe that you may be able to assist our enquiries into this most unfortunate incident. I understand that you were a visitor at the camp on that day, and that you left only hours before the attack.'

143

'That is correct, Commissioner.'

'Would you have any objection to making a statement to assist us? You know that there is no obligation for you to do so. You are fully protected by diplomatic privilege.'

'I will co-operate in any way possible. I particularly admired and liked the warden who was murdered. I will do all I can to help you apprehend the perpetrators of this foul crime.'

'I am most grateful to you, Your Excellency. May I send one of my senior inspectors to call upon you?'

The inspector was a burly Shona in plain clothes. He was accompanied by a sergeant in the smart uniform of the Zimbabwean police, and both of them were elaborately obsequious.

With profuse apologies the inspector took Cheng through a recital of his visit to Chiwewe, including his departure with the convoy of refrigerator trucks. Cheng had rehearsed all this and he went through it faultlessly. He was careful to mention his meeting with Daniel Armstrong.

When he had finished, the inspector fidgeted uncomfortably before asking, 'Doctor Armstrong has also made a statement, Your Excellency. His account confirms everything you have told me, except that he mentioned that he noticed there were bloodstains on your clothing.'

'When was that?' Cheng looked puzzled.

'When he encountered you and the Parks trucks, as he was returning to Chiwewe, after having seen the tracks of the raiders on the road.'

Cheng's expression cleared. 'Ah yes. I had been an interested spectator of the Parks elephant culling. As you can imagine, there was much blood about during the operation – I could easily have stepped in a puddle.'

The inspector was sweating with embarrassment by this stage. 'Do you remember what you were wearing that evening, Your Excellency?'

Cheng frowned as he tried to remember. 'I was wearing an open-neck shirt, blue cotton slacks, and probably a pair of comfortable running shoes. That is my usual casual attire.'

'Do you still have those items?'

'Yes, of course. The shirt and slacks will have been laundered by now, and the shoes will have been cleaned. My valet is very efficient . . .' He broke off and smiled as though a thought had only just occurred to him. 'Inspector, do you want to see these items? You might even wish to take them away for examination.'

Now the police inspector's embarrassment was painful. He squirmed in his chair. 'We have no right to ask for that kind of co-operation, Your Excellency. However, in view of the statement made by Doctor Armstrong. If you had no objection . . .'

'Of course not.' Cheng smiled reassuringly. 'As I told the commissioner of police, I want to co-operate in every possible way.' He glanced at his wristwatch. 'However, I am due at lunch with the president at State House in an hour. Do you mind if I send the clothing down to your headquarters with a member of my staff?'

Both police officers sprang to their feet. 'I am very sorry to have inconvenienced you, Your Excellency. We appreciate your help. I am sure the commissioner of police will be writing to you to tell you that himself.'

Without rising from his desk, Cheng stopped the inspector at the door. 'There was a report in the *Herald* that the raiders had been apprehended,' he asked. 'Is that correct? Were you able to recover the stolen ivory?'

'The bandits were intercepted at the Zambezi as they tried to cross back into Zambia. Unfortunately all of them were either killed or escaped, and the ivory was destroyed by fire or lost in the river.'

'What a pity . . .' Cheng sighed. 'They should have been made to answer for these brutal killings. However, it has simplified your work, has it not?'

'We are closing the file,' the inspector agreed. 'Now that you have helped us tidy up the loose ends, the commissioner will write to convey his appreciation and that will be the end of the matter.'

The packet of clothing that Cheng selected from his wardrobe and sent to police headquarters, although agreeing with the description he had given the inspector, had never been worn anywhere near Chiwewe or the Zambezi valley. Cheng sighed now as he thought about it. He replaced the ivory netsuke on his desk and stared at it morosely. But it was not the end of the matter, not now that Doctor Daniel Armstrong was nosing around, making trouble.

Could he rely on Chetti Singh once again, he wondered? It was one thing to get rid of two lowly Parks rangers, but Armstrong was game of a larger kind. He had international reputation and fame, there would be questions if he disappeared.

He touched the intercom button and spoke into the microphone on his desk in Cantonese.

'Lee, come in here please.'

He could have asked his question without ordering his secretary through, but he liked to look at her. Although she was of peasant stock from the hills, she was bright and nubile. She had done well at Taiwan University, but Cheng had not chosen her for her academic achievements.

She stood to the side of his desk, close enough for him to touch if he had wished to, in an attitude of servility and submission. Despite her modern accomplishments, she was a traditionally raised girl with the correct attitude to men, and in particular to her master.

'Have you confirmed the reservations with Qantas Airlines?' he asked. With Armstrong sniffing around in Lilongwe, it was as well that the return to Taipei was imminent. He would never have taken the risk of the Chiwewe adventure if he had planned to stay on at the embassy. Already his wife and family had left. He would follow at the end of the month, only eight days from now.

'Yes, the reservations have been confirmed, Your Excellency,' Lee whispered respectfully. To him her voice was as sweet as that of the nightingale in his father's lotus garden in the mountains. It stirred him.

'When are the packers coming in?' he asked, and touched her. She trembled slightly under his hand and that stirred him further.

'They will come in first thing on Monday, my lord.' She used the traditional title of respect. Her straight black hair hung to her shoulders and shimmered with light.

Cheng ran his fingers lightly up the thigh slit of her cheong-sam; her skin was as smooth as the ivory netsuke.

'You have warned them of the value and fragility of my art collection?' he asked, and pinched her beneath the skirt. He took a nip of that ivory skin between the nails of his thumb and second finger and she winced and bit her lower lip.

'Yes, my lord,' she whispered, with a catch of pain in her voice. He pinched a little harder. It would leave a tiny purple star on the flawless swell of her small firm buttock, a mark that would still be there when she came to him tonight.

The power of pain made him feel elated. He forgot about Doctor Daniel Armstrong and any trouble he might be brewing. For now, the police were off the track, and Lee Wang was lovely and compliant. He had eight days while he was separated from his wife in which to enjoy her to the full. Then he would return home, to his father's approbation.

 Daniel unlocked the rear door of the Landcruiser and packed the groceries and supplies that he had purchased from Chetti Singh's supermarket into his depleted tucker box. Then he went round to the cab and sat at the wheel. While he let the engine warm, he checked his notebook for the list of the Sikh's other business premises.

With help from a few obliging pedestrians he found his way into the light industrial area of the town, down near the railway line and the station. Here it seemed that Chetti Singh owned four or five acres of industrial sites. Some of these were undeveloped and overgrown with rank bush and weed. On one of the vacant lots a large signboard declared:

ANOTHER CHETTI SINGH PROJECT

SITE OF PROPOSED COTTON CARDING FACTORY

Development! Employment! Prosperity! Upliftment!
FOR MALAWI!

On one side of the open plot, behind a barbed-wire security fence, stood the workshops of Chetti Singh's Toyota agency.

At least a hundred new Toyota vehicles were parked in the front lot. They were still coated with the filth of the long rail journey up from the coast on open goods trucks. Clearly they were awaiting delivery service in the main workshop building. Through the open front doors Daniel could see a team of mechanics at work. Though the foremen appeared all to be Asians, some in Sikh turbans, most of the overalled mechanics were black. The enterprise appeared prosperous and well managed.

Daniel drove into the forecourt and left the Landcruiser parked at the reception bay. He spoke to one of the foremen in a blue dust-coat. Under the pretext of arranging a service for the Landcruiser he managed to get a good look around the workshop and administration building. There was no obvious place where a shipment of stolen ivory could be hidden.

While he made a booking to bring the Landcruiser in the following morning at eight o'clock, he chatted casually to the workshop foreman and learned that the sawmill and the Chetti Singh Trading Company warehouse were in the next street, backing on to the vehicle workshop.

He drove away and circled the block. It was easy to pick out the sawmill, even from the far end of the street. A dozen railway trucks stood at the private railway siding, every one of them piled high with heavy logs of indigenous timber cut in the heavily forested mountains. The shrieks of the circular saws carried clearly up the street.

As he drove past the gates he looked into the open sheds where the saws were housed. The spinning discs shone like quicksilver, and spurts of yellow sawdust flew from the rough logs as the blades bit into them. The resinous smell of freshly cut timber was pungent in the hot sunlight and mountains of raw planks were piled in the extensive yards, ready to be loaded on to the waiting railway trucks.

Daniel drove past slowly. Diagonally opposite the sawmill stood the warehouse complex. It was enclosed by a high diamond-mesh fence, green plastic-coated wire on sturdy concrete poles with offset tops angled out towards the street and festooned with barbed wire.

The warehouse was in five semi-detached units; the valleys

and peaks of the common roof formed a saw-tooth pattern of unpainted corrugated asbestos sheeting. The walls were also of the same corrugated asbestos. Each of the five units had separate doors of the roller type usually seen on aircraft hangars.

This time the signboard at the gates read:

CHETTI SINGH TRADING COMPANY
CENTRAL DEPOT AND WAREHOUSE

He was certainly not shy about advertising his name, Daniel thought wryly. There was a swinging boom and a brick-built gatehouse at the entrance and Daniel noticed at least one uniformed guard at the gate. As he drew level with the last building, he saw that the tall asbestos doors had been rolled open and he was able to look down the length of the cavernous warehouse.

Suddenly he leaned forward and his pulse accelerated as he recognised the huge pantechnicon parked in the centre of the warehouse. It was the vehicle that he had last seen on the Chirundu road four nights previously. The ten-wheel trailer with the green tarpaulin cover was still hitched behind it and the red dust that coated it matched that on his own Landcruiser.

The rear doors of the trailer were open and a team of a dozen or so black labourers assisted by a forklift truck were loading a cargo of brown sacks that could have contained maize, sugar or rice.

He could not see any of the distinctive dried fish bags that had been the cargo which he had seen in the Zambezi valley. He lowered the side window, hoping for a whiff of fish, but he smelled only dust and diesel fumes.

Then he was past. He thought about making a U-turn and another passing inspection.

'Hell, I've drawn enough attention already,' he told himself. 'Like the circus coming to town.'

He drove back to the Capital Hotel the way he had come, left the truck in the guests' car park and went up to his room. He ran a bath, as deep and hot as he could stand it, and soaked the dust and grime of the African roads out of his pores, while his skin turned a rich puce.

As the water cooled he twiddled the tap with his toe, adding fresh steaming gouts.

At last he stood to lather his nether regions and regarded himself seriously in the dewy mirror over the washbasin.

'Look here, Armstrong. The sensible thing to do is go to the police with our suspicions. It's their job, let them get on with it.'

'Since when, Armstrong,' he replied, 'did we ever do the sensible thing? Besides, this is Africa. It will take the police three or four days to stir their butts, and Mr Singh has had quite enough time already to get rid of any ivory he may just have lying around. By tomorrow it will probably be too late to catch him at it.'

'You are trying to tell me, Armstrong, that time is of the essence?'

'Precisely, old chap.'

'It couldn't be that you'd enjoy a touch of cloak and dagger, a bit of boy-scouting, a spot of amateur sleuthing?'

'Who me? Don't be silly! You know me.'

'Indeed I do,' he agreed with a wink at his image, and subsided back into the steamy suds, which slopped over the bath rim on to the tiled floor.

The dinner was a vast improvement on his last public meal.

The fillets of bream were fresh from the lake and the wine was a delicious Hamilton-Russell Chardonnay from the Cape of Good Hope. Reluctantly he rationed himself to half the bottle.

'Work to do,' he muttered ruefully, and went up to the room to make his preparations. There was no hurry. He couldn't move until after midnight. When he was ready he lay on the bed and enjoyed the sensation of excitement and anticipation. He kept looking at his wristwatch. It seemed to have stopped and he held it to his ear. The waiting was always the worst part.

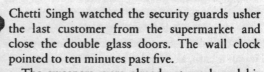

Chetti Singh watched the security guards usher the last customer from the supermarket and close the double glass doors. The wall clock pointed to ten minutes past five.

The sweepers were already at work and his daughters were busy at the tills, cashing up the day's receipts. The girls were as devout as virgins ministering at the altar of some arcane religion, and his wife stood over them as dignified as the high priestess. This was the high point of the daily ritual.

At last the procession left the tills and made its way across the shop floor, in strict order of precedence, his wife leading and her daughters following, the eldest first and the youngest last. They entered his office and laid the day's take on his desk, neatly banded bundles of currency notes, and canvas bags of coins, while his wife handed him the print-outs from the tills.

'Oh, good!' Chetti Singh told them in Hindi. 'The best day since Christmas Eve, I am sure.' He could recite the figures over the last six months without consulting his ledgers.

He entered the take in the day-book, and while his family watched respectfully, locked the cash and credit-card vouchers into the big Chubb safe built into the back wall.

'I will be late home for dinner,' he told his wife. 'I must go down to the warehouse to attend to certain matters.'

'Papaji, your meal will be ready when you return.' She clasped her hands to her lips in a graceful gesture of respect, and her daughters imitated her example and then filed from his office.

Chetti Singh sighed with pleasure. They were good girls – but if only they had been boys. It was going to be the devil's own job finding husbands for all of them.

He drove down to the industrial area in the Cadillac. The car was not new. Dearth of foreign exchange would not permit an ordinary citizen to import such a luxurious vehicle. Chetti Singh had, as always, a system. He contacted newly appointed members of the American diplomatic staff before they left Washington. Malawi customs regulations allowed them to import a new car and sell it locally at the end of their term. Chetti Singh paid them twice the US value of the Cadillac in Malawi kwacha on arrival. They could live in princely style on this amount for the full three years of their tour in Malawi while still retaining use of the car and saving their official salaries.

When they left, Chetti Singh took over the vehicle, ran it for a year, until the next arrangement matured at which time he placed the Cadillac on the showroom floor of his Toyota agency with a price tag of three times its original US value. It was usually sold within the week. No profit was too small to despise; no loss was too small to abhor. It was not by accident that over the years Chetti Singh had amassed a fortune the full extent of which not even his wife could guess at.

At the warehouse gates Chawe swung open the boom to allow him to drive the Cadillac through.

'Yes?' Chetti Singh asked the big Angoni.

'He came,' Chawe replied. 'As you said he would. He drove by on this road at ten minutes past four. He was in the truck with the man's arm painted on the door. He drove slowly and he was staring through the fence all the time.'

Chetti Singh frowned with annoyance. 'This chap is becoming an absolute pest. Never mind,' he said aloud, and Chawe looked bemused. His English was rudimentary.

'Come with me,' Chetti Singh ordered, and Chawe climbed into the back seat of the Cadillac. He would never be so presumptuous as to sit beside his master.

Chetti Singh drove slowly along the front of the warehouse complex. All the tall doors were already closed and locked for the night. There were no burglar alarms guarding the area; at night even the perimeter fence was unlit by floodlights.

There had been a period two or three years back during which he had suffered from repeated burglaries and break-ins. Alarms and floodlights had done little to prevent these depredations. In desperation he had consulted the most famous Sangoma in all the territory. This old witch-doctor lived in dread isolation up on the top of the misty Mlanje plateau attended only by his acolytes.

For a fee commensurate with his reputation, the witch-doctor descended from the mountain with his entourage and, with great fanfare and ceremony, he placed the warehouse under the protection of the most powerful and malevolent of the spirits and demons that he controlled.

Chetti Singh invited all the idlers and loafers of the town to witness the ceremony. They watched with interest and trepidation as the witch-doctor decapitated a black cockerel at each of the five doors of the warehouse and sprinkled its blood on the portals. After this, to suitable incantations, he placed the skull of a baboon on each corner-post of the perimeter fence. The spectators had been much impressed and the word spread swiftly through the townships and the beerhalls that Chetti Singh was under magic protection.

For six months thereafter there were no further break-ins. Then one of the township gangs worked up the courage to test the efficacy of the spell, and they got away with a dozen television sets and nearly forty transistor radios.

Chetti Singh sent for the witch-doctor and reminded him that his services carried a guarantee. They haggled until finally Chetti Singh agreed to buy from him at a bargain price the ultimate deterrent. Her name was Nandi.

Since Nandi's arrival there had been only a single break-in. The burglar had died in Lilongwe hospital the following day with his scalp ripped off his skull and his bowels bulging out of the rents in his belly. Nandi had solved the problem, permanently.

Chetti Singh drove the Cadillac around the peripheral pathway inside the fence. The fence was in good order, even the baboon skulls still grinned down from the tops of the cornerposts, but the infra-red alarms were gone. Chetti Singh had sold them at a good price to a Zambian customer. After Nandi's arrival they had become redundant.

Completing the circuit of the fence, Chetti Singh parked the Cadillac at the rear of the warehouse, beside a neat shed of the same corrugated sheeting as the main building. This was obviously a later addition, tacked on as an afterthought to the rear wall of the warehouse.

As Chetti Singh stepped out of the Cadillac, his nostrils flared to the faint but rank odour that wafted from the single small window in the shed. This was set high up and was heavily barred.

He glanced at Chawe. 'Is she safe?'

'She is in the small cage, as you ordered, *Mambo*.'

Despite the assurance, Chetti Singh peered through the peephole in the door before he opened it and stepped into the shed. The only light came from the high window and the room was in semi-darkness, made more intense by the contrast of the late sunshine outside.

The smell was stronger now, a pungent wild scent, and

suddenly from the gloom there was a spitting snarl so vicious that Chetti Singh stepped back involuntarily.

'My goodness,' he chuckled to hide his nerves. 'We are in absolutely foul mettle today.'

An animal moved behind the bars of the cage, a dark shape on silent pads and there was a gleam of yellow eyes.

'Nandi.' Chetti Singh smiled. '"The sweet one".' Nandi had been the name of King Chaka's mother.

Chetti Singh reached out to the switch beside the door and the fluorescent tube in the ceiling spluttered and then lit the shed with a cold blue light.

In the cage a female leopard shrank away against the far wall, crouching there, staring at the man with murderous eyes, her upper lip lifting in a creased and silent snarl to reveal her fangs.

She was a huge cat, over seven feet from nose to tail, one of the animals from Mlanje mountain forest, who would turn the scale at 120 pounds. A wild creature captured by the old witch-doctor in her maturity, she had once been a notorious goat-and dog-killer, terrorising the villages on the slopes of the mountain. Shortly before her capture she had savagely mauled a young herdboy who had tried to defend his flock against her.

The forest cats were darker than those of the open savanna, the jet-black rosettes that dappled her skin were close-set, so that she was close in coloration to the melanistic panther. Her tail curled and flicked like a metronome, the gauge of her temper. She watched the man unblinkingly. The force of her hatred was as thick as the wild animal stench in the small hot room.

'Are you angry?' Chetti Singh asked, and her lip lifted higher to the sound of his voice. She knew him well.

'Not angry enough,' Chetti Singh decided, and reached for the cattle prod on the rack beside the light switch.

The cat reacted immediately. She knew the sting of the electric prod. Her next snarl was a crackling rattle and she ran back and forth trying to escape from the torment she had come to expect. At the end nearest the main wall of the warehouse the steel mesh cage narrowed into a bottle-neck just wide enough to admit the leopard's body, a low tunnel that ended against a steel sliding door in the warehouse wall.

The prod was bolted on to a long aluminium pole. Chetti Singh slipped it between the cage bars and reached out to touch the leopard. Her movements became frantic as she tried to avoid the device, and Chetti Singh laughed at her antics as he pursued her around the cage. He was trying to drive her into the bottle-necked tunnel.

At last she flung herself against the bars of the cage, ripping at the steel with her claws as she tried to reach him, coughing and grunting with fury, but the length of the pole kept Chetti Singh out of range.

'Goodness gracious me!' he said, and touched the side of her neck with the points of the prod. Blue electricity flashed and the leopard recoiled from the sting of it and bounded into the tunnel at the end of the cage.

Chawe was ready for this, and he dropped the mesh door behind her. Now she was trapped. Her nose was against the steel hatch in the warehouse wall, while at her heels the mesh door prevented her backing away. The tunnel was so low that it almost touched her back and she could not rear up, it was so narrow that she could not turn her head to protect her heaving flanks. She was helplessly pinioned and Chetti Singh handed the prod to Chawe.

He returned to the table near the door and uncoiled the lead of a small electric soldering iron and plugged it into the wall socket. With the plastic-covered lead trailing behind him he came back to where the leopard crouched in the tunnel. He reached through the bars and stroked her back. Her pelt was thick and silky, and she could not avoid his touch. Her whole body seemed to swell with her fury and she snarled and tried to twist her neck to savage his hand but the bars prevented it.

Chetti Singh lifted the soldering iron and spat on the copper point to test its heat. His spittle sizzled and evaporated in a puff of steam. He grunted with satisfaction and reached through the bars once again. He grasped the leopard's tail and lifted it high, exposing her fluffy genitalia and the tight puckered black collar of her anus.

The leopard hissed with outrage and ripped at the cement floor with her claws fully extended. She knew what was coming and she tried to lower her tail and cover her delicate parts.

'Help me,' Chetti Singh grunted, and Chawe seized the tail. It writhed like a serpent in his grip but he forced it upwards, allowing his master free use of both hands.

Chetti Singh inspected the delicate flesh thoughtfully. It was dimpled and cratered with healed scars, some so fresh that the cicatrice was still pink and glossy. He reached out gently with the hot iron, choosing the spot to burn with care, avoiding the freshly healed skin. The cat felt the heat of the approaching iron and her body convulsed in anticipation.

'Just a little one, my beauty,' Chetti Singh assured her. 'Just enough to make you very angry if you should meet Doctor Armstrong tonight.'

Unmolested, leopards are not a serious threat to human beings. Man does not form a part of their natural prey, and their instinctive fear is enough to make them avoid rather than attack him. However, once injured or wounded, or particularly when they are deliberately tormented, they are amongst the most dangerous and vicious of all African animals.

Chetti Singh touched the glowing iron to the soft rim of the leopard's anus. There was a puff of smoke and the stink of burned skin and hair. The leopard shrieked with pain and bit at the steel bars.

Chetti Singh inspected the injury. With practice he could inflict a burn that was exquisitely painful, but which would heal within the week and would not damage the animal's appearance nor hamper her movements when she attacked.

'Good!' he congratulated himself. The iron had only superficially penetrated the outer skin. It was a shallow painful little wound, yet it had infuriated the golden cat.

He laid the soldering iron back on the table and picked up a bottle of disinfectant. It was raw iodine, dark yellow and pungent on the swab that he pressed against the open wound. The sting of it would increase her fury.

The leopard shrieked and hissed and struggled wildly against the restraining bars. Her eyes were huge and yellow and froth lined her open snarling lips.

'That's enough. Open the hatch,' Chetti Singh ordered, and the Angoni released the cat's tail. She whipped it down between her legs to protect herself.

Chawe went to the handle of the steel hatch and raised it. With one last snarl the leopard bounded through the opening and disappeared into the warehouse beyond.

At first it had been difficult to get the cat to leave the warehouse at dawn each morning, but with free use of the electric prod and the lure of the goat's meat on which she was fed, she had at last been trained to return to her cage in the shed on command.

It was the only training she had received. All night she prowled the warehouse, tormented and murderous. At dawn she returned to the shed and crouched there in the gloom, growling softly to herself and licking her deliberately inflicted injuries, awaiting the first opportunity to avenge her humiliation and pain.

Chawe closed the hatch behind the leopard and followed his master out into the last glow of the sunset. Chetti Singh mopped his face with a white handkerchief. It had been hot in the fetid little shed.

'You will remain in your guardhouse at the main gate,' he commanded. 'Do not patrol the fence or attempt to stop the white man from entering the warehouse. If he does get in, Nandi will warn you . . .'

They both smiled at the thought. They remembered the last intruder and his condition as they took him down to the casualty department of the general hospital.

'When you hear Nandi working on him, ring me from the main gate. The telephone is beside my bed. Do not enter the warehouse until I arrive. It will take fifteen or twenty minutes for me to get here. By that time Nandi may have saved us a great deal of trouble.'

His wife had one of her magnificent curries prepared for his dinner. She did not question where he had been. She was a good and dutiful wife.

After dinner he worked on his accounts for two hours. His was a complicated system of accountancy: he kept two separate sets of books, one for the civil tax collector which reflected a fictitious profit figure, and another authentic set which was meticulously correct. From this Chetti Singh calculated the tithe that he paid to the temple. It was one thing to cheat on income tax, but a prudent man did not mess around with the gods.

Before he went to bed he unlocked the steel safe built into the back of his wardrobe and took out the double-barrelled twelve-bore shotgun and a packet of SSG cartridges. He had an official police permit for the firearm, for, whenever possible and convenient, he was a law-abiding man.

His wife gave him a puzzled look, but made no comment. He did not satisfy her curiosity, but propped the weapon in the corner nearest the door, ready to hand. He switched out the lights and under the sheets made love to her with his customary dispatch. Ten minutes later he was snoring sonorously.

The telephone beside his bed rang at seven minutes past two in the morning. On the first peal Chetti Singh was awake, and before it could ring again he had the receiver to his ear.

'In the warehouse, Nandi is singing a pretty song,' said Chawe in Angoni.

'I am coming,' Chetti Singh replied, and swung his legs off the bed.

 There were no street lights, 'which makes the job a little easier,' Daniel murmured as he parked the Landcruiser on one of the open plots three hundred yards from the boundary fence of Chetti Singh's central depot. He had driven the last mile at walking speed without headlights. Now he switched off the engine and stepped out into the darkness. He stood listening for almost ten minutes before he checked his wristwatch. It was a little after one o'clock.

He already wore navy-blue slacks and a black leather jacket. Now he pulled a soft balaclava cap of dark wool over his head. He strapped a small nylon bag around his waist that contained the few items of equipment which he had selected from the tool-box.

Bolted to the Landcruiser's roof were two light aluminium extension ladders that he carried for laying as corduroy when negotiating soft sand or deep mud. They weighed less than seven pounds each. He carried both of them under one arm as he set out across the weed-choked wasteland towards the depot. He kept off the road, well back amongst the scrub.

The plot had been used as a rubbish dump. There were piles of garbage. A broken bottle or jagged piece of scrap iron could cut through the canvas and rubber boots he wore. He picked his way with care.

Fifty feet from the fence he laid down the ladders and crouched behind a rusty car body. He studied the depot. There were no lights burning in the warehouse, no floodlights illuminating the fence. That seemed odd.

'Too good? Too easy?' he asked himself, and crept closer. The only light was in the guardhouse at the front gate. It gave just sufficient back lighting with which to examine the fence. He saw at once that it was not electrified, and he could discover no trip-wire for an alarm system.

He moved stealthily to the corner-post at the rear of the property. If there were an infra-red alarm system, the eye would be mounted here. Something white gleamed on top of the post, but on closer inspection he realised that it was the bleached skull of a chacma baboon, and he grimaced. He felt vaguely uneasy as he went back to fetch the ladders from where he had left them beside the wrecked car.

Back at the corner of the fenced area, he settled down to watch for a guard making his rounds. After half an hour he had convinced himself that the fence was unguarded.

He moved in. The quickest and safest method of entry would have been to use the wire-cutters, but if possible he wanted to leave no trace of his visit. He extended both ladders to their full length. Then steeling himself for the squeal of a hidden alarm, he propped one of the ladders against the concrete corner-post. He let out his breath when no alarm sounded.

Carrying the second ladder, he scaled to the top of the fence. Balancing on the top rung, leaning backwards to avoid the offset barbed wire on the summit, he swung the spare ladder over and inwards. He had intended lowering it carefully on the far side, but it slipped from his grip.

Although it fell on grass, which cushioned the impact, the sound was like the report of a .357 magnum in his own ears. He teetered on the top of the ladder, his nerves screwed tight and waited for a shouted challenge or a shot.

Nothing happened, and after a minute he breathed again. He

reached into the front of his clothing under the polo-neck jersey, and brought out the roll of foam rubber which he used as a pillow when sleeping under the stars. It was an inch thick, just enough to pad the top strand of barbed wire. He spread it carefully over the top of the fence.

He took a firm grip between the spikes of the wire with his gloved hands and rolled smoothly over, dropping nine feet to the lawn on the far side. He broke his fall with a forward somersault and crouched low, listening again, peering into the darkness.

Nothing.

Quickly he set up the second ladder against the inside of the fence, ready for a speedy retreat. The unpainted aluminium gleamed like a beacon to catch the eye of a patrolling guard.

'Nothing we can do about that,' he told himself, and crossed to the side wall of the warehouse.

He slipped along the wall, thankful for the darkness, and reached the corner. He crouched there for a minute, listening. Somewhere far away a dog barked, and there was the distant sound of a locomotive shunting in the railway yards. Apart from that, nothing.

He glanced round the corner, and then crept down the long back wall of the warehouse. There was no opening here, except for a single row of the skylight windows very high up under the eaves of the saw-backed roof, at least thirty feet above him.

Ahead he made out a small shed in the gloom. It was attached to the rear wall of the warehouse, but its roof was much lower than that of the main building. As he approached it, he became aware of a faint but foul odour, like guano fertiliser or untanned hides.

The smell was stronger as he circled the shed, but he thought little of it. He was studying the shed. There was a downpipe in the angle where the shed's wall joined that of the main warehouse. He tested the pipe with his weight, and then went up it easily, hand over hand. Within seconds he was lying stretched out on the roof of the shed, looking up at the row of skylights in the main wall now only ten feet above him. Two of the panels stood open.

From the bag in the small of his back he brought out a coil

of nylon rope and quietly tied a Turk's head knot in one end to give it weight.

Balancing on the peak of the shed's roof he flicked the rope out and then got it swinging in an easy circle. With a snap of the wrist he shot the weighted knot upwards. It struck the jamb between the two open panels and then dropped back in a tangle around his shoulders. He tried again with the same result. At the fifth attempt the knot dropped through the open skylight, and immediately he tugged and it whipped back and made three natural turns around the jamb. He pulled back hard and the wraps held. Keeping pressure on the line he began to climb. He used the rubber soles of his canvas boots for purchase against the unpainted asbestos wall, and went up with the agility of a monkey.

He had almost reached the windows when he felt the end of the line start to unravel. With a sickening lurch he dropped back a foot and then it held again. Daniel gathered himself and lunged upwards. A gloved hand over the bottom frame of the open skylight steadied him.

He hung thirty feet above the ground, his feet kicking and slipping against the wall and the steel frame cutting into his fingers, even through the glove. Then with another convulsive effort he flung his right hand up and got a double grip. Now with the strength of both arms he was able to draw himself up smoothly and straddle the frame of the skylight.

He took a few seconds to catch his breath and listen for any sound from the dark interior of the building, then he unzipped the bag and groped for the Maglite flashlight. Before he left the hotel room he had screwed a red plastic shade over the lens. The shaft of light which he shot downwards was a discreet ruby glow that was unlikely to attract attention from outside the building.

Below him the warehouse floor was piled with towers and walls of packing cases in a multitude of sizes and shapes.

'Oh no!' he groaned aloud. He had not expected such abundance. It would take a week to examine all of them, and there were four other bays to the warehouse complex.

He flashed the torch-beam down the wall. The corrugated cladding was fixed to a framework of intricately welded angle iron. The frames formed an easy ladder for him to reach the cement floor thirty feet below. He swarmed down and switched off the flashlight.

Swiftly he changed position in the darkness. If a guard was creeping up on him he wanted to confuse the attack. He crouched between two cases, listening to the silence. He was about to move again, when he froze. There was something, a sound so small that it was just within the range of his comprehension, he felt it with his nerve ends rather than truly heard it. It ceased, if it had ever been.

He waited for a hundred beats of his racing heart but it did not come again. He switched on the torch and the light dispelled his unease.

He moved softly down the aisle between the masses of trade goods and bales and crates. He had seen the pantechnicon parked in the end bay. 'That's the place to start,' he assured himself and he sniffed the dark air for the smell of dried fish.

He stopped abruptly and switched off the torch. Once again he had sensed something, not definite enough to pin-point, not loud enough to be a sound – just a premonition that something was close by in the darkness. He held his breath and there was a whisper of movement, or of his imagination. He could not be certain, but he thought it might be the brush of stealthy footfalls perhaps, or the gentle sough of breathing.

He waited. No. It was nothing but his nerves. He moved on down the dark warehouse. There were no interior walls in the building, only pillars of angle iron supporting the roof, separating the spaces between each of the bays. He stopped again, and sniffed. There it was at last. The smell of dried fish. He went forward more rapidly, and the smell was stronger.

They were stacked against the end wall of the furthest bay, a high pile of sacks, reaching almost to roof level. The smell was strong. Printed on each sack were the words: 'Dried fish. Product of Malawi.' together with a stylised rising sun emblem with a crowing cockerel surmounting it.

Daniel groped in his bag and brought out a twelve-inch screwdriver. He squatted before the pile of fish sacks and began to probe them, stabbing the point of the screwdriver through the weave of the jute sacks, and then working it around to feel for any hard object packed beneath a layer of dried fish. He worked quickly, five or six quick stabs to each sack as he passed, reaching up to the sacks above his head, and then scrambling up the pyramid to reach the summit.

At last he stopped and thought about it. He had presumed that the ivory would be packed inside the fish sacks, but now he reconsidered and discovered the fallacy of his original theory. If Ning Cheng Gong had indeed transferred the ivory from the refrigerator trucks to Chetti Singh's pantechnicon, then there certainly would not have been the opportunity to repack it in the sacks and seal them during the few hours before Daniel had intercepted Chetti Singh on the Chirundu road. The very best they could have done was to lay the ivory on the floor of the cargo bed and pile the fish sacks over it.

Daniel clucked his tongue with annoyance at his own impetuosity. Of course, the fish sacks were too small to contain the larger tusks of the hoard, and they would make an impossibly flimsy packing in which to smuggle the ivory out of Africa to its final destination, wherever that might be. The heavy pointed tusks would surely work their way through the outer layer of fish and rupture the woven jute sacks.

'Damn fool.' Daniel shook his head. 'I had a fixed idea . . .' He flashed the shaded ruby beam of the torch about, and his nerves jumped tight. He thought he saw something big and dark move in the shadows at the extreme range of the beam, the glint of animal eyes, but when he steadied the torch and stared hard, he realised that it was his imagination again.

'Getting old and windy,' he rebuked himself.

He slid down the pyramid of fish sacks to the floor, then he hurried along the aisle between the mountains of goods. He examined the labelling on the packing cases as he passed. 'Defy Refrigerators', 'Koo Canned Peaches', 'Sunlight Soap Powder'. Each case consigned to 'Chetti Singh Trading Company'. It was all incoming cargo. He was looking for an outgoing cargo.

Ahead of him he made out the shape of a fork-lift truck standing high on the loading ramp near the main doors. As he moved towards it he saw a large case balanced on the fork arms of the truck. Beyond it, almost blocking the ramp, was a high pile of identical cases. They were ready for loading on to the empty railway truck that stood waiting in the bay below the ramp.

Obviously, this was an outgoing cargo and he almost ran down the length of the bay. As he approached he realised that they were traditional tea-chests, with sturdy plywood sides and solid frames, bound with flexible steel straps.

Then he felt an electric tickle of excitement lift the hair on his arms as he read the address stencilled on the side of the nearest chest:

LUCKY DRAGON INVESTMENTS
1555 CHUNGCHING S ROAD
TAIPEI

TAIWAN

'Son of a gun!' Daniel grinned happily. 'The Chinese connection! Lucky Dragon. Lucky for some!'

He crossed to the fork-lift truck and reached across to the controls. He clicked on the master switch and operated the controls. The electric motor purred and the chest rose silently. At head-height Daniel stopped it. He slipped beneath the suspended case. He did not want to leave any trace of his visit by interfering with the lid or sides of the case.

Working between the forked arms of the trunk, he thrust upwards into the bottom of the tea-chest with the screwdriver. The plywood crackled as he punched out a circular opening just large enough to admit his hand. He found that the interior of the case was lined with a heavy-duty yellow plastic sheet that resisted his efforts to tear through. He paused to find the clasp-knife in his bag, and then slit out a flap of the sheeting.

There was the familiar smell of dried tea leaves, and he began to dig into the compressed black vegetable mass, spilling the tea out on to the concrete floor. Soon he had dug into the full length of the screwdriver without encountering any alien object hidden in the case. He felt the first prickle of doubt. There were hundreds of tea-chests piled on the ramp; any of them could contain the tusks, or none of them.

He widened the hole with a few more blows of the screwdriver, then he drove the steel point up into the mass of tea with all the strength of his doubt and frustration.

It hit something solid with a force that jarred his wrist, and he almost shouted aloud with triumph. He ripped at the edges of the hole until he could get both hands into the chest, and he dug out lumps of tea that fell on to the ramp around his feet.

Now at last he could touch the hard object buried in the tea. It was round and smooth. Crouching under the chest he twisted his neck to look up into the aperture, slitting his eyes against the soft rain of dried tea leaves that trickled from the hole. In the beam of the torch he made out the soft creamy alabaster gleam.

With the point of the screwdriver he attacked the exposed surface of the object, stabbing and prising it, until at last a splinter lifted and he pulled it loose. It was the size of his thumb.

'No more doubts,' he whispered, as he examined the sample and picked out the distinctive chicken-wire pattern of the ivory grain. 'Now I've got you, you murdering bastards.'

Quickly he stuffed the torn flap of plastic back into the hole to prevent any more tea spilling out on to the ramp. Then he swept up the fallen leaves and scooped them into his pockets. It wasn't a very effectual job of tidying up, but he hoped that the loaders would be careless enough not to notice anything amiss when they started work again in the morning.

He went to the controls of the fork-lift and lowered the tea chest to its original place on the ramp. He flashed the beam of the torch around to make certain he had left no other evidence of his visit – and this time he saw it clearly.

A great dark shape crouched at the edge of the ramp, watching him with eyes that glowed like opals even in the muted beam of the torch. As the light struck it the creature seemed to dissolve like a puff of smoke, almost supernatural in its uncanny stealth. Daniel recoiled instinctively against the side of the fork-lift, trying to probe the darkness with the torch.

Then suddenly there was a sound that ripped across his nerve ends like an emery wheel. It echoed through the dark cavern of the warehouse and rang against the high roof. It was a hacking cadence, like a wood-saw cutting metal, and it set his teeth on edge. He knew what it was instantly, but he found it difficult to believe what he was hearing.

'Leopard!' he breathed, and with a chill in his guts he realised his danger.

All the advantage was with the beast. The night was its natural environment. Darkness made it bold; darkness made it aggressive.

He pulled the red filter off the lens of the torch and now the bright white shaft of light sprang out across the warehouse. He swept it back and around, and he glimpsed the cat again. It had moved in behind him, circling in. That was the most hostile manoeuvre. The predator circles its prey before rushing in for the kill.

As the light hit it, the leopard flashed away. With one lithe bound, it disappeared behind the wall of tea-chests, and its fierce chorus of hatred echoed through the darkness once again.

'It's hunting me!'

Whilst he was warden of Chiwewe one of his rangers had been mauled by a leopard, and Daniel had been first on the scene to rescue him. Now he recalled vividly the terrible injuries the beast had inflicted.

The other dangerous cat of Africa, the lion, does not have the instinctive knowledge of how best to attack the upright two-legged figure of a man. He will charge in and knock a victim down and then will bite and claw indiscriminately at whatever part of the man's body he can reach, often gnawing and crunching a single limb until the victim is rescued.

The leopard, on the other hand, understands the human anatomy. Baboons form a large part of the leopard's prey, and it knows how to go directly for the head and the vulnerable guts of the primate. Its usual attack is to leap on to its victim and hook into his shoulders with the front claws, while its back legs kick like those of a domestic cat playing with a ball of wool.

The long talons, unsheathed, will disembowel a man with half a dozen swift kicks, stripping his guts out. At the same time the leopard sinks his teeth into the face or throat and with one front claw reaches over to hook the back of its victim's scalp and tear it off the skull. Often the dome of the skull comes away with the scalp, like the top sheared off a soft-boiled egg, leaving the brain exposed. All this flashed through

Daniel's mind as the leopard circled him, its wild savage call echoing through the open bays of the warehouse.

Still crouched beside the fork-lift, Daniel zipped his leather jacket tightly up under the chin to protect his throat and slid the nylon bag around from the small of his back to cover his stomach. Then he shifted the screwdriver to his right hand, and with his left swung the torch to cover the leopard's menacing circles.

'My God, he's a huge brute!' Daniel realised, as he saw the true size of the cat. In the torchlight it was panther black. Bush-lore has it that the dark-coloured cats are the most ferocious of the breed.

It was impossible to hold the leopard in the beam of light. It was as elusive as a shadow. Daniel knew he would never make it back to where he had broken into the warehouse. It was too far to go with his back unprotected. The cat would be on him before he had covered half the distance. He flicked the torch-beam away for a second, seeking another avenue of escape.

The fish sacks. He saw the pyramid piled against the near wall, reaching as high as the windows, thirty feet above the warehouse floor.

'If I can just reach the skylight,' he whispered. There was a long drop down the outside wall, but he had the nylon rope to lower himself at least part of the way. 'Move!' he told himself. 'You're running out of time. It's going to rush you any moment now.'

He screwed up his nerve to leave the haven of the fork-lift. The machine covering his back was a solid comfort – while in the open he was vulnerable and puny against the speed and strength of the leopard. The moment he left the shelter of the fork-lift, the leopard sawed again, its savage cry more vicious and eager.

'Get out of it!' Daniel yelled at it, hoping to disconcert it with the sound of a human voice. The cat ducked sideways and disappeared behind a pile of packing cases – and Daniel made his mistake.

It was a stupid, unforgivable mistake. He, of all people, knew that you must never run from a wild beast. In particular you must never turn your back on one of the cats. Their instinct is to pursue. If you run, they must charge, just as a domestic cat cannot resist the flight of the mouse.

Daniel thought that he might just be able to reach the pyramid of fish sacks. He turned and ran, and the leopard exploded in a silent rush out of the darkness behind him. He never even heard it come. It landed with all its weight and the full momentum of its charge in the middle of his back, between his shoulder-blades.

Daniel was hurled forward. He felt its claws bite in and hold, and for a moment he thought they were hooked into his own flesh. Instead of bearing him down to the concrete floor the leopard slammed him into the pile of sacks. They cushioned the impact, but still it drove half the air from Daniel's lungs and he felt as though his ribs had collapsed.

The leopard was still mounted high on his shoulders, but as Daniel staggered under its weight he realised that its claws were hooked into the leather of his jacket and the thick woollen sweater beneath it.

Somehow Daniel managed to keep on his feet, supporting himself against the sloping wall of sacks. He could feel the cat on his back gather itself, bringing up its back legs, coiling its body like a spring, ready to lash downwards across his buttocks and the back of his thighs. It would open his flesh to the bone, slicing through blood vessels and arteries, a crippling injury from which he would probably bleed to death within minutes.

Daniel pushed off from the sacks with both arms, flipping backwards, rolling his body into a ball with his knees up under his chin. The leopard's claws tugged at the nylon belt of the bag and then kicked on downwards, but Daniel had drawn his legs up and clear. The cat's back paws with the curved claws outspread, struck at air, missing his flesh.

Now man and beast with their combined weight crashed to the concrete floor. Daniel was a big man and the leopard was underneath him. A single hissing snarl was forced from its lungs by the impact and Daniel felt its claws release their hold in the leather of his jacket. He twisted violently and reached over his shoulder with one hand, the screwdriver still clutched in the other. As he came to his knees, he seized a thick fold of skin at the scruff of the leopard's neck and, with the strength of his terror, tore the creature from his back and hurled it against the pile of packing-cases.

It rebounded at him like a rubber ball.

The torch had been knocked from his grip by the leopard's first charge. It rolled across the concrete floor until it came up against one of the packing-cases. Its beam was angled upwards now and reflected from the pale plywood case. The reflection gave Daniel just enough light to anticipate the leopard's charge.

Its jaws were open to their full gape, and its extended front paws reached for his shoulders. As it smashed into him, chest to chest, its back legs cocked up in the instinctive disembowelling movement and its head shot forward to sink its fangs into his face and throat. This was the classic leopard attack and Daniel countered with the screwdriver held sideways between both his hands, thrusting it like a curb bit into the leopard's open mouth.

One of the beast's front fangs broke off cleanly at the gum as it struck steel, and then Daniel was on his back holding the leopard off his face with the screwdriver. It snarled again and a hot mist of spittle blew into his face, the stink of carrion and death filled his nostrils.

He felt one forepaw stretch out over his shoulder, reaching out to the back of his scalp to rip it off his skull. At the same time the back legs jack-knifed up, claws fully extended to tear out the front of his belly. However, the back of Daniel's head was pressed up hard against one of the fish sacks and the leopard hooked its claws, not into the thin flesh of his scalp, but into the coarse jute of the sack only an inch from his ear. Then the cat slashed down with both back legs together, but instead of unzipping his belly, the claws bit into the tough nylon belt of the bag at his stomach.

For a moment the animal's attack was stalled. It ripped at the jute sack, seeming not to realise its error, and the back legs kicked downward spasmodically, tearing the nylon with a sharp rending sound.

As it struggled, the leopard pulled back its head, trying to avoid the steel shaft that Daniel was still forcing deeply between its open jaws. Instantly Daniel whipped the screwdriver back, releasing his grip on the sharpened end and then drove it forward again, aiming the point at one of the leopard's eyes.

His aim was wild, the point of the screwdriver shot into the cat's flaring nostril, but instead of finding the nasal channel into the brain, it deflected slightly, penetrated the gristle of the nose, and ran along the outside of the cheekbone below the dappled skin. The point emerged from beneath the leopard's ear, and the cat screamed with the shock and agony. For a moment it relaxed its attack. Daniel rolled over, and threw the leopard off him.

It seemed a miracle that up to now the leopard had not drawn blood, but as Daniel threw it backwards, the cat held on instinctively with one paw. The claws raked down Daniel's arm, slicing through the leather and wool and reaching the muscle of his forearm. It felt like a sword cut, and the pain goaded Daniel to throw in his last desperate reserve of strength.

He kicked out with both feet together, and his heels crashed into the feline body just as it gathered itself for the next charge. The kick drove it backwards in a snarling, snapping ball of dark fur that gleamed and rippled in the torchlight.

There was a space between the fish sacks at Daniel's back, it was just wide enough to admit his body. He flung himself backwards into the narrow cave. Now his back and flanks were protected, and the leopard could only attack from directly in front.

It thrust its head, growling and gaping into the narrow space, trying to reach him. Daniel stabbed for its eyes with the screwdriver. Again he missed, but the steel point lacerated the leopard's curling pink tongue, and it leaped backwards, hissing and spitting with pain.

'Go on! Get out of it!' he howled, more to bolster his own courage than with any hope of driving off the infuriated beast. He drew his legs up under him and worked his way as far as he could into the narrow gap between the fish sacks.

The leopard paced back and forth across the entrance, blotting out the feeble torchlight with each pass. Once it stopped and sat on its haunches, wiping its wounded nose with one paw, like a domestic cat, and then licking its own blood from the fur.

Then it bounded forward, blocking the entrance to the narrow cave, and stretched in one forepaw to try and reach

Daniel again. He stabbed at the groping limb and felt it hit and penetrate. The leopard spat explosively and pulled back. It began to patrol the entrance to his cave, pausing every few minutes to lower its head and let out one of those terrible sawing roars.

Daniel felt the blood sliming down his forearm under the sleeve and dripping from his fingers. He held the screwdriver between his knees, ready to fend off the next attack, and then, one-handed, bound his handkerchief around the torn arm to stem the bleeding. He pulled the knot tight with his teeth. The wound seemed superficial. The leather sleeve had saved him from serious injury, but the arm was already beginning to throb. Daniel knew how truly dangerous even the lightest scratch from a carnivore's teeth or claws could be, if untreated.

That was only one of his worries. The leopard had him trapped and soon it would be morning. It was a wonder that the roars of the animal had not yet attracted attention. He could expect a guard to arrive at any moment.

As he thought it, the warehouse was suddenly flooded with light. It was so brilliant that the leopard recoiled on to its haunches and blinked in confusion. Daniel heard the faint rumble as the main doors rolled open, driven by their electric motor. It was followed immediately by the sound of a motor car coming in through the opening.

The leopard snarled and slunk back towards the rear of the warehouse, carrying its head low and looking back over its shoulder.

Then somebody shouted, 'Hey, Nandi! Back to your cage! Back! Back!' Daniel recognised Chetti Singh's voice.

The leopard broke into a crouching run, and disappeared from Daniel's sight.

Chetti Singh spoke again. 'Lock the leopard in the cage quickly!' and there was the metallic clang of a cage door being slammed. 'Can you see the white man? Be careful, he may still be alive.'

Daniel shrank back as far as he could into the narrow opening between the sacks. He had no real hope of avoiding detection, and the screwdriver was not much of a weapon.

'There is a torch lying over there, still burning.'

'And over there, by the fish sacks. That looks like blood.'
Cautious footsteps approached.

'Nandi has done her work.'

'Give me the torch.'

The voices were closer.

Suddenly a pair of legs came into Daniel's view and then the man stooped and flashed the torch into the dark crack where Daniel squatted.

'My goodness!' the same voice said in English. 'Here the fellow is, and he is still in excellent fettle. How do you do, Doctor Armstrong? I am delighted to make your formal acquaintance at last.'

Daniel glared silently into the dazzling torch-beam and Chetti Singh went on in a jocular tone. 'You won't be needing that weapon, never mind. Please be good enough to hand it over.'

Daniel made no move to obey and Chetti Singh chuckled. 'This is a shotgun of fine English construction, dear sir, made by Mr Purdey, no less. It is loaded with bullshot cartridges. The Malawi police are very understanding on the little matter of defending self. I beg you most humbly to entertain my request for co-operation.'

With resignation Daniel tossed the screwdriver at his feet, and Chetti Singh kicked it away.

'You may now emerge from your kennel, Doctor.'

Daniel crawled out, and holding his injured arm to his chest, rose to his feet.

Chetti Singh pointed the shotgun at his belly and spoke to the uniformed guard in Angoni. 'Chawe, check the cases. See if the *malungu* has opened any of them.'

Daniel recognised the black guard from the supermarket. He was a big dangerous-looking brute. I prefer the leopard for a sparring partner, Daniel thought wryly as he watched the Angoni stride away down the ramp towards the fork-lift.

Before he reached the machine Chawe exclaimed and went down on one knee to scoop up a handful of spilled tea that Daniel had overlooked. Quickly he followed the trail of tea to the broached case on the fork-lift.

'Lift the case, Chawe!' Chetti Singh ordered and Chawe climbed behind the controls of the fork-lift and raised the case high.

A trickle of black tea leaves dribbled from under it. Chawe jumped down and thrust his arm into the hole that Daniel had gouged out of the plywood.

'You are a jolly clever fellow.' Chetti Singh shook his head at Daniel in mock admiration. 'Just like Sherlock Holmes, no less. But sometimes it is not wise to be too clever, my dear sir.'

Looking into the Sikh's eyes, Daniel discounted the man's stilted clownish speech. Those eyes were deadly. This was no clown.

'Chawe, where did the white man leave his truck?' he asked without moving the aim of the shotgun from the pit of Daniel's belly.

'He came without lights, but I heard the truck on the south side. I think he parked in the open land there.' They were speaking in Angoni believing that Daniel could not understand it, but his knowledge of Zulu and Ndebele allowed him to make sense of it.

'Go! Fetch the truck,' Chetti Singh ordered.

After Chawe had gone, Daniel and Chetti Singh confronted each other in silence. Daniel was looking for some sign of weakness or indecision. The Sikh was calm and contained, the shotgun steady in his hands.

'My arm is badly hurt,' Daniel said at last.

'My sincere commiseration, my dear Doctor.'

'There is danger of infection.'

'No.' Chetti Singh smiled. 'You will be dead before infection can manifest itself.'

'You intend killing me?'

'That is an amazingly facetious question, Doctor. What alternative do I have? You have been clever enough to discover my little secret. As I have often concluded, too much knowledge is a terminal disease. Ha, ha!'

'If I'm going to die, why don't you satisfy my curiosity and tell me about Chiwewe? Who proposed the raid, you or Ning Cheng Gong?'

'Alas, dear sir. I know nothing of Chiwewe or this other fellow. Besides I do not feel in a talkative frame of mind.'

'You have nothing to lose by telling me. Who owns the Lucky Dragon Investment Company?'

'I am afraid, Doctor, that you will have to take your curiosity to the grave with you.'

They heard the Landcruiser coming and Chetti Singh stirred. 'That did not take Chawe long. You could not have been at many pains to conceal your vehicle. Let us go to the main door to greet him. Will you lead the way, please, Doctor, and bear in mind that Mr Purdey's excellent firearm is only a foot from your spinal column.'

Still nursing his injured arm Daniel set off towards the warehouse doors. As they emerged from the aisle between the rows of packing-cases he saw a green Cadillac parked beside the empty railway truck.

Probably Chetti Singh had remained safely in the Cadillac until the leopard had returned to its cage. Daniel remembered the shed at the back of the building, and the foul animal smell that he had noticed earlier. He was piecing it all together, working out where the leopard was kept and how it was controlled. Even so, it was clear that neither Chetti Singh nor his henchman trusted the animal. On the contrary they had been extremely nervous when the leopard was loose.

When they reached the main doors, Chetti Singh motioned Daniel to a standstill. Then abruptly the heavy door began to roll aside, revealing Daniel's Toyota parked facing the entrance with its headlights burning. Chawe was standing at the external control box of the electrically operated door. When the door was fully opened, he withdrew his key-card from the lock of the control box. It was on a short key-chain and he dropped it into his hip pocket.

'Everything is ready,' he told Chetti Singh.

'You know what to do,' Chetti Singh replied. 'I don't want any birds to fly back to settle on my roof. Make sure you leave no sign. It must be an accident, a nice simple accident on the mountain road. You understand that?' They were speaking Angoni again, secure in the belief that Daniel could not understand.

'There will be an accident,' Chawe agreed. 'And perhaps a little fire.'

Chetti Singh turned his attention back to Daniel. 'Now, dear sir. Kindly mount to the controls of your automobile. Chawe will tell you where to go. Please obey him most faithfully. He shoots very well with the shotgun.'

Obediently Daniel climbed up into the cab of the Landcruiser and, at a word from Chetti Singh, Chawe took the seat directly behind him. Once they were settled, Chetti Singh passed the shotgun to the big Angoni. It was done as quickly and as neatly as an expert loader serving his gun in a Scottish grouse butt. Before Daniel could take any advantage, the double barrel was pressed firmly into the back of his neck, held there by Chawe.

Chetti Singh stepped back to the open window beside Daniel.

'Chawe's English is absolutely atrocious, never mind,' he said jovially, and then switched to the *lingua franca* of Africa. '*Wena kuluma Fanika-lo* – you speak like this?'

'Yes,' Daniel agreed in the same language.

'Good, then you and Chawe will have no difficulty understanding each other. Just do as he orders, Doctor. At that range the shotgun will make a most unsightly mess of your coiffure, no doubt.'

Chetti Singh stepped back, and at Chawe's command Daniel reversed the Landcruiser, swung it in a U-turn and drove out through the main gates into the public road.

In the rear-view mirror he saw Chetti Singh walk back to the green Cadillac and open the driver's door. Then the angle changed and Daniel could no longer see into the warehouse.

From the back seat Chawe gave curt directions, emphasising each with a jab of the shotgun muzzle into the back of Daniel's neck. They drove through the silent and deserted streets of the sleeping town, heading east towards the lake and the mountains.

Once they were out into the country Chawe urged him to increase speed. The road was good, and the Landcruiser buzzed along merrily. By now Daniel's wounded arm was stiff and painful. He nursed it on his lap, driving with one hand and trying to ignore the pain.

Within an hour the gradient changed and the road began a series of hairpins as it climbed the first slopes of the mountain. On each side the forest was denser and darker, pressing in upon the highway and the Landcruiser's speed bled off as she climbed.

The dawn came on stealthily, and beyond the shafts of the headlights Daniel saw the shapes of the forest trees emerging from the gloom. Soon he could see their high tops defined against the dawn sky. He turned his wrist and glanced at his watch. His sleeve was stiff with dried blood, but it was light enough now to read the dial clearly. Seven minutes past six.

He had had plenty of time to consider his predicament and to assess the man who held the gun to his head. He judged him to be a tough opponent. There was not the least doubt that he would kill without hesitation or compunction, and he handled the shotgun with a disheartening competence. On the other hand it was an awkward weapon to use in the confines of the Landcruiser's cab.

Daniel considered his alternatives. He quickly discarded the idea of attacking Chawe in the truck. He would have his head blown off before he could turn to face him.

He might kick open the side door and throw himself out of the cab, but that meant that he would have to reduce the Landcruiser's speed below fifty to avoid serious injury when he hit the ground. Gradually he lifted his foot from the accelerator. Almost immediately Chawe sensed the change in the engine beat and thrust the shotgun into the nape of his neck.

'*Kawaleza!* Go faster!'

That horse wouldn't run. Daniel grimaced and obeyed. On the other hand Chawe wasn't likely to shoot him at this speed and risk the sudden loss of control and the inevitable pile-up.

He expected an order to stop or pull off the road when they reached their destination, wherever that might be. That would be the time to make his play. Daniel settled down to wait until then.

Suddenly the road was steeper, and the bends sharper. The dawn was grey. As they came through each turn in the road, Daniel had glimpses of the valley below. It was filled with silver mist banks, through which he made out the white cascades of a mountain river, running deep in its gloomy gorge.

Another bend loomed ahead and as he braced himself to negotiate it, Chawe spoke sharply, 'Stop! Pull in to the edge. Over there.'

Daniel braked and pulled over, on to the verge.

They were at the top of a cliff. The edge of the road was guarded by a line of white-painted rocks. Beyond that the chasm gaped. It was a drop of two or three hundred feet to the rocky riverbed below.

Daniel pulled on the handbrake and felt his heart bounding against his rib cage. Would the shot come now? he wondered. It would be a stupid thing to do if they wanted to make it look like an accident, but then the big Angoni did not seem to be labouring under a heavy burden of brains. 'Switch off the engine,' he ordered.

Daniel did as he was told.

'Put your hands on your head,' Chawe ordered, and Daniel felt a small lift of relief. He had a few seconds longer. He obeyed and waited.

He heard the click of the door latch, but the pressure of the steel muzzle against his spine never slackened. He felt the cool draught of air as Chawe swung the back door open.

'Do not move,' he warned Daniel, and slid sideways from his seat still aiming the shotgun in through the open door. Now he was standing alongside the car.

'Open your door slowly.' The shotgun was aimed through the side window into Daniel's face. He opened the door. 'Now come out.' Daniel stepped down.

Still covering him with the shotgun, holding it in one hand like a horse pistol, Chawe reached out with his left hand through the open door. Daniel saw that he had the steel jack-handle lying on the rear seat. During the journey he must have taken it from under the front seat. In that instant Daniel understood how Chawe planned to get rid of him.

Chawe would prod him to the edge of the precipice with the shotgun, and then a single blow to the back of the skull with the jack-handle would tumble him two hundred feet into the rocky gorge. After that the Landcruiser, with the driver's door open and probably with a burning rag stuffed into the filler of the fuel tank, would be pushed over the cliff on top of him.

It would look like another tourist killed by negligent driving on a notorious stretch of mountain road. Nothing to excite police suspicion, or to tie the incident to Chetti Singh and a cargo of contraband ivory in Lilongwe a hundred miles from the scene.

At that moment Daniel saw his opportunity.

Chawe was reaching in through the open door, and he was just marginally off balance. Although the shotgun was still pointed at Daniel's guts, he would be slow to adjust his aim if Daniel moved quickly.

Daniel hurled himself forward, not at the man or the gun but at the door. He crashed into it with his full weight, and it slammed shut with Chawe's arm trapped between steel edge and jamb.

Chawe screamed in agony. The sound of it did not cover the crack of breaking bone, sharp as a stick of dry kindling snapped across the knee. His forefinger, thick as a blood sausage, slipped across the trigger, firing one of the barrels. The blast of shot missed Daniel's head by a foot, though the detonation fluttered his hair and made him wince. The recoil threw the barrel high.

Using his momentum Daniel charged him head on, seizing the shotgun with both hands, at buttstock and hot barrel. Chawe's grip on the weapon was single-handed and weakened by the agony of broken bone trapped in the door. He fired the second barrel, but the shot flew harmlessly into the sky.

Daniel slammed the side of the breech into his face, catching him across the upper lip, crushing his nose and shearing off all his upper teeth at the gum. Chawe bellowed through a mouthful of blood and broken teeth, as he tried to pull his arm from the steel trap of the door.

Daniel had the advantage of a double-handed grip on the shotgun and used it to tear the weapon from Chawe's right hand. He lifted the shotgun high, reversed it and drove the steel butt-plate into Chawe's face, catching him in the side of the jaw with the full force of the blow.

Chawe's jawbone shattered at the hinge and his face changed shape, sagging at one side as the bone collapsed. Stunned and uncoordinated he fell backwards, held only by his trapped arm. Daniel yanked the door handle and it flew open, releasing Chawe's arm when he was not expecting it.

Chawe reeled backwards, not in control of his legs, windmilling his arms to try and retain his balance, the shattered arm flapping uselessly below the joint of the elbow. One of the white-washed boulders at the edge of the cliff caught his heels and he jerked backwards, as though plucked on a wire, and disappeared over the precipice.

Daniel heard him scream. The sound receded swiftly as he fell and was cut off abruptly on the rocks at the bottom. The silence afterwards was profound.

Daniel found himself leaning against the Landcruiser with the shotgun still clutched to his chest, panting from those few seconds of wild exertion. It took a moment to gather himself and then he went to the edge of the cliff and looked over.

Chawe lay on his face on the rocks at the edge of the waterfall directly below, his limbs spread like a crucifix. There was no scuff mark at the brink of the precipice to mark his fall.

Daniel thought swiftly. Report the attack? Tell the police about the ivory? Hell, no! A white man had better not kill a black man in Africa, even in self-defence, even in a civilised state like Malawi. They would crucify him.

His mind was made up by the sound of a heavy vehicle descending the mountain road in low gear. Swiftly he slipped the shotgun on to the floorboards of the Landcruiser and pulled a light tarpaulin over it. Then he crossed to the edge of the cliff, unzipped the fly of his trousers and forced himself to urinate over the drop.

The descending truck appeared around the bend of the road above him. It was a timber lorry piled with cut logs that were chained to the cargo bed. There were two black men in the cab, the driver and his assistant.

Daniel made a show of shaking off the drops and zipping his fly closed. The black driver grinned and waved at him as the lorry rumbled past and Daniel waved back.

As soon as it was out of sight he ran to the Landcruiser and drove on up the mountain. Within two hundred yards he found a disused logging track that branched off the main road. He drove through the dense secondary growth that clogged the track until he was out of sight of the road. He left the Landcruiser there and went back on foot, ready to duck into cover at the sound of another vehicle.

At the top of the cliff he checked that Chawe's body still lay on the rocks below. His instinct was to leave him there and get far away from the scene as quickly as possible. He suspected that a Malawian prison was no great improvement on any other in Africa. His arm was very painful now. He could feel the first fires of infection kindling, but he didn't want even to look at it until he had cleaned up the evidence against himself.

He skirted the top of the cliff until he found a way down. It was a game path used by hyrax and klipspringer, steep and precarious. It took him twenty minutes to reach Chawe's body. The skin was cold as a reptile's when Daniel touched Chawe's throat. There was no need to check for a pulse. He was dead meat. Swiftly Daniel turned out his pockets. He found that a greasy well-thumbed pass-book was the only piece of identification. He wanted to get rid of that. Apart from a filthy tattered handkerchief and some loose coins, the only other items were four SSG shotgun cartridges and the key-card for the control box of the electric door on the warehouse that Daniel had seen him operate. That might come in useful.

Satisfied that he had made it as difficult as he could for the police to identify the corpse, if they ever found it, Daniel rolled Chawe to the river edge, his broken arm flopping and catching under him, and shoved him into the racing water.

He watched the body splash as it struck, then swirl and roll as it was carried swiftly downstream and disappeared around the next bend. He hoped that it would hang up on a snag somewhere in the inaccessible depths of the gorge long enough for the crocodiles to get a decent meal and further complicate the process of identification.

By the time he had climbed back up the cliff and reached the Landcruiser again, his arm felt as though it were on fire. Sitting at the driver's wheel, with his medical box on the passenger seat beside him, he stripped back the torn blood-caked sleeve and pulled a face at what he found beneath it. The claw wounds were not deep but already they were weeping yellow watery fluid and the flesh around them was swollen a hot crimson.

He packed the lacerations with thick yellow Betadine paste and bandaged it, then he filled a disposable syringe with a broad-spectrum antibiotic and shot it into the biceps of his own left arm.

All this took time. It was almost eight o'clock when he checked his wristwatch again. He reversed back down the logging trail and on to the main mountain road. He drove slowly past the top of the cliff, and the tracks of his tyres and the imprint of his feet showed clearly in the soft earth of the verge. He considered trying to obliterate them, and thought about the driver of the timber lorry who had seen him there.

'I've hung around here long enough,' he decided. 'If I'm going to stop Chetti Singh, I've got to get back to Lilongwe.' And he set off back towards the capital.

As he drew closer to the urban areas, the traffic on the road was heavier. He drove sedately, avoiding drawing attention to himself. Many of the vehicles he passed were Landrovers or Toyotas, so his truck was not remarkable. However, he regretted the touch of vanity that had led him to display his personal logo so prominently.

'Never thought I'd make a fugitive from justice,' he muttered, but still he knew that he could no longer parade around Lilongwe in the Landcruiser.

He drove to the airport and left the truck in the public carpark. He took his spare toilet-kit and a clean shirt from his sports grip and went to the men's washrooms in the airport building to clean up. He bundled his torn and blood-stained shirt and jersey and stuffed them into the refuse bin. Although it was still stiff and sore, he did not want to disturb the wound. After he had shaved, he dressed in a clean shirt whose long sleeves covered his bandaged arm.

When he checked his image in the washroom mirror he was reasonably respectable-looking and he headed for the public telephone booths in the main concourse.

A South African Airways flight from Johannesburg had just landed and the concourse was crowded with tourists and their luggage. No one paid him any attention. The police emergency number was prominently displayed on the wall above the payphone. He disguised his voice by muffling it with a folded handkerchief over the mouthpiece and by speaking in Swahili.

'I want to report a robbery and a murder,' he told the female police operator. 'Give me a senior officer urgently.'

'This is Inspector Mopola.' The voice was deep and authoritative. 'You have information of a murder?'

'Listen carefully,' Daniel told him, still in Swahili. 'I'm only going to say this once. The ivory stolen from Chiwewe National Park is here in Lilongwe. At least eight people were murdered during the robbery. The stolen goods are hidden in tea-chests which are being stored at the warehouses of the Chetti Singh Trading Company in the light industrial area. You had better hurry. They will be moved soon.'

'Who is this speaking, please?' the inspector asked.

'That isn't important. Just get down there fast and get that ivory,' Daniel told him, and hung up.

He went to the Avis car rental counter in the airport concourse. The Avis girl gave him a sweet smile and allotted him a blue Volkswagen Golf. 'I'm sorry. Without a reservation that is all we have available.'

Before he left the carpark, he stopped beside his dusty old Landcruiser and surreptitiously transferred the shotgun wrapped in tarpaulin to the boot of the Volkswagen. Then he retrieved his Zeiss binoculars and slipped them into the cubbyhole. As he drove away, he checked that the Landcruiser was tucked away at the furthest end of the crowded lot where it would escape casual observation.

He kept to the south side of the railway tracks, and found his way through the streets of the business area to the open-air market that he had noticed during his earlier explorations of the town.

At ten-thirty in the morning the market was crowded with vendors displaying their wares and shoppers haggling over them. Dozens of trucks and mini-buses thronged the area around it. They gave him cover. He parked the little blue Volkswagen amongst them, positioning her carefully. The market was on rising ground that overlooked the railway tracks and the light industrial area beyond.

He found himself less than half a mile from the Chetti Singh warehouse and the Toyota workshops, so close that he could read the huge lettering of the company signboard on the buildings with the naked eye. Through the nine-power lens of the Zeiss binoculars he had a fine view of the front of the warehouse and the main doors. He could almost make out the expressions on the faces of the men working on the loading ramps.

A regular stream of trucks passed in and out of the main warehouse gates, amongst them he recognised the big pantechnicon and trailer. However, there was no sign yet of any police activity and it was almost forty minutes since he had made his phone call to them.

'Come on, people! Get the lead out,' he muttered impatiently. As he said it he saw a shunting locomotive come puffing up the main line to the rail spur that entered the warehouse complex. It was running in reverse, the engine-driver leaning out of his side window.

As it approached, one of the warehouse guards swung open the mesh gate on the boundary fence and the loco rolled through, slowing as it entered the open doors of the warehouse. It passed out of Daniel's sight, but seconds later he heard the faint but characteristic clash of steel as the coupling engaged. There was another delay and then the loco re-emerged from the warehouse, drawing three trucks behind it. It gathered speed gradually as the heavily laden trucks gained momentum.

The goods trucks were each covered by heavy-duty canvas covers. Daniel stared at them through the Zeiss binoculars but could make out no definite indication that the tea-chests were under those covers.

He lowered the binoculars and hammered his clenched fist against the steering-wheel of the Volkswagen and groaned aloud with frustration. Where the hell were the police? It was at least an hour and a half since he had phoned them. Even in his agitation, he realised that it would certainly take them longer than that to obtain a search warrant.

'It just has to be the ivory,' he muttered to himself. 'There was no other outbound cargo stacked on that ramp. It's the ivory, I'd take any odds, and it's on its way to Taiwan.'

The loco was drawing the three trucks sedately down the curving rail spur towards the main line and the goods yards, but it had to pass very close to where Daniel was parked on the outskirts of the market-place.

Daniel started the Volkswagen and pulled out into the main road. He accelerated, passing a heavily laden lorry, and sped down to the level-crossing which the loco must cross to reach the main goods yard. The red warning lights were flashing, the warning bell trilling, and the swinging barrier came down in front of him to guard the crossing, forcing him to brake to a halt. The loco rumbled slowly over the crossing directly in front of the stationary Volkswagen, moving not much above walking speed.

Daniel pulled on the handbrake, and, leaving the engine running, jumped down into the road and slipped under the barrier. The first truck rolled past close enough to touch.

The railways consignment card was clipped into the holder on the side of the truck, and he read it easily as it came level and passed slowly in front of him.

CONSIGNEE: LUCKY DRAGON INVESTMENT CO
Destination: Taiwan via Beira
Cargo: 250 cases Tea

The last lingering doubt was dispelled. Daniel stared angrily after the departing train. They were going to get away with it, right under his nose.

The warning lights switched off, the bell fell silent and the barrier began to rise as the loco and its rolling stock pulled away. Immediately the drivers of the traffic backed up behind the Volkswagen began to sound their horns and flash their lights impatiently.

Daniel strode back to the hire car and drove on. He took the first road to the left, running parallel to the railway tracks and found another place to park from where he had a view into the railway goods yard.

He watched through the binoculars as the three trucks were shunted and coupled on to the end of a long goods train. The caboose was locked on behind them and, finally, the whole assembly of coaches and goods trucks pulled out of the yard. With a green mainline loco pulling them, it set off for Mozambique and the port of Beira five hundred miles away on the seaboard of the Indian Ocean.

There was nothing he could do to stop it happening. Wild fantasies flashed through his mind, of trying to hijack the loco, of rushing down to police headquarters and demanding that they take immediate action before it was too late and the train crossed the border. Instead, he drove back to his original vantage point beside the open-air market and resumed his vigil through the binoculars.

He felt tired and dispirited, and remembered that he had not slept at all the previous night. His arm was stiff and sore. He unwrapped the bandage and was relieved to see that there were no further obvious signs of infection. On the contrary the rips in his forearm were beginning to scab over as well as he could have hoped for. He replaced the bandage.

While he watched the warehouse, he tried to work out some means of stopping the ivory shipment, but he knew that his hands were tied. In the end it all came down to the death of Chawe. Chetti Singh had only to point at him, and he stood accused of murder. He dared not draw official attention to himself.

While he waited and watched, he thought about Johnny Nzou and Mavis and their children, mourning them and nursing his hatred for their murderers.

Almost two hours after the goods train had left, he noticed sudden activity around the warehouse. Chetti Singh's green Cadillac drew up at the main gates, followed by two grey-painted police Landrovers, each filled with uniformed constables.

There was a short discussion with the guards at the gates, then the three vehicles drove into the property and parked beside the open warehouse doors. Eleven police constables led by an officer climbed out of the Landrovers. The officer spoke briefly to Chetti Singh beside the Cadillac. Through the binoculars Daniel saw that the Sikh appeared dapper and unconcerned; his turban was crisp and white above his darkly handsome face.

The police officer led his men into the warehouse, only to emerge again an hour later, strolling along at Chetti Singh's side. The officer was gesticulating and talking persuasively, very obviously apologising to Chetti Singh, who smiled and waved away his protestations and finally shook his hand magnanimously.

The contingent of police constables reboarded their Landrovers and drove away. Standing beside the green Cadillac, Chetti Singh watched them go, and it seemed to Daniel through the binocular lens that he was no longer smiling.

'Bastard!' Daniel whispered. 'You haven't got away with it yet.' He finally got control of his anger and started to think rationally once again.

Could he stop the shipment before it left the country? he wondered. And almost immediately he abandoned the idea. He knew that the goods train was on a non-stop run and would reach the border within hours.

What about intercepting it at the port of Beira, before it was loaded on a tramp steamer bound for the Far East? This was a better bet, but still long odds. From what little he had learned about Chetti Singh so far, it was clear that he had a network of influence and bribery that extended over many countries in central Africa, certainly over Zimbabwe and Zambia, and why not over Mozambique, one of the most corrupt and chaotic states on the continent?

He was certain that a great deal of contraband passed through that warehouse over there, and Chetti Singh would have secured his pipeline to the outside world. As Malawi was a land-locked state, that pipeline must include the port captain and the Mozambiquan army, police force and customs service. They would be paid off by Chetti Singh and would protect him. Still, he decided, it was worth a try.

Daniel drove down to the main post office in the town centre. It was highly unlikely that the Malawi Police had the sophisticated equipment to trace a telephone call swiftly, but once again, he took the precaution of making his message short and of muffling his voice with a handkerchief and speaking in Swahili.

'Tell Inspector Mopola that the stolen ivory was shipped out of the warehouse at eleven thirty-five a.m. by goods train to Beira. It is hidden in a shipment of tea-chests consigned to Lucky Dragon Investment Company in Taipei.'

Before the operator on the police exchange could ask for his name he cradled the receiver, and crossed to a small general dealer's store on the opposite side of the street. If the police weren't going to do anything, it was all up to him.

He purchased a packet of safety-matches, a roll of Sellotape, a box of mosquito coils and two kilos of frozen minced meat, then drove back to the Capital Hotel.

As soon as he entered his hotel room he was aware that somebody had searched it. When he opened his canvas valise he saw that the contents had been disarranged.

'Nothing for Chetti Singh there,' he muttered with grim satisfaction. He had deposited his passport and traveller's cheques in the hotel safe at the cashier's desk downstairs, but the search of his possessions confirmed his estimate of Chetti Singh. 'He's not only a tough bastard, but a cunning one. He's organised and he hasn't missed a trick so far. Let's see if we can spoil his record, but first I need some shut-eye.'

He changed the dressing on his arm, and gave himself another shot of antibiotic and then fell on the bed.

He slept until dinner-time, then showered and changed. He felt refreshed and more cheerful. His arm was less painful and the stiffness had eased. It seemed that his mind had been busy even while he slept, for the details of his plan were clear as he sat down at the writing-desk and laid his small purchases out in front of him. He lit one end of a mosquito coil and left it smouldering as he worked, timing the rate at which it burned.

Using his clasp-knife he snipped the heads off the safety-matches. He used up the entire package of matches and discarded the decapitated sticks in the waste-paper bin. He stuffed the match heads back into the paper wrapping, and taped it all up.

It made a neat package the size of his fist, a very functional little incendiary bomb. He checked the burning rate of the mosquito coil. It was approximately two inches per half hour. The acrid insecticidal smoke made him sneeze, so he took the coil to the bathroom and flushed it down the toilet.

He returned to the desk and cut two fresh coils five inches long, to give a delay of a little over one hour. They were the time-fuses of his make-shift bomb, one as a back-up should the other fail. He pierced the paper packet of match heads, inserted the ends of the coils in the punctures and taped them carefully in place.

Then he went downstairs and stood himself a good dinner and half a bottle of Chardonnay.

After dinner he checked Chetti Singh's residential address in the telephone directory, and found the street in the town map provided so thoughtfully by the Lilongwe Chamber of Commerce.

Then he went down to the Volkswagen in the hotel parking lot and drove through the almost deserted streets. He passed the lighted shop-front of Chetti Singh's supermarket, then circled the block. In the alley behind the building he noted the bags of garbage and empty cardboard boxes piled against the rear wall of the supermarket, awaiting collection. He smiled with satisfaction as he noticed the smoke-detector of the fire-warning system high on the wall above the piles of garbage.

From there he drove out to the airport. The Landcruiser was now conspicuous in the almost deserted airport carpark. He gave the attendant a ten kwacha note and asked him to keep an eye on it. Then he opened the back doors of the truck and rummaged around in his medical box until he found the plastic canister of sleeping capsules.

Parked under a street light he opened the plastic bag of minced meat in his lap. By this time it had defrosted. With his thumbnail he split open the sleeping capsules and poured the white powder over the meat. He used fifty capsules.

That should be enough to stun a bull elephant, he decided with satisfaction, and thoroughly mixed the drug into the chopped meat.

Then he drove out to Chetti Singh's home in the elite suburb behind State House and the main government buildings. The house was the grandest on the street, set in two or three acres of lawns and flowering shrubs. He parked the Volkswagen further down the street in an unlit section and walked back along the sidewalk.

As he came level with the fence surrounding Chetti Singh's property, two dark shapes detached themselves from the shadows and hurled themselves against the wire mesh. German Rottweilers, Daniel noted, as the two guard dogs clamoured for his blood. My least favourite animals, after the hyena. On the other side of the fence, they kept pace with him as he followed the sidewalk to the end of the property.

As he passed the gates at the entrance to the driveway he noted that the padlock on the chain was of simple construction. Two minutes' work with a paper-clip.

He left the two Rottweilers staring after him hungrily and turned the corner into an unlit side street. From his pocket he brought out the packet of doped minced meat and divided it into two equal portions. Then he walked back the way he had come. The dogs were waiting for him. He tossed a portion of the meat over the fence and one of the dogs sniffed it and then gulped it down. Then he threw the second portion to the other dog and watched while it was devoured.

He returned to the Volkswagen and drove back into town. He parked a block away from the supermarket. Still sitting in the front seat, he lit the ends of the mosquito coils protruding from the packet of match heads. He blew on them gently to make sure they were burning evenly, then left the Volkswagen and sauntered down the alley behind the supermarket.

It was dark and deserted. With barely a check in his stride, he dropped the incendiary bomb into one of the cardboard cartons that made up the pile of rubbish and sauntered out of the alley.

Back in the Volkswagen he checked the time; it was a few minutes before ten o'clock. He drove back and parked three blocks away from Chetti Singh's home. He pulled on the black leather gloves. From under the driver's seat he brought out the twelve-gauge shotgun still wrapped in its sheet of light tarpaulin. He broke down the weapon into its three component parts and wiped them down meticulously, made certain there were no fingerprints. Then he refitted the forestock to the double barrels. When he stepped out of the Volkswagen he slipped the barrels down one leg of his trousers, while the breech and buttstock section he tucked under his leather jacket.

The barrels in his pants hampered his gait, but it was better to limp a little than parade fully armed through the streets. He had no idea how often the police patrolled this area. He checked his pockets to make sure that he had the spare cartridges and Chawe's warehouse keys. Then he limped on one stiff leg towards the Sikh's home.

There were no guard dogs to greet him when he reached the corner fence of the property, and neither of them appeared even when he whistled softly for them. The dosage of the drug he had given them might have put them out for good and all. At the gates to the driveway it took him even less than the two minutes he had estimated to deal with the padlock. He left the gates wide open and moved quietly across the lawns, avoiding the crunching gravel of the driveway.

Daniel was prepared for a challenge from a night-watchman; even though Malawi was not as lawless and uncontrolled as Zambia, there might have been a guard. However, Chetti Singh seemed to place more faith in animals than in humans.

No challenge came, and from the shelter of a spreading bougainvillaea arbour he surveyed the main house. It was in low ranch-house style with large picture windows, most of which were curtained and lit. Occasionally he saw the shadows of the occupants flit across the curtains and he could distinguish between the silhouettes of Mama Singh and her more sylphlike daughters.

The double garage was attached to the main house. One of the doors stood open and through it he made out the gleaming chrome work of the Cadillac. Chetti Singh was at home.

Still standing in shadow, Daniel reassembled the shotgun and slipped two SSG cartridges into the breeches. At close range they would almost cut a man in half. He closed the action, and set the safety-catch. Turning the dial of his wristwatch to catch the light from the windows he read the luminous numerals. In something under twenty minutes, depending on the burning rate of the mosquito coils, the packet of match heads would explode into bright phosphorous flame. The garbage pile should burn with a heavy outpouring of smoke and within seconds the fire alarms would detect it.

Daniel moved quickly across the open lawn, watching the windows of the house. The gravel crunched lightly under his feet and then he was into the garage. He tensed for any outcry, and when none came he checked the doors of the Cadillac. They were all locked.

In the garage wall nearest the driver's side of the Cadillac there was a door that obviously connected with the main house. Chetti Singh would have to come through that.

He probably had another fifteen minutes before the fire alarm was reported and Chetti Singh came rushing into the garage to drive to the scene of the fire. It was a long time for

Daniel to wait, and he tried to put from his mind any consideration of the morality of what he was about to do.

Killing Chawe had been an act of self-defence, but Daniel had killed deliberately before, during the bush war. However, he had never derived any pleasure or satisfaction from it, as some of the others had done. Even though it had been his duty as a soldier, the sickening guilt and remorse after each episode had built up slowly within him. That guilt had contributed overwhelmingly to the final revulsion and rejection of the whole ethic of the war which had led him to join the Alpha group.

Yet here he was preparing to kill again, in a much more cold-blooded and calculating manner. Those other nameless victims that he had left as blood-soaked bundles lying in the battle-scorched veld had been patriots too, in their own light, brave black men, almost certainly braver than he, who had been prepared to die for their own vision of freedom and justice. In the end they had succeeded where he had failed. Even though long dead, their vision still burned brightly where his had dimmed and faded away. The Rhodesia he had fought for no longer existed. For him those long-ago killings had been an obscene ritual, without passion and, he now realised, without morality.

On the other hand, could he justify what he was about to do by the memory of Johnny Nzou? Could he convince himself of the justice of it, become executioner when no judge had passed sentence? Was there enough angry fire in his belly to carry it through?

Then he remembered Mavis Nzou and her children, and the fire burned up brightly. He knew he could not turn away from it. He had to do it. He knew he would be sick with guilt after the fire of his anger had turned to cold grey ash, but he had to do it.

Somewhere in the house beyond the door he heard a telephone ring. Daniel stirred, shaking himself like a spaniel coming from the water on to the bank, throwing off the doubts and uncertainty. He tightened his grip on the stock of the shotgun and lifted it to high port.

There were hurried footsteps beyond the door, the lock

turned and then it was thrown open. A man came through. The light was behind him and for a moment Daniel did not recognise Chetti Singh without his turban. He stooped beside the Cadillac. His keys tinkled as he searched for the lock, and cursed softly when he could not find it and turned back to the light switch on the wall.

Light flooded the garage.

Chetti Singh was bare-headed. His long, never-trimmed hair and beard twisted up into a top-knot on his head were lightly streaked with grey. His back was still half-turned to Daniel as he fingered the bunch of keys, and then thrust one of them into the Cadillac's door lock.

Daniel stepped up behind him and poked the muzzle of the shotgun into his back. 'Don't do anything heroic, Mr Singh. Mr Purdey is looking down your spine.'

Chetti Singh's body froze, but his head swivelled slowly until he was gawking at Daniel over one shoulder.

'I thought . . .' he said, and then caught himself.

Daniel shook his head. 'It didn't work out that way. Chawe wasn't very bright, I'm afraid. You should have fired him long ago, Mr Singh. Now move around to the other side of the car, but move slowly. Please let us keep our dignity.'

He jabbed the gun into the Sikh's back, hard enough to bruise him through the thin cotton shirt which was all he wore above a pair of khaki slacks and sandals. Chetti Singh had obviously dressed in great haste.

They moved in close file around the front of the Cadillac's fancy radiator grille to the passenger door.

'Open the door. Get in,' Daniel instructed.

Chetti Singh settled himself on the gleaming leather upholstery, and looked up into the barrel of the shotgun only inches from his face. He was sweating more heavily than the warm night air warranted. Beads of sweat twinkled on his beaky nose and slid down his cheeks into the plaited beard. He smelt of curry spices and fear, but there was a tiny spark of hope in his eyes as he offered the keys of the Cadillac to Daniel through the open door.

'Are you going to drive? Here are the keys; take them. I place myself in your hands, absolutely.'

'Nice try, Mr Singh,' Daniel smiled coldly. 'But you and Mr Purdey are not going to be separated for a moment. Just slide across to the driver's seat, nice and slowly.'

Awkwardly Chetti Singh moved his big frame across the console between the seats, grunting with the effort, and Daniel prodded him with the shotgun.

'That's it. You are doing very well, Mr Singh.' He slid into the passenger seat as Chetti Singh settled at the wheel. He held the shotgun across his lap, out of sight of any casual observer, but with the muzzle still pushed hard into the Sikh's lower ribs. With his free hand he closed the door.

'All right. Start up. Drive out.'

As the headlights swept across the lawns, they lit the body of one of the Rottweilers lying on the grass.

'My dogs – my daughter is very fond of them.'

'She has my commiserations.' Daniel gave the taunt back to him. 'But the animal is doped, not dead.'

They drove out into the street. 'My shop – my supermarket in town is on fire. I think this is your doing, Doctor. It is an investment of several millions.'

'Again, you have my commiserations,' Daniel nodded. 'It's a tough life, Mr Singh, but worse for the insurance company than for you, I imagine. Now drive to the warehouse please.'

'The warehouse? Which warehouse?'

'Where you and Chawe and I met earlier today, Mr Singh. That warehouse.'

Chetti Singh turned in the correct direction, but he was still sweating. The smell of curry and garlic was very strong in the confined interior of the Cadillac. With his free hand Daniel adjusted the air-conditioning.

Neither of them spoke but Chetti Singh kept glancing in the rear-view mirror, obviously hoping for assistance. However, the streets were deserted until they stopped at a traffic light at the entrance to the industrial area. Then headlights flooded the interior from the rear, and a Landrover pulled up alongside them. It was painted grey and when Daniel glanced sideways at it, he made out the peaked cap brims of the two police constables in the front seat.

Beside him he felt Chetti Singh stiffen and gather himself. Stealthily the Sikh reached out for the door handle at his side.

'Please, Mr Singh,' Daniel said pleasantly. 'Don't do it. Blood and guts all over the upholstery will ruin your Caddie's resale value.'

Chetti Singh deflated slowly. One of the police constables was now staring across at them. 'Smile at him,' Daniel instructed.

Chetti Singh turned his head and snarled like a rabid dog. The constable looked away hurriedly. The lights changed and the Landrover pulled forward.

'Let them get ahead,' Daniel instructed.

At the next intersection the police vehicle turned left.

'You did that well,' Daniel congratulated him. 'I am pleased with you.'

'Why are you victimising me in such a barbarous fashion, please, Doctor?'

'Don't spoil your record by asking facetious questions,' Daniel advised him. 'You know why I'm doing this.'

'The ivory was no concern of yours, surely, Doctor?'

'The theft of the ivory is the concern of any decent man, but you are correct. That is not the main reason.'

'The business with Chawe. That was not personal. You brought that upon yourself. You should not blame me for trying to protect myself. I am a very wealthy man, Doctor. I would be glad to make up to you any injury to your dignity or person you might have suffered. Let us discuss a figure. Ten thousand dollars, US, of course,' Chetti Singh babbled.

'Is that your final offer? I find it miserly, Mr Singh.'

'Yes, you are right. Let's say twenty-five – no, make that fifty. Fifty thousand US.'

'Johnny Nzou was one of the best friends I ever had,' Daniel said softly. 'His wife was a lovely lady, they had three children, two girls and a little boy. They named the boy after me.'

'Now you have me at a loss, never mind. Who is Johnny Nzou?' Chetti Singh asked. 'Let's say fifty thousand for him, as well. One hundred thousand US dollars. I give it to you, and you walk away. We forget this foolishness. It never happened Am I correct, Doctor?'

'A little late for that, Mr Singh. Johnny Nzou was the warden at Chiwewe National Park.'

Chetti Singh let out his breath softly. 'I am terribly sorry about that, Doctor. Those were not my orders . . .' There was the brittle edge of panic in his voice. 'I had nothing to do with that. It was – it was the Chinaman.'

'Tell me about the Chinaman.'

'If I tell you, will you swear not to harm me?'

Daniel seemed to consider this at length. 'Very well,' he nodded at last. 'We will go to your warehouse where we can have a private uninterrupted chat. You will tell me all you know about Ning Cheng Gong, and afterwards I will release you, immediately, unharmed.'

Chetti Singh turned to stare at him in the reflected light from the instrument panel. 'I trust you, Doctor Armstrong. I think you are a man of integrity. I believe you will keep your word.'

'To the letter, Mr Singh,' Daniel assured him. 'Now just keep heading for the warehouse.'

They passed the sawmills. The lumber-yard was brightly lit and the teams of sawyers were at work in the long sheds. The squeal of the saw-blades slicing into timber carried clearly even into the air-conditioned interior of the Cadillac.

'Business must be good, Mr Singh. You are working night-shift.'

'I have a large consignment going to Australia at the end of the week.'

'You will want to survive long enough to enjoy those profits. Just keep co-operating.'

At the end of the street the warehouse stood in darkness. Chetti Singh stopped at the main gates. The gatehouse was deserted and unlit.

'Left-hand drive,' Chetti Singh remarked, indicating the controls of the Cadillac with an apologetic shrug. 'You must operate the gate from your side.' He handed Daniel a plastic-coated electronic key-card similar to the one retrieved from Chawe's corpse, and lowered the electric window.

Daniel leaned out and pressed the card into the slot of the control-box. The gate boom rose and Chetti Singh drove through. Behind them the boom dropped again automatically.

'Your guard leopard must save you a great deal in the way of wages.' Daniel's tone was mild and conversational but he kept a firm pressure of the shotgun into Chetti Singh's ribs. 'But I don't understand how you have made the animal so vicious. In my experience, leopards will not attack a man unless provoked.'

'That is true.' Chetti Singh was more relaxed since they had struck their bargain. He had stopped sweating and now he chuckled for the first time. 'I was advised by the man who sold it to me. Every once in a while it is necessary to give the brute a little gingering up, never mind. I use a hot iron under its tail . . .' He chuckled again, this time with genuine amusement. 'My goodness, it makes the animal very angry indeed. You never heard such a racket.'

'You deliberately torment it to make it vicious?' Daniel asked, shocked despite himself. His tone made evident his disgust and contempt, and Chetti Singh bridled.

'You English and your love of animals. It is merely a form of training to make it more efficient. The injuries are superficial and heal readily.'

They drew up outside the warehouse and once again Daniel used the electronic key-card to open the roller door. As they drove through, the door rumbled closed behind them.

'Park over there on the loading ramp,' Daniel ordered. The headlights swept powerfully down to the girders and corrugated sheeting of the wall at the far end of the cavernous building. The floor was as cluttered as before with a vast array of trade goods.

For an instant the leopard was caught in the full beam as the Cadillac drove on to the ramp and the headlights were deflected upwards. The great cat was crouched on the summit of a neatly squared pile of packing-cases. As the light struck it, the leopard crouched, yellow-eyed, and puckered its lips into a snarl. The light glinted on its exposed canine fangs. Then it dropped out of sight behind the pile of cases.

'Did you notice the injury to its face?' Chetti Singh asked virtuously. 'You did that, and yet you accuse me of cruelty, Doctor Armstrong. The brute is extremely aggressive and impossible to control at the moment. I may have to destroy it. It is too dangerous, even to me and my men.'

'This will do.' Daniel ignored the rebuke. 'We can talk here.

Switch off the engine and the headlights.' Daniel reached up to the cabin light in the centre of the roof and a soft glow replaced the harsh white glare as the headlights faded.

They sat in silence for a while longer, and then Daniel asked quietly, 'So, Mr Singh, how and when did you first meet Ning Cheng Gong?'

'It was about three years ago. A mutual friend told me he was interested in ivory and other commodities which I could supply,' Chetti Singh answered.

'What were they, these other commodities?'

When Chetti Singh hesitated, Daniel jabbed him sharply with the shotgun barrels.

'Let us both keep to our side of the bargain,' he suggested mildly.

'Diamonds . . .' Chetti Singh wriggled away from the shotgun. 'From Namibia and Angola. Emeralds from Sandwana. Rare Tanzanite gemstones from the mines at Arusha in Tanzania, some dagga from Zululand . . .'

'You seem to have access to many sources of supply, Mr Singh.'

'I am a businessman, Doctor. I think I am good, probably the best. That is why Mr Ning dealt with me.'

'It was mutually beneficial, then?'

Chetti Singh shrugged. 'He was able to use the diplomatic bag. Absolutely secure shipment . . .'

'Except when the products were too bulky,' Daniel pointed out. 'As was this last consignment of ivory.'

'As you say,' Chetti Singh agreed. 'But even then his family connections were abundantly useful. Taiwan is a convenient *entrepôt*.'

'Give me the details of your transactions. Dates, commodities, values . . .'

'There were many,' Chetti Singh protested, 'I cannot remember them all.'

'You have just told me that you are a good businessman.' Daniel prodded him again, and Chetti Singh tried to avoid the shotgun barrel but he was already hard up against the door and could move no further. 'I'm sure you remember every single transaction.'

'All right,' he capitulated. 'The first was in early February three years ago. Ivory, value five thousand dollars. It was a trial shipment. It went well. At the end of that month there was a second transaction, rhino horn and ivory, sixty-two thousand dollars. In May of the same year, emeralds, four hundred thousand . . .'

Daniel had trained his memory over the years as an interviewer. He knew he could retain the details until he had a chance to write them down. The recital went on for almost twenty minutes. Chetti Singh was quick and incisive until suddenly he ended on a home note.

'Then this last shipment, the one you know about.'

'Good.' Daniel nodded. 'We come to the Chiwewe raid, at last. Whose idea was that, Mr Singh?'

'The ambassador. It was his idea,' Chetti Singh blurted.

'I think you are lying. It is highly unlikely that he could have known about the ivory godown. Its whereabouts are not public knowledge. I think that it was more likely your area of expertise . . .'

'All right,' Chetti Singh agreed. 'I have known about it for some years. I was awaiting an opportunity. However, Ning told me he wanted a large *coup*. His term of office was almost expired. He was returning home and he wanted to impress his family, his father.'

'But you recruited the raiders, didn't you? Ning could not have done that. He did not have your contacts.'

'I didn't give the orders to kill your friend,' Chetti Singh's voice trembled. 'I didn't want that to happen.'

'You were just going to leave them alive to tell their story, to explain to the police about Ning?'

'Yes – no, no! It was Ning's idea. I do not believe in killing, Doctor.'

'Is that why you sent Chawe and me into the mountains together?'

'No! You gave me no choice, Doctor Armstrong. Please, you must understand. I am a businessman, not a brigand.'

'All right, let's leave that for the moment. Now tell me, what was your further arrangement with Ning? Surely you were going to continue such a lucrative partnership, even after he returned to Taiwan?'

'No!'

'Please don't lie to me. That is breaking our agreement.' Daniel jammed the steel muzzles into him so hard that he squealed.

'Yes, all right, please you are hurting me. I can't speak if you do that.'

Daniel relaxed the pressure a little.

'I must warn you, Mr Singh, that I would be delighted if you gave me an opportunity to break our contract. Johnny Nzou's two daughters were about ten and eight years old. Your men raped them. His son Daniel, my godson, was just four. They beat his brains out against the wall. It was not a pretty sight. Yes, I would enjoy it if you reneged on our bargain.'

'I don't want to hear these things, please, Doctor. I am a family man, myself. You must believe that I didn't want—'

'Let's talk about Ning rather than your delicate sensibilities, Mr Singh. You and Ning have plans for the future, don't you?'

'We have discussed certain possibilities,' Chetti Singh admitted. 'The Ning family have vast holdings in Africa. After this last shipment of ivory, Cheng's status in the family will be absolutely enhanced. Cheng has expectations that his father will place him in charge of the African division of Lucky Dragon, that is the family holding company.'

'You have a niche in these plans, don't you? Your expert services will be in demand. Surely you have discussed it with Ning?'

'No—' Chetti Singh squealed again as the steel eyes of the shotgun barrels burrowed into his flesh. 'Please don't do that, Doctor. I suffer from high blood pressure; this uncivilised behaviour is absolutely prejudicial to my health.'

'What are your arrangements with Cheng?' Daniel insisted. 'Where will you operate next?'

'Ubomo,' Chetti Singh squeaked. 'Lucky Dragon plans to move into Ubomo.'

'Ubomo?' There was surprise in Daniel's tone. 'President Omeru?'

The sovereign state of Ubomo was one of the few success stories of the continent. Like Malawi, it nestled on the escarpment of the Great Rift Valley, a country of lakes and mountains, on the eastern flank of Africa, where open savannah and primeval equatorial forest met. Like Hastings Banda, President Omeru was another benevolent despot, ruling in the age-old African fashion. Thanks to him his country was free of debt, and not as yet divided or ravaged by tribal warfare.

Daniel knew that Omeru lived in a small brick cottage with a corrugated-iron roof and drove his own Landrover. No marble palaces, no stretched black Mercedes, no executive jet for him. He flew to the meetings of the Organization of African Unity in the tourist class cabin of a commercial airline as a deliberate example to his people. He was a beacon of hope, not the type to deal with Lucky Dragon.

'Omeru? I don't believe it,' Daniel said emphatically.

'Omeru is yesterday's man. He is old, redundant. He resists change and development. Soon he will go. It is being arranged. Soon there will be a new man in Ubomo, young, dynamic . . .'

'And greedy,' Daniel suggested. 'What will Cheng and Lucky Dragon have to do with all this?'

'I do not know the details. Cheng does not trust me that far. All I know is that he has asked me to deploy my people in Ubomo, to make my dispositions. Ready for the day.'

'When will it be?'

'I do not know. I told you. But I think soon.'

'This year? Next year?'

'I do not know, you must believe me, Doctor. I have held nothing back from you. I have fulfilled my part of the bargain. Now you must keep yours. I think you are a man of honour, an Englishman, a gentleman. Am I correct, Doctor?'

'What was our bargain, Mr Singh? Refresh my memory,' Daniel asked, never relaxing the pressure of the shotgun for a moment.

'After I told you all I know about Cheng, you promised to release me immediately, unharmed.'

'Have I harmed you, Mr Singh?'

'No, not yet.' But Chetti Singh was sweating again now, more copiously than before. The expression on the white man's face was murderous.

Daniel reached across him, and seized the door handle. It was so unexpected, so quick that Chetti Singh had no chance to

200

react. He was hunched against the door, trying to get away from the shotgun.

'You are free to go, Mr Singh,' Daniel said softly. With one hand he wrenched open the driver's door of the Cadillac and placed his other hand in the centre of Chetti Singh's chest. With all the strength of his anger and disgust, he shoved.

The door flew open. Chetti Singh was leaning his full weight against it. The thrust of Daniel's arm hurled him outwards. He fell on his back on to the cement floor of the warehouse, and rolled over twice. He lay there stunned and paralysed with shock.

Daniel slammed the door of the Cadillac shut and locked it. He switched on the headlights. For a moment nothing changed. Chetti Singh lay on the floor outside the vehicle and Daniel stared down at him mercilessly through the shatterproof glass. Somewhere in the dim depths of the warehouse the leopard sawed hoarsely.

Chetti Singh bounded to his feet and threw himself against the side of the Cadillac, scrabbling at the window with his bare hands. His face contorted.

'You cannot do this to me. The leopard . . . Please, Doctor.' His voice was muted by the intervening glass, but still the raw panic was shrill in his voice and a dribble of saliva broke from the corner of his mouth.

Daniel regarded him dispassionately, his arms folded and his jaw clenched.

'Anything,' screamed Chetti Singh. 'I'll give you anything . . .' He glanced over his shoulder, and his expression was wild with terror as he turned back to Daniel. He had glimpsed that deadly shadow, circling silently in the gloom.

'Money,' he mouthed imploringly, slapping his pink palms on the glass. 'Please, I'll give you as much – a million dollars. I will give you anything. Just let me in. Please, please, I beg you, Doctor. Don't leave me out here.'

The leopard coughed, an abrupt explosion of sound filled with infinite menace. Chetti Singh spun round to face the darkness, cowering against the side of the vehicle.

'Get back, Nandi!' His voice was a high-pitched shriek. 'Back! Back to your cage!'

They both saw the leopard then, crouched in the alley between two walls of packing-cases. Its eyes reflected the head-lights, yellow and glittering. Its tail flicked back and forth with a mesmeric rhythm. It was watching Chetti Singh.

'No!' screamed Chetti Singh. 'No, you can't leave me to that brute. Please, Doctor. Please I implore you.'

The leopard raised its lip in a silent snarl of hatred and Chetti Singh urinated in a steady stream down the front of his khaki slacks. It puddled on the cement floor around his san-dalled feet.

'It's going to kill me! This is inhuman. Please . . . You can't allow this – please let me in.'

Suddenly Chetti Singh's nerve snapped. He pushed himself off the side of the Cadillac and ran for the closed main doors of the warehouse, a hundred feet away in the looming darkness. He had not covered half that distance before the cat was on him. It came from behind, snaking low across the bare cement floor, and rose to settle upon Chetti Singh's shoulders.

They looked like some grotesque hunchbacked creature with two heads, and then Chetti Singh was thrown forward by the leopard's weight and borne to the floor. In a kicking clawing tangle they rolled together, Chetti Singh's screams blending with the rattling growls of the leopard.

For a moment the man came to his knees, but instantly the leopard was on him again, going for his face. Chetti Singh tried to hold it off with his bare hands, thrusting them into its open jaws and the leopard clamped down on his wrist.

Even in the closed sedan Daniel heard the bones of the wrist go, crunching like dry toast, and Chetti Singh screamed on a shriller note. Goaded to superhuman effort by the pain he came to his feet with the leopard hanging on his arm.

He staggered in an erratic circle, beating at the cat with his fist, trying to break its grip on his other wrist. The leopard's back legs were slashing down the front of his thighs, ripping the khaki slacks, blood and urine mingling as the hooked yellow claws opened his flesh from groin to knee.

Chetti Singh blundered into a high pile of cardboard cartons, bringing them tumbling down around himself, and then his strength could no longer sustain the weight of the animal upon him. He collapsed again with the leopard still on top of him. The leopard ripped and bit and worried, and Chetti Singh's movements were becoming uncoordinated. Like an electric toy with a weakening battery he was slowing down. His screams were becoming feebler.

Daniel slid across to the controls of the Cadillac. As he started the engine, the leopard sprang back from its victim and stared at the vehicle uncertainly. Its tail lashed from side to side.

Daniel reversed slowly down off the loading ramp, and then manoeuvred the Cadillac so that its bulk would be between him and the leopard when he left the car and went to the door. He left the engine running and the headlights on and stepped out of the Cadillac. He watched the leopard steadfastly as he backed the few paces to the control-box. The leopard was almost thirty yards from him but he never took his eyes off it as he inserted the key into its slot and the heavy door rumbled open. He left the key in the slot, and then dropped the shotgun and backed out through the door.

He was careful not to run or to make any other hurried movement that might provoke the leopard, even though the body of the Cadillac should inhibit a charge, and the animal already had its victim. Daniel was now well out of the cat's attack circle.

Daniel turned at last and strode away into the night. He used Chawe's key-card to let himself out into the street, closed the main gates behind him and then broke into a jog-trot.

When they found Chetti Singh in the morning it would be apparent that for some unexplained reason he had gone to the wrong premises in response to the fire alarm call, and he had been attacked by his own animal while he was in the process of opening the warehouse door. The police would reason that left-hand drive controls of the Cadillac had made it necessary for him to leave the vehicle in order to operate the door controls. Daniel had left no fingerprints or other incriminating evidence behind him.

When he reached the furthest corner of the perimeter fence, Daniel paused and looked back. The glow of the Cadillac's headlights still lit the open warehouse door. He saw a dark feline shape, low and slinky, slip out through the door and streak to the high mesh of the perimeter fence. The leopard went over the fence with the ease of a bird taking flight.

Daniel smiled. He knew that the poor tormented brute would head unerringly for its home in the misty forested mountains. After what it had suffered, it deserved that freedom at least, he thought.

Thirty minutes later he reached the hired Volkswagen. He drove to the airport and parked it in one of the Avis bays. He dropped the keys in the return box of the locked and deserted Avis office and then went to his Landcruiser in the public car-park.

At the Capital Hotel he packed quickly, stuffing his few possessions into the canvas valise. He used one of his neckties as a sling for his arm. All that exertion had aggravated the injury. The sleepy night clerk at the hotel cashier's desk printed his credit card and he carried his own bag out to the Landcruiser.

Unable to restrain his curiosity he drove past the Chetti Singh supermarket. There was no damage to the main building, although in the back alley a couple of firemen were still hosing down the pile of scorched garbage and the smoke-stained rear wall, watched by a dozen or so local residents in their night-clothes.

He turned westwards and left Lilongwe, heading back towards the Zambian border post. It was a three-hour drive. He turned on the radio and tuned to the early-morning service of Radio Malawi, listening to the music and news reports.

He was approaching the border post when it came on the six o'clock news. It was the second item after a report on the breaching of the Berlin Wall and the flood of East Germans to the West.

'Meanwhile, here in Lilongwe we have just received a report that a prominent Malawi businessman and entrepreneur has been savagely mauled by his own pet leopard. Mr Chetti Singh was rushed to the Lilongwe General Hospital where he is now in the intensive-care unit. A hospital spokesman said that Mr Singh was suffering from extensive injuries and his condition is described as critical. The circumstances of the attack are unknown, but the police are seeking an employee of Mr Singh's, a certain Mr Chawe Gundwana, who they hope will be able to assist them with their enquiries. Any person knowing the whereabouts of Mr Gundwana is asked to report to the nearest police station.'

Daniel switched off the radio and parked outside the Malawi customs and immigration post. He was expecting trouble. There might be an APB out on him already, especially if Chetti Singh was in a condition to speak and had given Daniel's name to the police. Chetti Singh's survival had not been part of Daniel's calculations. He had expected the leopard to do a more thorough job. His mistake had been in moving the Cadillac too soon. It had distracted the leopard from its victim.

One thing was certain: Chetti Singh was going to need a few gallons of blood transfusion. In Africa that involved an additional hazard.

He hummed his own version of the old song:

> Ashes to ashes
> and dust to dust.
> If the leopard don't get him,
> then HIV must.

Then with some trepidation, he took his passport into the border post. He need not have worried. The law was all smiles and courtesy.

'Did you enjoy your holiday in Malawi? We are always pleased to see you, sir. Come again soon, sir.'

Old Hastings Banda had them well trained. They all appreciated the vital role that tourism played in their lives. There was none of the have-not resentment that was so evident in other parts of the continent.

He folded a five-dollar bill into his passport as he approached the post on the Zambian side, a hundred yards in distance but, it seemed to him, a mighty leap back into the dark ages as he passed between the two countries.

He telephoned Michael Hargreave within an hour of arriving in Lusaka, and Michael invited him to dinner that evening.

'Where are you heading next, you roving bedouin you?' Wendy demanded as she served him a second helping of her famous Yorkshire pudding. 'God, what a lovely adventurous, romantic life you lead. I really must find you a wife; you make all our husbands restless. How long will you be with us?'

'That depends on what Michael can tell me about a mutual acquaintance called Ning Cheng Gong. If he's still in Harare, that's where I will be heading. If not, well, it's back to London, or possibly Taiwan.'

'You're still chasing after the Chink?' Michael asked, as he pulled the cork from a bottle of reasonable *deuxième cru* claret that had come out in the diplomatic bag. 'Are we allowed to know what it's all about yet?'

Daniel glanced at Wendy, and she pulled a face. 'Do you want me to go to the kitchen?'

'Don't be an ass, Wendy. I've never had any secrets from you,' Daniel soothed her, and then turned back to her husband. 'I have proved to my own satisfaction that Ning Cheng Gong arranged the attack on the Chiwewe ivory godown.'

Michael arrested the claret glass on the way to his lips. 'Oh dear. Now I see what it's all about. Johnny Nzou was your pal, I remember. But Ning! Are you sure? He's an ambassador, not a gangster.'

'He's both,' Daniel disagreed. 'His hatchet man was a Sikh from Lilongwe, name of Chetti Singh. They have quite a few secrets between them. Not only ivory, but everything else from drugs to diamonds.'

'Chetti Singh. I've heard that name recently.' Mike thought for only a second. 'Yes, on the news this morning. He was mauled by his own pet leopard, wasn't he?' His expression changed again. 'Just about the time you were in Lilongwe. What a coincidence, Danny. Has it got anything to do with your arm being in a sling, and your smug expression?'

'I'm a reformed character, you know me,' Daniel assured him. 'Would never dream of any rough stuff, but I did find out something from Chetti Singh during my brief chat to him before the unfortunate incident with the leopard. It's something that might interest you spooks at MI6.'

Michael looked pained. 'Ladies present, old boy. We don't mention the firm like that. Never bruit it about. Bad form.'

Wendy stood up. 'On second thoughts, I *will* go and keep an eye on Cheffie. I'll be ten minutes, enough time for boy talk, I hope.' She took her wine-glass with her.

'Coast clear,' Michael murmured. 'Fire away, Danny.'

'Chetti Singh tells me that there is a *coup* being set up in Ubomo. Omeru is going to get the chop.'

'Oh, dear me; not Omeru. He wears a white hat. One of the good guys. That will never do. Have you any details?'

'Not many, I'm afraid. Ning Cheng Gong is in it, and his family, but not as principals, I suspect. I think they are merely eager sponsors of the proposed revolution, with expectations of rights and privileges later on.'

Michael nodded. 'Usual set-up. They get a slice of the pie when the new ruler of Ubomo divides it up. No idea who he will be?'

'None, I'm afraid, but it will be soon. My bet is within the next few months.'

'We'll have to get a warning to Omeru. The PM might want to fly in an SAS battalion to guard him. I know she's particularly pro the old boy and Ubomo is, after all, a member of the Commonwealth.'

'I'd be obliged if you could check up on Ning Cheng Gong while you're at it, Mike.'

'He's gone, Danny. Flown the coop. Spoke to my opposite number in Harare only this morning. Of course, I knew of your interest in him, so I dropped the question into the conversation. Ning held a farewell party at the Chinese embassy on Friday evening and flew home on Saturday.'

'Damn it,' Daniel exclaimed. 'That shoots down all my plans. I was going to go down to Harare—'

'Wouldn't have been a good idea,' Michael broke in. 'It's one thing feeding an ordinary law-abiding citizen to his own leopard, but one can't go around beating up ambassadors. It's considered very poor form indeed.'

'He's no longer ambassador,' Daniel pointed out. 'I could follow him to Taiwan.'

'Another very mediocre idea, if you don't mind my saying so. Taiwan is Ning's home wicket. From what I hear, his family all but owns the island. Whole place is sure to be bristling with Ning's uglies. If you're determined to play the avenging angel, best bide your time. If what you tell me is correct, Ning will be back in Africa soon. Ubomo is a nice neutral turf, better than Taiwan. At least I could back you up there. We've got an office in Kahali, the capital – in fact there is a chance that—' Michael broke off. 'Bit premature, but there is talk that I may be sent to Kahali on my next posting.'

Daniel stared into his glass, swilling the contents slowly as though admiring the ruby lights in the wine. At last he sighed and nodded.

'You're right, as always.' He grinned at Michael ruefully. 'I was getting carried away, besides which I'm terrifyingly short of cash. Doubt I could raise the airfare to Taipei.'

'Never have believed it of you, old boy. Thought you were rolling in the filthy stuff. Always been green with envy. All those million-dollar TV contracts.'

'Everything I have is wrapped up in those video cassettes you sent to London for me. Not worth a damn until I cut and dub them. That's what I'll have to do right now.'

'Before you go, you'd better give me a briefing on all you know about this pair, Singh and Ning. I'll follow up on my side, in case . . .'

'In case anything happens to me,' Daniel finished for him.

'Never said that, old boy. Perish the thought. Although this time you do seem to have picked on a pair of heavyweights.'

'I'd like to leave my Landcruiser and all my gear here in Lusaka with you in the usual way, if that isn't inconvenient?'

'Pleasure, dear boy. My home is your home. My garage is your garage. Feel free.'

The next morning Daniel returned to the Hargreaves' home. Michael was at work, but Wendy and her domestic staff helped him unpack the Landcruiser. His equipment was stiff with dust and the accumulated filth of six months' bush living. Between them they cleaned it all and repacked it into the vehicle. They threw away the perishables and Daniel made a list of replacements. Then he parked the Landcruiser in the spare garage, and put the battery on charge, ready for his next expedition, whenever that might be.

When Michael came home for lunch from the High Commission, he and Daniel spent an hour sequestered in his study. After that the three of them split a bottle of wine, sitting under the marula trees beside the swimming-pool.

'I passed on your message to London,' Michael told him. 'Apparently Omeru is in London at the moment. The Foreign Office had an urgent word with him, but it didn't do much good, by all accounts. Without chapter and verse – and your intelligence was rather vague – the old boy pooh-poohed the idea of a *coup*. "My people love me," he said, or words to that effect. "I am their father." Turned down the PM's offer of support. Nevertheless Omeru is cutting short his visit, and going back to Ubomo, so we might have done some good.'

'Probably sent him straight into the jaws of the lion,' Daniel said morosely, and watched Wendy heaping his plate with fresh salad grown in her own vegetable garden.

'Probably,' Michael agreed cheerfully. 'Poor old blighter. Speaking of lion's jaws, and that sort of thing, I have more news for you. I buzzed our man in Lilongwe. Your friend Chetti Singh is off the danger list. Hospital describes his condition as "serious but stable", although they did have to amputate one arm. Seems as though the leopard chewed it up rather thoroughly.'

'Wish it had been his head.'

'Can't have everything, can we? Must be thankful for small mercies. Anyway, I'll keep you posted while you are in London. Have you still got that flat in Chelsea, near Sloane Square?'

'It's not a flat,' said Wendy. 'Bachelor house of ill-repute, more like it.'

'Nonsense, old girl,' Michael twitted her. 'Danny is a monk; never touches the stuff – do you? Is the telephone number the same, 730-something? I've got it written down somewhere.'

'Yes, same address. Same number.'

'I'll ring you if anything comes up.'

'What can I bring you from London when I come back, Wendy?'

'You can bring me the entire stock of Fortnum's,' she sighed. 'No, I'm joking. Just some of those special biscuits in the yellow tin; I hallucinate about them. And some Floris soap, and perfume, Fracas. Oh! And undies from Janet Reger the same as you brought last time, and while you're about it, some real English tea, Earl Grey.'

'Easy, old girl,' Michael chided her. 'Lad's not a camel, you know. Keep it down to a ton.'

Later that afternoon, they drove Daniel out to the airport and put him on the British Airways flight. It landed at Heathrow at seven the next morning.

 That same evening the telephone in Daniel's Chelsea flat rang. Nobody knew he was back in town. He debated with himself whether to make the effort to answer it, and gave in after the tenth peal. He couldn't ignore such persistence.

'Danny, is it really you, or that cursed answering machine? I refuse to talk to a robot, matter of principle.'

He recognised Michael Hargreave's voice immediately.

'What is it, Mike? Is Wendy okay? Where are you?'

'Still in Lusaka. Both of us fine, old boy. More than I can say for your pal, Omeru. You were right, Danny. News has just broken. He's got the axe. Military *coup*. We've just had a signal from our office in Kahali.'

'What's happened to Omeru? Who's the new man in power?'

'Don't know to both questions. Sorry, Danny. It's all a bit confused still. Should be on the BBC news your end, but I'll ring again tomorrow as soon as I have any more details.'

That evening it was tucked in at the end of the news on BBC 1 over a file photograph of President Victor Omeru. Just a bare statement of the *coup d'état* in Ubomo, and the takeover by a military junta. On the TV screen Omeru was a craggily handsome man in his late sixties. His hair was a silver fleece and he was light-skinned, the colour of old amber. His gaze from the television screen was calm and direct. Then the weather forecast came on and Daniel was left with a sense of melancholy.

He had met Victor Omeru only once, five years ago, when the President had granted him an interview covering the dispute with Zaïre and Uganda over the fishing rights in Lake Albert. They had spent only an hour together, but Daniel had been impressed by the old man's eloquence and presence, and even more so by his obvious commitment to his people, to all the various tribal groupings that made up his little state, and to the preservation of the forest, savannah and lakes that were their national heritage.

'We see the riches of our lakes and forests as an asset that must be managed for posterity, not something that is to be devoured at a single sitting. We look upon nature's bounty as a renewable resource which all the people of Ubomo have the right to share, even those generations as yet unborn. That is why we resist the plunder of the lakes by our neighbours,' Victor Omeru had told him, and it was wisdom of a kind that Daniel had seldom heard from any other statesman. His heart had gone out to someone who shared his own love and concern for the land that had given them birth. Now Victor Omeru was gone and Africa would be a poorer, sadder place for his passing.

Daniel spent the whole of Monday in the City talking to his bank-manager and his agent. It went well and Daniel was in a far better mood when he returned to the flat at nine-thirty that evening.

There was another message from Michael on the answering machine. 'God, I hate this contraption. Call me when you come in, Danny.'

It would be two hours later in Lusaka, but he took Michael at his word.

'Did I get you out of bed, Mike?'

'No matter, Danny. Hadn't turned the light off yet. Just one bit of news for you. The new man in Ubomo is Colonel Ephrem Taffari. Forty-two years old. Apparently educated at London School of Economics and University of Budapest. Other than that, nobody knows much about him except that he has already changed the country's name to the People's Democratic Republic of Ubomo. Bad sign. In African Socialist-speak "democratic" means "tyrannical". There have been reports of executions of members of the former government, but one expects that.'

'What about Omeru?' Daniel demanded. It was strange how strongly his sympathies inclined towards someone he had known for such a short time so long ago.

'Not specifically mentioned on the butcher's bill, but presumed to be amongst those put to the wall.'

'Let me know if you pick up anything about my friends Chetti Singh or Ning Cheng Gong.'

'Will do, Danny.'

 Now Daniel put the events in Ubomo out of his mind and his world shrank down to the space enclosed by the four walls of the cutting-room at the studio in Shepherd's Bush. Day after day, he sat in the semi-darkness, concentrating his entire being on the small glowing screen of the editing console.

In the evenings, dizzy with mental exhaustion and red-eyed with strain, he staggered out into the street and caught a taxi back to the flat, stopping only at Partridge's in Sloane Street to pick up the makings of a sandwich supper. Each morning he awoke in darkness before dawn and was back at the studio long before the daily commuter invasion of the city was under way.

He was caught up in an ecstasy of creative endeavour. It heightened his emotional awareness to the point where all of his existence was in those lambent images that flashed before his eyes. The words to describe them bloomed in his mind so that he spoke into the microphone of the recorder with only occasional references to his notes.

He relived every moment of the scenes that unfolded before him to the point where he could smell the hot dusty musky perfume of Africa and hear the voices of her people and the cries of her animals ringing in his ears as he worked.

So great was Daniel's absorption in the creative process of dubbing and fine cutting his series that over the weeks that followed the recent events in Africa retreated into the mists of distance. It was only when, with a shock that started his adrenalin flowing, he saw Johnny Nzou's face looking at him out of the small screen and heard his voice speak from beyond the grave, that it all rushed back upon him and he felt his determination grow stronger.

Alone in the darkened cutting-room he replied to Johnny's image, 'I'm coming back. I haven't forgotten you. They haven't got away with what they did to you. I promise you that, old friend.'

By the end of February, three months after he had started the editing, he had a rough cut of the first four episodes of the series ready to show his agent. Elna Markham had sold his very first production and they had been together ever since. He trusted her judgement, and stood in awe of her business acumen.

She had an uncanny ability to judge to within a dollar just how much the trade would bear, and then to squeeze that very last dollar out of the deal. She wrote a formidable contract which covered every conceivable contingency, and several that fell outside that definition. She had once written a spin-off clause into one of his contracts. He had smiled at it when he read it, but two years later it had yielded a wholly unexpected royalty of fifty thousand dollars from Japan, a country that hadn't even entered into Daniel's original calculations.

At forty years of age, Elna was tall and willowy with dark Jewish eyes and a figure like a *Vogue* model. Once or twice over the years, they had almost become lovers. The closest they had come to it was three years previously, when they had shared a bottle of Dom Perignon in his flat to celebrate a particularly lucrative sale of subsidiary rights. She had drawn back from the very brink.

'You are one of the most attractive men I have ever met, Danny, and I'm sure we'd make tremendous music together, but still you're more valuable to me as a client than as just another good romp.' She had buttoned up her blouse and left him to the agonies of sexual frustration.

Now they spent the morning in the preview theatre at the studios watching the first four episodes straight through, back to back. Elna made no comment until the last tape was played out, then she stood up.

'I'll take you to lunch,' she said.

In the taxi she talked of everything but the production. She took him to Mosimann's in West Halkin Street. The club that Anton Mosimann had fashioned out of an old church was now a high cathedral of gastronomy. Anton himself, resplendent in his whites and his tall chef's hat, rosy-complexioned as a cherub, came out of his kitchens to chat to them at their table, an honour afforded only to his more favoured members.

Daniel was in a fever of anxiety to learn Elna's opinion of his work, but this was an old trick of hers to build up tension and expectation. He played along with her, discussing the menu and chatting unconcernedly about irrelevancies. Only when she ordered a bottle of Corton-Charlemagne did he know for certain that she liked it.

Then she flashed dark Jewish eyes at him over the rim of the glass and said in that husky sexy voice, 'Marvellous, Armstrong, bloody marvellous. Your best yet, I kid you not. I want four copies immediately.'

He laughed with relief. 'You can't sell it yet – it's not finished.'

'Can't I? You just watch my dust.'

 She showed it to the Italians first. They always favoured his work. The Italians had an historical and emotional interest in Africa, and over the years Italy had proved to be one of Daniel's best markets. He loved the Italians and they loved him.

A week later Elna brought the draft Italian contract around to his flat. Daniel contributed a plateful of smoked salmon sandwiches and a bottle to the proceedings and they sat on the floor, put Beethoven on the CD player and ate the sandwiches while Elna went over the contract with him.

'They liked it as much as I did,' she told him. 'I've jacked them up twenty-five per cent on the last advance they gave us.'

'You're a witch,' Daniel told her. 'It's black magic.' The Italian advance almost covered the entire cost of production of the series. The rest of it would all be profit. The big gamble had paid off handsomely, and he had no backers to share it with. After Elna had taken her commission, it was all his. He tried to estimate what his ultimate pay-off would be. Half a million certainly; probably a lot more, depending on the Americans. When all the world rights had been sold, it might be as much as three million dollars. He had impressed even himself.

After ten years of hard work, he had broken clear. No more overdrafts; no more taking his begging bowl from one arrogant sponsor to another. From now on he had charge of his own destiny; he had creative and artistic control over his work, and the rights to the final cut. In future it would be the way he wanted it, not the view imposed upon him by his backers.

It was a good feeling, a bloody wonderful feeling.

'What have you got lined up for the future?' Elna asked as she helped herself to the last of the smoked salmon.

'I haven't thought about it yet,' he lied. He always had two or three projects in the warming oven of his mind. 'I still have to finish the last two episodes.'

'I've had a few approaches from interested parties with money to invest. One of the big oil companies wants you to do a series on the South African apartheid society and the effect of sanctions on—'

'Hell, no!' It was marvellous to be able to turn down an offer of work in such a peremptory fashion. 'That's all cold porridge and last night's leftovers. The world is changing. Just look at Eastern Europe. Apartheid and sanctions are yesterday's news. They won't even exist by this time next year. I want something fresh and exciting. I've been thinking about the rain forests – not the Brazilian forests, that's been done and overdone, but the African equatorial region. It's one of the very few unknown parts left on this planet, yet ecologically it's of vast importance.'

'Sounds good. When will you start?'

'My God, you are a hard taskmistress. I haven't even finished the last one and you're on to me about the next.'

'Since Aaron divorced me, somebody has to keep me in the style to which I've grown accustomed.'

'All the duties of matrimony with none of the privileges and pleasures.' He sighed dramatically.

'You still on about that, silly boy. You could talk me into it yet, and you might not like it. Aaron didn't.'

'Aaron was a big prick,' Daniel said.

'That was part of the trouble,' she chuckled, huskily sexy. 'He wasn't.' Then she changed the subject. 'By the way, what happened between you and Jock? I had a very strange phone call from him. He said you'd had a major punch-up. He implied that you had blown your mind and gone over the top, nearly got him into all sorts of trouble. He said that you and he would not be working together again. Is that right?'

'Not to put too fine a point on it, yes, that's right. We have come to a parting of the ways.'

'Pity. He has done some fantastic work on this "Africa Dying" series. Do you have a replacement cameraman in mind?'

'I don't. Do you?'

She thought about it for a while. 'Would you have any objection to working with a female?'

'I can't think why I should, as long as she can stand the pace. Africa is a raw, rough country. It takes a certain resilience and toughness to cope with the physical conditions.'

Elna smiled. 'The lady I have in mind is tough enough and talented enough. You have my word on it. She's just done a piece for the BBC on the Arctic and the Inuit Indians, Eskimos to you. It's good, very good.'

'I'd like to see it.'

'I'll get you a print.'

Elna sent the tape round to the studio the next day but Daniel was so totally involved in his own work that he dropped it into a drawer of his desk. He meant to view it that evening, but instead he let it slide.

Three days after he had finished the series, the tape was still in his desk, forgotten in the excitement of all the other things which were happening around him.

Then Michael Hargreave called from Lusaka again. 'Danny, I'm going to send you a bill for these calls. Costing HM Government a ruddy fortune.'

'I'll buy you a case of bubbly next time I see you.'

'You must be in the chips, dear boy, but I'll accept the offer. The good news is that your friend, Chetti Singh, is out of hospital.'

'Are you sure, Mike?'

'Good as new. Remarkable recovery, so they tell me. I had our man in Lilongwe check it for me. Only one arm, but apart from that Chetti Singh is back in business. You'll have to send him another leopard for Christmas, the last one didn't work.'

Daniel chuckled ruefully. 'Did you hear anything of my other pal?'

'The Chink? Sorry, not a dickie bird. Gone home to Daddy and the Lucky Dragon.'

'Let me know if he pitches up. I won't be able to leave London for a couple of months at least. It's all happening here.'

Daniel was not exaggerating. Elna had just sold the 'Africa Dying' series to Channel 4 for the highest price ever paid for an independent production. They were also breaking their advance planning and screening the first episode at prime time on Sunday evening six weeks from now.

'I'm going to throw a viewing party for you on the big night,' Elna told him. 'Oh God, Danny, I always knew you were the tops. It's so good to be able to prove it. I've invited people from all the Continental and North American stations to watch it. This is going to take them by storm, believe me.'

The Saturday before the party she rang Daniel at his flat. 'Have you had a chance to look at that tape I sent you?'

'Which one?'

'Which means you haven't,' she groaned. 'The tape about the Arctic, "Arctic Dream", the one shot by that camerawoman, Bonny Mahon. Don't be obtuse, Danny.'

'Damn! I'm sorry, Elna, I just haven't had a chance to get around to it.'

'I've invited her to the party,' she warned him.

'I'll look at it now, right away,' he promised, and went to rescue the tape from his desk drawer.

He had been intending to skip-view the tape, but found that he was not able to give it such a cavalier treatment. From the opening sequence he found himself captivated.

It opened with an aerial sequence of the eternal ice of the far north, and the images which followed were striking and unforgettable. There was a particular sequence of a vast herd of barren ground caribou swimming across one of the open leads in the ice. The low yellow sun was behind them so that when the herd bull rose from the dark water and shook himself, he filled the air around him with a cloud of golden droplets which framed him in a precious nimbus like an animal deity from some pagan religion.

Daniel found himself enthralled to the point where his professional judgement was suspended. Only after the tape had run to its conclusion did he attempt to analyse how the camerawoman had achieved her effects. Bonny Mahon had understood how to use the extraordinary light to endow it with a texture and mood that reminded him overpoweringly of the luminous and ethereal masterpieces of Turner.

If he were ever to work in the gloomy depths of the equatorial forests, that use of available light would be critical. There was no doubt that she had the gift of exploiting it. He looked forward to meeting her.

For the viewing party Elna Markham had hired half a dozen extra television sets, and placed them in strategic positions in her flat, including the guest toilet. She was determined that no one should have an excuse for missing the event that they had all assembled to celebrate.

As befitted the guest of honour, Daniel arrived half an hour late and had to fight his way in through the front door. Elna's parties were extremely popular, and the large drawing-room was bulging at the seams. Fortunately it was a balmy May evening, and the guests had overflowed on to the terrace overlooking the river.

For six months Daniel had lived like a recluse. It was good to have human contact again. Of course, he knew most of those present and his reputation was such that they sought him out eagerly. He was the centre of an ever-changing circle of admirers, most of them old friends, and he was vain enough to enjoy the attention, although he knew just how ephemeral it could be. In this business, you were only as good as your last production.

Despite the gay and amusing company, Daniel felt his nerves screwing up tight as the hour approached, and he found it harder to concentrate on the clever conversation and repartee that flitted and sparkled in the air around his head like a flock of humming-birds. Not even the prettiest of the many lovely ladies present could hold his attention for long.

Finally Elna clapped her hands and called them to order. 'People! People! This is it!' And she went from room to room, switching on the television sets, tuning them to Channel 4. There was a noisy chatter of expectation as the opening credits began to roll and the theme music swelled and then the first sequence of Daniel's production opened with a view that was the spirit of Africa distilled to its essence.

There was a scorched sepia plain on which the scattered acacia trees stood dark green with twisted stems and flat anvil heads. A single elephant strode across the plain, an old bull, grey and wrinkled, his tusks stained with vegetable juices, thick and curved and massive. He moved with ponderous majesty, while around him fluttered a shining cloud of white egrets, their wings pearly and translucent. On the far horizon, against the aching African blue of the sky, floated the snowy pyramid of Kilimanjaro, detached from the burned ochre earth by the heat mirage. It had the same ethereal delicacy as the egrets' wings.

The tipsy laughter and chatter quietened and the crowded rooms fell silent, captivated by the timeless and eternal majesty of the vision that Daniel evoked for them.

Then they gasped with shock as the two old matriarchs of the Zambezi herd charged together headlong from the screen, tattered ears flapping, red earth dashed from under their great pads, until their wild infuriated squeals were cut off abruptly by the crash of gunfire. The bullet-strikes were an ostrich feather of dust dancing for an instant on the seared grey skin of each of their foreheads, and then the mountainous carcasses fell

219

to earth, twitching and shuddering in the dreadful palsy of the brain shot.

For forty-five minutes Daniel led his audience captive in golden chains of imagination through the majestic and ravaged continent. He showed them unearthly beauty and cruelty and ugliness, by contrast all the more shocking.

As the last image faded, the silence persisted for several seconds. Then they began to stir and come back to reality across six thousand miles. Someone clapped softly and the applause swelled and went on and on. Elna came to stand beside Daniel. She said nothing but took his hand and squeezed it.

After a while Daniel felt that he had to escape the crush of human bodies, and the boisterous congratulations. He needed space to breathe. He slipped out on to the terrace.

He stood alone at the railing and looked down, but did not see the boat lights on the dark Thames. Already he was experiencing the first reaction to the heady elation that had buoyed him up through the first part of the evening. His own images of Africa had moved him and saddened him. He should have been inured to them by now, but it was not so. Particularly disturbing had been the sequence with Johnny Nzou and the elephants. Johnny had been there all the time, at the periphery of his conscious mind all these months, but now his full-blown memory emerged again.

Suddenly, overpoweringly, the urge to return to Africa came upon Daniel with all its old force. He felt restless and discontented. Others might applaud what he had done, but for him it was over. His nomadic soul urged him onwards. Already it was time to move, to make for the next horizon, the next tantalising adventure.

Somebody touched his arm. For a moment he did not respond. Then he turned his head to find a girl beside him. She had red hair. That was the first impression he had of her, thick bushy, flaring red hair. The hand on his arm had a disconcerting, almost masculine, strength. She was tall, almost as tall as he was, and her features were generous – a wide mouth and full lips, a large nose saved from masculinity by the upturned tip and delicately sculpted nostrils.

'I've been trying to get to you all evening,' she said. Her voice was deep with a self-assured timbre. 'But you're the man of the moment.'

She was not pretty. Her skin was heavily freckled from sun and wind, but she had a clean outdoors glow. In the terrace lights her eyes were bright and green, fringed with lashes as dense and thick as bronze wire filaments. They gave her a candid and quizzical air.

'Elna promised to introduce us, but I've given up waiting for it to happen. I'm Bonny Mahon.' She grinned like a tomboy and he liked her.

'Elna gave me a tape of yours.' He offered his hand and she took it in a firm strong grip. All right, he thought, she's tough, as Elna said she was. Africa won't daunt her. 'You're good. You have an eye and an instinct for the light. You're very good.'

'So are you.' Her grin widened. 'I'd like to work with you some time.' She was direct, unaffected. He liked her even more.

Then he smelt her. She wore no perfume. It was the true undisguised smell of her skin, warm, strong and aphrodisiac.

'It could happen,' he told her. 'It could happen sooner than either of us suspects.' He was still holding her hand and she made no effort to withdraw it. They were both aware of the sexual ambiguity in his last remark. He thought that it would be exciting to take this woman to Africa with him.

Some miles north of where Daniel and Bonny stood on the terrace and appraised each other both professionally and physically, another person had watched the first episode of 'Africa Dying'.

Sir Peter 'Tug' Harrison was the major shareholder and CEO of British Overseas Steam Ship Co. Ltd. Although BOSS was still listed under 'Shipping' on the London Stock Exchange it had changed its nature entirely in the fifty years since Tug Harrison had acquired a controlling interest in it.

It had started out in the late Victorian era running a small fleet of tramp steamers to Africa and the Orient, but it had never prospered greatly and Tug had taken it over at the outbreak of the Second World War for a fraction of its value. With the profits of its wartime operation Tug had branched out in many directions and BOSS was now one of the most powerful conglomerates listed on the London Stock Exchange.

Tug had always been sensitive to the vagaries of public opinion and to the image that his company projected. He had as strong an instinct for these subtleties as he had for the commodity index and the fluctuations on the world stock markets. It was one of the reasons for his huge success.

'The mood is green,' he had told his board only a month ago. 'Bright green. Whether or not we agree with this new passion for nature and the environment, we have to take cognisance of it. We have to ride the green wave.'

Now he sat in his study on the third floor of his home in Holland Park. The house stood in the centre of a row of magnificent townhouses. It was one of the most prestigious addresses in London. The study was panelled in African hardwood from BOSS's concessions in Nigeria. The panels were selected and matched and polished so that they glowed like precious marble. There were only two paintings hanging on the panels, for the wood grain itself was a natural work of art. The painting facing the desk was a Madonna and Child from Paul Gauguin's first sojourn in the South Pacific islands, and the other painting, which hung behind him, was a Picasso, a great barbaric and erotic image of a bull and a nude woman. The pagan and profane set off the lyrical and luminous quality of the Mother and God-child.

Guarding the doorway was a set of rhinoceros horns. There was a burnished spot on one of the horns, polished by Tug Harrison's right hand over the decades. He stroked it each time he entered or left the room. It was a superstitious ritual. The horns were his good-luck charms.

As an eighteen-year-old lad, penniless and hungry, owning nothing but an old rifle and a handful of cartridges, he had followed that rhino bull into the shimmering deserts of the Sudan. Thirty miles from the banks of the Nile, he had killed the bull with a single bullet to the brain. Blood from a severed artery in its head had washed a little runnel in the desert earth, and from the bottom of the shallow excavation Tug Harrison had picked out a glassy stone with a waxy sheen that had almost filled the palm of his hand.

That diamond was the beginning. His luck had changed from the day of the rhino. He had kept the horns, and still he reached out to them every time he was within arm's length of them. To him they were more valuable than either of the fabulous paintings that flanked them.

He had been born in Liverpool's slums during the First World War, son of a drunken market porter, and had run away to sea at the age of sixteen. He had jumped ship at Dar es Salaam to escape the sexual attentions of a brutal first mate, and had discovered the mystery and the beauty and promise that was Africa. For Tug Harrison that promise had been fulfilled. The riches that he had wrested from the harsh African soil had made him one of the hundred richest men in the entire world.

The television set was artistically concealed behind the hardwood panelling. The controls were set into the intercom panel on his desk-top. Like most intelligent and busy men, he shunned the mindless outpourings of the television programmes, limiting his viewing to selected programmes, mostly the news and current affairs items.

However, anything African was his vital interest and he had noted the title 'Africa Dying' and punched the programme time into his desk-top alarm.

The discreet electronic chimes aroused him from his study of the financial statements which lay on the pigskin blotter in front of him. He touched the controls, and the panel in the wall directly across the figured-silk Qum carpet from his desk slid open.

He adjusted the volume of sound as the theme music floated into the room. Then the image of a great elephant and a snowy peak filled the screen, and instantly he was transported back fifty years and thousands of miles in time and space. He watched without moving until the final frame faded. Then he reached out to touch the controls. The screen went black and the silent panel closed like a sleepy eyelid.

Tug Harrison sat for a long time in silence. At last he picked up the eighteen-carat gold pen from the desk set and scribbled a name on his note-pad. 'Daniel Armstrong.' Then he swivelled his chair and took down his copy of *Who's Who* from the bookshelf.

Daniel walked from Shepherd's Bush to Holland Park. Just because he was a potential millionaire didn't mean he should toss away a fiver on a few minutes' taxi ride. The weather was bright and warm and the trees in the squares and parks were decked in early summer greenery. As he strode along, glancing with abstract appreciation at the girls in their thin dresses and short skirts, he was thinking about Tug Harrison.

Ever since Elna Markham had phoned him to pass on Harrison's invitation, he had been intrigued. Of course, he knew of the man. Harrison's tentacles reached into every corner of the African continent, from Egypt to the banks of the Limpopo river.

Daniel knew the power and wealth of BOSS and its influence in Africa but little about the man behind it. Tug Harrison was a man who seemed to have a knack for steering well clear of public controversy and the attentions of the tabloid press.

Wherever Daniel travelled in Africa these days he could discern Tug Harrison's influence, like the spoor of a cunning old man-eating lion. He left his tracks, but like the beast he was seldom seen in the flesh.

Daniel pondered the reasons for Harrison's peculiar success on the African continent.

He understood the African mind as few white men could. He had learned as a lad in the lonely hunting and prospecting camps in the remote wilderness, when his only companions for months on end had been black men. He spoke a dozen African languages but, more important, he understood the oblique and lateral reasoning of the African. He liked Africans, felt comfortable in their company, and knew how to inspire their trust. On his African travels Daniel had met men and women of mixed blood whose mothers were Turkana or Shona or Kikuyu, and who boasted that Tug Harrison was their true father. There was never any proof of their claims, of course, but often these people were in positions of influence and affluence.

There were very seldom news reports or photographs of Harrison's visits to the African continent, but his Gulfstream executive jet was often parked discreetly at the furthest end of the airport tarmac in Lusaka or Kinshasa or Nairobi.

Rumour placed him as an honoured guest and confidant in Mobutu's marble palaces or at Kenneth Kaunda's presidential residence in Lusaka. They said that he was one of the very few who had access to the shadowy Renamo guerrillas in Mozambique as well as to the guerrilla bush camps of Savimbi in Angola. He was also welcomed by the legitimate regimes that they opposed. They said that he could pick up the telephone at any hour of the day or night and within minutes be speaking to de Klerk or Mugabe or Daniel Arap Moi.

He was the broker, the courier, the adviser, the banker, the go-between, and the negotiator for the continent.

Daniel was looking forward to meeting him. He had tried many times before, without success. Now as an invited guest he stood outside the imposing front door and felt a little tickle of nerves. That premonition had served him well in the African bush; it had warned him so often of dangerous beasts and even more dangerous men.

A black servant in flowing white kanza and red fez opened the front door. When Daniel spoke to him in fluent Swahili, the wooden mask of his face cracked into a huge white smile.

He led Daniel up the wide marble staircase. There were fresh flowers in the niches of the landings, and Daniel recognised some of the paintings from Harrison's fabled art collection gracing the walls – Sisley, Dufy and Matisse.

Before the tall double doors of red Rhodesian teak, the servant stood aside and bowed. Daniel strode into the room and paused in the centre of the silk Qum carpet.

Tug Harrison rose from behind his desk. It was at once obvious how he had earned his nickname. He was big-boned but compact, although the exquisitely tailored pin-stripe suit smoothed the raw powerful angles of his frame and the heavy jut of his belly.

He was bald, except for a fringe of silver hair like that of a tonsured monk. His pate was pale and smooth while the skin of his face was thickened and creased and tanned where it had been unprotected by a hat from the tropical sun. His jaw was determined and his eyes were sharp and piercing, giving warning of the ruthless intelligence behind them.

'Armstrong,' he said. 'Good of you to come.' His voice was warm as molasses, too soft for the rest of him. He held out his hand across the desk, forcing Daniel to come to him, a subtle little dominance ploy.

'Good of you to ask me, Harrison.' Daniel took his cue and eschewed the use of his title, setting equal terms. The older man's eyes crinkled in acknowledgement.

They shook hands, examining each other, feeling the physical power of each other's grip without letting it develop into a boyish contest of strength. Harrison waved him to the buttoned leather chair beneath the Gauguin and spoke to the servant.

'*Letta chai*, Selibi. You will take tea, won't you, Armstrong?'

While the servant poured the tea, Daniel glanced at the rhino horns on the entrance wall.

'You don't see trophies like that often,' he said, and Harrison left his desk and crossed to the doorway.

He stroked one of the horns, caressing it as though it were the limb of a beautiful and beloved woman. 'No, you don't,' he agreed. 'I was a boy when I shot them. Followed the old bull for fifteen days. It was November and the temperature at midday was 120 degrees in the shade. Fifteen days, two hundred miles through the desert.' He shook his head. 'The crazy things we do when we are young.'

'The crazy things we do when we are older,' Daniel said, and Harrison chuckled.

'You are right. Life is no fun unless you are at least a touch crazy.'

He took the cup that the servant offered him. 'Thank you, Selibi. Close the doors when you leave.'

The servant drew the double doors closed and Harrison went back to his desk.

'I watched your production on Channel 4 the other night,' he said, and Daniel inclined his head and waited.

Harrison sipped his tea. The delicate porcelain cup looked fragile in his hands. They were battler's hands, scarred and ravaged by tropical sun and hard physical labour and ancient conflicts. The knuckles were enlarged but the nails were carefully manicured.

Harrison put the cup and saucer down on the desk in front of him and looked up at Daniel again.

'You got it right,' he said. 'You got it exactly right.'

Daniel made no comment. He sensed that any modest or deprecating comment would only irritate this man.

'You got your facts straight, and you drew the right conclusions. It was a refreshing change after all the sentimental and ill-informed crap that we hear every day. You put your finger on the roots of Africa's problems, tribalism and overpopulation and ignorance and corruption. The solutions you suggested made sense.' Harrison nodded. 'Yes, you got it right.'

He stared at Daniel thoughtfully. Harrison's faded blue eyes gave him a strangely enigmatic expression, like a blind man.

Don't relax, Daniel warned himself. Not for a moment. Don't let the flattery soften you up. This is what it's all about. He's stalking you like an old lion.

'Someone in your position is able to influence public opinion as others are never able to do,' Harrison murmured. 'You have a reputation, an international audience. People trust your vision. They base their view on what you tell them. That's good.' He nodded even more emphatically. 'That's very good. I would like to help and encourage you.'

'Thank you.' Daniel let a small ironical smile lift one side of his mouth. One thing he was certain of: Tug Harrison did nothing without good reason. He made no free gifts of his help and encouragement.

'What do they call you, your friends? Daniel, Dan, Danny?'

'Danny.'

'My friends call me Tug.'

'I know,' Daniel said.

'Our thinking is so much in accord. We share the same commitment to Africa. I think we should be friends, Danny.'

'All right, Tug.'

Harrison smiled. 'You have every reason to be suspicious I understand. I have a certain reputation. One should not always judge a man on his reputation, however.'

'That is true.' Daniel smiled back at him. 'Now tell me what you want from me.'

'Damn it!' Harrison chuckled. 'I like you. I think we understand each other. We both believe that man has a right to exist upon this planet, and that, as the dominant animal species, he has the right to exploit the earth for his own benefit, just as long as he does so on a basis of sustained and renewable yield.'

'Yes,' Daniel agreed. 'I believe that.'

'It is the balanced, pragmatic view. I would expect no less of a man of your intelligence. In Europe man has been farming the earth, felling the forests and killing the animals for centuries, and yet the earth is more fertile, the forests denser, the animals more numerous than they were a thousand years ago.'

'Except downwind of Chernobyl, or where the acid rain falls,' Daniel pointed out. 'But yes, I agree; Europe isn't in bad shape. Africa is another story.'

Harrison cut in, 'You and I love Africa. I feel that it is our duty to combat its evils. I can do something to alleviate the grinding poverty in some parts of the continent, and by investment and guidance offer some of the African people a better way of life. You, with your special gifts, are in a position to counter much of the ignorance that exists about Africa. You can clear the woolly-headed confusion of the armchair-conservationists and urban animal rights fanatics, those who are so cut off from the earth and the forests and the animals that they are actually menacing the elements of nature which they believe they are protecting.'

Daniel nodded thoughtfully and non-committally. It was weak tactics to disagree with the man until he had listened to everything he had to say, and heard the full proposal that Harrison was obviously working towards. 'In principle all you say makes excellent sense. However, if you could be a little more specific, Tug.'

'Right,' Harrison agreed. 'Of course you know the state of Ubomo, don't you?'

Daniel felt a little electric shock tickle the hair at the back of his neck. It was so unexpected and yet, in some bizarre manner, he felt that it was predestined. Something had been leading him inexorably in that direction. It took him a moment to recover himself, then he said, 'Ubomo, the land of the red earth. Yes, I have been there, though I can't claim to be an expert on the country.'

'Since independence from Britain in the sixties, it has been a little backwater.' Harrison shrugged. 'There wasn't much to know about it. It was the fief of an arrogant old dictator who resisted all change and progress.'

'Victor Omeru,' Daniel said. 'I met him once, but it was years ago, when he was bickering with his neighbours about the fishing rights in the lake.'

'That was typical of the man. He resisted all change on principle. He wanted to keep to the traditional ways and customs. He wanted to keep his people docile and compliant.' Harrison shook his head. 'Anyway, that is all history. Omeru has gone and there is a dynamic young man at the head of government. President Ephrem Taffari is there to open up the country and bring his people into the twentieth century. Apart from the fishing rights, Ubomo has considerable natural assets. Timber and minerals. For twenty years I have tried to convince Omeru that these should be developed for the benefit of his people. He has resisted with a blind intransigence.'

'Yes. He was stubborn,' Daniel agreed. 'But I liked him.'

'Oh, yes, he was a lovable old codger,' Harrison agreed. 'But that is no longer relevant. The country is ripe and ready for development and, on behalf of an international consortium of which BOSS is the leading member, I have negotiated the concession to undertake a major part of this development.'

'Doesn't sound as though you need me, then.'

'I wish it were as easy as that.' Harrison shook his head. 'We are being overtaken by the wave of hysteria that is sweeping the world. It is a psychological law that every mass popular movement is hi-jacked by fanatics and pushed beyond the dictates of reason and common sense. The pendulum of public feeling always swings too far in each direction.'

'You are running into opposition to your plans to develop

the natural resources of Ubomo. Is that what you are trying to tell me, Tug?'

Harrison cocked his head on one side. He looked like an eagle when he did that, a great bald-headed bird of prey. 'You are direct, young man, but I should have expected that.' He sat down behind his desk and picked up an ivory-handled duelling pistol which he used as a paper weight. He spun it on his forefinger and the gold inlay on the barrel sparkled like a Catherine-wheel.

'There was a female scientist working in Ubomo during Omeru's presidency,' he went on at last. 'She and the old man had a close relationship and he gave her all sorts of special privileges that he denied other journalists and researchers. She published a book on the forest-dwellers of Ubomo. You and I would call them pygmies, although that term is unfashionable in today's climate. The title was . . .' Harrison paused to think, and Daniel intervened.

'The title was *The People of the Tall Trees*. Yes, I have read the book. The author's name is Kelly Kinnear.'

'Have you met her?' Harrison demanded.

'No.' Daniel shook his head. 'But I would like to. She writes well. Her style reminds me of Rachel Carson. She is a—'

'She is a trouble-maker,' Harrison cut in bluntly. 'She is a shit-stirrer.' The coarse term seemed uncharacteristic of him.

'You'll have to explain that to me.' Daniel kept his voice even and his expression neutral. He didn't want to declare his sentiments until he had heard Harrison out.

'When he came to power, President Taffari sent for this woman. She was working in the forest at the time. He explained to her his plans for the advancement and development of the country, and asked for her support and her assistance. The meeting was not a success. Kelly Kinnear had some misguided sense of loyalty to old President Omeru and she resisted President Taffari's overtures of friendship. She is entitled to her views, of course, but then she began a campaign of agitation within Ubomo's borders. She accused Taffari of violations of human rights. She also accused him of planning to rape the country's natural resources by uncontrolled exploitation.' Harrison threw up those powerful scarred hands. 'In fact she went into female hysterics and attacked the new government in every way she was able. There was no logic nor reason nor even factual basis for these attacks. Taffari had no alternative but to send her packing. He chucked her out of Ubomo. She is, as you probably know, a British subject, and she ended up back here in the UK. However, she had not learned her lesson and she continues her campaign against the government of Ubomo.'

'BOSS has nothing to fear from someone like that, surely?' Daniel probed gently, and Harrison looked across at him sharply, searching for traces of irony in the question. Then he transferred his attention back to the duelling pistol in his right hand.

'Unfortunately, the woman has built up a foundation of influence on the strength of her writings. She is articulate and,' he hesitated, 'and personable. She manages to hide her fanaticism under a cloak of reasoned logic which is, needless to say, based on false assumptions and distorted facts. She has managed to recruit the support of the Green Party in this country and on the Continent. You are right, BOSS has nothing to fear from such an obvious charlatan, but she is a nuisance. She looks good on television. Now she has come to know of our interest in Ubomo and the plans that our consortium has to develop the area. She and her supporters are making a great deal of noise. You might have seen that piece in the *Guardian* recently?'

'No.' Daniel shook his head. 'I don't read the *Guardian*, and I've been pretty busy recently. I'm a little out of touch.'

'Well, take my word for it then, it is making life just a trifle uncomfortable for me. I have shareholders to answer to and an annual general meeting coming up. Now, I've just learned that this woman has acquired a small block of shares in BOSS, which gives her the right to attend the AGM and to speak. You can be certain she will have the radical press and a bunch of those lunatics from "Friends of the Earth" there with her, and she will make a circus of the occasion.'

'Awkward, Tug.' Daniel nodded, stifling his smile. 'How can I help you?'

'Your influence in public and scientific circles is far greater than Kelly Kinnear's. I have spoken to many people in various disciplines and diverse walks of life about you. You are well respected; your views on Africa are taken seriously. What I propose is that you go to Ubomo and make a documentary that sets out the true facts and examines the issues that this Kinnear woman has raised. It would blow her away like a puff of smoke. Television is a much more powerful medium than the printed word, and I could guarantee you maximum exposure. BOSS owns extensive media interests . . .'

Daniel listened to him with rising incredulity. It was like listening to a client propositioning a prostitute for the performance of a particularly lurid perversion. He felt the urge to laugh with outrage, to reject violently this insult to his integrity. This man truly believed that he was for sale. It took an effort for him to sit still and listen expressionlessly.

'Of course, I could also guarantee that you would receive the whole-hearted co-operation of President Taffari and his government. They would provide everything that you require. You need only ask and there would be military transport – helicopters, lake patrol boats – at your disposal. You could go anywhere, even into the closed area of the forest reservations. You could speak to anybody . . .'

'To political prisoners?' Daniel could not help himself. It slipped out.

'Political prisoners?' Harrison repeated. 'What the hell would you want to speak to politicals for? This will be a documentary on the environment and the development of a backward society.'

'Just suppose I did want to talk to political detainees,' Daniel insisted.

'Look here, young man. Taffari is a progressive leader, one of the few honest and committed leaders on the continent. I don't think he is holding any political prisoners. It isn't his style.'

'What happened to Omeru?' Daniel asked, leaning forward intently, and Harrison laid the duelling pistol on the blotter in front of him. Its barrels were pointing at Daniel's chest.

'Do I detect hostility towards the Ubomo government?' he asked softly. 'Towards my proposition?'

'No,' Daniel denied it. 'I just have to know what I'm getting myself into. I'm a businessman, like you, Tug. I want the hard

'That sounds to me like two thousand a week,' she said sweetly.

'Dollars?'

'This isn't New York, brother Dan. It's London. Pounds.'

'That's stiff. I don't get anywhere near that myself,' he protested.

'No, but you probably get twenty per cent of the gross, whereas I will have to be content with a lousy five per cent.'

'Five per cent of the gross on top of two thousand a week.' Daniel looked horrified. 'You have to be joking.'

'If I were joking, I'd be smiling, wouldn't I?'

'I've never given a cut to a cameraman – forgive me, a camera person before.'

'Once you get used to the idea, you won't find it unbearably painful.'

'I tell you what, let's call it twelve hundred a week, and forget about any percentage.'

'The acoustics are terrible in here. I can't believe what I thought I just heard. I mean, you wouldn't want to insult me, would you, Danny boy?'

'Would you do me a favour, Miss Mahon? Would you do up the top button of your shirt while we talk?'

The upper part of her chest was freckled like her face. It showed in the deep V of her open neck, but below a clear line where the sun had not stained it, her skin was as white as buttermilk. Under the thin cotton shirt her breasts, unfettered by any brassière, were tight and firm.

She glanced down into her deep cleavage. 'Is there something wrong with them?' She grinned slyly.

'No. Nothing at all. That's what I'm complaining about.'

She closed the button. 'Did I hear you say seventeen-fifty and four per cent?' she asked.

'You are right. There is something wrong with the acoustics,' he agreed. 'I said fifteen hundred and one and a half per cent.'

'Two per cent,' she wheedled him, and when he sighed and agreed, she added craftily, 'And a hundred a day location allowance.'

It took them almost three hours to hammer out the terms of her employment and at the end he found his liking for her tempered by respect. She was a hard lassie.

'Do we need a letter of intent?' he asked. 'Or will a handshake do?'

'A handshake will do fine,' she answered. 'As long as I have a letter of intent to back it up.'

He went through to his office and tapped out a draft of their agreement on his word-processor, and called her through to check the text on the screen. She stood behind him and leaned over his shoulder to read it. One of her breasts pressed taut and weightily on his shoulder. It was warm as a tsama melon that had lain in the desert under the Kalahari sun.

'You didn't put in the bit about first-class air tickets,' she pointed out. 'And the salary to commence from date of signature.'

The smell of her skin that he had noticed on their first meeting was more pronounced. He inhaled it with pleasure. It reminded him forcefully that he had been celibate for almost a year.

'Good boy,' she complimented him as he made the alterations she requested. 'That will do very nicely indeed.' The timbre of her voice had altered, it was softer and more resonant. There was also a subtle change in the odour of her body as well. He recognised the heady musk of female arousal; she was pumping the air full of pheromones which put his own hormones on red alert.

He was having difficulty concentrating as he ran off four copies of the agreement, one for each of them and another each for Elna and BOSS's legal department.

Bonny reached over him to sign all four copies, and now she pressed herself against his back and her breath was hot on his cheek. She handed the pen to him and he signed below her.

'Handshake?' he asked, and offered his open right hand. She ignored it, and instead reached over his shoulder and unbuttoned his shirt. She ran her hand down inside it.

'I can think of something more binding than a plain little old handshake,' she whispered, and pinched his nipple between her fingernails. He gasped; it was more pleasure than pain.

'Danny boy, you and I are going to be alone in the jungle for six months or so. I'm a girl of healthy appetites. It's going to happen sooner or later. It might as well be sooner. It would be hell if we waited until we got out there and then found that we didn't like it. Don't you agree?'

'Your logic is irrefutable,' he laughed, but it was shaky and rough. She took a pinch of his chest curls and used it as a goad to force him to his feet.

'Where's the bedroom? We might as well be comfortable.'

'Follow me.' He took her by the hand and led her to the door.

Standing in the centre of the bedroom floor she stepped back when he tried to embrace her. 'No,' she said. 'Don't touch me. Not yet. I want to draw it out until it's unbearable.'

She stood facing him, an arm's length between them. 'Do what I do,' she ordered, and began to unbutton her shirt.

Her nipples were tiny, like miniature rosebuds, carved from pale pink coral.

'You're as hairy and muscular as a grizzly bear. It gives me goose bumps,' she said, and he saw her nipples rise into rosy points. The colour darkened and the skin surrounding them puckered. His own flesh responded even more dramatically, and she stared at him shamelessly and chuckled as she unbuckled her own belt.

Her jeans were tight and she wriggled and squirmed to get them down.

'Exodus,' he said, 'chapter three.'

'That's not original.' She glanced down at herself complacently. 'I've had the quotation applied to myself before, the burning bush.' She combed her fingernails lingeringly through the thick mop of flaming curls at the base of her flat white belly. It was so crisp and dense that it rustled. It was one of the most excruciatingly erotic gestures he had ever watched.

'Come on,' she encouraged him. 'You're falling behind.'

He dropped his own trousers around his ankles.

'Who have we here?' She studied him frankly. 'Standing to attention and positively aching to sacrifice himself in the burning bush?' And she reached out to capture him expertly. 'Come along, my little mannikin,' she murmured throatily, grinning that sly tomboy grin and led him to bed.

BOSS's head office was at Blackfriars in the City, just opposite the pub that stood on the site of the old monastery that gave the area its name.

Daniel and Bonny came out of the main entrance of the tube station and paused to stare at the building.

'Shit!' said Bonny sweetly. 'It's imperial Roman rococo, with just a touch of Barnum and Bailey.'

BOSS House made the Unilever building down the street look insubstantial. For each of Unilever's Greek columns it had four, for each of Unilever's statues of the Olympian gods, it had a dozen. Where Unilever had used granite, BOSS had built in marble.

'If I'd seen this first I'd have held out for five thousand a week.' Bonny squeezed his arm. 'I think I've been done in more ways than one.'

They climbed the steps to the main entrance, while the statues of the gods frowned down at them from the pediment, and went in through the revolving glass doors. The floor of the entrance lobby was in a chessboard pattern of black and white marble. The roof was vaulted and gilded, with panels in the rococo style depicting either the Last Judgement or the Ten Commandments. It wasn't easy to tell which, but there was a great deal of action in progress between the nymphs and cherubs and seraphim.

'Bless us, Father, for we have sinned.' Bonny rolled her eyes at the ceiling cheerfully.

'Yes, but wasn't it fun!' Daniel murmured.

The senior public relations officer was waiting for them at the reception counter. He wore a dark three-piece suit and projected the BOSS image of the young executive.

'Hello, I'm Pickering,' he greeted them. 'You must be Doctor Armstrong and Miss Mahon.' He took Bonny's hand and eyed her quickly from the top of her flaming coiffure to her cowboy boots, clearly torn between disapproval of her denims and beaded leather waistcoat and hearty approval of her bosom. 'I'm supposed to set up a Ubomo briefing for you.'

'Fine. Let's get on with it then.' Daniel managed to divert his attention from Bonny's cleavage, and Pickering led them up the sweeping opera house staircase, giving them his tourist-guide patter as they went.

He pointed out the mirrored panels. 'French, of course, from Versailles after the Revolution. And those two are Gains-boroughs; the tapestry is Aubusson; that's a Constable . . .'

They left behind them the splendours of the public rooms and plunged into labyrinthine corridors in the upper rear of the building, passing scores of tiny offices divided by prefabricated partitions in which the BOSS battalions laboured under the humming air-conditioning units. Very few people raised their heads as the three of them passed.

'Cattle.' Bonny nudged Daniel. 'How can they stand life in this abattoir of the spirit?'

Eventually Pickering ushered them into a conference room. Clearly it was the venue of the lower and middle-ranking executives. The floors were covered with industrial stud-rubber tiles and the partition walls displayed charts of the company's administrative organisation and departmental structures. The furniture was laminate and chrome, with plastic upholstery.

Daniel smiled as he imagined how this room would probably contrast with the magnificence of the main boardroom that must be situated somewhere in the front of the building, close to Tug Harrison's personal office.

There were four men waiting for them, clustered around the table of snacks and refreshments in the corner. Pickering introduced them.

'This is George Anderson, one of our senior geologists; he is in charge of the Ubomo mineral developments. This is his assistant Jeff Aitkens. And this is Sidney Green who co-ordinates the timber and fishing concessions in Ubomo, and this is Neville Lawrence from our legal section. He will also be able to answer any questions you may have on the financial projections. Now, may I offer you a sherry?'

Bonny Mahon's presence did more than the cheap sherry to relax the atmosphere.

Pickering allowed them ten minutes, then he shepherded them to their plastic-covered chairs at the imitation-walnut-veneered conference table.

'Well, now. I'm not going to stand too much on ceremony here. This is *en famille*. My instructions are that this is to be a totally frank and open briefing. You must feel free, Doctor Armstrong, to ask whatever questions occur to you, and we will try our best to answer them. First of all just let me say how delighted and excited we are that BOSS is to be associated with this enormous project to uplift the Ubomo economy and to develop the rich natural resources of that beautiful little country for the good of all its citizens.' He allowed himself a sanctimonious smirk and then adopted a more businesslike tone. 'BOSS's concessions fall into four categories. Firstly, there are the mining and mineral deposits. Secondly, the timber and agricultural developments. Thirdly, the fishing and aquaculture projects, and lastly, the hotel, casino and tourist industry. We hope that the development of all these resources will eventually lead to Ubomo becoming one of the most prosperous little countries on the African continent. Before I ask our experts to discuss the economic potential of Ubomo in detail, I'm going to give you some background figures and facts. Let's put the map of Ubomo up on the screen.'

Pickering turned to the console of the audio-visual equipment and adjusted the overhead lighting.

'All right. Here we go.' The map of Ubomo appeared on the screen on the end wall. 'The People's Democratic Republic of Ubomo,' he intoned, 'is situated between Lakes Albert and Edward on the escarpment of the Great Rift Valley in eastern central Africa. It is bounded on the west by Zaïre, the former Belgian Congo, and on the east by Uganda . . .' Pickering pointed out the boundaries and the main features. 'The capital, Kahali, lies on the lakeshore below the foothills of the Ruwenzori range or, as they are more romantically known, the Mountains of the Moon. The first European explorer to chronicle the existence of these mountains was Captain John Hanning Speke who travelled in this area in 1862.'

Pickering changed the display on the screen. 'The total population of Ubomo is estimated at four million, although there has never been a census. You can see the breakdown into tribes. The largest tribe is the Uhali. However, the new President Taffari and most of his military council are Hita. In all a total of eleven tribal groups are represented in Ubomo, the smallest of which is the Bambuti, commonly known as the pygmies. About twenty-five thousand of these diminutive people live in the northern equatorial rain forests of the country. This is where BOSS's major mineral concessions are situated.'

Pickering was good at his job. He had assembled his information carefully and presented it in a lively and interesting fashion. However, there was very little he had to tell them that Daniel did not already know.

Bonny asked a few questions and Pickering addressed his replies to her bosom. Daniel found that Pickering's inability to take his eyes off those protuberances was beginning to irritate him. Daniel had conceived a proprietary interest of his own in this area.

After Pickering, the other company experts rose in succession to elaborate on BOSS's plans. Sidney Green showed them architect's impressions of the resorts and casinos that they would build upon the lakeshore. 'We anticipate the main tourist trade would come from southern Europe, particularly Italy and France. Flying time from Rome under eight hours. We are looking at an eventual half-million visitors a year. Apart from tourism we are planning a major aquaculture industry ...'

He went on to explain how the lake waters would be pumped into shallow dams in which freshwater shrimp and other exotic aquatic life would be cultured.

'We are aiming for an eventual annual harvest of a million tons of dried protein from aquaculture, together with another million tons of dried and frozen fish from the lakes themselves. We are considering the possibility of introducing high-yield fish populations to the lakes to augment the indigenous species.'

'What about the effect of these enterprises on the ecology of the lake itself?' Daniel asked diffidently. 'Particularly the construction of the marinas and yacht harbours and the introduction of exotic species such as carp and Asian shrimp to the lake waters.'

Green smiled like a second-hand car salesman. 'These are at present being fully investigated by a team of experts. We expect their report to be ready by the middle of the year. However, we do not anticipate any problems in that area.'

Quite right, Daniel thought. They aren't going to make waves if my new and good friend Tug is hiring and firing.

Sidney Green swept forward, still smiling, to discuss the agricultural potential.

'In the low-lying wooded savannah that covers the eastern half of the country the tsetse fly, *glossina morsitans*, closes a great deal of prime country to cattle-ranching. At the earliest opportunity we, in co-operation with the Ubomo government, will undertake a programme of aerial spraying to eradicate this insect menace. Once this is done, beef production will be of great importance to the economy.'

'Aerial spraying?' Daniel asked. 'What chemicals will be used?'

'I am pleased to say that BOSS has acquired several thousand tons of Selfrin at most favourable prices.'

'Would the favourable price have anything to do with the fact that Selfrin has been banned in the continental United States and in the European Common Market countries?'

'I assure you, Doctor Armstrong,' Green smiled blandly, 'that the use of Selfrin has not been banned in Ubomo.'

'Oh, that's good.' Daniel nodded, and returned his smile. He had smelled Selfrin in the Okavango swamps and the Zambezi valley. He had seen the devastation of entire insect species and the birds and small mammals that fed upon them. 'As long as it's legal, nobody can have any objection, can they?'

'Quite so, Doctor Armstrong.' Sidney Green changed the display on the lecture screen. 'Those areas of the savannah that are unsuitable for cattle-breeding will be planted with cotton and sugar cane. Irrigation water will be pumped from the lakes. The swamps and wetlands in the north will be drained – but these, of course, are long-term projects. Our immediate cash flow will be assured by logging operations in the timber-rich forests of the western mountain range.'

'The "Tall Trees",' Daniel murmured.

'I beg your pardon?'

'No, nothing of importance. Please continue. I'm finding this fascinating.'

'Of course, the logging operation will be carried out in concert with the mining operations. Neither project on its own would be profitable, but carried out in unison each becomes highly lucrative. In fact the timber will cover the direct cost of the development and the mineral recovery will be almost entirely profit. However, I will leave George Anderson, our senior geologist, to explain all this to you.'

Anderson's expression was as stony as one of his geological samples. His style was terse and dry.

'The only viable mineral deposits so far discovered in Ubomo lie in the north-western quadrant, below the forests that cover the lower northern slopes of the mountain range and lie within the basin of the Ubomo River.' He moved the cursor on the map display in a slow northern sweep. 'This forest cover consists of almost fifty varieties of economically significant trees, amongst which are the African oak, the African mahogany, the African walnut, the red cedar and the silk-cotton tree. I will not weary you with their botanical names, but suffice it to say that their existence holds out major economic advantages, as my colleague has pointed out.' He nodded wearily at Green, who flashed his bright salesman smile in return.

'The forest soils are for the most part leached laterites, the colour of which gives the Ubomo River its name, the Red River, and indeed the country itself, the Land of Red Earth. Fortunately, these soils are very thin, generally less than fifty feet in depth, and below them lies a folded pre-Cambrian formation.' He gave a dry and weary little smile. 'Again, I will not tax you with the technicalities, but these soils contain significant quantities of the rare earth, monazite, together with viable deposits of platinum almost evenly distributed in the upper levels. This series is unique. There is no other known formation that comprises this particular spectrum of minerals. Each of these individual minerals occurs in low concentrates, in some cases they are mere traces. Separately none of these would be workable, but taken together they will be highly lucrative, and their profitability will be enhanced by the valuable stands of timber harvested in the process of exposing the ore body.'

'Excuse me, Mr Anderson,' Daniel interrupted. 'Are you considering strip-mining the Ubomo river basin?'

George Anderson looked as though he had experienced a sudden stomach cramp.

'Doctor Armstrong, the term "strip-mining" is an emotionally charged one, filled with negative undertones. BOSS has never undertaken strip-mining operations anywhere in the world. I must be very firm on that issue.'

'I beg your pardon, I thought that the company's copper mines at Quantra in Chile were strip-mines.'

Anderson looked affronted. 'Open-cast mines, Doctor Armstrong, not strip-mines.'

'Is there a difference?'

'Of course there is. However, I think that this is neither the time nor the place to examine those differences. Just let me say that the open-cast mines that we intend developing in Ubomo will take full account of the sensitive environment of the area. We will operate on a refill-and-renew policy. BOSS has a green approach to nature. In fact, Doctor Armstrong, we are convinced that in the long term the environment will be significantly improved by what we are going to do for the country.'

He looked at Daniel challengingly, and Daniel almost rose to accept it. Then with an effort he forced himself to smile and nod. 'You must excuse me playing the devil's advocate, Mr Anderson. These are the kind of questions people will ask, and I must be able to answer them. That's what BOSS is paying me for.'

Anderson looked mollified. 'Yes, of course. However, I must reiterate. BOSS is a green company. It's Sir Peter's firm policy. I know he is even considering altering the company logo. As you know the present design is a miner's pickaxe and a ploughshare. Well, he intends adding a green tree, to show our concern for nature.'

'I think that's very tasteful.' Daniel smiled placatingly. He knew that this discussion would be reported to Tug Harrison – there was even a likelihood that at this moment it was being recorded. If he displayed open hostility and opposition to the company, his free ticket to Ubomo and his contact with the Lucky Dragon and Ning Cheng Gong would evaporate. 'With the assurances that you gentlemen have given me, I will be able to go to Ubomo with a clear conscience and I will endeavour to show the world the enormous benefits that will accrue to the country from the intensive development that the BOSS consortium is undertaking.'

He spoke for the benefit of the hidden microphones, and then paused for emphasis. 'Now, what I want from you is an architectural mock-up of the hotel and casino development on the lakeshore. I'd like to film the area as it is today, and then superimpose the concept over it, to bring out the best features of the design and how it blends into the natural background.'

'Sidney Green will take care of that, I'm sure.' Pickering nodded.

'Right, then I want details of the present per capita income of the average Ubomo citizen, and an estimate of what that income will be in, say, five or ten years' time, after the full benefits of the development programme begin to make themselves felt.'

'You'll see to that, won't you, Neville?'

The meeting ran on for another half hour before Daniel summed up with a note of finality. 'As a film-maker, I have to have a theme for this production. The general concept of Africa these days is one of a continent in trauma, plagued by seemingly insurmountable problems, demographic, economic and political. I want to strike a different note here. I want to show the world how it could be, how it should be. I see the theme of my production as . . .' He paused for dramatic effect, and then held up his hand to frame an imaginary screen. '"Ubomo, High Road to the African Future".'

The men at the table burst into spontaneous applause, and Pickering refilled the sherry-glasses.

As he escorted Daniel and Bonny back to the front of the building Pickering told them jovially, 'I say, that went rather well. I think you both made a very good impression.' He beamed like an approving schoolmaster. 'And now a little treat in store for you. Sir Peter Harrison, himself . . .' his voice took on a reverential tone, as though he had mentioned the name of a deity, 'Sir Peter in person has expressed the wish to have a word with you and Miss Mahon.'

He did not wait for their agreement but led them to the elevators.

They waited a mere five minutes in the antechamber to Tug Harrison's office, barely long enough to appreciate the priceless works of art displayed on the walls and in the glass-fronted cabinets. Then one of three comely secretaries looked up and smiled.

'Please follow me. Sir Peter is expecting you.'

As she led them towards the door at the far end of the antechamber, Pickering dropped away. 'I'll be waiting for you outside. Don't stay more than three minutes. Sir Peter is a busy man.'

The tall windows of Harrison's office looked out across the Thames to the National Theatre. As he turned from the window, the sunlight flashed off his bald head like a heliograph.

'Danny,' he said, offering his gnarled right hand. 'Have they looked after you?'

'Couldn't be better,' Daniel assured him. 'On the strength of what they've told me, I have come up with a theme for the production, "Ubomo, High Road to the African Future".'

'I like it!' said Tug Harrison without hesitation, but he was studying Bonny Mahon as he said it. The approbation could have been as much for her as for Daniel's title.

Exactly three minutes after they had entered the inner sanctum of BOSS, Tug Harrison drew back the cuff of his Turnbull and Asser shirt. Both his cuff-links and his wristwatch were of gold and diamonds.

'It was good to see you, Danny. Very pleasant meeting you, Miss Mahon, and now, if you'll excuse me . . .'

At the front doors of the BOSS building, Pickering had a taxi waiting for them.

'It's on the company account,' he said, shaking hands and giving Bonny's bosom a wistful farewell appraisal. 'It will take you wherever you want to go.'

'Caviar Kaspia,' Daniel told the driver recklessly, and when they were seated at a window table in the discreetly panelled front room of the lovely little restaurant, Bonny whispered, 'Who is paying?'

'BOSS,' he assured her.

'In that case I'll have 250 grams of the Beluga, with hot blinis and cream.'

'Spot on,' Daniel agreed. 'I'll join you and we'll split a bottle of bubbly. What do you fancy, Pol Roger, or the Widow?'

'What I truly fancy can wait until after lunch when we get

246

back to your flat, but in the meantime a glass of the Widow will help to pass the time – and build up your strength.' She slanted her eyes lewdly. 'You are going to need it. That's a direct threat.'

Bonny tucked into the caviar with the relish and appetite of a schoolboy at half-term.

'So what did you think of BOSS?' Daniel asked.

'I think Tug Harrison is one very sexy man. The smell of serious money and power is a stronger aphrodisiac than caviar and champagne.' She grinned at him with sour cream rimming the fine coppery down on her upper lip. 'Does that make you jealous? If it doesn't, it was meant to.'

'I am devastated. But apart from Harrison's sex appeal, what did you think of BOSS's plans for Ubomo?'

'Mind-boggling!' she enthused through a half-chewed blini. It was an expression that particularly irritated Daniel. 'Awesome!' That was even worse. 'If only you paid me enough to enable me to buy a block of BOSS shares! Someone is going to make a bagful of tom in Ubomo.'

'That's all there is to it?' Daniel smiled to make a joke of it. Yet was this the girl who had conjured up that hauntingly evocative sequence of caribou in the Arctic sunlight? 'A bagful of tom? Is that it?'

For a moment she looked mystified by the question, and then she dismissed it light-heartedly. 'Of course. What else is there, lover?' She mopped up the last grains of the Beluga with a scrap of blini pancake. 'Do you think that your newly acquired expense account could run to another pot of fish eggs? Not often a poor working girl gets a shot at them.'

Bonny Mahon was nervous. It was an unfamiliar sensation. The skirt and stockings felt just as unfamiliar. She was accustomed to the firmer embrace of denim. However, the occasion was sufficiently unusual to call for a change of her customary attire. She had even gone to the extraordinary lengths of visiting a hairdressing salon. Usually she managed or, she grinned at the thought, mismanaged her own hairstyle. She had to admit that the girl at Michaeljohn had done a better job.

She considered her reflection in one of the gilt-framed antique mirrors opposite where she sat in the lobby of the Ritz Hotel in Piccadilly.

'Not bad,' she admitted. 'I could pass for a lady at a hundred paces.' She preened her new curls which were fashionably anointed with gel. It was an uncharacteristic gesture, a symptom of the nervous anticipation with which she regarded the coming meeting.

The female secretary who had arranged the meeting over the telephone had suggested that the car pick her up at her lodgings. Bonny had shied away from the idea. She didn't want anybody to see her digs; she was economising and the area of south London where she presently resided was hardly salubrious.

The Ritz was the first alternative rendezvous that came to mind. It was more the image that she wished to project. Even though his secretary had arranged the date she had high hopes for what would come out of it.

'I mean, it just has to be a proposition, doesn't it?' she reassured herself. 'There was no doubt about the way he looked at me. I've never been wrong about that before. He's got a head of steam for me.'

She glanced at her wristwatch. It was exactly seven-thirty. He was the type who would make a point of being punctual, she thought, and when she looked expectantly towards the main doors a page was already coming towards her. She had taken the precaution of tipping the doorman and telling him where to find her.

'Your car has arrived, madam,' the page informed her.

A Rolls-Royce stood at the kerb. It was an iridescent pearly grey and the windows were smoked and opaque, giving the magnificent vehicle a surrealistic appearance.

The handsome young chauffeur, who wore a dove-grey uniform and cap with a patent-leather brim, greeted her as she came down the steps.

'Miss Mahon? Good evening.'

He opened the rear passenger door and stood aside for her.

Bonny settled into the sensual embrace of the soft grey Connolly leather.

'Good evening, my dear,' Tug Harrison greeted her in that dark-molasses voice that sent a shiver of unease and anticipation up her spine.

The chauffeur closed the door behind her, and sealed her in a cocoon of wealth and privilege. She inhaled the rich expensive smell of leather and cigar-smoke and some marvellous after-shave, the aroma of power.

'Good evening, Sir Peter. It was so good of you to invite me,' she said, and bit her own lip in anger. It sounded wrong, too gushing and subservient. She had planned to be cool and unimpressed by his condescension.

'Chez Nico,' Tug Harrison told the chauffeur, and then touched the button on the arm-rest that operated the sound-proof glass division between the driver and passenger seats.

'You don't mind my cigar, I hope?' he asked Bonny.

'No. I enjoy the smell of a good cigar. It's a Davidoff, isn't it?' It wasn't a guess. She had noticed the discarded band tucked into the ashtray. She had an eye for detail; it was the secret of her success as a photographer.

'Ah!' Tug Harrison acknowledged. 'A connoisseur.' He seemed amused. She hoped he had not noticed her little cheat, and she changed the subject quickly.

'I've never been to Chez Nico. Mind you, that's not surpris-ing. Even if I could get a reservation, I'd never be able to meet the bill. They say you have to book weeks in advance. Is that true?'

'Some people might have to.' Tug Harrison smiled again. 'I really don't know. I'll ask my secretary; she makes my arrange-ments.'

God, it was all going wrong. Every time she said anything, it came out sounding callow and gave him reason to despise her. For the remainder of the short journey she let him do the talking, yet despite her poor start to the evening, Bonny's imagination was running riot. If only she played her cards correctly from now on, this could be her future – Rolls-Royce and dinner at Nico's, a charge account at Harrods and Harvey Nichols and a flat in Mayfair or Kensington, holidays in

Acapulco and Sydney and Cannes and a sable coat. Pleasures and riches without end. 'This could be the big casino. Just cool it, girl.'

She had spent most of the afternoon tucked up in bed with Danny, but that seemed like a hundred years ago in another half-forgotten land. Now there was Sir Peter Harrison and a new world of promise.

The restaurant surprised her. She had expected a pompous dimly lit atmosphere, and instead it was gay and the lighting was cheerful. The lovely stained-glass ceiling was in green garden colours and captured a mood of *art nouveau*. Her own mood expanded and lightened in sympathy.

As they were ushered to the special table in the elbow of the L-shaped room, the conversation at the other tables faltered and all heads revolved to follow them and then came back close together to whisper his name and barter the latest gossip about him. Tug Harrison was the stuff of legend. It felt good to be at his side and savour the envious glances of other women.

Bonny knew just how striking were her tall athletic body and her flaming hair. She knew everyone would be jumping to conclusions about her status in Sir Peter's life.

'Please God, just let it come true. I'd better remember to take it easy on the wine. Perrier and a quick wit, those are the watch-words for this evening.'

It was easier than she expected. Tug Harrison was urbane and attentive. He made her feel pampered and very special by directing all his attention and charm upon her.

Nico Ladenis came up from his kitchen, especially to speak to Tug Harrison. With his dark satanic good looks Nico had a fearsome reputation. If he served the best food in England, he expected it to be treated with respect. If you ordered a gin and tonic to ruin your palate at the beginning of one of his celestial repasts you had to expect his wrath and contempt. Tug Harrison ordered a chilled La Ina for himself and a Dubonnet for Bonny. Then he and Nico discussed the menu with the same serious attention that Tug would give to BOSS's quarterly report.

When Nico left, sending one of his underlings to take their order, Tug turned to Bonny to ask what she had chosen, but she feigned a girlish confusion. 'Oh, it all sounds so gorgeous that I can't possibly make up my mind. Won't you order for me, Sir Peter?'

He smiled and she sensed that she was on the right track at last. She was getting the feel of the relationship, her intuition working up to cruise speed. Clearly, he liked to be in charge of any situation, even to choosing the meal.

She went very gently on the Chevalier-Montrachet that he ordered to complement her salmon. She encouraged him to relate the adventures of his young days in Africa. It was not difficult to show intense interest in his conversation, for he was a fine raconteur. His voice was like the caress of velvet gloves, and it didn't matter that he was old and that his skin was wrinkled and bagged and foxed by the tropical sun. Recently she had read somewhere, perhaps in the *Sunday Times Magazine*, that his personal fortune was over three hundred million pounds. At that price, what were a few wrinkles and scars?

'Well, my dear.' At last Tug dabbed his leathery lips with the folded table-napkin. 'May I suggest that we take coffee at Holland Park. There are a few small matters that I would like to discuss with you.'

Modestly she hesitated a moment. Could she afford to make herself too readily available? Shouldn't she play just a little hard to get? Should she hold out until the second time of asking? But what if there were no second time? She quailed at the thought.

Go for it now, honeychild, she counselled herself, and smiled at him. 'Thank you, Sir Peter. I'd love that.'

She was awed by the splendour of the Holland Park house. It was hard not to rubberneck like a tourist as he led her up to his study and settled her into a deep leather armchair. It was a masculine room with a set of rhinoceros horns on the panelled wall. She noticed the two paintings and shivered as she recognised their value.

'Are you cold, my dear?' He was solicitous and motioned the black servant in flowing white kanza to close the window. Sir Peter brought the coffee cup to her with his own hands.

'Kenya Blue,' he told her. 'Specially picked from my private plantation on the slopes of Mount Kenya.'

He dismissed the servant and lit a cigar.

'And now, my dear . . .' He blew a streamer of cigar smoke towards the ceiling. 'Tell me, are you sleeping with Daniel Armstrong?'

It was so unexpected, so brusque and alarming that she lost her equilibrium. Before she could prevent herself she flared at him, 'Just who the hell do you think you're talking to?'

He raised a beetling silver eyebrow at her. 'Ah, a temper to match the colour of your hair, I see. However, that's a fair question, and I'll answer straight. I think I am talking to Thelma Smith. That's the name on your birth certificate, isn't it? Father unknown. My information is that your mother died in 1975 of an overdose. Heroin, I believe. That was the period when a shipment of bad stuff got loose in the city.'

Bonny felt a cold nauseous sweat break out on her forehead. She stared at him.

'Like your mother's, your own career has been, shall we say, chequered. At the age of fourteen, a juvenile school of correction for shop-lifting and possession of marijuana. Then at eighteen, a nine-months' sentence for theft and prostitution. It seems you robbed one of your clients. While in women's gaol you developed your interest in photography. You served only three months of your sentence. Time off for good behaviour.' He smiled at her. 'Please correct me if I have got any of these facts wrong.'

Bonny felt herself shrinking down into the huge chair. She still felt sick and cold. She kept silent.

'You changed your name to the more glamorous version and got your first job in photography with Peterson Television in Canada. Dismissed in May 1981 for stealing and selling video equipment belonging to the company. They declined to press charges. Since then a clean record. Reformed, perhaps, or just getting a little more clever? Whichever is the case, it seems you are not burdened by too many moral qualms and that you'll do almost anything for money.'

'You bastard,' she hissed at him. 'You've been leading me on. I thought . . .'

'Yes, you thought that I was lusting after all that decidedly palatable flesh.' He shook his head with regret. 'I am an old man, my dear. As the flames burn lower, I find my appetite becomes more refined. With due respect for your obvious charms, I would class you as Beaujolais nouveau, a hearty young wine, tasty but lacking integrity or distinction. The wine for a younger palate, like Danny Armstrong's perhaps. At my age I prefer something like a Latour or a Margaux – older, smoother and with more class to it.'

'You old bastard! Now you insult me.'

'That was not my intention. I merely wanted us to understand each other. I want something other than your body. You want money. We can do a deal. It's a purely commercial arrangement. Now to return to my original question. Are you sleeping with Daniel Armstrong?'

'Yes,' she snarled at him. 'I'm screwing his arse off.'

'An expressive turn of phrase. I take it that no mawkish sentiments complicate this relationship? That is, not on your side at least?'

'There is only one person I love, and she's sitting right here in this room.'

'Total honesty,' he smiled. 'Better and better, especially as Danny Armstrong is not the type to treat it so lightly. You have a certain influence and leverage over him, so you and I can do business now. What would you say to twenty-five thousand pounds?'

The sum startled Bonny, but she screwed up her courage and followed her intuition. She dismissed the offer scornfully, 'I'd say "Up yours, mate!" I read somewhere that you paid ten times more than that for a horse.'

'Ah, but she was a thoroughbred filly of impeccable blood-lines. You wouldn't set yourself in that class, surely?' He held up his hands to forestall her furious response. 'Enough my dear; it was just a little joke, a poor one, I agree. Please forgive me. I want us to be business associates, not lovers, nor even friends.'

'Then before we talk about a price, you'd better explain what I have to do.' Her expression was bright and foxy. He felt the first vestiges of respect for her.

'It's very simple really . . .' And he told her what he wanted.

Daniel had spent every day that week at the Reading Room of the British Museum. This was invariably his practice before leaving on an assignment. In addition to books specifically on Ubomo, he asked the librarian for every publication that she could find on the Congo, the Rift Valley and its lakes, and the African equatorial forest.

He started with the books of Speke and Burton, Mungo Park and Alan Moorehead, re-reading them for the first time in years. He skipped through them rapidly, merely refreshing his mind on the half-forgotten descriptions of the nineteenth-century explorations of the region. He moved on to the more recent publications.

Amongst these he found Kelly Kinnear's book, *The People of the Tall Trees*, listed in the bibliography.

He called for a copy of her book and studied the author's photograph on the inside of the dust-jacket. She was rather pretty, with a strong and interesting face. The blurb did not give her birth date but it listed her honours and degrees. She was primarily a medical doctor, although she also had a Ph.D. in Anthropology from Bristol University. 'When not conducting research in the field, Doctor Kinnear shares a cottage in Cornwall with two dogs and a cat.' That was the only personal information that the blurb contained and Daniel returned to the photograph.

In the background of the photograph was a palisade formed by the trunks of large tropical trees. It seemed as though she stood in a forest clearing. She was bare-headed, dark hair pulled back from her face and twisted into a thick plait that had fallen forward over one shoulder and hung down her chest. She wore a man's shirt. It was difficult to tell what her figure was like, but she seemed slim and small-breasted. Her neck was long, with clean graceful lines, and her collar-bones formed a sculptured cup at the base of her throat.

Her head sat well on the column of her neck, strong square jaw and high cheekbones like an American Indian. Her nose was thin and rather bony and her mouth was determined, perhaps obstinate. Her eyes were probably her best feature, wide-set and almond-shaped, and she stared coolly at the camera. He judged that she had been in her early thirties when the photograph was taken, but there was no indication as to how old she was now.

'A handful,' Daniel decided. 'No wonder she has my friend Tug running scared. This is a lady who gets her own way.'

He flicked through to the first dozen pages of *People of the Tall Trees*, and read the introduction in which Kelly Kinnear explored the first references to the pygmies in the writings of antiquity.

This began with the report of the Egyptian leader Harkhuf to his child-Pharaoh Neferkare. Two thousand five hundred years before the birth of Christ, Harkhuf had led an expedition southwards to discover the source of the Nile river. In his field report, discovered four and a half thousand years later in Pharaoh's tomb, Harkhuf described how he had come to a mighty forest to the west of the Mountains of the Moon, and how in that dark and mysterious place he had encountered a tiny people who danced and sang to their god. Their god was the very forest itself and the description of their dancing and worship was so tantalising that Pharaoh despatched a messenger ordering Harkhuf to capture some of these tiny god dancers and bring them back to Memphis.

Thus the pygmies became familiar figures in ancient Egypt. Over the ages since then, many strange legends have grown up around these tiny forest people, and much that is fanciful and apocryphal has been written about them. Even their name was based on a misconception. 'Pugme' was a Greek unit of measurement, from elbow to knuckle, an imaginative estimate of their height by people who had never seen them.

Daniel had read all this before and he passed quickly to the more enjoyable portion of the book, the author's description of three years spent living with a pygmy clan in the depths of the equatorial forests of Ubomo.

Kinnear was a trained and professional anthropologist with a keenly observant eye for detail and the ability to marshal her meticulously garnered facts and extract from them reasoned conclusions, and yet she possessed the ear and heart of a storyteller. These were not dry scientific subjects she was describing but human beings, each with his own character and idiosyncrasies; here was a warm, loving and lovable people pictured against the awe-inspiring grandeur of the great forest, a merry people, wonderfully in tune with nature, expressing themselves with songs and dances and impish humour. At the end the reader was forced to share with the writer her obvious affection for and understanding of her subject, but even more, her deep concern for the forest in which they lived.

Daniel closed the book and sat for a while in the pleasant glow of well-being that it had inspired. Not for the first time he felt a desire to meet and talk to the woman who had created this small magic, but now at last he knew how and when to do so.

The annual general meeting of the shareholders of BOSS was set for a week before his departure for Ubomo, and Pickering in public relations arranged an invitation for Daniel and Bonny to attend.

The AGM was always held in the ballroom of BOSS's own magnificent headquarters in Blackfriars.

The AGM was always held on the last Friday of July and began at seven-thirty in the evening.

It ran for an hour and twenty-five minutes: ten minutes to read the previous minutes, an hour of sonorous prose from Sir Peter as he made his chairman's report and, finally, fifteen minutes of appreciation by the members of his board, capped by a vote of thanks and approbation, proposed by an individual planted in the body of the shareholders. The vote was always passed unanimously by a show of hands. That's the way it always went. It was company tradition.

Security at the door was very strict. The name of every person entering was checked against the current register of shareholders and special invitations were scrutinised by uniformed members of BOSS's security staff.

Sir Peter didn't want wild Irishmen or anti-Rushdie fundamentalists letting off bombs in the middle of his carefully rehearsed speech, nor did he want freelance journalists or trade unionists, or other free-loading riff-raff making pigs of themselves at the heavily laden buffet table and complimentary bar.

Daniel had mistimed their departure from the flat in Chelsea. They would have been at Blackfriars thirty minutes earlier but Bonny had, at the last minute, begun feeling very healthy. She had made a suggestion which Daniel, always the perfect gentleman, had been unable to refuse. Afterwards it had been necessary to take a shower together during which Bonny had started a water fight which had reduced the bathroom to a sodden shambles with water running out under the door into the passageway.

All this took time, and then they had battled to find a taxi. When they finally flagged one down in the King's Road they ran into traffic along the Embankment and only arrived at the BOSS building after Sir Peter was in full stride, mesmerising his audience with an account of BOSS's performance over the previous twelve months.

All seats were taken and the overflow crowded the back of the hall. They sneaked in, and Daniel shepherded Bonny into a corner near the bar, and pressed a large whisky and soda into her hand.

'That should hold you for half an hour,' he whispered. 'Just please don't start feeling healthy again until we get home.'

'Chicken.' She grinned at him. 'You can't take it, Armstrong.'

The shareholders around them frowned and shushed disapproval and they settled down contritely to an appreciation of Sir Peter 'Tug' Harrison's wit and erudition.

On the dais Sir Peter faced them from the centre of the long table with a microphone in front of him and the members of his board spread out on each side of him. Amongst them there was an Indian maharajah, an earl, an East European pretender and a number of run-of-the-mill baronets. All were names and titles that looked good on the company letter-head, but not a person in the room that evening had any illusion as to where the true power and might of BOSS lay.

Sir Peter stood with his left hand thrust into his jacket pocket, occasionally extending the forefinger of his right hand and pointing at his audience. As he made each point, he stabbed his forefinger like a pistol barrel at them, and even Daniel found himself flinching and blinking as though a shot had been fired at his head.

Everything Sir Peter had to tell them was good news, from the results of offshore oil drilling in the Pemba channel, to the cotton harvests and ground-nut crop of Zambia, and the increase in both pre-tax profits and declared dividends. The audience hummed with delight at each fresh revelation.

Sir Peter glanced at his watch. He had been running for fifty minutes – ten to go. It was time to move on to future plans and projections. He took a sip of water, and when he resumed, his voice was velvety and seductive.

'My lords, ladies and gentlemen, I have given you the bad news . . .' He paused for laughter and a volley of applause. 'Now let me move on to the good news. The good news is Ubomo, the People's Democratic Republic of Ubomo and your company's participation in a new era for that beautiful little country – the opportunity that we have, not only to provide employment but also prosperity for a sadly disadvantaged population of four million souls.' For nine minutes more he enthralled them with the promise of bright new profits and sky-rocketing dividends and then he ended, 'And so, ladies and gentlemen, what we see before us is Ubomo, the high road to the future of the African continent.'

'Hell!' Daniel whispered, his voice blanketed by the applause. 'That's a blatant case of plagiarism. The old bastard lifted it straight from me.'

When Sir Peter sat down the company secretary gave them two minutes to express their approval fully before he leaned over his microphone.

'My lords, ladies and gentlemen, I am now opening the meeting to the floor. Are there any shareholders' questions, please? Your chairman and board will endeavour to answer them to the best of their ability.'

His magnified voice was still reverberating through the hall when another voice cut in.

'I have a question for the chairman.' It was a feminine voice, clear, self-assured, and surprisingly loud – so loud that on the dais Sir Peter winced.

Up until then Daniel had been trying to identify Doctor Kinnear in the body of the crowded hall, but without success. She was either not present or she was obscured by the crush of other shareholders. He had given up the search.

Now there was no mistaking her. She was very much present, standing on her chair, three rows from the front. Daniel grinned with delight. The echoing volume of Kelly Kinnear's voice was explained. She had armed herself with an electronic bull-horn. How she had smuggled the device past the hawk-eyed security guards was a mystery, but now she was wielding it with telling effect.

So often at other meetings that Daniel had attended, the questions from the floor, no matter how pertinent or penetrating, had lost all their force simply because they were not audible to the bulk of the audience. 'What did he say?' and 'Speak up!' were the cries that greeted them, and the game was lost with the first delivery.

This was not happening to Kelly Kinnear. Perched high on her chair, in full view of the entire audience, she was lashing Sir Peter Harrison at a range of thirty paces in a ringing young voice.

She was smaller than Daniel had expected, but her neat little body was poised and graceful, almost birdlike, and there was a force and presence about her that transcended her physical size.

'Mr Chairman, BOSS has very recently included the image of a green tree in the company emblem. What I want to know is whether this is to enable you to cut it down?'

There was a stunned silence. Her sudden appearance had been greeted with amused and admiring smiles from most of the audience, the natural masculine reaction to a pretty girl, but now the smiles were replaced by puzzled expressions.

'For thirty years, Sir Peter,' Kelly Kinnear went on, 'ever since you have been chairman of BOSS, the slogan of the company has been "Dig it up!" "Chop it down!" or "Shoot it!"'

The puzzled expressions turned to frowns, shareholders exchanged worried glances.

'For many years BOSS employed professional hunters to massacre wild animals. The meat was used to feed the company's thousands of employees. The policy of cheap food was only discontinued relatively recently. That was the "shoot it" philosophy.'

The back of Kelly Kinnear's slim sun-tanned neck was flushing with her mounting anger. The thick dark braid of hair hanging down between her shoulder-blades twitched like the tail of a lioness.

'For thirty years, BOSS has been ripping the mineral riches from Africa's soil and leaving gaping craters and devastation in its wake. That's the "dig it up" mentality. For thirty years, BOSS has been slashing down the natural forests and putting the land to cotton and ground-nuts and other cash crops that drain the soil, that poison it with nitrate fertilisers, that contaminate the streams and rivers. That's the "chop it down" philosophy.'

Her whole body quivered with indignation, a phenomenon that intrigued Daniel.

'Those cash crops produce no food for the people who once lived upon the land. They are forced to trek away from the devastation that BOSS has created to live in the odious slums of Africa's sprawling new towns. These people are turned into outcasts by BOSS's greed.'

Sir Peter turned his head and raised an eyebrow at the company secretary. Obediently the secretary leapt to his feet.

'Will you please state your name, and put your question briefly and clearly?'

'My name is Doctor Kelly Kinnear, and I am putting my question. Will you just give me a chance?'

'That is not a question. You are haranguing . . .'

'Listen to me,' she ordered, and hopped around on the chair to face the ballroom filled with shareholders. 'For most of us, our personal welfare ranks far ahead of tropical forests and lakes in a faraway land. The princely dividends paid by BOSS are more important to us than exotic birds and unfamiliar animals and tribes of indigenous people. It's so easy to pay lip service to the environment as long as it doesn't affect our own pockets—'

'Order! Order, please!' bawled the company secretary. 'You are out of order, Doctor Kinnear. You are not asking a question.'

'All right,' Kelly rounded on him. 'I'll ask a question. Is the chairman of BOSS aware that while we sit here, the tropical rain forests of Ubomo are being destroyed?' She glared at him. 'Does the chairman realise that over fifty species of wildlife have become extinct in Ubomo as a direct result of the activities of BOSS?'

'Shame! Sit down!'

'The death of a species affects us directly. It will lead in the end to our own extinction, the death of man on earth.'

There was a hum of indignation and outrage from the shareholders. Sir Peter Harrison smiled and shook his head pityingly, making no attempt to respond to her attack. He knew where the loyalty of his shareholders lay.

'Sit down!' somebody shouted again. 'You silly bitch!'

'Doctor Kinnear,' the company secretary called, 'I must ask you to resume your seat at once. This is a deliberate attempt to disrupt our proceedings.'

'I accuse you, Mr Chairman,' Kelly pointed a quivering finger at Sir Peter, 'I accuse you of rape.'

There were shouts of protest, some of the other shareholders were on their feet.

'Shame!'

'The woman's a lunatic!'

One of them attempted to pull Kelly down off her chair, but it was obvious that she had surrounded herself with a small group of supporters of her own, half a dozen young men and women in casual dress, but with determined expressions. They closed up around her. One of the young men pushed her attackers away.

'Let her speak!'

'I accuse you of the rape of Ubomo. Already your bulldozers are ripping into the forests—'

'Get her out of here!'

'Doctor Kinnear, if you don't heed the chair I will have no alternative but to have you forcibly removed.'

'I'm a shareholder. I have every right—'

'Throw her out!'

There was confusion and uproar in the front of the hall, while on the dais Sir Peter Harrison looked bored and detached.

'Answer me!' Kelly yelled at him, surrounded by her struggling cohorts. 'Fifty species doomed to extinction so that you can drive around in your Rolls—'

'Ushers! Ushers!' yelped the company secretary, and from every corner of the room the uniformed security men leapt into the fray.

As one of them elbowed Daniel aside and charged forward, Daniel could not help himself. He thrust out his right foot, a cunning little ankle-tap that knocked one of the usher's large black boots across his own ankle. The man tripped himself and was hurled forward by his own momentum. He flew headlong into a row of chairs and, amidst loud cries of protest and outrage, knocked the occupants into a heap. Chairs crashed, and women screamed.

The press photographers loved it, and their flashes bloomed and lit the hall with a flickering like summer lightning.

'While you mouth your sanctimonious platitudes and put a little green tree on the BOSS emblem, your bulldozers are tearing the guts out of one of the most vulnerable and precious forests in the world.' Kelly Kinnear's amplified voice rose above the uproar. She was still on her chair, but swaying precariously in the storm that raged around her, a small heroic figure in the confusion.

'Those forests do not belong to you. They do not belong to the cruel military tyrant who has seized power in Ubomo and who is your accomplice in this atrocity. Those forests belong to the Bambuti pygmies, a tribe of gentle inoffensive people who have lived there since time immemorial. We, the friends of the earth, and all decent people everywhere say "keep your greedy hands off the—"'

Three of the BOSS ushers formed a scrimmage line; in their black uniforms they resembled a New Zealand front rank. They broke through her ring of defenders and reached up to drag Kelly Kinnear down from her perch.

'Leave me alone,' she yelled at them, and turned her bullhorn into an offensive weapon, raining blows upon them until the trumpet cracked and shattered and she was defenceless.

Between them they dragged her down off her perch and bore her, kicking and clawing and biting, from the hall. A kind of awed calm returned. Like the survivors of a bomb blast, the shareholders picked up the chairs and straightened their clothing and examined themselves for injuries.

On the dais Sir Peter rose unhurriedly to his feet and resumed his place at the microphone. 'Ladies and gentlemen, the floor show was unscheduled, I assure you. On behalf of BOSS and my board, I sincerely apologise for this outburst. If it served any useful purpose at all, it was as a graphic illustration of the difficulties we face when we try to improve the lot of our fellow men.'

Those who had been distracted gathered themselves and turned to listen to his rich dark seductive tones. After the shrill denunciations and accusations, it was a soothing balm.

'Doctor Kelly Kinnear is notorious for her intemperate views. She has declared a one-woman war on the government of President Taffari of Ubomo. She has, in fact, made as much of a nuisance of herself in that country as she did here tonight. You have seen her in action, ladies and gentlemen, so you will not be particularly surprised to hear that she was deported from Ubomo and formally declared an undesirable. The vendetta that she is waging is personal and spiteful. She sees herself as an injured party, and she is taking her revenge.'

He paused again, and shook his head.

'However, we must not make the mistake of believing that what we have witnessed tonight was the isolated act of some poor misguided soul. Unfortunately, ladies and gentlemen, in this crazy new world of ours we are surrounded by the loonies of the left. This lady, who has just left us . . .' They laughed uncertainly, beginning to recover from the effects of Kelly Kinnear's attempt at persuasion, 'this lady is one of those who prefers that tens of thousands of her fellow human beings suffer starvation and misery, rather than that a single tree be cut down, rather than that a single plough should run a furrow, rather than that a single animal should die.' He paused and scowled at them sternly, exerting the full force of his personality, reasserting his control that for a minute had been shaken by the small determined woman with the loud-hailer. 'This is a nonsense. Man has as much right to life as any other species on this planet. However, BOSS recognises its responsibility to the environment. We are a green company committed to the well-being of all creatures on this earth, men and animals and plants. Last year we spent over a hundred thousand pounds on environmental studies prior to proceeding with some of our enterprises. One hundred thousand pounds, ladies and gentlemen, is a great deal of money.' He paused for the applause from his audience. Daniel noted that he was careful not to compare this great deal of money to BOSS's taxable profits for the same period, profits of almost one billion pounds.

As the applause died away he continued. 'We spent that money, not to impress anybody, not as some grand public relations gesture, but in a genuine and sincere attempt to do the right thing by all the world. We know in our hearts that what we are doing is right and proper. So do you, who are the most important members of BOSS, the shareholders. Our conscience is clear, ladies and gentlemen! We can go forward with confidence and enthusiasm to keep our company what it has always been, one of the great forces for good in an otherwise sad and naughty world.'

The meeting overran its usual duration by almost twenty minutes, a great deal of extra time being devoted to a standing ovation for the chairman's impromptu speech.

For once the traditional vote of thanks was passed not by a show of hands, but by thunderous acclaim.

'Tug hammers loony Greens' was the headline in the tabloid press the following morning and the general consensus in the media was that it had been not so much a confrontation, as a massacre of the innocents.

There was no direct flight from Heathrow to Kahali in Ubomo. Although the airport had been renamed the Ephrem Taffari airport, and twenty-five million dollars had been loaned by the World Bank to extend the main runway to accommodate intercontinental jet aircraft and to refurbish the airport buildings, there had been a series of delays in the construction work due to the fact that much of the original loan capital seemed to have evaporated. Rumour in the streets of Kahali suggested that the missing funds had found a happy home in a numbered Swiss bank account. Another twenty-five million was needed to complete the project and the World Bank was demanding unreasonable assurances and guarantees before supplying it. In the meantime travellers were forced to travel to Ubomo via Nairobi.

Daniel and Bonny took the British Airways flight to Nairobi, and Daniel paid almost five hundred pounds in excess baggage charges for Bonny's video equipment. In Nairobi they were obliged to overnight at the Norfolk Hotel before they could catch the scheduled flight to Kahali on Air Ubomo which operated between the two capitals.

With a day to spare, Danny asked Bonny to shoot some background and filler footage. What he really wanted was the opportunity to watch her in action and to get used to working with her in the field. This was to be a dress rehearsal. He hired a combi with a cut-out roof and a Kikuyu driver. They drove out to the Nairobi National Park on the outskirts of the city.

The Park was another of Africa's surprises. Within a few miles of the Lord Delamere bar in the Norfolk Hotel, it was possible to witness wild lions making their kills. The boundary of the Park ran hard up against the Jomo Kenyatta Airport and the grazing herds of antelope did not even raise their heads as the great jet aircraft on final approach howled only a few hundred feet above them.

Daniel had filmed in the Park many times over the past few years. The Park warden was an old friend. They greeted each other in Swahili and shook hands with the double grip, palm then thumb, of brothers.

The warden delegated one of his senior rangers to escort and guide them, and gave Daniel *carte blanche* to go anywhere, even to disregard one of the strictest Park rules and leave the vehicle to film on foot.

The ranger led them to a stand of flat-topped acacia forest beside the river where a huge bull rhino was in ponderous courtship with a female in full oestrus. So absorbed were these antediluvian monsters with each other that Daniel and Bonny were able to leave the combi and creep up close.

Without making it obvious, Daniel was watching Bonny narrowly. The Sony video camera was a top-of-the-range model, sleek in design but heavy even for a man to carry. Daniel wanted to see how she handled it, and he made no offer to assist her. With a sharp warning in Swahili, he prevented the black ranger when he made an attempt to do so.

He had come to know Bonny's body in the most intimate way over the past weeks. He knew that there was no fat on her and that her limbs were clad in sleek hard muscle. She was in the prime physical condition of a trained athlete. In their playful wrestling contests he had been forced to extend his full strength to subdue her and get her to the bed when she challenged him outrageously to do so. She enjoyed her love-making with plenty of rough and tumble.

Still, he was surprised at the ease with which she lifted the camera and her lightness and agility on her feet even in the heat of the acacia forest and over the broken ground. The earth was studded with the spoor of rhino and buffalo that had been deeply trodden into the wet clay of the rainy season and was now baked hard as terracotta. It could turn an unwary ankle and the wait-a-bit thorns were viciously hooked to catch in flesh or cloth. Bonny avoided these snares with ease.

The bull rhino was displaying aggressively for the benefit of the female who had wandered into his territory and who he was now holding captive to his lust. Every time she attempted to reach the boundary of his territory he headed her off, snorting and blowing like a steam engine, raising gales of dust from under his high stamping feet.

The female swished her great grey backside from side to side in flirtatious refusal of his advances, affording him fleeting whiffs of her heady oestrus odours which drove him into further ecstasies of excitement. Every few minutes he rushed away to scent mark the borders of his territory and warn off any possible rivals who might be tempted to trespass on this ardent courtship.

As soon as he reached the boundary, he pointed his rump at one of the trees or shrubs which were his signposts, curled his tail up on to his back, unsheathed his massive pink penis from its scabbard of grey wrinkled skin and, aiming backwards

266

between his rear legs, released a cloud of urine with the force of a fire hose that almost flattened the target. Honour satisfied, he rushed back, grunting with passion to the bashful female, who immediately fled towards the furthest boundary of his domain with him in full pursuit.

At the best of times the rhino is afflicted with poor eyesight, but now these two were almost completely blinded by single-minded passion. Daniel and Bonny had to be alert and ready to run or dodge at any instant, for the rushes of the two inflamed creatures were wild and erratic. Unless they were quick on their feet, they could be trampled by those horny pads or gutted by a random thrust of one of the long polished nose horns.

It was hard dangerous work with death only an instant or a foot away, but Bonny showed no fear at all. Rather she seemed elated and excited by the danger. Her eyes shone and the sweat soaked her flaming hair and darkened the back of her shirt as they ran side by side through the forest or ducked behind one of the acacia trunks to avoid a sudden random rush by one of the animals.

Apart from her lack of fear, Bonny showed a physical stamina that impressed Daniel. He was unburdened by the equipment which she carried, and yet he was tiring in the heat and the dust while she seemed quite unaffected.

Suddenly the bull swirled without warning. Perhaps he had detected a breath of their body smell through the clouds of love perfume with which the female was filling his wide flaring nostrils. He charged straight at them and Daniel grabbed her arm.

'Freeze!' he whispered urgently, and they sank to their knees and froze into utter stillness.

From a distance of twenty feet the huge creature confronted them, blowing and huffing and snorting. His piggy eyes blood-shot with passion and fury, he peered myopically at them, waiting for some small movement that would convince him that they were neither a rock nor a bush, and thus worthy of the full weight of his jealous wrath.

Daniel tried to hold his breath, but his lungs were scalding from his exertions and he choked to breathe. Suddenly he was aware of a faint electric whirring sound close to his left ear, and he swivelled his eyes in their sockets without moving his head.

To his astonishment and incredulity, Bonny was still filming. The lens of the Sony was only feet from the rhino's nose. They could see right up his wide nostrils to the shiny wet pinkness of his nasal mucosa, and she was filming it. That impressed Daniel as nothing before had done.

I've got myself one hell of a camera jockey, he thought. Jock would have been on the next plane home by now.

Suddenly the rhino switched around, a movement so quick and agile that it seemed impossible in such a massive creature. Love had triumphed over aggression. He rushed back to his paramour, huffing and puffing with eagerness.

Bonny was laughing. Daniel could not believe what he was hearing. 'Come on!' She was on her feet again with a lithe bound.

By the time they caught up with the couple in a glade of pale grass beside the rocky watercourse, the cow had at last succumbed to the bull's persistent courtship. She allowed him to place his chin on her rump, and she stood quiescent and submissive under this significant caress.

'Get ready,' Daniel warned Bonny. 'It's going to happen at any moment.'

Suddenly the bull reared up over the female.

Bonny captured every titanic convulsion, every straining, thrusting drive of the enormous bodies. And then very swiftly it was over, and the bull dropped off the cow and stood heaving and blowing from the effort.

'You got it, and we've taken too many risks already,' Daniel whispered. 'Let's get out of here.'

He took her arm and drew her away. They retreated carefully, a pace at a time, watching the bull all the way.

A hundred yards from the two rhino, Daniel deemed them well out of harm's way and they set off towards the combi, still elated by the thrill and the danger, laughing and chatting, not bothering to look backwards, until Daniel snapped abruptly, 'Look out! He's coming again.'

The bull was charging straight at them, an ungainly gallop that did not swerve or deviate, glaring malevolently at them over the wickedly curved horn.

'I think he's got our wind.' Daniel grabbed Bonny's arm. He looked about them quickly. The nearest cover was a small thorn bush twenty paces ahead. 'Come on.' They ran for it together and crawled under the outstretched branches. The hooked thorns raked their shirts and exposed skin.

'He's still coming.' Bonny's voice was hoarse with dust and exertion.

'Get down. Keep still.' They crouched on the stony ground and watched in helpless horror as the rhino rushed straight at their hiding-place.

'This time, he's not going to stop.' For the first time Bonny showed signs of fear.

Four tons of prehistoric monster, horned and menacing, towered over them. It sniffed the thorn leaves that gave them such flimsy shelter and its breath rattled the branches and blew into their faces.

Then abruptly and unexpectedly, the bull switched around and presented them, at a range of only a few feet, with its fat rounded hindquarters. They stared in horror as its penis unsheathed from between its back legs.

'We are on his boundary,' Daniel breathed.

'He's going to mark this bush! Us!'

It pointed at them like a pink fire-hose.

'We're trapped,' Bonny wailed. The thorns hemmed them in. 'What can we do?'

'Just close your eyes, and think of England.'

A steaming cloud engulfed them, blowing over them with the force of a tropical hurricane, not a simple jet but a storm of scalding liquid that sent Daniel's bush hat flying from his head and soaked them both to the skin. The bull wriggled his tail with satisfaction, stamped his back feet and then charged away with the same impetuosity with which he had arrived.

Daniel and Bonny sat under the dripping thorn bush and stared at each other in horror. Their faces were running wet as though they had stood out in the monsoon rain and the odour was overpowering.

Daniel moved first. He wiped his face with the palm of his hand, a slow theatrical gesture beginning at the top of his forehead and ending at his chin. Then he inspected his hand.

'Now that . . .' he said in a sepulchral tone, 'really pisses me off!'

For a moment Bonny continued to stare at him, and then she let out a shriek of wild mirth and they fell against each other and laughed. Clinging together, sodden and stinking, they laughed until they couldn't stand up, and then they laughed some more. Rhino urine had lacquered their hair into sticky dreadlocks, and stained their clothing with interesting patterns.

They sneaked into the Norfolk Hotel through the rear entrance behind the kitchens and fled across the lawns to their cottage suite, where they stood under the shower for twenty minutes and, still giggling, shampooed and soaped each other until their bodies glowed.

Later, in a towelling bathrobe, Daniel sat in front of the television set while Bonny connected up her equipment.

He gave all his attention to the screen and, from the first minute, knew that he had made the right choice in hiring Bonny Mahon. Her technique was of superbly professional quality, and she had a fine eye and sense of timing. She knew when she needed to be close in and when to pull back, but more important, and infinitely rarer, she had a distinctive style, the style that he had first recognised in her Arctic film.

'You're good,' he told her when the screen went blank. 'You're damn good.'

'You don't know how good,' she grinned at him. 'I'm only just starting to get the feel of the light here. It's different, you know. Each place is different. Give me another week and I'll show you just how good I am.'

An hour later, dressed in clean clothing, they sauntered across the courtyard in the cool Kenyan dusk and stopped for a minute beside the aviary of wild birds in the centre of the lawn to admire the brilliant colours of the turacos and the gold-breasted starlings behind the wire. Other guests were also drifting in the direction of the grill room.

Daniel had paid no attention to the small figure standing near them, until she turned towards him and greeted him by name. 'Please forgive the intrusion. You are Daniel Armstrong, aren't you?'

Daniel started as he recognised her. 'Doctor Kinnear! The last time I saw you was at BOSS's annual general meeting.'

'Oh, were you there?' She laughed. 'I didn't notice you.'

'No, you did seem to have other things on your mind at the time.' Daniel smiled back at her. 'What happened to your bullhorn? Were you ever able to get it repaired?'

'Japanese rubbish,' Kelly Kinnear said. 'A couple of good shots to the head and it falls to pieces.'

She had a sense of humour of course – he knew that from her writing – but her eyes were even lovelier than the photograph on the dust-jacket had suggested. He liked her instantly. It must have been obvious, for Bonny pulled her hand out of his, and he felt a twinge of guilt.

'May I introduce you to my assistant, Bonny Mahon?'

'Actually, I'm a lighting cameraman, not an assistant,' Bonny corrected him tartly.

'Yes,' Kelly agreed. 'I know your work. You filmed "Arctic Dream". It was very good.' She had a disarmingly direct gaze and Bonny looked slightly abashed by the praise.

'Thank you. But I must warn you, I haven't read your book, Doctor Kinnear.'

'That puts you in a majority of several hundred million, Miss Mahon.' Kelly sensed the antagonism in the other woman but showed no sign of offence, and turned back to Daniel. 'I think I have seen every one of your productions over the years. In fact, you are responsible for me being in Africa at all. When I graduated I was going to Borneo to work with the Penan tribe. Then I saw one of your earlier series on the lakes of the Rift Valley. That changed my mind. After that I just had to come to Africa.' Kelly broke off and laughed softly with embarrassment. 'I know that this will sound terribly jejune, but I am a fan of yours. The truth is I've been hanging around here, just hoping to bump into you ever since I heard that you were in Nairobi. I just had to talk to you.'

'You aren't staying here at the Norfolk, then?' Daniel was feeling better disposed to her every minute. It is difficult to dislike someone who admits to being your fan.

'Good Lord, no.' Kelly laughed again with surprising gusto. She had perfect teeth, even her molars were free of fillings. 'I'm not a successful TV producer. I'm just a poor disadvantaged field researcher without a sponsor. The Smithsonian pulled my grant after I was slung out of Ubomo by Taffari.'

'Let me stand you a steak then,' Daniel offered.

'A steak! I salivate at the thought. I've been living on ground-nuts and dried lake-fish since I got back.'

'Yes, why don't you join us, Doctor Kinnear?' said Bonny in a voice of poisoned honey, placing emphasis on the plural pronoun.

'How sweet of you, Miss Mahon.' Kelly glanced at her coolly, and hostility flashed between them like a discharge of static electricity. Their method of communication was too esoteric for Daniel to appreciate, and he smiled amiably.

'Let's go and find some food,' he said, and led them towards the doors of the Ibis grill room that opened on to the court-yard.

'Are you going to film in Kenya?' Kelly asked. 'What are you doing in Nairobi, Doctor Armstrong?'

'Danny,' he invited her to drop the formalities. 'We are on our way to Ubomo, as a matter of fact.'

'Ubomo!' Kelly stopped dead and looked up at him. 'That's marvellous. It's a perfect subject for you, a microcosm of emerging Africa. You are one of the few people who could do it properly.'

'Your trust is flattering, but daunting.' Daniel smiled down at her. For a moment he had forgotten Bonny, until she squeezed his arm to remind him that she was there.

'I'll pay for my supper by telling you all I know about the country,' Kelly offered.

'Deal,' Daniel agreed, and they went into the mellow lighting and flowers and tinkling piano of the Ibis room.

As the two women studied the menu, Daniel surreptitiously compared one with the other.

The obvious difference between them was size. Bonny was almost six feet tall. Kelly was six inches shorter, and they were different in many other ways, from the colour of their hair and eyes to their skin tones. However, Daniel sensed that the differences extended far beyond physical characteristics.

Bonny was bold, direct and almost mannish in her attitude to life. Even from the earliest days of their relationship, Daniel had detected depths in her which he would rather leave unexplored. On the other hand Kelly Kinnear's manner seemed totally feminine, although he knew from her book that she was determined and fearless. It took a special kind of courage to live alone in the great forests with only the Bambuti for companions. He also knew from the book that she was intelligent and gentle, that her concern was for the spiritual rather than the material values of life, but in the ballroom at BOSS House he had witnessed a graphic demonstration of her contradictory, aggressive and warlike spirit.

Both women were attractive in totally different ways. Bonny was brazen, she hit you in the eye at fifty paces, a copper-headed Valkyrie. Kelly was shaded with delicate nuances. She was softer and more discreet, with facets that changed when viewed from different angles. In repose her face was almost plain, her nose and mouth austere, but when she smiled her entire face softened. As he had first noted from the photograph on the dust-jacket of her book, her eyes were her best feature. They were large and dark and expressive. They could glow with a merry impish light, or burn with a passionate sincerity and intelligence. And something else that the photograph didn't show, Daniel grinned to himself. Her boobs were miniature works of art.

Kelly looked up from the menu and caught the direction of his eyes. With a moue of disappointment, as though she had expected better of him, she moved the menu slightly to screen her bosom from his appraisal.

'When are you leaving for Ubomo?'

'We are flying in tomorrow,' Bonny answered for him, but Kelly did not acknowledge the interruption. She directed the next question at Daniel.

'Have you been in since the *coup*?'

'No, I was last there four years ago.'

'That was when Victor Omeru was president,' Kelly stated.

'Yes, I met Omeru. I liked him. What happened to him? I heard that it was a heart attack?'

Kelly shrugged non-committally, then changed the subject as the head-waiter came to take their orders. 'May I really order a steak, or were you just being cruel?'

'Have the porterhouse,' Daniel invited magnanimously.

When the food was in front of them Daniel returned to the subject. 'I heard that you and Omeru got on particularly well together.'

'Who told you that?' Kelly looked up sharply, and Daniel caught himself just in time. Tug Harrison was not a name to bandy about in front of this lady.

'I think I read it in an article somewhere ,' he hedged. 'It was some time ago.'

'Oh yes.' Kelly gave him release. 'Probably the *Sunday Telegraph*. They did a profile on Victor – on President Omeru – and they gave me an honourable mention.'

'That was it. What is happening in Ubomo? You promised to brief me. You said it was a microcosm of emerging Africa. Explain that.'

'Ubomo has got all the major problems common to every other African state: tribalism, population explosion, poverty, illiteracy. And now that President Omeru has gone and that swine Taffari has taken over, it's got itself another set of problems, such as one-party tyranny, a president for life, foreign exploitation and corruption and incipient civil war.'

'Sounds like the perfect society. Let's start with tribalism in Ubomo. Tell me about it.'

'Tribalism, the single greatest curse of Africa!' Kelly took a bite of underdone porterhouse and for a moment closed her eyes in ecstasy. 'Heaven,' she whispered. 'Bliss! All right, tribalism in Ubomo. There are six tribes but only two really count for anything. The Uhali are the most numerous, almost three out of four million. Traditionally they are an agrarian and lakeside people, tillers of the soil and fishermen. They are gentle, industrious people. Yet for centuries they have been enslaved and in the thrall of the much smaller tribe, the Hita. The Hita are fierce, aristocratic people closely related to the Masai and Samburu of Kenya and Tanzania. They are pastoralists and warriors. They live with and for their cattle, and despise the rest of humanity, including us Europeans, I may add, as inferior animals. They are beautiful people, tall and willowy. Any Hita *morani* under six foot three is considered a midget. Their women are magnificent with regal Nilotic faces;

they would grace the catwalk at any Paris fashion show. Yet they are a cruel, arrogant and brutal people.'

'You are taking sides. You are as much a tribalist as any of them, Kelly,' Daniel accused.

'Live long enough in Africa, as you know, Danny, and you come to be like them, a tribalist.' Kelly shook her head ruefully. 'But in this case, it's justified. Before the British pulled out of Ubomo back in 1969, they held a Westminster-style election and, of course, the Uhali by weight of numbers, took power and Victor Omeru became president. He was a good president. I'm not suggesting he was a saint, but he was as good as any other ruler in Africa, and a damned sight better than most. He tried to accommodate all his people, all the tribes, but the Hita were too proud and bloody-minded. As natural warriors and killers they gradually took over the army and, of course, the outcome was inevitable. Ephrem Taffari is now despot, tyrant and president for life. A million Hita totally dominate a majority of three million other tribes including the Uhali and my beloved little Bambuti.'

'Tell me about your Bambuti, the "people of the tall trees",' Daniel invited, and she smiled with pleasure.

'Oh, Danny, you know the title of my book!'

'Not only do I know it, but I've actually read it. More than once. Three times in fact, the last time a week ago.' He grinned at her. 'At the risk of sounding jejune,' he teased her with her own phrase, 'I'm a fan.'

'Yech!' Bonny spoke for the first time in fifteen minutes. 'Excuse me while I throw up.'

Daniel had almost forgotten her existence, and now he reached out to take her freckled hand that lay on the table cloth beside him. Bonny pulled it away before he could touch it and placed it in her lap.

'I'd like some more wine, if anybody is interested,' she pouted.

Daniel dutifully refilled her glass while Kelly concentrated tactfully on the last morsels of her steak.

At last Daniel broke the awkward silence. 'We were talking about the Bambuti. Tell me about them.'

Kelly looked up at him again, but did not answer immediately. She seemed to be struggling with a difficult decision. Daniel waited.

'Look here,' Kelly said at last. 'You want to know about the Bambuti. All right, what would you say if instead of talking about them I actually took you into the forest and showed you? How would you like to film them in their natural surroundings? I could show you things that nobody else has ever filmed, sights that very few Westerners have ever seen.'

'I'd jump at the chance, Kelly. Hell, I can't think of anything I'd like more, but isn't there just one little problem? President Taffari hates your guts and will hang you from the highest tree the moment you put one foot across the border.'

Kelly laughed. He was beginning really to enjoy the sound of her laughter. It had a delicious purring quality that made him feel good and want to laugh in sympathy. 'He's not much into hanging, is our boy Ephrem. He has other little tricks he prefers.'

'So, how would you manage the guided tour of Ubomo without Taffari's blessing?'

She was still smiling. 'I've lived in the forest for almost five years. Taffari's authority ends where the tall trees begin. I have many friends. Taffari has many enemies.'

'How will I contact you?' Daniel insisted.

'You won't have to. I'll contact you.'

'Tell me, Kelly, why are you risking your life to be back? What work is so important that you must do it without a field grant, without any kind of support, and under the threat of arrest, and possible death?'

She stared at him. 'That's an amazingly stupid question. There is enough work in the forests to keep me going for a lifetime. Amongst other things, I'm doing work on the physiology of the Bambuti. I have been studying the dwarfism of the pygmies, attempting to determine the cause of their stunted growth. Of course, I'm not the first to do this type of research, but I think I've come up with a new angle. Up until now everybody has concentrated on the growth hormone . . .' She broke off and smiled. 'I won't bore you with the details, but I believe it's the hormone receptors that are lacking.'

'Oh, we aren't bored.' Bonny made no effort to veil her

sarcasm. 'We're fascinated. Do you plan to give the pygmies an injection and turn them all into giants like the Hita?'

Kelly refused to be annoyed. 'The small stature of the Bambuti is a benevolent mutation. It makes them ideally suited for life in the rain forests.'

'I don't understand,' Daniel encouraged her. 'Explain how being small is a benefit.'

'Okay, you asked for it. Firstly, there is heat dissipation. Being so tiny they can shed the heat that builds up in the humid windless atmosphere beneath the forest canopy. Then again, their size makes them agile and nimble in the dense tropical growth. You will be astonished to see how the Bambuti move through the forest. The Egyptians and the early explorers truly believed that they had the power of invisibility. They can simply vanish before your eyes.'

Her own lovely eyes shone with enthusiasm and affection as she talked about these people whom she had made her own.

Daniel ordered dessert and coffee, and Kelly had still not exhausted the subject.

'The other area of my research is even more important than growth hormones and receptors. The Bambuti have a marvellous knowledge of plants and their properties, particularly medicinal properties. I estimate that there are well over half a million different species of plants growing in the rain forests, hundreds of them with already proven properties beneficial to man. I believe that the cure for most of our ills and diseases might be locked up in those plants, a cure for cancer, and for AIDS. I've had promising indications in all those directions.'

'Science fiction,' Bonny scoffed, and filled her mouth with chocolate ice cream.

'Do shut up, Bonny,' Daniel snapped at her. 'This is fascinating. How advanced is your research?'

Kelly pulled a face. 'Not as far as I'd like. I have the old women of the Bambuti helping me gather the leaves and barks and roots. They describe their properties and I try to catalogue and test them and isolate the active ingredient, but my laboratory is a thatched hut, and I am fresh out of money and friends . . .'

'Still I'd like to see it.'

'You will,' she promised, and she was so carried away by Daniel's interest in her work that she laid her hand on his arm. 'You'll come to Gondala where I live?'

Bonny was watching the other girl's hand on Daniel's tanned and muscular forearm. It was a small hand, like the rest of her body, neat and graceful.

'Sir Peter would be interested in the formula for curing AIDS,' Bonny said, still staring at the hand. 'BOSS could market it through their pharmaceutical company. It would be worth a billion—'

'BOSS? Sir Peter?' Kelly jerked her hand off Daniel's arm and stared at Bonny. 'Sir Peter who? Which Sir Peter?'

'Tug Harrison, ducky,' Bonny told her with relish. 'Tug is bank-rolling the production that Daniel is going to shoot in Ubomo. The idea is that Danny and I are going to show the world what a hell of a job BOSS are doing. They are going to call it "Ubomo, High Road to the African Future". Isn't that a cute title? It's going to be Danny's masterpiece—'

Kelly didn't wait for her to finish. She leapt to her feet and knocked over her cup. Spilled coffee spread across the tablecloth and cascaded into Daniel's lap.

'You!' Kelly stared down at him. 'You and that monster Harrison! How could you?'

She whirled and ran from the restaurant, shoving her way through a pack of American tourists who were blocking the aisle.

Daniel was on his feet mopping the coffee that had soaked his trousers. 'What the hell did you do that for?' he snarled at Bonny.

'You and the tree doctor were getting just a mite too chummy for my taste.'

'Damn you,' Daniel flared. 'You've screwed up a chance to film something unique. I'll talk to you later.'

He strode angrily after Kelly Kinnear. She was not in the hotel lobby. Daniel headed for the front entrance and called the doorman.

'Did you see a woman—' He broke off as he spotted Kelly on the far side of the road. She was astride a dusty 250 cc Honda motor cycle, and at that moment she jumped on the kick-starter and the engine shrilled to life. She swung the handlebars hard over, banking the cycle into a tight turn, the engine whining and popping jets of oily blue exhaust smoke.

'Kelly!' Daniel shouted. 'Wait! Give me a chance. I can explain.'

She wrenched the throttle grip fully open and the cycle reared up on its back wheel as it accelerated. She turned her face to him as she flew past where he stood. Her expression was at once angry and stricken and he could have sworn that there were tears on her cheeks.

'Hired gun!' she cried at him. 'Judas!' And then the motor cycle howled away. She banked it sharply, the steel foot-rest raised a shower of sparks as it grazed the tarmac, and she weaved into the traffic in Kimathi Avenue.

Daniel ran down to the corner. He caught one more glimpse of her two hundred yards down the avenue, leaning over the handlebars like a jockey, her braid standing out stiffly from the back of her head in the wind.

He looked around for a taxi to follow her, and then realised the futility of even trying. With the lead she had, and the Honda's manoeuvrability no car could hope to catch her.

He turned on his heel and marched back towards the hotel, intent on finding Bonny Mahon. Before he reached the entrance he realised the danger of confronting her in his present mood. It could only lead to bloody battle, and probably the break-up of their relationship. That did not worry him too much, but what restrained him was the danger of losing a cameraman. It might take weeks to find a replacement, and that could lead to a cancellation of his contract with BOSS, the end of his quest to follow the Lucky Dragon, and Ning Cheng Gong, into Ubomo.

He checked his stride and thought about it. It wasn't worth the pleasure of pinning back Bonny Mahon's ears.

'I'd better go and cool off somewhere.' He chose the Jambo Bar, one of the notorious bars down near the station.

It was full of black soldiers in camouflage, and male tourists and bar girls. Some of the girls were spectacular, Samburu and Kikuyu and Masai, in tight shiny skirts with beads and bright ribbons braided into their hair.

Daniel found a bar stool in the corner, and the antics of the middle-aged European tourists on the dance floor helped to alleviate his foul mood. A recent survey of the Nairobi bar girls had determined that ninety-eight per cent of them were HIV positive. You had to have a death wish to enjoy fully all that these ladies had to offer.

An hour and two double whiskies later, Daniel's anger had cooled sufficiently, and he headed back to the Norfolk Hotel. He let himself into the cottage suite and saw Bonny's khaki slacks and panties in the centre of the sitting-room floor where she had dropped them. This evening her untidiness irritated him even more than usual.

The bedroom was in darkness, but the lights in the courtyard shone through the curtains sufficiently for him to make out Bonny's form under the sheet on her side of the bed. He knew she was feigning sleep. He undressed in the darkness, slipped naked into his side of the bed, and lay still.

Neither of them moved or spoke for fully five minutes and then Bonny whispered, 'Is Daddy cross with his little girl?' She used her simpering childish voice. 'His little girl was very naughty . . .' She touched him. Her fingers were warm and silky down his flank. 'She wants to show him how sorry she is.'

He caught her wrist, but it was too late. She was cunning and quick and soon he didn't want her to stop.

'Damn it, Bonny,' he protested. 'You screwed up a chance . . .'

'Shh! Don't talk,' Bonny whispered. 'Little girl will make it better for Daddy.'

'Bonny . . .' His voice trailed away, and he released her wrist.

In the morning when Daniel checked the hotel bill before paying it, he noticed an item for 120 Kenya shillings. 'International telephone calls'. He taxed Bonny with it.

'Did you make an overseas call last night?'

'I called my old mum to let her know I'm all right. I know how stingy you are, but you don't grudge me that, do you?'

Something in her defiant manner troubled him. When she went ahead to see her video equipment safely packed into the taxi, Daniel lingered in the suite. As soon as she was gone he called the telephone exchange and asked the operator for the overseas number that was on his bill.

'London 727 6464, sir.'

'Please get it for me again now.'

'It's ringing, sir.'

A voice answered on the third ring.

'Good morning, may I help you?'

'What number is that?' Daniel asked, but the speaker was guarded.

'Who did you want, please?'

Daniel thought he recognised the voice, the strong African accent. He took a chance.

'Is that you, Selibi?' he asked in Swahili.

'Yes, this is Selibi. Do you want to speak to the *Bwana Mkubwa*? Who shall I say is calling?'

Daniel hung up the receiver and stared at it.

Selibi was Tug Harrison's manservant. So Bonny had telephoned Tug's flat the previous evening while he had been at the Jambo Bar.

'Curiouser and curiouser,' Daniel muttered. 'Miss Bonny isn't all she pretends to be – unless her old mum lives in Holland Park.'

 Every seat on the Air Ubomo flight to Kahali was taken. Most of the other passengers seemed to be businessmen or minor civil servants or politicians. There were half a dozen black soldiers in camouflage and decoration ribbons, berets and dark glasses. There were, however, no tourists – not yet, not before BOSS opened the new casino on the lakeshore.

The hostess was a tall Hita girl in flamboyant national dress. She handed out packets of sweet biscuits and plastic mugs of luke-warm tea with the haughty air of a queen distributing alms to her poor subjects. Halfway through the four-hour flight she disappeared into the toilet with one of the soldiers and all cabin service came to a halt.

They hit heavy clear-air turbulence over the eastern rim of

the Great Rift Valley and a corpulent black businessman in one of the front seats entertained them all with a noisy regurgitation of his breakfast. The air hostess remained ensconced in the rear toilet.

At last they were over the lake. Although like most names with colonial overtones, its name had been changed, Daniel still preferred Lake Albert to Lake Mobutu. The waters were pure azure, flecked with white horses and the sails of fishing dhows, and so wide that for a while there was no shore in sight. Then slowly the western shoreline emerged from the haze.

'Ubomo,' Daniel whispered, more to himself than to Bonny. The name had a romance and mystery that made the skin on his forearms tingle.

He would be following in the footsteps of the great African explorers. Speke had passed this way, and Stanley and ten thousand other hunters and slavers, soldiers and adventurers. He must try to instil some of that feeling of romance and history into his production. Across these waters had plied the ancient Arab dhows laden with ivory and slaves, the black and white gold that had once been the continent's major exports.

Some estimates were that five million souls had been captured like animals in the interior and herded down to the coast. To cross this lake they had been packed like sardines into the dhows, the first layer forced to lie on the bilge deck curled against each other, belly to back, like spoons. Then the removable deck planks were laid over them giving them eighteen inches of space, and another layer of human beings and another deck, until four decks were in place, crammed with howling, whining slaves.

With fair winds the crossing took two days and three nights. The Arab slave-masters were satisfied with a fifty per cent survival rate. It was a process of natural selection. Only the strong came through. On the eastern shore of the lake the living were lifted out of the holds coated with faeces and vomit. The dead were tossed overboard to the waiting crocodiles. The survivors were allowed to rest and gather strength for the last stage of the journey. When their masters deemed them fit, they were chained and yoked in long lines, each slave carrying a tusk of ivory, and they were marched down to the coast.

Daniel wondered if he could simulate some of the horrors of the trade with actors and a hired dhow. He anticipated the outcry that this would raise. So often he had been accused by reviewers and critics of depicting gratuitous violence and savagery in his productions. There was only one reply: 'Africa is a savage and violent continent. Anybody who tries to hide that from you is no true story-teller.' Blood was the fertiliser that made the African soil bloom.

He looked northwards across the shining waters. Up there where the Nile debouched from the lake there was a triangular wedge of land that fronted on to the river called the Lado Enclave. It had once been the private estate of the King of Belgium. The herds of elephant that inhabited those lands were more prolific and prodigiously tusked than anywhere else on the continent, and the Belgians had guarded and cherished them.

By international treaty the ownership of the Lado Enclave passed to the Sudan at the death of the Belgian king. When this happened the Belgian colonial service withdrew precipitately from the Lado, leaving a power vacuum. The European ivory-poachers swarmed in to take advantage. They fell upon the elephant herds and slaughtered them. Karamojo Bell describes in his autobiography how he followed a Lado herd from dawn until dusk, running to keep pace with them, shooting and running on again. In that single bloody day he killed twenty-three elephant.

Little had changed in the years since then, Daniel thought sadly. The slaughter and the rapine continued. And Africa bled. Africa cried to the civilised world for help, but what help was there to give? All the fifty member states of the Organization of African Unity combined were capable of generating only the same gross domestic product as little Belgium in the northern hemisphere.

How could the First World help Africa now? Daniel wondered. Aid poured into this vast continent was soaked up like a few raindrops upon the Saharan sands. A cynic had defined aid as simply the system by which poor white people in rich countries gave money to rich black people in poor countries to put into Swiss bank accounts. The sad truth was that Africa no longer mattered, particularly since the Berlin Wall had come down and Eastern Europe had started to emerge from the dark age of Communism. Africa was redundant. The rest of the world might give it passing sympathy, but Africa was beyond help. Europe would turn its attention to a more promising subject closer to home.

Daniel sighed and glanced at Bonny in the seat beside him. He wanted to discuss his thoughts, but she had kicked off her sandals and had her bare knees up against the back of the seat in front of her. She was chewing gum and reading a trashy science fiction paperback.

Instead Daniel looked out of the window again. The coast of Ubomo came up to meet them as the pilot began his descent. The savannah was red-brown as the hide of an impala antelope and studded with acacia trees. Upon the lakeshore the fishing villages were strung like beads, bound together by the narrow strip of green gardens and shambas that the lake waters nurtured. The village children waved as the aircraft passed overhead, and when the pilot turned on to final approach Daniel had a distant view of blue mountains clad with dark forest.

The air hostess re-emerged from the toilet, looking smug and adjusting her long green skirt, and ordered them in English and Swahili to fasten their seat-belts.

The unpainted galvanised roofs of the town flashed beneath them and they touched down heavily on the dusty strip. They taxied past the skeleton of steel and concrete beams that would have been the grand new Ephrem Taffari airport building if only the money had not run out, and came to a halt in front of the humbler edifice of unburnt brick that was a relic of Victor Omeru's reign.

As the door of the aircraft opened, the heat pressed in upon them and they were sweating before they reached the airport building.

A Hita officer in camouflage battledress and maroon beret singled Daniel out of the straggling group of passengers and came out on the field to meet him.

'Doctor Armstrong? I recognised you from the photograph on the dust-jacket of your book.' He held out his hand. 'I'm Captain Kajo. I will be your guide during your stay. The president, in person, has asked me to welcome you and assure you of our whole-hearted co-operation. Sir Peter Harrison is a personal friend of his, and President Taffari has expressed the wish to meet you as soon as you have recovered from the ill-effects of your journey. In fact he has arranged a cocktail party to welcome you to Ubomo.'

Captain Kajo spoke excellent English. He was a striking young man, slim and tall in the classical Hita mould. He towered over Daniel by a couple of inches. His jet eyes began to sparkle as he studied Bonny Mahon.

'This is my camera operator, Miss Mahon,' Daniel introduced them, and Bonny looked back at Captain Kajo with equal interest.

In the army Landrover, piled with their luggage and video equipment, Bonny leaned close to Daniel and asked, 'Is it true what they say about Africans being . . .' she sought the adjective, 'about them being large?'

'I've never made a study of it,' Daniel told her. 'But I could find out for you, if you'd like.'

'Don't put yourself out,' she grinned. 'If necessary, I can do my own research.'

Since he had learned about her secret phone call to Tug Harrison, Daniel's misgivings about her had increased. Now he didn't trust her at all, and he didn't even like her as much as he had only as recently as the previous day.

It was new moon, but the stars were clear and bright. Their reflections danced on the ruffled lake waters. Kelly Kinnear sat in the bows of the small dhow. The rigging creaked to the gentle push of the night breeze as they tacked across the lake.

The stars were magnificent. She turned her face up to them and whispered the lyrical names of the constellations as she recognised each of them. The stars were one of the few things she missed in the forest, for they were for ever hidden by the high unbroken canopy of the tree-tops. She savoured them now, for soon she would be without them.

285

The helmsman was singing a soft repetitive refrain, an invocation to the spirits of the lake depths, the *djinni* who controlled the fickle winds that pushed the dhow across the dark waters.

Kelly's mood was changeable as the breeze, dropping and shifting and then rising again. She was elated at the prospect of going once more into the forest, and the reunion with dear friends she loved so well. She was fearful of the journey and the dangers that still lay ahead before she could reach the safety of the tall trees. She was anxious that the political changes since the *coup d'état* would have destroyed and damaged much in her absence. She was saddened by the memory of damage already done, destruction already wrought upon the forest in the few short years since she had first entered their hushed cathedral depths.

At the same time, she was gladdened by the promises of support she had received and the interest she had been able to stir up during her visit to England and Europe, but disappointed that the support had been mainly moral and vocal rather than financial or constructive. She mustered all her enthusiasm and determination and forced herself to look ahead optimistically. We'll win through. We must win through.

Then suddenly and irrelevantly she thought of Daniel Armstrong, and she felt angry and unhappy again. Somehow his treachery was all the more heinous by reason of the blind faith and trust that she had placed in him before she had actually met him.

She had pre-judged him from what she had seen on the television screen and read in a few newspaper and magazine articles about him. From these she had formed a highly favourable opinion, not simply because he was handsome and articulate and his screen presence impressive, but because of the apparent depth of his understanding and his compassion for this poor wrecked continent which she had made her own.

She had written to him twice, addressing her letters to the television studio. Those letters could never have reached him or, if they did, they must have been overlooked in the huge volume of mail she was sure was addressed to him. In any event she had received no reply.

Then when the unexpected opportunity had presented itself

in Nairobi, Daniel Armstrong had, at first meeting, borne out all the high hopes she had placed in him. He was warm and compassionate and approachable. She had been aware of the instant *rapport* between them. They were people from the same world, with similar interests and concerns and, more than that, she knew that an essential spark had been struck between them. The attraction had been mutual; they had both recognised it. There had been a meeting and a docking of their minds as well as an undeniable physical attraction.

Kelly did not consider herself to be a sensual person. The only lovers she had ever taken were men whose intellects she admired. The first had been one of her professors at medical school, a fine man twenty-five years her senior. They were still friends. Two others were fellow students, and the fourth the man she eventually married. Paul had been a medical doctor like herself. The two of them had qualified in the same year and had come out to Africa as a team. He had died from the bite of one of the deadly forest mambas within the first six months and at every opportunity she still visited his grave at the foot of a gigantic silk-cotton tree on the banks of the Ubomo River deep in the forest.

Four lovers in all her thirty-two years. No, she was not a sensual person, but she had been intensely aware of the strong pull that Daniel Armstrong had exerted upon her, and she had experienced no great urge to resist it. He was the kind of man for her.

Then suddenly it was all a lie and a delusion, and he was just like the rest of them. A hired gun, she thought angrily, for BOSS and that monster Harrison. She tried to use her anger to shield herself against the sense of loss she felt at the destruction of an ideal. She had believed in Daniel Armstrong. She had given him her trust and he had betrayed it.

Put him out of your mind, she determined. Don't think about him again. He's not worth it. But she was honest enough to realise that it was not going to be that easy.

From the stern the helmsman of the dhow called softly to her in Swahili and she roused herself and looked forward. The shoreline was half a mile ahead, the low line of beach surf creaming softly in the starlight.

Ubomo. She was coming home. Her mood soared.

Suddenly there was a cry from the helm and she spun about. The two crew men, naked except for their loin-cloths, ran forward. In haste they seized the main sheet and brought the boom of the sail crashing down upon the deck. The lateen sail billowed and folded and they sprang upon it and furled it swiftly. Within seconds the stubby mast was bare and the dhow was wallowing low on the dark waters.

'What is it?' Kelly called softly in Swahili, and the helmsman answered quietly, 'Patrol boat.'

She heard it then, the throb of the diesel engine above the wind and her nerves sprang tight. The crew of the dhow were all Uhali tribesmen, loyal to old President Omeru. They were risking their lives, just as she was, by defying the curfew and crossing the lake in darkness.

They crouched on the open deck and stared out into the darkness, listening to the beat of the engine swelling louder. The gunboat was the gift of an Arab oil sheikh to the new regime, a fast forty-foot assault craft with twin cannon in armoured turrets fore and aft. It had seen thirty years' service in the Red Sea. It spent most of its time tied-up in the port of Kahali, with engines broken down, awaiting spare parts. However, they had picked a bad night for the crossing; the gunboat was for once seaworthy and dangerous.

Kelly saw the flash of foam at the bows of the oncoming patrol boat. It was heading up from the south. Instinctively she crouched lower, trying to shield herself behind the bulwark as she considered her position. On its present course the patrol boat must surely spot them. If Kelly were found on board the dhow, the crew would be shot without trial, one of those public executions on the beach of Kahali which were part of Ephrem Taffari's new style of government. Of course she would be shot alongside them, but that did not concern Kelly at that moment. These were good men who had risked their lives for her. She had to do all in her power to protect them.

If she were not found on board, and there were no other contraband, the crew might have a chance of talking themselves out of trouble. They would almost certainly be beaten and fined, and the dhow might be confiscated, but they might escape execution.

She reached for her backpack that lay in the bows. Quickly she undid the straps that held the inflatable mattress strapped to the underside of the pack. She unrolled the nylon-covered mattress and frantically blew into the valve, filling her lungs and then exhaling long and hard, all the time watching the dark shape of the patrol boat loom out of the night. It was coming up fast. There was no time to inflate the mattress fully. It was still soft and floppy as she closed the valve.

She stood up and slung the pack on her back and called back to the helmsman, 'Thank you, my friend. Peace be with you, and may Allah preserve you.' The lake people were nearly all Muslim.

'And with you be peace,' he called back. She could hear the relief and gratitude in his tone. He knew she was doing this for him and his crew.

Kelly sat on the bulwark and swung her legs overboard. She clutched the semi-inflated mattress to her chest and drew a deep breath before she dropped into the lake. The water closed over her head. It was surprisingly cold and the heavy pack on her back carried her deep before the buoyancy of the mattress asserted itself and lifted her back to the surface.

She broke through, gasping and with water streaming into her eyes. It took her a few minutes to master the trim of the bobbing mattress, but at last she lay half across it, her legs dangling, the strap of the backpack hooked over her arm. It held her head clear, but she was low down in the water. The waves dashed into her face and threatened to overturn her precarious craft.

She looked for the dhow and was surprised to see how far she had drifted from it. As she watched, the boom was hoisted and the sail filled. The ungainly little boat turned to run free before the breeze, trying to get clear of the forbidden coast before the patrol boat spotted her.

'Good luck,' she whispered, and a wave broke into her face. She choked and coughed, and when she looked again both the dhow and the patrol boat had disappeared into the night.

She kicked out gently, careful not to upset her balance, conserving her strength for the long night ahead. She knew that some monstrous crocodiles inhabited the lake; she had seen a photograph of one that measured eighteen feet from the tip of its hideous snout to the end of its thick crested tail. She put the picture out of her mind and kept kicking, lining herself up by the stars, swimming towards where Orion stood on his head upon the western horizon.

A few minutes later she glimpsed a flash of light far upwind. It may have been the searchlight of the patrol boat as it picked up the shape of the dhow. She forced herself not to look back. She didn't want to know the worst, for there was nothing more she could do to save the men who had helped her.

She kept swimming, kicking to a steady rhythm. After an hour she wondered if she had moved at all. The backpack was like a drogue anchor hanging below the half-inflated mattress. However, she dared not jettison it. Without the basic equipment it contained, she was doomed.

She kept on swimming. Another hour and she was almost exhausted. She was forced to rest. One calf was cramping badly. The breeze had dropped and in the silence she heard a soft regular rumbling, like an old man snoring in his sleep. It took her a moment to place the sound.

'The beach surf,' she whispered, and kicked out again with renewed strength.

She felt the water lift and surge under her as it met the shelving bottom. She swam on, torturously slowly, dragging herself and the sodden pack through the water.

Now she saw the ivory-nut palms above the beach silhouetted against the stars. She held her breath and reached down with both feet. Again the water closed over her head, but with her toes she felt the sandy bottom, six feet below the surface, and found enough strength for one last effort.

Minutes later she could stand. The surf knocked her sprawling, but she dragged herself up again and staggered up the narrow beach to find shelter in a patch of papyrus reeds. Her watch was a waterproof Rolex, a wedding gift from Paul. The time was a few minutes after four. It would be light soon. She must get in before a Hita patrol picked her up, but she was too cold and stiff and exhausted to move just yet.

While she rested she forced herself to open the pack with numb fingers and to empty out the water that almost doubled its weight. She wrung out her few spare items of clothing and wiped down the other equipment as best she could. While she worked she chewed a high-energy sugar bar and almost immediately felt better.

She repacked the bag, slung it, and started back northwards, keeping parallel to the lake, but well back from the soft beach sand which would record her footprints for a Hita patrol to follow.

Every few hundred yards there were the gardens and thatched buildings of the small shambas. Dogs barked and she was forced to detour round the huts to avoid detection. She hoped that she was heading in the right direction. She reasoned that the captain of the dhow would have come in upwind of his destination to give himself leeway in which to make his landfall so she must keep northwards.

She had been going for almost an hour, but reckoned that she had covered only a couple of miles when, with a surge of relief, she saw ahead of her the pale round dome of the little mosque shining like a bald man's head in the first pearly radiance of the dawn.

She broke into a weary trot, weighed down by the pack and her fatigue. She smelt woodsmoke, and saw the faint glow of the fire under the dark tamarind tree, just where it should have been. Closer, she made out the figures of two men squatting close beside the fire.

'Patrick!' she called hoarsely, and one of the figures jumped up and ran towards her.

'Patrick,' she repeated, and stumbled and would have fallen if he had not caught her.

'Kelly! Allah be praised. We had given you up.'

'The patrol boat . . .' she gasped.

'Yes. We heard firing and saw the light. We thought they had caught you.'

Patrick Omeru was one of old President Omeru's nephews. So far he had escaped the purges by Taffari's soldiers. He was one of the first friends that Kelly had made after her arrival in Ubomo. He lifted the pack from her shoulders, and she groaned with relief. The wet straps had abraded her delicate skin.

'Kill the fire,' Patrick called to his brother, and he kicked

291

sand over the coals. Between them they led Kelly to where the truck was parked in a grove of mango trees behind the derelict mosque. They helped her into the back and spread a tarpaulin over her as she lay on the dirty floorboards. The truck stank of dried fish.

Even though the truck jolted and crashed through the potholes, she was at last warm, and soon she slept. It was a trick she had learned in the forest, to be able to sleep in any circumstances of discomfort.

The sudden cessation of engine noise and movement woke her again. She did not know how long she had slept, but it was light now and a glance at her watch showed her it was after nine in the morning. She lay quietly under her tarpaulin and listened to the sound of men's voices close alongside the truck. She knew better than to disclose her presence.

Minutes later, Patrick pulled back the tarpaulin and smiled at her.

'Where are we, Patrick?'

'Kahali, in the old town. A safe place.'

The truck was parked in the small yard of one of the old Arab houses. The building was dilapidated, the yard filthy with chicken droppings and rubbish. Chickens roosted under the eaves or scratched in the dirt. There was a strong smell of drains and sewage. The Omeru family had fallen on hard times since the old president's downfall.

In the sparsely furnished front room, with its stained walls on which old yellowed newspaper cuttings had been pasted, Patrick's wife had a meal ready for her. It was a stew of chicken spiced with chilli and served with a bowl of manioc and stewed plantains. She was hungry, and it was good.

While she ate, other men came to speak to her. They slipped in quietly and squatted beside her in the bare room. They told her what had happened in Ubomo during her absence, and she frowned while she listened. Very little of it was good tidings. They knew where she was going and they gave her messages to take with her. Then they slipped away again as quietly and furtively as they had arrived.

It was long after dark when Patrick stood up and told her quietly, 'It is time to go on.'

The truck was now loaded with dried fish in woven baskets. They had built a small hiding-place for her under the load. She crawled into it and Patrick passed her pack in to her, then sealed the opening behind her with another basket of fish.

The truck started and rumbled out of the yard. This part of the journey was only three hundred miles. She settled down and slept again.

She woke every time the truck stopped. Whenever she heard voices, the loud arrogant voices of Hita speaking Swahili with the distinctive cutting accent, she knew they had halted at another military road-block.

Once Patrick stopped the truck along a deserted stretch of road and let her out of her hiding-place and she went a short distance into the veld to relieve herself. They were still in the open grassland savannah below the rim of the Great Rift. She heard cattle lowing somewhere close and knew that there was a Hita *manyatta* nearby.

When she woke again it was to a peculiar new motion and to the chant of the ferrymen. It was a nostalgic sound and she knew she was nearly home.

During the night she had opened a small peephole from her little cave under the baskets of dried fish into the outside world. Through it she caught glimpses of the expanses of the Ubomo River touched with the hot orange and violet of the breaking dawn.

The silhouettes of the ferrymen passed back and forth in front of her peephole as they handled the lines that linked the ferry-boat from one bank of the river to the other. The ferry across the Ubomo River was almost at the edge of the great forest. She could imagine it as clearly as if she were actually looking at it.

The wide sweep of the river was the natural boundary between savannah and forest. The first time she had stood upon its bank she had been amazed by the abruptness with which the forest began. On the east bank the open grass and acacia dropped away towards the lake, while on the far bank stood a gigantic palisade of dark trees, a solid unbroken wall a hundred feet high, with some of the real giants towering another fifty feet above those. It had seemed to her at once both forbidding and frightening. On the far bank the road tunnelled into the forest like a rabbit hole.

In the few short years since then, the forest had been hacked back as the land-hungry peasantry nibbled at its edges. They had toppled the great trees that had taken hundreds of years to grow and burned them where they fell for charcoal and fertiliser. The forest retreated before this onslaught. It was now almost five miles from the ferry to the edge of the tree-line.

In between lay sprawling shambas with fields of plantains and manioc. The worked-out ground was being abandoned to weeds and secondary growth. The fragile forest soils could bear only two or three years of cultivation before they were exhausted and the peasant farmers moved on to clear more forest.

Even when it reached the retreating forest edge, the road was no longer a tunnel through the trees, roofed over with a high canopy of vegetation as it once had been. The verges of the road had been cut back half a mile on each side. The peasants had used the road as an access to the interior of the forest. They had built their villages alongside the road and hacked out their gardens and plantations from the living forest that bordered it. This was the terribly destructive 'slash and burn' cultivation method by which they felled the trees and burned them where they fell. Those true giants of the forest, whose girth defied the puny axes, they destroyed by building a slow fire around the base of the trunk. They kept it burning week after week until it ate through the hardwood core and toppled two hundred feet of massive trunk.

The road itself was like a deadly blade, a spear into the guts of the forest, steeped in the poison of civilisation. Kelly hated the road. It was a channel of infection and corruption into the virginal womb of the forest.

Looking out of her peephole she saw that the road was wider now than she remembered it. The deep rutted tracks were churned by the wheels of logging and mining trucks and the other heavy traffic that had begun using it since President Omeru had been overthrown and the forest concession given to the powerful foreign syndicate to develop.

She knew from her studies and the meticulous records that she kept that already the road had altered the local rainfall patterns. The mile-wide cutline was unprotected by the umbrella of the forest canopy. The tropical sun struck down on this open swathe and heated the unshielded earth, causing a vast up-draught of air above the road. This dispersed the rain clouds that daily gathered over the green forest. Nowadays little rain fell along the roadway, although it still teemed down at the rate of three hundred inches a year upon the pristine forests only a few miles away.

The roadside was dry and dusty and hot. The mango trees wilted in the noonday heat and the people living beside the road built themselves *barazas*, thatched roofs supported by poles without walls, to shield them from the cloudless sky above the roadway. Without the forest canopy the whole Ubomo basin would soon become a little Sahara.

To Kelly the road was the Sodom and Gomorrah of the forest. It was temptation to her Bambuti friends. The truck-drivers had money and they wanted meat and honey and women. The Bambuti were skilled hunters who could provide both meat and honey, and their young girls, tiny and graceful, laughing and big-breasted, were peculiarly attractive to the tall bantu men.

The roadway seduced the Bambuti and lured them out of the fastness of the deep forest. It was destroying their traditional way of life. It encouraged the pygmies to over-hunt their forest preserves. Where once they had hunted only to feed themselves and their tribe, now they hunted to sell the meat at the roadside *dukas*, the little trading stores set up at each new village.

Game was each day scarcer in the forest and soon, Kelly knew, the Bambuti would be tempted to hunt in the heartland, that special remote centre of the forest where by tradition and religious restraint no Bambuti had ever hunted before.

At the roadside the Bambuti discovered palm wine and bottled beer and spirits. Like most stone-age people, from the Australian Aboriginals to the Inuit Eskimos of the Arctic, they had little resistance to alcohol. A drunken pygmy was a pitiful sight.

In the deep forest, there was no tribal tradition that restrained the Bambuti girls from sexual intercourse before marriage. They were allowed all the experimentation and indulgence they wanted with the boys of the tribe, except only that intercourse must not be with a full embrace. The unmarried couple must hold each other's elbows only, not clasp each other chest to chest. To them the sexual act was a natural and pleasant expression of affection, and they were by nature friendly and full of fun. They were easy game for the sophisticated truck-drivers from the towns. Eager to please, they sold their favours for a trinket or a bottle of beer or a few shillings, and from the lopsided bargain they were left with syphilis or gonorrhoea or, most deadly of all, AIDS.

In her hatred of the road, Kelly wished there was some way to halt this intrusion, this accelerating process of degradation and destruction, but she knew that there was none. BOSS and the syndicate were behemoths on the march. The forest, its soil, its trees, its animals, birds and its people were all too fragile. All she could hope for was to help retard the process and in the end to save some precious fragment from the melting-pot of progress and development, and exploitation.

Abruptly the truck swung off the road and in a cloud of red talcum dust drew up at the rear of one of the roadside *dukas*. Peering from her peephole, Kelly saw that it was a typical roadside store with mud walls and roof, thatched with ilala palm fronds. There was a logging truck parked in front of it and the driver and his mate were haggling with the store-keeper for the purchase of sweet yams and strips of dried game meat blackened with smoke.

Patrick Omeru and his brother began to unload some of the baskets of dried fish to sell to the store-keeper and as they worked he spoke without looking at Kelly's hiding-place.

'Are you all right, Kelly?'

'I'm fine, Patrick. I'm ready to move,' she called back softly.

'Wait, Doctor. I must make certain that it is safe. The army patrols the road regularly. I'll speak to the store-keeper; he knows when the soldiers will come.'

Patrick went on unloading the fish. In front of the *duka* the truck-driver completed his transaction and carried his purchases to the logging truck. He climbed on board and started up with a roar and cloud of diesel smoke, then pulled out into the rutted roadway towing two huge trailers behind the truck. The trailers were laden with forty-foot lengths of African mahogany logs, each five feet in diameter, the whole cargo comprising hundreds of tons of valuable hardwood.

As soon as the truck had gone, Patrick called to the Uhali store-keeper and they spoke together quietly. The store-keeper shook his head and pointed back along the road. Patrick hurried back to the side of the fish truck.

'Quickly, Kelly. The patrol will be coming any minute now, but we should hear the army vehicle long before it arrives. The store-keeper says that the soldiers never go into the forest. They are afraid of the forest spirits.'

He pulled away the fish baskets that covered the entrance to Kelly's hiding-place, and she scrambled out and jumped down to the sun-baked earth. She felt stiff and cramped, and she stretched her body to its full extent, lifting her hands over her head and twisting from the waist to get the kinks out of her spine.

'You must go quickly, Kelly,' Patrick urged her. 'The patrol! I wish I had someone to go with you, to protect you.'

Kelly laughed and shook her head. 'Once I'm in the forest, I will be safe.' She felt gay and happy at the prospect, but Patrick looked worried.

'The forest is an evil place.'

'You are also afraid of the *djinni*, aren't you, Patrick?' she teased him as she shrugged her pack on to her shoulders. She knew that, like most Uhali or Hita, Patrick had never entered the deep forest. They were all terrified of the forest spirits. Whenever possible the Bambuti were at pains to describe these malignant spirits and to invent horror stories of their own dreadful encounters with them. It was one of the Bambuti devices for keeping the big black men out of their secret preserves.

'Of course not, Kelly.' Patrick denied the charge a little too hotly. 'I am an educated man; I do not believe in *djinni* or evil spirits.' But even as he spoke his eyes strayed towards the impenetrable wall of high trees that stood just beyond the half-mile wide strip of gardens and plantations. He shuddered and changed the subject.

'You will get a message to me in the usual way?' he asked anxiously. 'We must know how he is.'

'Don't worry.' She smiled at him and took his hand. 'Thank you, Patrick. Thank you for everything.'

'It is we who should thank you, Kelly. May Allah give you peace.'

'*Salaam aleikum*,' she replied. 'To you peace also, Patrick.' And she turned and slipped away under the wide green fronds of the banana trees. Within a dozen paces she was hidden from the road.

As she went through the gardens she picked the fruits from the trees, filling the pockets of her backpack with ripe mangoes and plantains. It was a Bambuti trick. The village gardens and the villages themselves were considered fair hunting grounds. The pygmies borrowed anything that was left untended, but stealing was not as much fun as gulling the villagers into parting with food and valuables by elaborate confidence tricks. Kelly smiled as she recalled the glee with which old Sepoo related his successful scams to the rest of the tribe whenever he returned from the villages to the hunting camps in the deep forest.

Now she helped herself to the garden produce with as little conscience as old Sepoo would have evinced. In London she would have been appalled by the notion of shoplifting in Selfridges, but as she approached the edge of the forest she was already beginning to think like a Bambuti again. It was the way of survival.

At the end of the last garden there was a fence of thorn branches to keep out the forest creatures that raided the crops at night, and at intervals along this fence, set on poles were grubby spirit flags and juju charms to discourage the forest demons and *djinni* from approaching the villages. The Bambuti always howled with mirth when they passed this evidence of the villagers' superstition. It was proof of the success of their own subtle propaganda.

Kelly found a narrow gap in the fence, just big enough to accommodate the pygmy who had made it and she slipped through.

The forest lay ahead of her. She lifted up her eyes and watched a flock of grey parrots flying shrieking along the tree-tops a hundred feet above her.

The entrance to the forest was thick and entangled. Where the sunlight had penetrated to the ground it had raised a thicket of secondary growth. There was a pygmy track through this undergrowth, but even Kelly was forced to stoop to enter it. The average Bambuti was at least a foot shorter than she was, and with their machetes they cut the undergrowth just above their own head-height. When fresh, the raw shoots were easy to spot, but once they dried, they were sharp as daggers and on the level of Kelly's face and eyes. She moved with dainty care. She did not realise it herself, but in the forest she had learned by example to carry herself with the same agile grace as a pygmy.

It was one of the Bambuti's derisive taunts that somebody walked like a *wazungu* in the forest. *Wazungu* was the derogatory term for any outsider, any foreigner. Even old Sepoo admitted that Kelly walked like one of the real people and not like a white *wazungu*.

The peripheral screen of dense undergrowth was several hundred feet wide. It ended abruptly and Kelly stepped out on to the true forest floor.

It was like entering a submarine cavern, a dim and secret place. The sunlight was reflected down through successive layers of leaves, so that the entire forest world was washed with green, and the air was warm and moist and redolent of leaf mould and fungus, a relief from the heat and dust and merciless sunlight of the outside world. Kelly filled her lungs with the smell and looked around her, blinking as her eyes adjusted to this strange and lovely light. There was no dense undergrowth here, the great tree-trunks reached up to the high green roof and shaded away into the green depths ahead, reminding her of the hall of pillars in the mighty temple of Karnak on the banks of the Nile.

Under her feet the dead leaves were thick and luxuriant as a precious oriental carpet. They gave a spring to her step and rustled under her feet to give warning to the forest creatures of her approach. It was unwise to come unannounced upon one of the wicked red buffalo or to step upon one of the deadly adders that lay curled upon the forest floor.

Kelly moved swiftly, lightly, with the susurration of dead

leaves under her feet, stopping once to cut herself a digging-stick and to sharpen the point with her clasp-knife as she went on.

She sang as she went, one of the praise songs to the forest that Sepoo's wife, Pamba, had taught her. It was a Bambuti hymn, for the forest itself is their god. They worship it as both Mother and Father. They do not believe a jot in the hobgoblins and evil spirits whose existence they so solemnly endorse and whose depredations they recount with so much glee to the black villagers. For the Bambuti the forest is a living entity, a deity which can give up or withhold its bounty, which can give favours or wreak retribution on those who flout its laws and do it injury. Over the years she had lived under the forest roof Kelly had come more than halfway to accepting the Bambuti philosophy, and now she sang to the forest as she travelled swiftly across its floor.

In the middle of the afternoon it began to rain, one of those solid downpours that were a daily occurrence. The heavy drops falling thick and heavy as stones upon the upper galleries of the forest roared like a distant river in spate. Had it fallen on bare earth with such force, it would have ripped away the topsoil and raked deep scars, washed out plains and scoured the hillsides, flooding the rivers and wreaking untold harm.

In the forest the top galleries of the trees broke the force of the storm, cushioning the gouts of water, gathering them up and redirecting them down the trunks of the great trees, scattering them benevolently across the thick carpet of dead leaves and mould, so that the earth was able to absorb and restrain the rain's malevolent power. The rivers and streams, instead of becoming muddied by the torn earth and choked by uprooted trees, still ran sweet and crystal clear.

As the rain sifted down softly upon her, Kelly slipped off her cotton shirt and placed it in one of the waterproof pockets of her pack. The straps would cut into her bare shoulders so she rigged the headband around her forehead and kept her arms clear as the pygmy women do. She went on, not bothering to take shelter from the blood-warm rain.

Now she was bare-chested, wearing only a brief pair of cotton shorts and her canvas running shoes. Minimal dress was the natural forest way. The Bambuti wore only a loincloth of beaten bark.

When the first Belgian missionaries had discovered the Bambuti, they had been outraged by their nakedness and sent to Brussels for dresses and jackets and calico breeches, all in children's sizes, which they forced them to wear. In the humidity of the forest these clothes were always damp and unhealthy and the pygmies for the first time had suffered from pneumonia and other respiratory complaints.

After the constraints of city life, it felt good to be half-naked and free. Kelly delighted in the rain upon her body. Her skin was clear and creamy pale, almost luminous in the soft green light and her small taut breasts joggled elastically to her stride.

She moved swiftly, foraging as she went, hardly pausing as she gathered up a scattering of mushrooms with glossy domed heads and brilliant orange gills. These were the most delicious of the thirty-odd edible varieties. On the other hand there were fifty or more inedible varieties, a few of which were virulently toxic, dealing certain death within hours of a single mouthful. The rain ceased but the trees still dripped.

Once she stopped and traced a slim vine down the trunk of a mahogany tree. She dug its pure white roots out of the rain-soaked leaf mould with a few strokes of her digging-stick. The roots were sweet as sugar cane and crunched scrumptiously as she chewed them. They were nutritious and filled her with energy.

The green shadows crowded closer as the day died away and the light faded. She looked for a place to camp. She did not want to be bothered with having to build a waterproof hut for herself, the hollow at the base of one of the giant tree-trunks would do admirably as a hearth for a single night.

Her feet still rustled through the dead leaves, even though they were now dampened. Suddenly there was an explosive sound, a rush of air under pressure like a burst motor-car tyre, only ten feet or so ahead of her. It was one of the most terrifying sounds in the forest, worse than the bellow of an angry buffalo or the roaring grunt of one of the huge black boars. Kelly leaped involuntarily backwards, from a steady run she rose two feet in the air and landed as far as that back in her own tracks.

Her hand was shaking as she flicked the headband off her forehead and dropped the backpack to the leafy floor. In the same movement she dipped into one of the pockets and brought out her slingshot.

Because of her slingshot the Bambuti had given her the name 'Baby Archer'. Though they mocked her merrily, they were really impressed by her skill with the weapon. Even old Sepoo had never been able to master it, though Kelly had tutored him patiently. In the end he had abandoned the effort with a haughty declaration that the bow and arrow were the only real weapons for a hunter, and that this silly little thing was only suitable for children and babies. So she had become 'Baby Archer', Kara-Ki.

With one quick motion she slipped the brace over her wrist and drew the heavy surgical elastic bands to her right ear. The missile was a steel ball-bearing.

On the forest floor ahead of her something moved. It looked like a pile of dead leaves or an Afghan rug patterned in the colours of the forest, golds and ochres and soft mauves, striped and starred with diamonds and arrowheads of black that tricked the eye. Kelly knew that what seemed to be an amorphous mass was in reality a serpentine body, coiled upon itself, each coil as thick as her calf, but laced and camouflaged with cunning and seductive colour. The gaboon adder is, except for the mamba, Africa's most venomous snake.

In the centre of this coiled pyramid of body, the head was drawn back like a nocked arrow upon the S-bend of the neck. The head was pig-snouted, flattened and scaled, the eyes were raised on horny protuberances, the colour and lucidity of precious topaz. The pupils were bright as jet and focused upon her. The whole head was bigger than both her fists held together. The feathery black tongue flicked from between the thin grinning lips.

Kelly held her aim for only a fraction of a second and then let fly. The silver ball-bearing hummed as it flew, glinting like a drop of mercury in the soft green light. It struck the gaboon adder on the point of its snout and split its skull with such force that jets of blood spurted from the nostrils and the grotesque head was whipped over backwards. With one last explosive hiss the adder writhed into its death throes, the great coils of its body sliding and twisting over themselves, convulsing and contorting, exposing the pale belly latticed with diagonal scales.

Kelly circled the adder cautiously, holding the pointed digging-stick at the ready. As the shattered head flopped clear she darted forward and pinned it to the earth. Holding it down with all her weight while the adder wound itself around the shaft, Kelly opened the blade of her clasp-knife with her small white teeth and with a single slash lopped off the snake's head.

She left the headless body to finish its last reflexive throes and looked around her for a campsite. There was a natural cave in the base of one of the tree-trunks nearby, a perfect night shelter.

The Bambuti had never fathomed the art of making fire and the women carried a live coal with them when they moved from hunting-camp to hunting-camp, but Kelly flicked her plastic Bic lighter and within minutes she had a cheerful little fire burning at the base of the tree. She opened her pack and set up her camp. Then, armed with the digging-stick and clasp-knife, she returned to the carcass of the gaboon adder. It weighed almost ten kilos, far too much for her own needs. Already the red serowe ants had found it. Nothing lay long on the forest floor before the scavengers arrived.

Kelly cut a thick section from the centre of the carcass, scraped the ants away, and skinned the portion with a few expert strokes. The meat was clean and white. She lifted two thick fillets from the bone and placed them over the coals of her fire on a skillet of green twigs. She scattered a few leaves from one of the herby bushes over the fire and the smoke flavoured and perfumed the flesh. While it grilled, she strung the orange-gilled mushrooms on another green twig. Like a kebab she placed it on the fire, turning it regularly.

The mushrooms had a richer fungus flavour than black truffles and the flesh of the adder tasted like a mixture of lobster and milk-fed chicken. The exertions of the day had sharpened her appetite and Kelly could not remember a more delicious meal. She washed it down with sweet water from the stream nearby.

During the night she was awakened by a loud snuffling and gulping close to where she lay in her tree-trunk shelter. She did not need to see to know what had disturbed her. The giant forest hog can weigh as much as 650 pounds and stand three feet high at the shoulder. These pigs, the largest and rarest in the world, are as dangerous as a lion when aroused. But Kelly felt no fear as she listened to it gobbling the remains of the adder's carcass. When it was finished the pig came snuffling around her camp, but she tossed a few twigs on the coals and when they flared up the pig grunted hoarsely and shambled away into the forest.

In the morning she bathed in the stream and combed out her hair and replaited it while it was still wet into a thick dark glistening braid that hung down her naked back.

She ate the rest of last night's adder steak and mushrooms cold and was on her way again as soon as it was light enough. Although she had a compass in her pack, she navigated chiefly by the fungus plates and the serowe ant nests, which were attached only to the southern side of the tree-trunks, and by the flow and direction of the streams she crossed.

In the middle of the afternoon she cut the well-defined trail she was searching for, and turned to follow it in a south-westerly direction. Within the hour she recognised a landmark, a natural bridge across one of the streams formed by the massive trunk of an ancient tree that had fallen across the water-course.

Sepoo had told her once that the tree bridge had been there 'since the beginning of time', which meant in his living memory. Time and numbers were not concrete concepts in the pygmy mind. They counted 'one, two, three, many'. In the forest where the seasons made no difference to the rainfall or temperature, they regulated their lives on the phases of the moon, and moved from one camp to the next every full moon. Thus they never stayed long enough at one site to deplete the game or the fruits in the area, or to pollute the streams and sour the earth with their wastes.

The tree bridge was polished by generations of their tiny feet and Kelly inspected it minutely for fresh muddy tracks to judge how recently it had been used. She was disappointed and hurried on to the campsite nearby where she had hoped to find them. They were gone, but judging by the sign, this had been their last camp, they would have moved weeks previously at the full moon.

There were three or four other localities where they might be at this moment, the furthest almost a hundred miles away towards the heartland of the vast area which Sepoo's tribe looked upon as their own.

However, there was no telling which direction they had chosen. Like all tribal decisions, it would have been made at the last moment by a heated and lively debate in which all joined with equal voice. Kelly smiled as she guessed how the argument had probably been resolved. She had seen it so often. One of the women, not necessarily the eldest or most senior, fed up with the silliness and obstinacy of the men, not least that of her own husband, would suddenly have picked up her bundle, adjusted her headband, bowed forward to balance the weight, and trotted off down the trail. The others, many of them still grumbling, would have followed her in a straggling line.

In the Bambuti community there were no chiefs or leaders. Every adult male or female of whatever age had equal voice and weight. Only in a few matters such as when and where to spread the hunting-nets, the younger members would probably defer to the experience of one of the famous older hunters, but only after suitable face-saving argument and discussion.

Kelly looked around the deserted campsite and was amused to see what the tribe had abandoned. There were a wooden pestle and mortar used for pounding manioc, a fine steel mattock, a disembowelled transistor radio and various other items obviously purloined from the villages along the road. She was certain that the Bambuti were the least material people on earth. Possessions meant almost nothing to them, and after the fun of stealing them faded, they swiftly lost interest in them.

'Too heavy to carry,' they explained to Kelly when she asked. 'We can always borrow another one from the *wazungu*, if we need one.' Their eyes danced at the prospect, and they screamed with laughter and slapped each other on the back.

The only possessions they treasured enough to keep and

hand down to their children were the hunting-nets of woven bark. Each family had a hundred-foot length which they strung together with all the others to make the long communal net. The game was shared, with all the usual vehement debate, according to a time-honoured system amongst all those who had participated in the hunt.

Living within the bounty of the forest they had no need to accumulate wealth. Their clothing of bark-cloth could be renewed with a few hours' work, stripping and beating out the pith with a wooden mallet. Their weapons were disposable and renewable. The spear and the bow were whittled from hardwood and strung with bark fibre. The arrow and the spear were not even tipped with iron, but the points were simply hardened in the fire. The broad mongongo leaves roofed over their huts of arched saplings, and a small fire gave them warmth and comfort in the night.

The forest god gave them food in abundance, what need had they of other possessions? They were the only people Kelly had ever known who were completely satisfied with their lot, and this accounted for a great deal of their appeal.

Kelly had been looking forward to being reunited with them and she was downcast at having missed them. Sitting on a log in the deserted camp that was so swiftly reverting to jungle, she considered her next move. It would be futile to try and guess in which direction they had gone, and foolhardy to try and follow them. Their tracks would long ago have been obliterated by rain and the passage of other forest creatures, and she knew only this relatively small area of the forest with any certainty. There were twenty thousand square miles out there that she had never seen and where she might lose herself for ever.

She must give up trying to find them, and go on to her own base camp at Gondala, the 'place of the happy elephant'. In time the Bambuti would find her there and she must be patient.

She sat a little longer and listened to the forest. It seemed at first to be a silent lonely place. Only when the ear had learned to hear beyond the quiet did one realise that the forest was always filled with living sound. The orchestra of the insects played an eternal background music, the hum and reverberation like softly stroked violins, the click and clatter like tiny castanets, the wails and whine and buzz like the wind instruments. From the high upper galleries the birds called and sang and the monkeys crashed from branch to branch or lowed mournfully to the open sky, while on the leaf-strewn floor the dwarf antelope scuttled and scampered furtively.

Now when Kelly listened more intently still, she thought she heard far away and very faintly the clear whistle from high in the trees that old Sepoo solemnly swore was the crested chameleon announcing that the hives were overflowing and the honey season had begun.

Kelly smiled and stood up. She knew as a biologist that chameleons could not whistle. And yet ... She smiled again, settled her pack and stepped back on to the dim trail and went on towards Gondala. More and more frequently there were landmarks and signposts she recognised along the trail, the shape of certain tree-trunks and the juncture of trails, a sand-bank at a river crossing and blazes on the tree-trunks which she had cut long ago with her machete. She was getting closer and closer to home.

At a turning in the trail she came suddenly upon a steaming pile of yellow dung, as high as her knee. She looked about eagerly for the elephant that had dropped it, but already it had disappeared like a grey shadow into the trees. She wondered if it might be the Old Man with One Ear, a heavily tusked bull elephant that was often in the forest around Gondala.

Once the elephant herds had roamed the open savannah, along the shores of the lake and in the Lado Enclave to the north of the forest. However, a century of ruthless persecution, first by the old Arab slavers and their minions armed with muzzle-loading black powder guns and then by the European sportsmen and ivory-hunters with their deadly rifled weapons had decimated the herds and driven the survivors into the fastness of the forest.

It gave Kelly a deep sense of satisfaction to know that, although she seldom saw them, she shared the forest with those great sagacious beasts, and that her home was named after one of them.

At the next stream she paused to bathe and comb her hair and don her T-shirt. She would be home in a few hours. She had just tied the thong in her braid and put away her comb when she chilled to a new sound, fierce and menacing. She came to her feet and seized her digging-stick. The sound came again, the hoarse sawing that roughened her nerves like sandpaper, and she felt her pulse accelerate and her breath come short.

It was unusual to hear a leopard call in daylight. The spotted cat was a creature of the night, but anything unusual in the forest was to be treated with caution. The leopard called again, a little closer, almost directly upstream on the bank of the river, and Kelly cocked her head to listen. There was something odd about this leopard.

A suspicion flitted across her mind, and she waited, crouching, holding the sharpened digging-stick ready. There was a long silence. All the forest was listening to the leopard, and then it called again, that terrible ripping sound. It was on the riverbank above her, not more than fifty feet from where she crouched.

This time, listening to the call, Kelly's suspicion became certainty. With a blood-curdling scream of her own, she launched herself at the creature's hiding-place brandishing her pointed stick. There was a sudden commotion amongst the lotus leaves on the bank and a small figure darted out and scampered away. Kelly took a full round-armed swing with her stick and caught it a resounding crack on bare brown buttocks. There was an anguished howl.

'You wicked old man!' Kelly yelled, and swung again. 'You tried to frighten me.' She missed as the pixie figure leaped over a bush ahead of her and took refuge behind it.

'You cruel little devil.' She hounded him out of the bush, and he darted around the side, shrieking with mock terror and laughter.

'I'll beat your backside blue as a baboon's,' Kelly threatened, her stick swishing, and they went twice round the bush, the small figure dancing and ducking just out of range. They were both laughing now. 'Sepoo, you little monster, I shall never forgive you!' Kelly choked on her laughter.

'I am not Sepoo. I am a leopard.' He staggered with mirth and she nearly caught him. He made a spurt to keep just out of range and squealed merrily.

In the end she had to give up and lean, exhausted with laughter, on her stick. Sepoo fell down in the leaves and beat his own belly and hiccuped and rolled over and hugged his knees and laughed until the tears poured down his cheeks and ran into the wrinkles and were channelled back behind his ears.

'Kara-Ki.' He belched and hiccuped and laughed some more. 'Kara-Ki, the fearless one, is frightened by old Sepoo!' It was a joke that he would tell at every campfire for the next dozen moons.

It took some time for Sepoo to become rational again. He had to laugh himself out. Kelly stood by and watched him affectionately, joining in some of his wilder outbursts of hilarity. Gradually these became less frequent, until at last they could converse normally.

They squatted side by side and talked. The Bambuti had long ago lost their own language, and had adopted those of the *wazungu* with whom they came in contact. They spoke a curious mixture of Swahili and Uhali and Hita with an accent and colourful idiom of their own.

With his bow and arrow Sepoo had shot a colobus monkey that morning. He had salted the beautiful black and white pelt to trade at the roadside. Now he built a fire and cooked the flesh for their lunch.

As they chatted and ate, she became aware of a strange mood in her companion. It was difficult for a pygmy to remain serious for long. His irrepressible sense of fun and his merry laughter could not be suppressed. They kept bubbling to the surface, and yet beneath it there was something new that had not been there when last Kelly had been with him. She could not define exactly what had changed. There was an air of preoccupation in Sepoo's mien, a worry, a sadness that dimmed the twinkle of his gaze and in repose made his mouth droop at the corners.

Kelly asked about the other members of the tribe, about Pamba, his wife.

'She scolds like a monkey from the treetops, and she mutters like the thunder of the skies.' Sepoo grinned with love un-dimmed after forty years of marriage. 'She is a cantankerous old woman, but when I tell her that I will get a pretty young wife she replies that any girl stupid enough to take me, can have me.' And he chortled at the joke and slapped his thigh, leaving monkey grease on the wrinkled skin.

'What of the others?' Kelly pressed him, seeking the cause of Sepoo's unhappiness. Was there dissension in the tribe? 'How is your brother Pirri?'

That was always a possible cause of strife in the tribe. There was a sibling rivalry between the half-brothers. Sepoo and Pirri were the master hunters, the oldest male members of the small tribal unit. They should have been friends as well as brothers, but Pirri was not a typical Bambuti. His father had been a Hita. Long ago, further back than any of the tribe could remember, their mother while still a virgin had wandered to the edge of the forest where a Hita hunting-party had caught her. She had been young and pretty as a pixie and the Hita had held her in their camp for two nights and taken it in turns to have sport with her. Perhaps they might have killed her carelessly when they tired of her, but before that happened she escaped.

Pirri was born from this experience and he was taller than any other men of the tribe and lighter in colour and finer-featured, with the mouth and thin nose of the Hita. He was different in character also, more aggressive and acquisitive than any Bambuti Kelly had ever met.

'Pirri is Pirri,' Sepoo replied evasively, but although the old antagonism was still evident, Kelly sensed that it was something other than his elder brother that worried him.

Although it was only a few hours' journey to Gondala, the two of them talked the daylight away and evening found them still squatting at the cooking-fire with the threat of rain heavy in the air. Kelly used the last of the light to cut the thin supple wands of the selepe tree and, as Pamba had taught her, to plant them in a circle in the soft earth and bend them inwards and plait them into the framework of a traditional Bambuti hut. Meanwhile old Sepoo went off on his own. He returned just as she was completing the framework, and he was bowed under a burden of mongongo leaves with which to thatch the hut. The structure was complete within an hour of the work commencing. When the thunderstorm broke, they were huddled warm and dry in the tiny structure with a cheerful fire flickering, eating the last of the monkey steaks.

At last Kelly settled down on her inflated mattress in the darkness and Sepoo curled on the soft leaf mould close beside her, but neither of them slept immediately. Kelly was aware of the old man lying awake and she waited. With darkness as a cover for his unhappiness Sepoo whispered at last, 'Are you awake, Kara-Ki?'

'I am listening, old father,' she whispered back, and he sighed. It was a sound so different from his usual merry chuckles.

'Kara-Ki, the Mother and Father are angry. I have never known them so angry,' Sepoo said, and she knew that he meant the god of the Bambuti, the twin godhead of the living forest, male and female in one. Kelly was silent for a while in deference to the seriousness of this statement.

'That is a grave matter,' she replied at last. 'What has made them angry?'

'They have been wounded,' Sepoo said softly. 'The rivers flow red with their blood.'

This was a startling concept, and Kelly was silent again as she tried to visualise what Sepoo meant. How could the rivers run with the blood of the forest? she wondered. She was finally forced to ask, 'I do not understand, old father. What are you telling me?'

'It is beyond my humble words to describe,' Sepoo whispered. 'There has been a terrible sacrilege and the Mother and Father are in pain. Perhaps the Molimo will come.'

Kelly had been in camp with the Bambuti only once during the Molimo visitation. The women were excluded, and Kelly had remained in the huts with Pamba and the other women when the Molimo came, but she had heard its voice roaring like a bull buffalo and trumpeting like an enraged elephant as it rampaged through the forest in the night.

In the morning Kelly had asked Sepoo, 'What creature is the Molimo?'

'The Molimo is the Molimo,' he had replied enigmatically. 'It is the creature of the forest. It is the voice of the Mother and the Father.'

Now Sepoo suggested that the Molimo might come again, and Kelly shivered with a little superstitious thrill. This time

311

she would not remain in the huts with the women, she promised herself. This time she would find out more about this fabulous creature. For the moment, however, she put it out of her mind and, instead, concerned herself with the sacrilege that had been committed somewhere deep in the forest.

'Sepoo,' she whispered. 'If you cannot tell me about this terrible thing, will you show me? Will you take me and show me the rivers that run with the blood of the gods?'

Sepoo snuffled in the darkness and hawked to clear his throat and spat into the coals of the fire. Then he grunted, 'Very well, Kara-Ki. I will show you. In the morning, before we reach Gondala we will go out of our way and I will show you the rivers that bleed.'

In the morning Sepoo was full of high spirits again, almost as though their conversation in the night had never taken place. Kelly gave him the present which she had brought for him, a Swiss army knife. Sepoo was enchanted with all the blades and implements and tools that folded out of the red plastic handle, and promptly cut himself on one of them. He cackled with laughter and sucked his thumb, then held it out to Kelly as proof of the marvellous sharpness of the little blade.

Kelly knew he would probably lose the knife within a week, or give it away to someone else in the tribe on an impulse, as he had done with all the other gifts she had given him. But for the moment his joy was childlike and complete.

'Now you must show me the bleeding rivers,' she reminded him as she adjusted the headband of her pack, and for a moment his eyes were sad again. Then he grinned and pirouetted.

'Come along, Kara-Ki. Let us see if you still move in the forest like one of the real people.'

Soon they left the broad trail, and Sepoo led her swiftly through the secret unmarked ways. He danced ahead of her like a sprite and the foliage closed behind him, leaving no trace of his passing. Where Sepoo moved upright, Kelly was forced to stoop beneath the branches, and at times she lost sight of him.

No wonder the old Egyptians believed the Bambuti had the power of invisibility, Kelly thought, as she extended herself to keep up with him.

If Sepoo had moved silently she might have lost him, but like all the pygmies he sang and laughed and chattered to her and the forest as he went. His voice ahead guided her, and warned the dangerous forest creatures of his approach so that there would be no confrontation.

She knew that he was moving at his best pace, to test and tease her, and she was determined not to fall too far behind. She called replies back to him and joined in the chorus of the praise songs and when he stepped out on the bank of the river many hours later she was only seconds behind him.

He grinned at her until his eyes disappeared in the web of wrinkles and shook his head in reluctant approval, but Kelly was not interested in his approbation. She was gazing at the river.

This was one of the tributaries of the Ubomo that had its source high up in the Mountains of the Moon, at the foot of one of the glaciers above fifteen thousand feet, the altitude where the permanent snowline stood. This river found its way down through lakes and waterfalls, fed by the mighty rains that lashed this wettest of all mountain ranges, down through the treeless moors and heather, down through the forest of giant prehistoric ferns, until at last it entered the dense bamboo thickets which were the domain of gorilla and spiral-horned bongo antelope. From there it fell again another three thousand feet through rugged foothills until it reached these true rain forests with their galleried canopies of gigantic hardwoods.

The Bambuti called this river Tetwa, after the silver catfish that abounded in its sweet clear waters and shoaled on the yellow sandbanks. The Bambuti women shed even their tiny loin-cloths when they went into the waters of the Tetwa to catch the barbeled catfish. Each of them armed with a fish basket of woven reeds and bark, they surrounded the shoal and splashed and shrieked with excitement as they flipped the struggling slippery silver fish from the sparkling water.

That had been before the river began to bleed. Now Kelly stared at it in horror.

The river was fifty yards wide and the forest grew right to the edge and formed a canopy that almost, but not quite, met overhead. There was a narrow irregular gleam of sky high above the middle of the river-course.

313

From bank to bank the river ran red, not the bright red of heart blood, but a darker browner hue. The sullied waters seemed almost viscous. They had lost their sparkle and were heavy and dull, running thick and slow as used engine oil.

The sand spits were red also, coated with a deep layer of thick mud. The carcasses of the catfish were strewn on the red banks, thick as autumn leaves, piled upon each other in their multitudes. Their skulls were eyeless and the stench of their putrefying flesh was oppressive in the humid air below the forest canopy.

'What has done this, Sepoo?' Kelly whispered, but he shrugged and busied himself rolling a pinch of coarse black native tobacco in a leaf. While Kelly went down the bank, he lit his primitive cheroot from the live coal he carried wrapped in a pouch of green leaves around his neck. He puffed great clouds of blue smoke, squeezing his eyes tightly shut with pleasure.

As Kelly stepped out on to the sand spit, she sank almost knee-deep into the mud. She scooped up a handful of it and rubbed it between her fingers. It was slick as grease, fine as potter's clay, and it stained her skin a dark *sang de boeuf*. She tried to wash it off, but the colour was fast and her fingers were red as those of an assassin. She lifted a handful of mud to her nose and sniffed it. It had no alien smell.

She waded back to the bank and confronted Sepoo. 'What has done this, old father? What has happened?'

He sucked on his cheroot, then coughed and giggled nervously, avoiding her gaze.

'Come on, Sepoo, tell me.'

'I do not know, Kara-Ki.'

'Why not? Did you not go upstream to find out?'

Sepoo examined the burning end of his green-leaf cheroot with great interest.

'Why not?' Kelly insisted.

'I was afraid, Kara-Ki,' he mumbled, and Kelly suddenly realised that for the Bambuti this was some supernatural occurrence. They would not follow the choked rivers upstream for fear of what they might find.

'How many rivers are like this?' Kelly demanded.

'Many, many,' Sepoo muttered, meaning more than four.

'Name them for me,' she insisted, and he reeled off the names of all the rivers she had ever visited in the region and some that she had only heard of. It seemed then that almost the entire drainage area of the Ubomo was affected. This was not some isolated local disturbance, but a large-scale disaster that threatened not only the Bambuti hunting areas but the sacred heartland of the forest as well.

'We must travel upstream,' Kelly said with finality, and Sepoo looked as though he might burst into tears.

'They are waiting for you at Gondala,' he squeaked, but Kelly did not make the mistake of beginning an argument. She had learned from the women of the tribe, from old Pamba in particular. She lifted her pack on to her back, adjusted the headband and started up the bank. For two hundred yards she was alone, and her spirits started to sink. The forest area ahead was completely unknown to her, and it would be folly to continue on her own if Sepoo could not be induced to accompany her.

Then she heard Sepoo's voice close behind her, protesting loudly that he would not take another step further. Kelly grinned with relief and quickened her pace.

For another twenty minutes Sepoo trailed along behind her, swearing that he was on the point of turning back and abandoning her, his tone becoming more and more plaintive as he realised that Kelly was not going to give in. Then quite suddenly he chuckled and began to sing. The effort of remaining miserable was too much for him to sustain. Kelly shouted a jibe over her shoulder and joined in the next refrain of the song. Soon Sepoo slipped past her and took the lead.

For the next two days they followed the Tetwa River and with every mile its plight was more pitiful. The red clay clogged it more deeply. The waters were almost pure mud, thick as oatmeal porridge and there were dead roots and loose vegetation mixed into it already beginning to bubble with the gas of decay; the stink of it mingled with that of dead birds and small animals and rotting fish that had been trapped and suffocated by the mud. The carcasses were strewn upon the red banks or floated with balloon bellies upon the sullied waters.

Late in the afternoon of the second day they reached the far boundary of Sepoo's tribal hunting-grounds. There was no signpost or other indication to mark the line but Sepoo paused on the bank of the Tetwa, unstrung his bow and reversed his arrows in the rolled bark quiver on his shoulder, as a sign to the Mother and the Father of the forest that he would respect the sacred place and kill no creature, cut no branch nor light a fire within these deep forest preserves.

Then he sang a pygmy song to placate the forest, and to ask permission to enter its deep and secret place.

> Oh, beloved mother of all the tribe,
> You gave us first suck at your breast
> And cradled us in the darkness.
> Oh respected father, of our fathers
> You made us strong
> You taught us the ways of the forest
> And gave us your creatures as food.
> We honour you, we praise you . . .

Kelly stood a little aside and watched him. It seemed presumptuous for her to join in the words, so she was silent.

In her book, *The People of the Tall Trees*, she had examined in detail the tradition of the forest heartland and discussed the wisdom of the Bambuti law. The heartland was the reservoir of forest life which spilled over into the hunting preserves, renewing and sustaining them.

It was also the buffer zone which separated each of the tribes from its neighbours, and obviated friction and territorial dispute between them. This was only another example of the wisdom of the system that the Bambuti had evolved to regulate and manage their existence.

So, Kelly and Sepoo camped that night on the threshold of the sacred heartland. During the night it rained, which Sepoo proclaimed was a definite sign from the forest deities that they were amenable to the two of them continuing their journey upstream.

Kelly smiled in the darkness. It rained, on average, three hundred nights a year in the Ubomo basin, and if it had not done so tonight Sepoo would probably have taken that as even more eloquent assent from the Mother and Father.

316

They resumed the journey at dawn. When one of the striped forest duiker trotted out of the undergrowth ahead of them and stood to regard them trustingly from a distance of five paces, Sepoo reached instinctively for his bow and then controlled himself with such an effort that he shook as though he were in malarial ague. The flesh of this little antelope was tender and succulent and sweet.

'Go!' Sepoo yelled at it angrily. 'Away with you! Do not mock me! Do not tempt me! I am firm against your wiles . . .'

The duiker slipped off the path and Sepoo turned to Kelly. 'Bear witness for me, Kara-Ki. I did not trespass. That creature was sent by the Mother and Father to test me. No natural duiker would be so stupid as to stand so close. I was strong, was I not, Kara-Ki?' he demanded piteously, and Kelly squeezed his muscular shoulder.

'I am proud of you, old father. The gods love you.'

They went on.

In the middle of that third afternoon Kelly paused suddenly in mid-stride and cocked her head to a sound she had never heard in the forest before. It was still faint and intermittent, blanketed by the trees, but as she went on it became clearer and stronger with each mile until it resembled in Kelly's imagination the growling of lions on the kill, a terrible savage and feral sound that filled her with despair.

Now the River Tetwa no longer flowed, it was dammed with branches and debris, so that in places it had broken its banks and flooded the forest floor and they were forced to wade waist-deep through the stinking swamp. Then abruptly, with a shock of disclosure, the forest ended and they were standing in sunlight where sunlight had not penetrated for a million years.

Ahead of them was such a sight as Kelly could not have conceived in her most hideous nightmares. She gazed upon it until night fell and mercifully hid it from her and then she turned away and went back.

In the night she came awake to find herself weeping aloud and Sepoo's hand stroking her arm to comfort her.

The return journey down the dying river was slower, as though she were burdened by her sadness and Sepoo shortened his stride to match her.

Five days later, Kelly and Sepoo reached Gondala.

Gondala was a site unique in this part of the forest. It was a glade of yellow elephant grass less than a hundred acres in extent. At the south end it rose to meet a line of forest-clad hills. For part of the day the tall trees threw a shadow across the clearing, keeping it cooler than if it had been exposed to the full glare of the tropical sun. Two small streams bounded this wedge of open ground, while the slope and elevation disclosed a sweeping vista over the treetops towards the north-west. It was one of the few vantage points in the Ubomo basin from which the view was not obscured by the great forest trees. The cool air in the open glade was less humid than that of the deep forest.

Kelly paused at the edge of the forest, as she always did, and looked out at the mountain peaks a hundred miles away. Usually the Mountains of the Moon were hidden in their own perpetual clouds. This morning, as if to welcome her home, they had drawn aside the veil and stood clear in all their glistening splendour. The glaciated massif of Mount Stanley was forced upwards between the faults of the Great Rift Valley to a height of almost seventeen thousand feet. It was pure ice-white and achingly beautiful.

She turned away from it reluctantly and looked across the clearing. There was her homestead and laboratory, an ambitious building of log, clay plaster and thatch which had taken her almost three years to build, with a little help from her friends.

The gardens on the lower slopes were irrigated from the streams and fenced in to protect them from the forest creatures. There were no flowerbeds. The garden was not ornamental but provided the small community of Gondala with a large part of its sustenance.

As they left the forest, some of the women working in the garden spotted them and ran to greet Kelly, shrieking and laughing with delight. Some were Bambuti, but most were Uhali women in their traditional colourful long skirts. They surrounded her and escorted her up to the homestead.

318

The commotion brought a solitary figure out of the laboratory on to the wide verandah. He was an old man with hair as silver as the snows on Mount Stanley that faced him from a hundred miles away. He was dressed in a crisp blue safari suit and sandals. He shaded his eyes and recognised her and smiled. His teeth were still white and perfect in his dark intelligent face.

'Kelly.' He held out both hands to her as she came up on to the verandah, and she ran to meet him. 'Kelly,' he repeated, as he took her hands. 'I was beginning to worry about you. I expected you days ago. It's good to see you.'

'It's good to see you also, Mr President.'

'Come now, my child. I am no longer that, at least not in Ephrem Taffari's view, and when did we last stand on ceremony, you and I?'

'Victor,' she corrected herself. 'I have missed you so, and I have so much to tell you. I don't know where to begin.'

'Later.' He shook his handsome grizzled head and embraced her. She knew that he was over seventy years old but she could feel that his body had the strength and vigour of a man half that age. 'First let me show you how well I have taken care of your work during your absence. I should have remained a scientist rather than becoming a politician,' he said. He took her hand and drew her into the laboratory, and immediately they were engrossed in technical discussion.

President Victor Omeru had studied in London as a young man. He had returned to Ubomo with a Master's degree in electrical engineering and for a short time had been employed in the colonial administration until he had resigned to lead the movement towards independence. Yet he had always retained his interest in the sciences and his learning and skills had always impressed Kelly.

When he had been overthrown in Ephrem Taffari's bloody *coup*, he had fled into the forest with a handful of loyal followers and sought sanctuary with Kelly Kinnear at Gondala. In the ten or so months since then, the settlement in the glade had become the headquarters of the Uhali resistance movement against Taffari's tyranny, and Kelly had become one of his most trusted agents. When he was not receiving visitors from outside the forest and planning the counter-revolution, he made himself Kelly's assistant and in a very short time had become invaluable to her.

For an hour the two of them were happily engrossed with slides and retorts and cages of laboratory rats. It was almost as though they were deliberately putting off the moment when they must discuss urgent and ugly reality.

Kelly's research was handicapped by inadequate equipment and shortage of expendable supplies. All of this had to be portered into Gondala, and since Kelly's field grant had been rescinded and Victor Omeru deposed, she had been even more restricted. Nevertheless, they had made some exciting discoveries. In particular they had been able to isolate an anti-malarial substance in the sap of the selepe tree. The selepe was a common plant of the forest that the pygmies used for the dual purposes of building their huts and treating fever.

Malaria was a resurgent menace in Africa where more and more frequently there appeared strains resistant to the synthetic prophylactics. Soon malaria might rank, once again, as the greatest killer on the continent, apart from AIDS. It seemed ironic that both these scourges should have their origin in the cradle of man himself, in the Great Rift Valley of East Africa, where man had stood upright and taken his first uncertain footsteps into glory and infamy. Was it not possible that the ultimate cure for both these diseases might yet come from this same area of the globe? They both reasserted that hope, as they had done a thousand times before.

In addition to the malarial cure, there were the other possibilities that Kelly and Victor Omeru were considering. The one disease to which the Bambuti were susceptible was cancer of the pancreas. This was caused by some factor of their diet or environment in the forest. The women of the tribe used an infusion of the root of a vine that contained a bitter milky sap to treat the disease, and Kelly had witnessed some seemingly miraculous cures. She and Victor Omeru had isolated an alkaloid from the sap which they hoped was the active agent in the cure, and they were testing it with encouraging results.

They were using the same alkaloid to treat three of the Uhali men in camp who were suffering from AIDS. It was too soon to be certain, but once again the results were most encouraging and exciting. Now they discussed them avidly. This excitement and the pleasure of reunion lasted them through the frugal lunch of salads that they shared on the verandah of the thatched bungalow.

Kelly revelled in the joy of conversing with such a cultured and erudite man. Victor Omeru's presence had transformed her lonely isolated life at Gondala. She loved her Bambuti friends, but they came and went without warning, and though their simple happy ways were always a joy, they were no substitute for the stimulation of a superior educated mind.

Victor Omeru was a man she could respect and admire and love without reservation. As far as Kelly was concerned, he was without vice, overflowing with humanity and compassion for his fellow men, and at the same time with a deep and abiding respect and concern for the world in which they lived and the other creatures that shared it with them.

She saw in him the true patriot, completely devoted to his little nation. He was, in addition, the only African Kelly had ever met who was above tribalism. He had spent his entire political life trying to appease and ameliorate the terrible curse that was, in both their views, the single most tragic fact of the African reality. He should have been an example to the rest of the continent, and to his peers in the high councils of the Organisation of African Unity.

When, almost single-handed, he had obtained independence from the colonial administration, the preponderance of his fellow Uhali tribesmen had swept him into the presidential office and overturned at a single stroke the centuries of brutal domination by the proud Hita aristocracy.

The greatest crisis of his presidency had come within the very first days of independence. The Uhali tribe had turned upon the Hita in a savage orgy of retribution. In five terrible days, over twenty thousand Hita had perished. The mob had torched their *manyattas*. Those Hita who survived the flames were hacked to death with hoes and machetes. The tools with which the enslaved Uhali had tilled the fields and hewn the firewood for their masters were turned upon them.

The proud Hita women, tall and stately and beautiful, were

stripped of their traditional ankle-length robes, and the elaborately plaited locks in which they gloried were hacked roughly
from their heads. They were herded naked before the jeering
Uhali mob, and pelted with excrement. Some of the women
were lifted struggling and naked and impaled upon the poles of
the *manyattas'* outer stockade.

The younger women and girls had been yoked between two
of their own oxen, secured with rawhide thongs by each ankle.
Then the mob had urged the oxen forward and the girls had
been torn apart.

Kelly had not been there to witness these atrocities. She had
been a schoolgirl in England at the time, but the legend had
become history of how Victor Omeru had gone out to plead
with the mob and physically to interpose himself between them
and their Hita victims. With the sheer force of his personality
he had brought the slaughter to an end, and virtually saved the
Hita tribe from genocide and extinction. Nevertheless, thousands of Hita perished and fifty thousand fled for sanctuary
into the neighbouring countries of Uganda and Zaïre.

It had taken a major exercise of statesmanship over decades
of wise government for Victor Omeru to cool the terrible tribal
animosities of his people, to persuade the exiled Hita to return
to Ubomo, to restore their herds and their grazing lands to
them, and to bring their young men in from the traditional
pastoral ways to education and advancement in the modern
Ubomo nation he was trying to build.

In recompense for those terrible first days of independence
Victor had always thereafter erred on the side of leniency
towards the Hita tribe. To demonstrate his trust and faith in
them he allowed them gradually to take control of Ubomo's
little army and police force. Ephrem Taffari himself had
travelled abroad to complete his education on a special scholar-
ship provided by Victor Omeru out of his own meagre presidential salary.

Victor Omeru was paying for that generosity now. Once
again the Uhali tribe groaned beneath the Hita tyranny.

As so often happens in Africa, the cycle of oppression and
brutality had run its full course, but even now as they sat on
the wide verandah of the bungalow, immersed in discussion,

Kelly could still detect the suffering and concern for his nation and all his people in Victor Omeru's dark eyes.

It seemed cruel to add to his misery but she could no longer keep it from him.

'Victor, there is something awful happening up there, in the rivers of the forest, in the sacred Bambuti heartland. Something so terrible that I hardly know how to describe it to you.'

He listened without interruption, but when she had finished he said quietly, 'Taffari is killing our people and our land. The vultures smell death in the air and they are gathering, but we will stop them.'

Kelly had never seen him so angry before. His face was hard and his eyes were dark and terrible.

'They are powerful, Victor. Rich and powerful.'

'There is no power to match that of honest men and a just cause,' he replied, and his strength and determination were contagious. Kelly felt her despair slough away, leaving her feeling renewed and confident.

'Yes,' she whispered. 'We will find a way to stop them. For the sake of this land we must find a way.'

 'Formosa' meant beautiful. The name was appropriate, Tug Harrison conceded, as the Rolls-Royce Silver Spirit left the littoral plain and climbed up into the green mountains. The road swept around a shoulder of one of the peaks and for a moment Tug gazed out across the broad Formosa Straits and fancied he saw the loom of mainland China lurking like a dragon a hundred and more miles out there in the blue distance. Then the road turned again and they were back into the forests of cypress and cedar.

They were four thousand feet above the humid tropical plain and the bustle of Taipei, one of the busiest and most affluent cities in Asia. The air up here was sweet and cool; there was no need of the Rolls's superb air-conditioning system.

Tug felt relaxed and clear-headed. It was one of the joys of having your own jet aircraft, he smiled. The Gulfstream flew when he was ready, wherever he wanted to go. There was none of the aggravation of large airports and throngs of the great unwashed multitude. No miles of corridors to traverse nor luggage carousels at which to play the guessing game of 'will it come or won't it', no surly customs officials and porters and taxi-drivers.

Tug had taken it in easy stages from London. Abu Dhabi, Bahrain, Brunei, Hong Kong – he had spent a day or two in each of those centres in all of which he had major games in play.

The stop-over in Hong Kong had been particularly worthwhile. The richest and more prudent of the Hong Kong businessmen were intent on moving out their assets and relocating ahead of the termination of the treaty and the reversion of the territory to mainland China. In the permanent suite which he kept at the Peninsula Hotel, Tug had signed two agreements which should net him ten million pounds over the next few years.

When his chief pilot touched down at Taipei airport, ground control directed Tug's Gulfstream to taxi to a discreet parking billet behind the Cathay Pacific hangars and the Rolls-Royce was waiting on the tarmac, with the youngest son of the Ning family to meet him.

Customs and Immigration, in the shape of two uniformed officials, were ushered aboard, bobbing and smiling, by his host. They stamped Tug's red diplomatic passport and placed the 'in bond' seals on his private bar and departed, all within five minutes.

In the meantime Tug's matched set of Louis Vuitton luggage was being transferred to the boot of the Rolls by a team of white-jacketed and -gloved servants. Within fifteen minutes of touch-down, the Rolls whisked him out of the airport gates.

Tug felt so good that he was inclined to philosophise. He compared other journeys he had made when he was young and poor and struggling. On foot and bicycle and native bus he had crossed and recrossed the African continent. He remembered his first motor vehicle, a Ford V-8 truck with front mudguards like elephant ears, smooth tyres that never ran fifty miles without puncturing, and an engine held together with baling-wire and hope. He had been immensely proud of it at the time.

Even his first air flight on one of the old Sunderland flying boats that once plied the African continent, landing to refuel on the Zambezi, the great lakes, and finally the Nile itself, had taken ten days to reach London.

Truly to appreciate luxury it was necessary to have withstood severe hardship, Tug believed. The early days had been tough. He had revelled in each one of them but, hell, the touch of silk against his skin and the Rolls upholstery under his backside felt wonderful and he was looking forward to the negotiations that lay ahead. They would be hard and without quarter, but that was the way he liked it.

He loved the cut and thrust of the bargaining table. He enjoyed changing his style to match each adversary he faced. He could flash the cutlass or palm the stiletto as the occasion warranted. When called for he could shout and bang the table and curse with the same vigour as an Australian opal miner or a Texan rough-neck on an oil rig, or he could smile and whisper honeyed hemlock as skilfully as could the man he was now going to meet. Yes, he loved every moment of it. It was what kept him young.

He smiled genially and turned to discuss oriental netsukes and ceramics with the young man who sat beside him on the pale green leather back seat of the Rolls.

'Generalissimo Chiang Kai-shek brought the cream of China's art treasures with him from the mainland in 1949,' Ning Cheng Gong was saying, and Tug nodded.

'All civilised men must be thankful for that,' he agreed. 'If he had not done so, they would have been destroyed in Mao's cultural revolution.'

As they chatted, Tug was studying his host's youngest son. Even though he had not yet shown himself to be a force in the Ning financial dynasty, and up until now had been overshadowed by his elder half-brothers, Tug had a full dossier on Cheng.

There was some indication that Cheng, even as the youngest son, was his father's favourite, the child of his old age, by his third wife, a beautiful English girl. As often happens, the admixture of oriental and occidental blood seemed to have brought out the good traits of both parents. It seemed that

Ning Cheng Gong had bred true, for he was clever, devious, ruthless, and lucky. Tug Harrison never discounted the element of luck. Some men had it and others, no matter how clever, did not.

It seemed that old Ning Heng H'Sui was bringing him on carefully, like a fine thoroughbred colt, preparing him for his first major race with patience and diligence. He had given Cheng all the advantages, without allowing him to grow up soft.

After his master's degree at Chiang Kai-shek University, Ning Cheng Gong had gone straight into the Taiwanese army for national service. His father had made no effort to beat the draft on his behalf. Tug supposed that it was part of the toughening process.

Tug Harrison had a copy of the young man's military service record. He had done well, very well, and had ended his call-up with the rank of captain and a job on the general staff. Of course, the commander of the Taiwanese army was a personal friend of Ning Heng H'Sui, but his selection would not have been entirely based on preferment rather than ability. There had been only one small shadow on Cheng's service record. A civilian complaint had been brought against Captain Ning, and investigated by the military police. It involved the death of a young girl in a Taipei brothel. The full report of the investigating officer had been carefully removed from Ning's service record and only the recommendation that there was no substance in the accusation remained, together with an endorsement by the Attorney-General that no charges be pursued. Once again Tug Harrison scented the intervention of the Ning patriarch in this dossier. It increased Tug's respect for the power and influence of the family.

At the end of his national service, Ning Cheng Gong had gone into the Taiwanese diplomatic corps. Perhaps old Heng had not yet considered him ready to join the Lucky Dragon. Once again young Cheng's progress had been meteoric, and he had been given an ambassadorship within four years, admittedly it was to a small and insignificant little African country, but by all accounts he had done well. Once again Tug had been able to obtain a copy of his service record from the Taiwanese foreign office. It had cost him ten thousand pounds sterling in bribes, but Tug considered it a bargain. In this dossier he had again found some evidence of Cheng's unusual erotic tastes.

The body of a young black girl had been fished out of the Zambezi river only partially devoured by crocodiles. There was certain mutilation of the corpse's genital and mammary areas which had led the police to pursue further enquiries. They found that at the time the Chinese ambassador had been staying at a game lodge on the Zambezi south bank, near the girl's village. The missing girl had been seen entering Cheng's bungalow late on the evening before she disappeared. She had not been seen again alive. This was as far as the enquiry had been allowed to run, before being quashed by a directive from the president's office. Now the ambassador's term of office had run its course. He had resigned from the diplomatic service and returned to Taiwan to take up a position with the Lucky Dragon company, at last.

His father had given him the equivalent rank of vice-president, and Tug Harrison found him interesting. Not only was he clever but he was good-looking to the Western eye. His mother's influence was discernible in his features; although his hair was jet black there were no epicanthic folds in his upper eyelids. His English was perfect. If Tug closed his eyes he could imagine he was conversing with a young upper-class Englishman. He was suave and urbane, with just the slightest perceptible streak of ruthlessness and cruelty in him. Yes, Tug decided, he was a young man with prospects. His father could be proud of him.

Tug felt the familiar stab of regret as he thought of his own feckless offspring, weaklings and wastrels all three. He could only console himself by believing that the fault must lie in their maternal line. They were the sons of three different women all of whom he had chosen for their physical attractiveness. When you are young there is no reasoning with an erect penis, he shook his head regretfully, it seemed to inhibit the flow of the blood to the brain. He had married four women whom he would not have employed as secretaries, and three of them had given him sons in their mirror image, beautiful and lazy and irresponsible.

Tug frowned at this shadow across his sunny mood. Most

men give more thought and care to the breeding of their dogs and horses than they do to selecting a dam for their own children. Fatherhood was the only endeavour in his entire life in which Tug Harrison had failed dismally.

'I am looking forward to viewing your father's collection of ivory,' Tug told Cheng, putting unprofitable regret out of his mind.

'My father will be pleased to show it to you,' Cheng smiled. 'It is his chief delight, after the Lucky Dragon, of course.'

As he said it, the Rolls sailed around another hairpin and directly ahead stood the gates to the Ning estate. Tug had seen a photograph of them, but still he was not prepared for the actuality. They reminded him instantly of those gigantic garish sculptures in the Tiger Balm Gardens in Hong Kong.

The Lucky Dragon entwined itself around the gateway like a prehistoric monster, glittering with emerald-green ceramic tiles and gold leaf. Its talons were hooked and raised, its wings were spread fifty feet wide, its eyes glowed like live coals and its crocodile jaws were agape and lined with jagged fangs.

'My goodness!' said Tug mildly, and Cheng laughed lightly and deprecatingly.

'My father's little whimsy,' he explained. 'The teeth are real ivory and the eyes are a pair of cabochon spinel-rubies from Sri Lanka. They weigh together a little over five kilos. They are unique and are valued at over a million dollars, hence the armed guards.'

The two guards came to attention as the Rolls slid through the gateway. They were dressed in paramilitary uniform with blancoed webbing and burnished stainless helmets similar to those worn by the honour guard at Chiang Kai-shek's tomb in Taipei. They carried automatic weapons and Tug Harrison guessed that they had other duties apart from guarding the Lucky Dragon's jewelled eyes. Tug had heard that young Cheng, using his military experience, had personally recruited these guards from the ranks of the Taiwanese marines, one of the elite regiments of the world, to protect his father.

Old Ning Heng H'Sui had left more than a few widows and orphans behind him as he hacked his way to power. Rumour had it that he had once been head of one of Hong Kong's powerful secret societies, and that he still maintained close ties with the Tongs. He might now be an art collector and artist and poet, but there were many who remembered the old days and would dearly love to pay off a few ancient scores.

Tug felt no repugnance at all for the old man's personal history, just as he felt none for the youngest son's sexual foibles. Tug had a few secrets of his own, and knew the whereabouts of more than one unmarked grave in the African wilderness. He had lived his whole life in the company of, and in competition with, ruthless predatory men. He made no moral judgements. He accepted mankind as he found it, and looked instead for the profit to be made from its strengths or weaknesses.

Cheng returned the salute of the silver-helmeted guards with a nod and the Rolls passed beneath the Lucky Dragon's arched belly and entered a fantasy land of gardens and lakes, pagodas and arched Chinese bridges. Shoals of jewel-coloured khoi glided beneath the lake waters, and flocks of snow-white pigeons swirled about the eaves of the pagodas. The lawns were green and smooth as a silk kimono stretched over a pretty girl's thigh. The rhododendrons were in full bloom. It was peaceful and lovely, in contrast to the tasteless dragon sculpture at the main gateway.

The Rolls drew up at the entrance to a building that reminded Tug of a miniature of the Winter Palace in Peking. The fountains that surrounded it shot a sparkling lacework of foam high into the cool mountain air. A cortège of white-jacketed servants waited on each side of the entrance to welcome Tug, and they bowed deeply as Cheng led him into the vaulted interior.

The panelled walls had been slid aside so that the gardens seemed part of the décor. The furnishings were simple and exquisite. The floors of red cedar glowed and the cigar-box smell of the woodwork perfumed the air. A few ceramic treasures which would have graced any museum collection were arranged to full effect, and a single flower arrangement of cherry blossom was the centre-piece of the room.

'One of the maids will make tea for you, Sir Peter,' Cheng told him, 'while the other draws your bath and unpacks your suitcases. Then you will want to rest for an hour. My father invites you to take lunch with him at twelve-thirty. I will return a few minutes before that time to take you up to the main house.'

Tug realised that this was simply one of the guest houses, but he showed no sign of being impressed and Cheng went on, 'Of course, all the servants are at your command. If there is anything you should want,' Cheng placed a slight emphasis on the sentence, that turned it into a leer, 'you need only ask one of the servants. You are my father's honoured guest. He would be deeply humiliated if you were to lack anything at all.'

'You and your father are too kind.' Tug returned the young man's bow. There would have been a time, not too many years ago when Tug would have availed himself of the discreet invitation, but now he was thankful that the irrational and uncontrollable element of sexuality had faded from his existence. So much of his youthful time and energy had been spent in sexual pursuit. At the end he had very little to show for all the effort, apart from three useless sons and a couple of million a year in alimony payments. No, he was glad it was over. His existence now was calmer and saner. Youth was an over-rated period in a man's life, filled with so much confusion and anxiety and unhappiness.

The two Chinese girls who helped him down the tiled steps into the steaming perfumed bath wore only brief white kilts and he could look upon their pale creamy skins and cherry-blossom nipples with a connoisseur's appreciation and only a brief sweet nostalgic stirring of the loins.

'No,' he reiterated as he sank into the water, 'I'm glad I'm not young any more.'

Tug spurned the embroidered robes that the girls had laid out for him and chose instead one of his dark Savile Row suits with a Turnbull and Asser shirt and MCC tie that the valet had steamed.

'Damned fancy dress will make me feel like a clown. Old Heng knows it; that's why he tried to get me into it.'

Young Cheng was waiting for him at the appointed time. His eyes flicked over Tug's suit but his expression never changed. Didn't fall for it, did I? Tug thought smugly. I wasn't born yesterday, was I?

330

They strolled up the covered pathway, pausing to admire the lotus flowers and water-lilies and the rhododendrons until they turned through an arched gateway festooned with drapes of blue wistaria and abruptly the main house was disclosed.

It was stunning, a creation of unblemished white marble and ceramic roof-tiles in peaks and gables, modern and yet time-lessly classical.

Tug did not miss a stride, and sensed the young man's disappointment beside him. He had expected Tug, like all other visitors, to gawk.

The patriarch, Ning Heng H'Sui, was very old, older than Tug by ten years or more. His skin was dried and folded like that of the unwrapped mummy of Rameses II in Cairo Museum, and spotted with the foxing of age. On his left cheek grew a mole the size and colour of a ripe mulberry. It is a common Chinese superstition that the hairs growing from a facial mole bring good luck, and Heng H'Sui had never shaved his. A bunch of hair sprouted from the little purple cauliflower and hung down in a silver tassel below his chin above the simple tunic of cream-coloured raw silk he wore.

So much for the dragon embroidery he tried to rig me with, Tug thought, as he took his hand. It was dry and cool and the bones were light as a bird's.

Heng was desiccated with age; only his eyes were bright and fierce. Tug imagined that the giant man-eating dragons of Komodo might have eyes like that.

'I trust you have rested after your journey, Sir Peter, and that you are comfortable in my poor house.' His voice was thin and dry as the sound of the wind rustling the autumn leaves and his English was excellent.

They exchanged pleasantries while they measured and sized each other. It was their first meeting. All Tug's negotiations up until this point had been with the elder sons.

All the sons were here now, waiting behind their father, the three elder brothers and Cheng.

One at a time Heng H'Sui waved them forward with a bird-like flutter of his pale dry hand, and they greeted Tug cour-teously in strict order of seniority.

Then Cheng helped his father back to his cushioned seat

331

overlooking the garden. It was not lost on Tug that the youngest, rather than the eldest, was so honoured. Though there was no exchange of glances between the other brothers and no change of expression, Tug felt the sibling rivalry and jealousy so strong in the sweet mountain air that he could almost taste it. All this was good intelligence he was gathering about the family.

Servants brought them pale jasmine tea in bowls so fine that Tug could see the outline of his own fingers through the china. He recognised the cream on white leaf design, so subtle and understated as almost to elude casual examination. The bowl was a masterpiece of a fifteenth-century potter of the Ching Ti emperor of the Ming dynasty.

Tug drained the bowl and then, as he was about to set it down on the lacquered tray, he let it slip from his fingers. It struck the cedarwood floor and shattered into a hundred precious fragments.

'I am so sorry,' he apologised. 'How clumsy of me.'

'It is nothing.' Heng H'Sui inclined his head graciously, and gestured for a servant to sweep away the broken shards. The servant was trembling as he knelt to the task. He sensed his master's wrath.

'I do hope it was not valuable?' Tug asked, testing him, trying to unsettle him, paying him back for the trick with the dragon robe. An angry man, one with hatred in his heart, has his judgement impaired. Tug studied Heng H'Sui for a reaction. They both knew that Tug was fully aware that the bowl was priceless.

'It was of no value, I assure you, Sir Peter. A mere trifle. Think no more of it,' the old man insisted, but Tug saw that he had got to him. There was a man of passion lurking behind that dried-out mask with the tasselled cheek piece. However, the old man was exhibiting class and style and control. A worthy adversary, Tug decided, for he had no illusion as to any fiduciary relationship between them merely on account of the mutually convenient and probably transient partnership of BOSS and the Lucky Dragon.

With the breaking of the bowl he had achieved a momentary advantage over the patriarch. He had thrown him off balance.

The old man sipped the last of the pale tea from his own bowl which was identical to the one which Tug had broken, and then held out his hand with a quiet word of command. One of the servants knelt and placed a square of silk in his wrinkled paw. Heng H'Sui wiped out the bowl carefully and then wrapped it in the silk and handed it to Tug.

'A gift for you, Sir Peter. I hope that our friendship will not be as frail as this little bauble.'

Tug conceded that Heng had snatched back the advantage. Tug was left with no option but to accept the extravagant gift and the loss of face that the subtle rebuke entailed.

'I will treasure it for the generosity of the giver,' he said.

'My son,' Heng indicated him with a flick of his blue-veined hand, 'tells me that you have expressed a desire to see my collection of ivory. Do you also collect ivory, Sir Peter?'

'I don't, but I'm interested in all things African. I flatter myself that I know more than the average man about the African elephant. I know how much value your people place on ivory.'

'Indeed, Sir Peter, never dispute the efficacy of charms with a Chinese, especially those of ivory. Our entire existence is ruled by astrology and the courting of fortune.'

'The Lucky Dragon?' Tug suggested.

'The Lucky Dragon, certainly.' Heng's parchment dry cheeks seemed about to tear as he smiled. 'And the Dragon at my gate has fangs of pure ivory. I have been caught up in the spell of ivory all my life. I started my career as an ivory-carver in my father's shop.'

'Yes, I know that the netsuke that bears your personal chop fetches prices equivalent to those of the great master carvers of antiquity,' Tug told him.

'Ah, those were made when my eye was sharp and my hand steady.' Heng shook his head modestly, but did not deny the value of his own creations.

'I would dearly love to see some examples of your work,' Tug suggested, and Heng gestured to his youngest son to help him rise.

'So you shall, Sir Peter. So you shall.'

The ivory museum was at a distance from the main house.

They went slowly along the covered walkway through the gardens, holding back for Heng H'Sui's short laboured pace.

He stopped to feed the khoi in one of the ornamental pools, and as the fish roiled the water in a feeding frenzy, the old man smiled at their antics.

'Greed, Sir Peter; without greed where would you and I be?'

'Healthy greed is the fuel of the capitalist system,' Tug agreed.

'And the stupid unthinking greed of other men makes you and me rich, does it not?'

Tug inclined his head in agreement and they went on.

There were more paramilitary guards in silver helmets at the door of the museum. Tug knew without being told that their vigil was perpetual.

'Picked men.' Heng noticed his glance. 'I trust them more than all these modern electronic devices.'

Cheng relinquished his father's arm for a moment to punch the entry code into the control box of the alarm system and the massive carved doors swung open automatically. He ushered them through.

The museum was without windows. There was no natural light, and the artificial lighting had been skilfully arranged. The air-conditioning was set to the correct humidity to preserve and protect the ivory. The carved doors closed with a pneumatic hiss behind them.

Tug took three paces into the spacious antechamber and then halted abruptly. He stared at the display in the centre of the marble floor.

'You recognise them?' Heng H'Sui asked.

'Yes, of course.' Tug nodded. 'I saw them once, long ago, at the Sultan of Zanzibar's palace before the revolution. There has been speculation ever since as to what happened to them.'

'Yes. I acquired them after the revolution in 1964 when the Sultan was exiled,' Heng H'Sui agreed. 'Very few people know that I own them.'

The walls of the room were painted blue, that particular milky blue of an African noon sky. The colour was chosen to show off the exhibits to best effect and the dimensions of the antechamber had obviously been designed for the same purpose, to complement the pair of ivory tusks.

Each tusk was over ten feet long, and its diameter at the lip was larger than a virgin's waist. The legend inked on each tusk was in Arabic script written a hundred years ago by a clerk of the Sultan Barghash recording the weight when it arrived in Zanzibar. Tug deciphered the writing: the heaviest tusk had weighed 235 pounds, the other only a few pounds less.

'They are lighter now,' Heng H'Sui anticipated his question. 'Between them they have dried out by twenty-two pounds, but still it takes four men to carry one of them. Think of the mighty animal who originally bore them.'

They were the most famous tusks in existence. As a student of African history, Tug knew the story of these extraordinary objects. They had been taken a hundred years ago on the southern slopes of Kilimanjaro, by a slave named Senoussi. The slave's master was a villain named Shundi. He was one of the cruellest and most unscrupulous slavers and ivory-traders on the African east coast, an area notorious for the depredations of the slave-masters. When he had first come upon it, Senoussi had in awe delayed killing the old bull. He had crouched over his flintlock musket and studied this extraordinary creature with respect for several hours before he had summoned the courage to creep forward and send a lead ball through its heart.

According to Senoussi's later account to his master, the bull ran off only a hundred yards before collapsing. He was an extremely old elephant with his fourth and last molars almost worn away, on the verge of the slow starvation of great age. Although not particularly big-bodied, his neck and forequarters were overdeveloped to carry that great weight of ivory. Senoussi observed the bull had been forced to raise his head and lift the tips of his tusks free of the earth before he could move.

When Shundi displayed the tusks in the ivory market in Zanzibar they caused a sensation amongst traders accustomed to dealing with massive tusks. The Sultan had purchased the pair from Shundi for a thousand pounds sterling, which was a huge sum of money in those days. Tug had first seen them in the palace of the Sultan's successors overlooking the Zanzibar waterfront.

Now he approached them with awe and stroked one of them, staring up at the massive ivory arches that almost met high above his head. This was legendary treasure. To Tug, somehow, these tusks seemed to embody the history and the soul of the entire African continent.

'Now let me show you the rest of my poor little collection,' Ning Heng H'Sui suggested at last, and led the way past the towering ivory columns to the archway artfully concealed in the rear wall of the antechamber.

The interior of the building was a labyrinth of dimly lit passages. The floor was carpeted with midnight-blue Wilton, soft and soundless to the tread. The walls were the same colour, but set flush into them on each side of the passage were the showcases.

The proportions of each case were designed to the shape and size of the single exhibit it contained. The lighting of the cases was dramatically arranged so that each treasure was revealed in crisp detail and seemed to float airily and independently of the dim surroundings.

Firstly, there were religious and sacred objects, a Bible with covers of carved ivory and precious stones bearing the double-headed eagle of Imperial Russia.

'Peter the Great,' Heng murmured. 'His personal Bible.'

There was a copy of the Torah, the yellow parchment rolled on to an ivory distaff, and contained in an ivory case with the Star of David carved upon it.

'Salvaged from the great synagogue at Constantinople when it was destroyed by the Byzantine emperor Theodosius,' Heng explained.

Amongst other treasures there were icons of ivory set with diamonds and Hindu statuettes of Vishnu, a copy of the Koran covered with beaten gold and ivory, and ancient Christian statues of the Virgin and the saints, all carved from ivory.

Then, as they moved along the dim passageway, the nature of the exhibits became more profane, and secular. There were women's fans and combs and necklaces from ancient Rome and Greece, then an extraordinary object shaped like a two-foot rolling pin with a rooster head carved at one end. Tug did not recognise it and Heng explained expressionlessly.

'It belonged to Catherine the Great of Russia. Her physicians convinced her that ivory was a sovereign specific against syphilis. It is an ivory dildo, made to her own design.'

Occasionally Heng instructed his son to open one or two of the cases so that Tug could handle the exhibits and examine them more closely.

'The true joy of ivory lies in the feel of it in the hand,' Heng suggested. 'It is as sensuous as the skin of a lovely woman. See the grain, Sir Peter, that lovely subtle cross-hatching that no synthetic substance can duplicate.'

There was one object the size and shape of a football, carved like lacework. Within it were eight more balls, free and complete, one within the other like the layers of an onion. The artist had carved the inner balls through the minute apertures in the outer layers. In the centre of the ball was a carving of a rose bud, perfect in every detail.

'Three thousand hours of work. Five years from the life of a master craftsman. How can you place a value on that?' Heng asked.

Two hours after entering the museum they came at last to the room that contained the netsukes.

During the Tokugawa Shogunate in Japan, only the aristocracy were allowed to wear personal adornment. Amongst the newly emerging and affluent middle class the netsuke button, worn on the sash and used to secure a pill box or tobacco pouch, was an essential article of dress. The beauty and intricacy of the carving enhanced the owner's prestige.

Heng had assembled a collection of over ten thousand pieces. However, as he explained to Tug, he could only display a few of his favourites, and amongst them were his own creations. These were cased separately, and once again Tug was invited to take them in his hand and to admire the craftsmanship.

'Of course, I was obliged to seek out and buy back my own work.' Heng smiled and tugged at the tassel of hair that hung from his cheek. 'I have agents around the world still searching for my creations. I estimate there are at least a hundred that have so far eluded me. Ten thousand dollars if you find one, Sir Peter,' he promised.

'And worth every cent,' Tug agreed as he examined one of the tiny ivory buds. The detail and rendition was extraordinary and the subject matter covered a wide range of humanity and the animal world, from birds and mammals to men and beautiful women and children in every possible pose and indulging in every activity, from war to love, from death to childbirth.

Somehow, Heng the artist had managed to transform even the mundane into something remarkable and exciting. Subjects that might have been merely pornographic and coarse were instead spiritual, ethereal and moving.

'You have a rare gift,' Tug acknowledged. 'The heart and eye of a great artist.'

For a short while the two men were in accord, and then they left the treasure house and returned to the main house where servants had set out writing materials and light refreshments at a long lacquer-work table. They removed their footwear and settled themselves on cushions about the table and, at last, the real work began.

In London, Tug had negotiated and signed a document of intent with the elder Ning sons. This was subject to ratification by the patriarch. Tug had never expected this to be a simple procedure and he was not to be disappointed.

A little after midnight they adjourned and Tug was escorted back to the guesthouse by Cheng. The two female servants were waiting for him with tea and refreshments. They helped him change into his night clothes, then drew back the quilts on the low wide bed and waited expectantly.

Tug dismissed them and they left at once. He had not been able to discover where the video camera and microphone were concealed, but he was certain they were there. He switched off the light and lay for a while, well pleased with the progress he had made. Then he slept soundly and awoke eager for the fray.

In the middle of the following afternoon, Tug and Heng H'Sui shook hands. From all that Tug had learned about the old man, he believed that like himself Heng was a man of peculiar integrity. Between them that handshake was as good as any formal document. Of course, the lawyers on both sides would now come in and complicate and muddy the issues, but even they could never weaken the central pillars of the agreement. Between Tug and Heng it was sacrosanct, the honour of buccaneers.

'There is one other matter I would like to discuss with you,' Heng murmured, and Tug frowned.

'No, no, Sir Peter. It is a personal matter, not part of our agreement.' And Tug relaxed.

'I will do what I can to help you. What is it about?'

'Elephant,' Heng said. 'Ivory.'

'Ah.' Tug smiled and nodded. 'Why didn't I guess?'

'At the time that bloodthirsty madman Idi Amin took over Uganda, the largest elephant still alive on the African continent were in the Uganda National Park near the Murchison Falls at the headwaters of the Nile,' Heng explained.

'Yes,' Tug agreed. 'I saw a dozen animals in that Park that had tusks over a hundred pounds a side. They were wiped out by Idi Amin's henchmen and the ivory stolen by him.'

'Not all of them, Sir Peter. I have it on good authority that some of those animals, the largest of them, escaped annihilation. They crossed the border into Ubomo and reached the rain forests on the slopes of the Mountains of the Moon, that area which now forms part of our syndicate's concession.'

'It is possible,' Tug conceded.

'It is more than that. It is fact,' Heng contradicted him. 'My son Cheng', he indicated the man at his side, 'has a reliable agent in Ubomo. An Indian who has co-operated with us on many occasions. His name is Chetti Singh. Do you know him?'

'I have heard of him, vaguely.' Tug frowned again. 'Let me think ... Yes, he is connected with the illegal export of ivory and rhino horn. I have heard he is the mastermind behind all African poaching.'

'Chetti Singh has been in the forests of the Ubomo basin within the last ten days,' Heng went on. 'He has seen with his own eyes an elephant bull with tusks almost as large as those I showed you today.'

'How can I help you?' Tug insisted.

'I want those tusks,' Heng murmured, the passion of the collector barely concealed behind the time-eroded mask of his face. 'More than the ore and the hardwoods of the forest, I want that ivory.'

'President Taffari can sign a special Protected Game licence. I believe there is provision for that in the constitution. If there isn't, it can be changed. I presume that your man Chetti Singh will be able to arrange for the ivory to be harvested. He is the master poacher. If that is the case, I will send my Gulfstream to Ubomo to pick up the tusks and ferry them to you here. I can foresee no problems, Mr Ning.'

'Thank you, Sir Peter,' Heng smiled. 'Is there anything I can do for you in exchange?'

'Yes.' Tug leaned forward. 'As a matter of fact there is.'

'You only have to ask,' Heng invited.

'Before I do that, I must explain something of the new hysteria that is sweeping the Western world. Fortunately for you, you are not subject to the same pressures. There is a new thinking, especially amongst the young but also, regrettably, amongst those who should know better. This philosophy is that we have no right to utilise the natural assets of our planet. We cannot be allowed to mine the earth of its bounty, because our excavations will disfigure the beauty of nature. We cannot be allowed to cut the trees for timber, because they belong not to us but to posterity. We cannot be allowed to kill a living creature for its meat or fur or ivory, because all life is somehow sacred.'

'This is a nonsense.' Heng dismissed it with a brusque gesture, his dark eyes sparkling. 'Man is what he is today because he has always done these things.' He touched the cedar panels of the wall beside him, the hem of his silk tunic, the gold and ivory ring on his finger, the precious ceramic bowl on the table before him. 'All these were mined or felled or killed, as is the very food we eat.'

'You and I, we know that,' Tug agreed. 'But this new madness is a force to be reckoned with, almost an unreasoning religious fanaticism. A jihad, if you like, a holy war.'

'I mean no disrespect, Sir Peter, but the occidental is emotionally immature. I like to think that we of the east have more sophistication. We are not so readily caught up by such exaggerated behaviour.'

'That is why I appeal to you, sir. My company, BOSS, has recently become a victim of this campaign. The attention of the British public has been drawn to our operations in Ubomo by groups of these people who call themselves childish names such as "Greenpeace" or "The Friends of the Earth".'

Heng grimaced at the title, and Tug nodded. 'I know it

sounds silly and harmless, but one such organisation is led by a fanatical young woman. She has chosen my company as her target. She has already managed to do us some damage. There is a small but noticeable decline in sales and income that is directly attributable to her campaign. Some of our major markets in the United Kingdom and the United States are getting nervous, and asking us to back off from Ubomo, or at least to play down our involvement, and I personally have received hate mail and death threats.'

'You do not take those seriously?'

'No, Mr Ning, I do not, although these are from people who blow up animal experimentation laboratories and set fire to furrier's shops. However, I think it might be prudent to play down BOSS's role in Ubomo, or at least to give it better public relations.'

'What do you propose, Sir Peter?'

'Firstly, I have already hired an independent film-producer, quite well-known in Europe and America, to film a television feature on Ubomo with particular emphasis on the benefits to the country of our involvement.'

'You do not plan to expose all the syndicate's operations to the camera, Sir Peter?' There was a tone of alarm in Heng's question.

'Of course not, Mr Ning. The film-producer will be carefully guided to show our syndicate in the best possible light. It may even be necessary to prepare some exhibits for him to film.'

'To put on a little show for his benefit?' Heng suggested.

'Exactly, Mr Ning. We will keep him away from the sensitive areas of our operations.'

Heng nodded. 'That is wise. You seem to have arranged matters without my help.'

'You are in a better position than I am, Mr Ning. These so-called green people cannot reach you here in Taiwan. Your own Chinese people are too pragmatic to take up such an immature attitude to mining and forestry, especially as nearly all the products that we reap will be shipped here. You are invulnerable to this childish but dangerous influence.'

'Yes.' Heng nodded. 'I see that all you have said makes good sense, but where does it lead us?'

'I want Lucky Dragon to become the figurehead of the

syndicate. I want one of your best men, rather than one of mine, to go to Ubomo and take charge of the operations there. I will pull out my geologists and forestry experts and architects; you will put in Chinese experts. I will gradually sell off my share of the syndicate to Hong Kong front companies and other oriental nominees. Although you and I will meet regularly and discreetly direct the syndicate operations, BOSS will gradually withdraw from the scene.'

'You will become the invisible man, Sir Peter.' Heng chuckled with genuine amusement.

'The invisible man, I like that.' Tug laughed with him. 'May I know who it is that you would send to Ubomo to take charge there?'

Ning Heng H'Sui stopped laughing and tugged thoughtfully at the silver tuft that hung from his cheek.

His sons, sitting below him at the long lacquer table, leaned forward, trying not to display their eagerness, watching their father's face with impassive expressions that were betrayed by their eyes.

'Ha!' Heng coughed and wet his lips from the tea bowl. 'That will require some consideration, Sir Peter. Will you give me a week or so to decide?'

'Of course, Mr Ning. It is not a decision to be taken lightly. We will need somebody clever and dedicated and . . .' he hesitated as he weighed the adjective, discarding 'ruthless' as too explicit, 'and strong, yet diplomatic.'

'I will telephone you with my decision. Where will you be, Sir Peter?'

'Well, I am flying to Sydney tomorrow morning, and from there I will go on directly to Nairobi and Kahali in Ubomo to meet President Taffari. However, my aircraft has direct satellite communication. You can contact me in flight as easily as if I were in the next room.'

'These modern miracles.' Heng shook his head. 'Sometimes it is difficult for an old man to adjust.'

'It seems to me that you are old only in experience and sagacity, Mr Ning. In courage and dash you are young, sir,' Tug said, not entirely in flattery, and Ning Heng H'Sui inclined his head graciously.

Cheng had waited patiently for exactly the right moment to present his father with the gift that he had brought for him from Africa. It was almost two weeks since Sir Peter Harrison had visited Taiwan and still his father had made no announcement within the family as to which of his sons he was sending to run the syndicate's operation in Ubomo.

All the brothers knew it must be one of them. They had known it the moment that the Englishman had made the request. Cheng had noticed the others lean forward at the words, and he had seen his own excitement and expectation mirrored in their eyes. Ever since then, the brothers had been walking around each other like dogs with stiff legs. The extent of Lucky Dragon's investment in the Ubomo syndicate was unprecedented. When the project was fully financed and developed, the family would be committed to raising almost a thousand million dollars, much of it borrowed from banks in Hong Kong and Japan.

It must be one of the sons. Ning Heng H'Sui would never put so much trust in an outsider. Only his age forced him to delegate the task to one of them. Not long ago he would have taken command in Ubomo into his own hands, but now his sons knew he had to give it to one of them, and each of them would kill for the honour. That command would be the ultimate accolade which would show clearly whom Heng had chosen as his heir.

Cheng longed for the honour with a passion so intense that it denied him sleep and spoiled his appetite. In the two weeks since Sir Peter's visit, Cheng had lost weight and become pale and hollow-cheeked. Now, when he exercised in the gymnasium with his hired sparring partners, his body was lean to the point of emaciation. Every rib showed through the hard rubbery casing of muscle. However, his blows and kicks had lost none of their fury. As he fought, his dark eyes, sunken into bruised-looking cavities, glittered with a feverish intensity.

He found every excuse to be in his father's company. Even when the old man was painting, or meditating with the Confucian priests at the shrine in the gardens of the estate, or cataloguing his ivory collection, Cheng tried to be with him, keeping himself close. Yet he sensed that the moment was not exactly right to make the gift. He believed that his father's choice must in the end come down to that between his second brother, Wu, and Cheng himself.

The eldest brother, Fang, was tough and ruthless, but lacking in guile and cunning, a good hatchet man but not a leader. The third son, Ling, possessed an unreliable temperament. He was clever, as clever as either Wu or Cheng, but he was easily panicked and inclined to fly into a rage when things went against him. Ling would never head Lucky Dragon. He might become Number Two perhaps, but never Number One. No, Cheng reasoned, the choice must be between himself and Wu. As a child he had recognised Wu as his main rival and in consequence he hated him with a single-minded malevolence.

While she had been alive, Cheng's English mother had protected him from his half-brothers. But after she died he had been at their mercy. It had taken all these years to learn to hold his own and insinuate himself ever deeper into his father's favour.

Cheng recognised that this would be his chance, his only chance for supremacy. His father was old, more than old, he was ancient. Despite his seemingly boundless strength and energy, Cheng sensed that his father was near death. It might come at any moment of any day, and he went cold at the thought.

He knew that unless he consolidated his accession while his father still lived, Wu would wrest it from him with the help of his two full brothers, the moment his father died. He sensed also that his father was on the point of deciding on the Ubomo project. He knew that this was his moment. This was the slack water of the tide of his fortunes, and now they must turn and begin to flood, or he would be for ever stranded on the mudbanks.

'Honourable Father, I have something for you. A small and humble token of the respect and gratitude I feel for you. May I present it?'

Fortune seemed to conspire with Cheng to provide an appropriate opportunity. The old man was spry today, his mind quick and his waning bodily strength in some measure restored. He had eaten a ripe fig and an apple for breakfast, and had composed a classical stanza while Cheng walked him down to the shrine. It was an ode to the mountain peak that stood above the estate. The poem began:

> *Beloved of clouds*
> *who caress her face . . .*

It was good, although not as good as his father's paintings and ivory carvings, Cheng thought. However, when the old man recited it, Cheng clasped his hands.

'I am awed that so much genius resides in one person. I wish only that I had inherited a few grains of it for myself.'

He thought he might have overdone it a little, but the old man accepted the praise and for a moment tightened his grip on Cheng's arm.

'You are a good son,' he said. 'And your mother . . .' his voice trailed off mournfully, 'your mother was a woman . . .' He shook his head and Cheng thought incredulously that the old man's eyes had moistened. It must have been his imagination. His father was not prey to weakness and sentimentality. When he looked again his father's eyes were clear and bright, and the old man was smiling.

That morning Heng stayed on at the shrine much longer than he usually did. He wanted to inspect the work on his own tomb. One of the most famous geomancers on the island had come to position the tomb precisely and to orientate it so that it stood neither on an earth dragon's head nor on his tail. That would have disturbed the old man's death sleep. The geomancer had worked with a compass and a magic bag for almost an hour, directing the efforts of the priests and the servants to get the marble sarcophagus laid properly.

All this preparation for his own funeral put Heng into a pleasant relaxed mood, and when they were finished Cheng seized the moment and asked to be allowed to present his gift.

Heng smiled and nodded. 'You may bring it to me, my son.'

'Alas, father, the nature of the gift makes that impossible. I must take you to it.'

Heng's expression changed. These days he seldom left the

estate. He seemed about to refuse. However, Cheng had anticipated his reaction. All he needed to do was lift one hand and
the Rolls that was parked behind the clipped privet hedges
beyond the lotus pools slid silently forward.

Before the old man could protest, Cheng had helped him into
the back seat and settled him comfortably with a cashmere rug
over his knees. The chauffeur knew where to take them. As the
Rolls came down the mountain road on to the littoral plain,
Heng and Cheng were isolated and protected from the heat and
humidity, and from the teeming humanity that clogged the road
with Vespa motorcycles and buses, wild chicken taxis and
heavily laden trucks.

When they entered Chung Ching South Road in the Hsimend-
ing area of the city the chauffeur slowed and turned in through
the gates of the Lucky Dragon company's main city warehouse.
The guards jumped to attention as they recognised the couple
in the back seat.

One of the warehouse doors stood open and after the car
drove through, the steel shutter doors rolled closed behind it.
The Rolls parked on one of the loading ramps and Cheng
helped his father out of the back door and took his elbow to
lead him to a carved teak chair that stood like a throne,
covered with embroidered silk cushions, overlooking the floor
below the ramp.

As soon as his father was comfortable, Cheng signalled one
of the servants to bring freshly made tea. He sat on one of the
cushions lower than Heng and they drank tea and talked
quietly of unrelated subjects. Cheng was drawing out the
moment, trying to spice his father's anticipation. If he succeeded, the old man did not show it. He barely glanced towards
the floor below.

Ten brawny workmen knelt in a row facing the throne.
Cheng had dressed them in black tunics, with red headbands,
and the emblem of the Lucky Dragon embroidered on their
backs also in red. He had rehearsed them carefully and they
were motionless, heads bowed respectfully.

Finally, after ten minutes of talk and tea, Cheng told his
father, 'This is the present I have brought you from Africa.' He
indicated the rows of chests, arranged behind the workmen. 'It

is such a poor little present that now I am ashamed to offer it to you.'

'Tea?' Heng smiled. 'Cases of tea? Enough tea to last me the rest of my lifetime. It is a fine gift, my son.'

'It is a poor gift, but may I open the cases for you?' Cheng asked, and the old man nodded his permission.

Cheng clapped his hands and the ten workmen sprang to their feet and ran to seize one of the tea-chests and bring it forward. They worked swiftly, efficiently. With half a dozen blows of a slap-hammer and a twist of a jemmy bar, they lifted the lid off the first case.

Heng showed the first sign of animation and leaned forward in the high chair. Two of the workmen lifted out the first tusk from its bed of caked black tea.

Cheng had long ago arranged that it should be one of the largest and most finely shaped tusks in the entire shipment of stolen ivory. He had asked Chetti Singh to mark the case that contained it before the shipment left the Indian's warehouse in Malawi.

The tusk was long, over seven feet long, but not as thick and blunt as one of the typical massively heavy tusks from further north than Zimbabwe. Yet from an entirely aesthetic point of view this one was more pleasing, its girth more in proportion to its length and the curve and taper were elegant. It was neither cracked nor damaged and the patina above the lip was creamy yellow.

Involuntarily Heng clapped his hands with pleasure and exclaimed aloud.

'Bring it to me!' Two of the workmen, struggling under the burden, climbed the concrete steps and knelt before him offering the lovely tusk. Heng stroked the ivory and his eyes sparkled in the cobweb of wrinkles that surrounded them.

'Beautiful!' he murmured. 'The most beautiful of all nature's creations, more beautiful than pearls or the feathers of the brightest tropical birds.' He broke off abruptly as his fingers detected the rough patch on the tusk. He leaned closer and peered at it and exclaimed again. 'But this tusk bears a government stamp. "ZW". That is a Zimbabwe government number. This is legal ivory, Cheng.' He clapped his hands again. 'Legal ivory, my son, many more times more valuable for those numbers. How did you do it? How many more tusks are there?' His father's unrestrained pleasure was giving Cheng huge face. He must be careful to remain humble and dutiful.

'Every one of those cases is filled with ivory, honoured Father. Every tusk is stamped.'

'Where did you get them?' Heng insisted, and then raised his hand to prevent Cheng replying.

'Wait!' he ordered. 'Wait. Do not tell me!' He was silent, staring at his son for a while, and then he said, 'Yes. That is it. I know where this ivory comes from.' With a wave of his hand he sent the black-clad workmen out of earshot and leaned closer to Cheng, dropping his voice to a whisper. 'I read some time ago that there was a raid by a gang of poachers on a government ivory store in Zimbabwe. A place called Chiwewe? The gangsters were wiped out, but the ivory was not recovered, is that not so, my son?'

'I read the same newspaper article, honoured Father.' Cheng dropped his eyes and waited while the silence drew out.

Then Heng spoke again. 'The man who planned that raid was clever and bold. He was not afraid to kill for what he wanted,' he whispered. 'The kind of man that I admire. The kind of man that I was once, when I was young.'

'The kind of man that you still are, Father,' Cheng said, but Heng shook his head.

'The kind of man that I would be proud to have as my son,' Heng went on. 'You may present the rest of your gift to me now.'

Now Cheng's standing, in his father's eyes, was so enormous that he wriggled in his seat with pleasure and shouted for the workmen to open the other cases.

For the next two hours Heng examined the shipment of tusks. He gloated over every single piece, picking out a dozen or so of the loveliest or most unusual for his special collection. He was particularly interested in deformed ivory. The nerve of one of the tusks had been damaged, while it was still immature, by a hand-hammered lead ball from a native poacher's musket. The result was that the tusk had split into four separate shafts and these had twisted around each other in the same way as the strands of a hemp rope. The original lead musket-bullet, heavily corroded, was still embedded in the root of the tusk, and the entwined spirals of ivory resembled the horns of the legendary unicorn. Heng was delighted with it.

Cheng had seldom seen him so animated and voluble, but at the end of the two hours he was obviously fatigued, and Cheng helped him back into the Rolls and ordered the chauffeur to return to the estate.

Heng laid his head back on the soft Connolly leather and closed his eyes. When Cheng was sure the old man was asleep, he gently adjusted the cashmere rug over him. One of Heng's hands had dropped on to the seat beside him. Cheng lifted it into his lap and before he covered it with the cashmere he caressed it so gently as not to wake his father. The hand was thin and bony and the skin was cool as that of a corpse. Suddenly the long thin fingers tightened on Cheng's wrist and the old man spoke without opening his eyes.

'I am not afraid of death, my son,' he whispered. 'But I am terrified that all that I have achieved will be destroyed by careless hands. Your brother Wu is strong and clever, but he does not have my spirit. He does not care for fine and beautiful things. He does not love poetry or painting or ivory.'

Heng opened his eyes and turned his head to stare at his son with those bright implacable lizard's eyes.

'I knew that you had inherited my spirit, Cheng, but until today I doubted that you had the warrior's steel. That is the reason why I hesitated to choose between you and Wu. However, this gift that you have given to me today has changed that thinking. I know how you obtained that ivory. I know that it was necessary to squeeze the juice from the ripe cherry.' This was Heng's euphemism for drawing blood. 'And I know that you did not shrink from it. I know also that you succeeded in a difficult enterprise, whether by luck or cunning I do not really care. I prize both luck and cunning equally.'

He tightened his grip until it was painful but Cheng did not wince or pull away.

'I am sending you to Ubomo, my son, as the representative of the Lucky Dragon.'

Cheng bowed his head over his father's hand and kissed it. 'I will not fail you,' he promised, and a single tear of joy and of pride fell from the corner of his eye and sparkled like a jewel on the pale dry skin of his father's hand.

Ning Heng H'Sui made the formal announcement of his selection the following morning. He made it while seated at the head of the lacquer table overlooking the garden.

Cheng watched the faces of his brothers while the old man spoke. Wu remained as impassive as the ivory carving his father had made of him years ago. His face was bland, smooth and creamy yellow, but his eyes were terrible as he returned Cheng's stare across the table. When the old man finished speaking there was a moment's silence which seemed to last an eternity as the three elder brothers contemplated the world that had changed for them.

Then Wu spoke. 'Honourable Father, you are wise in all things. We, your sons, bow to your will as the rice stalks bow to the north wind.'

All four of them bowed so low that their foreheads almost touched the table-top, but when they straightened the other three were looking at Cheng. Cheng realised at that moment that it might be possible to attain too much face. His face was greater than that of all his half-brothers combined and he felt an icicle of fear slide down his spine, for his brothers were watching him with the eyes of crocodiles. He knew that he dare not fail in Ubomo. They would be waiting to rend him if he did.

Once Cheng was back in his own apartment, the fear fell away to be replaced by the elation of success. There was so much work to do before he returned to Africa, but for the moment he could not concentrate his mind upon it. Tomorrow certainly, but not now. He was too charged with excitement, his mind restless and unfocused. He needed to steady himself, to burn off the excess energy that made him both physically and mentally overwrought.

He knew exactly how to achieve this. He had his own special

ritual for purging his soul. Of course, it was dangerous, terribly dangerous. On more than one occasion before it had brought him to the very brink of disaster. However, the danger was part of the efficacy of the ritual. He knew that if anything went wrong he would have lost all. The monumental successes of these last few days, his father's selection and the ascendancy over his brothers would all be wiped away.

The risk was enormous, completely out of proportion to the fleeting gratification that he would achieve. Perhaps it was the gambler's urge to flirt with self-destruction. After each episode he always promised himself that he would never indulge in the madness again, but always the temptation proved too strong, particularly at a time such as this.

As soon as he entered his apartment his wife made tea for him, and then called the children to pay him their respects. He spoke to them for a few minutes and took his infant son on his lap, but he was distracted and soon dismissed them. They left with obvious relief. These formal interviews were a strain for all of them. He was not good with children, even his own.

'My father has chosen me to go to Ubomo,' he told his wife.

'It is a great honour,' she said. 'I offer you my felicitations. When will we leave?'

'I shall go alone,' he told her, and saw the relief in her eyes. It annoyed him that she made it so obvious. 'Of course, I will send for you as soon as I have made the arrangements.'

She dropped her eyes. 'I will await your summons.' But he could not concentrate on her. The excitement was fizzing in his head.

'I will rest for an hour. See that I am not disturbed. Then I have to go down to the city. There is much work to do before I leave. I will not return tonight, and I shall probably stay at the apartment in Tunhua Road. I shall send you a message before I return.'

Alone in his own room he teased himself with the telephone. He placed the cordless instrument on the table and stared at it, rehearsing every word he would say and his breathing was short and quick as though he had run up a flight of stairs. His fingers trembled slightly when at last he reached out for it. The telephone was fitted with a special coding scrambler. It could not be tapped and it was impossible for any other person, civil or military or police, to trace the special number that he punched into the key panel.

Very few people had this number. She had told him once that she had given it to only six of her most valued clients. She answered it on the second ring and she recognised his voice instantly. She greeted him with the special code name she had assigned him.

'You have not been to see me for almost two years, Green Mountain Man.'

'I have been away.'

'Yes, I know, but still I missed you.'

'I want to come tonight.'

'Will you want the special thing?'

'Yes.' Cheng felt his stomach clench at the thought of it. He thought he might be sick with fear and loathing and excitement.

'It is very short notice,' she said. 'And the price has risen since your last visit.'

'The price does not matter. Can you do it?' He heard the high strained tones of his own voice. She was silent, and he knew she was baiting him. He wanted to scream at her and then she said, 'You are fortunate.' Her voice changed. It became obscenely soft and slimy. 'I have received new merchandise; I can offer you a choice of two.'

Cheng gulped and cleared his throat of a plug of phlegm before he could ask. 'Young?'

'Very young. Very tender. Untouched.'

'When will you be ready?'

'Ten o'clock tonight,' she said. 'Not before.'

'At the sea pavilion?' he asked.

'Yes,' she replied. 'They will expect you at the gate. Ten o'clock,' she repeated. 'Not earlier, not later.'

Cheng drove to the apartment building in Tunhua Road. It was in the most prestigious part of the city and the accommodation was expensive, but it was paid for by Lucky Dragon.

He left his Porsche in the underground garage and rode up to the top floor apartment in the elevator. By the time he had showered and changed it was still only six o'clock and he had plenty of time in which to prepare himself.

He left the apartment building on foot and set off down Tunhua Road. He loved the *renao* of Taipei. It was one of the things that he missed most while he was away. *Renao* was a concept that was almost impossible to translate from the Chinese to any other language. It meant festive, lively, joyous and noisy all at the same time.

It was now the ghost month, the seventh lunar month when the ghosts return from hell to haunt the earth and have to be placated with gifts of ghost money and food. It was also necessary to keep them at a distance with fireworks and dragon processions.

Cheng paused to laugh and applaud one of the processions led by a monstrous dragon with a huge papier-mâché head and fifty pairs of human legs beneath its serpentine body. The jumping-jack fireworks popped with spurts of blue smoke about the ankles of the spectators and the band beat drums and gongs and the children shrieked. It was good *renao* and it heightened Cheng's excitement.

He threaded his way through the crowds and the bustle until he reached the East Garden area of the city and left the main thoroughfare to enter a back alley.

The fortune-teller was one Cheng had used for ten years. He was an old man with thin wispy grey hair and a facial mole like Cheng's father had. He wore traditional robes and a mandarin cap and sat cross-legged in his curtained cubicle with his paraphernalia around him.

Cheng greeted him respectfully and at his invitation squatted facing him.

'I have not seen you for a long time,' the old man accused him, and Cheng apologised.

'I have been away from Taiwan.'

They discussed the fee and the divination that Cheng required.

'I am about to undertake a task,' Cheng explained. 'I wish to have spirit guidance.'

The old man nodded and consulted his almanacs and star guides, nodding and mumbling to himself. Finally he handed Cheng a ceramic cup filled with bamboo rods.

Cheng shook this vigorously and then spilled the rods on to the mat between them. Each rod was painted with characters and emblems and the old man studied the pattern in which they had fallen.

'This task will not be undertaken here in Taiwan, but in a land across the ocean,' he said, and Cheng relaxed a little. The old man had not lost his touch. He nodded encouragement.

'It is a task of great complexity and there are many people involved. Foreigners, foreign devils.'

Again Cheng nodded.

'I see powerful allies, but also powerful enemies who will oppose you.'

'I know my allies, but I do not know who will be my enemies,' Cheng interjected.

'You already know your enemy. He has opposed you before. On that occasion you overcame him.'

'Can you describe him?'

The fortune-teller shook his head. 'You will know him when you see him again.'

'When will that be?'

'You should not travel during the ghost month. You must prepare yourself here in Taiwan. Leave only on the first day of the eighth lunar month.'

'Very well.' That suited Cheng's plans. 'Will I overcome this enemy once again?'

'To answer that question it will be necessary to make a further divination,' the old man whispered, and Cheng grimaced at this device for doubling the fee.

'Very well,' he agreed, and the fortune-teller replaced the bamboo sticks in the bowl and Cheng shook them out on to the mat.

'There are two enemies now.' The fortune-teller picked two rods out of the pile. 'One is the man that you know, the other is a woman whom you have not yet met. Together they will oppose your endeavours.'

'Will I overcome them?' Cheng asked anxiously, and the old man examined the fall of the bamboo rods minutely.

'I see a snow-capped mountain and a great forest. These will be the battleground. There will be evil spirits and demons . . .' The old man's voice trailed away, and he lifted one of the bamboo sticks from the pile.

'What else do you see?' Cheng insisted, but the old man coughed and spat and would not look up at him. The bamboo sliver was painted white, the colour of death and disaster.

'That is all. I can see no more,' he mumbled.

Cheng took a new thousand Taiwan dollar note from his top pocket and laid it beside the pile of bamboo rods.

'Will I overcome my enemies?' Cheng asked, and the note disappeared like a conjuring trick under the old man's bony fingers.

'You will have great face,' he promised, but still he would not look directly at his client, and Cheng left the cubicle with some of his good feelings dissipated by the ambiguous reply. More than ever now he needed solace, but it was still only a little after eight o'clock. She had told him not to come before ten.

It was only a short walk to Snake Alley, but on his way Cheng paused in the forecourt of the Dragon Mountain Temple and burned a pile of ghost money in one of the gaudy pyramid furnaces to placate the ancestral ghosts who would be prowling the night around him.

He left the temple and cut through the night market where the stall-holders offered a bewildering array of wares and the prostitutes plied their trade in flimsy wooden sheds in the back areas of the market. Both storekeepers and painted ladies haggled loudly with their potential customers, and the spectators joined in with comment and suggestion and laughter. It was good *renao*, and Cheng's spirits revived.

He entered Snake Alley down which the shê-shops were crowded closely together. Outside each stall were piled snake baskets of steel mesh and the front windows were filled with the largest and most spectacularly coloured of the serpents which gave the alley its name.

Many of the shops had a live mongoose tethered outside the front door. Cheng stopped to watch an arranged contest between one of these sleek little predators and a four-foot cobra. The cobra reared up as it confronted the mongoose, and the crowd gathered quickly and shrieked with delight. With its striped hood fully extended, the cobra revolved and swayed like a flower on its stalk to watch the circling mongoose with unblinking bright eyes while its feathery black tongue tasted the scent of its adversary on the air. The mongoose danced in and then leapt back as the cobra struck. For an instant the snake was off balance and fully extended and the mongoose darted in for the kill. It seized the back of the glistening scaled head and its needle teeth crunched into bone. The snake's body whipped and coiled in its death throes and the proprietor of the shê-shop separated the mongoose from its victim and carried the writhing reptile into his shop, followed by two or three eager male customers.

Cheng did not join them. He had his own special shê-shop, and he wanted a particular type of snake, the rarest, the most expensive, the most effective.

The snake-doctor recognised Cheng over the heads of the crowd that thronged the alley. His shop was famous. He did not have to stage mongoose fights to attract his customers. He beamed and bowed, and ushered Cheng through to the back room which was curtained off from the public gaze.

It was not necessary for Cheng to state his requirements. The shê-shop owner knew him well, over many years. It was Cheng who had arranged his supply of the most virulently poisonous reptiles from Africa. It was Cheng who had introduced him to Chetti Singh, and made the first consignments of snakes through the diplomatic bag. Of course, Cheng took a commission on each shipment.

Cheng had also persuaded him to deal in rare African birds. Once again these had been supplied by Chetti Singh and the trade was now worth over a quarter of a million US dollars a year. There were collectors in Europe and America who would pay huge sums for a pair of saddle-billed storks or bald ibis. The African parrots, although not as colourful as the South American varieties, were also much sought after. Chetti Singh could supply all these, and once again Cheng took his commission.

However, the main source of the snake-doctor's income was still the supply of venomous snakes. The more venomous, the more valuable they were to Chinese gentlemen with faltering potency. The African mamba had been entirely unknown in Taiwan or mainland China until Chetti Singh had made the first shipment. Now they were the most prized of all snakes on the island, and commanded a price of two thousand US dollars apiece.

The snake-doctor had a particularly beautiful specimen ready in a mesh cage on his stainless-steel-topped table. Now he drew on a pair of elbow-length gloves, a precaution that he would have scorned had he been dealing with a cobra.

He opened the sliding lid of the cage a crack and slipped in a long steel forked rod. Deftly he pinned the mamba's head and the snake hissed sharply and twined itself around the steel rod. Now the snake-doctor opened the lid fully and seized the mamba behind the head, careful to get thumb and forefinger aligned behind the protuberances of the skull so the snake could not pull free of his grip.

The instant he released the pressure of the forked rod, the snake wrapped itself in tight coils around his forearm. It was six feet long and angry. It exerted all its rippling scaled strength to pull its head free, but the snake-doctor prevented the points of the skull from being drawn through his fingers.

The mamba's jaws gaped wide open and its short fangs were erect in the pale soft mucous lining of its mouth. The clear venom oozed down the open channel in the fangs and dripped from the points like dew from a rose-thorn.

The snake-doctor held the reptile's head on a small anvil and with a sharp blow of a wooden mallet crushed the skull. The snake's body whipped around wildly in the death frenzy.

Cheng watched impassively as the snake-doctor hung the writhing body on a meat hook and then used a razor to slit open the belly cavity and drain the blood into a cheap glass tumbler. With a surgeon's skill he removed the venom sacs from the mamba's neck and placed them in a glass bowl. After that he lifted out the liver and gall bladder and placed them in a separate bowl.

Next he peeled off the snake's skin, ringing the neck with the razor and stripping the skin like a nylon stocking from a girl's leg. The naked body was pink and glistening. The snake doctor took it down from the meat hook and laid it on the steel table-top. With half a dozen blows of a cleaver he chopped it into pieces, and dropped them into a soup kettle that was already boiling on the burner of a gas stove at the rear of the shop. As he added herbs and spices to the kettle he intoned a magical incantation that had remained unchanged since the Han dynasty of 200 BC when the first snake-doctors had developed their art.

Once the soup was cooking, the snake-doctor turned back to his table. He spilled the gall bladder and liver into a small mortar and pounded them to pulp with a ceramic pestle. Then he looked up at Cheng enquiringly.

'Do you wish to take the tiger juice?' he asked. It was a rhetorical question. Cheng always drank the venom.

Again it was part of the gambler's thrill to flirt with death, for if he had a tiny gum boil or a scratch on his tongue, a bleeding rash in his throat or a raw spot in his guts, even a duodenal or gastric ulcer, the mamba venom would find it and kill him within minutes, and it would be an excruciating death.

The snake-doctor added the translucent sacs of venom to the mortar and pounded them in with the liver. Then he scraped the pulp into the glass tumbler of dark blood and while he stirred it he added a dash of medicine from each of three other bottles.

The concoction was black, and thick as honey. He handed the tumbler to Cheng.

Cheng drew a deep breath and then tossed back the liquid at a single gulp. It was bitter with gall. He placed the empty glass on the metal table-top, and folded his hands in his lap. He sat without showing any emotion, while the snake-doctor recited spells from his magic book over him.

If the venom did not kill him, Cheng knew that the potion would arm his manhood. It would transform his flaccid penis into a steel lance. It would turn his testicles into cannonballs of iron. He waited quietly for the first symptoms of poisoning. After ten minutes he felt no ill-effects, but his penis stirred and swelled into a semi-erection. He moved a little to give it space in his trousers and the snake-doctor smiled and nodded happily at the success of his treatment.

He went to fetch the soup kettle from the gas burner and poured some of the liquid into a rice bowl and then added a piece of mamba flesh, cooked white and flaking. He offered the bowl and a pair of ivory chopsticks to Cheng.

Cheng ate the meat and drank the soup and when he had finished he accepted a second bowl. At the end of the meal he belched loudly to show his appreciation, and again the snake-doctor nodded and smiled.

Cheng consulted his wristwatch. It was nine o'clock. He rose to his feet and bowed. 'Thank you for your assistance,' he said formally.

'I am honoured that my humble efforts have pleased you. I wish you a sword of steel and many happy hours in the velvet scabbard.'

There was no question of payment. The snake-doctor would make a deduction from Cheng's commission on the supply of African snakes and wild birds.

Cheng walked back quickly to the apartment building in Tunhua Road. He sat in the black leather driving seat of the Porsche and for a few minutes enjoyed the tight full sensation of his erection before he started the engine and drove out of the garage.

It took him forty minutes to reach the sea pavilion. The grounds were surrounded by a high wall topped with a ridge of ceramic tiles, except on the open sea side. Coloured paper lanterns hung from the traditionally-shaped pediment of the gate. It looked like the entrance to a pleasure garden or fairground. Cheng knew that the lanterns had been lit especially to welcome him.

The guards had been warned to expect him and they made no effort to detain him. Cheng drove through and parked above the rocky headland. He locked the Porsche and stood for a moment inhaling the kelp odour of the sea. There was a fast motor launch moored at the private jetty. It would be needed later. Cheng knew that in less than two hours the speed boat could be over the thousand-yard sounding, over the oceanic depths of the East China Sea. A weighted object, such as a human body, dropped overboard from there would fall into the primeval ooze of the seabed, never to be recovered. He smiled. His erection had abated only slightly.

He went up to the pavilion. It was also of traditional architecture. It reminded Cheng of the house in the willow-tree pattern on the blue porcelain plates. A servant met him at the door, led him into an inner room and brought him tea.

It was exactly ten o'clock when she entered the room from behind the bead curtain.

She was slim as a boy in her tight brocaded tunic and silk pantaloons. He had never been able to guess her age for she wore a mask of make-up like a player in a Peking opera. Her almond eyes were starkly outlined in jet black, while her lids and cheeks were hectically rouged to the carmine colour that the Chinese find so attractive. Her forehead and the bridge of her nose were ash white and her lips a deep startling scarlet.

'Welcome to my house, Green Mountain Man,' she lisped, and Cheng bowed.

'I am honoured, Myrtle Blossom Lady.'

She sat on the sofa beside Cheng and they exchanged formal and polite conversation, until Cheng indicated the cheap imitation leather briefcase he had placed on the table in front of him.

She appeared to notice it for the first time, but did not deign to touch it herself. She inclined her head and her assistant glided into the room on slippered feet. She must have been watching them from behind the beaded curtain. She left again as silently as she had entered, taking the briefcase with her.

It took her a few minutes to count the money in the back room and to put it in a safe place. Then she returned and knelt beside her mistress. They exchanged a glance. The money was all there.

'You say that there is a choice of two?' Cheng asked.

'Yes,' she agreed. 'But would you like to make sure the room is to your taste, and that the equipment is in order?'

She led Cheng through to the special room at the back of the pavilion.

The central piece of furniture was a gynaecologist's couch, complete with stirrups. It was fitted with a plastic cover that could be removed and destroyed after use, and there was also a plastic sheet laid over the floor. The walls and ceiling were tiled and washable. Like an operating theatre, it could be scrubbed down to its present sterile condition.

Cheng moved to the table on which the instruments were laid out. There was a selection of silk cords of various lengths and thicknesses arranged in neat coils on the tray. He picked up one of these and ran it through his fingers. His erection, which had softened, revived strongly. Then he turned his attention to the other items on the table, a full set of stainless steel gynaecological instruments.

'Very good,' he told her.

'Come,' she said, and took his hand. 'You may choose now.'

She led him to a small window in the near wall. They stood hand-in-hand in front of it and looked through the one-way glass into the room beyond.

After a few moments the female assistant led two children into the room. They were both dressed in white. In the Chinese tradition, white was the colour of death. Both the little girls had long dark hair and pretty little nut-brown pug faces. Cambodian or Vietnamese, Cheng guessed.

'Who are they?' he asked.

'Boat people,' she said. 'Their boat was captured by pirates in the South China Sea. All the adults were killed. They are orphans, nameless and stateless. Nobody knows they exist; nobody will miss them.'

The female assistant began to undress the two little girls. She did it skilfully, titillating the hidden audience like a strip-tease artiste.

One girl was at least fourteen. Once she was naked Cheng saw that she had full breasts and a dark tussock of pubic hair, but the other girl was barely pubescent. Her breasts were flower buds, and the fine haze of pubic down did not conceal the plump cleft of her pudenda.

'The young one!' Cheng whispered hoarsely. 'I want the young one.'

'Yes,' she said. 'I thought that would be your choice. She will be brought to you in a few minutes. You may take as long as you wish. There is no hurry.'

She left the room, and suddenly the music swelled from hidden speakers – loud Chinese music with gongs and drums that would cover any other sound, such as a little girl's screams.

The colonials of Victorian times had sited Ubomo's Government House with care on high ground above the lake, with a view out across the waters, and they had surrounded it with lawns and exotic trees brought out from Europe to remind them of home. In the evenings the breeze came down from the Mountains of the Moon in the west, with the memory of glaciers and eternal snows, to take the edge off the heat.

Government House was still as it had been in the colonial era, no more pretentious than a comfortable redbrick ranch house with high ceilings, enclosed on all sides by a wide fly-screened verandah. Victor Omeru had kept it that way. He would not spend money on grand public buildings while his people were in want. The aid that he received from America and Europe had all gone into agriculture, health and education, not personal aggrandisement.

Tonight the verandahs and lawns were crowded as Daniel Armstrong and Bonny drove up in the army Landrover that had been placed at their disposal. A Hita corporal in camouflage overalls, with a sub-machine-gun slung over one shoulder, waved them into a parking slot between two other vehicles with diplomatic licence plates.

'How do I look?' Bonny asked anxiously as she checked her lipstick in the rear-view mirror.

'Sexy,' Daniel told her truthfully. She had teased her hair out into a great tawny red mane and she wore a green mini-skirt tight around her buttocks and high on her thighs. For such a big girl she had shapely legs.

'Give me a hand. Damned skirts!' The Landrover stood high and her skirt rode up as she slid down. She showed a flash of lace pantie that rocked the Hita corporal on to his heels.

There were floodlights in the jacaranda trees and an army band belted out popular jazz with a distinctive African beat that lifted Daniel's spirits and put a spring in his step.

'All this in your honour,' Bonny chuckled.

'I bet Taffari tells that to all his guests.' Daniel smiled.

Captain Kajo, who had met them at the airport, hurried towards them as soon as they stepped on to the lawn. He was looking at Bonny's legs from twenty paces away, but he addressed Daniel.

'Ah, Doctor Armstrong, the president has been asking for you. You are the guest of honour tonight.'

He led them up the front steps on to the verandah. Daniel picked out President Taffari instantly, even though he had his back turned to them. He was the tallest in a room full of tall Hita officers. He wore a maroon mess jacket of his own design, although his head was bare.

'Mr President.' Captain Kajo addressed his back deferentially, and Taffari turned and smiled and displayed the medals on his chest. 'May I present Doctor Daniel Armstrong and his assistant Miss Mahon?'

'Doctor!' Taffari greeted Daniel. 'I am a great admirer of your work. I could not have chosen anybody more qualified to show my country to the world. Up until now we have been kept in obscurity and medieval isolation by the reactionary old tyrant we overthrew. It is time that Ubomo came into its own. You will help us, Doctor. You will help us bring my beloved country into the twentieth century by focusing world attention upon us.'

'I'll do all in my power,' Daniel assured him cautiously. Although he had seen photographs of him, Daniel was unprepared for Taffari's eloquence and presence. He was a striking-looking man, exuding power and confidence. He stood a full head taller than Daniel's six feet and had the features of an Egyptian pharaoh carved in amber.

His eyes slid past Daniel and settled on Bonny Mahon. She stared back at him boldly and wet her bottom lip with the tip of her tongue.

'You are the photographer. Sir Peter Harrison sent me a videotape of "Arctic Dream". If you can photograph Ubomo with the same understanding and craft, I will be well pleased, Miss Mahon.'

He looked down at her bosom, at the big golden freckles on her upper chest that gave way to a narrow strip of unblemished creamy skin above the top of her green dress. The exposed cleavage between her breasts was deep and tightly compressed.

'You are very kind, Mr President,' she said, and Taffari laughed softly.

'Nobody has ever called me that before,' he admitted, and then changed the subject. 'What do you think of my country so far?'

'We only arrived today,' Bonny pointed out. 'But the lake is lovely and the people are so tall, the men so handsome.' She made it a personal compliment.

'The Hita are tall and handsome,' Taffari agreed. 'But the Uhali are small and ugly as monkeys, even their women.' The Hita officers of his staff laughed delightedly and Bonny gulped with shock.

'Where I come from we don't talk disparagingly of other ethnic groups. It's called racism, and it's unfashionable,' she said.

He stared at her for a moment. Clearly he was unaccustomed to being corrected. Then he smiled, a thin, cool little smile. 'Well, Miss Mahon, in Africa we tell the truth. If people are ugly or stupid we say so. It's called tribalism, and I assure you it's extremely fashionable.'

His staff roared with laughter, and Taffari turned back to Daniel.

'Your assistant is a woman of strong views, Doctor, but I believe you were born in Africa. You have a keener understanding. It shows in your work. You have put your finger on the problems that face this continent, and poverty is the most crippling of those. Africa is poor, Doctor, and Africa is passive and supine. I intend to change that. I intend to endow my country with the spirit and confidence to exploit our natural wealth and to develop the strength and native genius of our people. I want you to record our endeavours.'

His staff officers, all in the same maroon-coloured mess jackets, applauded this statement.

'I'll do my best,' Daniel promised.

'I'm sure you will, Doctor Armstrong.' He was looking at Bonny again, but he went on speaking to Daniel. 'The British ambassador is here tonight. I'm sure you will want to pay your respects.' He summoned Kajo to him. 'Captain, please take Doctor Armstrong to meet Sir Michael.'

Bonny began to follow Daniel, but Taffari stopped her with a touch on the arm. 'Don't go yet, Miss Mahon. There are a

364

few things I would like to explain to you, such as the differences between the Uhali and the tall handsome Hita whom you so admire.'

Bonny turned back to him, thrust out one hip in a provocative stance and crossed her arms beneath her breasts, pushing them up so that they threatened to pop out of the green dress into his face. 'You should not judge Africa by the standards of Europe,' he told her. 'We do things differently here.'

From the corner of her eye Bonny saw that Daniel had left the verandah and followed Kajo down on to the floodlit lawn. She leaned close to Taffari, her eyes not much below the level of his.

'Goody!' she said. 'I'm always looking for new and different ways.'

Daniel paused at the bottom of the steps and began to grin as he picked out the familiar figure on the crowded lawn. Then he hurried forward and seized his hand.

'*Sir* Michael, forsooth! British ambassador no less, you sly dog. When did all this happen?'

Michael Hargreave gripped his elbow in a momentary display of un-British and undiplomatic affection. 'Didn't you get my letter? All very sudden. Hauled me out of Lusaka before you could say "Bob's your uncle". Sword on both shoulders from H.M. "Arise, Sir Michael", and all that. Shot me down here. But you *did* get my letter?'

Daniel shook his head. 'Congratulations, Sir Michael. Long overdue. You deserve it.'

Hargreave looked embarrassed and dropped Daniel's hand. 'Where's your drink, dear boy? Don't touch the whisky. Locally made. Convinced it's actually bottled crocodile piss. Try the gin.' He summoned a waiter. 'Can't think why you didn't get my letter. Tried to ring you at the flat in London. No reply.'

'Where's Wendy?'

'Sent her back to Lusaka to pack up. New chap there has agreed to look after your Landcruiser and gear. Wendy will be here in a couple of weeks. Sends her love, by the way.'

'Did she know you'd see me here?' Daniel was puzzled.

'Tug Harrison gave us the word that you'd be in Ubomo.'

'You know Harrison?'

'Everybody in Africa knows Tug. Finger in most pies. Asked me to keep an eye on you. Told me about your assignment here. You're going to film Taffari and make him and BOSS look good; that's what he told me. Right?'

'A little bit more complicated than that, Mike.'

'Don't I know it! Complications you haven't dreamed of yet . . .' He drew Daniel away to a deserted corner of the lawn, out of earshot of the other guests. 'But first of all, what do you think of Taffari?'

'I wouldn't buy a second-hand country from him without checking the tyres.'

'Check the engine as well, while you're about it,' Michael smiled. 'The indications are that he's going to make Idi Amin look like Mother Theresa. I saw him giving you fifty lyrical words on his plan for peace and prosperity in the land.'

'Rather more than fifty,' Daniel corrected him.

'What it actually amounts to is peace for the Hita, prosperity for Ephrem Taffari, and screw the Uhali. My pals at MI6 tell me that he already has his numbered bank accounts in Switzerland and the Channel Islands all set up, and nice little sums tucked away in them. American foreign aid.'

'That shouldn't surprise you. Everybody's doing it, aren't they?'

'Par for the course; got to admit it. But he is being rather naughty to the Uhali. Chopped old Victor Omeru, who was rather a decent sort, and now he's kicking the manure out of the rest of the Uhali tribe. Some nasty rumours flying about, dark deeds. We don't really approve. Even the PM is a bit browned off with him already, which reminds me – got some news of a pal of yours.'

'A pal of mine?'

'The Lucky Dragon. Rings a bell, doesn't it? And you'll never guess who they're sending out to run the operation here.'

'Ning Cheng Gong,' Daniel said quietly.

It had to be. That was the reason he was here in Ubomo. He had sensed it all along. This was where he would meet Cheng again.

'You've been reading my mail,' Michael accused. 'Ning Cheng Gong is right. He arrives next week. Taffari is giving another party to welcome him. Any excuse for a party with our Ephrem, even you.' He broke off and stared at Daniel. 'You all right, dear boy? Taking your anti-malarial, are you? Gone as white as a sheet.'

'I'm fine.' But Daniel's voice was hoarse and scratchy. He had a terrible mental image of the bedroom of the cottage at Chiwewe, and of the desecrated bodies of Mavis Nzou and her daughters. It left him feeling sick and shaken. He wanted to think of something else, anything but Ning Cheng Gong.

'Tell me everything about Taffari and Ubomo that I need to know,' he demanded of Michael Hargreave.

'Tall order, dear boy. Can only give you the headlines now, but if you drop in at the embassy, I'll give you a full briefing, and a peep at some of the files. Your eyes only, of course. Even got a couple of bottles of genuine Chivas tucked away.'

Daniel shook his head. 'We're going up the lakeshore tomorrow to start filming. Taffari has put the entire navy at our disposal. One clapped-out World War Two gunboat. But I could drop in at the embassy tomorrow evening.'

When it was time to go, Daniel looked around for Bonny Mahon but could not find her. He saw Captain Kajo with a group of other officers at the bar and went across to him.

'I'm leaving now, Captain Kajo.'

'That's all right, Doctor. President Taffari has left already. You are free to go.' You could only tell that Kajo was drunk by his eyes. They had that coffee-coloured haze over the whites. In a white man they would have been bloodshot.

'We will meet tomorrow morning, Captain? What time?'

'Six o'clock at the guest house, Doctor. I will pick you up. We must not be late. The navy will be waiting for us.'

'Have you seen Miss Mahon?' Daniel asked. One of the other Hita officers sniggered drunkenly and Kajo grinned.

'No, Doctor. She was here earlier on. But I haven't seen her in the last hour. She must have left. Yes, come to think of it now, I did see her leave.' He turned away, and Daniel tried not to scowl and look abandoned as he went out to the Landrover in the carpark.

The government guest house was in darkness when he drove up and parked under the verandah. She might be in bed, already asleep with the light out. Despite his altered opinion of her, he felt a stab of disappointment when he switched on the bedroom light and saw that the servants had turned down the beds and rigged the mosquito nets. She had given him the excuse to end it — why was he not more pleased that it was over?

He had drunk just enough of the local gin to have a headache. He picked up Bonny's bag from the foot of the bed and carried it through to the second bedroom. Then he went into the bathroom and swept her toiletries and cosmetics into her sponge bag and dumped them in the washbasin of the second bathroom down the passage. Then he held his head under the cold tap and took three Anadin tablets. He dropped his clothes on the floor and climbed naked under the mosquito net.

He woke with headlights sweeping the front of the guest house and shining through the curtains on to the wall above his bed. Tyres crunched on the gravel drive. There were voices, and then a car door slammed and the vehicle pulled away. He heard her come up the verandah steps and open the front door. A minute later the bedroom door opened stealthily and she crept into the room.

He switched on the bedside light and she froze in the middle of the floor. She carried her shoes in one hand and her bag in the other. Her hair was in a wild tangle, sparkling like copper wire in the light, and her lipstick was smeared over her chin.

She giggled and he realised she was drunk.

'Have you any idea of the risk you're taking, you silly bitch?' he asked bitterly. 'This is Africa. What you'll get is a four-letter word and it's not the one you're thinking of, sweetheart. It's spelt A I D S.'

'Tut! Tut! Jealous, are we? How do you know what I've been doing, darling?'

'It's no big secret. Everybody at the party knew. You've been doing what any good little whore does.'

She took a wild round-arm swing at his head. He ducked under the blow, and the momentum carried her on to the bed. She pulled the mosquito net down on top of herself and fell in a tangle of long legs. The mini-skirt pulled up almost as high as her waist, her buttocks were bare and white as ostrich eggs.

'By the way,' he said, 'you've left your knickers with Ephrem.'

She crawled up on to her knees and pulled down the green skirt.

'They are in my handbag, ducky.' She got unsteadily to her feet. 'Where the hell are my things?'

'In your room, your new room across the passage.'

She flashed at him. 'So that's the way you want it?'

'You didn't really think I'd want to pick up Ephrem's left-overs, did you?' Daniel tried to keep his tone reasonable. 'Off you go, there's a good little harlot.'

She picked up her handbag and shoes and marched to the door. There she turned back to him, swaying with a drunkard's dignity.

'It's all true, what they say,' she told him with vindictive relish. 'They *are* big. Bigger and better than you'll ever be!' She slammed the door behind her.

Daniel was on his second cup of breakfast tea when Bonny came out on to the verandah and, without greeting him, took her place at the breakfast table opposite him.

She wore her usual working uniform of faded blue jeans and denim top, but her eyes were puffy and her expression disgruntled with hangover. The guest house chef was an anachronism from the colonial era and he served a traditional English breakfast. Neither of them spoke while Bonny demolished her plateful of eggs and bacon. Then she looked up at him.

'So what happens now?'

'You make a film,' he said. 'Just the way it's written in your contract.'

'You still want me around?'

'As a cameraman, yes. But from now on it's a business relationship.'

'That suits me just fine,' she agreed. 'It was getting to be a bit of a strain; I'm not good at faking it.'

Daniel stood up abruptly, and went to fetch his gear from the bedroom. He was still too angry to risk getting into an argument with her.

Before he was ready, Captain Kajo arrived with three soldiers in the back of his Landrover. They helped carry out the heavy video equipment and load it into the back of the truck. Daniel let Bonny sit up in the cab beside Captain Kajo, while he rode in the back with the heavily armed Hita soldiers.

The town of Kahali was very much as he remembered it from his last visit. The streets were wide and dusty where the potholes had eaten, cancer-like, through the tarmac. The buildings looked like those from the movie set of an old-fashioned Western.

The main difference that Daniel noticed was the mood of the people. The Uhali women still wore their colourful ankle-length robes and turbans, the Moslem influence apparent in their demeanour, but the expressions on their faces were guarded and neutral. There were few smiles and no laughter in the open-air market where the women squatted in lines with their wares spread out on sheets of cloth in front of them. There were army patrols in the market-place and on the street corners. The populace averted their eyes as the Landrover passed.

There were very few tourists, and these were dusty, unshaven and rumpled, probably members of an overland safari making their way down the length of the African continent in a huge communal truck. They were haggling for tomatoes and eggs in the market. Daniel grinned. They were paying for a glimpse of purgatory. The overland safari meant amoebic dysentery and punctures, five thousand miles of potholes and army road-blocks, probably the only package holiday on the globe with no repeat customers. Once was enough to last a lifetime.

The gunboat was waiting for them at the wharf. Seamen in navy blue uniforms and bare feet carried the video equipment up the gangplank and the captain shook hands with Daniel as he came aboard.

'Peace be with you,' he greeted him in Swahili. 'I have orders to take you where you want to go.'

They left the harbour and turned northwards, parallel to the lakeshore. Daniel stood out on the foredeck and his good spirits returned swiftly. The water was a dark and lovely blue, sparkling in the sunlight. There was a single cloud on the northern horizon, as white as a seagull and not much larger. It was the spray column where the lake spilled over its rocky rim into a deep gorge and became the infant Nile.

The ultimate source of the White Nile had been debated for two thousand years and had still not been entirely agreed upon. Was it those falls where the Victoria Nile out of Lake Victoria joined the Albert Nile in Lake Albert and spilled over at the beginning of the incredible journey down to Cairo and the Mediterranean Sea? Or was it higher still, as Herodotus had written long before the birth of Christ? Did it spring from a bottomless lake lying between the two mountains Crophi and Mophi and fed by their eternal snows?

With the lake-spray in his face, Daniel turned to look westward, trying to make out the loom of the romantic mountain peaks in the distance, but today, as on most days, it was a diffuse blue cloud mass, blending with the blue of the African sky.

Many of the earlier explorers had passed close by the Mountains of the Moon without ever dreaming of their existence. Even Henry Morton Stanley, that ruthless, driven, Americanised Welsh bastard, had lived for months in their shadow before the perpetual clouds had opened and astonished him with a vista of snowy peaks and shining glaciers. It gave Daniel a mystic feeling to sail upon these waters that were the life-blood pumped from the heart mountains of this savage continent.

He turned and glanced up at the open bridge of the gunboat. Bonny Mahon was filming. She had the Sony camera balanced on her shoulder and pointed towards the shore. He grimaced with reluctant approval. Whatever their personal problems, she was a true professional. At the end she'd probably get a good shot of the devil on her way through hell, and the thought made him grin and took the edge off his antagonism towards her.

He went back to the chartroom below the bridge and spread the survey maps and architect's drawings that BOSS had provided for him on the table.

The site that had been chosen for the hotel and casino was seven miles up the coast from the port of Kahali. Daniel saw that it was a natural bay with an island guarding the entrance. The Ubomo River, pouring down the escarpment of the Rift Valley from the great forests and snowy mountain ranges, debouched into the bay.

On the map it looked an ideal site for the holiday complex that Tug Harrison hoped would make Ubomo one of the more desirable holiday destinations for tourists from southern Europe.

To Daniel there seemed to be only one drawback. There was already a large fishing village sited on the bay. He wondered what Tug Harrison and Ning Cheng Gong planned to do about that. European sunbathers would not want to share the beach with native fishermen and their nets, while the odour of sun-dried fish on the racks would not encourage the appetite or add much to the romantic attractions of Fish Eagle Bay Lodge, as the project had already been named.

The captain hailed Daniel from above. He left the chart-table and went out to the open deck, just as the gunboat rounded the headland and Fish Eagle Bay opened ahead of them.

Daniel saw at once why the name had been chosen. The island at the mouth of the bay was heavily forested. Nourished by the lake's sweet clear waters, the ficus and wild mahogany trees had grown into giants with branches spreading out high over the rocky shore and the surrounding lake waters. Hundreds of mating pairs of fish eagles had built their nests in the high branches. With russet and chestnut plumage and glistening white heads, these were the most spectacular of all the African raptors. The great birds sat on every prominent perch, while still others sailed overhead on wide pinions, throwing back their heads in flight to utter the wild yelping chant that is so much a part of the African pageant.

The gunboat anchored and launched an inflatable Zodiac to take Daniel and Bonny to the island. For an hour they filmed the eagle colony. Captain Kajo threw dead fish off the rocky cliff and Bonny captured exciting sequences of rival eagles contending for the offerings and engaging in ritual aerial combat by hooking each other's talons and spinning and swirling in flight.

Daniel helped her lug the Sony camera up the smooth, massive trunk of a wild fig tree to film the eagle chicks in the nest. The parent birds attacked them both on the exposed branch, coming in on screaming power-dives with talons extended and curved yellow beaks agape, pulling away at the last possible moment so that the draught of the great wings buffeted them on their exposed perch. By the time Bonny and Daniel reached the ground, their personal antagonism had·been shelved and they were operating as a professional film crew again.

They returned to the Zodiac and ran out to the gunboat. As they came aboard, the captain weighed anchor and pushed on slowly into the bay. It was a spectacular site with volcanic rock cliffs climbing sheer out of the blue water and bright orange sand beaches in between the black rock.

Once again they climbed into the Zodiac and landed on one of the beaches near the mouth of the Ubomo River. Leaving Captain Kajo and the two seamen on the beach with the boat, Daniel and Bonny climbed to the highest point on the cliffs and were rewarded with a panoramic view over the bay and the lake.

They could look down on the large fishing village at the mouth of the Ubomo River. Twenty or so dhow-rigged boats were drawn up on the beach while as many more were dotted out upon the lake waters. On gull-winged sails the fleet was bearing in towards the bay, the night's fishing over, coming in to land the catch.

Along the head of the beach the fishing-nets were spread out in the sunlight to dry and the smell of fish carried up to them, even on the top of the cliff. Naked black children played upon the beach and splashed in the lake. Men worked on the dhows or sat cross-legged with needle and palm to repair the festooned nets. In the village the women moved gracefully in their long skirts as they pounded grain in the tall wooden mortars, swinging rhythmically to the rise and fall of the pestles in their hands, or squatted over the cooking-fires on which stood the black three-legged pots.

Daniel pointed out the various features which he wanted filmed and Bonny followed his instructions and turned the camera lens to record it all.

'What will happen to the villagers?' she asked, still peering into the viewfinder of the Sony. 'They're scheduled to start digging the foundations of the casino in three weeks . . .'

'I expect they'll move them to another site,' Daniel told her. 'In the new Africa people are moved about by their rulers like chess pieces . . .' He broke off and shaded his eyes, peering out along the road that led back along the lakeshore towards the capital.

Red dust blew in a slow sullen cloud out across the blue lake waters, carried on the mountain breeze from up-country.

'Let me have a look through your telephoto lens,' he asked Bonny, and she handed him the camera. Swiftly Daniel zoomed the lens to full power and picked up the approaching column of vehicles.

'Army trucks,' he told her. 'And transporters ... I'd say those were bulldozers on the transporters.' He handed her back the camera, and Bonny studied the approaching column.

'Some kind of army exercise?' she guessed. 'Are we allowed to film it?'

'Anywhere else in Africa I wouldn't take the chance of pointing a camera at anything military, but here we've got President Taffari's personal *firman*. Shoot away!'

Quickly Bonny set up the light tripod she used only for long-range telephoto shots and zoomed in on the approaching military convoy. Meanwhile, Daniel moved to the edge of the cliff and looked down on the beach. Captain Kajo and the sailors from the gunboat were stretched out on the sand. Kajo was probably sleeping off the previous evening's debauch. Where he lay he was out of sight of the village. Daniel strolled back to watch Bonny at work.

The convoy was already approaching the outskirts of the village. A mob of children and stray dogs ran out to greet it. The children skipped along beside the trucks, laughing and waving, while the dogs yapped hysterically. The vehicles drew up in the open ground in the centre of the village which was both soccer pitch and village square. Soldiers in camouflage uniform, armed with AK 47 rifles, jumped down and formed up into their platoons on the soccer ground.

A Hita officer climbed on to the cab of the leading truck and began to harangue the villagers through a bull-horn. The sound of his electronically distorted voice carried intermittently to the crest of the cliff on which Daniel was standing. He lost the sense of some of the Swahili as the breeze rose and fell, but the gist of it was clear.

The officer was accusing the villagers of harbouring political dissidents, obstructing the economic and agricultural reforms of the new government, and engaging in counter-revolutionary activities. While he was speaking, a squad of soldiers trotted down to the beach and rounded up the children and fishermen there. They herded them back to the village square.

The villagers were becoming agitated. The children hid amongst the skirts of the women and the men were protesting and gesticulating at the officer on the cab of the truck. Now soldiers began moving through the village, ordering people out of the thatched huts. One old man tried to resist being dragged from his home, and a soldier clubbed him with the butt of an AK 47. He fell in a huddle on the dusty earth and they left him there and moved on, kicking open the doors of the huts and shouting at the occupants. On the beach another group of soldiers was meeting the incoming fishing fleet and prodding the fishermen ashore at bayonet point.

Bonny never looked up from the viewfinder of her camera. 'This is great stuff! God, this is the real thing. This is Emmy Award territory, I kid you not!'

Daniel did not reply. Her gloating excitement should not have offended him as much as it did. He was a journalist himself. He understood the need to find fresh and provocative material to stir the jaded emotions of a television audience reared on a diet of turmoil and violence, but what they were witnessing here was as obscene as scenes of SS troopers clearing out the ghettoes of Europe.

The soldiers were beginning to load the fisherfolk on to the waiting trucks, women were screaming and trying to find their own children in the throng. Some villagers had managed to collect a pathetic bundle of possessions, but most of them were empty-handed.

The two yellow bulldozers rolled down off their low trailer beds with engines pulsing and blue diesel smoke blowing from the exhaust stacks. One of them swung in a tight circle with a track locked, and lowered the massive frontal blade. Gleaming in the afternoon sunlight the blade sliced into the wall of the nearest hut and the thatched roof collapsed.

'Beauty!' Bonny murmured. 'I couldn't have staged it better. That was an incredible shot!'

The women were wailing and ululating, that peculiar chilling sound of African grief. One of the men broke away and ran towards the cover of the nearest field of sorghum. A soldier shouted a warning at him, but he put his head down and ran faster. A short burst of automatic rifle-fire popped like a string of fire-crackers and the man collapsed and rolled in the dust and lay still. A woman screamed and ran towards the fallen body carrying an infant strapped in a shawl on her back and an older child in her arms. A soldier barred her path with a bayoneted rifle and turned her back towards the truck.

'I got it!' Bonny exulted. 'The whole thing. The shooting and all. It's in the can. Shit, this is great!'

The soldiers were drilled and ruthless. It all went very quickly. Within half an hour the entire populace of the village had been rounded up, except for the fishermen still out on the lake. The first truck, fully loaded, pulled away, heading back the way it had come.

The huts were collapsing one after the other as the two bulldozers moved down the rows.

'God, I hope I don't run out of film,' Bonny muttered anxiously. 'This is a once-in-a-lifetime chance.'

Daniel had not spoken since the operation had begun. He was part of Africa. He had seen other villages wiped out. He remembered the guerrilla camp in Mozambique. Since then he had seen Renamo rebels work over a village, and he had witnessed forced removals by the minions of apartheid in South Africa, but he had never grown hardened to the suffering of the African people. He was sick to his guts as he watched the rest of the little drama unfold.

The remaining fishing-boats ran in unsuspectingly to the beach, where the soldiers were waiting to drag the crews ashore. The last truckload of villagers rolled away in a column of red dust, and as soon as it was out of sight, one of the yellow bulldozers waddled down on to the beach and swept the abandoned fishing-boats into a pile, like firewood kindling.

Four soldiers brought the body of the old man and the one who had tried to escape, carrying them by ankles and wrists, dead heads lolling backwards. They tossed them on to the funeral pyre of shattered hulls and torn sails. One of the soldiers hurled a lighted torch of thatch on to the top of the pile. The flames took hold and burned so fiercely that the soldiers were driven backwards, holding up their hands to protect their faces.

The bulldozers crawled back and forth over the remains of the huts, flattening them under the steel tracks. A whistle shrilled and the soldiers formed up quickly and re-embarked into the waiting troop-carriers. The yellow bulldozers crawled back on to their transporters, and the entire column wound away.

After they had gone, the only sound was the hushed whisper of the evening breeze along the cliff face and the distant crackle of the flames.

'Well,' Daniel tried to keep his tone neutral, 'the site is clear for the new casino. Taffari's investment in happiness for his people is secure . . .' his voice broke. He could not go on. 'The bastard!' he whispered. 'The murderous bloody bastard.'

He found that he was shaking with anger and outrage. It required an immense effort of will to bring his emotions under control. He strode to the edge of the cliff overlooking the beach. The gunboat was still anchored out in the deeper water in the middle of the bay and the Zodiac was drawn up on the beach with one of the soldiers guarding it, but Captain Kajo and the other sailor were no longer asleep on the sand. It was obvious that they had been awakened by the sound of gunfire and activity in the destroyed village.

Daniel looked around for Kajo and picked him out at last. He was climbing the cliff face half a mile away, and it was clear from his manner that he was agitated. He was searching for them, stopping every few minutes to shout through cupped hands and peer about him anxiously.

Daniel ducked back out of sight and snapped at Bonny. 'Nobody must know that we shot that footage. It's dynamite.'

'Gotcha!' she agreed.

'Give me the tape. I'll take care of it, in case they want to check what you've filmed.'

Bonny ejected the tape from the camera and handed it over. He wrapped it in a jersey and stuffed it into the bottom of his rucksack. 'All right, let's get out of here before Kajo finds us. He must never guess that we saw what we saw.'

Bonny gathered up her equipment swiftly and followed Daniel as he cut inland away from the remains of the village and the lakeshore. Within minutes they were into the tall grass and scrub of the savannah.

Daniel circled back through the elephant grass and scrub until he reached the lakeshore again near the mouth of the bay, opposite Fish Eagle Island. They scrambled down the cliff to the beach and Daniel paused to let Bonny catch her breath.

'I don't understand how they let a film crew loose in the area on the very day they were going to wipe out the village,' she gasped.

'Typical African screw-up,' Daniel told her. 'Somebody forgot to tell somebody else. The last *coup* attempt they made in Zambia, one of the conspirators broke into the radio station and announced the revolution while all his co-conspirators were still in barracks eating breakfast. He had the wrong day. It was supposed to be the following Sunday. AWA. Are you ready to go on?'

Bonny stood up. 'AWA?' she asked.

'Africa Wins Again,' Daniel smiled grimly. 'Let's go!'

Assuming a casual manner they set off side by side along the firm damp sand at the edge of the water.

They could see the beached Zodiac in the distance, but the demolished village was still hidden by the bulge of the cliff face.

They had not covered more than two hundred yards before Kajo hailed them from the cliff top. They stopped and looked up at him, waving as though they had only just noticed him for the first time.

'He's peeing in his pants,' Bonny murmured. 'He doesn't know if we witnessed the raid or not.'

Kajo came pelting down the cliff path, slipping and sliding on the steep places. He was out of breath when he reached the beach and confronted them.

'Where have you been?' he demanded.

'Out at the point,' Daniel told him. 'We filmed the casino site. Now we are going down to film the hotel site at the river mouth, where the fishing village is—'

'No! No!' Kajo grabbed Daniel's arm. 'That is enough. No more filming. We must go back to the boat. It is finished for today.' Daniel shrugged off his hand and argued with him for a while. Then finally, with a show of reluctance, he allowed himself to be led towards the Zodiac and ferried aboard the gunboat.

As soon as he reached the bridge, Kajo held a whispered discussion with the ship's captain and they both looked to the head of the bay. There were still streamers of smoke from the burning fishing boats drifting out over the water. The ship's captain looked worried and gave orders to get under way in unnecessarily loud and agitated tones.

Before Daniel could prevent her, Bonny walked to the stern rail and aimed the Sony camera back towards the shore. Captain Kajo scrambled down the bridge ladder and ran down the deck shouting.

'No! Wait! You must not film that!'

'Why not? It's only a bush fire, isn't it?'

'No! Yes! It's a bush fire, but it's classified material.'

'A top secret bush fire?' Bonny teased him, but she obediently lowered the camera.

As soon as they were alone Daniel scolded her. 'Don't get too damned clever. That little joke could have backfired on us.'

'On the contrary, I convinced Kajo that we are innocent,' she argued. 'When are you going to let me have my tape back?'

'I'll keep it,' he answered. 'Kajo's still suspicious. My bet is that when we reach Kahali, he'll check your equipment.'

It was after dark when the gunboat tied up at its berth. During the transfer of Bonny's video equipment from the vessel to the army Landrover on the wharf, the aluminium case that contained her tapes disappeared. Although she screamed at Kajo, and shook her finger in his face and threatened to report his inefficiency to President Taffari, Kajo just kept on smiling blandly. 'Don't worry, Miss Mahon. It will turn up. I give you my personal guarantee.'

Kajo arrived at the guest house the following morning, all smiles and apologies, carrying the missing case. 'All present and correct, Miss Mahon. One of those stupid Uhali porters mislaid it. Please accept my heartfelt apologies.'

'You can be damned certain they scanned every tape in the box,' Daniel assured her when Kajo had gone. He tapped the buttoned pocket of his bush jacket. 'I'm going to get this tape of the raid down to Mike at the British embassy. It's the only safe place for it. Are you coming?'

'I have an engagement.' She looked defiant.

'If you're going to visit your new boy friend, just be careful. That's my advice to you. You've seen his style.'

'Ephrem is an honourable man,' she flared. 'I can't believe he knew anything about that raid.'

'Believe what you want, but don't tell anybody about this tape. Not even Tug Harrison.'

Bonny froze and stared at him. She had gone very pale.

'What are you talking about?' she demanded.

'Come on, Bonny, give me some credit. I checked that phone call you made from the Norfolk Hotel in Nairobi. Of course you're reporting to Tug Harrison. How much is he paying you to spy on me?'

'You're crazy.' She tried to brazen her way out of it.

'Yes, I probably am. I fell for you, didn't I? But you'll be crazy if you tell Tug about this tape.'

He left her staring after him and he drove down the hill towards the British embassy. The grounds of the embassy were walled and the gates were guarded by soldiers of President Taffari's personal bodyguard in camouflage uniforms and maroon berets. Michael Hargreave came out of his office to greet Daniel.

'Morning, Sir Mickey.'

'Danny boy! I spoke to Wendy last night. She sends you her love.'

'When is she arriving?'

'Not for another few weeks, more's the pity. Her mother is unwell, so Wendy has to go home first instead of coming directly from Lusaka . . .'

Still chatting, he led Daniel into his office, but as soon as he closed the door his manner changed.

'News for you, Danny. The Chinaman has arrived. Landed this morning in BOSS's executive jet. My information is he came from Taiwan via Nairobi. Moved into BOSS headquarters in Lake House immediately to take over as head of the syndicate, and Taffari is throwing one of his bashes for him on

Friday evening. Expect you'll get an invitation from Government House.'

'That should be interesting.' Daniel smiled grimly. 'I'm looking forward to seeing that gentleman again.'

'That may be sooner than you think.' Michael Hargreave glanced at his wristwatch. 'Have to leave you, dear boy. Making a luncheon speech to the assembled Rotarians of Ubomo, would you believe? Those files I promised you are all with my secretary. She'll give you a room to work in. Have a peep at them, then give them back to her. No notes nor photostats, please, Danny. Eyes only.'

'Thanks, Mike; you're a hero. But one other favour, please?'

'Fire away. Anything to please. Hargreave family motto, don't you know?'

'Will you keep an envelope in your personal safe for me, Mike?'

Michael locked the sealed envelope containing the Fish Eagle Bay tape into his strong room, then shook hands and excused himself.

Daniel watched him from the verandah as he was driven away by his uniformed chauffeur in the ambassadorial car. Despite the Union Jack pennant on the bonnet, it was a ten-year-old Rover in need of a paint job. The ambassador to Ubomo did not rate a Rolls-Royce.

Daniel went back to the files that Michael's secretary had laid out for him in a back room. When he left the embassy three hours later, his original impression of Ephrem Taffari had been reinforced a hundredfold.

'He's a tough and wily bird,' Daniel muttered as he started the Landrover. 'He and Bonny Mahon should have fun together.'

 The motorcycle escort, sirens wailing, was forced to moderate its speed by the condition of the road through the new area of squatters' slums that had grown up around the capital. The tarmac was pitted with sharp-edged craters, while chickens and pigs scattered, cackling and grunting, ahead of the outriders.

The presidential car, another recent gift from the same middle eastern oil potentate, was a black Mercedes. It was a mark of his high regard that President Taffari had sent it down to Lake House on the waterfront to fetch his guest to the audience. Ning Cheng Gong sat behind the chauffeur and studied these first glimpses of Ubomo with interest.

After what he had observed in Asia and the other parts of Africa in which he had served, the poverty and degradation of the slums through which they drove neither repelled nor shocked him. From his father he had learned to look upon swarming humanity as either a source of cheap labour, or a market for the goods and services he had to sell.

'Without human beings there is no profit,' his father had pointed out on numerous occasions. 'The more people the better. Always when human lives are cheap, there are great fortunes to be made. We, the Lucky Dragon, must resist any effort to limit population growth in the Third World. People are our basic stock-in-trade.'

Cheng smiled at his father's wisdom, derived from a study of history. His father's view was that only when human populations had been checked and limited by extraneous factors had the common man regained dignity and a measure of control over his own destiny. The terrible depredations of the great plagues of medieval times had broken the slavery of the feudal system of Europe. They had reduced human populations to the point where men had scarcity value and could bargain for their labour once again.

The great wars of this century had smashed the class system of inherited privilege and fortune, and ushered in this aberrant age of human rights, in which the common men of inferior races were taught that they were the equal of their betters. In Cheng's view, and that of his father, common men had no such divine rights, any more than the antelope in the wild deserved special protection from the lion.

When the mass of humanity reached such proportions that human life was cheap, that was the age of opportunity for the great predators to emerge. Predators like Lucky Dragon. In Africa that time was fast approaching as populations swarmed like hiving bees.

He thought about the little Cambodian boat girl, whose

corpse now lay in the dark depths of the China Sea. There were millions and tens of millions more like her, in India and China and Africa and South America, for men like him.

Cheng had recognised in the burgeoning populations of Africa a unique opportunity. That was the main reason that Lucky Dragon was drawn so irresistibly to this continent. That was why he was going now to a meeting with the president of this country which would soon be made to render up its wealth to him. He would suck the juice from it, throw away the empty skin, and pluck another from the tree. He smiled at the metaphor and raised his eyes to the green hill above the town on which Government House stood.

President Ephrem Taffari had an honour guard in maroon uniforms and white sun-helmets drawn up to welcome him and a red carpet laid across the green lawn. He came down the carpet to meet Ning Cheng Gong personally and to shake his hand. He led him up on to the wide verandah and seated him in one of the carved armchairs under the revolving fan that hung from the ceiling.

An Uhali servant in ankle-length white robes, scarlet sash and tasselled fez offered him a silver tray of frosted glasses. Cheng refused the champagne and chose a glass of freshly squeezed orange juice.

Ephrem Taffari took the armchair opposite him and crossed one long leg clad in crisp white cotton trousers over the other. He smiled at Cheng with all his charm.

'I wanted our first meeting to be informal and relaxed,' he explained, and made a deprecatory gesture towards his own open-neck sports shirt and sandals. 'So you will excuse my casual attire and the fact that I have none of my ministers with me.'

'Of course, Your Excellency.' Cheng sipped the orange juice. 'I am also delighted by this opportunity to get to know you and to be able to speak freely without the inhibition of having other people present.'

'Sir Peter Harrison speaks very highly of you, Mr Ning. He is a man whose opinion I value. I am sure that our relationship will be mutually rewarding.'

For another ten minutes they traded compliments and protestations of friendship and goodwill. Both of them were at ease with this flowery circumlocution; it was part of their separate cultures and they understood instinctively the moves and countermoves as they circled and closed in on the real business of their meeting.

Finally Cheng took a sealed envelope from the inside pocket of his white silk tropical suit. It was a piece of expensive stationery, glossy and cream-coloured with a dragon motif embossed on the back flap.

'My father and I want you to believe, Mr President, that our commitment to your country is unswerving. We would like you to accept this as an earnest token of our friendship and concern.'

Cheng made his offering seem like a free and unsolicited gift, whereas both of them were aware that it had been the subject of intense and protracted bargaining. There had been other bidders in the market, not least of them the Arab oil sheikh who had provided the gunboat and the presidential Mercedes. It had taken all Sir Peter Harrison's influence to secure the deal for the BOSS and Lucky Dragon syndicate.

The envelope contained the second instalment due to Ephrem Taffari in his personal capacity. The first instalment had been paid over ten months previously, on signature of the original agreement.

President Taffari picked up the envelope and turned it over to examine the seal. His fingers were long and elegantly shaped, and very dark against the stiff creamy paper.

He split the corner of the envelope with his thumbnail and unfolded the two documents it contained. One was a deposit receipt to a numbered bank account in Switzerland. The amount of the deposit was ten million US dollars. The other was a share transfer document, notarised in Luxembourg. A total of thirty per cent of the syndicate's share equity was now registered in the name of Ephrem Taffari. The syndicate's formally registered name was 'The Ubomo Development Corporation'.

The president returned the documents to the open envelope and slipped it into the pocket of his flowered sports shirt.

'Progress has not been as rapid as I had hoped,' he said, his tone still courteous but underlaid with steel. 'I hope that will change with your arrival, Mr Ning.'

'I am aware of the delays. As you know, my field-manager has been in Kahali for the last week or so. He has given me a full report of the situation. I believe that some of the blame must attach to the previous management, put in place by BOSS. There has been some reluctance to exploit all the available assets.' Cheng made a delicately pejorative gesture. 'Mr Purvis of BOSS, who is now safely on his way back to London, was a sensitive man. You know how squeamish these Englishmen can be. My field-manager informs me that we are short of labour.'

'I assure you, Mr Ning, that you will have all the labour you require.' Taffari's smile became strained at the thinly veiled complaint.

'Thirty thousand,' Cheng said softly. 'That was the original estimate approved by you, Your Excellency. So far we have been given fewer than ten thousand.'

'You will have the rest before the beginning of next month.' Taffari was no longer smiling. 'I have given orders to the army. All political detainees and dissidents are to be rounded up and sent to the labour camps in the forest.'

'These will be members of the Uhali tribe?' Cheng asked.

'Of course,' Taffari snapped. 'You didn't think for a moment that I would send you Hita, did you?'

Cheng smiled at the absurdity of that notion. 'My field-manager tells me that the Uhali are good workers, hardy and intelligent and compliant. We will need most of them in the forest to begin with. It seems that we are experiencing problems there caused by the terrain and the climate. The roads are bad and machinery is bogging down. We will be forced to use more men.'

'Yes, I warned the BOSS people of that,' Taffari agreed. 'They were reluctant to use what they considered to be...' He hesitated. 'That man Purvis referred to our convict labour as slave labour.' He looked mildly amused by such pedantic definitions.

'These Westerners,' Cheng sympathised. 'The English are bad enough, but the Americans are even worse. They do not understand Africa or the orient. Their minds stop at Suez...' he broke off. 'I assure you, Mr President, that an easterner is now in control of the syndicate's operation. You will find that I do not suffer from these Western scruples.'

'It is a relief to be able to work with somebody who understands the necessities of life,' Taffari agreed.

'Which brings me to the hotel and casino project at Fish Eagle Bay. I understand from my field-manager that nothing has been done there, apart from the original survey of the area. He tells me that there is still a fishing village on the hotel site.'

'Not any longer,' Taffari smiled. 'The area was cleared two days ago, soon after Purvis left for London. The village was a hotbed of counter-revolutionary activity. My soldiers rounded up all the dissidents. Two hundred able-bodied prisoners are already on their way to the concession area in the forest to join your labour force. The hotel site is ready for construction to begin.'

'Your Excellency, I can see that you and I are going to work well together. May I show you the modifications that I have made to the schedule of works drawn up by Purvis?' He opened his briefcase and unfolded a large computer spreadsheet that covered the entire table between them.

Taffari leaned forward and listened with interest as Cheng pointed out the way in which he had restructured almost the entire syndicate operation.

At the end of the lecture Taffari's admiration was unconcealed. 'You have accomplished all this in the short time since you arrived in Ubomo?' he asked, but Cheng shook his head.

'Not all of it, Your Excellency. Some of the replanning was done before I left Taipei. I had the benefits of my father's advice and the assistance of his headquarters staff at Lucky Dragon. Only part of the planning was necessitated after my arrival in Kahali, on the advice of my field-manager, and his report on the conditions and problems we have encountered in the forest.'

'Remarkable!' Taffari shook his head. 'Sir Peter Harrison's opinion of you seems to be well founded.'

'Planning is one thing,' Cheng pointed out modestly. 'Execution is another thing entirely.'

'I am sure that you will bring the same energy and drive to that part of the operation.' Taffari looked at his wristwatch. 'I am expecting a guest for lunch . . .'

'I am sorry, Your Excellency. I have overstayed my welcome.' Cheng made as if to rise.

'Not at all, Mr Ning. I absolutely insist that you join us for lunch. It may amuse you to meet my other guest, a member of the film team which Sir Peter Harrison has hired.'

'Ah, yes.' Cheng looked dubious. 'Sir Peter explained to my father and myself why he had invited a film company to Ubomo. I am not certain that I agree with him, however. The English have a saying about sleeping dogs. In my view, it may be better not to draw world attention to our operations. I would like to cancel the project and send the film team out of Ubomo.'

'I am afraid it is too late for that.' Taffari shook his head. 'We have already received a great deal of adverse publicity. There is a woman, a protégée of the previous president, Omeru . . .'

For another ten minutes they discussed Sir Peter's plan to defuse Kelly Kinnear's propaganda campaign by a counter-campaign of their own.

'In any event,' Taffari pointed out, 'we can always suppress anything we don't like about this film production. Sir Peter Harrison has an approval clause written into the contract. We can even suppress the final product completely, and destroy all copies of the film, if we feel that is advisable.'

'Of course, you are taking precautions to make certain that these people do not get to see any of our sensitive areas? The convict labour camps, the main logging operations, and the re-fill mining?'

'Trust me, Mr Ning. They will see the pilot scheme only. I have a reliable military officer accompanying them at all times.' He broke off at the sound of an approaching vehicle. 'Ah! That would be the person we are discussing, the cameraman and Captain Kajo.'

'Cameraman?' Cheng asked, as they watched Bonny Mahon and Captain Kajo cross the lawn towards them.

'Inaccurate, I agree,' Taffari chuckled. 'But is there such a term as camerawoman, I wonder?' He stood up and went to meet his guest.

Captain Kajo came to attention and saluted. Taffari ignored him. Kajo's job was done. He had delivered Bonny. He turned on his heel and returned to wait in the army Landrover. He knew it might be a long wait.

Cheng studied the woman as Taffari led her down the verandah. She was too big and bosomy. She had no delicacy of bone structure nor refinement of feature. Both her nose and mouth were too large for his taste. Her freckled skin and coppery hair repelled him. Her voice and laughter, as she joked with Taffari, were loud and vulgar. Her confident attitude and powerful limbs made Cheng feel threatened as though she were challenging his masculinity. He did not like a woman to be as strong and assertive as a man. He compared her unfavourably with the dainty ivory-skinned women of his own race, with their straight black hair and submissive self-effacing manner.

However, he rose politely and smiled and shook her hand, and saw that Taffari was quite smitten by the woman.

He knew that Taffari had a dozen Hita wives who were amongst the most beautiful of the tribe, but he supposed that the president was attracted by the novelty of this gross creature. Perhaps he felt that it would add to his status to have a white woman as a plaything. However, Cheng guessed shrewdly that he would tire of her soon enough and discard her as casually as he had taken her up.

'Mr Ning is the chief executive officer of the Ubomo Development Corporation,' Taffari told Bonny. 'Technically he is your boss.'

Bonny chuckled. 'Well, I can report that we are doing a hell of a job, boss.'

'I am delighted to hear that, Miss Mahon.' Cheng was unsmiling. 'It is an important task that you are undertaking. What have you accomplished so far?'

'We've been working here in Kahali and on the lake. We've already filmed the site of the new hotel and casino.'

Both Cheng and Taffari listened seriously to her report.

'Where are you moving to after this?' Cheng wanted to know.

'After we finish here we are driving up-country to the forest area. A place called Sengi-Sengi. Have I got that right, Your Excellency?' She looked at Taffari.

'Quite right, my dear Miss Mahon,' Taffari assured her. 'Sengi-Sengi is the corporation's pilot scheme for utilising the forest assets.'

Cheng nodded. 'I will be visiting the project myself at the very first opportunity.'

'Why don't you come up to Sengi-Sengi while we are filming?' Bonny suggested. 'It would give much more weight to the production to have you in it, Mr Ning.' She paused as another thought struck her, and then with a boyish grin she turned to Ephrem Taffari. 'But it would really be terrific to have you in the production, Mr President. We could interview you on the site of the project at Sengi-Sengi. You could explain to us your hopes and dreams for your country. Just think of that, Your Excellency.'

Ephrem Taffari smiled and shook his head. 'I'm a busy man. I don't think I could spare the time.'

But she could see he was tempted. He was enough of a politician to relish the prospect of favourable exposure to a wide audience.

'It would be very valuable,' she urged him. 'For both Ubomo and your personal image. People out there in the big world have heard about you only vaguely. If they could see you, it would change their whole perception. I assure you from a professional point of view that you would look plain bloody marvellous on the screen. You are tall and handsome and your voice is sensational. I swear I'd make you look like a film star.'

He liked the idea. He liked the flattery. 'Well, perhaps . . .'

They both realised that he wanted to be persuaded just a little longer.

'You could fly up to Sengi-Sengi by helicopter,' Bonny pointed out. 'It would take half a day, no more . . .' She paused and pouted suggestively and touched his arm. 'Unless, of course, you decided to stay over for a day or two. That would be okay by me, also.'

 Daniel and Bonny, accompanied as always by Captain Kajo, drove up from Kahali. Although it was only a little over two hundred miles it took them two full days, for much of that time was spent not in travelling but in filming the changing countryside and the rural tribes in their traditional *manyattas* that they found along the way.

Captain Kajo was able to smooth the way and negotiate with

the tribal elders. For a few Ubomo shillings he arranged that they had the run of any of the Hita villages that they passed. They filmed the young girls at the water-holes, clad only in tiny beaded skirts as they bathed and plaited each other's hair. The unmarried girls dressed their coiffures with a mixture of cow dung and red clay until it was an intricate sculpture on top of their heads, adding inches to their already impressive height.

They filmed the married women as they returned to the village in long files clad in flowing red matronly togas, swaying gracefully under brimming calabashes of water drawn from the spring.

They filmed the herds of dappled, multi-coloured cattle with their wide horns and humped backs against a background of flat-topped acacia and golden savanna grasslands.

They filmed the herdboys bleeding a great black bull, twisting a leather thong around its neck to raise the congested vein beneath the skin, then piercing it with the point of an arrow and capturing the scarlet stream of blood in a bottle-shaped calabash. When the gourd was half filled they sealed the wound in the bull's neck with a handful of clay, and topped up the calabash with milk stripped directly from the udder. Then they added a dash of cow's urine to curdle the mixture into thick cheesy curds.

'Low cholesterol,' Daniel pointed out when Bonny gagged theatrically. 'And look at those Hita figures.'

'I'm looking,' Bonny assured him. 'Oh, hallelujah, I'm looking.'

The men wore only a red blanket over one shoulder, held with a belt at the waist. They allowed the skirts to flap open casually in the breeze, especially when Bonny was nearby. They let her film as much as she wished of everything they possessed, staring into the lens with masculine arrogance, the elongated loops of their earlobes stopped with bone and ivory earrings.

On the main road their Landrover passed ore trucks and logging trailers coming in the opposite direction. The weight of these massive vehicles, even though spread over a dozen axles and banks of massive tyres, rutted the road deeply and raised a fog of dust that covered the trees for a mile on both sides of the roadway with a thick coating of dark red talcum. Bonny gloried in the effect of the sunlight through the dust cloud and the shapes of the trucks lumbering out of it like prehistoric monsters.

When at last, on the second day, they crossed the river on the ferry and reached the edge of the great forests, even Bonny was awed by the height and girth of the trees.

'They're like pillars holding up the sky,' she breathed as she turned her camera upon them. The quality of the air and light changed as they left the dry savannah behind them and entered this humid and lush forest world.

At first they followed the main highway with its mile-wide open verges. Then, after fifty miles, they turned off on to one of the new development roads, freshly cut into the virgin forest. The deeper they journeyed into the forest, the closer the trees crowded the roadway, until at last their high branches met overhead and they were in a tunnel filled with dappled and greenish light.

Even the bellow of the truck engines that passed them seemed muted, as though the trees were blanketing and absorbing the alien and offensive sound. The surface of the road had been corduroyed with logs laid side by side, and over this was spread a layer of flinty gravel to give the great trucks footing.

'The returning ore trucks bring the gravel back from the quarries near the lakeshore,' Captain Kajo explained. 'If they did not, the road would become a bottomless swamp of mud. It rains almost every day here.'

Every mile or so there were gangs of hundreds of men and women working on the road, spreading gravel and laying new logs to hold the surface together.

'Who are they?' Daniel asked.

'Convicts,' Kajo dismissed them lightly. 'Instead of spending money keeping them locked up and fed, we let them work off their debt to society.'

'A lot of convicts for such a small country,' Daniel pointed out. 'You must have a lot of crime in Ubomo.'

'The Uhali are a bunch of rogues, thieves and troublemakers,' Kajo explained and then shuddered as he looked beyond the toiling lines of prisoners to the impenetrable forest behind them.

'I hate this place,' he said with abrupt and unusual vehemence. 'It is a dark and evil place, fit only for monkeys and their close relatives, the Bambuti pygmies.'

'Shall we see any pygmies?' Bonny demanded eagerly.

'Some of the tame ones trade along the road,' Kajo muttered. 'And their women whore with the truck-drivers. But the wild ones are forest animals. You won't see them; nobody does.' He shuddered again. 'I hate this place. We should cut down all these trees and sell them, and plant grass pasture in their place so that our cattle can multiply.' It was spoken with the fierce Hita love of cattle, the tribe's greatest treasure.

'If the trees were gone, the rains would cease. Then the rivers that flow down to the lake and water your herds would dry up. All things in nature depend upon each other. If you destroy one, you damage all,' Daniel began to explain, but Kajo snarled at him as he wrestled with the wheel of the Landrover as it bounced over the corduroy of logs.

'It is not necessary to patronise me, Doctor Armstrong. I have a university degree and, strange as it may seem, I can actually read. I know all these white elitist theories that you and people like you propound. It is all very well for you, rich white people, to tell us to starve ourselves and our cattle herds so that you can come here as tourists to stare for a few days at the beautiful view and admire the wild animals, then go home to your penthouses in New York and your mansions in England . . .' He broke off and drew a deep breath. 'Forgive me, Doctor. I did not mean to give offence but we Africans have to live here. We also have a right to a good life. These trees that you admire so much belong to us. We have a rapidly expanding population to care for, Ubomo's population is growing by six per cent every year. We need food and shelter and education, and we need land. Our people are crying out for land. These forests are useless to us unless we utilise them. We should cut them down and burn them and use the earth for gardens and pastures . . .'

Daniel was saddened as he listened. Kajo was an educated and intelligent young man. If he still clung to the traditional view, what hope was there of convincing the unsophisticated country people like those that they had filmed in the *manyattas*?

'Your white elitist theories,' Kajo had said. That was the viewpoint that could turn a continent into a desert. One day the Sahara might stretch from Cairo to the flat-topped mountain that guarded the Cape of Good Hope.

So they came eventually to Sengi-Sengi. The road ended at a considerable settlement in the midst of the forest. The larger trees had been left standing, but beneath them the undergrowth and lesser trees had been cleared to make way for the compounds that housed the labour force, for machine workshops and administrative buildings.

The huts in the compound that housed the labour force were made from materials gathered on the site. The walls were of raw timber, plastered with red clay and the roofs were of thatch. The workshops and offices were prefabricated structures, constructed in sections so that they could be taken down and moved to a new site with little effort or expense.

Kajo parked the Landrover in front of the main office building, another temporary structure set on brick piers to allow air to circulate below the floorboards and in that way to cool the interior and keep it dry during the daily rainstorms. He led them up the steps. 'I must introduce you to the field-manager of UDC.'

'What does UDC stand for?' Bonny wanted to know.

'Ubomo Development Corporation,' Kajo replied, and would have gone on to explain further, but the manager's secretary looked up from her typewriter as they entered the reception area of the building.

She was a Hita girl in her mid-twenties, probably a graduate of the new technical college in Kahali, dressed in Western-style clothing and wearing lipstick and eye shadow. Her apparel seemed incongruous after the natural beauties they had so recently filmed in the *manyattas*.

'You must be the film people,' she greeted them brightly in Swahili. 'We have been expecting you.'

'We were delayed—' Kajo started to explain, but broke off as the door to the inner office opened and the field-manager came out, smiling brightly.

'Welcome to Sengi-Sengi,' he said, as he came towards them. 'You should have been here yesterday, but better late than never!'

Kajo was standing in front of Daniel, obscuring him for the moment with his six foot six height. Now he moved aside, and Daniel and the field-manager confronted each other.

'Mr Chetti Singh,' Daniel said softly. 'I never expected to see you again. What a great pleasure this is.'

The bearded Sikh stopped as though he had walked into a glass wall and stared at Daniel.

'You know each other?' Captain Kajo asked. 'What a happy coincidence.'

'We are old friends,' Daniel replied. 'We share a common interest in wildlife, especially elephants and leopards.' He was smiling as he extended his hand to Chetti Singh. 'How are you, Mr Singh? Last time we met you had suffered a little accident, hadn't you?'

Chetti Singh had turned a ghastly ashen colour beneath his dark complexion, but with an obvious effort he rallied from the shock. For a moment his eyes blazed and Daniel thought he might attack him. Then he accepted Daniel's pretence of friendliness, and tried to smile, but it was like an animal baring its teeth.

He reached out to accept Daniel's proffered handshake, but he used his left hand. His right sleeve was empty, folded back and pinned upon itself. The blunt outline of the stump showed through the striped cotton. Daniel saw that the amputation was below the elbow. It was a typical mauling injury. The leopard would have chewed the bone into fragments that no surgeon could knit together again. Although there were no scars or other injuries apparent at a glance, Chetti Singh's once portly body had been stripped of every ounce of superfluous fat and flesh. He was thin as an AIDS victim, and the white of his eyes had an unhealthy yellowish tinge. It was obvious that he had been through a bad time, and that he was not yet fully recovered.

His beard was still thick and glossy, curled up under his chin, the ends tucked into his spotless white turban.

'Indeed, what an absolute pleasure to see you again, Doctor.' His eyes gave the lie to the words. 'Thank you for your kind sympathy, but happily I am fully recovered, except for my missing appendage.' He wiggled the stump. 'It's a nuisance, but

394

I expect to receive full compensation for my loss from those responsible, never mind.'

His touch was cool as a lizard's skin, but he withdrew his hand from Daniel's and turned to Bonny and Kajo. His smile became more natural and he greeted them cordially. When he turned back to Daniel he was no longer smiling.

'And so, Doctor, you have come to make us all famous with your television show. We shall all be film stars ...' He was watching Daniel's face with a strange greedy expression, like a python looking at a hare.

The shock of the meeting had been almost as great to Daniel as it had obviously been to the Sikh. Of course, Mike Hargreave had told him that Chetti Singh had survived the leopard attack, but that had been months ago and he had never expected Chetti Singh to turn up here in Ubomo, thousands of miles from where he had last seen him. Then, when he thought about it, he realised that he should really have been prepared for this. There was a strong link between Ning Cheng Gong and the Sikh. If Ning were placed in charge in Ubomo, he would naturally appoint as his assistant somebody who knew every wrinkle of the local terrain, and who had his networks securely in place.

In retrospect, it was obvious that Chetti Singh had been the perfect choice for Ning. The Sikh's organisation had infiltrated every country in central Africa. He had agents in the field. He knew whom to bribe and whom to intimidate. But most of all, he was totally unscrupulous and bound to Ning Cheng Gong in loyalty and fear and greed.

Daniel should have expected Chetti Singh to be lurking in Ning's shadow, should have been prepared to face his vengeance. It did not need the expression in Chetti Singh's eyes to warn him that he was in mortal danger.

The only escape from Sengi-Sengi was along the single roadway through the forest, every mile of which was controlled by company guards and numerous military road-blocks.

Chetti Singh was going to try to kill him. There could not be a single doubt of that. He had no weapon nor any other form of defence. Chetti Singh commanded the ground and could choose the time and the place to do it.

Chetti Singh had turned back and was chatting to Captain Kajo and Bonny. 'It is too late already for me to offer to show you around. It will be dark in a short while. You will want to move into the quarters we have prepared for you ...' He paused and beamed at them genially. 'Besides which, I have exciting news for you. I have just this minute received a fax from Government House in Kahali. President Taffari, in the very flesh, is coming to Sengi-Sengi by helicopter. He will arrive tomorrow morning and he has most graciously consented to a film interview on the site of our operation here. It is a great honour, I assure you. President Taffari is not a man to be taken lightly, and he will be accompanied by the chief executive officer of UDC, none other than our own Mr Ning Cheng Gong. He is another eminently important personage. Perhaps he will also consent to play a part in your production ...'

It was raining again as Chetti Singh's secretary showed them to the quarters that had been set aside for them. The rain rattled like birdshot on the roofs of the buildings and the already saturated earth steamed with a mist that was blue as smoke in the twilight beneath the forest canopy.

Wooden catwalks had been laid between the buildings and the secretary provided them with cheap plastic umbrellas gaudily emblazoned with the slogan: 'UDC means a better life for all'.

The guest quarters were a row of small rooms like stables in a long Nissen hut. Each room contained rudimentary furniture – bed, chair, cupboard and desk. There was a communal washroom and lavatory in the centre of the long hut.

Daniel checked his own room carefully. The door had a lock that was so flimsy that it would yield to any determined pressure, besides which Chetti Singh certainly had a duplicate key. The window was covered by a mosquito screen and there was a mosquito net hanging above the bed, none of which was any protection. The walls were so thin that he could hear Kajo moving around in the room beside his.

It was going to be a pleasant stay.

Okay, folks, we'll have a competition, he grinned ruefully to himself. Guess when Chetti Singh will make his first attempt to bump us off. First prize is a week's holiday at Sengi-Sengi. Second prize is two weeks' holiday at Sengi-Sengi.

Dinner was served in the mess for senior staff. It was another Nissen hut comfortably furnished as a bar and canteen. When Daniel and Bonny entered there was a mixed bag of Taiwanese and British engineers and technicians filling the mess with cigarette smoke and noisy chatter. Nobody took much notice of him, but Bonny caused a mild sensation, as usual, especially with the group of Brits playing darts and drinking lager at the bar.

The Taiwanese seemed to be keeping to themselves and Daniel sensed a tension between the two groups. This was confirmed when one of the British engineers told Daniel that since Ning had taken over UDC, he had been ousting the British engineers and managers and replacing them with his own Taiwanese.

Bonny was instantly adopted by the British contingent and after dinner Daniel left her playing darts with a couple of beefy mining engineers. She intercepted Daniel heading for the door and she grinned at him maliciously as she whispered, 'Enjoy your lonely bed, lover.'

He grinned back at her as icily. 'I never did like a crowd.'

As he made his way through the darkness along the slippery mud-caked catwalk, a spot in the centre of his back itched. It was the spot into which somebody sneaking up behind him might stick a knife. He quickened his pace.

When he reached the door of his room in the Nissen hut, he pushed it open but hung back for a minute. There could be somebody waiting for him in the darkened room. He gave them a chance to move before he slipped his arm around the door frame and switched on the overhead light. Only then did he venture in cautiously. He locked the flimsy door and drew the curtains and sat on the bed to unlace his boots.

There were just too many ways that Chetti Singh could choose to do it. He knew he couldn't guard against them all. At that moment he felt something move under the bedclothes on which he was sitting. It was a slow, stealthy, reptilian sliding movement beneath the thin sheet and it touched his thigh. An icy dart of fear shot up his spine, stiffening every muscle in his body.

He had always had an unreasoning fear of snakes. One of his earliest memories was of a cobra in his nursery. It had only been a few months after his fourth birthday, but he vividly remembered the grotesque shadow that the reptile's extended hood had thrown upon the nursery wall as it reared in the diffuse beam of the nightlight that his mother had placed beside his bed. He remembered the explosive hisses with which the snake had challenged his own wild and terrified screams, before his father had burst into the nursery in his pyjamas.

Now he knew with the utmost certainty that the thing beneath the sheet was a snake. He knew that Chetti Singh or one of his men had placed it there. It must be one of the more deadly species, one of the mambas, slim and glittering with their thin grinning lips, or a forest cobra, black as death, or one of the thick repulsive gaboon adders.

Daniel sprang from the bed and spun around to face it. His heart hammered wildly as he looked around for a weapon. He snatched up the flimsy chair, and with the strength of his fear tore off one of the legs. With this weapon in his hand he regained control of himself. He was still breathing rapidly and he experienced a quick rush of shame. As a game ranger he had stood down the determined charges of buffalo and elephant and the great killer cats. As a soldier he had parachuted into enemy territory and fought it out in hand-to-hand combat, but now he was panting and shaking at a phantom of his imagination.

He steeled himself to go back to the bed. With his left hand he took the corner of the sheet, raised the chair leg with the other hand and flung back the bedclothes.

A striped forest mouse sat in the centre of the white sheet. It had long white whiskers and its bright inquisitive button eyes blinked rapidly in the sudden light.

Daniel was barely able to arrest the blow that he had already launched at it, and he and the tiny creature stared at each other in astonishment. Then his shoulders sagged and shook with

nervous laughter. The mouse squeaked and leapt off the bed. It
darted across the floor and vanished into a hole in the wainscot-
ing and Daniel collapsed on to the bed and doubled up with
laughter.

'My God, Chetti Singh,' he gasped. 'You won't stop at
anything, will you? What other nefarious tricks have you got
up your sleeve?'

 The helicopter came in from the east. They
heard the *whoppity-wop* of its rotors long before
it appeared in the hole in the forest canopy high
above. It descended into the clearing with all the
grace of a fat lady lowering herself on to a
lavatory seat.

The helicopter was a French-built Puma and it was obvious
that it had seen many years of hard service, probably with a
few other airforces, before it had reached Ubomo.

The pilot cut the motors and the rotors slowed and stopped.
President Taffari vaulted down from the main hatch. He was
lithe and vitally handsome in combat fatigues and parachutist's
boots. Bonny moved in with the camera and he flashed a smile
as bright and almost as wide as the medal ribbons on his chest,
and stepped forward to greet the reception committee headed
by Chetti Singh.

Behind him Ning Cheng Gong used the boarding ladder to
descend from the Puma. He was dressed in a cream-coloured
tropical suit. His skin was almost a matching creamy yellow
that contrasted strongly with his eyes, dark and bright as
polished onyx.

He looked around quickly, searching for somebody or something, and he saw Daniel standing back, out of camera shot.
Ning Cheng Gong's eyes licked Daniel's face for only an
instant, like the black tongue of an adder, and then were past.
His expression did not change. There was not the least sign of
recognition, but Daniel knew with certainty that Chetti Singh
had managed to get a message to his master, to warn him of
Daniel's presence in Ubomo. Daniel was startled by his own

reaction. He had known that Cheng would be on the helicopter. He had steeled himself for the first sight of him, but still it was as much of a physical shock as a punch under the ribs. It required an effort to respond normally to President Taffari's handshake and greeting.

'Ah, Doctor; as you see, Mohammed has come to the mountain. I have set aside the afternoon to co-operate with your filming. What do you want me to do? I am yours to command.'

'I am very grateful, Mr President. I have drawn up a shooting schedule. In all, I will need about five hours of your time, that includes make-up and rehearsal . . .' Daniel resisted the temptation to glance in Cheng's direction, until Chetti Singh intervened.

'Doctor Armstrong, I'd like you to meet the managing director, head of UDC, Mr Ning.'

Daniel was almost overcome by a strange sense of unreality as he shook Ning's hand and smiled and said. 'We know each other. We met briefly in Zimbabwe, when you were ambassador there. I don't suppose you recall?'

'Forgive me.' Cheng shook his head. 'I met so many people in the course of my official duties.' He pretended not to remember and Daniel forced himself to keep smiling. It seemed incredible that the last time he had seen this man was on the escarpment of the Zambezi valley, only hours before he discovered the mutilated and abused corpses of Johnny and his family. It was as though all the sorrow and anger in him had grown stronger and more bitter for being bottled up all this time. He wanted to shout out his rage, 'You filthy, greedy butcher!'

He wanted to clench his fists and attack that smooth bland face, to batter it into pulp and feel the bones break under his knuckles. He wanted to gouge out those implacable shark's eyes and pop them between his fingers. He wanted to wash his hands in Ning Cheng Gong's blood.

He turned away as soon as he could. He could trust himself no longer. For the first time, he faced what he had to do. He had to kill Ning Cheng Gong, or be killed in the attempt.

He expected no personal gratification from it. It was the fulfilment of the oath he had sworn over the body of his friend.

It was a simple duty and a debt to the memory of Johnny Nzou.

 'You may think that I am standing on the bridge of a battleship . . .' Ephrem Taffari smiled into the lens of Bonny's camera, 'but I assure you that I am not. This is in fact the command platform of Mobile Mining Unit Number One, known here by the affectionate acronym MOMU.'

Although Taffari was the only person in camera-shot, the rest of the platform was crowded with company personnel. The chief engineer and the geologist had briefed the president on his spiel, making certain that he had a grasp of all the technical details. The crew of the unit were still at the command console of MOMU. The operation of the complex machine could not be interrupted even for such an important visitor as the state president.

Daniel was directing the sequence, and both Chetti Singh and Cheng were spectators, although they kept in the background. Bonny had seen to Taffari's make-up herself. She was as good as any specialist make-up artist that Daniel had worked with.

'I am standing seventy feet above the ground,' Taffari went on. 'And I am racing forward at the breathless speed of a hundred yards an hour.' He smiled at his own humour.

Daniel had to admit that he was a natural actor, completely at ease in front of the camera. With those looks and with that voice he could grab the complete attention of any female audience anywhere in the world.

'The vehicle on which I am riding weighs one thousand tons . . .'

Daniel was making editing notes on his schedule as Taffari spoke. At this point he would cut away to a full shot of the gigantic MOMU vehicle riding on its banks of tracks. There were twelve separate sets of steel tracks each of them ten feet wide to give it stability over the most uneven terrain. Steel hydraulic rams automatically adjusted the trim of the main platform keeping it on an even keel, tilting and dipping to

401

counterbalance the ponderous wallowing, pitching movements of the tracks as they climbed and fell over the contours of the forest floor.

The size of the machine was not much less than the battleship that Taffari had suggested in his opening remarks. It was over one hundred and fifty yards long and forty wide.

Taffari turned and pointed forward over the railing.

'Down there,' he said, 'are the jaws and fangs of the monster. Let's go down and take a look.'

It was easily said on camera, but it meant moving down to a new vantage point and setting up the angles, then rehearsing the new shot. However, Taffari was a joy to work with, Daniel admitted. He needed only one walk-through and he knew his lines. He delivered them with natural timing and without fluffing once, even though he was forced to raise his voice to a shout to compete with the noise of the machinery.

This shot was good cinema. The excavators were on long gantries. Like the necks of a herd of steel giraffe drinking at a water-hole, they moved independently, rising and falling. The excavator blades rotated ferociously, slicing out the earth and throwing it back on to the conveyor belts.

'These excavators can reach down thirty yards below the surface. They are cutting a trench sixty yards wide and digging out over ten thousand tons of ore an hour. They never stop. Day and night they keep on burrowing away.'

Daniel looked down into the cavernous trench that the MOMU was opening into the red earth. It would be a good place to dispose of a corpse, his corpse. He glanced up without warning; both Ning Cheng Gong and Chetti Singh were watching him intently. They were still standing on the command platform seventy feet above him. Their heads were close together, almost touching, and they were talking, their voices wiped out by the roar of the great spinning excavator heads and the thunder of the conveyor belts. From their expressions Daniel was left with no doubt about the subject of their discussion. For an instant he caught their eyes and then they both looked away and moved back from the rail. After that it was difficult for Daniel to concentrate on the work in hand, yet he had to take advantage of every minute that Ephrem Taffari was available to him.

Once again the camera crew climbed the steel ladder up to the central platform of the MOMU. Chetti Singh and Ning Cheng Gong had disappeared, and that made Daniel even more uneasy.

From the height of the platform they could look down on to the tube mills. These were four massive steel drums, lying horizontally on the deck of the MOMU, and revolving like the spin-dryer in a domestic washing-machine. However, these drums were forty yards long, and each one was loaded with one hundred tons of cast-iron cannonballs. The red earth coming up from the excavated trench on the conveyor belts was continually being dumped into the open mouths of the drums. As the earth passed down the length of the drum, the clods and rocks were pounded to fine talcum by the tumbling iron balls. The red powder that poured from the far end of the tube mills went directly into the separator tanks.

The film team moved down the steel catwalks until they were above the separators, and here Taffari continued his explanation for the benefit of Bonny's camera.

'The two valuable minerals that we are after are either very heavy or magnetic. The rare earth monazite is collected by powerful electromagnets.' His voice was almost drowned by the roar of the machinery. That didn't worry Daniel. Later he would have Taffari make another clear recording of his speech and in the studio he would dub the tape to give it good sound.

'Once we have taken out the monazite, the remainder goes into the separator tanks in which we float out the light material and capture the heavy ore of platinum.' Taffari went on, 'This is a very sensitive part of the operation. If we were to use chemical catalysts and reagents in the separator tanks we would be able to recover over ninety per cent of the platinum. However, the chemical effluent from the tanks would be poisonous. It would be absorbed into the earth and washed by rain into the rivers to kill everything that came in contact with it – animals, birds, insects, fish and plant life. As president of the Democratic People's Republic of Ubomo, I have given an inviolable instruction that no chemical reagents of any kind are to be used during platinum mining operations in this country.' Taffari paused and stared into the camera levelly. 'You have my absolute assurance on that point. Without using reagents, our recovery of ore drops to sixty-five per cent. That means tens of millions of dollars are lost from the process. However, my government and I are determined to accept that loss, rather than to run any risk of chemical pollution of our environment. We are determined to do all in our power to make this a safe and happy world for our children, and your children, to enjoy.'

He was utterly convincing. When you listened to that deep reassuring voice and looked at that noble face, you could not possibly doubt his sincerity. Even Daniel was moved, and his critical faculties were suspended for the moment. 'This bastard could sell pork pies in a synagogue.' He tried to get his cynical professional judgement functioning again.

'Cut,' he snapped. 'That's a wrap. That was marvellous, Mr President. Thank you very much. If you'd like to go back to the mess for lunch, we'll finish up here. Then this afternoon we'll film the final sequences with the maps and models.'

Chetti Singh reappeared, like a turbaned genie from a lamp, to usher Taffari down from the MOMU and to drive him back to the base camp where Daniel knew a sumptuous buffet lunch was awaiting him. The food and liquor had been flown up from Kahali in the Puma helicopter.

Once the others had left, Daniel and Bonny captured the last sequences on the MOMU which didn't require Taffari to be present. They filmed the heavy platinum concentrates pouring into the ore bins in a fine dark stream. Each bin had a capacity of a hundred tons and when it was full it dropped automatically on to the bed of a waiting trailer and was towed away.

It was three o'clock before they had wrapped up all the shots that Daniel wanted on the MOMU and by the time they got back to the base camp at Sengi-Sengi, the presidential lunch was just ending.

In the centre of the conference room of the headquarters hut was an elaborate scale model of a typical mining scenario, employing the MOMU unit. It was designed to illustrate the entire procedure. The model had been built by BOSS technicians in London. It was an impressive piece of work, complete in detail, authentic in scale.

Daniel planned to alternate between shots of the model and

helicopter shots from the Puma of the actual forest terrain with the real MOMU in action. He believed that on the screen it would be difficult to tell the difference between them.

The scale model showed the mining track, sixty yards wide, cut and cleared through the forest by the team of loggers and bulldozers working ahead of the MOMU. Daniel planned to devote a few days' filming to the logging operation itself. The felling of the tall trees would yield riveting footage. The ponderous arabesques of the yellow bulldozers dragging the logs out of the jungle, the gangs loading them on to the logging trucks, would all be good cinema.

In the meantime Daniel must take full advantage of the day's filming in which Taffari had agreed to participate. He watched Bonny fussing over him, whispering and giggling as she powdered his face. She was making it very obvious to anyone watching that they were lovers. Taffari had drunk enough to lower his inhibitions and he caressed her openly, staring at the big breasts that she thrust only inches from his nose.

She really sees herself as First Lady of Ubomo, Daniel marvelled. She hasn't the least idea how the Hita treat their wives. I'd love it to happen. She deserves anything that comes her way.

He stood up and interrupted the flagrant display. 'If you're ready, Mr President, I'd like you standing here, beside the table. Bonny, I want the shot from this side. Try to get both General Taffari and the model in focus . . .'

Taffari moved to his mark and they rehearsed the shot. He got it right at the first attempt.

'Very good, sir. We'll go for it now. Are you ready, Bonny?'

Taffari's military swagger-stick was of polished ivory and rhino horn, the shaft topped by a miniature carving of an elephant. It looked more like a field marshal's baton than that of a general officer. Perhaps he was anticipating the day when he would promote himself, Daniel thought wryly.

Now Taffari used the baton to point out the features of the model on the table in front of him. 'As you can see, the mining track is a narrow pathway through the forest, only sixty yards wide. It is true that along that track we are felling all the trees and removing the undergrowth for the MOMU to follow.'

He paused seriously, and looked up at the camera. 'This is not wanton destruction but a prudent harvest, like that of a farmer husbanding his fields. Less than one per cent of the forest is affected by this narrow strip of activity, and behind the MOMU comes a span of bulldozers to refill the mining trench and to compact and consolidate the soil. The trench itself is painstakingly following the land contours to avoid soil erosion. As soon as the trench is refilled, a team of botanists follows up to replant the open ground with seeds and saplings. These plants have been carefully selected. Some of them are quick-growing to act as a ground cover; others are slower growing, but in fifty years from now will be fully mature and ready to be harvested. I will not be there when this happens, but my grandchildren will. The way that this operation has been planned, we will never harvest more than one single per cent of the forest each year. You don't have to be a mathematician to realise that it will be the year AD 2090 before we have worked it all, and by that time the trees that we plant now, in 1990, will be a hundred years old and we can safely begin the whole cycle over again.' He smiled reassuringly into the lens, handsome and debonair. 'A thousand years from now the forests of Ubomo will still be yielding up their largesse to generations yet unborn, and offering a haven for the same living creatures that they do now.'

It all made sense, Daniel decided. He had seen the proof of it in operation. That narrow track through the forest could not seriously threaten any species with extinction. Taffari was proposing exactly the same philosophy in which Daniel himself believed so implicitly, the philosophy of sustained yield, the disciplined and planned utilisation of the earth's resources, so that they were always renewing themselves.

For the moment, his animosity towards Ephrem Taffari was forgotten. He felt like applauding him.

Instead he cleared his throat and said, 'Mr President, that was an extraordinary performance. It was inspirational. Thank you, sir.'

Sitting on the tailboard of the Landrover, Chetti Singh smoothed the document over his own thigh. He had developed a remarkable dexterity with his left hand.

'This scrap of paper takes all the fun out of it,' he remarked.

'It is not meant to be fun,' Ning Cheng Gong said flatly. 'It is meant to be a present for my honourable father. It is meant to be work.'

Chetti Singh glanced up at him and smiled blandly and insincerely. He did not like the change that was so apparent since Ning had returned from Taipei. There was a new force and strength in him now, a new confidence and determination. For the first time Chetti Singh found that he was afraid of him. He did not enjoy the sensation.

'Still, work goes better when it is fun,' Chetti Singh argued to bolster himself, but found he could not meet Ning's dark implacable stare. He dropped his eyes to the document and read,

PEOPLE'S DEMOCRATIC REPUBLIC OF UBOMO
Special Presidential Game Licence

The bearer, Mr Ning Cheng Gong, or his authorised agent, is hereby empowered by special presidential decree to hunt, trap or kill the following protected species of wild game anywhere in the Republic of Ubomo. To wit, five specimens of Elephant (Loxodonta Africana).

He is further empowered for reasons of scientific research to collect and have in his possession, to export or sell, any part of the aforesaid specimens including the skins, bones, meat and/or ivory tusks thereof.

Signed, Ephrem Taffari
President of the Republic.

The licence was a rush job. There was no precedent for the form or wording of it and at Cheng's request the president had scribbled it out on a scrap of notepaper and the government printer had set it up under the coat of arms of the Republic of Ubomo, and delivered it within twelve hours for President Taffari to sign.

'I am a poacher,' Chetti Singh explained, 'the best in Africa. This piece of paper turns me into a mere agent, an underling, a butcher's apprentice . . .'

Cheng turned away impatiently. The Sikh was annoying him. There were things other than this petty carping to occupy him. He paced the forest clearing, lost in thought. The ground was muddy and rutted underfoot and the humidity steamed up the lenses of his sunglasses. He removed them and slipped them into the breast-pocket of his open-neck shirt. He glanced around him at the solid green wall of jungle that hemmed in the clearing. It was dark and menacing and he suppressed the sense of unease that it evoked and instead glanced at his wristwatch.

'He is late,' he said sharply. 'When will he come?'

Chetti Singh shrugged and folded the game licence with one hand. 'He does not have the same sense of time that we do. He is a pygmy. He will come when it suits him. Perhaps he is already here, watching us. Perhaps he will come tomorrow or next week.'

'I cannot waste any more time,' Cheng snapped. 'There is other important work to do.'

'More important than your honourable father's gift?' Chetti Singh asked, and his smile was ironical.

'Damn these black people.' Cheng turned away again. 'They are so unreliable.'

'They are monkeys,' Chetti Singh agreed, 'but useful little monkeys.'

Cheng made another turn around the clearing, his feet squelching in the red mud, and then stopped in front of Chetti Singh again.

'What about Armstrong?' he asked. 'We have to deal with him.'

'Ah, yes!' Chetti Singh grinned. 'That will be fun, indeed.' He massaged the stump of his missing arm. 'I have dreamed about Doctor Armstrong every night for nearly a year. And yet I never thought to have him delivered so neatly to Sengi-Sengi. Like a trussed chicken, never mind.'

'You will have to deal with him while he is still here,' Cheng insisted. 'You can't allow him to leave here alive.'

'Perish the thought,' Chetti Singh agreed. 'I have been devoting much contemplation to the problem. I wish the good doctor's demise to be suitably symbolic and painful, and yet to be adequately explainable as a most unfortunate accident of fate.'

'Don't wait too long,' Cheng warned.

'I have five more days,' Chetti Singh pointed out complacently. 'I have seen the filming schedule. He cannot finish his work at Sengi-Sengi before that—'

Cheng cut in impatiently, 'What about the red-haired woman, his assistant?'

'At the moment President Taffari is having some bonking fun with her, but nevertheless I think it might be prudent to arrange for her to accompany Doctor Armstrong on the long journey—' Chetti Singh broke off abruptly and stood up. He peered into the forest and when Cheng opened his mouth to speak he silenced him with an imperative gesture. For another minute he stood listening with his head cocked before he spoke again. 'I think he is here.'

'How do you know?' Despite himself Cheng's voice was a cautious whisper and he cleared his throat nervously as he peered into the jungle.

'Listen,' said Chetti Singh. 'The birds.'

'I hear nothing.'

'Precisely.' Chetti Singh nodded. 'They have fallen silent.' He stepped towards the green wall and raised his voice, calling in Swahili. 'Peace be with you, son of the forest. Come forward, so that we may greet each other as friends.'

The pygmy appeared like a trick of the light in a hole in the wall of vegetation. He was framed in a wreath of shining green leaves, and a ray of sunshine through the top branches that surrounded the clearing danced upon his glossy skin and threw each muscle of his powerful little body into high relief. His head was small and neat. His nose was broad and flat and he wore a goatee beard of soft curling black wool, laced with silvery grey.

'I see you, Pirri, the great hunter,' Chetti Singh greeted him with flattery and the little man came into the clearing with a lithe and graceful step.

'Did you bring tobacco?' he asked in Swahili, with a childlike directness, and Chetti Singh chuckled and handed him a tin of Uphill Rhodesian.

Pirri unscrewed the lid. He scooped out a loose ball of yellow tobacco and wadded it under his top lip and hummed with pleasure.

'He is not as small as I thought he would be,' Cheng remarked as he studied him. 'Or as dark.'

'He is not a full-blooded Bambuti,' Chetti Singh explained. 'His father was a Hita, or so it is said.'

'Can he hunt?' Cheng asked dubiously. 'Can he kill an elephant?'

Chetti Singh laughed. 'He is the greatest hunter of all his tribe, but that is not all. He has other virtues, not possessed by his brethren, by reason of his mixed blood.'

'What are they?' Cheng wanted to know.

'He understands the value of money,' Chetti Singh explained. 'Wealth and property mean nothing to the other Bambuti, but Pirri is different. He is civilised enough to know the meaning of greed.'

Pirri was listening to them. Not understanding the English words, his head turned to each of them as they spoke, and he sucked his wad of tobacco. He was dressed only in a brief loincloth of bark cloth, his bow standing up behind his shoulder and his machete in a wooden scabbard at his waist. Abruptly he interrupted their discussion of him.

'Who is this *wazungu*?' he asked in Swahili, indicating Cheng with his woolly bearded chin.

'He is a famous chief, and rich,' Chetti Singh assured him, and Pirri strode across the clearing on muscular legs with bulging calves and looked up at Cheng curiously.

'His skin has the malaria colour and his eyes are the eyes of the mamba,' he announced without guile. Cheng understood just enough Swahili to bristle.

'He may know greed, but he does not know respect.'

'It is the Bambuti way,' Chetti Singh tried to placate him. 'They are like children; they say whatever comes into their heads.'

'Ask him about the elephant,' Cheng instructed, and Chetti Singh changed his tone of voice and smiled ingratiatingly at Pirri

'I have come to ask you about elephant,' he said, and Pirri scratched his crotch, taking a large handful of the contents of his loin-cloth and joggling it thoughtfully.

'Ah, elephant!' he said vaguely. 'What do I know about elephant?'

'You are the greatest hunter of all the Bambuti,' Chetti Singh pointed out. 'Nothing moves in the forest but Pirri knows of it.'

'That is true,' Pirri agreed, and studied Cheng reflectively. 'I like the bracelet on this rich *wazungu*'s wrist,' he said. 'Before we talk of elephant he should give me a gift.'

'He wants your watch,' Chetti Singh told Cheng.

'I understood!' Cheng snapped. 'He is impertinent. What would a savage do with a gold Rolex?'

'He would probably sell it to one of the truck-drivers for one hundredth of its value,' Chetti Singh replied, enjoying Cheng's anger and frustration.

'Tell him I will not be blackmailed. I will not give him my watch,' Cheng stated flatly, and Chetti Singh shrugged.

'I will tell him,' he agreed, 'but that will mean no gift for your honourable father.'

Cheng hesitated and then unclipped the gold bracelet from his wrist and handed it to the pygmy. Pirri cooed with pleasure and held the wristwatch in both hands, turning it so that the small diamonds around the dial sparkled.

'It is pretty,' he giggled. 'So pretty that suddenly I remember about the elephant in the forest.'

'Tell me about the elephant,' Chetti Singh invited.

'There were thirty elephant cows and calves in the forest near Gondala,' Pirri said. 'And two large bulls with long white teeth.'

'How long?' Chetti Singh demanded, and Cheng who had followed the conversation thus far leaned forward eagerly.

'One elephant is larger than the other. His teeth are this long,' said Pirri, and unslung his bow from his shoulder and held it above his head and stood on tiptoe. 'This long,' he repeated. 'As high as I can reach with my bow, from the tip of the tooth to the lip, but not counting the part concealed in the skull.'

'How thick?' Cheng asked in atrocious Swahili, his voice

coarse with lust, and Pirri turned to him and half-circled his own waist with his dainty childlike hands.

'This thick,' he said. 'As thick as I am.'

'That is a great elephant,' Chetti Singh murmured with disbelief, and Pirri bridled.

'He is the greatest of all elephants and I have seen him with my own eyes. I, Pirri, say this thing and it is true.'

'I want you to kill this elephant and bring me his tusks,' Chetti Singh said softly, and Pirri shook his head.

'This elephant is no longer at Gondala. When the machines of yellow iron came into the forest, he ran from their smoke and noise. He has gone into the sacred heartland where no man may hunt. It is decreed by the Mother and the Father. I cannot kill this elephant in the heartland.'

'I will pay you a great deal for the teeth of this elephant,' Chetti Singh whispered seductively, but Pirri shook his head firmly.

'Offer him a thousand dollars,' Cheng said in English, but Chetti Singh frowned at him.

'Leave this to me,' he cautioned. 'We don't want to ruin the trade with impatience.' He turned back to Pirri and said in Swahili, 'I will give you ten bolts of pretty cloth which the women love, and fifty handfuls of glass beads – enough to make a thousand virgins spread their thighs for you.'

Pirri shook his head. 'It is the sacred heartland,' he said. 'The Mother and the Father will be angry if I hunt there.'

'In addition to the cloth and beads, I will give you twenty iron axe-heads and ten fine knives with blades as long as your hand.'

Pirri wriggled his whole body like a puppy. 'It is against law and custom. My tribe will hate me and drive me out.'

'I will give you twenty bottles of gin,' Chetti Singh said. 'And as much tobacco as you can lift from the ground.'

Pirri massaged his crotch frantically and rolled his eyes. 'As much tobacco as I can carry!' His voice was hoarse. 'I cannot do it. They will call out the Molimo. They will bring down the curse of the Mother and Father.'

'And I will give you a hundred silver Maria Theresa dollars.' Chetti Singh reached into the pocket of his bush jacket and brought out a handful of silver coins. He juggled them in one hand, jingling them together and making them sparkle in the sunlight.

For a long moment Pirri stared at them hungrily. Then he let out a shrill yelp and sprang in the air and drew his machete. Chetti Singh and Cheng stepped back nervously, expecting him to attack them, but instead, Pirri whirled and, with the blade held high above his head, rushed at the wall of the forest and swung a hissing stroke at the first bush. Shouting with anger and temptation, he hacked and slashed at the forest growth. Leaves and twigs flew, and branches were sliced through. Slabs of bark and white wood rained down from the bleeding trunks under his onslaught.

At last Pirri stopped and rested on his blade, his muscular chest heaving, sweat pouring down his face and dripping into his beard, sobbing with exertion and self-loathing. Then he straightened up and came back to where Chetti Singh stood and said, 'I will kill this elephant for you, and bring you his teeth. Then you will give me all those things you promised me, not forgetting the tobacco.'

Chetti Singh drove the Landrover back along the rudimentary forest track. It took almost an hour for them to reach the main corduroy roadway on which the convict gangs were working, and over which the great ore-carriers and the logging trucks rumbled and roared.

As they left the overgrown logging track and joined the heavy flow of traffic towards Sengi-Sengi, Chetti Singh turned to grin at the man beside him.

'That takes care of the gift for your father. Now we must apply all our ingenuity and brains to a little gift for me – the head of Doctor Daniel Armstrong on a silver platter, with an apple in his mouth.'

Daniel had been waiting for this moment, praying for it.

He was high on the command deck of the MOMU and it was raining. The air was blue and thick with falling rain, and visibility was down to fifty feet or less. Bonny was sheltering in the command cabin at the end of the platform, keeping her precious video equipment out of the rain. The two Hita guards had gone down to the lower deck and for a moment Daniel was alone on the upper deck.

Daniel had become hardened to the rain. Since arriving at Sengi-Sengi he seemed always to be wearing wet clothing. He was standing now in the angle of the steel wall of the command cabin and the flying bridge, only partially shielded from the driving rain. Every now and then a harder gust would throw heavy drops into his face and force him to slit his eyes.

Suddenly the door to the command cabin opened and Ning Cheng Gong came out on to the flying bridge. He had not seen Daniel and he crossed to the forward rail under cover of the canvas sun awning and leaned on the rail, peering down at the great shining excavator blades that were tearing into the earth seventy feet below his perch.

It was Daniel's moment. For the first time they were alone and Cheng was vulnerable.

'This one is for Johnny,' he whispered, and crossed the steel plates of the bridge on silent rubber soles. He came up behind Cheng.

All he had to do was stoop and seize his ankles. A quick lift and shove, and Cheng would be hurled over the rail and dropped into the deadly blades. It would be instantaneous and the chopped and dismembered corpse would be fed into the tube mills and pounded to paste and mixed with hundreds of tons of powdered earth.

Daniel reached out to do it, but before he could touch him he hesitated involuntarily, suddenly appalled at what he was about to do. It was cold-blooded, calculated murder. He had killed before as a soldier, but never like this, and for a moment he was sick with self-loathing.

'For Johnny,' he tried to convince himself, but it was too late. Cheng whirled to face him.

414

He was quick as a mongoose confronted by a cobra. His hands came up, the stiff-fingered blades of the martial arts exponent, and his eyes were dark and ferocious as he stared into Daniel's face.

For a moment they were poised on the edge of violence, then Cheng whispered, 'You missed your chance, Doctor. There will not be another.'

Daniel backed away. He had let Johnny down with such weakness. In the old days it would not have happened. He would have taken Cheng out swiftly and competently and rejoiced at the kill. Now the Taiwanese was alerted and even more dangerous.

Daniel turned away, sickened by his failure, and then he started. One of the Hita guards had come up the steel ladder silently as a leopard. He was leaning against the rear rail of the bridge with his maroon beret cocked over one eye and the Uzi sub-machine-gun on his hip pointed at Daniel's belly. He had been watching it all.

That night Daniel lay awake until after midnight, unnerved by the narrowness of his escape and sickened by the savage streak in himself that allowed him to pursue such a brutal vengeance. Yet even this attack of conscience did not shake his determination to act as the vehicle of justice and in the morning he awoke to find his lust for revenge undiminished, and only his temper and his nerves shaky and uncertain.

This led directly to his final bust-up with Bonny Mahon. It began when she was late to start the day's assignment, and kept him waiting in the teeming rain for almost forty minutes before she finally sauntered out to meet him.

'When I said five o'clock, I didn't mean in the afternoon,' he snarled at her, and she grinned at him, all rosy and smug.

'What do you want me to do, commit hara-kiri, O Master?' she asked. He was about to let fly a verbal broadside, when he realised that she must have come directly from Taffari's bed without bathing, for he caught a whiff of the musky odour of their lovemaking on her, and had to turn away. He felt so furious that he could not trust himself not to strike her.

For Chrissake, Armstrong, get a hold on yourself, he cautioned himself silently, you're going to pieces.

They worked in brittle antagonism for the rest of the morning, filming the bulldozers and chainsaws as they cleared the mining track for the monstrous MOMU to waddle down.

It was heavy going in the mud and rain, and dangerous with falling tree trunks and powerful machinery working all around them. This did nothing to improve his mood but Daniel managed to keep a check on his tongue until just before noon when Bonny announced that she had run out of tape and had to break off to return to the main camp to fetch new stock from the cold rooms.

'What kind of half-baked cameraman runs out of stock in the middle of a shoot?' Daniel wanted to know, and she rounded on him.

'I know what's eating you up, lover boy. It's not shortage of film, it's shortage of good rich fruitcake. You hate me for what Ephrem is getting and you're not. It's the old green-eyed monster.'

'You've got an inflated idea of the value of what you sit on,' Daniel came back as angrily.

It escalated rapidly from there until Bonny yelled into his face, 'Nobody talks to me like that, Buster. You can stick your job and your insults up your left earhole, or in any other convenient orifice.' And she sloshed and slipped in the red mud back to where the Landrover was parked.

'Leave the camera in the Landrover,' Daniel shouted after her. It was all hired video equipment. 'You've got your return ticket to London and I'll send you a cheque for what I owe you. You're fired.'

'No, I'm not, lover boy. You're way too late. I resigned! And don't you forget it.' She slammed the door of the Landrover and raced the engine. All four wheels spinning wildly and throwing up sheets and clods of red mud, Bonny tore up the track and left him glaring after her. His bad temper increased as he belatedly thought of a dozen other clever retorts that he should have thrown at her while he had the chance.

Bonny was as angry, but her mood was longer-lasting and more vindictive. She racked her imagination for the cruellest revenge she could conjure up, and just before she reached the main camp at Sengi-Sengi it came to her in a creative flash.

416

'You are going to rue every single lousy thing you said to me, Danny boy,' she promised aloud, grinning mercilessly. 'You ain't going to shoot another tape in Ubomo, not you, nor any other cameraman that you hire to replace me. I'm going to make damned double sure of that.'

 His body was long and supple. In the dim light beneath the mosquito-net his skin shone like washed coal, still damp with the sweat of love. Ephrem Taffari lay on his back on the rumpled white sheet and she thought he was probably the most beautiful man she had ever seen.

Slowly she lowered her head and laid her cheek against his naked chest. It was smooth and hairless, and his dark skin felt cool. She blew softly on his nipple and watched it pucker and harden in response. She smiled. She felt aglow with well-being. He was a wonderful lover, better than any white man she had ever had. There had never been anyone else like him. She wanted to do something for him.

'There is something I must tell you,' she whispered against his chest, and with one lazy hand he stroked the thick glistening coppery bush of hair back off her face.

'What is it?' he asked, his voice soft and deep and replete, almost uninterested.

She knew she would have his complete attention again with her next statement, and she delayed the moment. It was too sweet to waste. She wanted to draw every last possible enjoyment from it. It was double pleasure – her revenge on Daniel Armstrong and her offering to Ephrem Taffari which would prove to him her loyalty and her worth.

'What is it?' he repeated. He took a handful of her hair and twisted it just hard enough to hurt. He was a master in inflicting pain, and her breath caught with masochistic pleasure.

'I'm telling you this to show you how completely I am yours, how much I love you,' she whispered. 'After tonight you'll never be able to doubt where my loyalties lie.'

417

He chuckled and shook her head gently from side to side, his fingers still locked in her hair, still hurting exquisitely.

'Let me judge that, my little red lily. Tell me this terrible thing.'

'It is a terrible thing, Ephrem. On the instructions of Daniel Armstrong I filmed the forced removal of the villagers from Fish Eagle Bay to make way for the new casino.'

Ephrem Taffari stopped breathing. For twenty beats of his heart under her ear he held his breath. Then he let it out softly, and his pulse rate was slightly elevated as he said quietly, 'I don't know what you are talking about. Explain this to me.'

'Daniel and I were on top of the cliff when the soldiers came to the village. Daniel ordered me to film them.'

'What did you see?'

'We saw them bulldoze the village and burn the boats. We saw them load the people into the trucks and take them away . . .' She hesitated.

'Go on,' he ordered. 'What else did you see?'

'We saw them kill two people. They clubbed an old man to death and they shot another when he tried to escape. They threw their bodies on the fire.'

'You filmed all that?' Ephrem asked, and there was something in his tone that made her suddenly uncertain and afraid.

'Daniel forced me to film it.'

'I do not know anything about these events, this atrocity. I gave no orders,' he said, and with a surge of relief she believed him.

'I was sure you didn't know about it.'

'I must see this film. It is evidence against those who perpetrated this atrocity. Where is the film?'

'I gave it to Daniel.'

'What did he do with it?' Ephrem demanded, and now his voice was terrible.

'He said that he had lodged it with the British Embassy in Kahali. The ambassador, Sir Michael Hargreave, is an old friend of his.'

'Did he show the film to the ambassador?' Ephrem wanted to know.

'I don't think so. He said that it was dynamite, that he wouldn't use it until the time was ripe.'

'So you and Armstrong are the only ones who know about it, who know that the film exists?'

She hadn't thought of it that way, and now it gave her an uneasy feeling.

'Yes, I suppose so. Unless Daniel has told anybody. I haven't.'

'Good.' Ephrem released her hair and stroked her cheek. 'You are a good girl. I am grateful to you. You have proved your friendship to me.'

'It is more than friendship, Ephrem. I have never felt about another man the way I feel for you.'

'I know,' he whispered, and lifted her head and kissed her on the lips. 'You are a wonderful woman. My own feelings for you grow stronger all the time.' Gratefully she pressed her own full body to his sleek feline length.

'We must get that film back from Sir Michael. It could do untold damage to this country and to me as the president.'

'I should have told you sooner,' she said. 'But only now I realise how much I love you.'

'It is still not too late,' he assured her. 'I will speak to Armstrong in the morning. I will give him my word that the guilty persons will be brought to justice. He must give me the film to be used in evidence.'

'I don't think he will do that,' she said. 'That tape is too sensational. It is worth a million to him. He won't want to give it up.'

'Then you will have to help me get it back. After all, it is your film. Will you help me, my beautiful red and white lily?'

'You know I will, Ephrem. I'll do anything for you,' she murmured, and without another word he made love to her, that beautiful devastating love of which only he was capable.

Afterwards she slept.

When she awoke it was raining again. It always seemed to be raining in this terrible green hell of jungle. The rain clattered and drummed on the roof of the VIP guest bungalow, and the darkness was complete.

She groped instinctively for Ephrem but the bed beside her was empty. The sheets on which he had lain were already cool. He must have left her some time ago. She thought he might have gone to the bathroom, and felt the pressure in her own bladder which had woken her.

She lay and listened for him to return, but after five minutes when he had not come, she crept out from under the mosquito-net and groped her way through the darkness to the bathroom door. She bumped into a chair and stubbed her bare toe before she reached it. She found the light switch and blinked in the sudden glare of white tiles.

The bathroom was empty, but the toilet seat was raised to prove he had been there before her. She flapped it down and perched naked upon it, still groggy with sleep, her red hair tangled over her eyes.

Outside the rain battered down and a sudden flare of lightning lit the window. Bonny reached across to the side wall for the roll of toilet paper in its holder and her ear was inches from the thin prefabricated partition wall of the bungalow. She heard voices, indistinct but masculine, from the room beyond.

She was slowly coming fully awake, and her interest was aroused. She pressed her ear to the wall and she recognised Ephrem's voice. It was crisp and commanding. Somebody answered him but the sound of the rain intruded and she could not recognise the speaker.

'No,' Ephrem replied. 'Tonight. I want it done immediately.' Bonny was fully alert now, and at that moment the rain stopped with dramatic suddenness. In the silence she heard the reply and recognised the speaker.

'Will you sign a warrant, Mr President?' It was Chetti Singh. His accent was unmistakable. 'Your soldiers could carry out the execution.'

'Don't be a fool, man. I want it done quietly. Get rid of him. You can get Kajo to help you, but do it. No questions, no written records. Just get rid of him.'

'Ah, yes. I understand. We will say that he went to film in the jungle. Later we can send a search party to find no trace of him. A great pity. But what about the woman? She is also a witness to our arrangements at Fish Eagle Bay. Do you want me to take care of her at the same time?'

'No, don't be an idiot! I will need her to recover the tape from the embassy. Afterwards, when the tape is safely in my hands, I will reconsider the problem of the woman. In the meantime just take Armstrong out into the jungle and get rid of him.'

'I assure you, Mr President, that nothing would give me more pleasure. It will take me an hour or so to make the arrangements with Kajo, but it will be all over before daylight. I give you my solemn promise.'

There was the sound of a chair being pushed back and heavy footsteps, then a door slammed and there was silence from the sitting-room of the bungalow.

Bonny sat frozen for a moment, chilled by what she had heard. Then she sprang to her feet and darted across the floor to the light switch and plunged the bathroom into darkness. Swiftly she groped her way to the bed and crept under the mosquito net. She lay rigid under the sheet, expecting Ephrem Taffari to return at any moment.

Her mind was racing. She was frightened and confused. She had not expected any of this.

She had thought that Ephrem might seize the videotape and arrest Daniel, then deport him immediately and declare him an undesirable alien, or something like that. She hadn't been too clear as to what Ephrem would do to Daniel, but she had never dreamed for a moment that he would have him killed, squashed like an insect without pity or remorse. With a jolt she realised just how naïve she had been.

The shock was almost too much to bear. She had never hated Daniel. Far from it, she had been as fond of him as she was capable of, until he had begun to bore and irritate her. Of course, after Ephrem had taken over Daniel had insulted and fired her, but she had given him some reason for that and she didn't hate him – not to the point of wanting him killed.

'Keep out of it,' she warned herself. 'It's too late now. Danny has to take his own chances.'

She lay waiting for Ephrem to come back to bed, but he did not come and she thought of Daniel again. He was one of the few men she had ever genuinely admired and liked. He was decent and good and funny and handsome . . . She broke that chain of thought.

Don't be a bleeding heart, she thought. It didn't turn out the way you expected but that's tough on Danny. And yet there had been a veiled threat to her in what Ephrem had said. 'When the tape is safely in my hands I will reconsider the problem of the woman.'

Ephrem still hadn't come. She sat up in bed and listened. The rain had stopped completely. Reluctantly she slipped out from under the mosquito-net and picked her robe from the foot of the bed. She crossed to the door that opened on to the verandah of the bungalow and opened it quietly.

She crept down the verandah. The light from the sitting-room windows beamed out on to the verandah floor. She moved into a position from where she could see into the sitting-room while remaining in shadow. Ephrem Taffari sat at the desk against the far wall. His back was to her. He was dressed in a khaki T-shirt and camouflage trousers. He was smoking a cigarette and studying the papers that were strewn across the desk-top. He seemed to be settled to his work.

It would take her less than ten minutes to reach the row of guest bungalows at the east side of the compound and get back to the bedroom.

The wooden catwalks were wet and red with mud. She was barefoot. Daniel might not be in his room. She thought of every excuse for not going to warn him.

I owe him nothing, she thought, and heard Ephrem's voice again in her imagination: 'Just take Armstrong out into the jungle and get rid of him.'

She backed away from the lighted window, not yet certain what she would do until she found herself running along the catwalk beneath the dark trees that dripped with rain. She slipped and fell on her knees but jumped up and kept running. There was red mud on the front of her robe.

She saw through the trees that there was one light on in the row of guest rooms. The rest of them were in darkness. As she came closer she saw with relief that the light was in Daniel's room.

She did not go up on to the verandah of the guest house, but jumped down off the catwalk and made her way around the back of the building. Daniel's window was curtained. She scratched softly on the mosquito-mesh screen that covered it, and at once heard a chair scrape back on the wooden floor.

422

She scratched again and Daniel's voice asked softly, 'Who is it?'

'For God's sake, Danny, it's me. I have to talk to you.'

'Come inside. I'll open the door.'

'No, no. Come out here. It's desperate. They mustn't see me. Hurry, man, hurry.'

Half a minute later his broad-shouldered form loomed out of the darkness, backlit by the lighted bungalow window.

'Danny, Ephrem knows about the Fish Eagle Bay tape.'

'How did he find out?'

'That doesn't matter.'

'You told him, didn't you?'

'Damn you to hell – I have come to warn you. He's issued orders for your immediate execution. Chetti Singh and Kajo are coming for you. They're going to take you into the jungle. They don't want any evidence.'

'How do you know this?'

'Don't ask bloody fool questions. Believe me, I know. I can't waste another minute. I've got to get back. He'll find I'm gone.' She turned away, but he seized her arm.

'Thanks, Bonny,' he said. 'You're a better person than you think you are. Do you want to make a break for it with me?'

She shook her head. 'I'll be all right,' she said. 'Just get out of here. You've got an hour, tops. Get going!'

She pulled out of his grip and hurried away through the trees. He caught one last glimpse of her: the lights from the bungalow transformed her tumbled hair into a roseate halo and the long white robe made her look like an angel.

'Some angel,' Daniel muttered, and stood for a full minute in the darkness deciding what he could do.

While there had been only Chetti Singh and Ning Cheng Gong to deal with he had stood a chance. Like him, they had been constrained by the necessity of working in secrecy. None of them had been able to attack the other openly, but now Chetti Singh had open sanction to kill him, a special presidential licence. Daniel grinned as mirthlessly as a wolf. He could expect the Sikh to act swiftly and ruthlessly. Bonny was right. He had to get out of Sengi-Sengi within the next few minutes, before the executioners arrived.

423

From the angle of the building he threw a quick glance down the verandah and around the compound. All was quiet and dark. He slipped back into his room, and lifted his small travel bag down from the cupboard. It contained all his personal documents, passport, airline tickets, credit cards and travellers' cheques. Apart from his clothing and toilet bag there was nothing else of value in the room.

He pulled on a light wind-cheater and checked that the key of the Landrover was in his pocket. He extinguished the lights and went out. The Landrover was parked at the far end of the verandah. He opened the door quietly and threw his bag on to the passenger seat. All the hired VTR equipment was packed into the rear compartment and there was a selection of basic camping and first-aid equipment in the lockers, but there was no weapon of any kind, apart from his old hunting-knife.

He started the Landrover. The engine noise seemed excessively loud in the darkness. He did not switch on the headlights and he let in the clutch gently, keeping the engine revs down. He drove slowly through the darkened compound towards the main gates. He knew that the gates were never closed at night, and that a single guard was on duty there.

Daniel was under no illusion as to just how far he was going to get in the Landrover. There was only one road from Sengi-Sengi to the Ubomo river ferry, and there was a road-block every five miles.

A radio call from Sengi-Sengi would alert every one of them. The guards would be waiting for him with their fingers on the triggers of their AK 47s. No, he would be lucky to make it through the first block, and then he would have to take to the jungle. He didn't relish that prospect. He had been trained for survival and warfare in the drier bushveld of Rhodesia, a long way further south. He would not be nearly as adept in the rain forest, but there was no other way open to him.

The first thing was to get clear of Sengi-Sengi. After that he would face each problem as it arose.

And this is number one, he thought grimly as suddenly the floodlights at the main gates switched on in a bright halogen dawn. The entire compound was brightly lit.

There were half a dozen figures running from the barrack

area where guards were quartered. It was obvious they had dressed hastily; some were in undervests and shorts. Daniel recognised both Captain Kajo and Chetti Singh.

Kajo was brandishing an automatic pistol and Chetti Singh was trotting along behind him, shouting and waving at the approaching Landrover, his white turban very visible in the glare of the floodlights. One of the guards was trying to shut the gates. He already had one wing of the steel-framed mesh gate half across the roadway.

Daniel switched on his headlights, put his hand flat on the horn and drove hard at him, the hooter blaring. The guard dived nimbly aside, and the Landrover slammed into the unlocked leaf of the gate and whipped it aside. He roared through.

Behind him he heard the rattling clamour of automatic rifle-fire. He felt half a dozen bullets slam into the aluminium bodywork of the Landrover, but he crouched low over the wheel and kept his foot hard down on the accelerator.

The first bend in the roadway rushed towards him in the headlights. Another burst of automatic fire splattered against the rear of the vehicle. The rear window exploded in a storm of glass splinters and something struck him high in the back within an inch of his spine. He had been hit by a bullet before, in that long-ago war, and he recognised the sensation. From the position of the wound, high and close to the spine, it had to be a lung shot, a mortal wound. He expected to feel the choking flood of arterial blood into his lungs.

Keep going as long as you can, he thought, and swung the Landrover into the bend at full throttle. She went up on two wheels but didn't roll.

When he glanced in the rear-view mirror the camp lights were obscured by forest trees, a dwindling glow in the darkness behind.

He could feel hot blood running down his back, but there was no choking, no weakness, not yet anyway. The wound was numb. He could think clearly. He could keep going.

He knew exactly where the first road-block was situated. 'Approximately five miles ahead,' he reminded himself. 'On the first river crossing.'

He tried to remember how the road ran to reach it. He had driven over it half a dozen times during the last three days' filming. He could remember almost every twist, every track that led off it.

He made his decision. He leaned back against the seat. The wound stabbed him like a knife in the back, but he wasn't losing much blood.

Internal bleeding, he thought. You aren't going to walk away from this one, Danny boy. But he kept going, waiting for the weakness to overcome him.

There were five logging roads branching off from the main highway before it reached the first road-block. Some of them were disused and overgrown, but at least two were still being subjected to heavy daily traffic. He chose the first of these, two miles from Sengi-Sengi and turned on to it, heading westwards. The Zaïre border was ninety miles in that direction, but the logging track only ran five miles through the forest before it intersected the MOMU excavation.

He would have to dump the Landrover and try to make the remaining eighty miles on foot through uncharted forest. The last part of the journey would be over high mountains, glaciers and alpine snowfields. Then he thought about the bullet wound in his back and knew he was dreaming. He wasn't going to get that far.

The logging track he was on had been deeply rutted and chopped up by the gigantic treaded tyres of the trucks and heavy trailers. It was a morass of mud the consistency and colour of faeces, and the Landrover churned through it in four-wheel drive, pounding through the knee-deep ruts. Flying mud stuck to the glass of the headlights and dimmed the beams to a murky glow that barely lit the roadway twenty paces ahead.

The wound in his back was beginning to ache, but his head was still clear. He touched the end of his own nose with his forefinger to check his co-ordination. No sign of losing it yet.

Suddenly he was aware of lights far ahead of him on the track. One of the logging trucks was coming towards him, and instantly he realised the possibility it offered. He slowed the Landrover and searched the verge of unbroken jungle that pressed in upon the track. He sensed rather than saw a break in the foliage and swung the Landrover boldly into it.

For fifty paces or so he forced his way through almost impenetrable undergrowth. It scraped along both sides of the bodywork, and small trees and branches thumped along beneath the chassis. The soft forest floor sucked at the wheels and the Landrover's speed bled off until at last she was high-centred and stranded.

Daniel cut the engine and switched off the headlights. He sat in the darkness and listened to the logging truck rumble past, headed eastwards towards Sengi-Sengi along the road he had come. When the sound of the huge diesel engine had dwindled into silence, he leaned forward in the seat and steeled himself to examine the bullet wound in his back. Reluctantly he twisted one arm up behind him and groped towards the centre of pain.

Suddenly he exclaimed and jerked his hand away. He switched on the interior lights and examined the razor scratch on his forefinger. Then quickly he reached behind himself again, and cautiously fingered the wound. He laughed aloud with relief. A shard of flying glass from the rear window had sliced open his back, and lodged against his ribs. It was a long superficial wound with the sharp glass still buried in it.

He worked it loose and examined it in the overhead light. It was bloody and jagged, and the bleeding had started again. But you aren't going to die from it, he reassured himself, and tossed the splinter out of the side window and reached for the first-aid kit which was under the VTR equipment in the back of the vehicle.

It was difficult to treat the wound in his own back, but he managed to smear it liberally with Betadine ointment and strap an untidy dressing over it and knot the ends of the bandage in front of his chest. All the time he was listening for other vehicles on the logging road, but he heard only the small jungle sounds of bird and insect and beast.

He found the Maglite in his kit and went back on foot to the road. From the verge he examined the muddy rutted tracks. As he had hoped, the logging truck had completely obliterated the Landrover's tracks with its own massive multiple wheels. Only the spot where he had driven over the verge still carried the Landrover's prints. He picked up a dead branch and swept them away carefully. Then he turned his attention to the foliage that the Landrover had damaged as it crashed into the forest.

He rearranged it as naturally as possible and smeared mud on the raw broken ends of branches and twigs so they would not catch the eye. After half an hour's work he was certain that nobody would suspect that a vehicle had left the road here and was hidden only fifty feet away in the dense undergrowth.

Almost immediately his work was put to the test. He saw headlights approaching from the direction of Sengi-Sengi. He drew back a little way into the forest and dropped flat. He smeared his face with a handful of mud and then covered the backs of his hands. His wind-cheater was dark forest green in colour; it would not show up in the lights.

He watched the vehicle approaching along the logging track. It was moving slowly and as it drew level with his hiding-place he saw that it was an army transport painted in brown and green camouflage. The rear was crowded with Hita soldiers and he thought he glimpsed Chetti Singh's white turban in the driver's cab, but he couldn't be certain. One of the soldiers in the rear was flashing a spotlight along the verges of the road. They were obviously searching for him.

Daniel dropped his face into the crook of his arm as the beam of the spotlight played over where he lay. The truck passed on without slowing and was soon out of sight.

Daniel stood up and hurried back to the stranded Landrover. Swiftly he made a selection of items from the lockers, most importantly the hand-bearing compass. He packed them into the small day pack. From the first-aid kit he took field dressings and antiseptic and anti-malarial tablets. There was no food in the truck. He'd have to live off the forest. He could not carry the pack the normal way without restarting the bleeding so he slung it over the other shoulder. He guessed that the wound really required stitching, but there was no way in which he could even attempt that.

I have to get across the MOMU track before first light, he thought. That's the one place I'll be in the open and vulnerable.

He left the Landrover and struck out westwards. It was difficult to orientate in darkness and the dense forest. He was forced to flash the torch and study the compass every few hundred yards. The going was soft and uneven and his progress was slow as he found his way between the trees. When he reached the MOMU excavation the open sky above it was flushing with dawn's first light.

He could make out the trees on the far side of the clearing, but the MOMU itself had passed on weeks before and was already working six or seven miles further north. This part of the forest should be deserted, unless Kajo and Chetti Singh had sent a patrol down the strip to cut him off.

It was a chance he had to take. He left the shelter of the forest and started across. He sank to his ankles in the red mud and it sucked at his boots. Every second he expected to hear a shout or a shot, and he was panting with exertion when at last he reached the far tree-line.

He kept going for another hour before he took his first rest. Already it was hot and the humidity was like a Turkish bath. He stripped off all his clothing, except for shorts and boots, rolled it into a ball and buried it in the thick soft loam of the forest floor. His skin was toughened by sun and weather and he had a natural resistance to insect stings. In the Zambezi valley he had been able to tolerate even the bite of the swarming tsetse fly. As long as he kept the wound on his back covered he should be all right, he decided.

He stood up and went on. He navigated by compass and wristwatch, timing his average stride to give him an estimate of distance covered. Every two hours he rested for ten minutes. By nightfall he calculated he had covered ten miles. At that rate it would take eight days to reach the Zaïre border but, of course, he wouldn't be able to keep it up. There were mountains ahead, and glaciers and snowfields, and he had abandoned most of his clothing. It was going to be interesting out on the glaciers in his present attire, he decided, as he made a nest in the moist leaf mould and composed himself for sleep.

When he woke it was just light enough to see his hand in front of his face. He was hungry and the wound in his back was stiff and painful. When he reached to touch it he found it was swollen and the flesh hot. All we need is a nice little infection, he thought, and renewed the dressing as best he could.

By noon he was ravenously hungry. He found a nest of fat white grubs under the bark of a dead tree. They tasted like raw egg yolks.

'What doesn't kill you, makes you fat,' he assured himself, and kept on towards the west, the compass in his hand. In the early afternoon he thought he recognised a type of edible fungus and nibbled a small piece as a trial. In the late afternoon he reached the bank of a small clear stream, and as he was drinking he noticed a dark cigar shape lying at the bottom of the pool. He cut a stake and sharpened one end, carving a crude set of barbs above the point. Then he cut down one of the hanging ant's nests from the branches of a silk-cotton tree and sprinkled the big red ants on the surface of the pool, taking care to stand well back from the edge with the crude spear in his right hand.

Almost immediately the fish rose from the bottom and began to gulp down the struggling insects trapped in the surface film. Daniel drove the point of his fish spear into its gills and brought it out flapping and kicking on to the bank. It was a barbeled catfish, as long as his arm. He ate his fill of the fatty yellow flesh and the rest of the carcass he smoked over a fire of green leaves. It should keep him going for a couple more days, he decided. He wrapped it in a package of leaves and put it in his pack.

However, when he woke the next morning his back was excruciatingly painful, and his stomach was swollen with gas and dysentery. He couldn't tell whether it was the insect grubs, the fungus or the stream water that had caused it, but by noon he was very weak. His diarrhoea was almost unremitting, and the wound felt like a red-hot coal between his shoulder-blades.

It was about that time that Daniel had the first sensation that he was being followed. It was an instinct that he had realised he possessed when he was a patrol leader with the Scouts in the valley. Johnny Nzou had trusted this sixth sense of his implicitly and it had never let them down. It was almost as though Daniel was able to pick up the malevolent concentration of the hunter following on his tracks.

Even in his pain and weakness Daniel looked back and felt a presence. He knew that he was out there, the hunter.

Anti-tracking, he told himself, knowing that it would slow his progress, but it would almost certainly throw off his real or imaginary pursuer, unless he was very good indeed, or unless Daniel's anti-tracking skills had atrophied.

At the next river-crossing he took to the water, and from then on he used every ruse and subterfuge to cover his tracks and throw off the pursuit. Every mile he grew slower and weaker. The diarrhoea never let up, his wound was beginning to stink, and he knew with clairvoyant certainty that the unseen hunter was still after him – and drawing closer every hour.

Over the years Chetti Singh, the master poacher, had developed various systems of contacting his hunters. In some areas it was easier than others. In Zambia or Mozambique he had only to drive out to a remote village and talk to a wife or brother, and rely on them to pass the message. In Botswana or Zimbabwe he could even rely on the local postal authority to deliver a letter or telegram, but contacting a wild pygmy in the Ubomo rain forest was the most uncertain and time-consuming of all.

The only way to do it was to drive down the main highway and stop at every *duka* or trading-store, to accost every half-tame Bambuti that he met upon the roadside and bribe them to get a message to Pirri in the forest. It was amazing how the wild pygmies maintained a network of communication over those vast and secret areas of the rain forest, but then they were garrulous and sociable people.

A honey-seeker from one tribe would meet a woman from another tribe who was gathering medicine plants far from her camp, and the word would be passed on, shouted from a forested hilltop in a high penetrating sing-song to another wanderer across the valley, or carried by canoe, along the big rivers, until at last it reached the man for whom it was intended. Sometimes it took weeks, sometimes, if the sender was fortunate, it might take only a few days.

This time Chetti Singh was extremely lucky. Two days after

he had given the message to a straggling group of pygmy women at one of the river crossings, Pirri came to the rendezvous in the forest. As always he appeared with the dramatic suddenness of a forest sprite and asked for tobacco and gifts.

'Have you killed my elephant?' Chetti Singh asked pointedly, and Pirri picked his nose and scratched himself between the legs with embarrassment.

'If you had not sent for me, the elephant would by now be dead.'

'But he is not dead,' Chetti Singh pointed out. 'And thus you have not earned those marvellous gifts I promised you.'

'Just a little tobacco?' Pirri pleaded. 'For I am your faithful slave, and my heart is full of love for you. Just a small handful of tobacco?'

Chetti Singh gave him half what he asked for and while Pirri squatted down to suck and enjoy it, he went on, 'All I have promised you – I will give you that much again if you kill another creature for me, and bring me its head.'

'What creature is this?' Pirri asked guardedly, narrowing his eyes suspiciously. 'Is it another elephant?'

'No,' said Chetti Singh. 'It is a man.'

'You want me to kill a man!' Pirri stood up with alarm. 'If I do that the *wazungu* will come and take me and put a rope around my neck.'

'No,' said Chetti Singh. 'The *wazungu* will reward you as richly as I will.' And he turned to Captain Kajo. 'Is that not so?'

'It is so,' Kajo confirmed. 'The man we wish you to kill is a white man. He is an evil man who has escaped into the forest. We, the men of the government, will reward you for hunting him.'

Pirri looked at Kajo, at his uniform and gun and dark glasses and knew he was a powerful government *wazungu*, so he thought about it carefully. He had killed white *wazungu* before in the Zaïre war when he was a young man. The government had paid him for it then and it had been easy. The white *wazungu* were stupid and clumsy in the forest. They were easy to follow and easy to kill. They never even knew he was there until they were dead.

'How much tobacco?' he asked.

'From me, as much tobacco as you can carry,' said Chetti Singh.

'From me also, as much tobacco as you can carry,' said Captain Kajo.

'Where will I find him?' asked Pirri, and Chetti Singh told him where to begin his search, and where he thought the man was heading.

'You want only his head?' Pirri asked. 'To eat?'

'No.' Chetti Singh was not offended. 'So that I know you have killed the right man.'

'First I will bring you this man's head,' said Pirri happily. 'Then I will bring you the teeth of the elephant, and I will have more tobacco than any man in the world.' And like a little brown ghost he disappeared into the forest.

 In the early morning, before the heat built up, Kelly Kinnear was working in the Gondala clinic. She had more patients than usual, most of them suffering from infectious tropical yaws, those great suppurating ulcers that would eat down to the bone unless they were treated. Others were malarial or had swollen eyes running with fly-borne ophthalmia. There were also two new cases of AIDS. She didn't need blood slides to recognise the symptoms, the swelling of the lymph glands and the thick white thrush that coated their tongues and throats like cream cheese.

She consulted Victor Omeru and he agreed that they should try the new treatment on them, the herbal extract of the selepi tree bark that was looking so promising. He helped her prepare the dose. The amount was necessarily an arbitrary decision, and they were discussing it when there was a sudden commotion outside the clinic front door.

Victor glanced out of the window and smiled. 'Your little friends have arrived,' he told Kelly, and she laughed with pleasure and went out into the sunshine.

Sepoo and his wife Pamba were squatting below the verandah, chatting and laughing with the other waiting patients. When they saw her they both squealed with delight and came running, competing with each other to take her hands and tell her all the news since their last meeting, trying to shout each other down to be the first to impart the choicest morsels of scandal and sensation from the tribe. One on each hand they led her to her usual seat on the top step of the verandah and sat beside her, still chattering in unison.

'Swilli has had a baby. It is a boy and she says she will bring it to show you at the next full moon,' said Pamba.

'There will be a great net hunt soon, and all the tribes will join . . .' said Sepoo.

'I have brought you a bundle of the special roots I told you about last time we met,' shrilled Pamba, not to be outdone by her husband. Her bright eyes were almost hidden in a cobweb of wrinkles and half her teeth were missing.

'I shot two colobus monkeys,' boasted Sepoo. 'And I have brought you one of the skins to make a beautiful hat, Kara-Ki.'

'You are kind, Sepoo,' Kelly thanked him. 'But what news from Sengi-Sengi? What about the yellow machines that eat the earth and gobble up the forest? What news of the big white man with curly hair and the woman with hair like fire who looks into the little black box all the time?'

'Strange,' said Sepoo importantly. 'There is strange news. The big man with curly hair has run away from Sengi-Sengi. He has run into the forest to hide.' Sepoo was gabbling it out to prevent Pamba from getting in before him. 'And the government *wazungu* at Sengi-Sengi have offered Pirri, my brother, vast treasure and reward to hunt the man and kill him.'

Kelly stared at him in horror.

'Kill him?' she blurted. 'They want Pirri to kill him?'

'And cut off his head,' Sepoo confirmed with relish. 'Is it not strange and exciting?'

'You have to stop him!' Kelly sprang to her feet, dragging Sepoo up with her. 'You must not let Pirri kill him. You must rescue the white man and bring him here to Gondala. Do you hear me, Sepoo? Go, now! Go swiftly! You must stop Pirri.'

'I will go with him to see that he does what you tell him, Kara-Ki,' Pamba announced. 'For he is a stupid old man, and if he hears the honey chameleon whistle or meets one of his cronies in the forest, he will forget everything you have told him.' She turned to her husband. 'Come on, old man.' She prodded him with her thumb. 'Let us go and find this white *wazungu* and bring him back to Kara-Ki. Let us go before Pirri kills him and takes his head to Sengi-Sengi.'

 Pirri the hunter went down on one knee in the forest and examined the tracks. He adjusted the hang of the bow on his shoulder and shook his head with reluctant admiration.

'He knows that I am here, close behind him,' he whispered. 'How does he know that? Unless of course he is one of the *fundis*.'

He touched the spoor where the *wazungu* had left the water. He had done it with great skill, leaving only traces that someone as good as Pirri could detect.

'Yes, you know I am following you,' Pirri nodded. 'But where did you learn to move and cover your tracks almost as well as a Bambuti?' he muttered.

He had picked up the *wazungu*'s tracks where he had crossed the broad road that the big yellow earth-eating tree-gobbling machine had left through the forest. The earth there was soft and the *wazungu* had left tracks that a blind man could follow on a dark night. He was heading westwards towards the mountains, as Chetti Singh had said he would.

Pirri thought immediately that it would be an easy hunt and a quick kill, especially when he had found where the *wazungu* had broken off a piece of poisonous fungus from a dead tree and eaten a little of it. He found the man's teeth marks in the piece of fungus that he had discarded, and Pirri laughed. 'Your bowels will turn to water and run like the great river, O stupid *wazungu*. And I will kill you while you squat to shit.'

Sure enough, he had found the place where the *wazungu* had slept the previous night and close by where he had voided his bowels for the first time. 'You will not go far now,' he chuckled, 'before I catch you and kill you.'

435

Pirri glided onwards, softly as a wisp of dark smoke blending with the gloom and shadows and sombre colours of the deep forest, following the easy trail at twice the speed of the man who had laid it. At intervals he found dribbles of his poisoned yellow dung, and then the trail reached the bank of a small stream and went into the water and vanished.

Pirri worked for almost half a day, casting both banks for a mile both upstream and down before he found where the *wazungu* had left the water again.

'You are clever,' he conceded. 'But not as clever as Pirri.' And he took the spoor again, going slowly now, for the man he was following was good. He laid back trails and false sign and used the water, and Pirri had to unravel each of his tricks, frowning while he worked it out and then grinning with approbation. 'Ah yes, you will be a worthy one to kill. You would long ago have got clean away from a lesser hunter. But I am Pirri.'

In the late afternoon of the second day he had reached a clearing and he caught his first glimpse of the *wazungu*. At first he thought it was one of the rare forest antelope on the opposite hillside. He caught just a tiny flicker of movement in one of the forest glades, almost a mile distant across the valley. For an instant even Pirri's phenomenal eyesight was cheated. It did not seem to be a man, certainly not a white man, and then as he disappeared into the tall trees at the edge of the forest he realised that the man had covered himself with mud from head to foot and wore a hat of bark and leaves which distorted the outline of his head and made it difficult to make out his human shape.

'Ha!' Pirri rubbed his belly with delight and granted himself another small pinch of tobacco under his upper lip to reward himself for the sighting. 'Yes, you are good, my *wazungu*. Even I will not be able to catch you before darkness falls, but in the morning your head will be mine.'

That night Pirri slept without a fire at the edge of the clearing where last he had seen the white man, and was moving again just as soon as it was light enough to make out the sign.

In the middle of the morning he found the *wazungu*. He was lying at the foot of one of the towering African mahogany trees and at first Pirri thought he was already dead. He had tried to cover himself with dead leaves, a pathetic last effort to thwart the remorseless little hunter.

Pirri moved in very slowly, taking every precaution, trusting nothing. He carried his broad-bladed machete ready in his right hand, and the weapon was honed to a razor edge.

When at last he stood over Daniel Armstrong he realised that although he was sick and wasted, he was not yet dead. He was unconscious, breathing with a soft bubbling sound in the back of his throat, curled like a sick dog under the blanket of leaf trash. His head was tilted at an angle, and the sweat had washed away the mud camouflage below his jaw line, leaving a white line. A perfect aiming mark for the decapitating stroke.

Pirri tested the edge of the blade of the machete with his thumb. It was sharp enough to shave his beard. He lifted it high above his head with both hands. The man's neck was no thicker than that of one of the forest duikers which were Pirri's usual prey. The machete would hack through meat and bone just as readily, and the head would spring away from the trunk with the same startling alacrity. He would hang it by its thick curly hair from a branch for an hour or so, to allow the blood to drain from the severed neck, then he would smoke it over a slow fire of green leaves and herbs to preserve it, before slinging it in a small carrying net of bark string and bearing it back to his poaching master, Chetti Singh, to collect his reward.

Pirri felt a little cold gust of regret as he paused at the top of his stroke before sending the blade hissing down. Because he was a true hunter he always experienced this sadness for his quarry at the moment of the kill, the creed of his tribe was to respect and honour the animals he killed, especially when the quarry had been cunning and brave and worthy.

Die swiftly, he made his silent entreaty.

He was on the point of slashing downwards when a voice said quietly behind him, 'Hold your blade, my brother, or I will put this poison arrow through your liver.'

Pirri was so startled that he leapt in the air and whirled to face about.

Sepoo was five paces behind him. His bow was arched and

the arrow was drawn to his cheek, the poison on the tip of the arrow was black and sticky as toffee and it was pointed unwaveringly at Pirri's chest.

'You are my own brother!' Pirri gasped with the shock. 'You are the fruit of my own mother's womb. You would not let your arrow fly?'

'If you believe that, Pirri, my brother, you are even more stupid than I believe you to be. Kara-Ki wants this white *wazungu* alive. If you tap a single drop of his blood, I will put this arrow through you, from brisket to backbone.'

'And I,' said Pamba his wife from the forest shadows behind him, 'I will sing and dance around you as you lie writhing on the ground.'

Pirri backed away sharply. He knew he could talk Sepoo into or out of almost anything, but not Pamba. He had a vast respect for and healthy fear of his sister-in-law.

'They have offered me great treasure to kill this *wazungu*.' His voice was shrill. 'I will share it equally with you. As much tobacco as you can carry! I will give it to you.'

'Shoot him in the belly,' ordered Pamba cheerfully, and Sepoo's arm trembled with the strain of his draw as he closed one eye to correct his aim.

'Wait,' shrieked Pirri. 'I love you, my dear sister; you would not allow this old idiot to kill me.'

'I am going to take a little snuff,' said Pamba coldly. 'If you are still here when I finish sneezing . . .'

'I am going,' howled Pirri, and took another dozen paces backwards. 'I am going.' He ducked into the undergrowth and the instant he was out of the line of fire he screamed, 'You foul old monkey woman . . .'

They could hear him slashing out with his machete at the bushes around him in fury and frustration. 'Only a decrepit venereal baboon like Sepoo would marry a drooling old hag . . .'

The sounds of his ranting fury gradually diminished as he retreated into the forest and Sepoo lowered his bow and turned to his wife.

'I haven't enjoyed myself so much since the day Pirri fell into his own trap on top of the buffalo that was already in the pit!' he guffawed. 'But he described you well, my lovely wife.'

Pamba ignored him and went to where Daniel Armstrong lay unconscious, half buried in dirt and dead leaves. She knelt beside him and examined him quickly but thoroughly, plucking the ants from the corners of his eyes and his nostrils.

'I will have to work hard to save him for Kari-Ki,' she said as she reached into her medicine bag. 'If I lose this one, I don't know where I will find another one for her.'

While Pamba ministered to Daniel, Sepoo built a hut over him where he lay and then lit a little fire to disperse the mosquitoes and the humidity. He squatted in the doorway and watched his wife work.

She was the most skilled medicine woman of all the Bambuti, and her fingers were swift and dextrous as she cleaned the wound in the *wazungu*'s back and applied a poultice of mashed and boiled roots and leaves. Then she forced him to drink copious quantities of a hot infusion of herbs that would bind his bowels and replace the fluid that his body had shed.

She crooned and muttered encouragement to the unconscious man as she worked, her bare dugs swinging wrinkled and empty as a pair of leather tobacco pouches from her bony chest and her necklace of ivory and beads clicking each time she moved.

Within three hours Daniel had regained consciousness. He looked up dazedly at the two little old people crouched over him in the smoky hut and asked in Swahili, 'Who are you?'

'I am Sepoo,' said the man. 'A famous hunter and a renowned sage of the Bambuti.'

'And I am Pamba, the wife of the greatest liar in all the forest of Ubomo,' said the woman, and cackled with laughter.

By the next morning Daniel's diarrhoea had dried up and he could eat a little of the stew of monkey meat and herbs that Pamba had prepared for him. By the following morning the infection of the wound in his back had abated and he was strong enough to begin the journey to Gondala.

Daniel went slowly at first, using a staff to steady himself, for his legs were still wobbly and his head seemed to be filled with wool and floating clear of his shoulders. Pamba kept him company, leading him at a gentle pace through the forest and keeping up a constant chattering punctuated with shrieks of merry laughter, Sepoo ranged afar hunting and scavenging in the usual Bambuti manner.

Daniel had already guessed the identity of the mysterious Kara-Ki who had sent the pygmies to rescue him, but as soon as Pamba gave him an opportunity he questioned her further, trying to get her to describe her patron in detail.

'Kara-Ki is very tall,' Pamba told him, and Daniel realised that to a Bambuti everybody else in the world is very tall. 'And she has a long pointed nose.'

All Bambuti noses were flat and broad. Pamba's description could apply to any *wazungu*, so Daniel gave up and hobbled on after the little woman.

Towards dusk Sepoo suddenly appeared again from the forest with the carcass of a duiker he had killed hanging over his shoulder. That night they feasted on grilled liver and fillets. The next morning Daniel was strong enough to discard his staff and Pamba increased the pace of the march.

They reached Gondala the following afternoon. The pygmies had given Daniel no warning that they had arrived, and as he stepped out of the forest he was presented with the dramatic view of the little community. Its open gardens and streams, and the high snow-capped mountains forming a grand backdrop to the scene.

'Daniel,' Kelly Kinnear greeted him as he climbed the verandah steps, and even though he had half expected it, Daniel was unprepared for his own pleasure at meeting her again. She looked fresh and vital and attractive, but he sensed a reserve in her as she came to him and shook his hand. 'I was so worried that Sepoo might not get to you in time . . .' Then she broke off and stood back. 'God, you look awful. What on earth happened to you?'

'Thanks for the compliment,' he grinned ruefully. 'But to answer your question – a great deal has happened to me since we last met.'

'Come into the surgery. Let's have a look at you, before we do anything else.'

'Couldn't I have a bath first? I find it difficult even being near myself.'

She laughed. 'You are rather strong on the nose, but so are most of my patients. I'm used to it.'

She took him into the surgery and laid him on the examination table. After she had gone over him thoroughly and inspected the wound on his back, she remarked, 'Pamba has done a pretty good job. I'll give you a shot of antibiotic and I'll put a fresh dressing on your back after your bath. It should have had stitches but it's too late for that now. You'll have a new interesting scar to add to all the others.'

As she washed her hands in the basin, she smiled at him over her shoulder. 'You look as though you've been in a fight or two.'

'Always the other guy's fault,' he assured her. 'Talking about fights, you never let me explain myself at our last meeting. You jumped on your motorbike before I had a chance.'

'I know. It's my Irish blood.'

'Can I explain now?'

'How about a bath first?'

The bathroom was a thatched hut, and the bath was a galvanised iron tub just large enough to contain him if he kept his knees up under his chin. The camp servants filled it with buckets of steaming water heated on the fire outside. There was clothing laid out for him: khaki shorts and shirt, faded and worn but clean and crisply ironed, together with a pair of rawhide sandals. One of the servants took away his stinking blood-stained shorts and muddy boots.

Kelly was waiting for him in her surgery when he had dressed.

'What a transformation,' she greeted him. 'Let's fix that back.'

He sat on the single chair and she stood behind him. Her fingers were cool and light and quick on his skin. When she spoke he could feel her breath on the back of his neck and smell her. He liked the feel of her hands and the sweet clean smell of her breath.

'I didn't thank you for sending your pygmies to save my life,' he said.

'All in the day's work. Think nothing of it.'

'I owe you one.'

'I'll call on you.'

'You were the very last person I'd have expected to find here,' Daniel told her. 'But when Pamba described you I began to suspect who you were. How did you get into the country? And what the hell are you doing here? If Taffari gets hold of you it will be a shooting party on the beach or a head-dress of hornets.'

'Oh, so you're beginning to find out the truth about Ephrem Taffari, that he's not the saint and saviour you thought he was?'

'Don't let's fight again,' he pleaded. 'I'm still too weak to defend myself.'

'You're as weak as a bull. Look at all that muscle. Okay, now it's time for your shot. Lie on the bed and drop your shorts.'

'Hey! Can't I have it in the arm?'

'You haven't got anything I haven't seen before. Get on the table.'

Grumbling he lay face down, and lowered his shorts halfway.

'Nothing to be ashamed of, in fact, not bad at all,' she assured him, and slid the needle home. 'Okay, that does it. Get dressed and come to dinner. I've got another surprise for you. A dinner guest, somebody you haven't seen for years.'

In the sunset they crossed from the clinic to Kelly's living quarters at the end of the clearing. On the way they stopped for a minute to watch the sunset turn the Mountains of the Moon to a splendour of gold and flames.

'I carry the memory of this beauty wherever I travel in the world,' Kelly whispered. 'It's one of the things that draws me back.'

And Daniel was moved as much by her reaction to it as by the grandeur of the scene itself. To express his accord with her he wanted to take her arm and squeeze it, but he kept his distance and after a while they moved on.

There was a dinner-table laid on the verandah of Kelly's bungalow and a solitary figure seated at it, who rose as they approached.

'Doctor Armstrong. How good to see you again.'

Daniel stared at him in astonishment and then hurried forward. 'I heard that you were dead, Mr President, that you had died of a heart-attack or been shot by Taffari.'

'The news of my death was slightly exaggerated.' Victor Omeru chuckled and took Daniel's hand.

'I found a flask of whisky in my medical chest,' Kelly said. 'Tonight seems like an auspicious occasion to administer it.' She poured a little of the golden liquid into each of their glasses and offered them the toast. 'To Ubomo! May it soon be released from the tyrant.'

Dinner was a simple meal of fish from the river and vegetables from the gardens of Gondala, but there was plenty of it and the conversation at the table never slackened or palled.

Victor Omeru explained to Daniel all the circumstances of the revolution and his overthrow, his escape into the forest and his activities since then.

'With Kelly's help, I have been able to turn Gondala into the headquarters of the resistance to Taffari's brutal dictatorship,' he ended, but Kelly pressed him eagerly.

'Victor, tell Daniel what Taffari has done to the country and its people since he seized power. Daniel has been duped into believing that Taffari is a black Christ figure. In fact, Daniel is here to shoot a production that was to extol Taffari's virtues . . .'

'No, Kelly,' Daniel interrupted her. 'That's not the way it was. It's far more complicated than that. Originally I accepted the commission to make the film for personal and private reasons.' He went on to explain the murder of Johnny Nzou and his family. He told them of Ning Cheng Gong's involvement and how he had traced the Lucky Dragon to Ubomo. He told them about Chetti Singh.

'I'll be frank with you both,' he said at last. 'I wasn't concerned with Taffari and Ubomo's real problems when I came here. I wanted my revenge and the film contract was only a means to that end. Then, after my arrival, I began to find out more about what was really going on in the country . . .'

He told them about the atrocity at Fish Eagle Bay and the forced labour he had witnessed and filmed. Victor Omeru and

Kelly exchanged glances, and then Victor nodded and turned back to Daniel.

'Taffari has seized at least thirty thousand of the Uhali people to work in the mines and the logging camps. They are slaves, kept in the most appalling conditions. They are dying like flies in the camps, starved, beaten, shot. I cannot begin to describe to you the horror of it.'

'And he is devastating the forest,' Kelly cut in. 'He is destroying millions of acres of the rain forest.'

'I saw the mining unit at work,' Daniel said. 'Actually, what he is doing there at least is in line with my own convictions on controlled use of a country's natural assets on a renewable and sustainable yield basis.'

Both Kelly and Victor stared at him in disbelief, and then Kelly blurted out angrily, 'You approve of what he is doing to the forest? Are you out of your mind? It's rape and pillage. I was right about you the first time! You *are* one of the plunderers!'

'Hold it, Kelly.' Victor held up his hands. 'Don't use inflammatory language. Let Daniel tell us what he saw and what he filmed.'

With an obvious effort Kelly brought herself under control, but she was still pale with anger and her eyes blazed.

'All right, Daniel Armstrong, tell us what Taffari showed you and let you film.'

'He showed me the MOMU unit at work . . .'

'*The* MOMU,' Kelly interjected. 'MOMU *singular*—'

'Kelly, please.' Victor stopped her again. 'Let Daniel finish before you interrupt.' She was breathing heavily, but she nodded and sat back as Daniel went on.

'Bonny and I filmed the MOMU and Taffari explained how the track of the vehicle would be replanted after it had passed.'

'Replanted!' Kelly snapped, and Victor shrugged helplessly and let her continue. 'My God! Did he tell you about the chemical reagents they've started using in the past few weeks to refine the platinum as it passes through the tube mills of the MOMU?'

'No.' Daniel shook his head. 'He told us of his determination that no reagents nor catalysts were to be used during the mining process. Even though it meant a forty per cent drop in the production of platinum and monazite.'

'And you believed him?' Kelly demanded.

'I saw it with my own eyes,' Daniel told her. He was starting to get angry. 'I filmed it. Of course I believed him.'

Kelly jumped up from the table and fetched a map of Ubomo from the next room. She spread it in front of Daniel.

'Show me where you saw the MOMU in action,' she ordered. Daniel considered the map and then placed his finger on a spot just north of Sengi-Sengi.

'Hereabouts,' he said. 'A few miles north of the camp.'

'Sucker!' Kelly blazed at him. 'Taffari set you up. He showed you the pilot scheme. It was a little show for your benefit. The main mining operation is here.' She placed her fist over an area fifty miles further north. 'Here at Wengu. And it's a damned sight different from what Taffari showed you.'

'How is it different?' Daniel demanded. 'And by the way, I don't like being called a sucker.'

'You let yourself be conned.' Kelly moderated her tone. 'But I'll tell you how the main operation is different from the pilot. First of all, it is—'

'Hold on, Kelly,' Victor Omeru intervened gently. 'Don't tell him about it. It would be much more impressive, and he'd be more likely to believe you if you showed him.'

For a moment Kelly stared at Victor and then she nodded. 'You're right, Victor. I'll take him up to Wengu and show him. And while we are there, you can film just what that bastard is doing to the forest, and show it to your great pal Sir Tug Bloody Harrison, if he doesn't know already.'

'I'm not a cameraman,' Daniel objected.

'If you don't know how to use a VTR after being around them for so many years, then you aren't very bright, Doctor Daniel.'

'All right, I could use a camera. Not very artistically but adequately, if only I had one. Where do you suggest I find a VTR in the middle of the forest?'

'What happened to the one your red-haired girlfriend had?' Kelly demanded.

'Bonny isn't my girlfriend. You're a great one for hurling

445

accusations,' he began, and then broke off and stared at Kelly. 'Damn it!' he said. 'You're right. I left the VTR in the Land-rover. If Taffari's lads haven't found it yet, then it's still there.'

'Why don't you go back and fetch it?' Kelly enquired sweetly. 'I'll send Sepoo with you.'

'I have brought you the head of the white *wazungu*,' Pirri, the hunter, announced dramatically and unslung the net bag of plaited bark fibre from his shoulder and dropped it in front of Chetti Singh.

The head rolled out of the bag and Chetti Singh jumped back and exclaimed with revulsion. There was no skin left on the head. The raw meat was putrefying and the stench was fierce enough to make him gag.

'How do I know that this is the head of the white *wazungu*?' Chetti Singh demanded.

'Because I, Pirri the hunter, say it is so.'

'That's not the highest recommendation, never mind,' Chetti Singh said in English, and then reverted to Swahili. 'This man has been dead a long time; the ants and the worms have half eaten him. You did not kill him, Pirri.'

'No,' Pirri admitted. 'This stupid *wazungu* had eaten a poison mushroom and died in the forest before I could find him and kill him. The ants had eaten him, as you say, but I have brought you his head, and that was our bargain.' Pirri mustered all his dignity and drew himself up to his full four foot six inches. 'Now you must give me what you promised me, especially the tobacco.'

It was a long and forlorn hope. Even Pirri realised that. To obtain this head Pirri had exhumed one of the mass graves that the Hita guards had dug in the forest for the corpses of the slave labourers who died in the camps.

'You are certain that this is the head of the white *wazungu*?' Chetti Singh demanded. He did not believe the pygmy, but on the other hand he had to placate both Ning Cheng Gong and

446

President Taffari. He dared not admit to them that there was a possibility that Armstrong had escaped. Pirri was offering him an easy exit from his dilemma.

'It is the *wazungu*,' Pirri affirmed, and Chetti Singh thought about it for a while.

'Take this . . .' he touched the reeking head with his toe, 'take it back into the forest and bury it.'

'What about my reward? Especially the tobacco?' Pirri's tone became an ingratiating whine.

'You did not bring me the whole head. The skin and hair were missing. Therefore I cannot give you the whole reward. And I will give it to you only when you bring me the teeth of the elephant, as we agreed.'

Pirri let out a shout of anger and drew his machete.

'Put that knife away,' said Chetti Singh reasonably. 'Or I will shoot your head off with this.' He showed the pygmy the Tokarev pistol concealed in the pocket of his bush jacket.

Pirri's scowl became a beatific smile. 'It was only a little joke, O master. I am your slave.' And he sheathed the machete. 'I will go and fetch the teeth of the elephant as you command.' He picked up the severed head. But as he skipped away into the forest Pirri's guts and chest were filled with so much anger that he thought they might burst.

'Nobody cheats Pirri,' he whispered, and slashed at a tree-trunk with the machete as he ran. 'Pirri will kill the man who cheats him,' he promised. 'You want a head, O one-armed and greasy man. I will give you a head. Your own.'

'Daniel Armstrong is dead,' Chetti Singh told them. 'The Bambuti brought me his head. He died in the forest.'

'There can be no doubt?' President Taffari demanded.

'None at all,' Chetti Singh affirmed. 'I saw the head with my personal eyes.'

'That means the woman is the only living witness.' Ning Cheng Gong looked relieved. 'You should get rid of her immediately, Your Excellency. She should disappear in the forest, just the way that Armstrong did.'

Ephrem Taffari picked up his empty glass and rattled the ice cubes. Captain Kajo hurried across the room and took the glass from his hand. At the small bar in the corner of the president's office he poured gin and tonic.

'Aren't you forgetting the videotape?' Taffari asked, as Kajo respectfully handed him the drink.

'Of course not,' Cheng said. 'But once she has recovered the tape from the embassy we must get rid of her.' He hesitated. 'I could arrange that personally.'

Ephrem Taffari smiled at him over the rim of the glass. 'Ah, yes.' He nodded. 'I have heard that you have a rather unusual hobby, Mr Ning.'

'I am not quite sure what you are implying, Mr President,' he answered stiffly. 'I was merely offering to make certain that the job was done properly. We don't want any more loose ends.'

'Quite right, Mr Ning,' Taffari agreed. 'The woman is becoming a bore. I have lost interest in her. Once we have recovered the tape, she is yours. Just make certain that there are no mistakes.'

'Trust me, Mr President.'

'Oh yes, Mr Ning, I trust you just as completely as you trust me. After all, we are partners, are we not?'

'My arrangement with Danny was that he would pick it up personally.' Sir Michael Hargreave inspected his fingernails with some interest and then placed his hand in his pocket and went to the window of his office in the British embassy. He looked out over the lake. 'Daniel didn't say anything about handing it over to a third party. You must understand my position, Miss – ah – Miss Mahon.'

The punkah fan on the ceiling squeaked and whirled and Bonny thought quickly. She knew that she must not appear too eager, even though she was acutely aware of what the consequences might be if she returned to Ephrem empty-handed.

448

'I didn't realise it would be a problem.' She stood up. 'Danny asked me to pick it up. He'll probably be bitter with me for not bringing it back, but I don't imagine the tape is of any real importance. I'm sorry I didn't think to ask Danny for a note. Anyway, thank you for your time and I'll explain to Danny that you couldn't see your way clear to handing the tape to me.'

She held out her hand and gave him her sexiest smile, thrusting out her bosom. Sir Michael's gaze wavered from her eyes, and then he seemed to make up his mind.

'Look here, I suppose it will be all right. I mean, you are Danny's assistant. Not as though you were a total stranger . . .' He hesitated.

'I don't want you to do anything you feel is not right,' Bonny told him. 'I'm sure Danny will understand that you didn't trust me.'

'Good Lord, my dear young lady, it isn't a case of not trusting you.'

'Oh, that's what I thought it was.' She fluttered her eyelids at him.

'Would you mind signing a receipt? Sorry to be so awkward, but I must cover myself with Danny.'

'I understand, Sir Michael.'

He scribbled out a receipt on a sheet of the embassy stationery and she signed it and wrote out her full name and passport number at the foot of the page.

Sir Michael went into the adjoining room and she heard him put a key into a lock and then the metallic sound of the door lugs of a steel safe opening and closing. A few minutes later he returned and handed her a bulky manila envelope with Daniel's name printed on it. She tried not to make her relief apparent, but her hand shook as he handed it to her.

'Please give Danny my best salaams.' Sir Michael walked her to the front door of the embassy. 'When is he coming back from Sengi-Sengi?'

'I'm flying up to join him this afternoon . . .'

Bonny had her nerves under control and chatted easily. They shook hands at the door.

'Having one of our regular cocktail parties next Saturday,'

Sir Michael said. 'If you and Danny are back in town by then, you must come along. I'll have Miss Rogers send you an invitation to the guest house.'

The news of Daniel Armstrong's disappearance had not yet been reported to the embassy. Ephrem Taffari wanted all the loose ends tidied up before the alarm was raised.

Bonny went out to where Captain Kajo was waiting at the wheel of an army Landrover. She clutched the envelope in her lap, but managed another smile and wave for Sir Michael as they pulled out of the embassy gates.

Then she let out a deep breath and fell back against the seat.

'President Taffari is waiting for you on his yacht, Miss Mahon,' Captain Kajo told her, and took the lakeside road down to the harbour.

The yacht was moored at the naval jetty beyond the fish factory. The vessel had been the toy of a wealthy Asian businessman, one of those whom Taffari had deported and sent back to the United Kingdom when he came to power. Of course, he had confiscated all the Asian's property, and this vessel was now the presidential yacht.

It was a forty-five-foot Camper and Nicholson with lovely lines, equipped with every luxury, although most of the electronic equipment had long ago failed and had not been replaced, and the paintwork and sails were no longer pristine. However, the bar was well stocked and since the yacht very seldom left its berth, the lack of navigational and sailing gear was not critical.

There were two men in the main cabin, seated at the red teak saloon table facing each other.

President Taffari was perusing the monthly operating report and profit-and-loss accounts of UDC, smiling and nodding as he did so. Ning Cheng Gong was watching him expectantly. When Taffari lowered the document and looked up, Cheng answered his smile.

'I am impressed, Mr Ning. It is only a very short time since you arrived in Ubomo to take control of the company, but the results are really quite spectacular.'

'You are very gracious, Your Excellency.' Cheng bowed slightly. 'But I can truthfully say that I expect an even greater improvement in the months ahead. There were many problems that my English predecessor left for me, but these are being resolved.'

'What about the vehicle maintenance depot? This is one of my major areas of concern.' Taffari's smile faded.

'And rightly so, Mr President. We have over a thousand heavy vehicles in service, not counting the actual MOMU installations. Our maintenance costs were running at over three million dollars a month when I took over. As you can see, I have managed to reduce these by almost forty per cent . . .'

Their discussion lasted another hour before there were footsteps on the deck outside and a polite knock on the cabin door.

'Who is it?' Taffari called.

'Captain Kajo, Mr President, and Miss Mahon.'

Taffari glanced at Cheng significantly and the Chinaman nodded. This was the reason that the meeting was being held on board the yacht, rather than in the boardroom at Lake House.

'Come in!' Taffari ordered, and the door slid aside. Kajo stooped his long frame into the cabin and saluted awkwardly.

'I have Miss Mahon waiting in the Landrover on the dock,' he reported.

'Did she pick up the packet?' Taffari asked anxiously.

'Yes, sir. She has it with her.'

Again Taffari and Cheng exchanged glances, but now both of them were smiling again.

'All right, Captain.' Taffari nodded. 'You have your orders.'

'Yes, Mr President. I am to accompany Mr Ning and Miss Mahon on the expedition to Lamu Island and I am to—'

'No need to repeat them, Captain,' Taffari interrupted. 'Just carry them out to the letter. Now you may bring Miss Mahon aboard.'

She burst into the cabin and went directly to Ephrem Taffari, ignoring the other man at the table.

'I've got it, Ephrem,' she gloated. 'Here it is.' She laid the envelope in front of him and he picked it up, tore it open and shook out the video cassette.

'Are you sure this is the one?'

'Yes, that's my notation on the label. My handwriting. It's the one, all right.'

'Well done. I am extremely pleased with you,' Taffari told her. 'Come and sit beside me, my dear.'

She accepted the offer with alacrity and Taffari laid his hand on her thigh below the table-top.

'Captain Kajo,' Taffari ordered. 'There is a bottle of champagne in the refrigerator. This calls for a celebration.'

Kajo went to the bar and busied himself with the bottle. The cork popped and a little froth gushed on to the carpet. It was Australian rather than French, but none of them complained. Kajo turned back to the bar, screening the row of glasses on the bar top while he poured the wine. He gave Bonny her glass first, and then served the others in order of their seniority.

Taffari lifted his glass towards Bonny. 'To you, my dear. You have saved me and my country from a potentially damaging situation.'

'Thank you, Mr President.' Bonny took a mouthful of the champagne. She noticed but did not remark on the slightly bitter aftertaste, for she had learned not to give him the least pretext for offence. And when Kajo refilled her glass, she drank it without question. The unpleasant taste was less noticeable now.

'I thought we might go for a sunset cruise on the lake,' Taffari told her, and Bonny smiled at him but her cheeks felt strangely numb.

'That would be fun,' she tried to say, but it came out slurred and jumbled. Bonny broke off and stared at them. Their faces were receding and there was a ringing sound in her head. It became louder and her vision was darkening. There was only a tiny hole in the centre of the blackness in which she could see Ephrem's face, as though through the reverse end of a telescope, small and remote.

His voice boomed and echoed in her drugged brain. 'Goodbye, my dear,' he said, and her head dropped forward on to the table-top.

There was silence in the cabin for a full minute after Bonny Mahon had collapsed. Then President Taffari gathered his papers and placed them in his briefcase. He stood up and Kajo hurried to open the door for him. Taffari paused in the doorway and looked back. Ning Cheng Gong was still seated opposite the unconscious girl. He was watching her with a strange pale intensity.

At the head of the gangplank Taffari paused to talk to Captain Kajo. 'Make sure the yacht is washed down thoroughly before you bring her back to port. You know how to use the pressure hose?'

'I do, Your Excellency.'

Taffari went down the gangplank to his Mercedes and Kajo stood to attention and saluted as he drove away.

The yacht's diesel engine was already running, the exhausts bubbling softly under the stern. Kajo cast off the lines and went to the wheel. He eased the yacht away from the jetty and turned her bows towards the harbour entrance.

It was a two-hour run out to Lamu Island, and the sun had already set when he dropped anchor in the lee of the uninhabited horseshoe-shaped rock.

'We have arrived, Mr Ning,' he said into the voice tube.

'Help me, please, Captain.'

Kajo went down into the cabin. Bonny Mahon was lying, still unconscious, on the carpeted deck. Between them they carried her up into the open cockpit and while Kajo held her upright Ning strapped her wrists and ankles to the stainless steel railings. He spread a nylon sheet under her with the end hanging over the stern, to make it easier to hose down the deck later.

'I don't need any further assistance,' he told Kajo. 'Take the rubber dinghy and go ashore on the island. Stay there until I call you. No matter what you may hear you will remain ashore. Do you understand?'

'Yes, Mr Ning.'

Cheng stood by the stern rail and watched Kajo in the stern of the dinghy disappear into the darkness. The little three hp outboard puttered softly, and the beam of Kajo's flashlight threw an erratic beam in the darkness. At last he reached the island and the outboard motor cut out into silence. The flashlight was extinguished.

Cheng turned back to the girl. She sagged against her bonds. She looked very pale in the cockpit lights and her hair was an untidy copper bush.

Cheng took a few moments longer to savour the moment. Physically the woman was unattractive to him, and she was much older than he liked, but none the less he felt his excitement mounting. Soon he would be so absorbed and transported that such small adverse considerations would be of no account.

He looked around him carefully, taking his time, considering the circumstances. Lamu Island was twelve miles from the mainland and the lake crocodiles infested the waters around it. They would immediately devour any offal that was dropped overboard. On top of which he was under the protection of President Taffari.

He went back to the girl and adjusted the tourniquet around her upper arm, massaging the veins in the inside of her elbow until they stood out thick and blue in the cockpit lights. He had used the drug on many previous occasions, and he kept the antidote and disposable syringe available at all times.

Only seconds after he injected the antidote, Bonny Mahon opened her eyes and peered at him groggily.

'Good evening, Miss Mahon.' Cheng's voice was throaty with excitement. 'You and I are going to have a little fun together.'

There had been an almost immediate *rapport* between Daniel and Sepoo. It was strange for in every way they were completely different: in size and colour and shape and mentality there was no similarity whatsoever.

It had to be a thing of the spirit, Daniel decided as he followed Sepoo through the forest. They were children of Africa, its pulse beat in both of them, its soul was their soul. They understood and loved this land's beauty and savagery and treasured its bounty. They understood and loved its creatures and counted themselves merely one amongst this multitude of species.

When they camped that night they sat close to each other beside the fire and talked quietly. Sepoo spoke to him of the secrets and the mystery of the forest and the deeply felt beliefs of his people, and Daniel understood. In some measure they were his beliefs too and he accepted the reasons for the customs of these people as Sepoo explained them, and admired the wisdom and virtue of their lore. Sepoo called him 'Kuokoa', which meant 'The one I rescued'. Daniel accepted the name, even though he knew it was meant as a monument to Sepoo's deed and a reminder of his debt to the old man.

They came to the MOMU track through the forest near Sengi-Sengi in the late afternoon and lay up at the forest edge until it was dark. Then they crossed the open ground in the night.

Sepoo led Daniel to the logging road where he had abandoned the Landrover almost ten days previously but even Sepoo could not lead him directly to the stranded vehicle. It was only the following day that they at last found the Landrover exactly as Daniel had left it behind its screen of dense undergrowth, sunk to its axles in the soft forest floor.

There were no fresh human tracks around it and the video equipment was still in its aluminium carrying cases. Daniel laid it out on the tailboard of the vehicle and checked it quickly. The camera was not working. Either the batteries were flat after standing so long, or else the moisture had penetrated the mechanism. Daniel noticed droplets behind the glass of the lens and condensation beaded the casing.

It was a bitter disappointment, but Daniel could only hope that the batteries could still be recharged or that a rudimentary cleaning and drying, once he reached Gondala, would get the camera serviceable again. He gave Sepoo the case of cassettes to carry while he took for himself the camera, the lens and the spare battery packs, a burden of almost seventy pounds to lug through the steaming forest.

Heavily laden as he was, the return took almost twice as long as the outward march and it rained most of the time. As soon as he reached Gondala, Daniel recruited Victor Omeru's assistance. He knew that Victor was a qualified electrical engineer.

Victor had built and installed a turbine generator beneath the waterfall at the head of the Gondala glade. It generated 220 volts and almost ten kilowatts of power, sufficient to supply the community with lighting and to operate Kelly's laboratory equipment.

So Victor was able to place the battery packs for the video on charge and found only one of them was defective. The camera and the lens were a different problem altogether. Daniel would not have known where to begin to look for the fault, but Victor stripped the camera and cleaned the condensed moisture. He checked the circuits and found one of the transistors was blown. He replaced it with one that he cannibalised from Kelly's gas spectroscope. Within twenty-four hours he had the VTR functioning again, then he took down the lenses and cleaned and dried them out and reassembled them.

Daniel realised just what a difficult task the old man had undertaken in such primitive conditions.

'If you never get your country back, I've always got a job for you, sir,' he told Victor.

'That's not such a good idea,' Kelly warned him. 'You'd probably end up working for him.'

'All right,' Daniel said. 'I've got a camera. Now what do you want me to film?'

'We leave tomorrow morning at first light,' Kelly told him.

'I'm coming along, Kelly,' Victor Omeru told her.

'I don't think that is very wise, Victor.' She looked dubious. 'You're much too valuable.'

'After all my hard work, I deserve a little reward, don't you think?' He turned to Daniel. 'Besides which, you might have another breakdown in the equipment. Come on, Doctor Armstrong, put in a good word for me.'

'Chauvinists, both of you,' Kelly protested. 'You're ganging up on me just because I am a female. I'll have to call Pamba to my aid.'

'Hell no!' Daniel shook his head. 'That is using too much gun!' But he shared Kelly's misgivings. Victor Omeru was over seventy years of age and the going would be tough. It was almost fifty miles to Wengu. He was about to say so when Victor intervened quietly.

'Seriously, Ubomo is my country. I cannot rely on second-hand reports. I have to see for myself what Taffari is doing to my people and my land.'

Neither of them could argue with that, and when the safari started out from Gondala the following morning, Victor Omeru was with them.

Sepoo had recruited eight men from his clan to act as porters and Pamba appointed herself as caravan manager to make certain that they applied themselves and did not lose interest in the typical Bambuti fashion, dropping their bundles to wander off fishing or honey hunting. Every man in the clan stood in awe of Pamba's tongue.

On the third day they reached the first of the bleeding rivers and the Bambuti men lowered their loads to the ground and huddled on the bank. There was no laughter nor banter. Even Pamba was silent and subdued.

Daniel climbed down into the stinking morass of red mud, dead animals and poisoned vegetation, and scooped a handful of it. He sniffed it and then threw it from him and tried to wipe the filth from his hands.

'What is it, Kelly?' He looked up at her on the bank above him. 'What caused this?'

'It's the reagent that Taffari swore to you that he would never use.' She was dressed only in a cotton T-shirt and shorts with a coloured headband around her brow, and her small neat body seemed to quiver with outrage.

'Victor and I have been monitoring the effluent from the mining operation. At first it was pure mud. That was bad enough. Then recently, in the last few weeks, there's been a change. They have begun using a reagent. You see, the platinum molecules are coated with sulphides. The sulphides reduce the efficiency of the recovery process by forty per cent. They are using a reagent to dissolve the sulphide coating and to free the platinum.'

'What does the reagent consist of?' Daniel demanded.

'Arsenic.' She spat the word like an angry cat. 'They are using a two per cent solution of white arsenic to break down the sulphide coating.'

He stared at her in disbelief. 'But that's crazy.'

'You said it,' Kelly agreed. 'These aren't sane or responsible people. They are poisoning the forest in a murderous orgy of greed.'

He climbed up out of the dead river and stood beside her. Slowly he felt her outrage seep into his own conscience.

'The bastards,' he whispered. It was as though she realised the moment of his total commitment to her cause, for she reached out and took his hand. It was not a gentle or an affectionate gesture. Her grip was fierce and compelling.

'You haven't seen it all yet. This is just the beginning. The real horror lies ahead at Wengu.' She shook his arm demandingly. 'Come!' she ordered. 'Come and look at it. I challenge you to remain on the sidelines after you have seen it.'

The little column moved on, but after another five hours' march the Bambuti porters abruptly halted and dropped their packs and whispered together.

'Now what is the trouble?' Victor wanted to know, and Kelly explained.

'We have reached the boundary of the clan hunting area.' She pointed ahead. 'From here onwards we will be entering the sacred heartland of the Bambuti. They are deeply troubled and perplexed. So far only Sepoo has seen what is happening at Wengu. The others are reluctant to go on. They are afraid of the wrath of the forest god, the Mother and Father of the forest. They understand that a terrible sacrilege has been committed and they are terrified.'

'What can we do to persuade them?' Daniel asked, but Kelly shook her head.

'We must keep out of it. It is clan business. We must leave it to Pamba to convince them.'

The old lady was at her best now. She spoke to them, sometimes haranguing them shrilly, at others dropping her voice to a dovelike cooing and taking one of their faces in her cupped hands to whisper into an ear. She sang a little hymn to the forest and smeared ointment on each of their bare chests to absolve them. Then she performed a solitary dance, shuffling and leaping as she circled. Her withered breasts bounced against her belly and her skirt of bark cloth flipped up at the back to expose her surprisingly neat and glossy little buttocks as she cavorted.

After an hour one of the porters suddenly picked up his load and started along the path. The others, grinning sheepishly, followed his example and the safari went forward into the sacred heartland.

They heard the machines at dawn the next morning and as they went on the sound became louder. The rivers they crossed were waist-deep and thick as honey with the fearful red-poisoned mud. Apart from the distant growl and roar of the machines, the forest was silent. They saw no birds or monkeys or antelope, and the Bambuti were silent also. They kept close together and they were afraid, darting anxious glances into the forest around them as they scurried forward.

At noon Sepoo halted the column and conferred with Kelly in a whisper. He pointed towards the east and Kelly nodded and beckoned Daniel and Victor to her.

'Sepoo says we are very close now. Sounds in the forest are very deceptive. The machines are working not more than a few miles ahead. We dare not approach closer for there are company guards at the forest edge.'

'What are you going to do?' Victor asked.

'Sepoo says there's a line of hills to the east. From there we'll be able to overlook the mining and logging area. Pamba will stay here with the porters. Just the four of us, Sepoo and I, you, Daniel, and Victor, will go up on to the hills.'

Daniel unpacked the VTR and he and Victor checked it.

'Come on,' Kelly ordered, 'before the light goes or it begins to rain again.'

They climbed the hills in Indian file with Sepoo leading. However, even when they came out on the top they were still hemmed in by the forest. The great trees soared high overhead and the undergrowth pressed in closely about them, limiting visibility to twenty or thirty feet. They could hear the bellow of diesels below them, closer and clearer than before.

'What now?' Daniel wanted to know. 'Can't see a damned thing from here.'

'Sepoo will give us a grandstand view,' Kelly promised, and almost as she said it, they reached the base of a tree that was a giant amongst a forest of great trees.

'Twenty pygmies holding hands can't encircle this tree,' Kelly murmured. 'We've tried it. It's the sacred honey tree of the tribe.' She pointed at the primitive ladder that scaled the massive trunk.

The pygmies had driven wooden pegs into the smooth bark to reach the lowest branches and from there they had strung liana ropes and lashed wooden steps that ascended until they passed out of sight into the forest galleries a hundred feet above where they stood.

'This is a Bambuti temple,' Kelly explained. 'Up there in the high branches they pray and leave offerings to the forest god.'

Sepoo went first for he was the lightest and some of the pegs and steps were rotten. He cut new ones and hammered them into place with the hilt of his machete, and then signalled the others to follow him.

Kelly went next and reached down to give Victor a hand when he faltered. Daniel came last, carrying the VTR slung over his shoulder and reaching up to place Victor's feet on the ladder rungs when he could not find them for himself.

It was slow progress, but they helped the old man up and reached the upper gallery of the forest safely.

This was like the land at the top of Jack's beanstalk, an aerial platform formed by interlinked branches and fallen debris. New plants had taken root in the suspended leaf mould and trash and formed a marvellous hanging garden where strange and beautiful flowers bloomed and a whole new spectrum of life flourished closer to the sun. Daniel saw butterflies with wings spread as wide as his hands, and flying insects that sparkled like emeralds and princely rubies. There were even lilies and wild gardenias growing in this fairyland. Daniel caught the flash of a bird so jewelled and splendid that he doubted his own eyes as it vanished like a puff of brilliant smoke amongst the foliage.

Sepoo barely allowed them to rest before he began to climb again. The trunk of the tree was half as thick at this level, but still as huge as its neighbours had been at their bases. As they went higher so the light changed. It was like coming up from the depths of the ocean. The green submarine glow brightened until abruptly they burst out into the sunlight and exclaimed with wonder.

They were on the top branches of the sacred honey tree. They looked down upon the carpet of the forest roof. It spread away, undulating like the billows of the ocean, green and unbroken on every side, except in the north. All their eyes turned in that direction and their cries of wonder faded and they stared in horror and disbelief.

In the north the forest was gone. From the base of the green hill below them, as far as they could see to the north, to the very foothills of the snowclad mountains the forest had been erased. A red plain of desolation lay where once the tall trees had stood.

None of them could speak or move. They clung to their lofty perch and stared speechlessly, turning their heads slowly from side to side to encompass the enormity of the bare devastated expanse.

The earth seemed to have been raked by the claws of some rapacious beast, for it had been scoured by the torrential rain waters. The topsoils had been torn away, leaving stark canyons of erosion; the fine red mud had been washed down to clog and choke the rivers through the forest. It was a desolate lunar landscape.

'Merciful God!' Victor Omeru was the first to speak. 'It is an abomination. How much land has he defiled? What is the full extent of this destruction?'

'It's impossible to calculate,' Kelly whispered. Even though she had seen it before, she was still stunned by the horror of it. 'Half a million – a million acres, I don't know. But remember, they've been at work here for less than a year. Think of the destruction in another year from now. If those monsters . . .' she pointed at the line of MOMU vehicles that were strung along the edge of the forest at the foot of the hill, 'if those monsters are allowed to continue.'

It was an effort for Daniel to drag his eyes from the wide vista of destruction and to concentrate on the line of yellow machines. From their high vantage point they seemed as tiny and innocuous as a small boy's toys left in the sandbox. The MOMU were in a staggered formation, like a line of combine-harvesters reaping one of those endless wheat fields on the Canadian prairie. They were moving so slowly that they appeared to be standing still.

'How many?' Daniel asked, and counted them aloud. 'Eight, nine, ten!' he exclaimed. 'Running side by side that gives them a cutline almost four hundred yards wide.'

461

'It doesn't seem possible that just ten machines have been able to inflict such terrible damage.' Victor's voice shook uncertainly. 'They are like giant locusts – remorseless, insensate, terrible.'

The caterpillar tractors were working ahead of the line of MOMUs, scything the forest to make way for the monstrous earth-eating machines to follow.

Even as they watched, one of the tall trees quivered and swayed. Then it began to move, swinging ponderously as the steel blades ate through the base of its trunk. Even at this distance they heard the scream of living timber rending. It sounded like the death throes of a wounded animal. The falling tree gathered momentum, its death cry rose higher and shriller, until the trunk thudded into the red earth and the mass of foliage shivered, then lay still.

Daniel had to look away. Sepoo was perched beside him on a high branch, and he was weeping. The tears ran very slowly down his wrinkled old cheeks and dripped unheeded on to his naked chest. It was a terrible intimate grief, too painful for Daniel to watch.

He looked back just in time to see another tree fall and die, and then another. He unslung the VTR from his shoulder and lifted it to his eyes, focused the telephoto lens, and began to film.

He filmed the devastated bare red plain on which not a living thing remained, not an animal, or bird, or a green leaf.

He filmed the line of yellow machines grinding inexorably forward, keeping their formation rigidly, attended by an endless horde of container trucks, like worker ants behind the queen ant, carrying away the succession of eggs she laid.

He filmed the red poison spewing from the dump chutes at the rear of the MOMU, falling carelessly upon the savaged earth where the next rainstorm would carry it away and spread it into every stream and creek for a hundred miles down the contour.

He filmed the fall of the trees ahead of the line of yellow machines and the giant mechanical saws mounted on specially modified caterpillar tractors. Fountains of wet white sawdust flew high into the air as the spinning silver blades bit in and the tree-trunks fell into separate logs.

He filmed the mobile cranes lifting the logs on to the trailer beds of the logging vehicles.

He filmed the hordes of naked Uhali slaves working in the red mud to keep the roads open for the massive trucks and trailers to pass over, as they bore away the looted treasures of the forest.

He had hoped that the act of manipulating the camera and viewing the scene through the intervening lens might somehow isolate him from reality, might allow him to remain aloof and objective. It was a vain hope. The longer he watched the destruction, the more angry he became until his rage matched that of the woman who sat on the branch beside him.

Kelly did not have to give voice to her outrage. He could feel it like static electricity in the air around her. It did not surprise him that he was so in tune with her feelings. It seemed only right and natural. They were very close now. A new bond had been forged between them, to reinforce the attraction and sympathy that they had already conceived for each other.

They stayed in the treetop until nightfall, and then they remained another hour, sitting in darkness as though they could not tear themselves away from the terrible fascination of it. They listened to the growl of engines in the night and watched the floodlights and the swinging headlights turn the forest and the devastated red plain to daylight. It never stopped, but went on and on, cutting, digging, roaring, spilling out poison and death.

When at last it began to rain again and the lightning and the thunder crashed overhead, they crept down from the treetop and made their way slowly and sadly back to where Pamba waited in the forest with the porters.

In the morning they started back through the steaming silent forest towards Gondala, stopping only for Daniel to film the polluted, bleeding rivers. Victor Omeru went down into the muck and stood knee-deep in it and spoke into the camera, giving articulate voice to all their sorrow and rage.

His voice was deep and compelling and filled with concern and compassion for his land and its people. His silver hair and dark noble features would hold the attention of any audience, and his credentials were impeccable. His international reputation was such that nobody could seriously doubt that what he described to them was the truth. If Daniel could show this to the outside world, he knew that he would be able to communicate his own sense of outrage.

They moved on slowly. The Bambuti porters were still subdued and dismayed. Although they had not witnessed the mining, Sepoo had described it to them and they had seen the bleeding rivers. Yet even before they reached the boundary between the heartland and their traditional hunting grounds they were given even greater cause for sorrow.

They cut the tracks of an elephant. They all recognised the spoor of the beast, and Sepoo called him by name. 'The Old Man with One Ear,' he said, and they all agreed. It was the bull with half his left ear missing. They laughed for the first time in days as though they had met an old friend in the forest, but the laughter was short-lived as they studied the spoor.

Then they cried out and wrung their hands and whimpered with fear and horror.

Kelly called urgently to Sepoo. 'What is it, old friend?'

'Blood,' Sepoo answered her. 'Blood and urine from the elephant. He is wounded; he is dying.'

'How has this happened?' Kelly cried. She also knew the elephant like an old friend. She had come across him often in the forest when he had frequented the area round Gondala.

'A man has struck and wounded him. Somebody is hunting the bull in the sacred heartland. It is against all law and custom. Look! Here are the tracks of the man's feet lying over the spoor of the bull.' He pointed out the clear imprints of small bare feet in the mud. 'The hunter is a Bambuti. He must be a man of our clan. It is a terrible sacrilege. It is an offence against the god of the forest.'

The little group of pygmies were shaken and horrified. They clustered together like lost children, holding each other's hands for comfort in these dreadful days when all they believed in was being turned upside down – first the machines in the forest and the bleeding rivers, and now this sacrilege committed by one of their own people.

'I know this man,' Pamba shrieked. 'I recognise the mark of his feet. This man is Pirri.'

They wailed then and covered their faces, for Pirri had made his kill in the sacred places and the shame and the retribution of the forest god must come down upon all of them.

Pirri the hunter moved like a shadow. He laid his tiny feet down gently upon the great pad marks of the elephant, where the bull's weight had compacted the earth and no twig would snap and no dead leaf would rustle to betray him.

Pirri had been following the elephant for three days. During all that time Pirri's entire being had been concentrated upon the elephant, so that in some mystic way he had become part of the beast he was hunting.

Where the bull had stopped to feast on the little red berries of the selepe tree, Pirri read the sign and could taste the tart acidic juice in his own throat. Where the elephant had drunk at one of the streams, Pirri stood upon the bank as he had done and felt in his imagination the sweet clear water squirt and gurgle into his own belly. Where the elephant had dropped a pile of yellow fibrous dung on the forest floor, Pirri felt his own bowels contract and his sphincter relax in sympathy. Pirri had become the elephant, and the elephant had become Pirri.

When he came up with him at last, the bull was asleep on his feet in a matted thicket. The branches were interwoven and covered with thorns that were hooked and tipped with red; they could flay a man's skin from his limbs. As softly and slowly as Pirri moved, yet the elephant sensed his presence and came awake. He spread his ears, one wide and full as a mainsail, the other torn and deformed, and he listened. However, he heard nothing, for Pirri was a master hunter.

The elephant stretched out his trunk, sucked up the air and blew it softly into his mouth. The olfactory glands in his top lip opened like pink rosebuds and he tasted the air, but he tasted nothing, for Pirri had come in below the tiny forest breeze and he had smeared himself from the top of his curly head to the pink soles of his feet with the elephant's own dung. There was no man-smell upon him.

Then the elephant made a sound, a gentle rumbling sound in his belly and a fluttering sound in his throat. It was the elephant song. The bull sang in the forest to learn if it was another elephant or a deadly enemy whose presence he sensed.

Pirri crouched at the edge of the thicket and listened to the elephant sing. Then he cupped his hand over his mouth and his nose and he gulped air into his throat and his belly and he let it out with a soft rumbling and fluttering sound.

Pirri sang the song of the elephant.

The bull sighed in his throat and changed his song, testing the unseen presence. Faithfully Pirri replied to him, following the cadence and the timbre of the song, and the elephant bull believed him.

The elephant flapped his ears, a gesture of contentment and trust. He accepted that another elephant had found him and come to join him. He moved carelessly and the thicket crackled before his bulk. He came ambling forward to meet Pirri, pushing the thorny branches aside.

Pirri saw the curved shafts of ivory appear high above his head. They were thicker than his waist and longer than he could reach with his elephant spear.

The elephant spear was a weapon that Pirri had forged himself from the blade of a truck spring that he had stolen from one of the *dukas* at the roadside. He had heated and beaten it until the steel had lost its temper and he was able to work it more easily. Then Pirri had shaped and sharpened it, and fitted it to a shaft of hard resilient wood and bound the blade in place with rawhide. When the rawhide dried it was hard and tight as the steel it held.

As the elephant's head loomed above him, Pirri sank down and lay like a log or a pile of dead leaves on the forest floor. The elephant was so close that he could make out clearly every furrow and wrinkle in the thick grey hide. Looking up he could see the discharge from the glands in the elephant's head running like tears down his cheeks, and Pirri gathered himself.

Even with the spear he had made, which was sharp and heavy and almost twice as long as Pirri was tall, he could never drive the point through the hide and meat and the cage of ribs to pierce the bull's heart or his lungs. The brain in its bony casket was far beyond his reach. There was only one way that a man of Pirri's size could kill an enormous beast like this with a spear.

Pirri rolled to his feet and bounded up under the elephant's belly. He stood between the bull's back legs and he braced himself and drove the point of the spear upwards into the angle of his groin.

The elephant squealed as the blade sliced through the baggy skin that hung around his crotch and lanced up into the sac of his bladder. The razor steel split his bladder open and the hot urine sprayed out in a yellow jet. He convulsed with agony, hunching his back, before he began to run.

The elephant ran screaming through the forest, and the foliage crashed and broke before him.

Pirri leaned on his bloody spear and listened to the elephant run out of earshot. He waited until the silence was complete and then he girded up his loincloth and began to follow the dribbled trail of blood and urine that steamed and reeked on the forest floor.

It might take many hours to die, but the elephant was doomed. Pirri, the hunter, had struck a mortal blow and he knew that before tomorrow's sunset the elephant would be dead.

Pirri followed him slowly, but he did not feel the fierce hunter's joy in his heart. There was only a sense of emptiness and the terrible guilt of sacrilege.

He had offended his god, and he knew that now his god must reject and punish him.

 Pirri the hunter found the carcass of the elephant bull the next morning. The elephant was kneeling, with his legs folded up neatly beneath him. His head was supported by the massive curves of ivory that were half buried in the soft earth. The last rainstorm had washed his hide so that it was black and shiny and his eyes were open.

He appeared so lifelike that Pirri approached him with great

467

caution and at last reached out with a long thin twig to touch the open staring eye fringed with thick lashes. The eyelid did not blink to the touch and Pirri noticed the opaque jelly-like sheen of death over the pupil. He straightened up and laid aside his spear. The hunt was over.

By custom he should now sing a prayer of thanks to the forest god for such largesse. He actually uttered the first words of the prayer before he broke off guiltily. He knew that he could never sing the hunter's prayer again, and a profound sadness filled his being.

He made a small fire and cut the rich fatty meat out of the elephant's cheek and cooked it on a skewer over the coals. For once this choice morsel was tough and tasteless in his mouth. He spat it into the fire and sat for a long time beside the carcass before he could rouse himself and shrug off the sense of sorrow that weighed him down.

He drew his machete from its sheath and began to chop one of the thick yellow tusks from its bony canal in the elephant's skull. The steel rang on the skull and the bone chips flew and fell about his feet as he worked.

That was how the men of his clan found him. They were drawn to Pirri by the sound of his machete hacking through bone. They came out of the forest silently, led by Sepoo and Pamba, and they formed a circle around Pirri and the elephant.

He looked up and saw them, and he let the machete fall to his side, and he stood with blood on his hands, not daring to meet their eyes.

'I will share the reward with you, my brothers,' he whispered, but nobody answered him.

One at a time the Bambuti turned from him and disappeared back into the forest as silently as they had come, until only Sepoo remained.

'Because of what you have done the forest god will send the Molimo to us,' said Sepoo, and Pirri stood with despair in his heart and could not raise his head to meet his brother's eyes.

Daniel began a review of the videotapes as soon as they reached Gondala.

Kelly set aside a corner of her laboratory for him to work in and Victor Omeru hovered over him, making comments and suggestions as he compiled his editing notes.

The quality of the material he had gathered was good. As a cameraman he rated himself as competent but lacking the artistry and brilliance of somebody like Bonny Mahon. What he compiled was an honest sober record of the mining and logging operation in the Wengu forest reserve, and of some of the consequences.

'It has no human warmth to it,' he told Victor and Kelly at dinner that evening. 'It appeals to reason, not to the heart. I need something more.'

'What is it you want?' Kelly asked. 'Tell me what it is and I'll get it for you.'

'I want more of President Omeru,' Daniel said. 'You have presence and style, sir. I want much more of you.'

'You shall have me.' Victor Omeru nodded. 'But don't you think it is time we dispensed with the formalities, Daniel? After all, we have climbed the sacred honey tree together. Surely that entitles us to use each other's Christian names?'

'I'm sure it does, Victor,' Daniel agreed. 'But even you won't be enough to convince the world. I have to show them what is happening to human beings. I have to show them the camps where the Uhali forced labour units are housed. Can we arrange that?'

Victor leaned forward. 'Yes,' he said. 'You know that I am the leader of the resistance movement to Taffari's tyranny. We are growing stronger every day. At present it is all very much underground, but we are organising ourselves and recruiting all the most important and influential people who reject Taffari. Of course, we are mostly Uhali, but even some of Taffari's own Hita people are becoming disenchanted with his regime. We will be able to get you to see the labour camps. Of course, you won't be able to get into the camps, but we should be able to get you close enough to film some of the daily atrocities which are being perpetrated.'

'Yes,' Kelly asserted. 'Patrick and the other young resistance leaders will be arriving here within the next few days for a conference with Victor. He will be able to arrange it.' She broke off and thought for a moment. 'Then there are the Bambuti. You can show your audience how the destruction of the forest will affect the pygmies and destroy their traditional way of life.'

'That's exactly the type of material I still need,' Daniel replied. 'What do you suggest?'

'The Molimo ceremony,' Kelly said. 'Sepoo tells me that the Molimo is coming and he has agreed that you may witness it.'

 Patrick, Victor Omeru's nephew, arrived at Gondala a day earlier than was expected. He was accompanied by a retinue of a dozen or so Uhali tribesmen. The pygmies had guided them through the forest. Many of the delegation were also relatives of Victor Omeru, all of them educated and committed young men.

When Daniel showed them the tapes he had already filmed and described the material he still required, Patrick Omeru and his men were enthusiastic.

'Leave it to me, Doctor Armstrong,' Patrick told him. 'I'll arrange it for you. Of course, there will be some danger involved. The camps are well protected by the Hita, but we'll get you as close as is humanly possible.'

When Patrick and his men left Gondala, Daniel and Sepoo went with them.

The two of them returned to Gondala nine days later. Daniel was thin and gaunt. It was obvious that they had travelled hard and unremittingly. His clothing was mud-stained and tattered and Kelly saw at once that he was near the point of exhaustion as he stumbled up on the verandah of the bungalow.

Without thinking she ran to greet him and the next moment they were in each other's arms. It startled both of them. They clung to each other for a moment, but when Daniel turned his mouth down towards hers, Kelly broke away and shook his hand instead.

'Victor and I were so worried,' she blurted, but she was blushing a deep rose colour that Daniel found enchanting, and she released his hand quickly.

That afternoon, after Daniel had bathed and eaten and slept for two hours, he showed them the new material. There were sequences of the forced labour gangs working along the logging roads. They had obviously been filmed from a distance with a telephoto lens.

The Hita guards stood over the gangs with clubs in their hands, and they struck out seemingly at random at the half-naked men and women toiling in the mud and slush below them.

'I've got much too much of this,' Daniel explained, 'but I'll edit it down, and keep only the most striking sequences.'

There were sequences of the gangs being marched in slow exhausted columns back to the camps at the end of the day's work, and other shots, taken through wire, of their primitive living conditions.

Then there were a series of interviews, shot in the forest, with prisoners who had escaped from the camps. One of the men stripped naked in front of the camera and displayed the injuries that the guards had inflicted upon him. His back was cut to ribbons by the lash, and his skull was criss-crossed with scars and half-healed cuts where the clubs had fallen.

A young woman showed her feet. The flesh was rotting and falling away from the bone. She spoke in soft Swahili, describing the conditions in the camp. 'We work all day in the mud – our feet are never dry. The cuts and scratches on them fester like this, until we cannot walk. We cannot work.' She began to weep softly.

Daniel was sitting beside her on the log. He looked up at the camera which he had previously set up on a tripod. 'This is what the soldiers in the trenches of France during World War One called "trench foot". It's a contagious fungoidal infection that will cripple the sufferer, will literally rot his feet off if it is not treated.' Daniel turned back to the weeping woman and asked gently in Swahili, 'What happens when you can no longer work?'

'The Hita say that they will not feed us, that we eat too

471

much food and are no longer of any use. They take the sick people into the forest . . .'

Daniel switched off the VTR and turned to Kelly and Victor. 'What you are about to see are the most shocking sequences I have ever filmed. They're similar to the scenes of the Nazi death squads in Poland and Russia. Some of the quality might be rather poor. We were filming from hiding. It's horrible stuff. You might prefer not to watch it, Kelly?'

Kelly shook her head. 'I'll watch it,' she said firmly.

'Okay, but I warned you.' Daniel switched on the VTR and they leaned forward towards the tiny screen as it flickered and came alive again.

They were looking into a clearing in the forest. One of the UDC bulldozers was gouging a trench in the soft earth. The trench was forty or fifty yards long and at least ten feet deep, judging by the way the bulldozer almost disappeared into it.

'Patrick was able to find out from his spies where they were doing this,' Daniel explained. 'So we could get into position the night before.'

The bulldozer completed the excavation and trundled up out of the trench. It parked nearby. The shot was cut off.

'This next sequence is about three hours later,' Daniel told them.

The head of a column of prisoners appeared out of the forest, chivvied on by the Hita guards on the flanks. It was apparent that all the prisoners were sick or crippled. They staggered or limped slowly into sight. Some were supporting each other with arms around the shoulders, others were using crude crutches. A few were carried on litters by their companions. One or two of the women had infants strapped on their backs. The guards marched them down into the trench and they disappeared from sight.

The guards formed up in a line on top of the excavation. There were at least fifty of them in paratrooper overalls with sub-machine-guns carried on the hip. Quite casually they began firing down into the trench. The fusillade went on for a long time. As each paratrooper emptied his Uzi machine-gun, he reloaded it with a fresh magazine and recommenced firing. Some of the men were laughing.

Suddenly one of the prisoners crawled up over the bank of the pit. It was almost unthinkable that he could have survived this long. One of his legs was half shot away. He dragged himself along on his elbows. A Hita officer unholstered his pistol and stood over him and shot him in the back of his head. The man collapsed on his face and the officer put his boot against his ribs and shoved him over the lip of the trench.

One at a time the soldiers stopped shooting. Some of them lit cigarettes and stood in groups along the edge of the grave, smoking and laughing and chatting.

The driver of the bulldozer climbed back on to his machine and eased it forward. He lowered the blade and pushed the piles of loose earth back into the trench. When the excavation was refilled he drove the bulldozer back and forth over it to compact the earth.

The soldiers formed up into a column and marched away along the track they had come. They were out of step and slovenly, chatting and smoking as they went.

Daniel switched off the VTR and the screen went blank. Kelly stood up without a word and went out on to the verandah of the bungalow. The two men sat in silence until Victor Omeru said quietly, 'Help us please, Daniel. Help my poor people.'

The word went through the forest that the Molimo was coming, and the clans began to gather at the tribal meeting place below the waterfall at Gondala.

Some of the clans came from two hundred miles away, across the Zaïre border, for the Bambuti recognised no territorial boundaries but their own. From every clan area and from every remote corner of the forest they came, until there were over a thousand of the little people gathered together for the terrible Molimo visitation.

Each woman built her leafy hut with the doorway facing the doorway of a particular friend or a close and beloved relative, and they gathered in laughing groups throughout the encampment, for not even the threat of the Molimo could quench their high spirits or dull their cheerful nature.

The men met old cronies and hunting companions that they had not seen since the last communal net hunt, and they shared tobacco and tall stories, and gossiped with as much relish as the women at the cooking-fires. The children squealed and ran unchecked amongst the huts, tumbling over each other like puppies, and they swam in the pool below the waterfall like sleek otter cubs.

One of the last to arrive at the meeting place was Pirri the hunter. His three wives staggered under the heavy sacks of tobacco they carried.

Pirri ordered his wives to build his hut with the doorway facing the doorway of his brother Sepoo. However, when the hut was finished, Pamba closed in the doorway of Sepoo's hut and built another opening facing in the opposite direction. In Bambuti custom this was a terrible snub, and it set the women at the cooking-fires chattering like parrots at roosting time.

Pirri called to old friends, 'See how much tobacco I have. It is yours to share. Come, fill your pouches. Pirri invites you, take as much as you wish. See here! Pirri has bottles of gin. Come drink with Pirri.' But not a man of all the Bambuti took advantage of the offer.

In the evening, when a group of the most famous hunters and story-tellers of the tribe were gathered around a single fire with Sepoo in their midst, Pirri came swaggering out of the darkness with a bottle of gin in each hand and elbowed a place for himself at the fire. He drank from the open gin bottle and then passed it to the man on his left. 'Drink!' he ordered. 'Pass it on, so that all may share Pirri's good fortune.'

The man placed the untouched bottle on one side and stood up and walked away from the fire. One after the other, the men stood up and followed him into the darkness until only Sepoo and Pirri were left.

'Tomorrow the Molimo comes,' Sepoo warned his brother softly, and then he also stood up and walked away.

Pirri the hunter was left with his gin and his bulging tobacco pouch, sitting alone in the night.

Sepoo came to the laboratory to call Daniel the following morning, and Daniel followed him into the forest, carrying the camera on his shoulder. They went swiftly, for Daniel had by now learned all the tricks of forest travel, and even his superior height and size were no great handicap. He could keep up with Sepoo.

They started off alone, but as they went others joined them, slipping silently out of the forest, or appearing like dark sprites ahead or behind them, until at last there was a multitude of Bambuti hurrying towards the place of the Molimo.

When they arrived there were already many others before them, squatting silently around the base of a huge silk-cotton tree in the depths of the forest. For once there was no laughter nor skylarking. The men were all grave and silent.

Daniel squatted with them and filmed their sombre faces. All of them were looking up into the silk-cotton tree.

'This is the home of the Molimo,' Sepoo whispered softly. 'We have come to fetch him.'

Somebody in the ranks called out a name. 'Grivi!' And a man stood up and moved to the base of the tree.

From another direction another name was called. 'Sepoo!' And Sepoo went to stand with the first man chosen.

Soon there were fifteen men at the base of the tree. Some were old and famous, some were mere striplings. Young or old, callow or proven, all men had equal right to take part in the ceremony of the Molimo.

Suddenly Sepoo let out a shout and the chosen band swarmed excitedly up into the tree. They disappeared into the high foliage and for a time there was only the sound of their singing and shouting. Then down they came again, bearing a length of bamboo.

They laid it on the ground at the foot of the tree and Daniel went forward to examine it. The bamboo was not more than fifteen feet long. It was cured and dried out, and must have been cut many years before. There were stylised symbols and crude animal caricatures scratched on it, but otherwise it was simply a length of bamboo.

'Is this the Molimo?' Daniel whispered to Sepoo while the men of the tribe gathered around it reverently.

'Yes, Kuokoa, this is the Molimo,' Sepoo affirmed.

'What is the Molimo?' Daniel persisted.

'The Molimo is the voice of the forest,' Sepoo tried to explain. 'It is the voice of the Mother and the Father. But before it can speak, it must be taken to drink.'

The chosen band took up the Molimo and carried it to the stream and submerged it in a cool dark pool. The banks of the pool were lined with ranks of little men, solemn and attentive, naked and bright-eyed. They waited for an hour and then another while the Molimo drank the sweet water of the forest stream, and then they brought the Molimo to the bank.

It was shining and dripping with water. Sepoo went to the bamboo tube and placed his lips over the open end. His chest inflated as he drew breath and the Molimo spoke from the tube. It was the startlingly clear sweet voice of a young girl singing in the forest, and all the men of the Bambuti shuddered and swayed like the top leaves of a tall tree hit by a sudden wind.

Then the Molimo changed its voice, and cried like a duiker caught in the hunter's net. It chattered like the grey parrot in flight and whistled like the honey chameleon. It was all the voices and sounds of the forest. Another man replaced Sepoo at the tube, and then another. There were voices of men and ghosts and other creatures that all men had heard of but none had ever seen.

Then suddenly the Molimo screamed like an elephant. It was a terrible angry sound and the men of the Bambuti swarmed forward, clustering around the Molimo in a struggling heaving horde. The simple bamboo tube disappeared in their midst, but still it squealed and roared, cooed and whistled and cackled with a hundred different voices.

Now a strange and magical thing took place. As Daniel watched, the struggling knot of men changed. They were no longer individuals, for they were pressed too closely together. In the same way that a shoal of fish or a flock of birds is one beast, so the men of the Bambuti blended into an entity. They became one creature. They became the Molimo. They became the godhead of the forest.

The Molimo was angry. It roared and squealed with the

voice of the buffalo and the giant forest hog. It raged through the forest on a hundred legs that were no longer human. It revolved on its axis like a jellyfish in the current. It pulsed and changed shape, and dashed one way and then the other, flattening the undergrowth in its fury.

It crossed the river, kicking up a white foam of spray, and then slowly but with awakening purpose began to move towards the gathering place of the tribe below the waterfall at Gondala.

The women heard the Molimo coming from a long way off. They left the cooking-fires and seized the children and ran to their huts, dragging the little ones with them. Wailing with terror, they closed the doors of the huts and crouched in the darkness with the children clutched to their breasts.

The Molimo rampaged through the forest, its terrible voice rising and falling, crashing through the undergrowth, charging one way and then the other, until at last it broke into the encampment. It trampled the cooking-fires and the children screamed as some of the flimsy huts were knocked askew by its ungoverned anger.

The great beast raged back and forth through the camp, seeming to quest for the source of its outrage. Suddenly it revolved and moved purposefully towards the far corner of the camp where Pirri had built his hut.

Pirri's wives heard it coming and they burst from the hut and fled into the jungle, but Pirri did not run. He had not gone to the silk-cotton tree with the other men to fetch the Molimo down from its home. Now he crouched in his hut, with his hands over his head and waited. He knew there was no escape in flight, he had to wait for the retribution of the forest god.

The Molimo circled Pirri's hut like one of the giant forest millipedes, its feet stamping and kicking up the earth, screaming like a bull elephant in the agony of a ruptured bladder.

Then abruptly it charged at the hut in which Pirri was hiding. It flattened the hut, and trampled all Pirri's possessions. It stamped his tobacco to dust. It shattered his bottles of gin and the pungent liquor soaked into the earth. It kicked the gold wristwatch into the fire and scattered all his treasures. Pirri made no attempt to fly its wrath or to protect himself.

The Molimo trampled him; squealing with rage it kicked and

pummelled him. It crushed his nose and broke his teeth; it cracked his ribs and bruised his limbs.

Then suddenly, it left him and rushed back into the forest from whence it had come. Its voice had changed, the rage was gone out of it. It wailed and lamented as though it mourned the death and the poisoning of the forest and the sins of the tribe that had brought disaster upon them all. Slowly it retreated and its voice became fainter, until at last it faded into the distance.

Pirri picked himself up slowly. He made no effort to gather up his scattered treasures. He took only his bow and his quiver of arrows. He left his elephant spear and his machete. He limped away into the forest.

He went alone. His wives did not go with him, for they were widows now. They would find new husbands in the tribe. Pirri was dead. The Molimo had killed him. No man would ever see him again. Even when they met his ghost wandering amongst the tall trees, no man or woman would acknowledge it.

Pirri was dead to his tribe for ever.

'Will you help us, Daniel?' Victor Omeru asked.

'Yes,' Daniel agreed. 'I will help you. I will take the tapes to London. I will arrange to have them shown on public television in London and Paris and New York.'

'What else will you do to help us?' Victor asked.

'What else do you want of me?' Daniel countered. 'What else is there I can do?'

'You are a soldier, and a good one, from what I have heard. Will you join us in our fight to regain our freedom?'

'I was a soldier, long ago,' Daniel corrected him, 'in a cruel unjust war. I learned to hate war in a way that no one can until they have experienced it.'

'Daniel, I am asking you to take part in a just war. This time I am asking you to make a stand against tyranny.'

'I am no longer a soldier. I am a journalist, Victor. It is not my war.'

'You are a soldier still,' Victor contradicted him. 'And it is your war. It is the war of any decent man.'

Daniel did not reply immediately. He glanced sideways at Kelly, on the point of asking for her support. Then he saw her expression. There was no comfort for him there. He looked back at Victor, and the old man leaned closer to him.

'We Uhali are a peaceful people. For that reason we, alone, do not have the skill necessary to overthrow the tyrant. We need weapons. We need people to teach us how to use them. Help me, please, Daniel. I will find all the young brave men you need, if only you will promise to train and command them.'

'I don't want—' Daniel began, but Victor forestalled him.

'Don't refuse me outright. Don't say anything more tonight. Sleep on it. Give me your answer in the morning. Think about it, Daniel. Dream of the men and women you saw in the camps. Dream of the people you saw killed or deported at Fish Eagle Bay, and the mass grave in the forest. Give me your answer in the morning.'

Victor Omeru stood up. He paused beside Daniel's chair and placed his hand on his shoulder.

'Good night, Daniel,' he said, and went down the steps and crossed in the moonlight to his own small bungalow beyond the gardens.

'What are you going to do?' Kelly asked softly.

'I don't know. I really don't know.' Daniel stood up. 'I'll tell you tomorrow. But right now, I'll do what Victor suggested, I'm going to bed.'

'Yes.' Kelly stood up beside him.

'Good night,' he said.

She was standing very close to him, her face tilted up towards him.

He kissed her. The kiss held for a long time.

She drew back only a few inches from his mouth and said, 'Come.' And led him down the verandah to her bedroom.

It was still dark when he woke the next morning under the mosquito net with her.

Her arm was thrown over his chest. Her breath was warm on his neck. He felt her come softly awake.

'I'm going to do what Victor wants,' he said.

She stopped breathing for a few moments then she said, 'It wasn't meant as a bribe.'

'I know,' he said.

'What happened between us last night is a thing apart,' she said. 'I wanted it to happen from the first day I met you – no, from before that. From the first time I saw your images on the screen, I was half in love with you.'

'I've also been waiting for you a long time, Kelly. I knew you were out there somewhere. At last I've found you.'

'I hate to lose you so soon,' she said, and kissed him. 'Please come back to me.'

Daniel left Gondala two days later. Sepoo and four Bambuti porters accompanied him.

He paused at the edge of the forest and looked back. Kelly was on the verandah of the bungalow. She waved. She looked very young and girlish, and he felt his heart squeezed. He did not want to go – not yet, not so soon after he had found her. He waved and forced himself to turn from her.

As they climbed the lower slopes of the mountain the forest gave way to bamboo, which was so dense that in places they were forced to their hands and knees to crawl through the tunnels which the giant hog had burrowed. The bamboo was solid overhead.

They climbed higher and came out at last on to the bleak heath slopes of the high mountains, twelve thousand feet above sea level, where the giant groundsel stood like battalions of armoured warriors, their heads spiked with red flowers.

The Bambuti huddled in the blankets that Kelly had provided, but they were miserable and sickening, totally out of their element. Before they reached the highest pass, Daniel sent them back.

Sepoo wanted to argue. 'Kuokoa, you will lose your way on the mountains without Sepoo to guide you and Kara-Ki will be angry. You have never seen her truly angry. It is not a sight for any but the brave.'

'Look up there.' Daniel pointed ahead to where the peaks showed through the cloud. 'There is cold up there that no Bambuti has ever experienced. That shining white is ice and snow so cold that it will burn you like fire.'

So Daniel went on alone, carrying the precious tapes inside his jacket close to his skin, and he crossed below the moraine of the Ruwatamagufa glacier and came down into Zaïre two days after leaving Sepoo. He had frostbite on three of his fingers and one of his toes.

The Zaïrean district commissioner at Mutsora was accustomed to refugees coming across the mountains, but seldom with white faces and British passports and fifty-dollar bills to dispense. He did not turn this one back.

Two days later, Daniel was on the steamer going down the Zaïre River and ten days after that he landed at Heathrow. The tapes were still in his pocket.

 From his Chelsea flat Daniel telephoned Michael Hargreave at the embassy in Kahali.

'Good Lord, Danny. We were told that you and Bonny Mahon disappeared in the forest near Sengi-Sengi. The army has had patrols out searching for you.'

'How secure is this line, Mike?'

'I wouldn't stake my reputation on it.'

'Then I'll give you the full story when next we meet. In the meantime, will you send me that packet I gave you for safe-keeping? Get it to me in the next diplomatic bag?'

'Hold on, Danny. I gave the package to Bonny Mahon. She told me that she was collecting it on your behalf.'

Daniel was silent for a beat as he worked it out. 'The little idiot. She played right into their hands. Well, that settles it. She's dead, Mike, as sure as fate. She handed over the package and they killed her. They thought I was dead, so they killed her. Nice and neat.'

'Who are "they"?' Michael demanded.

'Not now, Mike. I can't tell you now.'

'Sorry about the package, Danny. She was very convincing. But I shouldn't have fallen for it. Must be getting senile.'

'No great harm done. I have some stronger medicine to replace it.'

'When will I see you?'

'Soon, I hope. I'll let you know.'

Despite the short notice, the studio gave him a cutting-room to work in. He worked without a break – it helped to allay his sadness and guilt at what had happened to Bonny Mahon. He felt responsible. The final cut of the videotape did not have to be perfect, and it was not necessary to dub the Swahili dialogue into English. He had a copy ready to show within forty-eight hours.

It was impossible to get through to Tug Harrison. All Daniel's calls were intercepted on the BOSS switchboard and were not returned. Of course, the number of the Holland Park address was not listed, and he could not remember the number that he had telephoned from Nairobi to check on Bonny Mahon. So he staked out the house, leaning against a car with a newspaper as though he were waiting for someone, and watching the front of the building.

He was fortunate. Tug's Rolls-Royce pulled up at the front door that same day a little after noon, and Daniel intercepted him as he climbed the front steps.

'Armstrong – Danny!' Tug's surprise was genuine. 'I heard that you had disappeared in Ubomo.'

'Not true, Tug. Didn't you get my messages? I telephoned your office half a dozen times.'

'They don't pass them on to me. Too many freaks and funny bunnies in this world.'

'I must show you some of the material I have been able to shoot in Ubomo,' Daniel told him.

Tug hesitated and consulted his wristwatch dubiously.

'Don't mess me around, Tug. This stuff could sink you. And BOSS.'

Tug's eyes narrowed. 'That sounds like a threat.'

'Just a friendly piece of advice.'

'All right, come in,' Tug invited, and opened the front door. 'Let's have a look at what you have for me.'

Tug Harrison sat behind his desk and watched the tape run through from beginning to end without moving, without uttering a word. When the tape was finished and the screen filled with an electronic snowstorm, he pressed the remote control

482

button, ran the tape back and then played it a second time, still without comment.

Then he switched off the tape and spoke without looking at Daniel. 'It's genuine,' he said. 'You couldn't have faked it.'

'You know it's genuine,' Daniel told him. 'You knew about the mining and logging. It's your bloody syndicate. You gave the orders.'

'I meant the labour camps, and the use of arsenic. I knew nothing about that.'

'Who is going to believe that, Tug?'

Tug shrugged and said, 'So Omeru is still alive.'

'Yes. He is alive and ready to give evidence against you.'

Tug changed the subject again. 'Of course, there are other copies of this tape?' he said.

'Silly question,' Daniel agreed.

'So this is a direct threat?'

'Another silly question,' Daniel said again.

'You are going to go public with this?'

'That's three in a row,' Daniel said grimly. 'Of course, I'm going public. Only one thing will stop me. That is if you and I can make a deal.'

'What deal are you offering?' Tug asked softly.

'I will give you time to get out. I will give you time to sell out your interest in Ubomo to Lucky Dragon or anyone else who will buy.'

Tug did not answer immediately but Daniel saw the faintest gleam of relief in his gaze.

Tug drew a breath. 'In return?'

'You will finance Victor Omeru's counter-revolution against Taffari's regime. After all, it won't be the first *coup* in Africa that you have orchestrated, Tug, will it?'

'How much will this cost me?' Tug asked.

'Only a small fraction of what you would lose if I were to release the tape before you have a chance to pull out. I could get a copy around to the Foreign Office and another to the American ambassador within thirty minutes. It could be on BBC 1 at six o'clock . . .'

'How much?' Tug insisted.

'Five million in cash, paid into a Swiss account immediately.'

'With you as the signatory?'

'And Omeru as a counter-signatory.'

'What else?'

'You will intercede with the president of Zaïre. He is a friend of yours, but no friend of Taffari's. We want him to allow clandestine passage of arms and munitions across his border with Ubomo. All he has to do is turn a blind eye.'

'Is that all?'

'That's the lot.' Daniel nodded.

'All right. I agree,' Tug said. 'Give me the account number and I'll deposit the money before noon tomorrow.'

Daniel stood up. 'Cheer up. All is not lost, Tug,' he advised. 'Victor Omeru will be very kindly disposed towards you once he is reinstated in his rightful position. I am sure he will be prepared to renegotiate the contract with you – with the proper safeguards in place this time.'

After Daniel had left, Tug Harrison sat staring at his Picasso for fully five minutes.

Then he glanced at his watch. There was a nine-hour time difference in Taipei. He picked up the telephone and dialled the international code, followed by Ning Heng H'Sui's private number. The old man's eldest son, Fang, screened the call, and then passed him on to his father.

'I have a very interesting proposition for you,' Tug told the old man. 'I want to fly out to speak to you face to face. I can be in Taipei within twenty-four hours – will you be there?'

He made two other phone calls. One to his chief pilot's home number to warn him to get the Gulfstream ready, and the second to the Crédit Suisse Bank in Zurich.

'Mr Mulder, I will be making a large transfer from the number two account within the next twenty-four hours. Five million sterling. Make certain there is no delay once you receive the code card instruction.'

Then he hung up the telephone and stared at the painting again without seeing it. He had to decide what reason he would give Ning for wanting to sell his share in UDC. Should he say that he was in a cash bind? Or that he needed to be liquid for a new acquisition? Which would Ning fall for more readily?

What was his price? He mustn't set it too low, for that

would arouse the cunning old oriental's suspicions immediately. Not too high either. Low enough to excite his greed, high enough not to alarm him. It was a nice calculation. He would have the duration of the flight to Taipei to consider it.

'That young fool Cheng has dropped me in it. It's only right that his father be made to pay.'

He thought about Ning Cheng Gong. He has been too good a choice, Tug smiled bitterly. He had asked for a ruthless one, and got more than he bid for.

Of course, Tug had known about the forced labour, but not the details of their treatment. He had not wanted to know. Neither had he known for certain about the use of the arsenic reagents, though he had suspected that Cheng was using them. The platinum recovery figures had been too high, the profits too good, for it not to be so. He had not wanted to know any of the unpleasant details. But, he thought philosophically, the enhanced profitability of the mining venture would make it easier to sell out his interests to Lucky Dragon.

Ning Heng H'Sui would think he was getting the bargain of his life.

'Good luck, Lucky Dragon,' Tug grunted. 'You're going to need all of it.'

Three months to the day since his last crossing Daniel stood on the moraine below the Ruwatamagufa glacier. This time he was properly equipped for the alpine conditions; there would be no more frostbite. And this time he was not alone.

The line of porters, each man bowed forward against the headband of his pack, stretched back as far as Daniel could see into the mountain mist. They were all men of the Konjo tribe, dour mountaineers who could carry heavy loads at these high altitudes. There were six hundred and fifty porters, and each man carried an eighty-pound pack.

In all, that made twenty-six tons of arms and ammunition. There were no sophisticated weapons in the loads, only the tried and true tools of the guerrilla and the terrorist, the ubiquitous AK 47 and the Uzi, the RPD light machine-gun and the RPG rocket-launcher, Tokarev automatic pistols and American M26 fragmentation grenades, or at least convincing copies of them made in Yugoslavia or Romania.

All of these were readily obtainable at short notice in any quantity required, as long as the buyer had cash. Daniel was amazed how easy it had been. Tug Harrison had supplied him with the names and telephone numbers of five dealers, one in Florida, two in Europe and two in the Middle East.

'Take your pick,' Tug had invited. 'But check what you're getting before you pay. Some of that stuff has been floating around for forty years.' Daniel and his instructors had personally opened every case and laboriously checked each piece.

Daniel had calculated that the very minimum number of instructors he needed was four. He went back to Zimbabwe to find them. They were all men he had fought with or against during the bush war. They were all Swahili speakers and they were all black. A white face attracted a lot of attention in Ubomo.

The leader of the group of four was an ex-sergeant-major in the Ballantyne Scouts, a man who had fought with men like Roland Ballantyne and Sean Courtney. He was a magnificent figure of a Matabele warrior called Morgan Tembi.

There was another recruit in the party, a cameraman to replace Bonny Mahon. Shadrach Mbeki was a black South African exile who had done good work for the BBC, the best man that Daniel could find at such short notice.

To the north Mount Stanley was hidden in clouds, and the cloud dropped down to form a grey cold ceiling only a hundred feet above their heads, but to the east below the cloud it was open. Daniel gazed down upon the forest almost ten thousand feet below. It looked like the ocean, green and endless, except to the north where a dark cancer had bitten into the green. The open mined area was deeper and wider than when Daniel had last seen it from this vantage point only a few short months ago.

The cloud and the mist dropped over them abruptly, blotting out the distant carnage, and Daniel roused himself and started down, the long column of porters unwinding behind him. Sepoo was waiting for him where the bamboo forest began at the ten thousand foot level.

'It is good to see you again, Kuokoa, my brother. Kara-Ki sends you her heart,' he told Daniel. 'She asks that you come to her swiftly. She says she can wait no longer.'

The men of Sepoo's clan had cut out the trail through the bamboo, widening it so that the porters could pass through without having to stoop.

Below the bamboo where the true rain forest began at the six thousand foot level, Patrick Omeru was waiting with his teams of Uhali recruits to take over from the Konjo mountaineers. Daniel paid off the Konjo and watched them climb back through the bamboo into their misty highlands. Then the Bambuti guided them on to the newly opened trail, back towards Gondala.

After Kelly's message Daniel could not restrain himself to the pace of the heavily laden convoy, and he and Sepoo hurried ahead. Kelly was on the trail coming to meet them, and they came upon each other suddenly around a bend in the forest path.

Kelly and Daniel came up short and stared at each other, neither of them seemed able to move or even to speak until Kelly said huskily, without taking her eyes from Daniel's face, 'Go on ahead, Sepoo. Far, far ahead!'

Sepoo giggled happily and went without looking back.

 During Daniel's absence, Victor Omeru had built his new headquarters in the edge of the forest beyond the waterfall at Gondala where it would be hidden from any possible aerial surveillance. It was a simple *baraza* with half walls and a thatched roof. He sat with Daniel on the raised dais at one end of the hut.

Daniel was meeting the resistance leaders, many of them for the first time. They were seated facing the dais on long split-pole benches, like students in a lecture theatre. There were thirty-eight of them, mostly Uhali tribesmen, but six were influential Hita who were disenchanted with Taffari and had thrown in their lot with Victor Omeru as soon as they heard that he was still alive. These Hita were vital to the plan of action that Daniel had devised and discussed with Victor.

Two of them were highly placed in the army and one was a senior police officer. The other three were government officials who would be able to arrange permits and licences for travel and transport. All of them would be able to supply vital intelligence.

At first there had been some natural objection to Daniel's new cameraman filming the proceedings, but Victor had interceded and now Shadrach Mbeki was working so unobtrusively that they soon forgot his presence. As a reward for his assistance Victor Omeru had agreed that Daniel could make a film record of the entire campaign.

Daniel opened the meeting by introducing his four Matabele military instructors. As each man rose and faced the audience, Daniel recited his curriculum vitae. They were all impressive men, but Morgan Tembi in particular they regarded with awe.

'Between them they have trained thousands of fighting men,' Daniel told them. 'They won't be interested in parade-ground drills or spit and polish. They will simply teach you to use the weapons we have brought over the mountains and to use them to the best possible effect.' He looked at Patrick Omeru in the front row. 'Patrick, can you come up here and tell us how many men you have at your disposal, and where they are at the present time?'

Patrick had been busy during Daniel's absence. He had recruited almost fifteen hundred young men.

'Well done, Patrick, that's more than we need,' Daniel told him. 'I was planning on a core of a thousand men – four units of two hundred and fifty, each under the command of one of the instructors. More than that will be difficult to conceal and deploy. However, we will be able to use the others in non-combatant roles.'

The staff conference went on for three days. At the last session Daniel addressed them again.

'Our plans are simple. That makes them good – there is less

to go wrong. Our whole strategy is based on two principles. Number one is that we have to move fast. We have to be in a position to strike within weeks rather than months. Number two is total surprise. Our security must be iron-clad. If Taffari gets even a whiff of our plans he'll crack down so hard that we'll have no chance of success whatsoever. There it is, gentlemen, speed and stealth. We will meet again here on the first of next month. By then President Omeru and I will have a detailed plan of action drawn up. Until then you will be taking orders from your instructors in the training-camps. Good luck to all of us.'

Pirri was confused and angry and filled with formless despair and hatred.

For months now he had lived alone in the forest with not another man to talk to, or woman to laugh with. At night he lay alone in his carelessly built leaf hut far from the huts of other men and he thought of his youngest wife. She was sixteen years of age, with plump little breasts. He remembered the wetness and lubricious warmth of her body, and he moaned aloud in the darkness as he thought that he would never again know the comfort of a woman's body.

During the day he was lethargic and without care. He no longer hunted with his old intensity. Sometimes he sat for hours gazing into one of the dark forest pools. Twice he heard the honey chameleon call and he did not follow. He grew thin and his beard began turning white. Once he heard a party of Bambuti women in the forest, laughing and chattering as they gathered mushrooms and roots. He crept close and spied upon them, and his heart felt as though it would break. He longed to join them, but knew he could not.

Then one day while wandering alone, Pirri cut the trail of a party of *wazungu*. He studied their tracks and read that there were twenty of them, and that they moved with purpose and determination as though on a journey. It was exceedingly strange to find other men in the forest, for the Hita and Uhali were afraid of hobgoblins and monsters, and never entered the tall trees if they could avoid doing so. Pirri recovered a little of his old curiosity, and he followed the tracks of the *wazungu*. They were moving well, and it took him many hours to catch up with them. Then he discovered a most remarkable thing.

Deep in the forest he found a camp where many men were assembled. They were all armed with the *banduki* that had a strange banana-shaped appendage hanging from beneath – either a tail or a penis, Pirri was not certain. And while Pirri watched in astonishment from his hiding-place, these men fired their *banduki* and made a terrible clattering clamour that frightened the birds into flight and sent the monkeys scampering away across the forest galleries.

All this was extraordinary, but most marvellous of all was that these men were not Hita. These days only Hita soldiers in uniform carried *banduki*. These men were Uhali.

Pirri thought about what he had seen for many days, and then the acquisitive instinct, which had been dormant in him since the coming of the Molimo, began to stir. He thought about Chetti Singh, and wondered if Chetti Singh would give him tobacco if he told him about the armed men in the forest. He hated Chetti Singh who had cheated and lied to him but as he thought about the tobacco, the saliva jetted from under his tongue. He could almost taste it in his mouth. The old tobacco hunger was like a pain in his chest and his belly.

The next day he went to find Chetti Singh and he whistled and sang as he went. He was coming alive again after the Molimo death. He stopped only once, to hunt a colobus monkey that he spied in the treetops eating the yellow fruit of the mongongo tree. His old skills came back to him and he crept to within twenty paces of the monkey without it suspecting his presence, and he shot a poisoned arrow that struck one of its legs.

The monkey fled shrieking through the branches, but it did not go far before it fell to earth, paralysed by the poison, its lips curled up in the dreadful rictus of agony as it frothed and trembled and shook before it died. The poison on Pirri's arrow was fresh and strong. He had found the nest of the little beetles only days before and had dug them up and crushed them to paste in a bark crucible and smeared his arrow-tips with the juices.

With his belly full of monkey meat and the wet skin folded into his bark-fibre bag, he went on towards the rendezvous with the one-armed Sikh.

Pirri waited two days at the rendezvous, the clearing in the forest that had once been a logging camp but was now overgrown and reverting to jungle. He wondered if the Uhali storekeeper who kept the little *duka* on the side of the main highway had passed on his message to Chetti Singh.

Then he began to believe that Chetti Singh had received the message but would not come to him. Perhaps Chetti Singh had learned of the Molimo death and was also ostracising him. Perhaps nobody would ever speak to Pirri again. His recent high spirits faded as he sat alone in the forest waiting for Chetti Singh to come, and the sense of despair and confusion overwhelmed him all over again.

Chetti Singh came on the afternoon of the second day. Pirri heard his Landrover long before it arrived and suddenly his anger and hatred had something on which to focus.

He thought how Chetti Singh had cheated and tricked him so many times before. He thought how he had never given him everything he had promised; always there was short-weight of tobacco, and water in the gin.

Then he thought how Chetti Singh had made him kill the elephant. Pirri had never been as angry as he was now. He was too angry even to lash out at the trees around him, too angry to shout aloud. His throat was tight and closed, and his hands shook. Chetti Singh was the one who had brought the curse of the Molimo down upon him. Chetti Singh had killed his soul.

Now he forgot about the armed *wazungu* in the forest. He even forgot about the tobacco hunger, as he waited for Chetti Singh to come.

The mud-streaked Landrover butted its way into the clearing, pushing down the thick secondary growth of vegetation ahead of it. It stopped and the door opened and Chetti Singh stepped down.

He looked around him at the forest and wiped his face with a white cloth. He had put on much weight recently. He was

491

plumper now than he had been before he had lost the arm. His shirt was stained dark with sweat between his shoulder-blades where he had sat against the leather seat.

He mopped his face and adjusted his turban before he shouted into the forest, 'Pirri! Come out!'

Pirri sniggered with laughter and whispered aloud, mimicking the Sikh. 'Pirri! Come out!' And then his voice was bitter, 'See how he oozes grease like a joint of pork on the coals. Pirri, come out!'

Chetti Singh strutted around the clearing impatiently. After a while he opened his fly and urinated, then he zipped his trousers and looked at his wristwatch.

'Pirri, are you there?'

Pirri did not answer him, and Chetti Singh said something angrily in a language that Pirri did not understand, but he knew that it was an insult.

'I am going now,' Chetti Singh shouted, and marched back to the Landrover.

'O master,' Pirri called to him. 'I see you! Do not go!'

Chetti Singh spun around to face the forest. 'Where are you?' he shouted.

'I am here, O master. I have something for you that will make you very happy. Something of great value.'

'What is it?' Chetti Singh asked. 'Where are you?'

'Here I am.' Pirri stepped out of the shadows with the bow slung over his shoulder.

'What stupidity is this?' Chetti Singh demanded. 'Why do you hide from me?'

'I am your slave.' Pirri grinned ingratiatingly. 'And I have a gift for you.'

'What is it? Elephant teeth?' Chetti Singh asked, and there was greed in his voice.

'Better than that. Something of greater value.'

'Show me,' Chetti Singh demanded.

'Will you give me tobacco?'

'I will give you as much tobacco as the gift is worth.'

'I will show you,' Pirri agreed. 'Follow me, O master.'

'Where is it? How far is it?'

'Only a short distance, only that far.' Pirri indicated a small arc of the sky with two fingers, less than an hour's travel.

Chetti Singh looked dubious.

'It is a thing of great beauty and value,' Pirri wheedled. 'You will be very pleased.'

'All right,' the Sikh agreed. 'Lead me to this treasure.'

Pirri went slowly, allowing Chetti Singh to keep close behind him. He went in a wide circle through the densest part of the forest, crossing the same stream twice. There was no sun in the forest; a man steered by the fall of the land and the run of the rivers.

Pirri showed Chetti Singh the same river twice from different directions. By now, the Sikh was totally lost, blundering blindly after the little pygmy with no sense of distance or direction.

After the second hour Chetti Singh was sweating very heavily and his voice was rough. 'How much further is it?' he asked.

'Very close,' Pirri assured him.

'I will rest for a while,' Chetti Singh said and sat down on a log. When he looked up again, Pirri had vanished.

Chetti Singh was not alarmed. He was accustomed to the elusive comings and goings of the Bambuti. 'Come back here!' he ordered, but there was no reply.

Chetti Singh sat alone for a long time. Once or twice he called out to the pygmy. Each time his voice was shriller. The panic was building up in him.

After another hour he was pleading. 'Please, Pirri, I will give you anything you ask. Please show yourself.'

Pirri laughed. His laughter floated through the trees and Chetti Singh sprang to his feet and plunged off the faint track. He stumbled towards where he thought he had heard the laughter.

'Pirri!' he begged. 'Please come to me.' But the laughter came from a new direction. Chetti Singh ran towards it.

After a while he stopped, and looked about him wildly. He was streaming sweat and panting. Laughter, mocking and faint, trembled in the humid air. Chetti Singh turned around and staggered after it. It was like chasing a butterfly or a puff of smoke. The sound flitted and flirted through the trees, first from one direction, then the other.

Chetti Singh was weeping now. His turban had come loose and hooked on a branch and he did not stop to retrieve it. His hair and beard tumbled down, streaming down his chest and flying out behind him. His hair was soaked with sweat.

He fell and dragged himself up and ran on, his clothing stained with mud and leaf mould. He screamed his terror to the trees, and the laughter became fainter and fainter, until at last he heard it no more.

Chetti Singh fell on his knees and held up his hand in supplication. 'Please,' he whispered, with tears streaming down his face. 'Please don't leave me alone here.'

And the forest was silent with dark menace.

Pirri followed him for two days, watching him stagger haphazardly, ranting and pleading, through the forest, watching him grow weaker and more desperate, stumbling over dead branches, falling into streams, crawling on his belly, shaking with terror and loneliness. His clothing was ripped off him by branch and thorn. Only a few rags still hung on his body. His skin was scratched and lacerated, and the flies and the stinging insects buzzed around the wounds. His beard and long hair were tangled and matted, and his eyes were wild and mad.

On the second day, Pirri stepped out of the forest ahead of him and Chetti Singh screamed like a woman with the shock and tried to drag himself to his feet again.

'Don't leave me alone again,' he screamed. 'Please, anything you ask, but not again.'

'Like you, I am alone,' Pirri said with hatred in his heart. 'I am dead. The Molimo has killed me. You are talking to a dead man, to a ghost. You cannot ask mercy from the ghost of a man you murdered.'

Deliberately Pirri fitted an arrow to his little bow. The poison was black and sticky on the point.

Chetti Singh gaped stupidly. 'What are you doing?' he blurted. He knew about the poison, he had seen animals die from Bambuti arrows.

Pirri lifted his bow and drew the arrow to his chin.

'No!' Chetti Singh held up his hand to ward off the arrow just as Pirri released it.

The arrow, aimed at his chest, hit Chetti Singh in the palm of his open hand and stuck firmly, its point buried between the bones of the first and second fingers.

494

Chetti Singh stared at it.

'Now we are both dead,' said Pirri softly, and vanished into the forest.

Chetti Singh stared in horror at the arrow in his palm. The flesh around it was already stained purple by the poison. Then the pain began. It was stronger than anything that Chetti Singh had ever imagined. It was fire in his blood, he could feel it running up his arm into his chest. The pain was so terrible that for a long anguished moment it took his breath away and he could not scream.

Then he found his voice and the sound of his agony rang through the trees. Pirri paused for a while to listen to it. Only when the forest was silent again did he move on.

'We are ready,' Daniel said quietly, but his voice carried to every man seated in the headquarters hut at Gondala.

They were the same men who had gathered here a month ago, and yet they were different. There was an air of confidence and determination about them that had not been there before.

Daniel had spoken to his Matabele instructors before the meeting. They were pleased. No man had been dropped from the training camps for any reason except sickness or injury.

'They are *amabutho* now,' Morgan Tembi had told Daniel. 'They are warriors now.'

'You have done well,' Daniel told them. 'You can be proud of what you have achieved in so short a time.'

He turned to the blackboard on the thatched wall behind him and pulled aside the cloth that had covered it. The board was covered with diagrams and schedules.

'This, gentlemen, is our order of battle,' Daniel said. 'We will go over it, not once but until every one of you can recite it in your sleep,' he warned them. 'Here are your four cadres, each of two hundred and fifty men. Each cadre is assigned different targets and objectives – the main army barracks, the airfield, the harbour, the labour camps . . .' Daniel worked down the list. 'Now, most important of all, the radio and television studio in Kahali. Taffari's security forces are good. Even with initial surprise we cannot hope to hold all our objectives longer than the first few hours, not without popular support. We have to secure the studio. President Omeru will be moved to the capital well ahead of time and will be in hiding in the old quarter, ready to come out and broadcast an appeal to the people. As soon as the populace sees him on television and realises that he is alive and leading the rising, we can expect every man and woman to join us. They will come out on to the streets and join the battle. Taffari's storm-troopers may be better armed than we are, but we will crush them by sheer weight of numbers.

'However, there is one other condition that we have to fulfil in order to ensure success. We have to take out Taffari himself within the first hour. We have to crush the head of the snake. Without Taffari they will collapse. There is nobody to replace him. Taffari himself has seen to that. He has murdered all possible rivals. He is a one-man band, but we have to get him with the first surprise stroke.'

'That won't be so easy.' Patrick Omeru came to his feet. 'He seems to have a kind of sixth sense. He has already survived two assassination attempts in the short time he has been in power. They are beginning to say he is using witchcraft, like Idi Amin—'

'Sit down, Patrick,' Daniel interrupted him sharply.

'Witchcraft' was a dangerous word to use, even to a group of educated and intelligent men such as this. They were still African, and witchcraft was rooted in the African soil.

'Taffari is a cunning swine. We all know that. He seldom sticks to any routine. He changes plans at the very last moment. He cancels appointments without reason and he sleeps at the home of a different wife each night, in random order. He's cunning, but he is no wizard. He'll bleed good red blood, I promise you that.'

They cheered him for that and the mood of the gathering improved. They were confident and eager again.

'However, there is one routine that Taffari has established. He visits the mining operation of Wengu at least once a month.

He likes to see his treasure coming out of the earth. At Wengu he is isolated. It is the one place in the entire country where he is most vulnerable.' Daniel paused and looked down at them. 'We are fortunate to have some good intelligence from Major Fashoda.' He indicated the Hita officer on the dais beside him. 'As you all know, Major Fashoda is the transport officer on Taffari's staff. He is the man responsible for arranging Taffari's personal transport. Taffari always uses a Puma helicopter to visit Wengu. He has ordered a Puma to stand by for Monday the 14th. This indicates a high probability that his next inspection tour to Wengu will be on that date. It gives us five days to make our final preparations.'

Ning Cheng Gong sat beside President Taffari on the padded bench in the fuselage of the airforce Puma helicopter. Through the open hatch he could see the green blur of the treetops as the Puma sped low across the forest. The wind buffeted them and it was noisy in the cabin. They had to raise their voices and shout to be heard.

'What news of Chetti Singh?' Ephrem Taffari shouted, his mouth close to Cheng's ear.

'Nothing,' Cheng shouted back. 'We found his Landrover, but no sign of him. It has been two weeks now. He must have died in the forest, as Armstrong did.'

'He was a good man,' Taffari said. 'He knew how to get work out of the convict labour. He was good at keeping costs down.'

'Yes,' Cheng agreed. 'He will be very hard to replace. He spoke the language. He understood Africa. He understood . . .' Cheng bit his lip. He had been on the point of using a derogatory term for black people. 'He understood the system,' he ended lamely.

'Even in the short time since his disappearance there has been a marked drop in production and profits.'

'I'm working on it,' Cheng assured him. 'I have some good men coming to replace him. Mining men from South Africa, as good as Chetti Singh. They also know how to get the most work out of these people.'

Taffari nodded and stood up. He made his way down the length of the cabin to speak to his companion.

As usual, Taffari was travelling with a woman. His latest flame was a tall Hita girl, a blues singer in a night club in Kahali. She had a face like a black Nefertiti. Taffari was also accompanied by a detachment of his presidential guard. Twenty crack paratroopers under the command of Major Kajo. Kajo had received promotion after the disappearance of Bonny Mahon. Taffari appreciated loyalty and tact, and Kajo was a man on the way up.

Cheng had come to detest these presidential inspection tours of the mining and logging concessions. He hated low-flying in one of the ancient Pumas of the Ubomo airforce. The helicopter pilots were notorious daredevils. There had been two fatal crashes in the squadron since his arrival in Ubomo.

More even than the physical danger, Cheng was uncomfortable with Taffari's searching questions and penetrating eye for figures and production details. Under his dashing martial exterior he had an accountant's mind. He understood finance. He could form a shrewd judgement as to when profits were falling below estimate; he had an instinct for money, and he could sense when he was being cheated.

Of course, Cheng was milking the syndicate, but not excessively, not blatantly. He was merely showing a benign bias towards the Lucky Dragon. He had done it skilfully. Not even a trained auditor would have picked it up, but President Taffari was already suspicious.

Cheng used this respite, sitting between two heavily armed paratroopers, feeling slightly queasy with air sickness, to go over all his financial dispositions and to search for any weak spots in his system that Taffari might be able to pin-point.

At last he decided that, at least temporarily, it might be prudent to reduce the amount he was skimming. He knew that if Taffari's suspicions ever became certainty he would not hesitate to terminate his contract, permanently, with the seal of a Kalashnikov No. 47. There would be another unmarked grave in the forest along with those of Chetti Singh and Daniel Armstrong.

At that moment the Puma banked sharply and Cheng clutched at his seat. Through the open fuselage hatch he had a glimpse of the bare red earth of the mining cut and the line of yellow MOMUs strung out along the edge of the forest. They had arrived at Wengu.

Daniel watched the Puma circle the landing-pad, slow down in flight and at last hover, nose-heavy, against a backdrop of purple cumulus cloud. There were puddles of rainwater on the concrete pad and the windsock flapped, sodden on its pole.

A small delegation of Taiwanese and black managers and officials were gathered in front of the main administrative building, confirming that Daniel's intelligence had been correct. Ephrem Taffari was on board the hovering helicopter.

Daniel's perch in the middle branches of the mahogany tree was three hundred and twenty yards from the landing pad. He had climbed to his perch during the night. Sepoo had waited at the base of the tree and when Daniel lowered the light nylon rope, he had hooked on the bundle of sniper's equipment.

By dawn Daniel was settled close in against the main trunk of the tree, beneath a tangle of vines and leafy climbing plants. He had cut a narrow window in the foliage which gave him a clear view of the helicopter pad. He wore a full camouflage sniper's coverall and mesh face-mask. His hands were covered with gloves.

His rifle was a 7mm Remington Magnum and he had chosen a 160 grain soft-point bullet, a compromise between velocity and high ballistic coefficient that would not be too severely affected by a cross-wind. He had tested the rifle extensively and it was shooting consistent four-inch groups at 350 yards. That wasn't good enough for any fancy head shots. He would aim for the centre of the chest. The expanding bullet could be expected to rip out Taffari's lungs.

It felt vaguely obscene to be thinking like this again. The last time had been ten years previously when the Scouts had staked out a ZANU cadre leader's kraal in Matabeleland. The man had been too wily and elusive for them to attempt an arrest. They had culled him without warning. Daniel had fired the shot and had felt sick for days afterwards.

Daniel thrust the memory aside. It might dilute his determination. Thinking like that might make his trigger finger just that crucial thousandth of a second slow when the image in the Zeiss lens was right.

If Taffari was on board the Puma, then Cheng must be with him. Cheng was the chief executive officer of UDC and he had accompanied every other presidential tour of the workings. If he could take Taffari with the first shot, then he could rely on a moment of utter astonishment and paralysis amongst his retinue. There would be a chance to get Cheng with the second shot, if he were quick enough.

There would be no hesitation about that kill. Deliberately he conjured up the memory of Johnny Nzou and his family to steel himself. He recalled every dreadful detail of the murder scene at Chiwewe and felt the sour hatred and rage swell in his chest. Ning Cheng Gong was his real reason for being in Ubomo at all. The second bullet was for him.

Then there was Chetti Singh. Daniel doubted that even if the Sikh were a member of the presidential party he would get the opportunity of a third shot. The paratrooper guards were trained soldiers. He might get a second shot, but not a third before they reacted.

Chetti Singh would be taken care of later, once the rising succeeded. He was in charge of the labour camps. Daniel's film of the executions in the forest would be damning evidence at his trial. He could afford to wait for Chetti Singh.

In the short time that it took the Puma to sink down towards the landing-pad, Daniel reviewed his dispositions, even though it was too late to change them now.

Victor Omeru was in Kahali. He had travelled down to the lakeside in one of the logging trucks, disguised as the mate of the Uhali driver. The arms and ammunition had been distributed in the same manner, transported in the UDC trucks. It was a nice irony, using the tyrant's own system to defeat him.

At this moment there were two revolutionary commandos in the capital, waiting for the word to strike. As soon as it was received, a detachment would storm the TV and radio studios. Victor Omeru would broadcast to the nation, calling upon them to rise. He would tell them that Taffari was dead and promise them an end to their suffering.

Meanwhile the other two commandos were deployed here at Wengu and Sengi-Sengi. Their first objectives would be to wipe out Taffari's Hita escort and to release the thirty thousand captives.

The signal for the rising to begin would be the shot that Daniel fired through Ephrem Taffari's lungs. Victor and Patrick Omeru would be informed by radio the moment that happened. There was a powerful radio in the UDC administrative building beside the landing-pad, but they would probably not be able to reach that immediately. As a back-up Daniel had a portable VHF transmitter, with which they could contact the headquarters at Gondala. Kelly was the radio operator who would transmit the signal that the rising had begun.

Daniel had drawn up four fall-backs and alternative plans to deal with every foreseeable contingency, but everything hinged on getting Taffari with the first shot. If Daniel failed there, he could expect Taffari to react with the speed and fury of a wounded lion. He would rally his men – it didn't bear thinking about. Daniel put the possibility out of his mind. He had to get Taffari.

The Puma was only fifty feet above the concrete landing-pad, sinking towards it slowly.

Daniel laid his cheek against the buttstock of his rifle and stared into the brilliant field of the telescopic sight. It was set to nine magnifications. He could see the expressions on the faces of the little reception committee at the landing-pad.

He lifted his aim, and captured the image of the helicopter. The lens was too high-powered to show him more than the hatchway in the Puma's fuselage. The flight engineer stood in the opening, directing the aircraft's descent. Daniel focused his attention on him, keeping the cross-hair of the telescope on his chest, using the buckle of his safety strap as an aiming point.

Suddenly another head appeared over the engineer's shoulder. Beneath the maroon beret with its glittering brass cap-badge were Ephrem Taffari's noble aquiline features.

'He's come,' Daniel exulted. 'It's him.'

He lifted the cross-hairs of the sight and tried to hold between Taffari's dark eyes. The movement of the helicopter, his own heart beat and hand shake, the inherent inaccuracy of the rifle all made it an impossible shot, but he concentrated all his mind and his will on Taffari. He purged himself of any last vestige of conscience and of mercy. Once again he forced upon himself the cold hard determination of the assassin.

At that moment the first raindrop struck the back of his neck. It startled him, his aim trembled, then another raindrop splashed against the lens of the Zeiss scope, and a soft wavering line of rain water ran down across the glass and dimmed the brilliance of the telescopic image.

Then it started to rain in real earnest, that sudden tropical deluge that seemed to turn the air to mist and blue water. It was like standing beneath a torrent in a mountain stream.

Daniel's vision dissolved. The crisply detailed human shapes he had been watching an instant before became dim blurs of movement. The men waiting on the landing-pad raised coloured umbrellas, and swarmed forward to meet the president, to offer him protection from the roaring rain.

There was misty movement and confusion. The colours of the umbrellas ran and starred and confused his eye. He saw a distorted image of Ephrem Taffari vault down lightly from the hatchway. Daniel had expected him to pose theatrically above the heads of the crowd and perhaps make a brief speech, but he vanished instantly. Though Daniel tried desperately to keep the cross-hairs on him, somebody raised a wet umbrella and held it over him.

Ning Cheng Gong's misty figure appeared in the hatchway, distracting Daniel's concentration. He swung the sights back towards Cheng, and then stopped himself. It had to be Taffari first. Desperately he swung the telescope back and forth, questing for a view of his target. The welcoming delegation had crowded around Taffari, umbrellas raised, obscuring him completely. The rain struck the concrete pad with such force that each drop exploded in a burst of spray.

Rain was splattering against the lens of the telescopic sight and streaming down Daniel's face beneath the mask.

Hita paratroopers were jumping down from the helicopter and clustering around their president. No sign of Taffari now, and everybody was running towards the waiting Landrovers, crouched down under the lofted umbrellas, splashing through the pools of rain water.

Taffari appeared again, stepping out fast in the slanting rain, heading for the leading vehicle. Even at a walking pace and taking into account the velocity of the 7mm bullet, Daniel would have to lead him by two feet or more. He could barely distinguish him through the clouded lens. It was an almost impossible shot, but he tightened up on the trigger, just as one of the Hita bodyguards ran forward to assist his master.

The shot went off before Daniel could stop himself. He saw the Hita paratrooper spin round and go down, shot through the chest. It would have killed Taffari as cleanly, if the man had not covered him.

The whole pattern of moving men in the rain exploded. Taffari threw down the umbrella he carried and darted forward. All around him men were running in confusion.

Daniel jacked another round into the chamber of the rifle and fired again, a snap shot at Taffari. It had no effect, a clean miss. Taffari kept running. He reached the Landrover and before Daniel could reload, he had jerked open the door and thrown himself into the front seat of the vehicle.

Daniel glimpsed Ning Cheng Gong in the thick of it, and fired again. He saw another paratrooper go down on his knees, hit low in the body, and then the other soldiers were blazing away wildly towards the edges of the forest, uncertain from which direction Daniel's shots were coming.

Daniel was still trying desperately to get another shot at Taffari, but the Landrover was pulling away. He fired at the head he could see behind the windscreen, not certain whether it was Taffari or a driver. The windscreen shattered, but the vehicle did not check or swerve.

He emptied the magazine at the accelerating vehicle. Then as he tried to reload from the bandolier at his waist, he saw three or four of the Hita guards and the civilian officials take hits and go down sprawling in the rain. There was the swelling clatter of small-arms fire.

The men of his own commando had opened fire from their positions in the forest outside the perimeter.

The uprising had begun, but Taffari was still alive.

Daniel saw the Landrover make a wide circle, swinging past the office building and come back round under the hovering helicopter. The Puma was hanging twenty feet above the ground, almost hidden by the falling curtains of rain. Taffari was leaning out of the driver's window, signalling frantically for the pilot to pick him up again.

At that moment a man appeared out of the jungle on the far side of the clearing. Even at that distance Daniel recognised Morgan Tembi, the Matabele instructor. He carried the tube of an RPG rocket-launcher on his shoulder as he raced forward.

None of the Hita bodyguard seemed to have spotted him. A hundred paces from the hovering Puma, Morgan dropped on one knee, steadied himself and fired a rocket.

It rode on a tail of white smoke, whooshing in to hit the Puma well forward, almost in line with the perspex pilot's canopy.

The cockpit and the pilot in it were obliterated by the burst of smoke and flame. The Puma performed a lazy cartwheel in the air and fell to earth on its back. The spinning rotors smashed themselves into tiny fragments on the concrete landing-pad. An instant later a ball of fire and black smoke devoured the machine.

Morgan Tembi jumped to his feet and ran back towards the edge of the forest. He never made it. The Hita bodyguards shot him down long before he could reach cover, but he had cut off Taffari's escape.

It had taken less than a minute but already the Hita were recovering from the shock of the surprise attack. They were piling into Landrovers and following Taffari as he drove for the roadway beyond the office building. Taffari must have realised the strength and numbers of the attackers and decided that his best bet would be to try and break out and reach the nearest road-block on the Sengi-Sengi road which was manned by his own men.

Three Landrovers filled with his own guards were flying after him. Most of the civilian officials were lying flat on the ground, trying to keep below the wild cross-fire, although some of them were running for the shelter of the office buildings. Daniel saw Cheng amongst them. His blue safari suit was distinctive, even in the rain mist. Before he could get a shot at him Cheng reached the building and ducked through the front door.

Daniel turned his attention back to the four escaping Landrovers. They had almost reached the main road into the forest and the fire that the Uhali commando was turning upon them was furious but inaccurate. It seemed to be totally ineffectual. With Morgan Tembi dead they were blazing away without aiming, like the raw untried recruits they truly were.

Taffari was already out of range from where Daniel was perched in the mahogany tree. He was going to get clear away. The whole attack was becoming a fiasco. The Uhali were forgetting all their training. The plan was falling to pieces. The rising was doomed within minutes of beginning.

At that moment a huge yellow D10 caterpillar lumbered out of the forest.

'At least somebody has remembered his orders,' Daniel snarled to himself. He was angry at his failure, taking the full blame on himself.

The caterpillar tractor waddled forward, straddling the roadway, cutting off the flying convoy of Landrovers.

A small band of Uhali emerged from the forest and ran behind it, dressed in blue denim and other civilian clothing. They used the tractor as a barricade and opened fire on the leading Landrover as it raced towards them.

At close range their concentrated fire was at last effective. Taffari, in the leading Landrover, saw his escape cut off and spun the truck in a hard 180-degree turn. The other trucks followed him round.

They came back across the open ground in a line, and they were within range again. Daniel fired at Taffari's head, but the Landrover was doing sixty miles an hour and bouncing over the rough track. Daniel never saw the strike of his bullets, and the line of the Landrovers tore away down the track that led to where the MOMU units were working. That direction was a dead end. The road ended at the mining excavation. The situation had been retrieved from total disaster by the driver of the caterpillar tractor.

By now the column of Landrovers was out of sight from where Daniel was perched in the mahogany tree.

He left the rifle hanging on its strap and swung out of the branch. He used the nylon rope to abseil down the trunk of the tree, kicking himself outwards with both feet, dropping so swiftly that the rope scorched the palms of his hands. As he hit the ground Sepoo ran forward and handed him his AK 47 assault rifle and the haversack that contained the spare magazines and four M26 grenades.

'Where is Kara-Ki?' he demanded, and Sepoo pointed back into the forest. They ran together.

Two hundred yards further into the forest Kelly was crouched over the VHF radio transmitter. She jumped up when she saw Daniel.

'What happened?' she shouted. 'Did you get him?'

'It's a total balls-up,' Daniel told her grimly. 'Taffari's still out there. We haven't got control of the radio station at Wengu.'

'Oh God, what happens now?'

'Transmit!' He made the decision. 'Give Victor the go-ahead. We are committed now. We can't turn back.'

'But if Taffari—'

'Damn it, Kelly, just do it! I'm going to try and retrieve the ball. At least Taffari didn't get clear away. We are still in with a chance. For the present we've got him bottled up here at Wengu.'

Kelly did not argue again, she knelt beside the radio set and lifted the microphone to her lips.

'Forest Base, this is Mushroom. Do you read me?'

The portable transmitter did not have the range to reach Kahali on the lakeshore direct. They must relay through the more powerful set at Gondala.

'Mushroom, this is Forest Base,' the voice of Kelly's male nurse from the Gondala clinic came back immediately. He was a trusted Uhali retainer of many years' standing.

'This is a relay for Silver Head in Kahali. Message reads, "The Sun has Risen". I say again, "The Sun has Risen".'

'Stand by, Mushroom.'

There was a few minutes' silence, then Gondala came back on the air. 'Mushroom, Silver Head acknowledges "The Sun has Risen".'

The revolution was launched. Within the hour Victor Omeru would be on television announcing it to his nation. But Taffari was still alive.

'Kelly, listen to me.' Daniel took her arm and dragged her up to face him, making sure he had her full attention. 'Stay here. Try and keep in contact with Gondala. Don't go wandering off. Taffari's storm-troopers will be scattered everywhere. Stay here until I come back for you.'

She nodded. 'Be careful, darling.'·

'Sepoo.' Daniel looked down at the little man. 'Stay here. Look after Kara-Ki.'

'With my life!' Sepoo told him.

'Kiss me!' Kelly demanded of Daniel.

'Just a quick one. More to follow,' Daniel promised.

He left her and ran back towards the UDC buildings.

Before he had gone a hundred yards he heard men in the forest ahead. 'Omeru!' he shouted. It was the password.

'Omeru!' they shouted back. 'The Sun has Risen!'

'Not yet, it bloody hasn't,' Daniel muttered, and went forward.

There were a dozen men of the commando, the blue denim jackets were almost a uniform.

'Come on!' He gathered them up.

Before they reached the road that ran down to the mining cut he had thirty men with him. The rain had stopped by now, and Daniel paused on the edge of the forest. Before them stretched the endless plain of churned earth that the MOMU units had devoured. The line of machines was ahead of them, ranged along the boundary where forest and red mud met. They looked like a line of battleships in a storm.

Closer still were the four Landrovers, scattered at abandoned angles on the muddy plain. As Daniel watched, the Hita guards were straggling across the open ground towards the nearest MOMU.

Daniel recognised Ephrem Taffari's tall uniformed figure leading them. It was clear that he had selected the nearest MOMU as the most readily defensible strong-point available to him, and Daniel conceded grimly that it was a good choice.

The steel sides of the gigantic machine would offer almost complete protection from small-arms fire. Even the RPG rockets would make no impression on its massive construction.

To reach it an attacker would have to cross soft open ground

507

that could be covered by fire from the upper platforms of the MOMU. Just as important, the steel fortress was manoeuvrable. Once he was in control of it, Taffari could drive it anywhere.

Daniel looked about him quickly, by now there were fifty or so Uhali guerrillas congregated around him. They were noisy and over-excited, behaving like green troops after their first taste of fire. Some of them were cheering and firing at the distant figures of Taffari and his guards. They were well out of range, and it was a dangerous waste of their precious stocks of ammunition.

There was no point in trying to get them under control. He had to attack before they lost their wild spirits, and before Taffari reached the MOMU and organised its defence.

'Come on!' Daniel shouted. 'Omeru! "The Sun has Risen"!'

He led them out on to the open ground, and they followed him in a rabble, cheering wildly.

'Omeru!' they yelled. Daniel had to keep the momentum going.

The mud was ankle-deep in places, knee-deep in others. They passed the abandoned Landrovers. Ahead of them Daniel saw Taffari reach the MOMU and haul himself up one of the steel boarding ladders. As they ploughed on through the mud, their progress slowed to a plodding walk.

Taffari was organising his men as they came aboard the MOMU. They were taking cover behind the massive steel machinery. Bullets started slashing amongst the attackers, plugging into the mud, cracking around their heads. The man beside Daniel was hit. He went down face first in the mud.

The attack slowed, bogging down in the mud. The Hita on the MOMU were lodging in, hidden behind steel bulkheads. They were shooting accurately, and more of Daniel's men were falling.

The attack stalled, some of the Uhali broke and started to stumble back towards the forest. Others crouched behind the stranded Landrovers. They were not soldiers. They were clerks and truck-drivers and university students faced by crack paratroopers in an impregnable steel fortress. Daniel could not blame them for breaking, even though the revolution was dying in the mud with them.

He could not go on alone. Already the Hita had singled him out. Their fire was concentrating on him. He stumbled back to the nearest Landrover and crouched behind its chassis.

He saw the crew of the MOMU desert their stations and huddle helplessly on the lower platform. One of the Hita paratroopers gestured to them imperiously and with obvious relief they swarmed down the steel ladder and dropped into the mud like sailors abandoning a sinking ocean liner.

The engine of the MOMU was still running. The excavators were chewing into the earth, but now with no direction the gigantic rig was wandering out of its formation. The crews of the other rigs in the line saw what was happening and they too abandoned their posts and streamed overboard, trying to escape the bursts of gunfire that rattled and clanged against the steel plating.

It was a stand-off. Taffari's men had command of the MOMU and Daniel's commando were stalled in the mud unable to advance or retreat.

He tried to think of some way to break the *impasse*. He could not expect his shattered and demoralised survivors to mount another charge. Taffari had fifteen or twenty men up there, more than enough to hold them off.

At that moment he became aware of another eerie sound, like the mewling of seagulls or the cry of lost souls. He looked back and at first saw nothing. Then something moved at the edge of the forest. At first he could not make it out. It was not human, surely?

Then he saw other movement. The forest was coming alive. Thousands of strange creatures, as numerous as insects, like a column of safari ants on the march. They were red in their myriads, and the wild plaintive cry rose louder and more urgently from them as they swarmed out of the forest into the open.

Suddenly he realised what he was seeing. The gates of the labour camps were open. The guards had been overwhelmed and the Uhali slaves had risen out of the mud. They were red with it, coated with it, naked as corpses exhumed from the grave, starved to stick-like emaciation.

They swarmed forward in their legions, in their thousands,

women and men and children, sexless in their coating of mud, only their white and angry eyes glaring in the muddy red masks of their faces.

'Omeru!' they cried, and the sound was like a stormy sea on a rocky headland.

The fire of the Hita paratroopers was blanketed by the roar of their voices. The bullets of the AK 47 assault rifles made no impression on the densely packed ranks, where one man fell a dozen more swarmed forward to replace him. On the MOMU fortress the Hita guards were running out of ammunition. Even at this distance Daniel could sense their panic. They threw aside their empty rifles, the barrels hot as though from the furnace.

Unarmed they climbed the steel ladders to the highest platform of the ungainly yellow rig. Helplessly they stood at the railing and watched the naked red horde reach the machine and climb up towards them.

Daniel recognised Ephrem Taffari amongst the Hita on the upper deck. He was trying to speak to the slaves, spreading his arms in an oratorial gesture, trying to reason with them. In the end, when the front rank was almost upon him Taffari drew his pistol and fired down into them. He kept firing as they engulfed him.

For a time Daniel lost him in the struggling red mass of naked humanity. He was like a fry absorbed by a gigantic jelly fish. Then he saw Taffari again, lifted high above the heads of the mob by hundreds of upraised arms. They passed him forward struggling wildly.

Then they hurled him from the top of the MOMU.

Ephrem Taffari turned in the air, ungainly as a bird trying to fly with a broken wing. He dropped seventy feet, into the spinning silver blades of the excavator head. The blades sucked him in and in a single instant chopped him to a paste so fine that his blood did not leave so much as a stain on the wet earth.

Daniel stood up slowly.

On the MOMU they were killing the Hita paratroopers, tearing them to pieces with their bare hands, swarming over them screaming and exulting.

Daniel turned away. He started back towards where he had left Kelly. His progress was slow. Men of the commando clustered around him, shaking his hand, thumping him on the back, laughing and shouting and singing.

There was still some desultory small-arms fire in the forest. The administrative offices were on fire. Flames leapt high, crackling and pouring out black smoke. A roof collapsed. People were trapped in there, burning to death. The mob raged everywhere, chasing the guards and officials and engineers and clerks of the company, black and Taiwanese, anybody connected with the hated oppressor. They caught them and killed them, kicking and beating them as they writhed on the earth, hacking at them with spades or machetes, throwing their dismembered bodies into the flames. It was savage. It was Africa.

Daniel turned away from the horror. One man could not stop the orgy. They had suffered too long; their hatred was too fierce. He left the track and went into the forest to find Kelly.

He had not gone a hundred yards before he saw a small figure running towards him through the trees.

'Sepoo!' he called, and the pygmy darted to his side and seized his arm and shook it.

'Kara-Ki!' he screeched incoherently, there was a gash in his scalp and he was bleeding heavily.

'Where is she?' Daniel demanded. 'What has happened to her?'

'Kara-Ki! He has taken her. He has taken her into the forest.'

 Kelly knelt in front of the radio set, gently manipulating the fine-tuning knob of the receiver. Although her transmitter did not have the range to reach the capital of Kahali on the lakeshore, Sepoo had climbed into the silk-cotton tree above her and strung the aerial wire from the top branches. She was picking up the transmission of Radio Ubomo on the twenty-five metre band with very little atmospheric disturbance.

'This next request is for Miriam Seboki of Kabute who is

eighteen years old today, from your boy friend, Abdullah, who wishes you many happy returns and says he loves you very much. He has requested, "Like a Virgin" by Madonna, so here it is just for you, Miriam ...' The harsh cacophony of the music was aberrant in the forest silences and Kelly turned down the volume. Immediately she was aware of other sounds even more obscene, the distant fusillade of gunfire and the wild screams of fighting and dying men.

She tried to blot the sounds from her mind, tried to calm her anxiety and fear for the progress of the rising. She waited, powerless and afraid, for something to happen.

Suddenly the music was cut off, and the only sound from the speaker was the whistle and crackle of static. Then abruptly a new voice came on the air.

'People of Ubomo. This station is now under the control of the Freedom Army of Ubomo. We bring you the President of Ubomo, Victor Omeru, speaking to you in person from the radio studio in Kahali.'

There was a burst of martial music, the old national anthem, that Ephrem Taffari had banned when he seized power. Then the music ended. There was a pause and at last the thrilling voice that Kelly loved so well reverberated from the speaker.

'My beloved people of Ubomo, you who have suffered so much beneath the yoke of the oppressor, this is Victor Omeru. I know that most of you believed that I was dead. But this is not a voice from the grave. It is indeed I, Victor Omeru, who call upon you now.' Victor was speaking in Swahili, and he went on, 'I bring you tidings of hope and of great joy. Ephrem Taffari, the bloody tyrant, is dead. A loyal and true band of patriots has overthrown his cruel and brutal regime and given him the punishment he so justly deserves. Come forth, my people, a new sun rises over Ubomo ...' His voice was so compelling, so sincere, that for a moment Kelly almost believed what he was saying – that Taffari was already dead and the revolution was secure. Then she heard the sound of gunfire and she glanced over her shoulder.

There was a man standing close to her. He had come up soundlessly behind her. He was an Asian, almost certainly Chinese. He wore a blue safari suit damp with rain or sweat and stained with mud and blood. His long straight black hair hung down over his forehead. There was a shallow cut in his cheek from which the blood had dripped to stain the front of his jacket.

He carried a Tokarev pistol in one hand, and there was a wild and hunted look in his eyes – eyes so dark that there was no division between iris and pupil, black eyes like a mako shark. His mouth was contorted with fear or anger, and the hand that held the pistol twitched and trembled.

Although she had never seen him before, Kelly knew who he was. She had heard Daniel speak of him so often. She had seen his photograph in the out-of-date copies of the Ubomo *Herald* newspaper that occasionally reached Gondala. She knew that he was the Taiwanese managing-director of UDC, the man who had murdered Daniel's friend, Johnny Nzou.

'Ning,' she said, and scrambled to her feet trying to back away from him, but he sprang forward and seized her wrist.

She was shocked by his strength. He twisted her arm up behind her back.

'A white woman,' he said in English. 'A hostage . . .'

Sepoo rushed at him, trying to help her, but Cheng swung the pistol in a short vicious arc and the barrel struck the little man above the ear, splitting open his scalp. He dropped at Cheng's feet. Still holding Kelly with the other hand, Cheng stretched down and aimed the pistol at Sepoo's temple.

'No,' screamed Kelly, and threw herself back against Cheng's chest. It spoiled his aim, and the bullet ploughed into the earth six inches from Sepoo's face. The shot roused him, and Sepoo rolled to his feet and darted away. Cheng fired another shot at him as he ran, but Sepoo vanished into the undergrowth.

Cheng twisted her arm savagely, pulling her up on to her toes with the agony in her shoulder-blade.

'You're hurting me,' she cried.

'Yes,' Cheng agreed. 'And I will kill you if you resist me again. Walk!' he ordered. 'Yes, like that. Keep going if you don't want me to hurt you again.'

'Where are we going?' Kelly asked, trying to keep the pain out of her voice, trying to be calm and persuasive. 'There is no escape into the forest.'

'With you there is,' Cheng said. 'Don't talk. Be quiet! Keep going.'

He pushed and dragged her onwards, and she dared not resist. She sensed that he was desperate enough to do anything. She remembered what Daniel had told her about him, about the murdered Matabele family in Zimbabwe, about the rumours of children and young girls tortured for his perverted pleasure. She realised that her best chance, perhaps her only chance, was to comply with anything he ordered her to do.

They covered half a mile, staggering and stumbling, made clumsy by the wrist-lock that Cheng had on her, and by his wild haste. When they came out suddenly on to the bank of a narrow stream she realised that it was the Wengu, the small river that gave the area its name. It was one of the tributaries of the main Ubomo River.

It was also one of the bleeding rivers, clogged with the poison effluent from the MOMU vehicles. It was stinking and treacherous. Even Cheng seemed to realise the danger of trying to wade across it.

He forced Kelly to her knees, and stood over her, panting and looking about him uncertainly.

'Please . . .' she whispered.

'Be silent!' he ranted at her. 'I told you not to speak!' He screwed her wrist to enforce the order, and despite herself she whimpered aloud.

After another few moments, he asked suddenly, 'Is this the Wengu River? Which direction does it run? Does it go southwards towards the main road?'

Instantly she realised which way his mind was working. Of course, he would have an intimate knowledge of the area. It was his concession. He would have studied the maps. He would certainly know that the Wengu made a circle to the south, an ox-bow that intersected the main road. He would know that there was a Hita military post at the bridge.

'Is it the Wengu?' he repeated, twisting her wrist until she screamed, and she almost answered truthfully before she caught herself.

'I don't know.' She shook her head. 'I don't know anything about the forest.'

'You lie,' he accused, but he was obviously uncertain. 'Who are you?' he demanded.

'I'm just a nurse with the World Health Organization. I don't know about the forest.'

'All right.' He hauled her to her feet. 'Get going!'

He shoved her forward, but now they turned southwards following the bank of the Wengu River. Cheng had made up his mind.

Kelly deliberately kicked and scuffed the soft earth as he pushed her along. She put all her weight on her heels, trying to lay as good a spoor as possible for Sepoo to follow. She knew Sepoo would be coming, and with him must come Daniel.

She tried to snap any green twig that came within reach as Cheng forced her through the undergrowth. She managed to tear a button off her shirt and drop it, an identification for Sepoo to pick up. At every opportunity she tripped over a dead branch or fell into a hole and dropped to her knees, holding him up as much as possible, slowing down their progress, giving Sepoo and Daniel a chance to catch up.

She began whining and whimpering loudly and when Cheng raised the pistol threateningly, she screamed, 'No, please! Please don't hit me!'

She knew her cries would carry, that Sepoo with his sensitive, forest-trained ears would hear her at a distance of quarter of a mile and pin-point her position.

Sepoo picked the shirt button out of the leaf trash of the forest floor, and showed it to Daniel.

'See, Kuokoa, Kara-Ki is laying sign for us to follow,' he whispered. 'She is clever as the colobus, and brave as the forest buffalo.'

'Keep going.' Daniel prodded him impatiently. 'Make your speeches later, old man.'

They went on along the spoor, quick, silent and alert. Sepoo pointed out the sign that Kelly had left, the broken twigs, the heel marks and the places where she had deliberately fallen to her knees.

'We are close now.' He touched Daniel's arm. 'Very close . . .'

'Be careful not to run into him. He might lay an ambush . . .'

Kelly screamed in the forest ahead of them. 'No, please! Please don't hit me!' And for an instant Daniel lost control. He lunged forward, rushing to her defence, but Sepoo seized his wrist and hung on doggedly.

'No! No! Kara-Ki is not hurt. She is warning us. Don't rush in like a stupid *wazungu*. Use your head now.'

Daniel pulled himself together, but he was still trembling with rage.

'All right,' he whispered. 'He doesn't know I am here but he has seen you. I'm going to circle round them and lie-up downstream. You must drive him on to me, just as you drive the duiker in the net hunt. Do you understand, Sepoo?'

'I understand. Give the call of a grey parrot when you are ready.'

Daniel screwed the folding bayonet off the muzzle of his AK 47 and propped the rifle against the tree beside him. Cheng was using Kelly as a shield. The rifle was useless. He abandoned it.

Armed only with the bayonet, he circled out swiftly away from the river-bank. Twice more he heard Kelly's voice, pleading and whining, giving him a pin-point on her position.

It took him less than five minutes to get downstream of Cheng and Kelly and to flatten himself against the bole of one of the trees growing on the bank. He cupped his hands over his mouth and gave an imitation of the squawk of a roosting parrot. Then he crouched down with the bayonet at the ready.

Sepoo's voice shrilled through the trees. He was using the high ventriloquist's tone that would deceive the listener as to direction and distance. 'Hey, *wazungu*. Let Kara-Ki go. I am watching you from the trees. Let her go, or I will put a poison arrow into you.'

Daniel doubted that Cheng could understand the Swahili words, but the effect would be the same, to concentrate Cheng's attention upstream while driving him down to where Daniel was waiting.

He crouched and listened. A few minutes later, Sepoo called again, 'Hey, *wazungu*, do you hear me?'

516

Silence fell again and Daniel strained his eyes and his hearing.

Then a branch rustled just ahead of him, and he heard Kelly's voice, muffled and terrified.

'Please don't . . .' she began, but was cut off by Cheng's brusque whisper.

'Shut your mouth, woman, or I will break your arm.'

They were very close to where Daniel waited. He tightened his grip on the hilt of the bayonet. Then he saw movement in the undergrowth, and a moment later made out the blue of Cheng's jacket.

Cheng was moving backwards, holding Kelly against his chest, facing the direction of Sepoo's voice, aiming the Tokarev pistol over Kelly's shoulder, ready to fire the moment Sepoo showed himself. He was backing directly towards the tree where Daniel waited.

Daniel knew that Cheng was an exponent of the martial arts. In any hand-to-hand combat, Daniel would be at a terrible disadvantage. There was one sure way. That was to drive the point of the bayonet into his kidneys from behind. It would cripple him instantly.

He stepped out from behind the tree with the bayonet held low and underhand. He launched the stroke, but at the same instant Cheng twisted violently sideways. Daniel never knew what had alerted him, for he had made no sound. It could only have been the almost supernatural instinct of the Kung Fu fighter.

The bayonet caught Cheng in the flank, an inch above the hip bone. It went in to the hilt, but Cheng's turn tore the weapon from Daniel's grip.

Cheng released Kelly, shoving her away from him and brought the Tokarev round to fire into Daniel's face. Daniel grabbed the wrist of his pistol hand and forced it upwards. The first shot went into the branches above their heads.

Cheng twisted in Daniel's grip, and as Daniel tried to hold him, he whipped his body back again and his knee came up, aimed for Daniel's crotch. Daniel caught the kick on his thigh, but the force of it paralysed his leg.

From the corner of his eye he saw Cheng's left hand, stiff as an axe-blade, flick towards his head, aimed at his neck below the ear. He hunched his shoulders and caught it on the thick muscle of his upper biceps. The strength and power of it sickened him. His grip on Cheng's pistol hand slackened.

The hand flicked at him again, and this time Daniel knew it would snap his neck like a dry twig. Kelly had not fallen, despite the vicious shove Cheng had given her between the shoulder-blades. She gathered herself and hurled herself back at him, shoulder first into Cheng's side, into the flank that the bayonet had laid open. The force of it turned the blow aside from Daniel's exposed neck and Cheng stumbled against him and dropped the pistol with a shout of pain.

Desperately Daniel locked his free arm around the back of Cheng's head and threw himself backwards, in the direction in which Cheng had been thrown by Kelly's charge. Cheng could not resist and they fell, locked together, down the sheer bank of the river, dropping six feet into the thick red ooze, going under completely.

Almost immediately their heads broke out through the surface. Both of them were gasping for breath, still locked together.

Daniel's leg was still paralysed. Cheng was wiry and quick. Daniel realised that he could not hold him. Kelly saw he was in distress and stooped. She picked up the bayonet, and in the same movement threw herself feet first down the bank, sliding on her backside, the bayonet poised.

Cheng squirmed over the top of Daniel, whipping one arm around his neck from behind. His back was turned to Kelly, the jacket of his safari suit shining wetly with red mud.

Kelly stabbed from as high as she could reach. Her first blow struck one of Cheng's ribs and was deflected. Cheng grunted and convulsed. She lifted the bayonet and stabbed again and this time the point found a gap between his ribs.

Cheng released the armlock from Daniel's neck and wriggled around to face Kelly in the mud. The bayonet was still lodged high in his back, the blade half buried.

Cheng reached out for Kelly with both hands, his mud-daubed features contorted with an animal ferocity. Daniel recovered and threw himself forward on to Cheng's back, locking both arms around his throat, bearing him down with all his weight. The hilt of the bayonet was trapped between them and the blade was forced all the way home. A mouthful of blood burst over Cheng's lips and poured down his chin.

Daniel heaved and shoved his head below the surface, and held it there. As Cheng was struggling in the red mud, one of his arms broke out and groped blindly for Daniel's face, trying to reach his eyes with hooked fingers. Daniel held on grimly, and the hand fell away. Cheng's movements in the mud became feebler and more erratic.

Kelly waded to the bank and crouched there, watching in fascinated horror.

Suddenly a rush of slow fat bubbles rose out of the red ooze and burst upon the surface as Cheng's lungs emptied. Only Daniel's head was clear of the mud. He lay there for a long time, never relaxing his grip on Cheng's submerged throat.

'He's dead,' Kelly whispered at last. 'He must be dead by now.'

Slowly Daniel released his grip. There was no movement below the surface. Daniel dragged himself to the bank, like an insect moving through treacle.

Kelly helped him up the bank. His injured leg trailed behind him. On the top the two of them knelt together clinging to each other. They stared down into the riverbed.

Slowly something rose to the surface like a dead log. The mud coated Cheng's corpse so thickly that it almost obscured the human shape. They stared at it for fully five minutes before either of them spoke.

'He drowned in his own cesspool,' Daniel whispered. 'I couldn't have chosen a better way.'

extracts reading groups
competitions books new
discounts extracts extracts
competitions reading groups discounts
books new events
reading groups extracts events
new events books reading groups
extracts discounts
books new title reading groups
interviews
reading groups events extracts extracts new books
books discounts events interviews
extracts new books events new
events events new
discounts extracts discounts interviews new books extracts
www.panmacmillan.com
extracts events reading groups
competitions books extracts new